MW00942081

THE MALJA CHRONICLES

VOLUME 1

Stuart Jaffe

The Malja Chronicles is a work of fiction. Names, characters, places, and incidents either are the product of the author's imagination or are used fictitiously, and any resemblance to any persons, living or dead, business establishments, events, or locales is entirely coincidental.

THE MALJA CHRONICLES

Copyright © 2015 by Stuart Jaffe

ISBN-13: 978-1514833636
ISBN-10: 1514833638

First Edition: July, 2015

Also by Stuart Jaffe

Introduction

It is a strange and humbling feeling to be writing this introduction. Strange that what began as an idea for a podcast would twist and turn over many years to become a six book series with an off-shoot short story series that led to a comic book limited series and whatever else may yet come. Humbling that all you readers have made this possible, that you all enjoyed Malja's story enough to keep the books coming, and that you stuck through it with me all these years.

The creation of Malja and her world took a long time. So long, in fact, I often thought it would never happen. About a decade ago, I was getting started on this writing career thing (this was long before ebooks existed as a viable option), had myself an agent shopping around a few manuscripts, and had several short stories published in small press magazines and anthologies. I had been a guest panelist at several conventions and heard about this new one starting up called Ravencon. It was only a four-hour drive from my home, so I contacted them and got on the guest list.

It was there that I met Tee Morris. He was raving about this new-fangled thing called podcasting. Well, the idea intrigued me so much that when I went home, I told my wife I was starting a podcast. Only one problem: I had no clue what to do it about. And here's where the first seeds of The Malja Chronicles were planted. I thought I'd do a science-fiction drama as an old radio-play. It was a post-apocalyptic revenge tale called The Way of the Sword and Gun, and it followed a young man named Owl who traveled the wastelands with a mute boy, Tommy, and an ex-police officer named, Dana.

I wrote eight or nine episodes of a planned twelve, grew in excitement over the whole idea of podcasting, and proceeded to produce nothing. Two things got in the way. First, I realized that to produce these shows the way I wanted them to be done would require more people and equipment than I had access to. I could have, of course, done them on the cheap, but something in me balked at the idea. Not because I'm against shoestring theater, but in retrospect, I think part of me knew I had the seeds of a special story, and I wanted it done right. Second, my wife got the podcasting bug and wanted to do a show with me. So, I shelved the audio-play, and with my wife, we created *The Eclectic Review* which, I'm proud to write, became one of the longest running genre-related podcasts.

Over the years, I would pick up the story of Owl and Tommy and Dana, re-read it, and wonder. Maybe I could turn these scripts into a graphic novel. That sounded cool and fun, so I contacted various artists. Several of them expressed great interest in the project, but one thing or another got in the way, and The Way of the Sword and Gun remained nothing more than words on my hard drive.

But still I wondered

Though the original story was a science-fiction tale, as I let it stew in my brain, I thought it would be fun to introduce magic. But I didn't want to make an outright fantasy tale, either. Rather, I wanted to mix both science-fiction and fantasy together, the way it had been done back at the start of the genres. As I pondered these possibilities, I found myself staring at the tattoos I have on my arm. And poof, the idea of tattoo magic arrived.

It would still be a few years before I wrote the whole thing into a novel. It was after my favorite novel (up to that point) had been rejected because the publishers loved it so much (I'm not joking, I wish I was), that I decided to write this crazy idea and the heck with everything else. I had burned out on science-fiction and knew my short stories were leaning more and more heavily into fantasy. Plus, I just loved all the ideas I'd built in my head. So, I started out writing several short stories to see how the old audio-play might translate into prose.

Not very well, it turned out.

Dana didn't work. Oh, I could have made her work. I'm the one writing the story, after all. I could have forced her to do what I wanted and make her more appealing to a prose way of storytelling. But everything I tried with her came out feeling either flat or like a female version of Judge Dredd. Yet the world the story took place in was still really cool.

Enter Malja.

She popped into my head close to fully-formed, and when I finished writing three short stories with her and Tommy, she was complete. I tackled *The Way of the Black Beast* and had a blast in the process. The only thing missing was Owl. He was such an awesome, butt-kicking dude, and I missed him. So, I promised myself that I'd introduce him in the second book, and obviously, I took the old title as well.

The Owl that ended up in the book is far different than the one from the podcast scripts. The original Owl played more like a Clint Eastwood stranger on a horse. There's still a bit of that lurking in him, but I love the Owl that you'll read in here. Far more interesting.

The final book (or so I thought), *The Way of the Brother Gods,* gave me the opportunity to follow through on Tommy's story, which had been building since the opening pages of *The Way of the Black Beast.* I wrote a lot of that tale to satisfy myself and what I wanted for the characters. Based on reader reactions, you all wanted the same things. Needless to say, this pleases me.

In fact, it was due to your reactions that the story didn't end here. I do quite a few convetion appearances, and at every one, I would come across some of you fans who would ask when Book 4 was coming out. I had no idea.

I knew a general arc of what I would do for books 4-6, and I also knew that if I started Book 4, I would commit to writing all three books in two years. I didn't want to "George R. R. Martin" you. Not only is it not necessary to have you waiting for decades between each book, but it would be no fun for me either. At some point, the call for more Malja reached a critical mass, and I sat at my desk to figure out what would happen next.

I had one big image for the final book and a few key moments for the entire arc, but that was about it. However, once I started moving on the project, it built an amazing amount of momentum. The story raced out of me, and I had a blast writing it.

The hardest part came when I had to write *The Way of the Soul,* but more on that in Volume 2. For now, you have the first half to *The Malja Chronicles* and it's plenty to get you started.

One last thing. It's important. None of this was possible without you, so thank you for reading and enjoying all Malja has had to offer. And if this is your first outing with Malja, hold on tight!

- North Carolina, 2015

THE MALJA CHRONICLES

VOLUME 1

THE WAY OF THE
BLACK BEAST

BOOK 1 OF THE
BEST SELLING SERIES
THE MALJA CHRONICLES

STUART JAFFE

THE WAY OF THE

BLACK BEAST

Book 1 of The Malja Chronicles

For Glory and Gabe

CHAPTER 1

Malja had followed the killer for hours. She hid amongst the shadows of the forest pines and birches, careful not to alert him with any sound. Though he acted as if out for a stroll, all her instincts told her a confrontation neared.

He stepped into an open clearing. The broken macadam of a four-lane highway long dead cut through only to disappear in an overgrowth of weeds and vines. Insects meandered in the tall grass. A rusting signpost — NO FLYER LANDING — held a lonely vigil in the center.

The killer stopped near the sign and raised his face to the clouds. The hot Krysstaprime season neared its end, but the sun still cooked the ground.

"Don't you think it's 'bout time we talk?" he said. His dark skin obscured the brown eyes underneath his little round hat. He wore a strange suit — all black, trim cut, black shirt, gold buttons — and carried a beaten guitar on his back. Unusual clothes but not unheard of, not like Malja's long coat and black assault suit. "Or do you plan on following me forever?"

Malja cursed and stepped away from the trees. She stopped at the clearing's edge, reached behind, and pulled Viper from its custom-made sheath. The large sickle-shaped weapon with both its inner- and outer-crescents sharpened was unique amongst the world's fine straight edges.

"Weapons already?" the killer/guitarist said. "No talk?"

"We'll talk." She scanned the trees, searching for an ambush. Light and shadow sprinkled the ground. He had picked this spot for a reason. "You killed two people before I could talk with them. Why?"

"It's my job. Why else?"

She saw movement off to the right — just a bird. The guitarist grinned as he pulled a sleek, balanced sword from the neck of his guitar. Sunlight glinted off its clean blade. "You want to kill me for those I killed?"

"I want to know who hired you."

He chuckled. "I can't tell you that."

"The two people you murdered had information for me."

"I imagine so. I was told to kill them before they could speak with you."

So it hadn't been a coincidence. Her body slipped from cautiousness to warrior with nothing more than a shift of her foot. Her grip on Viper tightened as anger heated her chest. Her senses grabbed every detail — the rustle of the leaves, the movement of his blade, the uneven macadam, the broken branches, the sweat trickling down his neck, the sun baking the earth.

With a sadistic grin, the guitarist pointed to the left edge of the forest. "Come out, boy," he said, his voice losing all of its playful tone.

Malja's anger boiled hotter. A lanky, twelve-year-old took three furtive steps into the clearing. He had scraggly blond hair and misfit clothes. *Tommy*. Malja had told him to stay at their camp.

"Doesn't look much like you," the guitarist said.

Now she saw why he had picked this place. He knew the boy had followed them, and he thought she was the mother. He had traveled such an odd, circuitous route in order to force Tommy's position — too far away for Malja's protection.

She glanced at Tommy. Despite the hot sun, he was shivering. She studied the guitarist, searching for the flicker of motion that gave an enemy away — a twitch of the shoulder, a change in attention, a lowering of the body. When she saw it, she knew he was about to attack the boy.

Like two wolves smelling the same meal, Malja and the guitarist broke into sprints to reach Tommy. Her straight black hair, braided to the middle of her back, slapped left and right. The thick heat made the run brutal. Malja's legs pumped hard only to travel a short way. Everything in her felt slow and labored while the guitarist appeared to glide through the grass.

Tommy stood his ground.

He thinks I'll get to him first, but he's wrong. Breathing in dust and heat, Malja found enough air to yell once, "Tommy!"

Her urgency cut through his confidence. Recognizing his miscalculation, he dashed towards her. Too late. He only managed a few steps. The guitarist grabbed his arm, yanked him close, and put the sword against his neck.

Tommy grunted and kicked, but the guitarist had a firm grip. Malja rushed up and snapped into a fighting stance. Tommy saw this and became still — quiet and cold. To Malja's surprise, his eyes dropped to the lightning arc tattoo on his forearm.

No, don't do that. "I'd love to kill you," the guitarist said, dripping sweat.

"Let the boy go, and you can give it a try."

"Not my orders, sadly, and I must follow my orders." Honest regret flashed across the man's face. "Of course, if you really are who you say — *the* Malja — well, maybe I ought to bend the rules a little."

Don't, Tommy. I can handle this.

The guitarist readjusted his hold on Tommy, breaking the boy's concentration for a moment. A chilling sparkle lit in the guitarist's eye. "Y'know, if you really are her, then I know how to get you what you're after. Or should I say *who* you're after, hmm?"

No matter how much she wished otherwise, Malja's shock raced through her like a feverish disease. "You lie," she finally managed.

The guitarist shook his head with patronizing mirth. "You're looking to find two magicians. Brothers. Go by the name of Jarik and Callib."

Malja's chest constricted. "Anybody who knows even a little about me knows I'm going to kill those bastards."

"Not a very nice thing to call your fathers."

"I can think of a lot worse to call them. They ripped me from my mother's arms, taught me only to fight, and then tossed me away because I didn't turn out like they wanted. Left me in the woods to die. I was ten." Tommy would be ready anytime now. If he succeeded, she would have no choice but to strike. "Now tell me what you know or die."

"An empty threat while I have the boy."

"Never made an empty threat in my life."

With amusement, the guitarist weighed her words. "Perhaps I've said too much. Let's end this in the best way possible. We each go off on our own. You can go back to your camp, and I'll go a different direction. I'll send the boy when I'm safe. Then you —"

A ball of crackling electricity appeared before the guitarist. *No, not yet,* she thought as the guitarist stared, befuddled by its sudden formation. Angry understanding gradually creased his forehead. He looked at Tommy.

Before he could slash the boy's neck, the entire electric ball blasted into the guitarist. Violent shaking sent him a few steps backwards, throwing Tommy aside. Malja wanted to rush to Tommy — his body shook as well — but she could do nothing for him. The guitarist, however — with him she could do plenty.

She struck fast like another ball of electricity. Cutting upward from the knee, out across the forearm, and back through the neck. Three distinct cuts in one fluid maneuver as she stepped forward. She finished a pace beyond the guitarist and listened like an animal expecting another attack. Only when she heard his body slush to the ground in several pieces could she relax.

With careful, controlled motions, she removed a stained cloth from her pocket and wiped Viper. Her pulse calmed as she cleaned. When she finished with the cloth, she pulled out an apple.

Malja loved apples. She had grown up eating them and for her, they were the perfect food. Her blade was perfect, too. It needed to be sharpened and oiled but it did the job, slicing more people than she dared to think about. Easier to think about apples. Each bite calmed her, brought her back from the animal she had just been.

She tossed the core aside, spun Viper and settled the blade in its special sheath. She walked over to Tommy who sat in the grass playing with a rock.

"You okay?" she asked.

Tommy squinted against the sun, tapped his chest twice, and brought his hand to his forehead — a military salute. A brave face, but Malja caught the tremors in his hands. She also saw the tattoo on his arm. She often tried to forget that Tommy was a magician. Most of the time, she only saw a sweet boy who had suffered at the world's callousness. But when she glimpsed that tattoo, she glimpsed the other side of him.

Magicians bore one tattoo for each spell they mastered, using it as a focal point. Some said the magic came from the tattoo itself. If that was true, then Tommy could never be rid of it. Under her scrutiny, he rolled his sleeve down.

"Don't do that again," she said. "If he had realized you were conjuring, he would've killed you. He almost did."

Flashing a cute smile, Tommy pointed to Malja.

"You can't know I'll win. I make mistakes."

Tommy popped to his feet and skipped toward the body. Even after caring for the boy over several months, Malja found some of his behaviors disturbing. Maybe because of his abusive past, maybe because of his magician blood, maybe because he needed her protection — whatever the reason, he seemed to find comfort in her violence.

As she approached the dead guitarist, Tommy motioned for her attention. He held up the old acoustic and pointed to the pick guard. The word *Bluesman* had been etched in with a graceful hand.

"Means nothing to me. And don't think you're forgiven. No more magic. Understand?"

Tommy saluted, but his body language said he doubted her.

To hide her frustration, she inspected the body pieces. The first thing to strike her was the suit. This close up, she saw that it had been well made and well cared for — looked almost new if not for being slashed to pieces and soaked in blood. Nobody made clothes like this anymore.

Long ago, centuries maybe, before the Devastation, everybody wore such suits. The world thrived under the spell of success and civilization. Magicians provided unlimited energy, bountiful harvests, and all the raw power needed to fuel industry and technology. But some magicians grew too powerful. They abused their magic, striving to dominate people instead of helping society, seeking the secrets that might turn them into gods. And the Devastation leveled it all, casting the people into generations of scavengers and survivors. Yet another gift of the magicians.

The guitarist might have found scraps of a suit in one of the many city ruins, but a well-tailored, crisp and clean one? That stretched reality too far. Yet here he lay. The only answer she could think of was magic. But magic supposedly only worked in the natural realms. A magician could conjure a cotton plant or a herd of wooly torsles to sheer, but someone would still have to turn it all into cloth and tailor the suit.

Then again, Jarik and Callib had conjured her assault suit, and without a doubt, it was magic. She had worn it from her earliest memory — it grew with her, always conforming to her changing body. It stayed cool in the heat of Krysstaprime and warm in the icy rains of Korstraprime. It allowed her to move free and smooth.

"Look at this," she said, spreading open the Bluesman's coat. Tucked in his waistband, Malja found a small handgun — a relic from before the Devastation. Finding ammunition would be challenging, but in the right hands, a well-placed shot could end a fight very fast. The gun had a clean barrel and a wooden body with a minor crack down the side — and no trigger. That's why he didn't use it.

Malja considered pocketing the find. However, experience told her the weapon would never work well again. She'd be better off having one made from scratch, except no one did that. The magicians had made them. Like so many other secrets, the Devastation took that art as well.

"This man," she said, "was an assassin with a suit that could only have been conjured, and the only magicians I know who can do that are Jarik and Callib. So they hire him, kill off my way of finding them, but don't kill me? Maybe they have some feelings for me after all." Tommy grunted and shook his head. "No? Because they don't need to hire an assassin. So, who would hire this man?"

Tommy pulled his hand from the Bluesman's inside pocket. He held up a gold coin for Malja to see. On either side, the same name had been engraved — NOLAN.

Malja let out a disappointed sigh. "Wonderful."

Chapter 2

After the morning's excitement, neither Malja nor Tommy wanted to trek farther through the forest. They silently decided to take the rest of the day off in front of their campfire. Tommy played with some sticks, watched birds, and tended the fire. Malja pulled a tattered book from her pack and settled down to read.

Though just a torn cover and eight pages remained (numbered 127-134), the book never failed to capture Malja's imagination. It was called *Astronomical Wonders*. A two-page spread sat in the middle of the text, diagramming the solar system. The book explained that the stars in the night sky were actually enormous fireballs, and that people lived on a planet that circled one such fireball. Their planet, Geth, was second from their star and one of only four in the system, but that every star had planets.

Malja peered up into the night. As much as she believed the book to be true — it matched what she had been taught growing up — she found it difficult to comprehend. Corlin was only one of five large countries in the world, and if Geth could be big enough to hold five countries, why couldn't the universe be as big as the book suggested?

She put the book away. It made her feel small and insignificant. On some days that was a good thing. But not when she killed. She didn't want to think that taking the life of another meant so little.

From her pocket, she pulled out the Nolan coin. As the hours passed, Malja twirled the gold coin between her fingers.

"Teala Nolan," she said, barely raising an eyebrow from Tommy. She kicked dirt in his direction, startling him. "You almost died today. I don't want you in a situation like that again. Understand? If I choose to confront Nolan—" Tommy cocked his head and grunted. "Okay, when I confront Nolan, it'll be my choice. But you're stuck with me. It's not right for you to be in danger so much because of me. Violence follows me. You don't need that."

Tommy lifted his shirt to reveal the criss-cross pattern of scars left from repeated lashings.

"That's my point. You've already seen enough. Those bastards using you to power their boat, chaining you in that small room ..." She grew quiet as she recalled the blood on the walls, the raging storm, and her decision to save the boy. Shaking off the memory, she said, "I couldn't just leave you there. But I'm no mother, and this is no way to grow up."

Scowling, Tommy strode toward Malja. He snatched the Nolan coin away and began packing their travel gear. Malja closed her eyes for a moment, not sure if she should be thankful or sad.

"For the longest time, I've been on my own. I'm not good at being responsible for another."

Tommy slapped his hands against his sides and frowned. He pointed at her with one finger, at himself with another, and put the fingers together.

"We're a team, huh? A team has to be able to trust. You know I don't want you using magic. It's dangerous, and I can fight fine for myself. So, you want to be a team, you start by listening to the leader. Trusting the leader's decisions. And I'm the leader."

Tommy crossed his arms and produced a familiar scowl. Not only did this mean that he didn't agree with her, but it also added a connotation of *Go ahead, try to live without me. I'll just stand here.*

The boy had courage. Malja gave him that. He could brave the idea of facing Nolan or any threat without a visible hesitation. Moreso, he could stand up to her. And while she wanted to protect him, she had to admit that to survive in this world, one needed to be brave and strong. The safest way for Tommy to achieve that was by her side. Without her, he might get injured or die, and she hadn't gone through all the trouble of saving his life just to let the world rip him apart.

"Okay," she said. "But you listen to your leader."

With a happy double-tap salute, Tommy continued to pack their things.

They stood before the iron gate. Drizzling rain did little to wash away the four grueling days spent hiking to the Nolan mansion. Torches burned in sconces on either side offering little light and less warmth. Four northern konapols growled at them. They were the smaller, domesticated version of the wild konapol, but like their relatives, they had thin gray fur that highlighted toned muscles, powerful front legs, and comical, wrinkled faces that hid vicious teeth. They were like pudgy, old men who would be glad to tear apart anyone dumb enough to cross them. Though tired and grumpy with hunger, Malja forced her mind to remain alert.

As the gate opened, the clanking of old metal died along the muddy ground. One man appeared. A burly fellow wearing a torn tunic adorned with a white sash — an attempted uniform.

"What you want?" he said, clearly unhappy at having to answer a night call in the rain.

Malja held out the coin. The guard squinted, harrumphed, and headed away. He herded the northern konapols into two cages.

"Come on," he yelled over his shoulder. "I ain't gonna carry ya."

As they entered the grounds, Malja observed closely — marking exits and ambush points. Everywhere her eyes fell, she saw the simple miracles of civilization that the world had lacked since the Devastation. The pathway leading to the house had not been thrown together from scavenged concrete but rather had been meticulously laid with red and brown brick alternating in a subtle yet lovely pattern. Four enormous columns, good for defense, reached from the ground all the way to the overhanging roof three stories above. The foyer did not have the marks of decay and neglect but rather showed the tender care of a house staff working with meticulous pride every day. Even in the huge main room where they waited, claw-shaped sconces buzzed with lightning balls pointing to the employment of magicians — just like in ancient days. They cast a brash, pale light on the stone walls.

Tommy took interest in a marble statue standing in an alcove. Two waterways in the floor trickled small streams down the center of the room, and Tommy hopped over them in several boyish bounces. The statue that had caught his eye depicted a hefty, bald man with a beard reaching to his feet — the Prophet Galot who learned the will of Korstra, brother god of Kryssta, and brought it to the enlightened. Malja knew nothing more of the story. She never had a use for religion.

"That's over two thousand years old," Nolan said, entering the room in a crimson gown as if waiting to host a grand ball. The lines on her face suggested she had been waiting a long time. Though stark and cold in demeanor, she had a disarming, pleasant voice. "My apology for the lack of welcome, but my staff is asleep. They work hard for me, keep this place running and I give them a roof and a full belly. But if I push too hard, they'd probably leave."

"I suspect people would put up with a lot to live here," Malja said.

Clasping her hands together, Ms. Nolan said, "So you're the great

Malja. I half expected flames to burn from your eyes."

"That's a new one. Usually I'm ten-feet tall with the muscles of a betron."

Ms. Nolan's mouth opened in a hideous grin. "Stories of me are equally exaggerated ... mostly. Now, what do you want?"

"I'd like to know why you're trying to have me killed." Malja had not intended to be so blunt, but the old lady had a way about her that opened things up. Magic? Malja wondered. Other than in fairy tales, she had never heard of mind-controlling spells, but few people knew the full extent of magic and its uses.

Ms. Nolan appeared puzzled. "I assure you, I don't wish you dead. I have no reason to."

Malja reached behind her and gripped Viper, but a thought stopped her from pulling the weapon out. Nobody had frisked her. Nobody had even asked her to give up her weapons. Malja found herself, once again, wishing she had listened better to Gregor, her adoptive father. He had tried to teach her about magicians, but at such a young age and having been tossed aside by the bastard magicians Jarik and Callib, Malja had no desire to be educated on that topic.

"Why do you believe I want to kill you?"

Malja held out the Nolan coin. "I found this on the body of your assassin."

"I see," Ms. Nolan said with a distasteful frown. "Follow me, please."

The two women walked through a hall lined with ornate paintings of the Corlin countryside. Tommy flitted around them, never taking his eyes off Malja for too long. This time the attention pleased her — it meant the boy would not notice the open booths built into the walls. She had never seen a focus booth before but had heard about them in every starving town she visited.

Before the Devastation, wealthy people owned private collections of magicians to provide electricity, food, heat, everything. These heartless closets were where the magicians slaved away their days — easy to access by the Masters but out of view to guests. One booth had its door closed. Malja thought Ms. Nolan was about to comment on this, but she closed her mouth while observing Tommy. *She's noticed the tattoo.*

"In here," she said and opened a heavy door carved with the Korstrian symbol — four lines intersecting to form an intricate M. At least, Malja always thought it looked like an M.

Ms. Nolan took one step, stopped, and faced Malja with a look of concern more unnerving than her contorted grin. "We call this the Dry Room. Perhaps," she said, tapping her lips like a worried grandmother, "the boy should wait out here."

"He goes with me."

"I understand; however, in this room—"

"He goes with me," Malja said, her patience dying.

"Very well."

As Malja entered, she saw the horrible reason Ms. Nolan wanted Tommy outside. An emaciated woman clung to the thick, wooden bars of a cage. The cage, shaped like an enormous egg, had wooden spikes pointing in and out — the woman could not escape and nobody could help her. Madness drenched her. She howled as if calling the moon and followed the mournful sound with an abrasive cough. She tore a strip of gray cloth from her shredded dress and coughed mucous into it. When she attempted to reach through the bars, Malja saw the tattoo — a bluish swirling like the wind blowing through clouds or a tide splashing the rocks.

Malja glanced down at Tommy. He spied the woman from behind Malja — curious, but scared. Not for the first time, she wondered how old he really was. Based on his height, the little bit of fuzz on his upper lip, and his odor, she placed him at twelve, on the cusp of puberty. His reactions, though, ranged from the cold pragmatism of a seasoned warrior to the trembling fear of an abused child. The latter appeared to be winning out now.

"Enough," Malja said, her firmness snapping Tommy from his fear as well as re-focusing her own purpose. "Tell me why you sent that man, or I'll just kill you and forget about it all."

"Do you solve all your problems by killing?"

Malja held still. The question had plagued her thoughts for some time now. She hated killing. She believed that. Each time she cut open an enemy, part of her became less than before, made her smaller. Yet, if she wanted to be honest, killing did solve a lot of her problems. She often eased her worries by remembering that violence ruled the world around her. No governments. No laws. She killed to survive.

Ms. Nolan walked to the cage with an arrogant stride, but stopped just shy of the madwoman's reach. Speaking firmly but in a calm, controlled tone — a warrior's tone used to command but not agitate — she said, "I didn't hire anyone to kill you."

"This coin calls you a liar."

"No, it calls you naïve. Do you think I'm stupid? Why would I pay an assassin with a coin that identifies me?"

"You think someone wanted me to think it was you?"

For a breath, Ms. Nolan's eyes lost focus as if she had lost herself in some indulgent memory. With a sudden sadness, she said, "I wish you were right, but I think the answer is less tricky. The coin was the mark, the assignment. The killer was sent to kill me. You just got in the way."

Malja shook her head. "He was assigned to kill certain people before I could speak with them. But I had no reason to seek you out."

"Maybe not yet."

"I don't understand."

Ms. Nolan pointed to the cage. "That shadow of a woman in there was ... is ... my sister. Audrex was born two years to the day after me." Ms. Nolan paused, and Malja had the presence to wait quietly. From the side, she saw Tommy had the presence, too. "My sister was the wild one. She would run through the woods, yelling silly words, not worrying about whose attention she might garner. She would pick up a plant or eat a berry without worrying what it was or if it might be harmful. She never seemed to notice the painful lives we all led. We were struggling to survive, and she would play. If there was no food, she would sing a song. If there was no water, she would dance and twirl. And she was beautiful. When she hit her teens, men showered us with gifts — food, clothing, anything. Father had died and her beauty made life easier, so we let it happen. But no matter how generous the bribe, Audrex would only flirt or offer a little kiss. They wanted a wife; they got a memory. That all changed when the magicians came.

"There are so few people in the world now, and they're spread so far apart. If you find a few good ones, you're lucky. But we had a whole town of good people — solid people, real law and order, all Korstrian, no magicians. Blissgar was a good town. Actually built the town ourselves rather than live in the ruins and rubble like so many do. Of course, here in Corlin, too many roving gangs want to destroy such towns. It's safer to be in the ruins. We found that out when a gang of them arrived. Magicians. Yes, I see it in your face. I thought the same thing — magicians don't form gangs. I knew something bigger was at hand. The two leaders stepped forward and declared that Blissgar now belonged to them. Two brothers. You know them."

Malja nodded. "Jarik and Callib."

"No other magicians are so brazen. We resisted, but it was a foolish thing to do. We had no hope of winning. They overpowered us the first day. It only took one week for them to notice Audrex and only one day to seduce her. They were handsome, powerful, and different from everything Blissgar had ever offered her. She willingly became their consort. The idea alone nearly killed Mother. The day she went off with them was the last I saw of her for thirty-four years.

"I went on with my life. What else could I do? I thought of her all the time, but it became like a mourning period, like I had to accept that she was dead. A few years later, I married Ven Nolan. We tried to consolidate the towns in the area — form a government, but there were never enough people. Still, my husband was respected and we ran several farms. When he died, I took control.

"Then, as the Korstraprime rains fell, she appeared at my door — changed. It's been hard. The cage protects her and us. But it's hard."

Audrex prowled her cage and stared at her tattoos. Whatever her magic needed, the cage kept her from it. Malja tensed as a thought hit her with frightening force. "Magic ability is a family trait."

"And yet I'm not a magician." Ms. Nolan shuddered. As she spoke on, her voice cracked. "Nor were my parents. Nor our grandparents. That's why she's insane. They stole her from me and did Korstra alone knows to turn her into a magician. But we are what we are born to. It can't be changed."

"So they threw her aside," Malja said as the coals in her heart burned.

Nolan's eyes dropped to Tommy. "Your boy is a magician. Be careful around him."

"He's not like that."

"Not yet. But every magician is unique in how much talent they possess. He has one spell now. But as he grows older, if he learns more, well, magic takes its toll."

Malja knew that price. She had seen it first hand in Jarik and Callib. Each time a magician cast a spell, it ate away at the brain. Little by little. The more powerful spells took away more of a magician's sanity. The weakest magicians, the ones that could only create electricity, became feeble old men and women lost in delirium. The strongest magicians ended up mad long before they became old. That madness had led to the lunatic thoughts that brought on the Devastation. It led to two brothers stealing a little girl.

Malja glanced down at Tommy. *He's not like that.* Besides, if he doesn't use his magic, he won't suffer any damage.

With a sharp, cleansing breath, Ms. Nolan stepped away from her sister. "Your assassin tried to cut off a trail you have followed and his next target was me. If my information is correct, and it is, you seek Jarik and Callib. I can help."

"Then help."

"I want a promise, first. Promise me that whatever you do to them, promise me you'll make them suffer extra for Audrex."

Malja bared her teeth. "With pleasure."

Chapter 3

Tommy clutched the saddle's pommel as they headed west through the forest. His tense heartbeat pattered against Malja's skin. She had tried letting him ride in back of her, wrapping his arms tight around her waist, but he near-wet himself. His anxiety subsided only slightly when seated in front, protected by her arms. How anyone could grow up not knowing how to ride a horse — never mind absolute terror of the experience — baffled her. Then again, a slave on a thief's boat had little call for horsemanship.

The chestnut quarter horse Ms. Nolan had supplied (Orla was its name, but Malja tried not to put names to horses — they never lasted long around her) did not react to Tommy's fear, although Malja swore the animal took care to provide a smoother ride than usual. She just hoped they wouldn't need to gallop. Tommy would have a heart attack.

The morning air smelled crisp as the sun poked through the trees. Already the heat rose, and Malja wondered how long the horse could endure. Later the air would be stifling. The horse better hold out. Ms. Nolan gave the impression that time mattered in this case.

Fawbry, she had said, was a minor nuisance in Terrgar. All the surrounding towns belonged to Ms. Nolan (according to her), but Terrgar remained a dark hole on her map. It caused problems getting supplies to the far-end towns, caused problems with communications, and caused problems forming a solid front to her greater enemies in the western countries. Allowing Fawbry to continue to disrupt her holdings or escalate his activities invited an attack.

"Fawbry knows who you need to see. Bring him to me, and I'll get the information you want," Ms. Nolan had said.

The politics didn't matter to Malja. Warlords, politicians, businessmen, magicians — all the same. They sought to rule over others using the laws of people as tools for their personal advancement. They hid beneath lofty ideals and utopian promises they never intended to keep. Or they simply bullied their way from behind a sword. Malja had no use for it. Anarchy worked just fine.

They camped in the shade of a fractured bridge. Half the bridge spanned the far side of a dry bed. The other half was a mere skeleton. Its concrete pillars rose to hold up nothing like musicians standing on stage without their instruments — awkward and wrong.

Malja let the heat of their campfire soothe her weariness. Tommy nestled by her leg, wrapping his arms around her calf and resting his head on her knee. With a tentative touch, she stroked his hair, recalling the first time he had hugged her knee — the night she rescued him. It was such a simple act of affection, the very act that had won her over, yet she found it difficult to reciprocate more than her gentle touch on his hair.

Like horses, people didn't stay with her long. If she managed to keep Tommy alive long enough to become an adult, she expected him to go off for a life of his own. She couldn't expect him to stay. And she refused to force him to be what she wanted — that was Jarik and Callib's way.

Before she could spiral down into blistering memories, Malja cleared her thoughts with several deep breaths. She watched Tommy's hair trickle through her fingers. She listened to his slumber. She fought off all other concerns until an hour later, she fell asleep.

After another day traveling, Tommy had relaxed a little around the horse. By the time they reached Noograff, he could act like he had been born riding. But it was an act. He put on a brave face for the townspeople, yet Malja felt his tensed muscles clinging to the saddle.

The town of Noograff looked like many towns Malja had seen. An amalgam of single-story buildings cobbled together with materials from the nearest ruins. Rock, wood, and concrete chunks formed the foundation of materials. Old pavement, metal bars and pipes, and sharp bits of glass were more typical for extravagant homes. Noograff appeared to be more foundation and less extravagant.

The two roads were dirt with the odd bit of macadam poking through. Food and labor seasoned the air with a savory, rich aroma. Two wells marked sources of healthy water. To Malja — all signs of hearty, honest folk who understood these wild lands.

Good, she thought. She wanted to be around people that made sense.

She had heard rumors about the North countries that they had many carpenters and stoneworkers. They had towns cleared of the ruins and even a city or two. But those lands were elsewhere and they were governed. She preferred these towns. What they lacked in beauty they made up for in heart.

When they reached the main road through town, Malja's initial assessment faltered. A crowd of forty men and women congregated in the road. Many were absent limbs. Some bore deep scars and one woman had lost a chunk of her left ear. They carried makeshift weapons and sweated under makeshift armor. Some wore animal hides and others wore stained and patched clothing from long ago. Everyone wore something bright yellow around the head, arm, or neck. Despite their roughened exteriors, they looked like children playing at war.

Standing on a table made from a door laid across four large rocks, a heavy-set man with salt-and-pepper hair spoke to the exuberant crowd. In one hand, he waved a pearl-grip handgun. In the other, he clutched a yellow cloth. "I say it is enough that we struggle to eat, it is enough that we labor our meager fields. Why should we pay this scoundrel, too?" The townspeople roared their agreement. "This isn't our first time facing some idiot that thinks we'll be easy to bully. Nor is it our second or even our third. Warlords come and go. We've faced them, fought them, and in the end, we remain. What makes this different—" The crowd roared and hooted again. "What makes this different, what makes this unique, is that for the first time we will bring the battle to them. We will not wait for the evils of the world to pick upon us, to try to tear us apart. We will not watch our children shiver with the fear of what might come our way. No. We will take on the evil where it lives. And when we're done, Mayor Fawbry and all his ilk will never bother the town of Noograff again!" The loudest explosions of support erupted complete with the banging of swords, stamping of feet, and fluttering of yellow.

Malja had seen plenty of armies do the same. She had even stood before a few, spouting similar lines about how great they were and how righteous their cause. In the end, blood flowed the same color.

The heavy man paused in his speech and squinted toward Malja. "You there. You've picked the wrong day to visit."

"I'm passing through, but I think I can help you."

"Help us? Why would the mother of a young boy want to help fight with strangers?"

"Ms. Nolan has sent me after Mayor Fawbry."

All eyes were on Malja and Tommy. The faces were firm but not threatening — not yet. The man on the table made a show of his confusion. "Don't know any Nolan, and we don't want your help."

Damn. Ms. Nolan's power had appeared authentic, but obviously she claimed more than she truly held. That clouded the matter of

Mayor Fawbry. If Ms. Nolan's claim of information turned out to be a lie, Viper would make her pay.

"Go away," the man said. "Pass through tomorrow."

With one hand, Malja eased Tommy to the ground. He didn't want to let go at first, but Malja shook him off. Pouting, he scampered to the side as she urged the horse forward.

"My name is Malja," she said, noting the stunned look on a few faces. "Those who know of me, know that I am an army within myself. We have a common enemy today. I will be in Terrgar. I will fight to get to the Mayor. There is no changing that. The question you face is whether to fight with me or to get in my way."

The man scanned the crowd. Malja felt his confidence drain away like snow melting in her hands. "Y-You're a liar," he said. "You could be anybody. You could be one of Fawbry's people. Prove you're Malja."

"No."

The man waited for her to say more, to justify her refusal, but the longer he waited, the stronger she became. She sensed the shift as it rippled behind her. A lackey of the enemy would stage some kind of display in order to prove herself. The angry crowd understood that Malja would do what she said, that only the real Malja would attack a town by herself, that they had no choice.

"I'm Pressig," the man said, trying to regain some ground through bluster. "You may join us, but do not impede us or you'll be brought before our judges."

Malja smirked. "Nice to see a town with some laws."

Pressig frowned, unsure if she mocked them. A second later, with smooth political ease, he broke into thick laughter. The townspeople followed suit, and Malja withstood the onslaught of merriment like a small animal caught in a storm. Another wave of yellow followed and more hollers. When they finished, Pressig raised his hands and said, "We have an ally, and that's good. But the battle still waits. Get what you can. Prepare your hearts and souls. We leave at second bell."

The town rushed to life as everyone handled their final business before war — providing for loved ones in case the worst happened and saying goodbye. Though she knew Tommy could take care of himself, Malja arranged for Pressig's wife to look after him. This act would gain Pressig's trust more than any display — she had given him a hostage.

Pressig's wife took the boy's hand with a melancholy nod. The woman's eyes spoke of deep sadness, and Malja suspected she had lost a child awhile back. It was common enough. Tommy brought a slight smile to her face that surprised Pressig enough to stare slack-jawed for a moment.

Nearby a small group of Korstrians knelt in a circle. One chanted a prayer and the rest bowed until their heads touched. The Kryssta followers were, no doubt, off alone praying in a quiet corner.

As Malja prepped her horse, she listened to the droning chants. She failed to see how people could think a little singing would influence the world, but she did like the rumbling of the sound. It seemed to soothe her horse, too.

When the second bell rang, warm goodbyes turned into passionate cries. Weeping and arguing snaked through the town. She helped Pressig gather people up, forcing them from their families, reminding them of the reason for the battle. Malja had expected this — she'd seen it before. She did not expect, however, to see Tommy astride her horse.

"You're not coming," she said, gritting at the parental tone she heard coming from her mouth.

Tommy pointed to the amassing force.

"No."

He made a muscle and when that failed to impress, he pulled back his sleeve and pointed to the tattoo.

"Absolutely not," she said in a low growl. "You don't understand anything about this, and I don't want you to start. You will stay here, and I'll come back for you. Now get off that horse."

With a dirty look, he climbed down. He lifted a defiant chin and crossed his arms.

She drew upon all her will not to shout at the boy. "Stay here. If you disobey me this time, if you come after me—"

She didn't have to finish. Tommy rushed towards her and gave a short hug. She stiffened at the embrace but also warmed inside. Something told her she should kiss the top of his head, but she held back. Thankfully, he did not cry.

Later, astride her horse and moving with the small force, she hoped Tommy believed she would come back. She should have been gentler with him; however, things had been moving too fast. That was her life. Always too fast. Except if she wanted to be honest, she preferred the fast pace. The slow times, like marching hill after hill towards battle, these were the times she dreaded — stuck with only her thoughts and the faces of those she had killed.

Paying them their honor, Gregor had called it.

Ever since he found her alone and half-wild in the woods, he wanted her to slow down, to think about the lives she touched, to consider her place in the world. Most mornings he would wake early in their two-room shack, take a walk amongst the pines, and pick a choice vegetable from their small garden. He'd prepare breakfast while she set the table or played war with her doll (its left leg missing), and he would talk in his rich, booming voice. She didn't understand back then, but these morning talks were his way of sneaking in an education — a little history, a lot of agriculture, some math and reading, and endless discussions of philosophy.

"You're a tough girl," he said while cracking a korkor egg he had filched from a nearby nest. "You've already been through more than many seasoned soldiers experience in a lifetime." She could hear his concern, but also detected a touch of pride. "So I want you to learn something right now. You may not understand it all today, but you learn it, you remember it, and that'll be enough."

"Okay, Uncle Gregor," she said, setting her doll on the wood-plank floor.

"This is a dangerous world," Gregor said, chopping the onion he had picked and tossing it in with the eggs. "It's a violent world. With what those bastard magicians did to you, I don't think you can expect a quiet life. But that doesn't mean you've got to embrace it either. It doesn't mean you've got to find pleasure in killing. If you do that, you may well lose your soul. I don't want that to happen. So when you kill, I want you to remember to pay them their honor. Anything living that falls at your hand — good, evil, whatever — anything once living deserves at least a moment of thought — calm, peaceful, sincere thought. Pay them their honor, sweetheart, and you'll find the dead won't haunt your dreams."

But it wasn't her dreams that troubled her. It was the quiet moments with nothing to occupy her mind that brought back the ghosts. Thankfully, her most recent kill, the Bluesman, didn't trouble her. She could honor his skill and gracefulness without guilt. However, thinking of those she had failed to save — the Bluesman's victims who died because of her — these ghosts haunted her thoughts like stingbeetles swarming over their disturbed nest.

And then there was Tommy. She could still smell the brine that tainted every inch of that thief's ship. Brine and blood. She felt the storming sea roll her stomach one more time, and she heard the begging as she pressed her foot down, sending the ship's captain under.

He had been an bestial man who had harmed Tommy for no other purpose than turning the boy into a battery. But no death could be worse than drowning. The slow helplessness of it.

At the front of the line, Pressig raised his hand and everyone halted. He gestured for Malja. Before them, a wide hill rose. "Other side of that," Pressig said, "is Terrgar. Any suggestions on the best way to do this?"

"You don't have a plan of attack?" Malja whispered so as not to worry the tired men and women — calling them *troops* did not feel right to her.

"To be honest, I didn't think it'd get this far. We're just a bunch of farmers. I knew people were mad, but this is more than I expected. I thought I'd stir up their anger and we'd, I don't know, protest. Maybe get a little something."

"And then what? They'd elect you to run the town? Give you a stupid title like Mayor or Duke? I once met a fool who called himself President. Is that what you want?"

At least Pressig had the brains to look ashamed. "Please believe me, I care about these people. I don't want them hurt. I was going to call the attack off. I was. Except you showed up, and then it all just, sort of, happened. I guess I thought with you, maybe we'd actually win."

With the disapproval of a parent forced to clean up her child's mess, she said, "Stay here. Order your people to rest. I'll scout and when I get back, I'll have a plan."

"Oh, thank you. Thank you so much."

"Stop it. Act like you're in control or you'll lose them."

"Right," he said, regaining his composure.

"Does that thing work?" She pointed to the handgun.

"Not even if it had bullets." He turned away, and as Malja headed up the hill, she heard him barking out commands.

Near the crest, Malja tethered her horse to an oak and crawled on her belly to get a closer look. She pulled out her spyglass — a reward she had taken from a pompous fool in the Freelands. He had thought magicians conjured the object. She knew better. It bore the marks of being hand-made — the imperfections and artistic flourishes of a craftsman at work. However, since the spyglass came from the ruins of a pre-Devastation town, she would have to admit that, at the least, magic-powered tools may have played a part in its creation.

Peering through the cracked eyepiece, Malja gazed upon Terrgar — empty Terrgar. A few barricades had been erected at the obvious entry points and sniper nests had been set up in the two tallest buildings. But no people manned either location. Four main roads wound through the town to form a large square in the center. There she spied a crude throne atop a mountain of rubble. A man sat on the throne — presumably, Mayor Fawbry. Twelve griffle guards surrounded the rubble pile, each armed with a sword, pike, or an improvised weapon.

Griffles were once human. The Devastation had destroyed more than just the land. The mutations to the living were numerous. Those who survived often did so because their mutations provided advantages in such a harsh world. For the griffles, this meant strength and speed. They were short, muscular, and ugly — mottled skin, stringy hair, and flattened faces. Fawbry must have hired them cheap — griffles weren't known for their brains.

One griffle, though, looked oddly small. The runt of the litter. It had little tufts of white hair growing from its joints and it followed Fawbry's every step. She even watched it climb upon his back. He must have a serious hold on the griffles if they allow one of their own, even the runt, to be treated like a pet.

None of this posed a problem, though. The problem sat a few sword-lengths in front of the griffles and the Mayor. Two oxters. Large, brown beasts with four muscular legs — excellent for farm work except for the forked tail lined with poisonous barbs. Usually the poison glands were removed at birth. Malja suspected that was not the case with these two. Their faces were smudged, bumpy things like the patterns in a muddy footprint. Just to make matters more interesting these oxters were female — highly aggressive and armed with two sharp horns curving out of the snout. They struggled against thick chains.

By the time Malja returned to the group, the situation had worsened. Half of Pressig's mini-armed force had run off. Those remaining looked as if they just waited for an excuse to leave with a clear conscience. Two angry oxters could rip them apart with ease. She needed a better plan than relying on numbers.

With a resigned sigh, she nodded to herself. Deep within, she had known her real plan all along. The sight of the oxters made her wish for another route, but so be it.

"Look here," she said. She didn't need to. All eyes already watched her. "I am a true warrior, and a true warrior walks the path of death. When I set out for this Mayor, I did not expect you people. So, I have a plan, and I want you to do as I say. Follow me, and I might live another day. I assure you, though, you all will."

Pressig frowned. "I don't understand. What's your plan?"

"There are two oxters protecting the Mayor." Before the worried moans died down, she raised her voice. "I'll handle them alone."

Chapter 4

When it came to fighting, Malja preferred it this way — alone. She had hoped to convince Pressig's people to provide support, but after learning of the oxters, they just wanted to crawl home. Fine by her. They would've been a hindrance. It was better this way. No concerns but for her own skin. It felt good for a change.

A long time had passed since she traveled without another. Though she enjoyed Tommy's quiet companionship, she also worried about him whenever danger threatened. She told herself not to — after all, she had been two years younger than him when she had to survive on her own in the wild. And she couldn't defend him all the time. He had to learn to survive. That's why she left him back in town. Still, walking along Terrgar's empty streets, only having to care about herself — the corners of her lips raised a fraction.

As she came closer to the town's center, a strange tingling crossed her skin. At first, she thought of it as anticipation, but each dirt-crunching step dispelled this idea. It hit her like a sudden blast of air — the town was empty. Not just of people, she had expected that, but empty of all signs of life.

Terrgar had been built among the ruins of an ancient town, yet no sign of rebirth existed. Broken doorways rotted. Burned-out windows sagged. The remnants of grounders and flyers, transports that once ran on magical power, rusted under the elements. She had seen more evidence of life in the desolate Freelands. That thought resonated strong — this Mayor was little more than a failed Freelands warlord. He had no town here. He had no base of power. He only had his griffle guards and his oxters. He just wanted to bully the weak for easy food or women or whatever pleased him.

As she approached the town square, she heard an oxter bellow its deep, croaking moan. Malja unsheathed Viper and cleared her mind. She kept expecting an ambush from the empty buildings, kept expecting her assumptions to be wrong, but nothing challenged her progress. The shadows remained dark and empty. Nothing dared to pop out at her. She didn't even need to look for an escape route (not that she expected to use one) because every direction provided escape. Of course, that meant that every route could also be used to attack. Further proof that Mayor Fawbry had no tactical sense at all, that he was just a fool making a pompous stand.

She stopped at the square's edge. The animals' musty odors reminded her of mucking out Gregor's stables. A cool breeze blew by — a cue of the changing season, the passing time, the need to find Jarik and Callib.

From atop his throne, Mayor Fawbry said, "Are you serious? This is all they're sending? One little woman?"

"I'm not from Noogruff," Malja called back.

Fawbry sat forward and the runt griffle peeked over his shoulder. "Oh, really? Then what do you want?"

Attempting the most businesslike posture she could manage while still holding Viper, she said, "Ms. Nolan would like to speak with you at her residence."

Fawbry stroked his wiry, unkempt hair like a crazed teacher. He wore a tattered but colorful robe that rippled as he paced. "You hear that, Tufts? Ms. Nolan would like me to visit her? Well, Ms. Nolan can rot," he said and Tufts let out a high-pitched laugh. "I'm not leaving here."

At least he knows her. With a shrug, Malja said, "Then I'll have to come up and get you."

One griffle, stockier than the rest and wearing a breastplate (really a piece of metal with the faded words THE BEST DRINK painted sideways), broke ranks and whispered to Fawbry. Fawbry's face dropped as he shook his head. The griffle pushed Fawbry toward the ground. The other griffles stayed silent and Tufts scurried to hide amongst the ranks.

Fawbry protested once more, but the griffle growled and pointed off to a red-brick building. Fawbry nodded as if it hurt his heart. Satisfied, the griffle returned to his place in line as Fawbry stood and brushed off his robe.

"Go away. Tell Nolan I'm not interested," he said, and Malja swore she heard pleading in his voice.

"I can't go without you."

Fawbry's shoulders drooped as he let out a dismayed breath. Two griffles emerged from the red-brick building, leading two men and a woman — all three were bound and wore square cloths covering their faces, each secured with coarse twine. They were lowered to their knees.

A sickly quiet overtook the square. As if to shut out the world, Fawbry closed his eyes. The griffle who appeared to be in charge, Drink, stepped out once more and walked toward the condemned. The soft clicking of his armor echoed across the open square. He slid out his sword.

Too far away to strike, Malja could think of only one thing to do. She shouted. "Hey. Moron. Oh my, look. The squat griffle is going to be tough killing defenseless people."

Drink watched her. She couldn't be sure he understood her words, but he clearly comprehended her tone. "Poor baby. Did I make you feel sad?"

Some of those in line snickered. The stocky griffle snarled at them. They quieted down. With a snort as if to say, "Watch this," he broke into a full-on charge at Malja.

She stood ready with giddiness. Drink closed in and swung his sword. Malja met the clumsy attack, locking his blade in Viper's crescent. As he strained to free it, Malja kicked his kneecap. She heard the bone crunch. He fell to the street, his sword clattered next to him, and Malja sliced open his belly.

"Is that it?" she asked to the stunned enemy on the mound.

Tufts climbed Fawbry's robe and shivered on his back. Fawbry's eyes shared the same fear. One of Fawbry's griffle guards stepped forward. With a stoic face, he raised his blade and brought it down on the chains that kept the oxters at bay.

"No," Fawbry said, panic edging into his voice, but nobody listened.

It took the guard four sparking hits, but the chains broke. Like dogs let out of a kennel, the two beasts stampeded towards Malja.

She could never withstand such a blow, so holding her ground was not an option. Instead, she brandished Viper, let out a fierce battle cry, and charged. She had hoped to startle them. Such a move might have confused a human, but the raging animals stayed their course. As they neared Malja, they lowered their snouts, positioning their horns at deadly angles.

Malja sprinted on, the adrenaline rush boosting her speed. She could feel the thunderous vibrations of the beasts trampling the ground. She heard the griffles cheer and holler from the safety of their rubble mound. She focused on the oxters' legs. Timing would be crucial. She blocked out all distractions as she closed in. The moment had come.

Malja slid low.

One oxter had lifted its head, expecting her to vault upward. The other had barreled forward. Neither anticipated her sliding underneath.

Malja's assault suit eased the friction with the street, letting her slide as if on ice. She resisted the urge to cut the oxters open from below. She couldn't risk one of the enormous beasts collapsing and clipping her in the head as it fell. She popped to her feet behind them and dashed to the right.

The oxters spun, croaked their anger, regrouped, and observed her while hissing and displaying their yellow-black teeth. She moved fast, trying to keep one oxter between her and the other at all times. This way she only had a single opponent to deal with directly, and the other oxter had to work hard to get around its peer — exhausting work that Malja planned to take advantage of later. *If I make it that far.* The oxters, however, had other plans.

The one in the back, the one Malja now noticed had a red rash around its eyes, shot straight ahead, planted its forelegs on the other's haunches, and leapt over its head. It swiped at Malja as it landed, connected with her shoulder, and threw her into a pile of bricks.

Which hurt more — the beast's blow or the bricks — she couldn't tell. Both just hurt and made her angry. She scrambled back to her feet and rushed forward, swinging Viper with calculated fervor. Before she could take control of the fight, Red Rash flanked her. She stepped back, parrying horns and claws more than attacking. Each step she tried to reposition for a fairer fight. Frustration and rage played out on the oxters' ugly faces. They wanted to slow her enough for a poisonous tail strike.

From the corner of her eye, she saw Not Red go for a wide swipe meant to finish her. Malja ducked and came up hard, thrusting Viper into its chest. The oxter yelped and yanked back, causing Viper's curved blade to cut more as it ripped out.

Without hesitation, Malja spun to face Red Rash, but the beast had already attacked. She met the blow full on, taking it on her side, and being thrust into more rubble. Not what she had planned, but in battle, improvisation ruled. At this point, Red Rash made a critical mistake — it should have struck with its tail, but first, it glanced at the other oxter. Malja did not want to miss such an opportunity. She rolled to the left, ignoring her bruised side, and positioned behind Red. It attempted to snap her with its tail. Malja sliced it off. Blood and cries erupted. Malja skewered the barbed slice onto Viper, and armed with the poisonous tail, she slammed it into each oxter. In seconds, they moved no more.

Panting as sweat dripped from her face, Malja straightened and tossed the bloody tail aside. Before she could face Fawbry, however, she heard him whimper and protest. Though he garbled his words, she understood — the griffle guards would no longer follow him. They would no longer wait.

They yelled as they charged into battle like a chorus of berserk madmen. Malja sneered, bracing for a tough fight. She did not dream of surviving. She never did in any fight. She thought only of inflicting damage.

They picked up speed and pointed their weapons at her. Malja readied Viper once more and took slow, controlled breaths. Channeling all her rage, she roared at her stampeding enemy.

With only a few steps to go before reaching the killing zone, the guards skidded to a halt. Surprise and perplexed fear covered their monstrous faces as they backed up and staggered away. Malja wanted to laugh. Her battle roar never had such a response before.

Then she heard the tidal wave break behind her. Pressig and his town flooded the square in pursuit of the guards. Pressig glanced over his shoulder and said, "They watched you fight. They wanted to help." He smiled in victory and pressed onward.

A few townspeople rushed over to free the three prisoners. The prisoners stood with the confused joy of those who had accepted the fate of Death — Malja had felt that way many times. She could not be sure if the newly freed people belonged to the town, but she could tell by their effusiveness that they would probably be joining soon.

Malja let her body relax for a few breaths. She looked at Fawbry, alone on his throne, yelling at his abandoning guards, reaching out as Tufts scurried away, and she thought of Jarik and Callib.

The people of Noogruff couldn't hold back their excitement. Three riders galloped ahead to tell the town of their success. By the time Malja, Pressig, and the rest arrived, a full-blown celebration filled the main street.

Fire pits blazed and savory aromas of roasting meat touched every grumbling stomach. Warmed breads and hot vegetables were doled out to every plate. A handful of men and women brought out patched-together instruments and played one raucous tune after another.

Couples danced under torchlight, their bodies shimmering with the flames.

Tommy showered Malja with hugs. She tried not to stiffen up under his affections, but she had no doubt he noticed her discomfort. He broke away and rubbed down her horse. Later, he played with her hair while she ate. This she handled better.

A little girl with straight, blond hair looked up at her with eager eyes and asked to hear the story of the battle. "You don't want to hear that," Malja teased before telling the story to the girl's rapt attention. By the time Malja finished, a crowd of children had formed around her.

"Tell it again!" they shouted, clapping their hands and banging the ground until Malja put down her plate and described the battle once more. She had never enjoyed trading stories with adults — it was just competition — but with children, the experience took on the purity of inspiration.

Tommy sat beside her, beaming with the pride of being her trusted ally. As she finished retelling the story, she decided to help Tommy's status a little more. Though they'd probably never see these people again, he deserved at least one night of fun playing the hero.

"You know Tommy helps me stay sharp, so I'm prepared for whatever threats might come our way," she said to the amazed faces. "We play a game I call The Reflex Game."

"Show us," the kids cried out.

Before Malja said another word, Tommy jumped to his feet and put his hands behind his back. Malja laughed and Tommy gave her a rare, genuine smile.

"Pair off," she said, and the kids rushed around to find their best friends. "Now one person do just like Tommy. The other do as I do." Malja faced Tommy and brought her hands together as if in prayer. The kids followed along. "Tommy's going to try to slap my hand. If he gets me, he keeps going, but if he misses, then we switch and it's my turn to slap his hands. But there are rules. I can only move my hands up or down, and they must stay together all the time. Tommy can try to fake an attack but if his hand comes around enough to be seen, he must follow through. And last, the most important rule — if he fakes a strike, but I react anyway, he gets a free slap. I can only try to evade a real attack. Understand?"

Some of the children launched right into the game. Others appeared to be afraid. Malja looked at them and said, "A warrior must learn to face down a threat and only react to true dangers. Play this game enough, and you'll be on your way to being a great warrior."

The little blonde girl had her hands out and concentrated on her partner's shoulders. "Then we can defend ourselves, right?" she said.

"That's right." Tommy and Malja played a few rounds and soon all the children were giggling, slapping, feigning, and smiling. With a nod, Malja sent Tommy off to play with the others. She returned to her meal, grinning at the playful sounds around her. She swore she even heard a giggle sneak out of Tommy's lips, but when she turned around he was silent. But smiling.

Later, parents broke up the game to send their children to bed. Though there were many complaints, most of the children were tired and some moved with sluggish steps. A few uttered words of thanks before heading home. With his eyes growing too heavy to stay awake, Tommy curled around Malja's knee. Pressig's wife, however, swooped in and carried him to her house.

A handsome, young man climbed onto a table. "Drinks for the victors," he said, raising two frothing jugs in the air.

Malja observed the eager townspeople line up to get drunk on fermented whatever, and she let a new smile drift across her face. She rarely got to see this side of battle. Often while others celebrated, she traveled onward. This time, however, she had little choice. With Tommy asleep in the house and Fawbry locked away, she would have to wait for things to settle down before she could say goodbye.

Besides, she thought, eyeing the young man doling out drinks, *I don't want to leave just yet.*

A rapid-fire giggle soared over the general party noise, and Malja's eyes spotted a young gal being wooed by one of the rescued prisoners. She searched for the others and spotted them standing near the musicians. That suited her fine. It was interesting, maybe even pleasant, to see everyone so happy, but she didn't want to be forced into an awkward bout of praise from those individuals.

"We certainly owe you a big thanks," Pressig said as he approached Malja. He offered her a cup of the drink which she took without a word. It tasted sour, but the alcohol kick more than made up for its lack of flavor. "Oh, and don't worry about the ex-Mayor Fawbry," he went on. "He's tied to a chair in the Wilk's house. He won't go anywhere."

"I'm just glad nobody died."

"A couple broken bones and plenty of bruises is all. Thank you for everything."

Malja took another swig of her drink and put her mouth to Pressig's ear. Quiet and cold, she spoke. "You were lucky. You ever send these people into a fight like that again, you'll have nothing but corpses to celebrate with." Pressig tried to pull away, but Malja clamped down on his hand. "And if I ever hear that you let such a thing happen, especially because we both know you did this for politics, I'll hunt you down."

She released his hand but locked eyes with him until she saw the shock fade into resignation. She had no delusions that her threat would protect Noogruff from Pressig's ambitions for too long, but he would be cautious for a while. He left his cup behind when he made his exit.

Malja looked about for the handsome man who had supplied the alcohol. Before she could find him, a loud warbling emitted from the trees coupled with a buzzing, electric crackle. The music stopped as all eyes turned toward the forest.

From the shadows emerged a dirt-spackled, flatbed flyer loaded with salvaged items and things brought from far away. Each corner of the roofless vehicle had a cylinder blazing electric energy that kept it floating on air. At the front sat the magician who supplied the electricity and a filigoto driving.

The filigoto waved his stumpy hand as he brought the vehicle to the ground. He was short, wide, and bald with no neck to speak of. Another mutated version of humans, the filigoto had no homeland other than whatever they traveled in. They became traders by necessity.

"Good evening, all. I'm Weyargo. Here to trade," he said with his melodic, lilting voice.

Many townspeople encircled his flatbed to see what he had brought. Malja knew a few filigoto. They were fine enough creatures. Never bothered her much. And they often brought tales from other countries.

"Corlin," most would say, "is the only place to be. The others are empty of everything. Towns are so far apart, and there are so few people."

Indeed, Malja heard Weyargo speaking a similar line to his new customers. He probably praised whatever country he was in. "It's what I've always told those from other lands. You must come to Corlin. It seems most of the people in the world live in this wonderful country. Now, ma'am, doesn't that look lovely? I'll make a fair deal with you."

While Weyargo made one fair deal after another, his magician rested. Malja watched that one closely. Just in case. He twitched a few times and seemed unsure of his surroundings, but all went well.

The townspeople were so high on their success that they bought more than they should — fabrics and spices from Penmorvia to the north, shovels and hoes from Corlin towns to the east, and more alcohol from wherever (no one cared). When the last purchase had been made, Weyargo blew kisses to the people as he climbed into the driver's seat. "Thank you all," he said. "Enjoy your new things, and I promise to stop by when I come back this way later in the year. May Korstra and Kryssta smile upon you all."

The magician concentrated on his tattoo. With a bang, the flyer's engines ignited. The people stepped back, making a commotion of startled laughter as it lifted into the air and flew away.

To see a working flyer like that had been quite an event. Most people went their entire lives without ever seeing anything move that wasn't hitched up to horses. For these townspeople, this day had become far more memorable than any battle victory in the past.

Once the trader left, the musicians started up again, and the party resumed with even greater enthusiasm than before thanks to the extra alcohol. Malja surveyed the townspeople, searching for the handsome man. She found him dancing with a plump gal, twirling and laughing and flashing a charming smile. Malja didn't dance which was exactly why he caught her eye and waved her over.

When she stood, her alcohol-soaked head spun. She played it up and begged off the dancing. To her surprise, and the plump girl's ire, the man left the dance floor and walked over to her.

"You didn't have to stop dancing for me," she said.

"Well, you are the guest of honor," he said. Then in a mock-conspiratorial whisper, he added, "Besides, Nalli is a nice girl, but she talks a lot and steps on my feet."

Malja finished her drink in two gulps. "I'm not much of a dancer. Your feet might be safer with Nalli."

"You trying to say I should be nicer to her?"

Malja laced her fingers behind her head and stretched back. She didn't miss his eyes snatching a peek at her breasts. "I've seen a few towns and I'll tell you this much — most are far less friendly."

"Well, we like being friendly," he said as he stroked her knee.

"That's a bit bold."

"You don't get anywhere waiting for things to just happen."

Malja licked her lips. Traveling such an empty land meant she often went without human contact for long periods, and though she couldn't picture settling down in one town for any length of time, she wondered if a girl like Nalli had it better. Safer, certainly, but safer didn't mean much. She felt far more alive during the dangerous times in her life than the calm ones. Except for sex, nothing quite matched.

But sex often did. And with the life she led, that kind of contact rarely found her. No way would she miss a good opportunity — especially a good-looking good opportunity. "Let's go," she said, pulling on his wrist.

"What?"

"Will we be bothered in the stables?"

As Malja led the way, the man's face shifted from confusion to excitement. "By the way," he said, "my name is —"

"Don't care."

The closer they came to the stables, the hotter Malja's blood burned. The second they stepped inside, she wrenched him around and pressed her lips against his. They stood and kissed while music played in the distance. But her mind refused to shut off its game of remembering horrors. She saw the bleeding head of Duke Brotta as she tossed it into a swarm of hungry konapols.

"Something wrong?" the man asked.

"Harder," she said, smushing her mouth into his. She grasped his body, squeezing and rubbing. She leaned back, letting him lick her neck. But she saw the emaciated magician Lexip as she burned him alive.

She ripped open her lover's shirt and fumbled off his pants. She heard the wet slush of the Bluesman's sliced body. With a push, she sent her man to the ground. The scent of seawater and bile attacked her nose. She slipped out of her assault suit, straddled her partner, took hold of him and thrilled to his startled gasps as she guided him inside.

For a few minutes, her drunken mind shut down. The flashes of her violent past went dark and only the rough pleasure between her legs remained. She lifted slow and dropped hard, grinding her pelvis toward the ground, trying to think only of her technique and the sheer delight of skin on skin.

She had no illusions of a grand climax. For all his bravado, she could tell her lover lacked experience. The man tried to say something, but she ignored him. She simply took what he could offer and collapsed when he had nothing left.

With her head on his chest, she listened to his heavy breathing and pounding heartbeat. Those memories itched to return, but she refused to give in. She rolled onto her back, pulled her man on top, and pressed down on his head until he got the message. She would not let him come up for air until she had her release.

Malja woke to the sound of a horse being saddled. The rider shushed and cursed and snapped at the horse. With her head throbbing, Malja sat up, careful not to disturb the man next to her, and investigated the noise.

Fawbry.

She sneered as she pulled Viper from her clothes pile. She walked straight into view, letting Viper lead as her threat. Fawbry startled at her approach. His face dropped in disbelief.

"You're naked," he said.

"And you're trying to escape. Question is — will you sit down and let me tie you up or are you going to do something stupid and let me kill you?"

Chapter 5

The first cool day of the Postkryssta season had arrived. It wouldn't be long before the mornings began with a light frost and the chilly Korstraprime rains would follow soon after. Tommy nestled in front of Malja as she guided the horse back to Ms. Nolan's mansion. A second horse trailed behind with Fawbry bound in rope. She had intended for Fawbry to walk but the people of Noograff wanted to give her the bay in thanks. She still considered making Fawbry walk — especially after his attempted escape; however, she succumbed to the lure of faster travel. Especially with colder weather coming.

"I ought to thank you," Fawbry said. He had a north-country voice now that he wasn't playing Mayor — a slight accent as if educated from an early year. "Really," he continued. "I wasn't very good at that Mayor-leader thing, but I couldn't get out of it. I thought my incompetent leadership would've ended it, but those griffles refused to go and I didn't want them angry with me. They would've torn me apart. Literally. But they're loyal, I guess. Anyway, they probably think I'm dead now. By Kryssta, I would've been dead, if not for you."

Tommy pressed against Malja, trying to sleep despite Fawbry's ramblings. She rested a hand on the boy's thin shoulder.

"Anyway, thanks," Fawbry said. "And I'm sorry about this morning. I'm sure you understand. I've got to take the opportunities as they come. Nothing personal. So tell me about Ms. Nolan. You work for her long? What's she like?"

"Fawbry."

"Yes?"

"Stop talking."

As they traveled on, Malja fought against her mounting excitement. She had explored too much of the Corlin countryside, battled too many of its inhabitants, and suffered too greatly at its callous hand — all just to find Jarik and Callib. She had never felt closer. Yet she had grown accustomed to her best leads drifting into the air like dust. Fawbry, though, seemed to be the right kind of coward — the kind that worried about an immediate threat more than one far away. She expected her pressure on him to bring results.

Then she'll have Jarik and Callib. She'll track them down. Confront them. And before she sinks Viper down their throats, she'll get answers.

Tommy startled awake and looked at Malja with concern. She must have tensed her muscles without realizing. Patting his shoulder, she eased him back into slumber. It wasn't so easy to calm her thoughts.

That night they camped against a burnt-out home — only two stone walls remained. Fawbry tried to engage her in conversation, but she ignored him. No point in talking when she would be rid of him soon enough. Tommy, perhaps still high from the party, approached Fawbry with his hands together.

"What?" Fawbry asked. "You want to pray? You know about Kryssta?"

Malja snorted. "He wants to play The Reflex Game." To Tommy, she said, "It's okay. You can untie him."

Tommy did so and eagerly pantomimed how to play. Malja pulled out her eight-page book and read a little, but mostly she watched Fawbry. She had no fear of untying him. She recognized weakness and knew he wouldn't dare use Tommy as an escape. Still, she watched.

Though not as fun as the night before, she could see that Tommy enjoyed playing with Fawbry. And, to her surprise, Fawbry appeared equally amused. The sight of her cowardly prisoner slapping hands with her sweet boy made her feel odd because it seemed so normal. The boy amazed her. After all he had been through, he could still be a kid. She wished she could know his secret.

"Want to play?" Fawbry asked, while rubbing his red hands.

She was about to say *No* when Tommy pulled her over by the arm. They played the game, teasing and striking and feigning, until Tommy went to sleep. Without a word, Malja tied Fawbry up — a coward like him would run when she fell asleep. She returned to her book.

Fawbry shook his head. "I got no place to go, y'know." She didn't answer. "Right. I'll just be over here if you need me." He managed a few more sarcastic comments but eventually quieted down.

For awhile, Malja just soaked in the silence.

* * * *

Late the next day, they reached Ms. Nolan's mansion. Malja's heart sank. The main gate had been smashed open and bullet holes marred the concrete pillars. The number of bullet holes spoke to a large group attacking with great purpose — one doesn't waste bullets on a small target. Ms. Nolan was important, yet Malja couldn't help but wonder — *maybe they had expected me to be there.*

The gate guard lay dead on the ground, his white sash spattered in crimson. The four northern konapols never made it out of their cages. Their lifeless eyes stared at Malja, mocking her.

She dismounted, and with Tommy's help, untied Fawbry.

"You're letting me go?" he asked, rubbing his arms.

Malja checked the guard's body for weapons or anything useful, but found nothing. He'd already been searched. "You can go, but you won't."

"Really now? Why's that?"

"Because Ms. Nolan is probably dead. Somebody's working hard to kill off anybody who can help me with information. Who do you suppose is next?"

"Who? Me?" Fawbry hugged himself, looking smaller than ever before. "I don't know anything."

"You do, and you'll help me."

"But—"

"Do you think you're safer alone or by my side?" Malja asked and trudged into the mansion. She said nothing when she heard Fawbry follow.

The interior faired worse than the exterior. The intruders had run out of ammunition or working guns and resorted to melee weapons. Fires burned low in the corners offering enough light to see. Five people hung from the foyer beams — the staff.

"Perhaps the boy and I should wait outside," Fawbry said, but Tommy sped up, passing them all for the large room where they had first met Ms. Nolan.

The statue of Prophet Galot lay in three large pieces and thousands of tiny marble shards as if the Devastation had happened again. Furniture had been piled into meager barriers working toward the back hall. Ms. Nolan had mounted a noble defense though outnumbered and inexperienced.

Stepping over the cracked waterways, Malja saw a dark spot on the floor. Though she knew the answer, she leaned in to be sure — blood. Fawbry interrupted her thoughts. "You think anybody lived through this?"

Glass shattered down the hall followed by an anguished cry. The sound echoed throughout the mansion. The cry of a burning soul.

"Never mind," Fawbry said. "I don't want to know."

Tommy settled against a wall, pouting at Malja's body language. She needed him out of the way and safe. Though he clearly wanted to come with her, she was pleased that he knew what times called for what actions. Fawbry would have to learn.

"Stay here," she said. Fawbry opened his mouth, probably to protest any plan other than leaving right away, but Malja glowered at him.

With a nervous nod, he raised a finger as if making an intellectual point. "I'll stay here."

Malja slunk down the hall, wielding Viper and watching every flickering shadow. The intricately carved door to the Dry Room had been blasted outward as if a giant fist had punched through it. Inside, she found Ms. Nolan, a guard, and another man — their bodies stacked in the corner like a cord of wood. The cage that held Ms. Nolan's sister, Audrex, no longer held anyone. The bars had been torn apart. Splintered wood and twisted metal littered the expensive floor.

Malja examined the corpses. Ms. Nolan's face had locked in a final expression of agony. Or *maybe betrayal,* Malja considered while glancing at the empty cage. Bruises covered the guard's body and his clothes were soaked. Drowned or beaten to death. Malja hoped for beaten — drowning ... no, she couldn't think about the thief's ship. Not now.

The third corpse caused Malja's stomach to squeeze tight. He wore a suit — all black, trim cut, black shirt, gold buttons. She looked closer at the wood scattered on the floor. Not too far away she found it — little pieces of guitar. One chunk had the letters BLU carved in it. The rest of the word lay elsewhere on the floor, but Malja knew it well.

"Ms. Nolan, looks like you were right. They did come for you," she said with a bitter chuckle. The evidence troubled her, though. She could see well enough that these Bluesmen attacked (she didn't want to get stuck on the fact that the Bluesmen had shifted from a lone assassin to an organized group) and that Ms. Nolan's people defended hard. In the end, the Bluesmen won out. The most troubling part — Audrex's cage. If Ms. Nolan had let the madwoman loose as some last desperate weapon, she would have opened it without destroying it. Besides which, Malja could not see Ms. Nolan using her sister like that. Not if her story was true. The Bluesmen, however, would be idiots to rip open the cage. They would have unleashed an insane magician upon themselves. Judging from the Bluesman she had killed in the woods, they were not idiots. The only other explanation she could see involved a stray gunshot. But such a blast would have pushed the bars inward not outward.

Unless ...

Malja's heart raced as she envisioned a deadly possibility — a trap. The Bluesmen kill Nolan. They know Malja will be returning. They want to kill her, but they don't want to be around for it. Why? Because they're not supposed to kill her. But she killed one of theirs, and they're mad. They set some kind of explosive device to Audrex's cage, or perhaps they have a magician who can do such a spell. They leave. The explosion blasts the door, rips up the bodies, and frees an insane magician. Audrex is a trap.

Before Malja heard the scream, she dashed toward the main room. She flew in and saw Fawbry curled in a ball, hiding in his multi-colored robe, blubbering for help. A column of water stood over him, its body shifting from basic shapes to hideous faces to tortuous blades. Malja slashed through the water, and the twisting column fell like a deluge of rain.

"Are you hurt?" she asked while looking for Tommy. She found him where she had left him — against the wall.

Fawbry stood on teetering legs. "I'm fine. There was this crazy woman—"

"I know."

A tendril of water shot out from the waterways, a monstrous mouth drooling water at its tip. Malja cut it down but another rose farther on. As she cut through the new threat, another appeared. She spun toward the latest tendril but one more snuck from the side and slammed her head with water. The force hit like solid ice, knocking her down and rattling her skull. The water continued to shower her. It wouldn't let up. She struggled for air. Her lungs strained. Her chest burned.

Without enough air for her full strength, she still struck out at the tendril drowning her. She didn't slice through it but hit it hard enough to break off its assault. When it stopped, she gasped and coughed and spit up water.

Audrex entered at the far end of the room. Her bloodshot eyes refused to blink. She stepped into the waterway. If she had any sanity while in the cage, it too had escaped. She looked like an abstract drawing — every feature askew, every detail off-kilter. In a high-pitched cackle that pricked their skin, she said, "This is my home."

She stared at the tattoo on her arm and the water trembled. Her previous conjuring had taken its toll. Malja had a small window to act. Still coughing and off-balance, she used a smashed chair to help get on her feet. Her brain thrummed as if someone had wrapped her head in a blanket and smacked it.

"They're almost ready," Audrex said. The lustful yearning in her voice told Malja who *they* were — Jarik and Callib. "Soon the brothers will have the power to fix this blighted world. They'll emerge from hiding and save us all." Four dragonfly wings issued from her back and fanned out as if preparing to fly. "But no matter what — this is my home."

As Malja reoriented herself, she caught Fawbry watching like a spectator, his mouth as wide as his eyes. She had moved too slowly. She could read it on Fawbry's face. She braced for a fierce blow when she spotted Tommy — *Oh no,* she thought.

A crackling bolt of lightning arced from the air near Tommy and struck the water. A screech poured out of Audrex like a foul wind filling the room with its revolting presence. Malja spun — her head dipped and weaved. A column of water, jagged like knives, froze in place. Electricity coursed through it and reached out for Audrex. Her body jittered as if performing a possessed dance. Her eyes rolled back. Smoke rose from her arms and wings.

"Tommy, stop!" Malja said, but the boy continued. She could see the determination on his face — he meant to kill.

Summoning her remaining strength, Malja sprinted across the room, pulled back Viper, and swung through the madwoman's neck. Her head splashed in the water, the jagged column collapsed, and her screeching silenced. Tommy let out a breath and clambered to his feet. The smell of burnt air mixed with burnt skin. He swaggered toward Malja and offered a proud smile. Without pause, she slapped it away.

Catching her breath and forcing herself not to yell, she said, "You are not a killer."

An enraged grimace formed on his tight lips, and he bolted outside but not fast enough. Malja saw his tears. She waited a moment to compose herself. The boy needed time to calm — they both did. Besides, she still had things to do. While cleaning Viper before sheathing the blade, she said, "Okay, Fawbry, time to speak."

"What?" he said, still shaken by all that had happened.

"The late Ms. Nolan said you had information that would help me find Jarik and Callib. I didn't go through all this to come out with nothing."

Fawbry tugged at his hair. "No, no, no. That's not fair. You can't do this to me."

"I am doing this."

"Go find someone else."

"Sorry. You've got the information."

"Is this how you deal with everything in your life — threats, coercion? You should try being nice to people. Didn't your mother ever teach you to be nice?"

Malja punched Fawbry in the gut. "Watch what you say."

"Sure," Fawbry groaned. "The hell with nice. This is much better."

"I'm not interested in anything else about you except what you know."

"Right. Jarik and Callib. Do you know what those lunatics will do to me if I help you? Have you any clue what their capable of?"

"More than you know."

"Then why ask me? You should know I can't."

"Stay by me, and you'll be safe."

"Like I was safe here?" he said, ending in a squealing scream. "No, and no again." He froze at the sight of blood on his hand. Not his, but Malja suspected that only made matters worse. He plunged his hands into the waterway without Audrex's body and scrubbed. "You," he said, snapping out his words, "are not safe."

Malja resisted the urge to throttle the man. Instead, she spread her hands and said, "Then tell me. What do you need to feel safe?"

"To feel safe enough to tattle out Jarik and Callib? You're joking, right?" Malja glared at him, and he shrunk back. He muttered to himself, and his chest sagged. "You don't really want me. Trust me. I know only one thing, one person who might know where they are. That's it. That's all I know. Hardly worth all this effort."

"If it's so meaningless, then give me the name."

Fawbry's face contorted as he strained for an escape. He looked from one side to the other. No answer appeared. His wild hair made him look cornered, and for a moment, Malja thought he might strike out like one of his oxters.

But he brightened a fraction. Then a bit more. An idea had formed. "Fine, fine. You want me to talk? Take me to Barris Mont. He can keep me safe. You get me to him, and I'll tell you the name."

"Thought I wasn't safe."

"I'm not stupid," Fawbry shouted. "You're better than nothing.

And I'm marked now. Right? So, you take me to Barris, okay? That's the deal."

Malja nodded. "So where is this guy?"

"He's not a guy. He's a ... well, he owes me. He lives near Lyngrovet. At Dead Lake."

Wonderful.

Chapter 6

The rich campfire aroma did little to soothe Malja. Though Tommy and Fawbry had been snoring loudly since sundown, Malja couldn't quiet her tired head long enough to fall asleep. They had been riding west for several days, but not making good time. The horses needed extra rest. They had been pushed hard, and the Postkryssta coolness had given way to a surprising, late blast of heat. Malja figured it would be better to go slowly, if it meant still having the horses in the long run. Besides, if she rode the horses into the grave, Tommy would be even angrier with her. For a boy who didn't talk, he had become even quieter since their fight.

She stood, stepped to the side, and faced away from the fire before stretching her sore body. She didn't think about the motions, designed to keep her night vision clear and her awareness toward possible danger, she just moved. Her popping joints blended with the snapping fire. Stifling a yawn, she walked to a wide stream nearby. The conjured assault suit she wore never needed cleaning, but she did. She removed her clothes and stepped into the cold water. Her over-heated body relished the sensation, and she carefully undid the braids in her long hair, letting the water seep in all the way to her scalp. If only everything in knots could be undone so easily.

As she washed off dirt and sweat, her hands felt the ridges and valleys of her numerous scars. *They're my tattoos.* Except these didn't turn a person into an object of power. These didn't drive a person mad. It was so unfair — an innocent boy like Tommy doomed for nothing. Nobody asked him if he wanted to be a magician. He had no choice.

Nobody gave me a choice either.

Gregor had tried to build a normal life for her. He had given her dolls and dresses. Took her flower-picking. Built her a dollhouse, even. But the magicians had done their damage. She ignored the dollhouse and played with the kitchen knives. She dirtied the dresses with mud and blood. She sliced through hordes of pansies and violets. *When those bastards are dead,* she thought, *then I'll have a choice. And Tommy will, too.*

She remembered reaching out to Tommy's cowering form, offering to rescue him — *No, I can't allow myself to rewrite the past.* The night she found him should remain a night she paid honor.

Bending backward so her head cooled in the water but her ears stayed just above and always aware, Malja opened the gates on this one particular memory. Not to pay any honor, she decided, but simply to be honest with herself.

She remembered waking to urgent banging on the cabin door. She remembered the churning sea rolling her stomach like a thoughtless mother rocking her baby too hard. She remembered the young crewman standing in the corridor.

He wore blue, threadbare trousers, a filthy, torn shirt, and a round, white cap — what passed for a uniform on a thief's ship. He took her to see Captain Wuchev, and when they stepped into the narrow corridor, she saw blood decorated the metallic walls in long slashes. Through one cabin door, a crewman slumped over dead, his hair matted and gooey. Mage-rats, the crewman explained, had conjured the storm and raided the ship.

She had chosen to take the boat to avoid this very thing. She thought she could cut across the water to save time and lives in her effort to find Jarik and Callib. But the violent world always followed her like a foul dog.

Captain Wuchev stated it all clearly. The salvaged-metal ship had a rounded back like a half-shell and a wide main deck thrusting forward with three makeshift masts cut into the rusting deck. In a heavy storm they were useless, but before leaving shore, he had a magician conjure electric power and stored it in batteries.

"Up there," he said nodding to the front of the ship, "you'll find the battery station. I've got one left. There's a lever to switch over to the full battery."

"No problem. I'll cut through the cargo hold and —"

"If it were that simple, I'd have this weasel do it." He pointed to the young crewman. "The hold is armed with spells I had installed for this trip. It even held off those thieving pirates. They got everything else, but they didn't get my prize. So, no, you can't go in there. You got to go outside."

Crossing the main deck had been brutal. Powerful winds screamed in her ears and shoved her around. The rain bounced off her assault suit like impatient fingers beating a random rhythm. Icy water found its way down her neck and underneath the suit. It drenched her in seconds. Lightning flashed and thunder cracked. The smell of salty, ocean water blended with her nausea.

She worked her way from one key point to the next. A stack of containers lashed to the deck. A door level with the deck. The first mast. When it came time to run for the second, the ship lurched upward and she fell.

On the rain-soaked deck, Malja swooshed down and gained too much momentum. She slid right by the second mast and rolled on her back only to see the third mast coming upon her like an immovable wall hungry to break her bones. *Viper!* She spun onto her stomach, snatched Viper from her back, and slammed the blade into the deck. With a trail of sparks and the shriek of metal grinding metal, Viper dug in and slowed Malja's descent.

The ship crested. Malja jumped to her feet and stumbled for the door. Every muscle moved, but with maddening sloth. She pried it open, and once inside, heat enveloped her. She leaned back against the door and took a moment to shiver in the darkness.

The room smelled foul like rotting food and feces. Even with no light, she felt cramped. Soon her body would move again. As her heart calmed and her breathing slowed, she heard breaths she had not taken. They were quick and shallow — fearful. Someone hid here.

She listened close, building a mental picture of what she heard — breathing in the corner, scuffing feet as the person tried to melt into the wall, metal rattling. Malja stepped forward, holding Viper back, ready to attack. A spark popped from the corner followed by a ball of sizzling electricity. A magician. Though blinded by the sudden light, Malja swung Viper in front of her.

Often in battle, time slowed. This moment, it slowed enough to see that her enemy was not an enemy. It slowed enough for her to pull Viper back before beheading a child.

All went dark again as the spell dissipated. Malja took a few steps back, staring at the black space where a little boy cowered.

"It's okay," she said. "I won't hurt you. I thought you were a pirate. I'm sorry. I promise I won't hurt you."

With another pop, a small electric ball ignited in the air near the boy. He wore remnants of clothing and had been chained to a large pipe passing through the room. To her left, Malja saw a light switch. She flicked on the dim bulbs so the boy didn't have to maintain his spell. A gentle humming came from Malja's right. Looking that way, she saw two batteries, each towering over her. At eye level, a meter read full on one and three-quarters on the other. Her forehead wrinkled as she turned to the boy.

"He uses you for electricity?"

The boy said nothing.

"He said we were running out of power." Malja thought over the treacherous crossing of the main deck. *Wuchev expected me to die out there.* "Is Captain Wuchev working with the mage-pirates?"

The boy said nothing.

Magician or not, Malja refused to let a little boy be treated like property. "Close your eyes," she said, and flipped Viper so it would strike on the outer-crescent. With careful aim, she swung onto the chains. After three solid hits, the metal gave way, falling to the floor with a freeing clatter.

Rubbing his sore hands, the boy gazed up at Malja and offered a grateful nod.

"I'm Malja."

A smile crept onto the boy's face.

"You got a name?"

The boy returned to his sullen silence.

"No? How about ... Tommy? It's a bit unusual, but then again, so are you."

Again, the boy smiled, and Malja found a glimmer of pleasure warm her.

Listening to Fawbry and Tommy snore as she dried off, Malja felt that same glimmer inside. She just hoped she hadn't snuffed out the matching one in Tommy. He did his jobs — took care of the horses, collected firewood, helped find water — but he barely glanced in her direction.

"I'm sorry," she whispered before settling in to sleep. "But I hope you'll understand. Someday."

Morning arrived with the appetizing aroma of eggs cooking in sweet milk and onions. Malja kept her eyes closed, letting the flavors in the air tempt her tongue. For a moment, she thought she would hear Gregor's deep melodies telling her about planting seasons or Corlin history or why evil must be fought by good people. When she opened her eyes, she found Tommy, and while she missed Gregor terribly, the boy was a welcome sight. He pulled a skillet from the fire and offered her a plate. He then took his own plate and sat facing away.

"Where did all this come from?" she asked, hoping the tears welling inside her did not fall.

Fawbry appeared from behind a tree, buttoning his fly, and said, "I figured Ms. Nolan wouldn't miss a few items. You know, your boy is quite handy with a skillet."

Sitting up, Malja said, "He's not my boy."

"Oh. Sorry."

"I can't have children. I don't menstruate."

The shock on Fawbry's face matched her own. Maybe she had not fully awakened, maybe the weight of the last few days had finally hit her, but the words just blurted out.

Fawbry stood, plate in hand, unable to speak.

"I think Jarik and Callib did it to me. Makes me a better warrior, I guess." She dug into her breakfast and Fawbry followed. "Parents do that kind of thing sometimes. They can be harsh to try to make you better." Tommy didn't react, so she focused on her food. It warmed her belly and calmed her body. Afterwards, she acted as if she had not said anything so personal. Fawbry played along.

"We'll get there today," Fawbry said while saddling his horse.

"Good."

"We just have to cross the Yad."

She knew this would be required, but she hated it regardless. The Yad River cut through the Corlin countryside like an old bone fracture. Its waters ran deep and fast. There were no bridges but plenty of bridge remains. Officially (not that there were any officials), nobody knew why the bridges always failed along the Yad. Some thought the fish used their natural connection with magic to fight what they perceived as an invasion. Some thought the warring brother gods, Korstra and Kryssta, caused the destruction. Most, however, believed every attempt to bridge the river failed because of sabotage.

The Muyaza magicians controlled all crossings of the Yad. They had their lives tied to it. As long as they existed, no bridges would last. They had established villages at all the key points and sent teams up and down the riverbank looking for anybody stupid enough to start constructing a bridge. They never left enough proof that they were responsible for the accidents that followed.

Long before reaching the Muyaza village, Malja smelled them. They did not bathe out of contempt for water. It was something to be controlled and dominated — nothing more. The other smell cutting through the air balanced out the rank odor — cooking meats. Soon the trees thinned out, and Malja saw the village forming a half-circle facing the river.

The Yad stretched off into the distance. Its waters sped along, creating a dull rumble. The massive amount of moving water cooled the air with its fishy odor. One look vanquished any hope of crossing without the Muyaza.

A small line of people formed outside the village. Two boys sat up front. They collected the toll. They had rich, golden-brown skin and striking, dark eyes. Muscular arms and chiseled chests found unlikely pairings with ripples of fat around the neck and round potbellies. Waddles of loose skin hung below wide lips. Along their sides grew thick bumps that moved like the stumps of amputated limbs.

They wore dark, heavy animal skins which, Malja admitted, looked better than some of the ad hoc creations people muddled together. Each also wore a carved piece of wood in the hair. Some wore cubes. Some wore a swooping curve. Others wore a jagged bolt.

"I'd hate to give up a horse," Malja whispered as they took their place in line, "but what else do we have?" This type of negotiation never worked well for her. She knew how to bargain when holding Viper at somebody's throat. The finesse required for a less threatening situation often eluded her.

Fawbry puffed up. "Don't worry. I know these creatures."

The line moved slowly while the boys inspected each offering with care. Most customers were quiet, humble, and knew what to bring. Food held the most value. Using magic to cross the river burned a lot of energy. Offering a chicken, a dazku, or such got fast, respectful service. Items that could be traded for food at a later date were met with grumbling and negotiating.

One man offered his services as a cook. The boys said no. He argued and pleaded. "We got cooks," they said and pointed for him to leave. The man got angry and yelled obscenities. In no time, three adults walked from the village, each carrying a club adorned with rusty nails and flexing their oversized arms. Before they reached the line, the man had slinked away.

"You sure about this?" Malja asked Fawbry. She didn't want to end up having to kill those three men because Fawbry wanted to take responsibility and screwed up.

"I'm not a brave man," Fawbry said. "Trust me. I want to get across the river without any trouble."

Malja couldn't argue — partially because of his brazen honesty and partially because their turn in line came up.

The two boys looked bored and petulant. "How many?" one said with a thick, guttural accent.

Like a traveling merchant, Fawbry raised his hands to punctuate his words. His multi-colored robe fanned out, mesmerizing the boys for an instant. "The three of us, plus the two horses."

"What you pay?" one boy said, fighting his urge to smile at Fawbry's entertaining form.

Fawbry moved closer to the boys while checking over his shoulder. "Look here," he said. The boys peered into his hand and exchanged an unsure look. One boy motioned to the other. The other jogged off to confer with one of the adults. The way the adult scowled gave Malja an itch to grab Viper and prepare for slaughter. Though she could control her hands, her eyes still sought out battle information. The longer the boy and the man talked, the more she saw the fight coming.

She noted how flat the land lay. The hill they came down was too far back for any initial advantage. She observed those in line, gauging if any posed a serious threat. The boy trotted back and whispered to his cohort. Malja focused on the adult watching from a distance. Any sign of an attack and she would take out the boys first. She hated the idea but the shock might gain her enough time to save Tommy and herself. Maybe even Fawbry.

The boy giving orders swiped the object from Fawbry's hand and said, "We see you again, food or no cross."

"Of course, of course. Thank you," Fawbry said. He even added a slight bow and waved to the adult glaring at them. "Thank you," he yelled.

As they walked toward the village proper, Malja asked, "What did you give them?"

"Nolan's coin."

Malja let a grin escape and swore she heard Tommy snigger.

A young Muyaza woman stood by a small hut. She asked how many were crossing and if the horses would go, too. With an unreadable face, she led them into the inner-yard. The constant activity exhausted Malja just to watch.

The tribe worked hard all day. Each member had a specific task, all designed to get people across the river. In front of the small huts, the women cooked non-stop, using large cauldrons and whatever food came there way. Some plucked feathers, some butchered a carcass, while some stirred and stirred. Mangy correts and squeaking phengmice scampered for bones and gristle amongst the waste piles. A long table stretched toward the shore. Sitting on the gravelly sand, the men surrounded the table and shoveled in food like starving orphans. Meats and vegetables piled high in bowls kept arriving. The older ones received deference while eating, but the extra food did not help. All the elderly men were skeletal, wasting away. They looked lost and confused.

Malja missed the signal, but somehow three men were assigned to them — two young, one old. This was always the combination. The two men lifted a wooden litter from a tall stack. They placed it next to the old man and waited with patience as the young woman guided him to the center. With the grace and expertise of people who have done this for a lifetime, they lifted the litter and rested its arms on their fat-padded shoulders. The young woman gestured for Malja and her group to follow the men to the river.

Malja started at the sight before her. She heard Tommy gasp. All across the river, dotting the waters from shore to shore, Malja saw these three-man teams, each surrounded in a shimmering bubble of air. The Muyaza magicians practiced only this one spell, and they did it well. The old ones sat on the litters, focused on their tattooed legs, and created the protective bubble so the others could walk across.

"Come on," Fawbry said, for their team already had walked to the shore. As impatient as Fawbry sounded, Malja caught him running his forefinger across his forehead — a sign of prayer to Kryssta.

Why not? They were stepping into a river, a rushing body of water, something which under other circumstances she avoided. To make it worse, the only thing protecting them was an old man's magic.

Magic ability varied from magician to magician. Part of it was training. Part of it was innate. Some could glance at their tattoos and have a solid spell in a few seconds. Others worked harder. And others strained the whole time. Likewise some spells required more effort even from the best magicians.

The Muyaza tried to use only the best among them — drownings were bad for business — but Malja didn't know this magic well enough to judge the quality of their assigned magician. Her mouth dried as she neared the water. She tried not to think about magicians, magic, or madness. *Just keep walking.*

Water rose around them, as did Malja's tension, but the field did not puncture. The Muyaza had lined this section of the riverbed with wood planks so they could walk without stumbling over slippery rocks and uneven terrain. Spotted fish swam up, stared at the people and horses, mouthed a few O's, and swam away.

Malja tentatively ran her fingers across where she expected the field to be. Her fingers vibrated and the sensation rushed up her arm, shaking her bones. She snatched back her hand and rubbed it on her leg. It didn't hurt, but it was not something she wanted to experience again.

The farther they walked, the higher the water rose. Despite her assault suit's attempt to regulate her temperature, Malja shivered and sweat prickled a line down her neck. She worried about the bubble having enough air. She worried about the old man dying suddenly. She thought about the pain of drowning.

And she thought of the thief's ship and the way she had killed Captain Wuchev. *Tommy better appreciate this.*

About halfway across, the river became shallow, and the Muyaza halted for the old magician to rest a moment. Water passed over their feet and splashed on their ankles. Malja glanced back to see the village had become tiny. That's when she saw the Bluesman.

She whipped out her spyglass to check — another dark-skinned, dark suited fellow with a guitar. This one had a gray beard and one eye clouded over. He argued with the Muyaza. Probably wanted them to hurry.

"Something wrong?" Fawbry asked.

"No," she said, closing the spyglass. "Not yet."

When they reached the opposite shore, they thanked the Muyaza. The men nodded. The village on this side mirrored the one they had left as if the river had cut one village in half. The two litter-carriers set the old magician down with great care as a young woman arrived to guide him to the food table.

Malja mounted her horse, invigorated to be on an animal on solid ground again. "Let's get moving."

Chapter 7

The hours that followed threatened to bring about the ghosts of Malja's memory, but she managed to deflect such thought by focusing on Dead Lake. Fawbry called it a reminder of how the Devastation had changed the world. Before, the area had been composed of hills and forests, roads and towns, houses and families. Children played in their yards, climbing trees and throwing balls. Mothers and fathers worked to better their families and society. Magicians strolled the streets like holy leaders of peace and prosperity.

In the instant of the Devastation, the town vanished. A giant hole engulfed the land and rains filled it in. Those unfortunate enough not to disappear with the land and roads and homes floated in the new lake, adding their blood to the water.

All these years later, little life had returned. The innocent blood poisoned the shores. Nothing grew. Gray rocks littered the ground and the occasional bone washed up in the limp tides. It reminded Malja of the Freelands — a dark, wet version.

Hazy fog rolled off the waters bringing on night a few hours early. Tommy shifted in the saddle, and Malja tried to comfort him with a firm hold, but he shirked off her arm. The horses' various sounds — hoof against stone, air forced through nostrils, headshakes jingling reins — amplified in the narrowing visibility. Malja's eyes never ceased searching for threats.

"Almost there," Fawbry said, his eagerness unmistakable.

All of what counted for civilization lay so far back that Malja understood why Fawbry might feel safe here. Desolate and destroyed, the area would be lonely, but alone and alive sounded better than surrounded by others and dead. A figure appeared in the haze causing Malja to reconsider the "alone" part.

"It's okay," Fawbry said. "They're just the Chi-Chun."

"I thought they were a story."

"No, the Chi-Chun have existed for a long time. I'm not saying they really have the magic to ward off the dead. Frankly, I don't really believe the dead are going to rise. But they believe."

As they rode by, Tommy's hand trembled. Malja fought off the urge to respond. The Chi-Chun presented a frightening figure. He stood six feet tall, but seemed bigger, framed by bony trees and thin foliage. He wore a frayed, black robe — tattered cloth that draped him like seaweed. He stood motionless with his hooded head hung low and his arms outstretched. Malja imagined the pain his arms would radiate after only a few minutes. If the stories were true, he would stand like that for several hours.

Fawbry explained that the Chi-Chun were a sect of Korstrians that had few but highly devoted followers. They believed Dead Lake was the epicenter of the Devastation and if not constantly kept in check, a second blast would occur, strong enough to ensure extinction for every living thing. "According to their texts, the first sign of this blast will be the return of all the dead at Dead Lake," Fawbry said with a derisive snort.

"Wait, wait," Malja said. "You can read?"

"No, of course not," he said with a fumbling cough. "And if I could, I wouldn't waste my time with Chi-Chun nonsense. I mean, they spend hours like that for what? Another will come along to relieve them. Then they go to their little commune, pray, eat, sleep, start all over. Nothing else. What kind of life is that?"

Malja settled back in the saddle. She didn't care about the Chi-Chun, but to find another who could read thrilled her. He could deny it all he wanted, but she had heard the education in his voice earlier, and now he let slip that he could read.

Gregor had taught her and if for nothing else, she loved him for that infinite gift. Jarik and Callib had taught her much as well but only what served them — never what would solely benefit her. Teaching a child should be an act of love in many ways. For Jarik and Callib, it was an act of control.

Over the next hour, they saw three more Chi-Chun. One stood unsteady, his arms shaking. Fawbry said that one must be new. Malja thought they looked like creepy scarecrows. They existed, after all, to scare away the dead.

"We're here," Fawbry said, but to Malja, this patch of gray looked much the same as any other they had traveled across.

Tommy nudged her and pointed to the one difference. A decrepit, wooden dock poked out into the water like a splinter. The lake lapped against it with a steady, dull clap. A Chi-Chun stood her outstretched vigil at the tip of the dock like a ghost forever waiting a lover's return.

After dismounting and tethering the horses, Malja and Tommy stood back while Fawbry approached the lake. For a coward, he seemed to be quite gutsy. Fawbry squatted and slapped the water three times, paused, slapped three times, paused, and continued the pattern for a full minute. The Chi-Chun stiffened at the disruption but did not break her pose.

Fawbry straightened, cupped his mouth, and called out, "Barris! Barris Mont!"

Malja kept close watch on the motionless Chi-Chun and readied for an attack. Fawbry called out again, his voice fading in the fog but still crossing the water. The Chi-Chun lowered her arms, turned around, and removed her hood.

Her night-black skin hid most of her features like the dark lake hid its depths. Only her deep-set eyes — a bold, sickly yellow — and her matted hair — knotted with weeks of grime — revealed the dangerous mind beneath. She looked like the dead returned. Malja thought these Chi-Chun had taken the idea of studying the enemy a bit too far.

The woman advanced towards Fawbry, her agile and speedy feet surprising all. Malja started to retaliate but Fawbry put out his hand, motioning for her to wait. When the Chi-Chun reached him, she widened her eyes, pointed at him, and said, "Do not call upon the damned."

"Barris is not damned."

"Blasphemy! Do not speak such names or I shall call the power of Korstra, and with His might I shall lay a curse upon your head."

"Fine, fine. Just do it and get out of here, so I can call Barris Mont in peace."

The Chi-Chun woman sucked in air as if she might explode should she hear anything more. "You vile heathen."

"No, ma'am. You are the heathen. I follow the right and just Kryssta, the greater brother god, the true leader of all mankind."

"Blasphemy!" The woman pressed her thumb against Fawbry's chin. He did not move away, though he rolled his eyes and huffed disdain. "I curse thee," she said, her words seething hatred. "I curse thee in the name of Korstra, the wise and powerful brother god. Change your path, heathen, or this curse shall follow you always." She put her hood back on and kneeled at the edge of the shore. In seconds, her body swayed as she mumbled words Malja could not make out.

Fawbry waved Malja and Tommy over. "Don't worry," he said.

"I've been cursed before by the Chi-Chun. If they have any real power, curses aren't it. Now that I say that, I can't think of anybody ever suffering from a curse. Must not be real."

"She's dangerous," Malja said, her wary eyes hawking the woman.

"Do you really think I'd stand up to her if she were?"

"Good point."

"Come. Onto the dock."

Malja waited. "I'm fine here." Having just crossed the Yad, even standing on a rickety dock overlooking a large lake felt too close to water.

Fawbry shook his head as if mocking a child but wisely left it at that. He walked out on the dock and tapped the water once more. Malja noticed that Tommy had left her side. He hovered near the Chi-Chun. *Facing his fears. Good.* Before she could say anything, a low groan bubbled up from the lake. Fawbry hurried back to the shore.

"He's here. He's here," he said, giddy and impatient.

The Chi-Chun woman inched back but continued her praying.

From the water, a dark object emerged. Malja thought, at first, she saw the head of a man, but as it moved closer, as it rose higher, she saw nothing that resembled a human form. The head-like shape became an eye, one of many, and its large size hinted at the creature coming.

To say Barris Mont was enormous was to say a grain of sand was small. The word failed to convey any real sense of proportion and power. Barris was massive. Taller than the trees and wider than a house, he moved with slow yet powerful grace. A monstrous, lumpy shape — soft and wet and malleable. Good for underwater living. Waves of fish odor pulsed off him. His purplish-black skin looked like an enormous bruise, and his eyes popped open at random points like blemishes. Worse were his legs. More than a tentacle but not as sturdy as a foot, Barris had so many he looked like a mound of dark meat atop thick, never-ending noodles.

The Chi-Chun let out a cry and pressed her head to the stony ground. Tommy watched in gasping disbelief. Fawbry danced about like a child expecting a new toy.

"Barris," he said when he finally regained a little control, "this is the warrior Malja and her companion, Tommy."

A gray appendage wormed out of Barris. Its prehensile tip settled on Fawbry's head. Fawbry closed his eyes and, with a relieved grin, grew rigid like a corpse shortly after a battle. Two similar appendages emerged and took hold of Tommy and the Chi-Chun. It had not happened quickly, yet Malja did not react. The sheer size of Barris had stunned her. But when she saw another gray snake coming for her, she snapped free from her awe.

She brandished Viper and took on a fighting stance. "Let go of them," she said.

In a deep, indecipherable voice, Barris spoke. His tones shook the ground. Leaves fell off trees. Two birds darted into the sky, cawing a frightened warning to others. Malja dropped to her knees and clutched her ears. Her bones radiated pain from the marrow outward as they vibrated against her muscles.

"Stop! Stop talking!" Her words sounded muffled, and she feared she might go deaf. He spoke no more. For now. Wiping at the tears in her eyes, she looked up at the sky and saw no end to Barris. She wobbled back to her feet. Weaving like a drunkard, she swung Viper toward the gray appendage attached to Tommy. Another splashed from the lake and slapped her down. As she hit the ground, a sharp rock poked the small of her back.

The gray tube, for she could think of nothing nicer to call it, still waited for her, its tip motioning for her to join. She stumbled to her feet, her body complaining at each movement. If Barris chose to speak again, Malja knew her ears would bleed and her body would fail. Death would come swiftly. But still that disgusting tube beckoned.

She wanted to check on Tommy, but her heart told her not to bother. She had failed the boy. Alive or dead, she had failed the boy.

No. I only fail if I do nothing.

She grabbed that gray tube so hard Barris let out a startled complaint — loud enough for Malja's legs to buckle, but she managed to stay upright. She pulled the tube closer. Another tube tried to strike her, but she wouldn't fall again. She dodged the attack with one step and with a second step, she planted her legs solidly.

"I don't want to hurt you," she said, knowing how absurd her words sounded, "and since Fawbry wanted to be here, I think you don't want to hurt us. So, you just let go of the boy, and I'll let go of you. We'll leave you in peace. Okay?"

Nothing happened.

"Fine. I'll go first," she said and let go of the gray tube.

Barris spoke. The ground shook as vibrations radiated outward with explosive force. A dying tree splintered and fell. Distant animals screeched and fled.

Malja collapsed as blood dribbled from her nose and ears. The pressure on her head brought spots to her eyes. She felt like the brother gods had each taken a side of her skull and pushed.

She rolled on the ground, clutching her head, trying to focus. She saw Tommy. Despite the vibrations shooting endless jolts straight through to her bones, she reached for the boy. Her breathing labored and her vision clouded. She rolled onto her back, fighting for air. She found Viper and tried to think of a way to strike back. But part of her mind began wondering what form Death would take.

Barris finally stopped. All fell into silence. Malja couldn't even hear her own heartbeat. She felt the gray tube slither across her leg. She held Viper now but could not find the strength to left her weapon. The tube entered her field of vision.

Barris did not hesitate. The tube lowered onto Malja's head.

Chapter 8

Malja, come here now," a voice called from behind. She knew that thin timbre — Callib. A terrified yelp surged up Malja's throat, but she clamped her mouth against it. Brutal lashings waited for her should she turn around. "Malja," Callib said, exasperated and harsh, "did you kill my dolyan birds?"

"Yes, sir," a little girl answered through her bawling.

Malja whirled around to see a four-year-old girl clad in a black assault suit. The dead lake, the barren trees, the overcast sky — gone. Tommy, Fawbry, the Chi-Chun, Barris — gone. Before she could say a word, little Malja vanished.

Another Malja appeared in the distance. Eight-years-old. The younger version of her practiced with a new sword she had been given for her birthday. Malja remembered the day well. Lunges, parries, sweeps, and slices. Over and over she went through her forms — each choreographed step a tutorial for battle. No windows to distract her. No warmth to lull her. Just cold, echoing stone and damp, musty odors. Warm tears stung in her eyes, but she kept practicing.

Then she was ten, crouched at the door to her room listening to her fathers argue in the hall. "She's a complete failure," Callib said. "There's not a bit of magical ability in her. Nothing."

"Failure?" Jarik said, his deeper tones always more striking than Callib's shrill rants. "It's a success she's survived this long."

"Obviously, but—"

"You continue to think you can change her, but look at what she is. Look at what she can do."

"What? The fighting?"

"Yes, the fighting. She's by far the most talented warrior this world has ever seen. We did that. That's success."

"That's your success. It has nothing to do with finding safe passage, and quite frankly, it's a waste of our valuable time and resources. She's nothing but a failure to me."

She stared at the door. Burning tears streamed down her face, but she wiped them back.

Again the world dissolved. Malja gasped as her vision flooded with memory after memory. She saw her days training, her days being yelled at, her days being beaten. She saw the morning they tossed her in a sack and abandoned her in a forest.

She felt the fear and the loss and the betrayal. Yet she also had the context of an adult looking back to aid her. She admired little Malja's pluck. That girl refused to give in.

She saw the week she had struggled to survive, scavenging for the mere basics — eating grubs, enduring freezing rain, fighting off hungry konapols. She saw the day she thought she would die of starvation, the same day Gregor found her on his morning walk and decided to take her in.

The years with Gregor were pleasant but never secure. She listened closely and tried to obey his rules. But no matter how often he professed his love for her, she kept an eye out for any change to come. At some point, she expected, he would grow tired of her burden and dump her.

With a jolt like riding in a wagon run by a spooked horse, she saw a seventeen-year-old Malja returning from a three-day hunt. She had a load of meat to store for Korstraprime. She called Gregor to give her a hand. She really just wanted to show him how well she had done. He always praised her accomplishments, and she never tired of hearing him.

When he didn't answer, she cupped her mouth and said, "Wake up, Lazy-head. I'm home." The concern on her face lacked any humor. Both Maljas — old and young — tensed as the seventeen-year-old approached their tiny shack.

The older Malja closed her eyes, knowing what awaited the younger. Gregor — ripped to pieces. Blood and tissue strewn about like sloppy decorations. Burn marks on the walls and a sour stench marring the air — sure signs of magic.

Only two magicians would have cared about an old man and his daughter living alone in peace. Jarik and Callib. The younger Malja, her eyes cold and dry, tripped on her way outside to throw-up. The older knew what happened next. She could never forget about the man hiding in the second room. She braced herself for the coming confrontation, for the moment that changed so much, but the vision skipped ahead, cheating her from watching her truly discover her strength and saving her from having to deal with it. Now, she saw herself standing before the shack as she burned it and Gregor's remains to the ground. And she made her oath. She would find her fathers. She would unleash the beast for Gregor's sake.

More years soared by her — all the dark, dreadful places she had seen. The barbarians of the Freelands, the criminal magicians holding towns hostage, the constant battle against roving groups of killers and cretins — all of it washed her in the blood of memory.

But then she stood in a gleaming, white room. Not a memory. She had never seen such a room before. A window encompassed an entire wall letting the sun glitter off the white marble floor. A white desk and chair occupied one side of the wide room. Far across on the other, Malja saw a white couch. She had seen furniture before but never in such pristine condition. Two white birds chased each other around the ceiling.

"I'm sorry it took so long to settle on a meeting location," said a man in a gray suit with a brilliant green tie. He touched his desk and the birds vanished. "Usually I can find a memory that's happy, warm, and above all else, safe. I could not find such a place in you. Admittedly, I'm pressed for time, but still, you've lived a bitter life."

Malja thought hard on what she had seen and heard. She offered the most intelligent reply she could muster. "Huh?"

The man smiled, revealing just how handsome he could be — and clean. His skin, his hair, his clothes — everything smelled as clean and clear as the spotless room. "I apologize again. This can be a bit disorienting the first time." He raised a finger. "Let's begin with introductions. I'm Barris Mont." He offered his hand.

As Malja shook, she said, "But you were that huge thing."

Barris laughed. "Yes, I was. Still am. All this is going on in my head."

"Your head?"

"Well, it was meant to be yours, but as I said, your life has been rather dark. So I brought you into my mind instead."

"Then this is your memory?"

"Back when I was human. Before the Devastation."

With timid steps, Malja approached the window. Never had she felt so shy, so unsure of what she would do with what she would see. Before she felt ready, the world opened up.

The office she stood in must have been miles in the air, for she could see the city spread out to the horizon. Far below people scurried about and grounders zipped along the road. Other offices floated in the air while some buildings simply stacked upon each other, reaching for the clouds. Lights of every shape and color winked and flashed and dazzled.

A scarlet bird with white-tipped wings slid along the air and settled on the window ledge. It seemed nonplused by this amazing, breathing city. It seemed at peace.

Malja saw that the city was at peace, too. Despite the speeding grounders and bustling people, despite the airborne offices and the numerous advertisements, despite it all, the city moved with a quiet, peaceful grace. The engines, the food, the lights — all powered by magicians, silently doing their job from the shadows.

"It had elegance, don't you think?" Barris said.

Malja could not hide her wonder. "It was beautiful."

"This is the city of Winsal, one of the great cities of the Southern Countries."

Though she wanted to see more — indeed, she could have stared at it for hours as if she were a magician casting a massive spell — she pulled away and put on a thoughtful look. "So, Mr. Mont, what is all this for? What do you want?"

"You, of course. But I need you to be honest, and honesty often requires comfort. So, I suppose you could say that all this—" Barris pointed to the world around them. "—is about your comfort." With a smile that suggested a surprise, he pressed another button on his desk.

A young man entered with a stiff walk. He wore black pants, a white shirt and jacket, and had a funny, little tie. He carried a silver, covered tray. When he approached Malja, he bent towards her as if in solemn reverie.

"A little gift," Barris said.

The man lifted the tray cover to reveal one firm, red apple. Malja thanked the young man as she took the apple. Before the young man had left, she bit the fruit.

Delicious. Exquisite. Perfect.

For an instant, she could believe in the world outside the window — she did not stand at the edge of a putrid lake, and the sun gleamed off life like the bursting juice in her apple.

"Good," Barris said as he settled on the couch and patted a spot at his side. She sat, marveling at how the cushion felt softer than a moss bed. He placed his hand on her shoulder and said, "We have much to discuss."

Malja pressed him back like a young girl fending off a kiss yet not wanting to hurt the boy's feelings. "What are you talking about? 'Much to discuss.' I brought you Fawbry. He's the one who wanted to be with you. Though you sure are cute." *What did I just say?* Malja's head felt fuzzy. "Did you ... do something to this apple?"

"No," Barris said, his face filled with worry. "You're reacting to being in my mind. You're not supposed to be here. The experience can be euphoric — and sometimes disrupting. So, listen. I need you to focus. This is important."

"Sure. No trouble. Stay focused. But just know I'm good at a lot more than fighting." Malja lurched forward and whispered quite loudly, "I'm talking about sex."

Barris held Malja's chin and said, "I want ..."

With a drunken slur, Malja said, "You want ..."

"I want you to ..."

"You want me to ..."

"I want you to kill the brothers, Jarik and Callib."

No words, no magic, no concoction of any kind could have snapped her sober faster. "What?" she said, all traces of euphoria flushed from her system. Her skin wriggled like someone had plucked out her dirtiest desire and spoke it out loud just so she could feel its slime dribble down her chest. Maybe that's exactly what happened. Maybe he plucked it right from her head.

She put some distance between them. She couldn't understand how he had made her feel violated. She never had kept quiet about her hatred for Jarik and Callib. Ms. Nolan had known. The Bluesmen knew. Yet she couldn't shake the feeling that she had been severely wronged.

Barris reclined, crossed his legs, and said, "Good, you're clear-headed again. It won't last long though, so focus. Now I know you want to kill them. I want it, too. For different reasons, of course."

"What reasons?"

"No time for that. What matters is that you complete your task. That's why you're here. I have to know with absolute certainty you won't back off at the end. I have to be sure you won't afford them any sliver of compassion."

"You think I won't do it?"

"I think part of you is still a little girl who wants her daddies to love her."

"Gregor loved me."

"But Gregor is not Jarik. Gregor is not Callib. Gregor can't tell you about your mother."

Malja threw her apple at Barris. He ducked and the apple exploded against the wall, leaving behind a wet spot and splatters of fruit. "I'll kill them. It's that simple. I certainly don't need you to motivate me."

"Okay," Barris said, cautiously sliding to the far end of the couch. "Let's move on, then. The boy, Tommy, you must leave him with me."

Malja let a laugh burst out of her, but she had no idea if it was the effect of this place or her honest astonishment. "You were just in my head, you idiot. You should know I won't let him go."

"And yet, you must. If you truly care for him, then you know he is not safe with you. Not with the task you have ahead. He is a liability to you. Jarik and Callib may feel some sense of caring towards you — in fact, I'm counting on it — but they won't care about the boy. They'll use him against you. And that cannot be allowed to happen."

"You're wasting my time. Tommy stays with me."

"You don't understand. The boy is growing, and he'll be vulnerable."

Malja wrinkled her eyebrows. "He's young. He's supposed to grow."

"He's a magician, too," Barris said. Malja's stomach twisted. "And I have given him a second spell."

"You've *given?*"

"In the old days, before the Devastation, before I mutated into the lumbering thing I am, I was a Sotnol. There were many back then. We're not really magicians, yet we're not really just people either. We're the spell givers. More accurately, we unlock spells. I enter a magician's mind and help him or her unlock the potential that resides there."

"And you did this to Tommy."

"He did it to himself. I merely showed him the doorway."

Malja kicked the desk, careening it into the wall with a screech. "If any of this were real, I'd kill you right now."

Barris shrugged. "Lucky for me, then, that I'm big enough to squash you." Barris stood, brushed his pants, and once more rested his arms on Malja's shoulders. She giggled at the thought of dancing with him. "Stay focused," he said.

She snapped back her attention. "I'm not leaving him. I've protected him this long. I'll continue to protect him."

"I expected this. Hoped for otherwise, but expected it nonetheless. So, I'm sending the Chi-Chun woman with you. Her name is Tumus. She'll know how to care for the boy as he adjusts to his new ability."

Malja wanted to argue, but she felt the drunken state just on the edges of her control. "Anything else?"

"Cole Watts will tell you where Jarik and Callib are. Watts is your key." Barris placed a finger on her open lips. "Shh. Patience. Fawbry knows how to find Watts. I do not, and I don't want to know."

"This is ridiculous. Why should I listen to any of this?"

The walls rippled as if seen through a waterfall. Barris lowered his head. "I'm sorry. If we stay any longer, your brain may be damaged."

"Then answer quickly. Why should I listen? And what exactly did you do to Tommy? And why do I need your Chi-Chun? And —"

Barris became transparent even as he sighed all too real. "You'll have to answer it for yourself. Goodbye, Malja."

"Wait. Tell me something. Anything. Why are the Bluesmen trying to stop me?"

The jolt of fear and surprise that hit Barris spread across the fading office. He said something, but only an odd childlike voice — several steps out of synch and speaking in a language that sounded made-up — followed his moving lips. When he disappeared completely, Malja felt a giant force shove her through darkness. Another force grabbed her inside the chest and yanked hard enough to cause an unheroic squeal.

Malja opened her eyes. Fawbry, Tommy, and Tumus were all lying by the dock. Malja sat up and scanned the hazy lake. Barris was gone.

Chapter 9

Nobody was happy. Tommy crouched on the rocks clutching his arm as if it had been broken. Tumus, the Chi-Chun woman, stood near the dock watching the lake — her mouth open, her face stoic, her mind lost in disbelief. Knee-high in the water, his worn but flashy robe soaking, Fawbry kicked and splashed and screamed.

"You bastard! Come back here. You can't do this to me. This isn't right. Come back here."

Malja didn't care about Fawbry, and she didn't care about Tumus. At that moment, she wanted only to hold Tommy and ease any suffering Barris had caused him. Yet she could not move. She watched Tommy rubbing his arm and wondered if this marked the beginning, if the magician in him would now take over, if the little boy she had rescued would cease to exist, if madness waited to consume him. She tried not to look across his skin for the new tattoo. She snuck a peek anyway — not a brave approach but she couldn't bear to let Tommy see her face if he, indeed, had a new marking. A wave of relief crashed over when she did not see it. But if he lacked the tattoo, then Barris had done something else to him. Perhaps something worse.

"I won't do it," Fawbry said, now sobbing into the lake. "I don't care about what you want."

The sun rose. Malja wondered how long they had been unconscious and how long they had been in communion with Barris. A new day awoke around them, and for her part she wanted to make it worthwhile. Cole Watts. Find him to find Jarik and Callib. Find them and put an end to the constant gnawing, constricting, worrying tension in the middle of her chest that even thoughts of Gregor could not ease.

"I refuse," Fawbry went on. "You hear that, you big bastard? I refuse!"

With a tinge of pleasure, Malja turned toward Fawbry. This she could handle. "Fawbry, get out of the water."

Her voice cut through his panic. He stopped screaming at the lake and looked over his shoulder. Dripping with confusion and fear like an abused pet, he shook his head. "He was supposed to keep me safe. Not send me off with you."

"Where do I find Cole Watts?"

Fawbry pouted at the lake. "I don't want to go there. I don't want to go to the Freelands."

"You don't have to. Tell me where in the Freelands, and I'll go by myself. You can stay here. All of you can. Just stay here where it's safe."

Everyone stopped their personal mourning and stared at Malja. Fawbry even stumbled a few steps away from her. Nobody said a word.

Tommy broke the silence first. Pushing himself to his feet, he let out a single, puppyish whimper. He walked to her side, cold determination set in his eyes, and huffed as if to say *Don't even think about arguing.* Malja had no such intention. She had expected Tommy to come. No matter how angry he might be, he wouldn't leave her. Not yet. But she needed Fawbry for information — not just Cole Watts's location, but his connections, his importance. Everything Fawbry could provide, she wanted.

Tumus's dark face twisted in a tug-of-war. Her lips quivered, and for a moment, Malja feared she would have two blubbering fools to contend with. But with a garbled shout and a rude gesture to the lake, Tumus stomped over to Tommy.

One more.

Fawbry still shook his head. "I'm not a fighter. I'm not brave. I'm not smart. I'm just trying to survive."

"You're more than that," Malja said. "You're the one who got us across the river. You're the one who fed us so well that morning. And as for brave, the only reason we're here at this lake is because you stood up to me. Now, you know where Cole Watts is, and you know Barris wants you to help me."

He crossed his arms. "Okay. I'll tell you. Then you can go off and take care of it all and it doesn't matter to me. I'll be here."

"Except Barris wants you with me. Can you guarantee he'll protect you when you go against his wishes? I don't know. I don't think you'll be as safe with him as you think. Come with me, and you know I'll protect you. And it's what he wants. Really, your situation hasn't changed that much. I'm still your safest bet."

Fawbry thought this over for a second and slapped the water hard. While wiping his eyes, he trudged out of the lake. "I hate you."

＊ ＊ ＊ ＊

As they approached the last hill before reaching the Muyaza village, Malja's concern for Tommy's welfare grew. Illness had set in fast. His face burned with fever while his body shuddered against her. Holding the horse's reins in one hand and clutching Tommy to her breast with the other, Malja made the silent promise that should anything happen to Tommy, she would kill Barris Mont.

Fawbry and Tumus shared the other horse a few feet behind. Neither said much except for the occasional complaint against the placement of one's hand or the smell of the other's body.

Cresting the hill, Malja saw the Muyaza village already buzzing in the morning's work. A short line formed outside the village where the requisite two boys sought payment for the crossing. One spied the horses and their riders. Recognition ignited astonishment. With frantic gestures, he pointed them out to the adult males standing in the distance.

"Guess word's gotten out about us," Fawbry said — his first words since they had left the lake.

Malja reached over, flipped open the saddlebag, and produced a dead rabbit. She had caught it when the little thing made the mistake of crossing the dirt road they rode on. It wasn't much, but she hoped it would be enough. If it wasn't, then she knew other ways to get what she wanted.

Before the fierce Muyaza male had stopped his approach, he waved them off. "No," he said. "No welcome here."

Malja tossed the dead rabbit onto the ground.

The Muyaza scoffed at the offering, the stumps on his sides bristling. "No good."

"The horse," Fawbry said.

Malja looked over her shoulder in shock as Fawbry dismounted and pulled Tumus off. He walked the horse up to the Muyaza and handed him the reins. The Muyaza looked at the reins in his hand with even greater shock than Malja.

Fawbry glanced up to Malja. "We can always get another horse." For a fleeting moment, the words unnerved her — people rarely thought the way she did, let alone actually acted upon such thoughts.

The Muyaza looked back at the village and then at Malja. He inspected the horse, licking his lips as he ran a hand over the meaty rump. Something at the village made him hesitate, though. With an incredulous shake of the head, he bent down, picked up the dead rabbit, and walked the horse back to the village. The others followed.

They entered the main circle of homes, and the village stopped. The cooking stopped. The talking stopped. Even the ceaseless eating stopped. Only the sizzle of meat and the rumble of boiling stew disrupted the uneasy silence. At length, a woman assigned a Muyaza team to Malja and her friends. Nobody seemed eager to move, but the woman spat out a few words and business returned to its usual pace.

With the old Muyaza upon his litter and the protective bubble formed, Malja's group entered the river. The villagers snuck glances but refused to meet Malja's eyes. The air felt colder than the previous crossing, the water less welcoming, the bubble less secure. The litter carriers exchanged worried looks. Malja gripped Tommy tighter and tried to ignore the rising water. After a few minutes, Malja noticed Tumus had edged her way to the right side of the horse and placed her hand on Tommy's foot. Fawbry walked ahead near the litter.

Something was wrong.

Malja felt it vibrating deep within like the coming of an earthquake. More than just fear of drowning — this was her warrior instincts shooting off. When the river had risen to the point that only her head and that of the old Muyaza on the litter broke the surface, she saw it. There were no other litters in the water. Despite people bustling and cooking and trading, nobody else had entered the river.

She looked back at the shore. Searching. The tall Bluesman stood out clearly against the little Muyaza village — gray beard and clouded eye. The Muyaza stayed far behind him. They fretted about, but none would challenge the strange man. He raised a lengthy pipe — no, not a pipe — a rifle. Before Malja could warn anybody, the muzzle flared and a crack rolled across the air. The bullet splashed a few feet upriver.

"Faster," Malja said but she didn't need to — the carriers had picked up the pace. She checked the shore. The Bluesman went through the reloading process with the careful and efficient motions of a trained soldier. When he lifted the rifle to aim, Malja leaned over Tommy, pushing him lower to the horse's neck. The shot snapped out and the head of the old man on the litter exploded.

The bubble surrounding them tore apart like strands of saliva pulled away by water. Anguished cries erupted from the Muyaza on the shore. And the river reclaimed its territory with a powerful thrust. It swept Malja from her horse. It ripped Tommy from her grasp. Water spun her, flipped her, tossed her aside. She couldn't tell which way was up, and each time she thought she had it right, the river spun her into disorientation again.

She smacked into a rock, her back scrapping against the jagged surface, the force of the blow knocking out what little air she had in her lungs. And then — light. A glint of sunlight from above. Pushing off the rock, she swam hard for the surface. Her lungs burned, and a dark thought crossed her mind — *I'm not going to make it*. The surface didn't seem to be getting closer. She was going to drown. Each stroke felt as if a giant pressed its enormous fist against her ribs. But when she burst into the air, gasping for every lungful she could manage, her surprise cost her. She missed grabbing hold of a log.

Striving to stay above water, she swam hard with little to show for it. The river fought her, its unmerciful hands pushing her chest and pulling at her legs. She searched for Tommy but only saw Fawbry. He had found purchase on a large boulder and hugged it like a crying child to his mother's breast.

The river yanked Malja into its muddy jaw, filling her vision with browns and greens, grit and sand. Sounds mutated into bubbled nonsense. Three strong strokes brought her back to the surface. She spun around, seeing water and the shore and Fawbry falling away from view. Something else, too. A small, dark shape limp in the water. *Tommy*.

Swimming away from the shore, Malja battled the waters for every stroke. The boy's body bumped against some rocks but did not react. *Don't think about that. Just get him.* Water crept down her throat — a dirty trick of the river, but as she coughed and spit, she swam. She saw Tommy on that thief's ship, his cautious eyes, his small hand in hers as she made her promise. So she swam. Deeper into the river's angry flow.

Bracing on a nearby rock, she grabbed the body. Blood drenched it as much as water. She turned him over. Not Tommy. The Muyaza litter carrier — cracked open his skull on the rocks.

As she dropped the Muyaza back into the current, she saw the shattered litter within reach. It took several tries, but she snagged it and floated her way downriver.

Soon the waters began to ease, and the river's grip relaxed. She paddled toward shore — it took a hard effort, but the river put up less of a fight.

A dark stone formed in her belly. As she stepped out of the river, her assault suit dotted with beads of water, her body dry, her long hair sopping wet, she bit back against the urge to cry. Still no Tommy.

Her eyes scanned the river once more. She saw the small figure of Fawbry leaping from his mama boulder to the river's edge. One foot landed in the water and he scrambled the rest of the way to safety. Nothing else. Nobody. Not even the horse.

"Over here," a breathless voice called out.

Malja looked behind her. About twenty feet inland, Tumus waved for help as she bent over a small body. Despite her exhaustion, Malja sprinted across the grass. The stone in her belly lifted to her chest where fear and hope tugged at each other like two wild animals ravaging the same piece of meat.

Tommy lay underneath Tumus. She slapped his face, trying to bring normal color back to his bluish skin. Pushing Tumus aside, Malja sat Tommy up and reached around him from behind. She squeezed hard just below his ribs, hoping to force out anything. Brackish water vomited from him with each squeeze. By the time Fawbry had joined them, Tommy had coughed the last out and began to breathe.

"What the hell happened?" Fawbry said.

Malja ignored him. She hugged Tommy and asked, "You okay?"

Tommy nodded. Normal color returned to his face. "He's okay," she said and let a few tears fall. She hugged him tighter, as if the river could jump the bank and take him away. "I'm here for you. You understand? Forget about Nolan's place and all that. I'm sorry about it. Okay? I'm always here for you."

Tommy squirmed from her tight grasp and verbal bombardment. He reached out to Tumus and held her hand. Tumus snatched her hand back and moved a short distance away. As she wiped water from her face, she said, "He'll be fine. Cold water probably helped with the fever."

Malja knew she should say thanks, that she should sound a little grateful — after all, Tommy was alive. But, though she loathed the idea, a new pain plucked in her chest when Tommy had reached for Tumus. She should have been the one to save him, not this Chi-Chun crazy. Worse still, Tumus had the nerve to pull away her hand.

Malja walked a few steps from the group and tried to cool off. However, seeing the smoke of cooking food from the distant Muyaza village only fueled her fire. And that target she could focus on with less confusion.

Once Tommy could walk, Malja led them back to the Muyaza. Nobody argued with her. Tumus probably didn't care. Fawbry took one look at her seething anger and kept quiet. And Tommy always trusted her. That's all she really needed.

She trudged on, each step strengthening her as she felt the warm coat of the warrior enfold her. If she had the time and knowledge, she would have built a bridge crossing the Yad, and she would've done it right next to the Muyaza village. They would try to stop her, and she would cut them down. But she lacked that much time. She would have to be content with getting across the river and putting the villagers in their place.

The Bluesman had run off. No surprise there. And the Muyaza seemed eager to return to their normal lives. They were not ones for open confrontation. They would mourn their losses at night, in private. At the sight of Malja and her party, one woman cried out and the tribe froze.

They watched her as if she were a ghost — unsure if they could believe their eyes. With Viper in her hand, Malja pointed at the nearest old man and at two younger men. She gestured toward the litters. They needed nothing more. In a few tense seconds, the old man sat atop the litter and attempted to calm himself enough to form the protective bubble. The tribe watched. A few men squinted in impotent rage. Many looked down in shame.

They crossed the river with speed, not even stopping at the halfway point. The two men carrying the litter rushed along as if Malja had poked them with Viper. When they reached the other side, the Muyaza at that village halted everything — even the babies were hushed. Five horses were tied to a post, awaiting their turn at becoming dinner stew. Malja pointed to three, and under her watchful eyes, Fawbry and Tumus untied and saddled them.

"No," snapped a male sitting at the dining table. Three horses represented a lot of hard work. He stood, revealing his chiseled, muscular body and white scar across his chest. He stormed toward them, throwing a konapol bone to the side. A woman motioned towards him only to collapse in tears at his stern, determined face. He opened his mouth, displaying long, sharp teeth, and again said, "No."

Malja no longer bothered with words. She grabbed the man's wrist, twisted it, ducked underneath his arm, and pulled up, pinning his arm behind his back. With two swift kicks, she popped his knees forward, sending him to the ground. She raised Viper, cutting the air with a low whoosh, and swung down with every intention of watching that blade sink into the man's chest. But the blade never made it.

Tommy blocked her arm with his. They locked eyes. It took only a few seconds, but for Malja, those eyes spoke for years. Years of abuse, of strain and hurt, and of betrayal. She had no idea whose years she saw — his or her own.

She released the male. He walked off, trying to regain face in his angry steps. The woman who had wept for him approached, and he spit out harsh words and raised his hand but did not strike. Malja mounted a dappled gray and pulled Tommy into her arms. She cradled him, and like a child, he settled into his familiar position. Fawbry and Tumus each took a horse and followed Malja's lead out of the village. Nobody dared even to look at them.

Soon, she would need Fawbry to lead the way, but for now, she knew where to go. The Freelands. A barbaric dead land she had hoped never to return to. A place that made the Muyaza look like the friendliest of neighbors.

"I hate the water," she said.

Chapter 10

During her youngest years, while under the magical protection of Jarik and Callib, Malja never suffered from sickness — not a cold, not a fever, not a rash, not a bellyache, nothing. Health surrounded her like a golden aura. When they tossed her away, she slogged through the next few years contracting every possible bug Corlin had to offer. Gregor did his best to comfort her during times of sickness, but he also explained that fighting her way to health would train her body to defeat the bugs in the future.

"Sometimes," he said, "a good fight is the best lesson." Watching Tommy sweat and shiver in her arms, she wondered how Gregor ever had the strength to let sickness run its course.

She held Tommy, wiped his brow, talked to him — anything she could think of. She told him about Gregor's tiny shack and how she loved the place. She talked of the way Gregor played *Find the Apple* and in doing so, helped her discover the endless nooks of the small, two-room home. He made it feel bigger. She described Gregor's laugh, his stern voice, and even the way his belches chirped out instead of a loud boom.

Tommy mustered a weak grin. She wanted to read for him, but they lost *Astronomical Wonders* in the Yad. Instead, she described the solar system as best she could recall. He listened well, but she thought it all sounded made up.

Malja talked on for he seemed to like it. But she was no doctor, and this illness she did not understand. She tried to warm him and make him feel safe.

Fawbry and Tumus fumbled through constructing camp. Though slow and inefficient, they did get the job done. Soon the warmth of the campfire helped calm Tommy. He closed his eyes and slept to the rich aroma of burning pine.

Malja watched his shallow breathing, his weakened body, his trembling lips. *Make it better,* she commanded but nothing changed. She longed to do something active — kill something, defeat someone, run somewhere. Anything would be better than sitting here watching Tommy burn away.

"Let me hold him," Tumus said.

Malja started and cursed under her breath — she should never let anybody sneak up on her. "Go away," she said.

"Barris ordered me—"

"Barris isn't here."

Tumus's yellow eyes narrowed. Tossing her hands up, she said, "Stupid." To Malja's relief, Tumus stormed away. To her disappointment, Fawbry slipped in place.

"You should be nicer to her," he said, squatting near the campfire. "It's not her fault. Besides, imagine what she's going through. Raised her whole life to think she's saving the world as some magic protector against the dead, that Korstra has it all planned out. Then Barris comes along and suddenly nothing she believed in is true. It's sad."

Tumus flew back with a fury Malja wished to see in most warriors. "You be quiet, you Kryssta-loving fool. You know nothing of my people but the lies your pathetic priests tell you."

Fawbry put some distance between them but laughed. "Oh, really. So what are you doing here? Did Korstra tell you to convert us or something?"

"Shut your filthy mouth. Don't you speak the Lord's name."

"The Lord is not Korstra."

"Blasphemy!"

Malja snapped in a harsh whisper. "Both of you, stop it. You'll wake Tommy."

"My apologies," Fawbry said, adding a silly bow. "I can't educate such a heathen when she so excitable."

"You're the heathen," Tumus said, pacing as she spoke, flexing her fingers, rolling her head — all actions Malja recognized. If Fawbry kept pushing, she expected Tumus to strike out. "You have brought the curse of blasphemy upon us," Tumus continued. "You should go away."

"I didn't want any part of this. But I trust Barris, and I trust Kryssta. And Kryssta help me, I might be starting to trust Malja. So I'm staying. Besides, if I'm cursed, you're the one who put it on me. Remember?"

Tumus's head pulled back like a cat smelling rancid meat. "Are you saying this is my fault? Do you really want—"

Malja cringed as they geared up for more arguing. Tommy didn't stir, so she figured she should let them get it out. However, she suspected these two could keep fighting all night and most of the next day.

But then Tommy began to shake.

Just a short spasm in the arm. Then the leg. Then his body bucked in a wild display. He moaned and flailed. With surprising force, he belted Malja off of him. She scrambled back, trying to hold yet not hurt him. She called his name.

"This can't be," Fawbry said. "Barris can't be right."

Malja had never seen anything like this. White, foamy spittle pooled in Tommy's mouth. Her heart pounded. She tried to hold down his limbs but couldn't keep him still. Her mind blanked. She struggled to hold him. No other part of her could move. *Is this panic?* Tommy was dying before her eyes and she had frozen. *Is this how people feel when I attack with Viper?*

From her dazed fog, she heard a voice — an authoritative voice. "Pull her off."

"I'm trying," Fawbry said. Malja felt hands on her shoulders, and she let them lead her back a few paces. Like snow dropping down her back, shocking her with its cold, the situation became clear and chilling again. She started for Tommy but Fawbry blocked her path. "No, Malja. If you want Tommy to live, let Tumus help. Barris warned me that when the time came, Tommy might need her."

Standing at Tommy's feet, Tumus spread her robed arms like black wings while Tommy thrashed about below her. Malja broke Fawbry's grip with ease and stormed ahead. Tommy kicked out and stiffened like he had been petrified. She let out a sharp cry. *He's dead,* she thought.

The boy arched, his belly lifting to the sky, and a hot blast of energy shot out of him. It exploded in all directions, lighting up the night like a golden funeral pyre. But the energy curved — literally shifted directions as if an invisible wall had formed amongst the trees and rocks. The energy turned in on itself until it found the one open release — Tumus.

Like a sword thrust straight through an opponent, the energy pierced into the Chi-Chun woman. She staggered but remained standing. It poured in, and she cried out. When the last of it had entered her, the forest darkened into night. Nothing radiated out of her. She had absorbed it all.

She lowered her head and rubbed her belly like a newly pregnant woman. Malja crawled to Tommy who sat, awake and looking healthy but tired. He pointed to his mouth. *I'm hungry.*

Bursting into joyous laughter, Malja wiped her eyes. She gazed up at

Tumus. "Thank you."

Tumus let out a satisfied breath. "This was only the first. There will be more."

"More? What's the matter with him?"

"Nothing. He's just becoming a magician."

As Malja handed Tommy some nuts, she looked at his right wrist. Three swirling lines that had not been there before now marred his skin. She felt nausea. They were faint lines, could've been mistaken for dirt, but clear to her — the beginnings of a tattoo.

She wanted to shout but said nothing. She remained by Tommy's side while he inhaled his food. Tumus also sat next to Tommy, observing every motion, every breath. When he winced before belching, Malja witnessed the anticipation in Tumus. Whatever her exact part in all this, the Chi-Chun woman wanted it to happen again.

Later that night, Tommy slept with a full belly, and Fawbry snored nearby. Malja stood watch. The closer they came to the Freelands, the more vigilant they would have to be. Luxuries like a full night's sleep would have to wait until this ended.

Malja hated guard duty. Not enough to occupy her mind. Too much time for her memories to return. After her experience with Barris Mont, she knew her memories would overwhelm her if given the chance. Too many walls she had built up, Barris had knocked down.

As if it had only just happened, she could feel the ground as she threw up outside the shack — Gregor's mutilated body just out of her sight. Taking a long, raking breath, she rolled to the side and screamed. When her voice died out, she heard the whine of the wooden floor. Somebody was still inside the shack. Jarik or Callib, it didn't matter. Malja intended to make them pay.

She didn't have Viper back then, but the short sword she wielded had been with her for many years. She knew its weight well. Coupled with the over-confidence of a seventeen-year-old, she found no problems with her plan of bursting into the shack and slicing apart anything living she saw. The man hiding inside, however, thought fighting back to be a better idea.

Tommy moaned and kicked out in his sleep. Malja watched him for several minutes, her eyes glistening in the firelight, and she waited. One more moan or whimper or cry, any sign of distress, and she would wake him. She knew the nightmare he suffered. She had seen it in his eyes when she rescued him.

She remembered the cold rain rattling the tiny battery room Tommy had been locked in. She had cut his chains, and he had smiled. But she picked up the chains and examined them. They were old and rusty like the ship. She looked at the boy's wrists and saw where prolonged binding had left its marks.

"Well, Tommy," she said, trying to figure out what still troubled her. "The Captain doesn't appear to be a friend to either of us. He tried to drown me and he keeps you locked up here." Malja bolted up as her thoughts connected. "Why didn't the mage-pirates kill you? Or, at least, take you with them? And Wuchev must've seen me make it across the deck. He knows now that I know something's going on. He'll be coming. He has to. But he doesn't want to cross outside, and his precious cargo ... there is no cargo."

With a scowl and a grunt, Tommy snatched the chains and threw them across the tiny room. He stepped in the opposite direction and, pushing a box out of the way, revealed an access hatch in the floor. He opened it, a rusty whine echoed around them like an aged alarm, and descended on a ladder.

Malja hesitated. Though he appeared to be little more than an abused boy, Tommy was a magician. However, being stuck on a ship in a raging storm left her with few alternatives. She sheathed Viper and climbed down.

The ladder ended in a narrow corridor. She caught sight of Tommy at the far end, opening a doorway. By the time she reached the door, he had stepped inside and stood on a wide platform overlooking the empty, cavernous cargo hold. Empty, except for a simple box at the center of the hold floor.

"What's in there?" she asked.

Tommy stared at it, his eyes blazing hatred.

"Is that what the mage-pirates wanted?" Malja shook her head. "No. Because there were no mage-rats."

A loud bang echoed in the hold and the entire ship groaned to the side. Tommy pointed to the rusting hull. Malja climbed down to the cargo hold's floor and inspected the hull. She knew nothing about ships, but even her untrained eye could see the ancient metal dying. The bang repeated and the metal whined as the storm battered the hull.

Squatting to Tommy's level, Malja looked him over and said, "Wuchev killed his crew, didn't he? He drugged us and killed them. That's why I slept through everything."

Tommy nodded. Not a moment's hesitation. He knew the answer. She wondered how he could be so clear when he was chained in the battery station — unless by some magical means he could spy on the world outside. But that sounded paranoid to her. Magic didn't work like that. At least, not any magic she had ever come across.

She stepped back from the boy, her heart pounding against her ribs as if Callib had rebuked her for some minor infraction, reminding her that this little boy would grow up to be a ruthless magician. From the corner of her eye, she saw the box. Something about the box had bothered the boy.

Moving closer, her stomach rolled as the ship took another trip along a steep wave. With her hand resting on the rough wooden lid, she gazed back at the boy. If he proved to be more magician than boy, then she would have to defend herself. *Can I really kill a child?* She wanted to say *no* without hesitation, but she didn't know. She understood that deep within her the capability to perform such a vile act existed if it turned out to be necessary. She just didn't know if the rest of her would protest.

She lifted the lid and gazed in the box. A robe. A ripped, dusty robe.

Malja looked back at Tommy. His face gave nothing away. Before she could say a word, Captain Wuchev stepped out of the shadows. He held a single-shot handgun. From the dented barrel to the chipped wood body, Malja figured he would be lucky if the gun fired without exploding, luckier if it came near its target.

"You're not being very cooperative," Wuchev said.

"Not really trying."

To Tommy, he gestured with the gun. "Come join us, little maggot." Tommy rushed to Malja's side. Wuchev glanced at the box. "Do you know how much that's worth?"

"Don't care," Malja said.

"People would give me everything they had just to look at it. I could stop running this ship. I could build a mansion, pay for guards and a few magicians to power the place. I could live like our great ancestors once did. All because a bunch of backwards Korstra zealots think that has spiritual powers. They really believe Korstra wore that. As if a brother god had need for mortal clothing. Kryssta forgive me for dealing with such heretics, but it's worth it."

In Wuchev's eyes, Malja saw more than sheer greed. "When I approached you, you couldn't turn me down without causing suspicions amongst the crew."

Wuchev sneered. "They already were on edge because I wouldn't allow them in here. If I turned away easy money like you ... well, I'll tell you something, though — I never thought you'd make it across the deck in this storm. You're reputation is well earned."

"The storm," Malja said, another point clicking in her brain. "No mage-rats. You conjured it."

"Remarkable, isn't it?" he said and lifted his shirt with his free hand. A design like seven blades spinning in the wind tattooed his stomach. "Spent my whole life working on only the one spell. Takes a lot out of me, that's why I kept the one crewman alive. I needed a partner."

"So, what now?"

Wuchev sauntered back and forth in front of the box, waving the gun in lazy motions. His pleasure at holding somebody in his power filled the air with an arrogant stench. His eyes twitched and searched with paranoid fervor — mad from magic. "Now, my pretty dear, I'm going to—"

The hull screamed as a long crack formed near the floor. Water spewed into the air like a fountain gone berserk. Wuchev jumped, and Malja took full advantage of the precious seconds afforded her. She hurdled the box and blocked Wuchev's arm as he tried to aim. The gun fired into the air, flame licking out of the damaged barrel, and the burnt smell swirled around them. He spun away from Malja and attempted a few jabs, but she far exceeded his limited skills. She feinted to the side and punched him hard on the temple. His eyes rolled back and he dropped to the floor.

To Malja's surprise, Tommy also had taken advantage of Wuchev's initial distraction. While she had been disarming the foolish Captain, Tommy had snatched the robe. He stood on the edge of the shadowed hold as water blanketed the floor.

"Wait," she called, and despite his worried expression, he did not run away.

Malja bent down and shouldered Wuchev. As the frigid water rushed around her feet, she stood and groaned like the old ship. He was lighter than she had expected but still a burden. She looked at Tommy's questioning face and said, "If I don't have to kill, I won't." *I'm glad I don't have to kill you.*

Tommy led the way through the hold and into the narrow corridors. Wuchev's head dragged on the walls, but Malja had enough trouble lugging the fool to worry about his forehead getting cut up. Water followed them, and when they reached the first set of stairs, Malja could feel the little heat left being sucked away by the ravenous sea.

Stepping out onto the main deck, sheets of rain covered them. The waves had become mere foothills in the sea, and the wind had eased back to a strong breeze, but the storm had not abated. Wuchev could get the thing going but he couldn't control it.

Malja placed Wuchev on the deck, resting against the door frame. With reverence, Tommy approached the port railing. He held the robe over the side. He dropped it into the sea. Walking back, he wore a solemn grin. Behind him, light blue painted the horizon as dawn approached, promising a warm sun and a pleasant day.

The ship took a long time to sink. There was no rush. With Tommy's help, Malja lowered a lifeboat into the water after laying Captain Wuchev inside. She searched the cabins for the young crewman, called out for him, but she never found him and he never answered.

Later, when the storm had vanished into the distant horizon and the ship had disappeared into the sea's darkness, Malja rowed under the soothing morning light. Tommy stood in the boat for a while, displaying excellent balance.

That's when Wuchev let out an enraged roar and swiped Tommy's legs. The boy splashed into the ocean as Wuchev lunged for Malja. Malja fell back, posted her foot in the air, and caught Wuchev in the gut. His eyes bulged as the air in his lungs forcibly shot out of his mouth. She tossed him overboard.

Tommy scratched and clawed at the edge of the lifeboat. Malja rushed over and reached for him — his skin paling and his body shivering in the cold water. As she pulled him up, Wuchev splashed to the surface and latched onto the boy. He punched the boy's ribs. He grabbed at the boy's hair. Madness painted his face as he tried anything to break that boy's grip.

"I'll drown you, maggot!"

Malja swung her leg over the side and pressed her foot against Wuchev's head. She looked straight at Tommy and said, "I promise you, I won't let go." Pulling on Tommy and pushing on Wuchev, she started to separate the two.

Wuchev screamed, but Malja did not stop. "I'm sorry," he blubbered. "I'm sorry. Don't let me die. I'll take it all back. I didn't mean to hurt anybody. I wasn't going to drown the boy."

Malja raised her foot and for a second, Wuchev smiled as if he had won. With her teeth clenched and her top lip lifted in a snarl, she slammed her heel into his nose, breaking it with a gush of blood, and sending him into the water. His muted screams were strong enough to come through the water for longer than she had expected. She yanked Tommy aboard, and without pause, returned to the oars.

Tommy looked at her, his eyes shimmering with such a blend of emotion, Malja couldn't tell what he thought. She stared right back at him, unwavering, not giving him an alternative but to deal with his thoughts. She saw fear in those eyes. And anger. And newborn freedom. She thought she saw tremors of the magician within him. And she knew he saw the monster within her.

But he stepped over to her. He sat at her knees. And he rested his head against her leg.

Tumus joined her, snapping Malja from her memories. Malja couldn't decide if that was any better. They were quiet at first. Malja wished she would leave and chose to scan the trees rather than risk inviting conversation. She tried to clear her mind, but Tommy's eyes would not leave her. She even tried to think about Gregor's attacker, but doing so with Tumus right there left Malja feeling wrong as if she had defiled his memory a little. She hoped Tumus would give up, but such hopes were dashed as Tumus cleared her throat.

She began with some dull talk about Fawbry, the cooling weather, and horses. Malja answered in as few words as possible. She knew Tumus was building up the courage to say something and just had to wait it out.

At length, Tumus said, "What do you know about the Chi-Chun? Other than the superstitious nonsense Fawbry spouts."

"Not much."

"Well, let me teach you some things."

"No, thanks. Don't mean to be offensive, but I don't really care what you believe. Korstra, Kryssta — all that religious stuff never served me well."

"Then I feel sadness for you," Tumus said with honest pity in her voice. "Listen, though, please. I'm not seeking a convert. I do think what I have to say is important for you and our task — it's about Cole Watts."

Though Malja did not look away from the woods, her skin prickled. "I'm listening."

"Thank you," Tumus said. "First, you must see that those who follow Korstra and those who follow Kryssta were not always enemies. Long ago, the brother gods ruled as one, and the world lived in glorious peace. All existed in perfect balance. All was as it should be. Trouble came along with Elatria — an exquisite princess. Some say a goddess as well. The brothers each fell in love with her and each sought to win her over the other. But they are gods and immortal. The world suffered under their endless battle. Until one day, Korstra made a bold and gracious gesture. To save the world, he would give up Elatria and dominion over half the people, and in exchange he called upon Kryssta to do the same."

"Split control of the world and nobody gets the girl. Nobody's happy, but their pain is equal."

"Exactly. But Kryssta betrayed Korstra and stole Elatria away. What neither god knew was that they had formed Elatria themselves. And so she required both of their love to exist. Without Korstra, she perished. Now, Fawbry will no doubt tell you this was all Korstra's fault, but —"

"What does any of this have to do with Cole Watts?"

Tumus smiled as if pitying a naïve child. "Elatria's death brought about the Devastation."

Malja shook her head. "I don't believe that."

"It doesn't matter if you believe or not. It is true. Elatria died, and the Devastation came, erasing most of the world and reshaping the rest. Korstra wept at this loss, but he still had control over half the remaining souls. That included the magicians. Korstra looked down and saw a man drowning in Dead Lake. He pulled together all the matter he could grab quickly and transformed that man into a conduit — a godlike creature, but a damned one, who would someday aid in Korstra's return to power, yet never enjoy peaceful bliss."

"Barris Mont?"

"Yes."

"Are you saying that through Barris Mont a brother god has sent us on a mission to find Cole Watts?"

"Patience. I'm almost finished. Korstra promised there would be signs to tell his followers if the brother god taking control was him or Kryssta. One of these signs, one that tells us Kryssta is coming, is called the Rising of the Dead. Don't listen to Fawbry. We don't think corpses will come back to life. That is nonsense. We circle Dead Lake so that Korstra can speak to us through Barris Mont at any time. But as for the dead — well, what do you know of science?"

"Almost as much as I know about religion."

"Before the Devastation, mankind created many wondrous things. Buildings that could fly, ways to communicate across oceans, and machines that could think and work and talk. It took a tremendous amount of magical energy, but they succeeded. These are the dead we worry about. The machines. If they rise again, Korstra will have lost. So, Korstra made us, the Chi-Chun. We absorb the energy, we redirect it if needed, we keep the dead dead, and help prevent Kryssta from victory."

"Sounds like more superstition."

"Except that Cole Watts, the one we seek, builds these machines."

Chapter 11

Of all the land in Corlin, the Freelands had been hit hardest by the Devastation. Though it had never been good land for farming, it had flourished with rugged trees and dangerous wildlife. After the Devastation, it transformed into barren rocks. Those creatures that survived did so by the most ruthless means. No day passed without the death of something. And oftentimes death was preferred. By the time trees grew again and more animals returned, those that dwelled in the Freelands had grown accustomed to the area. They understood and accepted its rules. Many saw no other way to live.

Malja led her team along the remains of an ancient road. Every so often they came across a sign marking the way. The signs varied in size. Some were like a shield posted on a metal rod. Some were enormous, mounted on metal framework, spanning the distance across the pocked pavement and beyond.

"The road used to fill up the whole space," Fawbry said. "I've seen a few up North still intact. I can't imagine what the world must've been like to need a road this wide. I mean, look there." The skeleton of a grounder long ago stripped of anything valuable rusted off to the side. "These grounders weren't big. A road this wide — you could've fit five, six, maybe seven or more across. Can you even begin to picture the numbers of people a world like that had?"

Malja didn't have to. Thanks to Barris Mont, she had seen it. That world had been breathing and vibrant. It overflowed with exuberance for human life that literally floated amongst the clouds. Surely a world like that would never allow monsters like Jarik and Callib. She didn't lie to herself — evil must have existed. But in her world, especially in the Freelands, people tolerated evil. People tried to strike bargains with evil just to be left alone, to survive.

In the Freelands, evil thrived. Here, such things held a twisted logic. But in that glistening, peaceful world she had witnessed, it made no sense. Evil lived off want. There was no want in that world. *Don't be an idiot. People always want what they don't have.*

The road hugged the sides at each hill and found every crevice as a detour. Half the time chewed-up pavement disappeared leaving only a dirt path to follow. Sometimes the road vanished completely. In fact, Malja realized they could have picked up a different road by mistake. According to the sun, though, they still headed in the right direction. That would have to suffice.

"You're pushing my tolerance," Tumus said.

Fawbry had been making little comments all day — praising Kryssta for fresh air or cursing Korstra for a sore muscle. Malja wondered what offense had brought Tumus to the point of threats. The answer forced her to suppress a laugh. Sitting in his saddle, scrunching his features with studious concentration, Fawbry silently read from a tiny book.

"Put away that vile affront or I'll be forced to put it away for you," Tumus said.

Feigning confusion, Fawbry looked up from his text. "This? The Book of Kryssta? It's hardly an affront. The fact that Kryssta's guiding hand kept this book safe when I nearly drowned in the Yad should tell you that much. Besides which, even if you don't follow its wisdom, the poetry in these pages is beautiful." Fawbry held the book out. "Here, try it."

Before Malja even saw Tumus's frustrated, hurt features, she knew Fawbry had done a nasty thing. Odds were that Tumus could not read. No shame there — most people couldn't read. But for Fawbry to flaunt his education, to literally shove it at her, that lacked any sense of respectability.

Perhaps he recognized his error because, in a solemn voice, he said, "I know you don't believe, but let me share with you one thing from this —

> *My brother, my earth, my home, my world —*
> *The endless angles of ourselves —*
> *We inhale what others exhale —*
> *We are formed from others' dust.*

— Do you see? We are all one to the brother gods. After all, even Korstrians believe the goddess Elatria was formed by the brother gods together. We are all one."

Tumus led her horse ahead, but her hostility lessened for awhile.

As the day wore on, Tommy's fever returned. Malja dismissed her concerns at first, but when dusk approached, there could be no denying. He had begun the day bright and joyful — sitting upright in the saddle, pointing at trees and birds, smiling. Now, he curled in Malja's arms, shivering and sweating, pale and pained.

Tumus had noticed, too. She never stopped watching him, and every little groan or shift or sigh he made elicited an overbearing response. In seconds, her horse would ride alongside and she bombarded Malja with questions about the boy that had no answers. She touched the boy's brow with the back of her hand, touched his shoulder to readjust his shirt, and touched her own lips mumbling prayers. Malja bit back her desire to knock Tumus off her horse.

The sun lowered turning the gray rocks milky blue. The air grew colder. Ahead, they saw a dilapidated structure — a welcome sight amongst the endless rocks.

The one-story building had a wide roof that jutted out several feet creating a covering for the horses. *Probably meant for grounders,* Malja thought. Shaped like two cylinders smashed together, the building appeared to have been a way station. Old batteries were piled against the wall, each one so empty of magically-created electricity that its power gauge lacked enough power to give a reading. No surprise, of course. Those things hadn't been charged in over a generation. For that matter, the only thing keeping Nature from reclaiming the space was the barren remoteness of the area — that and the occasional travelers fixing it up for a night or two.

"We'll stay here tonight," Malja said. Tumus dismounted and hurried to help Tommy down. Malja turned the dappled gray away and said, "See if you can find some firewood." Before Tumus's confused pout found a voice, Malja spied Fawbry near the doorless doorway. "Be careful."

Fawbry stepped away. "Don't worry. I'm not going in there until you do."

Once Tumus left on her futile errand (Malja would be shocked if she found more than a sapling or two), Malja eased Tommy off the horse and handed Fawbry the reins. Tommy stood by one of the dented posts holding up the overhang. Any minute he might collapse. She pulled out Viper and approached the doorway. Something smelled horrible like urine-soaked rags.

Inside, Malja saw a dusty, marble-topped counter with holes smashed through it. Behind the counter, an archway opened up to another room. Rubble lined the paint-peeled walls. In the center, a circle of stones marked the spot many had used for a campfire. Malja peered at the domed ceiling — black with soot. She couldn't see an air vent, but there had to be one, otherwise a campfire would choke the room.

Just in front of the campfire, she found the source of the stench — four rabbits and a hawk, blood drying on the floor. Her thought — blood sacrifice of one of the smaller religions. When she turned to leave, however, she saw that her thought was severely incorrect.

"What in Kryssta is that?" Fawbry asked. "It sure stinks."

"I told you to stay outside," Malja said.

Tumus entered with Tommy. "It started pouring out there and the overhang is full of leaks. Cold rain is the last thing Tommy needs."

"Go back outside. I'll take care of this," Malja said with a glance at the undulating, brown mass pasted high on the wall.

Tumus stepped closer. "Is that an egg sac?"

"Cocoon. Now get out before anything breaks free of that."

Fawbry raised an eyebrow. "Looks like someone threw a crap at the wall."

Tumus pointed at the dead animals. "Those are for the baby when it gets out."

"It's a snake-cutter," Malja said, "and when it leaves that cocoon, it'll eat everything in sight."

Fawbry scratched his head. "So can't you kill it now while it's stuck in there? We'll get a fire going and have baby snake-cutter for dinner."

"I told you to wait outside. When I strike, if it survives the first blow, I don't want it coming after any of you."

"I don't want that, either. You've convinced me. We'll wait outside."

"It's too wet, too cold," Tumus said. "Tommy can't take that."

"It'll be just a moment," Fawbry said. "Just pray to your Korstra to protect the boy."

"I do. All the time."

Malja pointed to the doorway. "Go. Let me get this done." Tumus scowled, but she followed as Fawbry headed out. Tommy, however, stepped forward. He placed his hand on top of Malja's — the one gripping Viper. His hand felt clammy and ill, but his eyes cut into her with icy clarity. She tried to pull away, but he held fast. "I don't like killing," she said, unsure of why she spoke, hating the little girl she heard. "And I've killed more things in my life than I ever wish on anybody. Everyday I live with it. Everyday I know I've got more killing ahead. Right or wrong doesn't matter. Justified or not doesn't matter. I do it because it's all I know. And it kills me."

Tommy released her hand and collapsed. Tumus hurry to his side. Malja wiped her face — tears glistened off her cheeks.

Breaking the silence, Fawbry said, "Um, I think it's hatching."

Malja did not move. She searched Tommy's unconscious face for an answer as to what had just happened. Behind her, she heard the cracking cocoon. He had touched her and she could not stop her talking. She heard the kittenish cry of the baby snake-cutter. He had pierced her with his eyes, and she revealed so much of herself. She heard an odd crinkling as the baby snake-cutter ate its cocoon. The only answer she saw — Tommy had used magic on her.

"Malja," Fawbry said as he clambered on top of the counter, "it's almost out."

She spun around to face the baby beast. White like snow and covered in mucus, the four-foot snake-cutter flopped to the cracked, tile floor. Its tubular body and hundreds of tiny, slithering legs gave it the snake illusion. Its head, however, lacked any such image. It didn't even have a face. Instead, its front end closed tight like a sphincter. Eyes on either side and a long-hair mane made this one of the ugliest creatures Malja had ever seen.

Righting itself, the baby shook off the fall, eyed one dead rabbit, and launched into it with abandon. It slurped and groaned and mewed. Each sound flipped Malja's stomach. She clenched her teeth and snarled. The snake-cutter's eyesight may have been poor, but its hearing worked just fine. Its head shot up, searching for a threat.

Malja looked back at Tommy. He had used magic. On her.

With a raw, primal scream unlike any war cry she had ever made before, Malja swung Viper. The tip hooked the snake-cutter. It cried out like a child strangling its tears and jerked away causing its skin to tear. Malja kicked it to the wall, shredding its skin as it ripped free from Viper. Wriggling against the wall, it moaned and screeched as its blood pooled. Malja moved forward. It cringed at her approach.

Again she struck hard with Viper, launching the baby into a new frenzy of cries.

Again she struck hard. Holding his ears, Fawbry yelled, "Just finish it." But she didn't want to. She wanted it to fight back.

Again she struck. Blood sprayed against the wall. Tumus cried out at each blow, her shocked voice melding with the dying creature's.

Again. Malja's arm shook as Viper cut straight through to the floor.

The cries weakened. The blood flow lessened. Still, Malja struck.

When she finally stopped, she let Viper clatter on the tile floor. She stumbled backward. Rain and thunder played a double rhythm. Her frenzied fury still echoed along her skin, pulsing with her heartbeat. Lightning flashed. She looked at Tommy — the magician. He gazed up, shivering next to Tumus.

"Don't ever use magic on me again," Malja said and walked into the rain.

Chapter 12

As night edged in, Malja worked on the horses. Under fluttering torchlight, she slid her hands along the withers, kneading when required. She scooped the rib cage and massaged the chest, working the rubdown all the way to the legs. She cleaned out a metal container and collected rainwater so the horses could drink. She talked to them and combed their manes. By the time she had finished, most of her anger had dissipated.

Fawbry spent this time clearing out the mess she had made. He built a pile of rabbit, hawk, and smoke-cutter bits and covered it with stones and mud to keep scavengers away. He built a fire using the charred remains in the campfire circle — not enough for a good blaze, but it would keep them warm.

Malja had watched this as she worked. Now, she stood by her dappled gray, stared out at the rain, and listened to its drum rattle on the overhang. She heard Fawbry behind her — sounded like he made extra noise so as not to startle her into a swift attack.

"You okay?" he asked.

She shrugged.

"You can come back in, you know."

She glanced at the doorway. "I don't think that's a good idea."

"Don't be stupid. We're your friends." Malja raised an eyebrow and Fawbry laughed. "I am, at least. I'm trying. Tommy is, you know that. Tumus probably not. The point is, we'll listen to you. We understand."

"I doubt you could ever understand."

"Oh, really? Just because I know when to run, doesn't mean I don't know anything about anger, about rage so powerful it takes over all of your thoughts."

"This was more than just being really mad."

"I know. I do. You think of me as I am, but even a coward will fight if there's no other choice."

Lightning flashed against the wet, rocky landscape. Fawbry rested a hand on his black mare. Malja watched as he tried to rub out a harsh memory swimming just below the surface of his words. An authentic smile crept upon her lips. Any more anger and these horses won't want to be touched again.

Fawbry said, "Years ago, when I was a young man, I lived up north with my parents. I worked our farm in the mornings and went to school the rest of the day. Things up there are a little better, a little more stable, and my father thought some kind of education would set me up for a good life.

"I did enjoy school. I miss it. It was simpler. You just had to show up and learn. At least, that's how it was until I started noticing girls."

"We do have a way of complicating each other's lives."

Fawbry grinned. "Yes, we do. I've often thought men and women would be better off living in separate colonies that only get together once in a while to procreate."

"I can think of a lot of men and quite a few women who'd hate that idea."

"Well, they never went after the wrong girl. It sounds silly now, but back then I would've done anything for Yolen. She possessed me with a fire I've never felt for another woman. But she was not a good person. I put up with her using me and tolerated her infidelity. I was a real idiot. My parents saw through her, and they tried to make me see, but I ignored them. What kid is going to listen to his parents when they're telling him to give up on someone he wants?

"Things changed when I met Pung Kirkle. Big guy. Always had two big friends with him. Yolen left me for Pung, and I couldn't do anything about it. As hurt and sad and betrayed as I was, I would've just gone off and cried and maybe, someday, moved on. But Yolen was cruel, and Pung was her new dog. It began with simple teasing, then they started hitting me in passing, and then ... well, then we get to the whole point of this."

Thunder rumbled. "I take it you fought back," Malja said, "and you felt bad about it. This is different."

"I didn't just fight back. I lured them. I waited until Pung and his two thug friends were alone. And then I called them names — I knew that's all it would take to get them to chase me. I ran down a dead-end alley. They slowed down, knowing I couldn't escape, thinking they had all the time. But I had planted a metal pipe with jagged scrap attached.

"My first two swings caught them by surprise. Both of Pung's buddies fell. One lost his nose. The other took it in the side and was bleeding bad. Pung — I saw him become afraid. That made me feel good. Really good. Like I had exposed him in front of the world. Like I was powerful. Euphoria and—"

"I know it well."

"I suppose you do. Anyway, he swung at me. The problem for him was that I had been hit by him many times. What was one more? I didn't flinch, and I didn't turn away. I took the fist."

"And then you were in range."

"Exactly. I smashed out his kneecaps. He curled up and cried — may have even wet himself. But I didn't stop. I couldn't. All my hatred and anger and jealousy and everything poured out with each strike. I just kept hitting. I screamed and kicked and I couldn't find a way to stop. He almost died. Had I been stronger, he would be dead.

"I ran away that day. Headed South. Trouble for me was that the South was more barbaric than I could handle. Brains got me far, but in the end, people down here solve everything with a sword."

"Is this meant to make me feel better?"

Fawbry patted his horse and headed toward the door. "No. Just wanted you to know you're not alone."

The rain picked up, and the wind shifted. Malja backed up, but the storm reached her no matter where she stood. From the doorway, Fawbry said, "Come back inside."

"Maybe later."

With an angry howl, the wind shifted again taking the rain with it. The sudden drop in noise filled up with Malja's laughter. It came out in short bursts, initially, but when Fawbry joined in, the floodgates released. She laughed hard, not even sure why, but letting the wondrous sensation run its course. Tears formed and her chest ached, but each time she thought she had control the laughter exploded again. It seemed like it would never end. Until she heard Tommy cry in pain.

A bright light flashed through the doorway. Malja dashed over to Fawbry. Inside, Tumus sat against the wall holding Tommy in her arms. Both were covered in sweat. Tommy's eyes were closed.

"He's okay," Tumus said. "This one was rough, but he's fine now."

Seeing Tommy secure in the Chi-Chun's embrace twisted a hot spear through Malja's chest. With a sharp motion, she waved Tumus outside. Easing away from Tommy took some maneuvering, but Tumus managed not to wake him. As she stepped outside, Malja said, "How much more of this does he have to go through?"

"I don't know. If he were back at the lake, Barris could guide him. Alone like this — he has to find his own path to each spell."

Malja stepped back as if slapped. "How many spells does he have?"

"I don't know. Barris didn't tell me. But the power I've been absorbing from him is more than anything I've ever experienced."

She watched Tommy curl up. Her heart pounded unlike anything she ever felt before battle. When he woke, she hoped he would understand and not think she had broken her promise. She clasped her hands so she could feel the tight grip that she imagined kept Tommy safe. With a curt nod, she said, "Then we can't wait. Fawbry, saddle up our horses. Tumus, you stay here with Tommy. You'll be safe enough inside. The smell of that dead snake-cutter should keep most things away. We'll leave what food we have, but ration it. And when we get back, I expect him to be in good shape. You let anything happen to him, you better run. Understand?"

Tumus nodded. Malja suppressed a grin — good to see her authority voice still held its power.

"Where are you going?" Tumus twisted the black shreds of her robe. "In case Tommy asks."

"To find Cole Watts, of course."

Chapter 13

By the time the rainstorm had passed and the morning sun breached the sky, Malja and Fawbry had crossed nearly ten desolate miles. The horses were exhausted. Two long treks with little rest in between left them sore and irritable. Malja shared the sentiment.

She pictured Tommy waking up to find her gone. She knew she had made the right choice — he needed close care right now. Care which, it galled her to admit, she could not provide. But even if Tumus could help him with his magic, he would also miss her. He had to. When she returned, he'll sprint towards her, his arms open wide, ready to wrap around her legs. Maybe then she'll get him to listen to orders more often.

They stopped for an early-morning break and let the horses wander free for a bit. Not too far, though. Malja kept eyeing them like a worried parent watched a toddler. This was the Freelands, after all. Not a place to be caught without a horse.

Later, when her bladder demanded attention, she asked Fawbry to watch the horses. She found a boulder to get behind and relieved herself. Afterward, she didn't move. She remained squatting as her mind flashed through the memories Barris Mont had churned up.

I'll kill that damned thing for what it's done to me. She'd rather have Gregor's voice pestering her about paying the dead their honor. She considered those thoughts for a moment. Perhaps it was as simple as that. If Gregor had been right, and he often was right, then by paying them their honor, she had been able to bury her memories safely. Barris Mont dug them all up again. If she paid the honor once more, she hoped that might be enough to stop these flashes.

Except Barris didn't unearth the horrors of her years as a warrior. He dug into her formative years. There weren't any deaths to pay honor to. In fact, he pulled her into his head after seeing her at seventeen on the day Gregor ...

She stood fast and nearly toppled from the head rush. With one hand against the boulder, she took several deep breaths.

Gregor.

That day had started out so well. After three days hunting, she had accumulated enough meat to last them through the first quarter of the Korstraprime season. Not only had she caught and butchered the meat, she even smoked it herself. Usually Gregor insisted she return with her catches so he could smoke it in the little smokehouse he had built out back. But this time, she had done it all on her own.

She constructed a sled from fallen logs and loaded it with all the meat. Lugging all these pounds had not been easy, but as she neared home, the energy within her rose to the occasion.

"Gregor," she called out. "Come give me a hand."

She couldn't wait to see his face when he laid eyes on all this food. When he didn't come out, she cupped her mouth and bellowed, "Wake up, Lazyhead. I'm home."

Nothing. Her body tensed as she approached the shack. *He's probably asleep,* she tried to assure herself, but her innate warrior's sense, something she had yet to really understand at seventeen, warned her that the situation felt wrong.

She opened the front door and let out a sharp gasp. Blood covered the walls and floor and furniture. An animal had forced its way in and attacked and shredded Gregor. No. On the walls, Malja saw burn marks, and the air smelled sour. Magic.

Her stomach flipped and she rushed outside to vomit. She heaved until nothing more would come. Rolling on her back, clutching her stomach, she fought for a breath that didn't shake with tears. *Gregor. It's not fair.*

She heard something — a sound of movement from the shack. Malja got to her feet and lowered her stance. Caution, hatred, anger, and sorrow swirled around her heart. She pulled out her short sword. *Just like hunting dinner.*

Moving slowly, carefully, she stepped into the shack. The bedroom door was closed. She positioned in front of it with her sword ready to thrust forward should anybody attempt to open the door and bolt out.

Again she heard movement. Her prey hid in the bedroom. No doubt in her mind.

Her nerves jangled and her hand shook. It was one thing to spar an opponent where there were set rules of conduct. To fight for real — she had never experienced such a thing. But one glance at the bloody mess on the floor ignited her rage.

"For Gregor," she yelled and kicked the door in. She rushed forward, looking for anyone or anything to slaughter.

A man jumped from the side. Without thought, she lunged at him, thrusting her sword into his gut and twisting the blade for maximum damage. His face froze in astonishment as blood dribbled from his mouth. She stared back, her own mind stunned by the act of her first kill.

But the door slammed behind her and a blow to her back thrust her against the opposite wall. In the surprise, she dropped her sword, leaving the dead man skewered on the floor.

A man pushed his fist in the exact spot he had struck her, forcing her to arch away from the pain. He grabbed her arm and wrenched back and upward. With his other hand, he kept her face shoved into the wood. She could hear his heavy breath in her ear and felt his bristled cheek against her head. He smelled of fish and alcohol.

"You're not supposed to be back yet," he said.

"I'm going to kill you," she said, trying to fight back. He raised her arm and the pain stopped all struggle.

"Now, now. You just calm down, and we'll get out of this fine. See, you shouldn't be here. We were told only to kill the old man. Not the girl. Specifically not the girl."

"What? Somebody hired you to do this?"

The man chuckled, and it sounded like alley sex with a whore. "Oh, stupid girl, see that? You got far worse things to worry about than me. I mean, you don't want to be on the bad side of the brothers. And if they're killing off somebody you care about but letting you live to stew in it, well, you must've done something pretty bad to them."

Malja stomped on the man's toe. He screamed out but held on to her arm. With his free hand, he punched her in the side.

"Don't do that again," he said. "There's no need. I just want to get out of here alive. I've told you who's responsible, so there's no need to bother with me. Think of me as just the messenger. I'm sorry the news was so bad, but I got my own problems and now that I've done this, I'm hoping a lot of my problems will go away."

"You killed Uncle Gregor."

"And you killed my friend."

"I'm going to find you. You understand? I'll find you."

"Shut up, now," he said.

Only then did Malja realize the man had hardly moved since putting her against the wall. She thought of the burn marks and the sour stench. She felt his hands grow warm, the smell grew worse, and she felt a blow to her head that knocked her unconscious.

Hours later, she woke and gathered her things. She made a funeral pyre out of the shack, and over Gregor's burning body, she vowed to kill Jarik and Callib for this and all the misery they had brought to her life.

"Malja?" Fawbry called. "You okay?"

"I'm fine," she said and leaned her head against the cool boulder. Whenever she thought about that day, the day that started everything, she rarely considered the man she killed. Her first. She always thought of Gregor and the vow and the man that got away. But her first kill had also been that day. That's the honor she had failed to ever pay.

She took a moment to remember his face — hook nose, small eyes, and a dark hatred on his brow. She knew nothing more about him than that frozen look, but it sufficed. She could feel the memory easing down inside her to a place where it would not plague her thoughts.

"How much farther?" she asked Fawbry as she walked around the boulder.

"A couple miles, I think, and we'll see the cabin."

Fawbry stretched out on the ground, and Malja sat next to him. Playing with a few rocks in the dirt, she knew her mind needed to refocus. She said, "The other night Tumus mentioned something about machines. That Cole Watts makes machines."

"Yeah, she did."

"She? I thought Cole Watts was a man."

"Not in the least," Fawbry said with a snicker.

"Oh? Did you have a relationship with her? Is that how you know her?"

"Absolutely. She's an incredible woman. I met her when I first came down here. She helped get me on my feet, helped me work through all my guilt over Pung."

"You're not together now. What happened?"

Fawbry's eyes darkened. "She's ambitious. I tried to be, too, but you know what? Nolan was right. Some parts of us can't be changed. I don't have the ruthless instinct required. By Kryssta, I couldn't even keep a gang of griffles together."

Neither spoke for a while. At length, Malja left to retrieve the horses. When she returned, she said, "So what about the machines? Is it true? Cole Watts is making machines."

Fawbry swung up onto his horse. "Probably."

* * * *

The ride was short. The afternoon sun barely began its descent. Fawbry pointed to the last hill, and when they crossed over, Malja saw the cabin.

The base had been built of gray and white stone. The rest used wood and a flimsy metal not often found this far from a city — Cole Watts would have had to carry it in on horseback. A gated, metal fence formed a perimeter. One floor, a porch, some windows, even a chimney. In a town or countryside, a cabin like this would be enviable even with the rust, the dirt, and the dents. Out here, such a thing was unfathomable. If Malja had not seen it, she would never have believed it.

They walked the horses a short way back and tied them to a tree out of eyesight. Then they approached on foot. Malja had Viper out and ready. She heard the wind, saw the shadow of a little creature darting under a rock, smelled the Freelands' usual odors of mold and decay. A patch of tilled soil made a rough square in front of the home, but nothing grew and nothing rotted. Just empty soil.

"Don't touch the fence," Fawbry said as they approached the gate. He picked up a rock and tossed it at the fence. The entire gate brightened as if reflecting the sun. A second later, when it had returned to normal, only a pile of dust remained of the rock.

"She's a magician," Malja grumbled.

"No. But she's always been fascinated by magic, and she's always tried to find ways for regular people to make use of it."

"So how do we get in?"

"As long as the password's the same, that'll be no problem." Fawbry winked as he pulled out his small copy of the Book of Kryssta. He searched for the correct page, leaned towards a meshed, circular object next to the gate, and said, "Password start —

> *We are fragile —*
> *Without wonder, we languish —*
> *Without knowledge, we suffer —*
> *Without purpose, we perish."*

The gate clicked open. Fawbry flashed a smile and led the way onward. They walked the yard without incident, but the fence and gate had heightened Malja's alertness. She would have pounced upon a bird if it had flown near her.

As they stepped on to the creaking porch, Malja listened for any signal of attack. She stopped at the front door and motioned for Fawbry to stay still. She listened. She scanned. She sniffed.

"I don't think anyone's here," she said.

"Of course not. That would've let me out of this mess." Fawbry banged on the door. "Cole? You in there?"

Malja shoved Fawbry to the side. "Just 'cause nobody's here doesn't mean you can't be heard."

"I'm going to assume you're referring to either hungry animals or Kryssta himself, both of which don't matter in this case. Let's just try the door."

The door opened without trouble, and after feigning shock, Fawbry entered. Malja scanned the outside one last time before following.

Inside, the cabin was sparse but tasteful. It reminded Malja a little bit of the shack she had lived in with Gregor. Though far more roomy, the place felt comfortable like a true home. It also felt wrong — the comfort did not exist for them. They were trespassers.

"This is Cole Watts's place?"

"I know it doesn't seem like it, but this is it." Fawbry pointed to a torn, yellow couch. "I slept there for almost three months. And that fireplace hated me — it always sent sparks flying in my direction. I swear it used magic. Didn't matter where I stood in here, a spark always found its way to me."

"How sweet. Where's Cole Watts?"

"Not here, apparently."

"I can see that much. Where would she go?"

"Could be anywhere."

Malja heard a clicking — a steady sound like a bird repeatedly poking between rocks in search of food. *Click. Click. Click.* Slow and silent, Malja edged around the room listening for the source. *Click. Click.* Fawbry heard it, too. He moved just behind Malja as she neared a closet door. Making as little noise as possible, she tried to lift the door latch. It popped up with surprising ease.

As she opened the door, the clicking grew louder. Old wood-plank stairs led into a dark basement. "We'll need torches, if we're going down there," she said.

Fawbry peeked over her shoulder. "Then let's not go down there."

"Just get some wood."

"Wait. She probably has something rigged for light." Taking

tentative steps, Fawbry climbed down the stairs, all the while feeling along the walls with his hands. "Here we are." He pushed a button and the basement flooded with the pale light of magical electricity.

Malja went downstairs. The basement reminded her of being in Barris's mind — stark white room, stark white couch, stark white tables. This was no office, though. The tables overflowed with metal parts, colored wires, and strange equipment. All showed various levels of decay — some just tarnished, some rusting away. The air was cooler than above and smelled oily.

From a back corner, Fawbry called out. "Found that noise."

Malja walked over, careful not to disturb any of the metal contraptions. At Fawbry's feet Malja saw what looked like a metal arm ending in a sphere, the whole thing mounted on a wide, flat stand. The clicking noise appeared to correspond with the arm moving in a circle.

"What is that?" Malja asked.

"Don't know. Just another of Cole's machines."

"I'm glad Tumus isn't here. She'd think this is the end of everything."

Fawbry chuckled.

Browsing amongst the tables, Malja came across a doll's head. Wires poured from the neck and connected to a metal box with several buttons. Like water raging over a levee, a memory of Jarik and Callib splashed into her.

She had thought it no more than a toy. At seven-years-old she couldn't be expected to understand. Besides, her fathers presented it as such.

"See here, little Malja? See this button? This brings the machine to life," Jarik said, pushing a green button, and indeed, the machine sprang into motion.

It looked like a stick man with a doll's head on top. Over the coming years, she would learn its true purpose. It stood firm on its platform, but it could thrust attack, side parry, and weave its torso with amazing agility.

"Every day," Callib said, standing at her doorway, "you are to practice with this machine. This is in addition to the rest of your training."

"Cole Watts," Malja said, and Fawbry looked up. "She made all this?"

"She's very bright. But she thinks she can save the world. Bring us back to before the Devastation. I told her that there aren't enough people anymore. Cities like those of before — they need people to operate them. Lots of people. I doubt we have enough left in the world to man even one city."

"Is that why you left her?"

"She started trying to contact Jarik and Callib. Said she worked for them before, that they understood her, that they would help her change everything. It was pretty clear she didn't need me anymore."

"Doesn't look like she's been gone long."

"She might've gone to stock up on supplies. Maybe we should wait. See if she returns."

"Maybe," Malja said, wondering first if the doll head would sound like the one she practiced on long ago, and then if she wanted to hear that sound ever again.

"Look at this." Fawbry lifted a rusty frame from a pile of rusty frames.

"Looks like scrap."

"That's why it isn't. Cole likes to hide her work in plain sight. The shiny, impressive machines usually do the least. Something like this, though — it could be great. Maybe some super weapon for you."

"Or maybe just a frame for a painting."

"Who paints anymore?"

"Somebody must, otherwise, where do the paintings come from?"

"Very true. But in this case, very wrong. See here? There's a button on this frame."

"Don't —"

Too late. Fawbry pushed it. A high-pitched whine emitted from the frame. Fawbry placed it on the table like a father handling his baby and backed away. A clipped beeping began.

"That doesn't sound good," Fawbry said. The beeping quickened. "I think maybe we should —"

"Run!"

They raced up the stairs. As they reached the top, a loud whomp reverberated the floor and hot air pressed against their backs. Fawbry fell hard while Malja stumbled but regained her footing. Dust filled the air. Crackling like a healthy campfire seeped up through the floorboards along with thick smoke and intense heat.

Malja helped Fawbry to his feet and shoved him towards the door. He pushed back in the opposite direction. The smoke thickened fast. She saw only a hazy outline of the cabin. She tried to turn Fawbry around, but he swatted her hands away. He tried to speak and merely coughed into a hacking fit. But even as he coughed, he managed to point and Malja finally understood. She had been the one going in the wrong direction.

As they staggered outside, flames climbed the walls. She forced Fawbry to keep walking until she thought they had reached a safe distance, several feet beyond the fence. There they both collapsed — coughing, gasping, wheezing, and eventually breathing.

Fawbry sat up first. Malja watched as his face broke into the smile of someone relieved to be alive. She had seen that look many times; probably had it cross her own face, too. Often, the next expression became serious — either a heartfelt gratitude or a sober recognition of mortality. Neither came to Fawbry's face, though. Instead, he looked into the distance with dismay. And he raised his hands.

She knew it was too late but instinct propelled her to her feet. Five Bluesmen covered them with three handguns, a shotgun, and a guitar.

"Care for a song?" the guitarist said.

Chapter 14

They rode in on horseback. Malja and Fawbry's hands tied behind their backs. The shotgun-wielding Bluesman towed them along, holding both of their horses' reins in one hand. Their captors made no effort to hide their destination. That troubled Malja more than anything.

From afar, the place appeared like an oasis — an extra-large farmhouse surrounded by acres of working farmland nestled amongst barren mountains. Two men handled livestock in a small but sufficient pasture. Farm hands tilled land, harvested food, fixed fences. A well-maintained stable stood near a wide barn. In every direction beyond — gray rocks, straining trees, dust and death.

The closer they came the more Malja smelled the fragrant farm aromas — most pleasant, a few rank. Even as she noted numbers of men and women, exit windows and doors, easy to climb terrain and dangerous spots to avoid, the smells lifted memories of Gregor into her mind. He knew a farmer nearby and would trade for manure to fertilize their garden. He would take their food scraps and dump them around their apple tree. If she wrinkled her nose at the odor, Gregor would look askance and say, "Just wait 'til you taste an apple from here. You'll want to toss everything onto the pile." Gregor said he had picked the spot for the shack because of the tree. Wide and gnarled, wrinkled with age, unlike any apple tree Malja had ever seen. And he had been right. It created the most delicious fruit.

One outbuilding they passed harbored three men working amongst a mountain of sawdust. Guitars in various stages of construction hung from every available wall, post, and rafter. Next, a row of well-kept but cheaply-made buildings lined the way. Each appeared to be packed with people sleeping.

They rounded a corner and approached the stables. One squat building on the right Malja took for an outhouse, but when she peeked inside, she saw a man in a black suit standing on a stool before a cracked and smudged mirror. Another man circled his legs, making marks on his clothes with a white stone while nearby two women used needles and thread on some cut cloth. Malja had seen Gregor mend his shirts and pants before, but never had she seen such fine threads and delicate work.

Three stable boys hurried forward and walked all seven horses away, leaving Malja and Fawbry heading with the men toward the house. A chubby fellow rocked on a wooden chair and smoked a pipe. His pale skin stood out amongst all his darker brethren.

"Get out of my chair, Suzu," the guitarist said.

Suzu bounced out and lowered his head. "Sorry, Willie."

Willie took his seat and strummed a few chords. "Go tell her we're back. Tell her I got two birds. Ask her what she wants with them."

"You got it, Willie. I'll be right back." Suzu hurried inside while the group listened to Willie play — nothing fancy, but a pleasant tune with a steady rhythm like a trotting horse.

A sweating laborer walked by with a basket of potatoes on his shoulder. "Hey, Willie," he said with a booming voice.

"Hey, Rev. We gonna have a feast tonight?"

"You know it. Might even gut a knonol in honor of our guests."

"Oh, that'd be great. I love what Cook can do with a knonol."

"That's the truth."

The men laughed, and Rev rounded the house with a joyous step. Malja had seen towns filled with people who found peace and happiness in a special harmony they built between each other and working the land — rare but she had seen them. She had also seen towns ruled by madmen and followers who thrived on abducting the unfortunate and carving up their bodies and souls for survival. But never had she seen both co-exist. How Willie could be an assassin, a Bluesman, and also carry on with Rev like a happy farmer baffled her.

Suzu returned with a glass of some gold-brown drink. Little clear cubes bobbed in the glass, making odd chiming clinks. He leaned his bulk over and whispered to Willie. Eyeing Malja with both fascination and trepidation, Suzu went back inside.

With a nod at Shotgun, Willie said, "She wants them locked up. Don't take any guff, but keep them alive."

Malja didn't know the word *guff*, but she got the idea. She stayed silent and Fawbry only grunted as they were roughly handled. Shotgun guided them to the stables — ten stalls, five on each side, and a wide path down the middle. Shotgun opened a stall and tied them to the barred door. As he backed out, he tipped his head with a contrite but firm expression. He pulled a stool over and lowered with a relieved exhale.

"I don't play guitar as good as Willie, but if you want, I'll play awhile for you."

Malja turned away. She had worried that Fawbry's cowardly streak would cause her trouble, but looking at him, she saw rage. She nodded at him — *I feel the same.*

"I hate you," he said. Her surprise must have shown because he continued. "I may not have been doing great, but my life was a lot better before I met you."

"I didn't ask for you to come along here. I wanted to leave you at Dead Lake."

"Well, don't worry. When we get out of here, I'm leaving you and all your stupidity."

"I'm not the one who blew up that house."

Fawbry rattled the gate and kicked at the hay floor. "Hey, can I be put in another stall? Please. I can't stand to be with her."

Shotgun raised his hands and shrugged.

With another kick at the door, Fawbry said to Malja, "Y'know, if you would just let this all go, so many people would be alive right now. Death is all over you like perfume, and you don't care. Poor, little Malja is mad at her daddies so everybody must suffer. Have you ever stopped long enough to think about what a mess you've made of all this?" While he barked out all his frustration, Malja wanted to defend herself but felt as if Gregor, not Fawbry, criticized her actions. She stood like a scolded schoolgirl. She could see his disapproving frown and wanted to hug him. *This is for you, Uncle Gregor. I do this for what they did to you.* But as the figure before her pounded the stable door, she saw Fawbry once again.

His voice rose as he continued his rant. "Jarik and Callib — clearly they don't want you finding them. They don't love you. And for most of us scattered around the world, Jarik and Callib don't matter. They're just names."

"You're wrong 'bout that," Shotgun said. "Those magicians are nothing good, but they're far more than just names."

"Great. Thanks. Now I can't even argue without somebody interfering."

Malja took a sharp look at Shotgun. "What do you know about Jarik and Callib?"

"Kryssta help me," Fawbry said. "Have you heard nothing I've said?

Let it go or we'll all be killed. You want Tommy dead?"

Malja shoved Fawbry aside. Swiping her hair away from her eyes, she returned to Shotgun. "You were going to say something about the magicians."

"Me? I got nothing to say." Shotgun stood and scratched his chin. He sauntered out of view for a moment, every step infused with a cockiness that under different circumstances Malja would find attractive. When he returned, he held Viper. He practiced a few swipes, inspected the blade, and even ran his thumb on the edge. "This is a fine weapon."

"I know," she said, gritting her teeth.

"Lots of chinks in it, though. Must've tasted a lot of action."

"Keep playing with it, and I'll see it gets a taste of you."

His confidence faltered, but he brought it back quickly. He did place Viper gently on the ground, though. Refusing to meet Malja's eyes, he settled on his stool and crossed his arms. Malja called to him and banged the gate, but he refused to answer. He cast his gaze outside.

I couldn't have scared him that much. But something had shifted. Fawbry crouched as far from her as his bonds would allow. Malja leaned back against the gate. *Wait, listen, and observe.* The more information she had about her opponents, the more chances she'll have at success — Gregor taught her that.

Hours later, after the sun had set, Suzu appeared. He whispered to Shotgun, who stretched his legs. "Time to go," he said. As Fawbry rose, Shotgun shook his head. "Just her. You stay with me for now."

"Of course," Fawbry said and slumped down.

Suzu led Malja along the dirt path to the house. Little bags with candles lined the path. Two armed men guarded the porch. Even from halfway down, Malja could hear the party. Giddy yelps, explosive laughter, shouted names — all riding the crest of a thundering music wave.

Off to the side, a group of people formed a large circle. Two dogs were let loose, growling and barking and fighting. People cheered and laughed.

At the porch, however, Suzu turned away from the door, leading her around the side. A rusting ladder connected to metal stairs that jutted from the wall ended at a platform and door high above. "Go," Suzu said, pointing upward.

"Can't climb with my hands tied behind my back." Suzu pursed his lips and searched for someone to help him decide what to do. Though

Malja enjoyed watching him wiggle in discomfort, she had more important matters at hand. "Relax. I want to go up there to meet your boss."

"She ain't my boss. She's just—"

"Shut up, Suzu," Willie called as he turned the corner. He had taken off his suit coat, and his fine shirt stuck to his chest with sweat. "I'll take her up." Suzu relinquished Malja with grateful relief and scurried away.

Willie escorted her into a small, sumptuous apartment. The pounding party downstairs reverberated in the floor and walls. Willie directed her to an overstuffed chair and waited by the door. Low candlelight and deep-red paint closed the room in. All the furniture had been carved with intricate patterns and several portraits of guitarists hung on the walls. In the distance, Malja heard a dog yelp followed by a huge cheer erupting from the circle of onlookers.

A woman entered from a dark hall. At first, Malja only saw the dress — a slinky, red cloth that hung loose and low. It sparkled off the candles. As the woman closed in, her dark skin finally contrasted enough to be seen. She was exquisite. Malja rarely found women appealing, but this time she thought she saw what men found so interesting. Though flat-chested and more straight than curvy, sexuality slid off this woman like lava burning down a mountainside.

She flowed into a chair opposite Malja and with a rich, silken drawl said, "My. Look at you. All grown up."

"You're Cole Watts?" Malja knew the answer, felt it the second she saw the woman, but she had to ask anyway. Gregor had many sayings on the subject of assumptions.

"I am," Cole said. "And you're a very special young lady."

"Is that why your people have been trying to kill me? Because I'm so special?"

If Malja's abrasiveness rattled Cole, she never showed it. In fact, the more tension Malja felt, the smoother Cole seemed to become. Crossing her legs, showing off her strong, tone calf, Cole said, "Sweetie, think about it. I've had you under guard for quite awhile. If I'd been trying to kill you, why would you still be alive?"

"You've certainly been trying to stop me from finding Jarik and Callib."

"That I have been doing. But not for any reasons you might think of."

"Then why don't you tell me."

"Mmm, yes, we'll get to that. But first, Willie, please excuse us."

Willie leveled his hard eyes on Cole. "I think it best I stay. To protect you."

"That's very thoughtful," Cole said, her voice harder than his eyes. "However, it's entirely unnecessary. Malja's a seasoned fighter. She won't harm me until she knows such an action will help her. She's not rash. Willie dear, you could learn quite a bit from a woman like this."

"Maybe so, but —"

"Willie. This office don't belong to you, yet. So leave now." As an afterthought, she flashed a faux smile. "Please."

Clenching his hands, Willie said, "Of course. My apologies."

Cole watched him until he turned and walked out, closing the door with a loud bang. Returning her seductive smile, she faced Malja. "It's never easy being a leader, is it? Something we have in common, I imagine, considering Fawbry."

"He can be trying."

"Why that's an understatement."

Raucous laughter pushed up from party. Malja asked, "What's the celebration?"

Cole rose and poured a drink at a small counter. Her hands moved smooth and sure, but they were calloused and scarred. "Dear sweet Malja, you ain't ready for that party. No, ma'am, not just yet."

"Okay. Since you won't answer my questions, I guess your pal Willie might help me out."

"A little patience, please. This is our 'getting friendly' phase. Or if you prefer, this is foreplay. We'll get to the hard action soon enough. And as for Willie — well, I suppose that's part of what this is about. That is to say, just who is it you're going to support?"

"I have no interest in your games."

"'Course you do. You want Jarik and Callib, don't you? Well then, you'll have to help me out."

"Fawbry warned me you were ambitious."

"Oh, I'm a lot of things."

"So what is it you want? How do I help you?"

Cole returned to her chair like a spider that knows its prey is caught. "Right now, patience. I've got a party to attend or I'll lose some support. Next time we meet, you'll understand, and then we'll see if you'll help me." Cole finished her drink. "I'm off now. Willie's waiting outside to take you back. Goodnight."

Walking back down the candlelit path with Willie just behind her,

Malja tried to digest her brief meeting with Cole. The woman certainly intrigued her, but Cole's strangeness worried her more — in this case, strange meant unpredictable. If Malja wanted to get free but also obtain the whereabouts of her fathers, she'd have to find a way to make Cole predictable. Or get real lucky. When Willie placed a firm hand on her shoulder and guided her away from the stables, she knew luck had abandoned her.

He took her into the middle of the fields where only the moonlight revealed them. Two men joined up — he called one Robert and the other Lonnie. More oddball names — and she thought Tommy was a funny name.

"Is he ready?" Willie asked.

Lonnie kept his eyes on the house. "He's the best he's gonna be. I don't promise anything beyond that."

"I know. Thanks for doing what you could."

Robert kicked a clump of dirt. "C'mon, let's get this done before anybody wonders where we gone to."

Grabbing Malja's arm, Willie led the group toward a rundown shack on the far end of the field. Next to the shack, the necessary equipment for making alcohol sat. Heat radiated outward and with it a sour odor — the machine rarely got rest, Malja guessed. They didn't stop there, however. They walked for several minutes — well beyond the tilled land and into the harsh world just outside the oasis. They came upon two men seated before a rock face. One of the men strummed a sad tune on a beaten guitar while the other blew a soft accompaniment into a mouth harp. Neither stopped playing as Willie approached, but the guitarist did acknowledge him with a nod.

Willie shoved Malja to the steep rocks. Lonnie rushed ahead and walked right through the stone — just disappeared. As they led Malja through the false wall, she tried to determine which of her captors was the magician.

A cool, stone passageway led to a round room — probably had been an old cave. Years of usage showed many improvements including cots, table and chairs, a metal stove made from old cars, and even an aluminum chimney that bored into the stone ceiling.

Robert pushed Malja into a chair. Willie opened his hands and said, "I'm going to be honest with you — as best I can. But in the end, you're going to have to choose which of us to support."

"If this is all you've got," Malja said, surveying the cave, "then Cole's already won."

"Oh, we've got more. We've got Old McKinley for one. Lonnie, bring him out."

Lonnie went deeper into the cave. He returned pushing a chair on wheels. A bony, old man sat in the rickety chair with a stained, blue and white blanket covering his legs. His curly white hair made a drastic contrast to his dark skin. The left side of his body drooped — eye, mouth, shoulder, arm. His right eye quivered and drool slid from his mouth.

They brought Old McKinley beside her. He lifted his right arm and touched her face like a blind man. His hand traced her throat and shoulder, then settled on her breast.

Malja slapped him away. "No way," she said and stood.

An invisible force yanked her back into the seat. She growled as she tried to move, but her body had become locked to the chair. The old man's hand fondled her again. This time she saw the tattoo on his palm — *he's the magician.* And considering how fast he pulled off that spell and how destroyed he looked, he had to be quite talented.

"Now," Willie said, "you may not want to help us, but I can't have you helping Cole Watts."

"Don't you think you've jumped ahead a bit? I mean, I never said I wouldn't help you."

"I tend to do that. Jump ahead. 'Specially when I know the outcome. See, I can read it on your face. You won't help me. At least, not yet. So why waste the time yapping?"

Old McKinley groaned and slobbered.

Malja wriggled but couldn't move enough to avoid the old man. "Look, Cole didn't tell me anything. Maybe you can explain to me what's going on and then I can—"

"No, you won't believe if I tell you. Understand this is about a lot more than just who runs this farm. This is about real power. Big power. You got to see the party to get it."

"Then what am I here for? Just giving the old man a thrill? Take me to the party."

Willie motioned to Lonnie who wheeled Old McKinley back into the dark. Malja felt the pressure holding her to the chair release, but she made no attempt to get up — not with Willie and Robert holding the advantage.

Willie said, "That old man is more than a magician. He's seen things — and now he sees things. This wasn't about him getting a thrill. By Korstra, he's so old, I doubt anything works down there. No, this meeting was so he could touch into you, gauge what I should expect from you."

"You sure? Because his hand seemed very happy."

"He ain't no joke. He's a great, powerful man. He sees you now. He knows you won't help me. He tells me so, but I still find it hard to believe he's never wrong. I mean, we're all wrong once in a while."

"I don't understand what you people want but—"

"I know." Willie backed away. "Don't worry. Tomorrow. We'll try again."

Without another word, Robert escorted Malja back to the stables.

Chapter 15

Fawbry grumbled as he tried to find a comfortable position for sleep. With his hands secured to the door and fresh manure clogging the air, he failed. Malja stood as far from him as her bindings allowed. Since her return, Fawbry hadn't said a word to her. He hadn't even shown the slightest bit of curiosity as to what had happened when they took her away.

Not that she could tell him much if he did ask. Clearly, some kind of struggle for rule had become quite serious. Cole Watts and Willie had followers, bases of operations, and mounting pressure. Why they wanted her and what went on at those parties troubled her, but for the moment, she saw little recourse other than to wait and gather more information.

Waiting, however, would be torture.

More than any other, two thoughts plagued her mind. First, she kept picturing Old McKinley — his dead left side, his drooling mouth, his eager bony hand. He smelled like a rotten fruit — a sharp, sour odor of sickness. Every time Malja saw his visage in her head, she thought of Tommy.

Her overactive mind leapt ahead and formed a hideous image — Tommy as a withered man. Crazed by magic, palsied and helpless. Old McKinley's brother in insanity.

Whenever she managed to obliterate this line of thinking, a second powerful thought hit her. Shotgun snored from his stool. Good. She didn't want an eavesdropper.

"Fawbry," she said, her voice soft. Fawbry leaned against one wood wall and closed his eyes. "That's okay. You don't need to talk. But, please listen." She paused, her trepidation like new food in her mouth. "I-I'm sorry."

Fawbry raised an eyebrow. "Excuse me?"

"You're right. I've dragged every one of you into this, and now you're stuck here because of me. For that, I apologize."

Looking away, he said, "Doesn't really do me much good now, does it?"

"I just thought I should say that. When you told me about Pung and Yolen, I understood more than you realize. You did what you did out of the need to satisfy the Black Beast."

"What's that?"

"Something Gregor, my guardian growing up, once told me about. I talked often to him about what I would do if I ever found Jarik and Callib — how I wanted them to suffer for all they had done to me. 'Vengeance,' he said to me, 'is the Black Beast that never lets you free.' He pointed to the charred wood in the fireplace. He told me the Black Beast was like that wood. On the surface, it's cold and harsh. But its desire burns quietly inside, waiting for the opportunity to reignite. Then it'll fiercely consume itself and all around it until nothing remains but ash. 'Let go of all your hatred,' he said to me. 'Be careful,' he said. He warned me."

"So why don't you listen to him?"

"I did. I tried. But the Black Beast never lets go. When I was seventeen, Jarik and Callib had my Uncle Gregor murdered. That's when I made my vow to the Beast. That's when my search really began. So, I'm sorry that you got caught in this."

"You really think that's enough?" Fawbry said. He kept his gaze on the dark ground. "Saying you're sorry is just words. You should've listened to Gregor. The man sounds smart. Had you listened to him, we'd have never met, and I'd be a lot happier. So I don't really care that you feel bad about any of it."

Malja could think of nothing else to say that would make things better, so she let silence cover them. It didn't last long. A minute later, Fawbry turned a challenging look at her and said, "If you're truly sorry, then change. If not for yourself, then do so for Tommy. Change your ways of doing things. Otherwise, you ought to shut up."

"You mean I should put away Viper and become a farmer or something? No. I'll always be a warrior."

"True. But *why* you kill is more important than just being a warrior. Change that and you change everything."

The next morning, they took Fawbry away. They came in, gave Malja a bowl of oatmeal, and left with Fawbry. All throughout the day, she waited but he never returned and no explanation came. She thought of Tommy often and of Fawbry's words, and she wished she believed in one of the brother gods so she'd have somebody to pray to. Instead, she waited. Alone.

When night arrived, so did Suzu. The walk up to Cole's office was quieter. No party this time. No candles lining the path. No drunken dog fights. All appeared calm and sleepy.

Entering the office, Malja came upon Cole and Willie — anything but calm and sleepy. They glared at each other like enemies on the battlefield. One raised an eyebrow. One clenched teeth. An entire argument occurred without a word spoken. At length, Willie let out an exasperated sigh and stomped out, rattling the windows with the slam of the door. Cole dismissed the tension with a wave and poured Malja a drink.

"I'm sorry about him. He's a fool. He's got his friends and his magician, but he's a fool. Yes, I know about Old McKinley. I'm sorry you had to meet that lecherous scum, but as a result, you've already helped me."

"Oh?"

"Until last night, I only had rumors and deductions to figure out Willie's strength."

"You followed us. Then the whole meeting between you and me was just a way to flush out Willie's hiding place?"

"I did want to meet you, and I do still want your help. But bless your heart if you think each step I take revolves around you. You've come here at a complex time, and I must capitalize on any opening my opponents leave me."

"*That* I can understand."

"I thought a fighting metaphor might help." Cole tapped her painted nails on the arm of her chair. "Do you know how magic works?"

"You're born to it."

"But that doesn't mean you can't understand how it works, even if you can't do it."

"Then I guess, no, I don't know how it works."

Cole tapped her nails faster. "It works by vibrations. Some of it does, anyway. Little, rapid movements that grow together, feed off each other, until you have a reaction. It's called sympathetic vibration. Magicians and many animals can create these initial vibrations. But it also occurs all around us. Music, say for example the kind created from a guitar, also creates sympathetic vibrations — not nearly to the magnitude needed for magic nor the right frequency for that matter. Unless, of course, you brought together a lot of musicians, built a device that could increase the power of their total vibrations, and knew what frequencies to emit. Why, then you might be able to create your own magic."

"Are you saying you've done this? Created your own magic?"

While Malja sipped her drink — something fruity with a hint of alcohol and amazingly cold — Cole slipped out of her chair and sauntered toward a stout cabinet. She pulled out a metal contraption that looked like a crab with its legs wrapped around a ball. She set the thing on the little, wood table before Malja.

"Creating magic is easy," Cole said. "The real challenge is creating machines that can work with or even enhance magic."

"So what does this machine do?"

"That one can tell if you're lying. It can read your body signals at a mere touch and then interpret those signals as to whether or not you've been a naughty girl and lied to me."

"I take it you want to use it on me."

"When you're ready to pledge your aid to me, then we'll use it. After that, you'll get all you want and more."

"More?"

"My sweet little Malja, oh, yes more. After all, it's not enough to find Jarik and Callib, is it? That would be nothing, but for blood. Don't you want to know why you are so special? Don't you want to know where you come from? Who you really are? Or is it all just about killing them?"

Malja sprang to her feet and put out her arm. "Fine. Hook up your machine. I'll take your pledge."

"Dear me, no. Not like this. Why that would be extortion — well, it would if there were any law in this world. Besides, I can't show you tonight anyway. But there'll be another party tomorrow night. If you really want to pledge yourself to me, we'll do it then."

"Pledge *myself*? You said it was just my help."

"See that. You're not ready. You don't get it yet. But you will." Cole headed down the dark hall. "Be sure to tell Willie I give him my fondest."

When Malja left the room, more confused than when she had arrived, Willie grabbed hold of her. She didn't resist. She wanted to go this time. Without a word, he guided her into the fields.

Robert and Lonnie were less agitated this time, and all three escorted her to the magic wall that camouflaged their cave. The two men guarding the way smiled and gave Malja a casual salute before starting up a new song. Once inside, they sat her down and Lonnie rushed off to fetch Old McKinley.

The old man started with her legs this time. He inched close to her, sniffing her thighs through his mucous-filled nose. As he worked toward her face, his white stubble poked at her neck. He leaned back, his head at an awkward angle, spittle dancing on his lips, and whispered to Willie.

"You're lucky you didn't make that pledge," Willie said. "If you'd been lying, the magic in her machine would have fried you up in seconds. And if you really meant your pledge, the magic would have enslaved you to her will."

Malja laughed. "Right. Sure. You guys aren't very good at conning people. I mean of course I'll believe in fire magic. Everybody knows magic is based on the elements. And while you're fake wall trick is arguable, I'm sure many would reason it out for themselves — but sniffing me and suddenly knowing what happened and then throwing in magic that can enslave people. Nobody's going to believe that."

Willie didn't change his attitude at all. "There's far more magic in the world than you'll ever know." Malja thought of how Tommy had made her talk so bluntly. "If you give Cole what she wants, you'll see some of the worst."

"Then you tell me what I want to know."

"And what is that?"

"Cole knows where Jarik and Callib are. Finding them is why I came here. That's all I want."

Old McKinley coughed hard. As he hacked away, Lonnie rubbed his back and looked at Willie with a hopeless expression.

Willie rested a hand on Old McKinley's shoulder when the coughing fit ended. He turned back to Malja. "I can't tell you where to find the magicians."

"But you do know. Until now, you've been Cole's second-in-command. From what I've seen, you still are in many ways. It's not possible that she would hide that bit of information from you. So you choose not help me."

"It's not that simple."

"Then I guess I'll go see Cole."

"You can't go to any of them. You don't understand what they're trying to do. Cole, Jarik, Callib — they've all gone too far."

"Then tell me."

"How can I tell you of powerful magic when you don't even believe in the smaller stuff?"

Old McKinley groaned and raised a hand to Willie. After some whispering Willie nodded to Lonnie, who wheeled the old man away, but not before Old McKinley pointed a shaking finger at Malja. He almost spoke but started coughing, and Lonnie rushed him out before it could become another full-on fit.

Willie consulted Robert next. Robert didn't like what he heard but relented under Willie's stern eye. He dug into his coat and produced a vial of yellowish-green liquid. Willie took the vial and handed it to Malja.

"Tomorrow night," he said, "when Suzu comes for you, drink this. It only lasts a short time but it'll deaden many of your readings so Cole's machine will fail. The machine will say you speak the truth but its magic will be blocked."

Malja examined the sickly liquid. "Why would I trust you? This could be poisoned."

"Old McKinley said you'd take it. He said you're a great warrior and once you've thought through the strategies involved, you'll see we have no better alternative except to kill you. But we don't want to kill you. It would keep you out of Cole's hands and Jarik and Callib's, but then there'd be nobody bold enough to fight them."

"Do you always speak so vaguely?"

"Just drink it tomorrow. Cole will think she has control over you. She'll tell you everything and show you more. You'll see then. You'll understand. Then I expect you'll very much want to kill her."

She spent the night alone. Fawbry had not been brought back. The idea that he might be dead weighed her down in between thoughts of magical machines, crazed old magicians, and strange liquids. Only her goal kept this bizarre place in perspective.

Listening to Shotgun snore while he should be guarding her only reinforced her will. She could have busted free many times, but that would send her back to the beginning — and Fawbry would be right about her creating a mess. Stuck in the middle of two power-hungry factions had brought her no closer to answers. Of course she would drink the liquid to gain Cole's trust. The real question was simply how much information could she get before blood had to be spilled.

Tommy flashed in her mind but she pushed him away. She knew what she had to do. It had to be kept that simple.

Chapter 16

Stuck in the stall throughout the day, Malja had nothing to do but rest, sit, and listen. She heard a lot of activity, more so than any previous day. They were preparing for something special. She heard Rev and Willie walking by outside. They were engrossed in a debate over which animals could be slaughtered for the party without damaging the needs of the farm. She heard plenty of guitars being tuned and plenty of joyful voices building in excitement as the day wore on.

But she couldn't be distracted by these sounds all day. At some points, her mind would wander. Inevitably, she would see and think of those she had killed. And she thought of the Black Beast.

She had not told Fawbry everything. She had spoken of Gregor's warnings and her rage-filled vows and all that one would say to dissuade another from the Beast. But the truth she withheld could not be hidden from herself — the Beast satisfied a part of her soul. Every step closer to her prey felt good inside like a brief intoxication. She would never turn away from it. The purity of her hatred promised an equal ecstasy when the bastard magicians fell. The Black Beast may be all that Gregor had warned, but it gave her so much, too. It gave her a purpose, a reason to live.

That was something Jarik and Callib had taken away. They denied her any chance to discover who she wanted to be. They molded her as they desired. But they didn't expect her to be so strong willed. She learned what she wanted and shunned the rest — but only of what they made available.

It all sounded good in her head, full of righteous bluster and woe-is-me anger. But underneath all that lay two stones of truth embedded in her bones. The first told her she could never get her fathers to see her as anything more than their failure. That's why they got rid of her.

The second stone reminded her of the coldest truth — she had been free from them since age ten. They wanted nothing to do with her and had no control over her actions. At some point, she had to stop blaming them and accept that all her actions are her own. But the Black Beast always answered that one with its raspy growl — *when they're dead.*

That night, when Suzu arrived, he acted differently. He spoke with greater care and even added a polite "Yes, ma'am" and "No, ma'am" when answering her. He fumbled with the locks and walked with a stiff back that pushed his belly out even further.

"Wait," Malja said, clenching her legs together. "Before we go anywhere, may I ... you know?"

Suzu's cheeks reddened. "Of course, ma'am. I-I'll turn around, but don't try nothing. There's lots of people out tonight. You wouldn't get far. And I'd hate to see you get hurt."

"Thank you," Malja said. Once Suzu had his back to her, Malja downed the bitter liquid in the vial Willie had provided. Hoping the metallic taste wouldn't coat her throat long, she squeezed out what little pee she had so Suzu would hear. "All done," she said, and with a warm smile, added, "You're a real sweetheart."

Suzu giggled. "Follow me, ma'am. I'll get you there safe."

They walked up to the house, the party sounds loud but not as raucous as before. Suzu's demeanor returned to his earlier formalness. Those mulling around the grounds whispered and exchanged darting glances. Whatever Cole had planned for tonight, it seemed everyone knew.

By the time they reached the office, Malja's body had become numb. The potion had begun to take hold. She still retained control; she just didn't feel anything as if all her nerve-endings had been frozen in a Korstraprime ice storm. Cole entered the room, showing no sign that Malja appeared any different.

"Well, my dear Malja, normally I'd be a better host, but the party's waiting on you," she said, dressed in a black gown with a white sash — ready for a party, indeed. "Let's just get the unpleasantness over with. Then we can go join the fun downstairs. That is, if you're ready to pledge to me."

"If it means I'll find Jarik and Callib, I am."

Cole beamed. "Well, bless your heart, that's simply wonderful." She wasted no time getting her machine. She pulled one of its crabbish arms outward and said, "You just hold onto this and speak the truth."

Gregor taught her about bravery and heroics once. It had been a summer morning and he cooked up talma root and tomatoes for breakfast. He said that true heroes act without self-regard in battle because they have controlled their fear. "See, sweetie, if you worry about getting hurt or dying, you'll be too cautious and too slow. The brave accept death, and therefore are free. After all, if failure means death, then you'll never live to regret failure. So, heroes charge in, knowing that if they live, they will win the prize, and if they die — then nothing. They rest."

Without pause, Malja grabbed the metal arm. "Cole Watts, I pledge myself to your service."

Cole concentrated on the machine, but she made no reaction. Malja's hands tingled. "Try again," Cole said.

Malja cleared her throat and repeated, "Cole Watts, I pledge myself to your service."

Cole frowned, and Malja's hands tingled more. Her feet began to tingle as well. The potion was wearing off. It had to be. And while she knew in her heart that Gregor's words on heroism were true, the idea of dying in Cole's office instead of in battle turned her stomach.

"Thank you," Cole said in a monotone that gave away nothing. She packed up the machine and left it on the small table. Lifting her eyebrows and spreading her hands open, she said, "As promised, I will tell you where the magicians hide. You'll find Jarik and Callib in the City of Ashes."

City of Ashes — a massive cemetery of a city covering endless miles of the western mountains. Remote, difficult terrain, and inconvenient as a place from which to command. If Cole spoke the truth, they really picked the last place Malja would have ever looked. "You can be a little more specific. That city is enormous. I can't even be sure you're telling the truth. In fact, why don't you grab your machine and prove your honesty."

"Now, now. Patience. Once we're ready I'll walk you right up to them."

"I don't trust you."

"You don't have to. Just know that those brothers have hurt many people besides you. Some of us are willing to go far in order to see them pay." As Cole spoke, her eyes darkened. "I have no interest in betraying you. If I'm to harm Jarik and Callib, I need you."

"Then what are we waiting for?"

"First, we have to stop the Willie fracas. Once this group is united, we'll have our army. Then I'll show you the exact location of those nasty magicians' hideaway."

Malja sat back with a disapproving sigh. "You people think magic can do anything. It's not like that."

"Oh, but it is," Cole said, her eyes firing up as she rose. "Before the Devastation, magic was used like most people think. Government and law kept it limited to the simple elements. They feared its power, so they controlled its users. After a few generations, magicians were born into thinking that's all they could do. But the Devastation came and wiped away the rules — no governments, no laws. Before, with billions of people, anarchy would have been madness. But with only a few scattered millions, anarchy is freedom. And that kind of freedom means nobody can stop a magician from reaching the fullest potential."

She walked into the dark hall. She turned, revealing her lovely profile, and said, "Come along now. Let me show you what I'm talking about."

Malja launched to her feet and rushed down the hall. Cole waited at another door. Colored lights seeped through its edges. Sorrowful, mourning music drifted in with the light.

With a suggestive roll of her shoulder, Cole opened the door. A vast hall spread out before them as if the house had been gutted of all its little rooms. A balcony wrapped around the hall, and Malja saw a stage at the far end below. Two guitarists and a drummer played a slow but powerful tune while a man who rivaled Suzu in size belted out the words. Like a Kryssta congregation at worship, the packed audience swayed and called and cried. They were a mix of humans, griffles, raggers, and cholohs — others, too that Malja had never laid eyes on before. She didn't know what to make of Cole's sympathetic vibrations, but she could see the magical way this music moved its people.

"It's called the Blues," Cole said.

"I should've guessed. They are the Bluesmen, after all."

"Watch now, dear. You're going to see something amazing."

They went down a flight of stairs ending on a landing overlooking the stage. The music stopped. The crowd stilled. All eyes turned to Cole.

Four wide flags unfurled from the ceiling. Each pale-brown one dropped down about seven feet and flowed as if a gentle breeze cascaded from above. Malja first thought of magic, but then realized these were not flags at all. They were living creatures.

On an unspoken cue, Willie entered from the back carrying a guitar quite different from any Malja had ever seen. Rather than a deep body made of light-colored wood, Willie's guitar appeared to be a shallow, solid chunk painted with rich, dark colors blending into each other. Unlike a normal guitar, this one lacked a hole for the sound and was adorned with silver knobs and switches.

Willie stepped onto the stage. Robert wheeled out a large black box with a thick, black rope coming out of it. Willie picked up the end of the rope and stuck it into his guitar. He touched the box and suddenly the guitar came to life. Willie played a few notes and the sound wailed out of the box like a crying brother god. The crowd roared its approval.

Four Bluesmen brought out chairs and guitars — normal looking ones. They took up a steady, pulsing rhythm which the drummer joined in on. Willie played over this, his guitar making one long cry after another. Watching Willie perform mesmerized Malja, and she missed the moment when still other guitarists joined. Looking around the stage, she now counted twenty men playing including Lonnie and Robert. Others in the crowd also strummed. They clearly yearned for the stage but no more space was opened.

The noise level increased as did the tempo. Willie's playing grew frantic, but his notes were precise. He pushed the others faster and louder. More energy. More power. The music broke down into a cacophony of dissonance. Despite the sheer mayhem of sound, the crowd moved as one to a rhythm Malja could not discern. Her skin prickled as sensation continued its slow return to her body. The music grew louder and the hair on her body stiffened. The higher notes that Willie hit shivered her teeth. She peeked over at Cole. The sexuality had vanished, replaced with a maniacal anticipation.

Following the erratic drumbeat, the crowd split down the middle, backing away enough to reveal a metal frame built flush into the floor. The wood inside the frame shimmered with each note Willie played. The air smelled of sweat and lust and something Malja could not place. As the air crackled with little electric arcs, it hit her. The smell — a memory of Callib attempting to teach Malja magic. Not the sour smell of violent casting, but a crisp aroma unique to special magic.

The flag-like creatures flapped with vigor, always in time to Willie's playing. Holes opened up — mouths that stretched enough to swallow a person. They sang in harmony — loud enough to remind her of Barris Mont. An enormous explosion of sound blasted the room as if the air itself had been shattered. Malja fell to the floor, covering her ears, controlling her breathing, trying hard to stay conscious. People passed out around her. She pressed her ears tighter. She closed her eyes to stay focused.

Somebody tapped her shoulder. She looked up. All was still. Cole rested her slender hand on Malja's head and pointed to the frame in the floor.

The metal frame pulsed an orange glow that kept time with the slow moan that the musicians had settled into. Inside the frame, the floor no longer existed. Instead, Malja saw a room as if she hung from the ceiling. A round table covered in fuzzy green material dominated the room while dark wood shelves and darker rugs filled the rest. Malja thought they had blown a hole into the floor and looked upon some basement room. Except bright, noonday sunlight cut across the table.

"What is this?" she whispered.

"This," Cole said, savoring each word as it crossed her tongue, "is real magic. This is a hole into another world." Raising her arms like a prophet before her people, she climbed down the stairs and crossed the stage. "Long ago, perhaps not as long as you think, before the Devastation, magicians who knew the truth the governments denied them practiced in secret so that their power would grow and their ways would not die. They sought to improve their dominion over the world. Like little children playing with guns, they attempted to open a doorway into another world. They succeeded. Only for a second. Then they lost control, and we've all paid for that."

Malja gripped the banister. "What are you saying? This is the magic that caused the Devastation?"

Cole whispered, "Don't worry. We've not caused another Devastation."

"Well, what have you done?"

"Sympathetic vibrations. We create our own magic — just like them."

"Who?"

"Those from the other side. They came to us first, opened a portal right here. It only lasted a short while but it was enough to start talking with us. They call their magic a séance and they think of us as ghosts. Through them, we learned the Blues music and their way of life. We pattern ourselves after them for we have seen what great power exists — after all they opened a hole to our world without destroying theirs."

A portal into another world. She had no idea if such a thing were possible or if this was a hoax. Gregor certainly never mentioned it.

From their ceiling view, everyone in the house craned to see into the portal. Malja watched as a woman wearing a pink dress walked in to the séance and set the green table. She moved faster than normal as if time itself moved differently on that world. The golden-pink hues of sunset cascaded across the floor and a few minutes later night arrived.

A commotion erupted behind her. Malja turned to find Fawbry being physically moved into the hall by Shotgun and another big fellow. Shotgun had looped a rope around Viper, and the weapon dangled at his side. Fawbry looked tired and frightened but not bruised or broken.

Cole stepped forward. "Malja, I've watched you grow for many years. I've waited for you to be ready, for you to be able to see this and understand it without fear causing you to ruin this incredible opportunity we have before us. The time has come. Watch closely now."

"Cole?" Fawbry said, his face lighting up even as Shotgun pushed him toward the glowing frame in the floor. "Cole, honey, it's me. It's Faw-Faw. Remember Faw-Faw?"

The crowd mocked him, and Cole spoke to them even as she offered Fawbry a solemn glance. "Those days are gone. The Bluesmen came to me so I could build them a way through. We want to do more than just talk to this other world. We want to travel there. We want to live there. Tonight, we may finally succeed."

Several people now sat at the séance table. They all held hands and one seemed to be chanting. Their jerky, rapid motions would have been comical under different circumstances.

A dark man in a fine, gray suit sat nearby. He strummed a guitar with a gentle hand. Malja looked around the stage at all the guitarists, all the suits — all learned from this other world. Impossible.

"This isn't real," Malja said. "If you had this portal, if you had this magic without a magician, you would've left the Freelands long ago. I don't believe this is anything more than a trick."

"My, my, it seems your pledge to me may not have been all that strong. I'll have to fix my machine. As for the portal — it is very real, and you'll now see our very real problem."

Shotgun moved Fawbry closer to the frame. "No, no, no. You don't have to do this to me."

"Watch, Malja. Watch what happens to Fawbry."

"Cole, my love, don't do this to me. Please."

"Love? You left me for a pack of griffles."

Malja said, "Stop this."

"Relax," Cole said. "We're not sending him through. But you need to see to understand."

"Let me go," Fawbry said, pulling back but not strong enough to stop them.

Malja wanted to rush in and save him, but her body had become numb again. She didn't know if she'd be fast enough or have enough control to help. Her thoughts swirled and her head throbbed.

While the one man held Fawbry tight, Shotgun grabbed his hand and edged him toward the floor. Blubbering, pleading, begging — Fawbry watched as they plunged his hand into the framed hole.

He howled — a ghastly, chilling cry that caused several in the crowd to flinch. Malja heard the hand sizzle and smelled burning flesh. When they pulled Fawbry back, only a cauterized stump remained. Gray wisps of smoke drifted up like paper-thin tendrils. Fawbry cradled his stump and rolled on the floor. Tears and spit and mucous covered his open-mouthed anguish, but he made no sound.

Though she tried to be cold and stoic, Cole winced at the few gasps escaping Fawbry. She took a breath, plastered on her faux smile, and said, "Now, Malja, it's time for you to understand just how special you are."

Two men took hold of Malja and pushed her toward the portal. Her head dipped and her body followed, but the men kept her upright. She yanked her arms back. The men held on.

Too numb.

Looking down, she saw the séance magic — silly and frightening at the same time. The men each grabbed one of her feet and the world flipped over. Vomit rushed up and out — burning into nothing as it hit the portal. When Malja finally regained her bearings, she was suspended over the portal frame.

She couldn't feel her arms and legs — she just floated like driftwood on a lake. She closed her eyes, enjoying the sensation. Until they dropped her.

Her body swung — both men clamped down on her legs — so that her head went in first. The shock to her skin jolted straight to her toes like ice cold water on burning hot skin. The sudden cold reignited her numbed senses, clearing her mind even as it tortured her body.

She screamed.

Opening her eyes, she saw those around the séance table staring at her — some amused, some terrified. They moved at a normal pace now. The walls were high like a prison but a tall window showed Malja another world — buildings pressed against each other as wheeled vehicles pulled by horses clip-clopped by. Streetlamps of flame lit the area. Two children smooshed their faces against the window, looking wide-eyed with her.

A woman dressed in veils and holding a heavy book rose from her seat. Those seated around the table paled and shivered, a few mouths quivering. The guitarist slipped out of the room, muttering a strange prayer not to the brother gods but to a deity Malja never heard of — Geezuz. The veiled woman raised one hand and said, "Oh, Spirit from the Afterworld, long we have tried to meet you, to see you as more than a voice. Oh, wondrous apparition, guide us, please. Show us the way to our greatest fortunes."

Something pulled at Malja's ankles. Before she could speak, her body receded into the ceiling. And she was back home.

The band launched into a lively tune, and Cole Watts gyrated and twirled to the music. The entire crowd roared its excitement. People toasted their success and guzzled their drinks. With the change in music, the portal spell collapsed — popping and clicking until nothing remained but an empty frame, the wood floor, and the strong aroma of vinegar. They shoved Fawbry on stage, and Cole danced around him. He held his stump and gazed in the distance like a slave enduring a master's punishment.

Malja felt the majority of her numbness had vanished. The congested atmosphere closed in on her but she didn't move. She suffered disorientation, and nausea crept up her throat. She waited for it to pass and wondered if after experiencing the portal, it ever would.

The song finished and Cole, perspiration beading on her skin, calmed the rowdy crowd. "I told you all the truth. I promised you that Malja would be the key, that she alone held the secret within her. Tonight she proved it. Tonight, our sweet Malja safely slipped into another world. Oh my, and will you look at her face. She has no idea. That's okay, dear, soon you very much will."

"Let Fawbry go."

"No, no. He's our insurance for your co-operation. Now that I've proved what you can do, I need to study you. I need to figure out the process, so I can build a machine to let all of us travel through. And when we have that, we can access all the wonders that the world has. We can be great powers of this world. Jarik and Callib will bow at our feet, and we shall destroy them. But don't worry. You're far too precious. We'll test the machine on Fawbry first."

No.

In seconds, the hall became a tumultuous cavern of violence. Two brutes had closed in on Malja, and she wasted no effort in dispatching them. Blows to the head. Blows to the gut. She fought through the crowd with one focus — save Fawbry.

Suzu blocked her path. She elbowed his chest, bending him over, locked his head in her arms, kicked back to ward off those trying to sneak up on her, and propelled Suzu like a siege engine tearing apart a tower wall. Three people were knocked aside.

"Malja, stop," Cole said. "You won't be harmed."

The fury state had taken over. Malja dodged, attacked, and surged ahead. A battle cry from the stage slashed through the commotion — Willie. He pulled a sword from the neck of his guitar and plodded towards her.

Watching Willie, Malja never saw the attacker on her left. Two punches to her stomach took her by surprise. She doubled over and saw Viper hanging on a rope — Shotgun. Instead of straightening up, Malja jabbed her elbows skyward. Though her right met only air, her left caught Shotgun with a satisfying crunch. Before he recovered, she tore Viper free and swung up to meet Willie's attack.

The blades clanged and a metal chip flipped through the air, flickering light in all directions. The sound echoed across the hall. The chaos ebbed as the crowd settled, backing up a respectful distance. Malja had experienced this before. The people wanted to watch a show. From the look in Willie's eyes and the strength of his attack, Malja suspected they would put on quite a show indeed.

Willie ignited a flurry of blows that Malja should have parried with ease — her spinning head and sudden exertions worked against her. Twice she locked his straight sword in the curve of her blade, but could not snap it loose from his hand. They circled, each feigning attacks to feel out the other's counters, waiting for the other to overreach. Malja knew a good fighter when she saw one. Willie took his time, searched with his eyes, moved with grace and agility. He displayed patience and balance. A good fighter — definitely. Perhaps even an excellent fighter.

Wrapped in her thoughts, she failed to notice he had taken smaller steps for the last few, closing their distance by her own doing. He jabbed forward. When she blocked, he used her power to spin in the opposite direction and land a blunt chop on her side. The hit shocked her. Before she could get over her mistake, he swung through, catching Viper and nearly disarming her. The momentum knocked her off balance and onto the floor. Willie's sword tip caressed her neck.

"Stop," Cole called out, her voice trembling.

Malja kept her eyes on Willie as she breathed deep, sweat drenching her face and hair.

"Malja? You okay?"

Fawbry? Malja searched for where his voice had come from. Fawbry must have snuck off during the fight. At the same moment as Willie, she found Fawbry, his good hand leveling a handgun at Cole Watts.

"Malja?"

"I'm okay."

Willie helped her to her feet. The cut on her side looked worse than it felt and would hamper her until it healed.

Fawbry cleared his throat, and in his most powerful voice, he said, "Malja and I are leaving here. Nobody'll follow us. If anything happens, I'll kill Cole. When we feel safe, she'll be set free."

Willie said, "What about —"

"No talk. Get three horses ready. Do as I say or she dies."

"Kill her, then. We got on just fine before she came along, we'll be fine if she's gone."

Fawbry hesitated. Malja said, "Then we'll shoot someone else until we find one that matters."

"Come now, Malja," Willie said with a half-cocked grin, "Why do you think I went to the trouble to get you in here?"

"You *want* me to kill her? Then why are you fighting me?"

"You were hacking away at everybody. That, and I needed time to get my men in place. I figured everybody would want to watch us fight. See, Old McKinley is in charge now. Look around."

Malja, Fawbry, Cole, and many of Cole's supporters surveyed the still room. Willie's men guarded all the exits. Others formed a barrier around the portal frame. Still others occupied key locations should Cole's people try to fight. All of Willie's soldiers were armed, many with guns.

Willie sauntered onto the stage and retrieved his guitar. With great care, he slid his sword back into the guitar's neck. As he wiped the fretboard with a thin cloth, he said, "I thank you, Malja. We needed you to prove there was a way through the portal, and we needed Cole to show everybody how power-mad she really is. Now we can follow Old McKinley as he learns from your body the magic we will all use to leave this world for one far greater." He kissed his guitar and rested it in its case.

Malja's lip lifted a tiny fraction. "Let her go, Fawbry."

"What?"

"Do it," she said and leveled her icy glare on Willie, "And then pick up Willie's guitar."

"No," Willie said, moving toward Fawbry. Malja lunged for the stage, hooked Viper around Willie's knee, and the arrogant bastard fell. Fawbry lifted the guitar and held it like a club.

Malja said, "Anything happens, Fawbry, and you smash that guitar. Then you destroy any others you can get your hands on." She closed in on Willie. "No guitar, no magic. Right?"

Shivering with impotent rage, Willie grumbled, "Let them go." A path parted toward the front door. "When I see either of you again—"

"I expect no less," Malja said, as she and Fawbry edged off the stage. To Cole, she said, "You're coming, too."

Before Cole could move, Willie said, "She stays. Break all our guitars and all our bones. Doesn't matter. Cole stays."

Malja saw truth in his eyes. He would throw away everything that mattered to him, fight until he lacked the strength to move, all to make sure Cole did not leave the farm. Old McKinley wanted to fondle her no doubt. Besides, politics don't end just because Malja wrecked the place. "Fine," she said. "You're on your own, Cole. I'd say I'm sorry I couldn't help you here, but we both know that would be a lie."

Cole rolled her eyes. "Just go."

Backing out, Viper poised for work, Malja and Fawbry exited the hall.

Chapter 17

All through the night, they rode. They had to go slowly or else endanger their horses with a nasty fall in the dark, but still they rode. From time to time, Fawbry would look back with anxious jittering eyes. Malja looked back, too. Even after they left the guitar by a tree, they looked back.

Malja wanted them to follow, wanted them to appear — especially Willie. Every minute they traveled further away, she thought about him. When they stopped by a creek to let the horses rest, she had decided. "I'm going back."

"What?"

"You go meet up with Tommy and Tumus. Look after them."

"You can't go back there. We almost died."

"I still don't know where to find Jarik and Callib. The City of Ashes is too huge. But Cole Watts knows."

"Cole Watts is dead."

"Not yet. She had a lot of supporters. If Willie kills her right away, he'll have a civil war on his hands. He wants to be their leader. So, he's got to convince them first. Rile them up until they only see her death as a release from her tyranny. He'll convince them that doing what he says is true freedom."

"How do you know what he'll do?"

"It's what I'd do."

Fawbry paused for a moment. "I don't believe you," he said finally. "You don't care about Cole. We could find out that information some other way. No, you want to go back because you're ticked off that Willie got the better of you. You want a little revenge."

"I want—"

"Go. I don't care anymore. You and your Black Beast and your screwed-up fathers and all of it — I don't care. I'm done with you."

Malja stayed motionless, her face devoid of expression. She stared at Fawbry until he broke eye contact. He shook his head, mounted his horse, and trotted off. She listened as the dull clops of horse hooves receded in the distance, and only then did she relieve her tension with a drawn-out sigh.

Fawbry had spoken a fraction of truth — it angered her that Willie had won their conflict. But she had no intention of hunting him down. Not yet. She sought Cole Watts. She sought information.

Riding back took even longer than getting away. Several times she heard noises and had to hide — Willie and his men might have tried to pursue them or simply patrol the area. Caution was critical. Malja exercised greater patience than she ever thought possible. By the time she edged toward the open compound, the noonday sun blazed overhead.

Sitting against a large rock, she observed the area through her spyglass. The farm appeared to be running in full force — just another day. Closer to the house, however, the tension ramped up. Willie stood on the porch with fists pressed against his hips like an arrogant general, while Lonnie and three others sat on horses, waiting for orders. Shotgun paced behind Willie, his weapon resting on one shoulder. Suzu flitted about, his energy revealing the true degree of fear simmering. Not Willie, though. No fear there. Just the controlled anger of the true warrior.

Whenever possible, Malja kept her attention on Suzu — who he talked with, what he might have said, where he went. Suzu was the main lackey. Sure enough, at length, he stepped out of the house carrying a tray of food and a glass of water — lunch. He headed for the stables. An armed guard checked over the tray before letting him in.

Well, well. No office prison for Cole. Malja hunkered down amongst the rocks. For now, she had nothing more she could do until night. Nothing but sit quiet with her thoughts spinning around Fawbry's words.

She waited until the party grew raucous, until the only people leaving the house were amorous couples seeking dark privacy. Only then did Malja leave her position and scuttle in the shadows toward the stables. The sticky air warned of heavy showers, but the sky harbored only a few clouds. With any luck, the storm would arrive soon. Heavy rains would aid her escape.

Crouching low, she hurried across open land, stopping when she could press her back against the stable wall. She slid along the wall, reached the corner, and peeked around — still just a single armed guard. She released Viper from its sheath and readied to rush the guard.

Suzu slammed open the house door. He held a bottle high in the air and stumbled a few steps. "Long live Willie," he said before taking a tumble down the stairs and passing out.

While the guard watched Suzu, Malja took advantage of the distraction. She acted with swift confidence like a magic shadow stealing in the darkness. The guard never heard her approach, and in seconds, she had him out of view on the side of the stable. She raised Viper but the guard's face stopped her. He couldn't have been much older than Tommy. His eyes pierced her much like Tommy's eyes.

"Fine," she grumbled and hit the guard's temple with Viper's hilt. He passed out.

Taking a moment to check the area once more, she noticed the top half of the stall door above her was open. She climbed in. Peeking through the main stall door, she saw Shotgun's empty stool. The guard must have been all they thought they needed — after all, Malja would never dare come back. Not this soon, at least.

She crept across the stable in dark silence. Cole Watts had been tied to a gate similar to the way the Bluesmen had tied Fawbry and her only days before. She had been allowed to change clothes. Gone was her party dress. Instead, she wore a more practical pair of pants and a dirty men's shirt — clothes for field work. Despite the darkness, Cole's wet cheeks stood out in the cuts of light that broke in from the house.

Cole perked up. "Hello?"

"Be quiet."

"Malja? What are you doing?"

"Jarik and Callib. Where in the City of Ashes?"

Disappointment lowered Cole down. "I thought you'd figured this out. Thought you came back to try the portal on your own."

"I don't really care about your little magic games here."

"You should. It's little magic games that caused the Devastation. And it's little magic games that'll restore the world. It's where the power is to make a real difference."

Malja pictured the glowing metal frame, the green round table, the portal to another world. She had been given no time to think about any of what she had seen. *And not now either.* She checked to make sure nobody was coming. Shotgun and a man with milky-white hair weaved down the dirt path, but they stopped half-way, turned to the side, and pissed on the grass.

"I'm not interested in making a difference. I just want Jarik and

Callib. Tell me where they are or I'll kill you."

Cole shook her tied bonds. "Look at me. When they finish their party, *they'll* kill me. If not tonight, then tomorrow's party. So, if you want to find your fathers, then you best get me out of here. I'll take you right to them or wherever you want, just get me out of here."

Malja hadn't slept in a long time and lacked the energy to argue. Besides, this situation could go sour very fast. Best to get Cole Watts out and get the information later.

Using Viper, Malja snicked Cole's ropes open. "Follow me, do what I say, no questions. Understand?"

"Since we're talking about keeping me alive, I'll understand anything you say."

Malja checked outside once more — Shotgun and White Hair had returned to the party. Malja led the way out of the stable. They passed the tailors — door closed. They passed the guitar workshop — a couple embraced against a post. They crossed the open land. Their feet crunching the dirt road echoed in Malja's ears, but she knew others could not hear it. Such sounds were illusions created by tension. All seemed to go well as they scrambled back up the hill.

Until the ground shook.

Cole looked back as men poured outside with guns and women screamed in drunken fear. Malja tugged Cole's arm, but Cole wrenched her arm free. Blood drained from her face.

"This can't be," she said.

Malja watched the chaos below. "What's wrong? It's just a quake. Isn't it?"

"No. They're coming."

Willie stepped outside and fired a round into the air to regain control. Malja couldn't help but think of the wasted bullet. The ground settled and Willie said, "See? Just a quake. Now everybody back to the par — Where's T-bone?"

Shotgun and Lonnie dashed toward the stables. Malja pulled Cole further up the hill. "Come on. They're going to find you've escaped."

"No," Cole said, resisting with her meager strength. "They're here. Your fathers are here."

The ground shook once more. The fierce fighting dogs whimpered and scurried away, tails tucked between their legs. The horses whinnied and kicked their stalls. Even the bravest Bluesmen moved closer to the house and Willie.

"Everybody calm down," Willie said.

Shotgun and Lonnie rushed back. "She's gone," Shotgun said. "And T-Bone's out cold round the back."

"It's okay, everybody," Willie said, but Malja heard the worry of a leader facing his first big test. "Robert, take three men and check the perimeter. Mud and Rev, get a few more and check all the out-buildings — make sure she ain't hiding out there."

"Right," the men said, but they never got to follow through on the orders.

The ground cracked open. A hole formed the size of Suzu. It buckled as something below pushed hard, swelling higher and growing wider until it exploded in a shower of rocks and dirt. Five maxdins punched around the hole until they could climb out. Eight feet tall, covered in bristling hair, and with more teeth than brains, the maxdins were Jarik and Callib's personal thugs. They lumbered on two feet, striking with sharp claws.

"They're really here," Malja said.

The maxdins pressed forward, herding the people away from the fissure in the ground. With another rumbling quake, the ground surrounding the hole tumbled inward. The maxdins let loose a low bellow that caused the skin to quake.

Two men rose from the smoke and dust. They ascended like graceful dancers and continued into the sky. A circle of ten magicians, male and female, rose beneath the two men — each cross-legged on air and locked in concentration. Balls of electricity spread around, casting the area in stark light.

Malja's stomach felt like she had been punched. The men looked nothing like the Jarik and Callib she remembered from childhood, yet she knew to her core they were. Both were bald and shirtless, and tattoos covered every bit of skin. Despite their age, both looked to be in their prime — young, strong, commanding. The only difference between them — Callib's tattoos formed harsh, block-like patterns whereas Jarik's formed delicate webs of intricate designs.

The Bluesmen had recovered from their shock. They aimed their weapons and approached with calculated steps, fanning out with impressive unity. Willie stepped down from the porch, putting out his hand to caution his men. With a similar gesture (and, no doubt, some magic), the magicians halted the maxdins.

"Welcome to the Bluesmen's home," Willie said, opening his arms and bowing.

Callib's mouth turned down with scorn. "Give us the portal frame."

On the hill, Cole dropped to her knees, one hand covering her mouth, the other holding her stomach. "They mustn't. Sweet child, they mustn't get that frame."

A gun fired. Malja couldn't tell who shot, but the release let loose all the others. Gunfire blazed like the dragon fire of ancient stories, but the bullets never reached their targets. Concentrated wind bursts like two-second hurricanes knocked the bullets away. The air in Malja's lungs chilled until she gasped a breath — she never knew magic could do such things.

The snapping gunfire ceased — eight weapons had jammed and the rest needed reloading. As if toiling through a tedious day, Jarik floated behind Callib and focused on Callib's back tattoos. Callib gazed upon the people below like they were bugs he longed to hear pop.

By an unspoken command, the maxdins attacked. Those unfortunate enough to have been standing in front of the beasts never had the chance to fight back. The maxdins scooped up their victims and devoured them raw.

"Take cover and fight back," Willie yelled. His men scattered for cover and enough distance so they could reload.

Jarik lifted his head to the sky and let out an ecstatic, pleasurable moan as magic rippled along his veins and tensed his muscles. Vines darted from the open ground — thorny, gray vines. They moved fast like hyperactive snakes, wrapping around legs and arms and weapons before the Bluesmen could react. A few vines squeezed their victims' throats and dragged the blue-faced bodies back underground.

"How did they do that?" Malja asked Cole. "How can a magician use another's tattoo? And so fast. They're so fast."

Cole shook her head like a child both afraid and in denial. "Don't let them get the frame. Not the frame. Nothing else matters."

Malja picked her way down the steep hill even as her mind raced to digest a fraction of the moment. Jarik and Callib — her fathers — hovered in the air unleashing carnage upon those who had become her enemy, yet her soul told her to defend the Bluesmen. Her mind warned her that she had not yet prepared for this, that despite years of searching she never dealt with any emotion regarding her fathers beyond anger. Still, her legs charged on.

Two maxdins spotted her assault. One tore off to meet her. The other first finished chewing an arm.

Malja leapt from a rock and surprised the first maxdin — it never expected her attack to be so high. She cleaved its head half-off. The other tried to rush her, but when she hit the ground, she rolled right up against its legs and severed the backs of its knees. The hairy beast howled while its blood muddied the ground.

The remaining maxdins turned toward Malja. They bared their numerous teeth and growled from the throat. Malja launched toward them, cutting every vine within reach as she approached.

Her eyes kept snatching glimpses of Jarik and Callib — the two frowning and a bit confused at her appearance. She trained her attention back to the maxdins. Still her eyes wanted to linger on her fathers. She wondered if they even recognized her or if they had been so consumed by her failure that they could not comprehend their daughter's current ability.

A maxdin threw its arms high above and stomped towards her like a towering giant squashing the villagers. Four gunshots rang out followed by something bursting. The beast toppled to the darkening ground. Behind it stood Suzu, his face as pale-gray as the smoke seeping from his handgun's ruined barrel. He had been lucky to get two shots off, let alone four, before the weapon busted. Shotgun and Robert disposed of the remaining two maxdins with several more gunshots.

A chorus of anguish rose from the circle of magicians floating underneath Jarik and Callib.

"Willie?" Suzu called out. He stood amongst the blood and bodies. The others also stood in the destruction while each passing second deflated them like leaking balls. They had beaten the magicians' forces, yet they acted defeated.

The right corner of Callib's mouth lifted and his eyes narrowed. He slid behind Jarik to focus on one of the spidery tattoos.

"No," Malja said. Ignoring her conflicting thoughts and roiling emotions, she sprinted towards her fathers and let out her war cry.

Callib took no notice of her. He remained focused on the tattoo. Jarik, however, flicked his hand at her as if shooing away a fly.

Yanked by an unseen force, Malja flew back twenty feet. The impact knocked the air from her lungs and slowed her from getting back up.

"Gahhh!" Callib said, and a sudden storm approached. A blast of wind and bolts of red magic smashed into the house. Those inside screamed and some abandoned the building in panic. Everything but the floor — walls, roof, stairs, doors, everything — cracked, splintered, and shattered. The cacophony washed out all other sounds of the house. Pieces blew off into the distance like a pile of dead leaves carried on a stormy gale. When the last of the house, a brick chimney, crumbled and blew away, the storm ceased.

Like a floating fortress, the mass of magicians cruised across the air until they hovered above the houseless floor. Jarik moved his hands in a circular pattern and the portal frame ripped out of the floor. It drifted toward Jarik like a hawk returning to its master. Callib stroked the frame as if consoling it — promising the worst had passed.

"Magicians!" a defiant voice called out.

Everyone turned toward the fields. Willie and Lonnie stood there with their guitars in hand. Between them stood Old McKinley. The old man's bent body and vacant expression clashed with the shock and hesitation seen in Jarik and Callib.

"We've got what we came for," Jarik said, waving the frame. "There's no need for further tragedy."

Callib elbowed Jarik aside. "McKinley? Are you such an idiot that you'd try to face us again? Look at yourself. Drooling like a baby. You can barely stand. Where's your wheelchair? And you've pissed yourself. I can smell you from here. You're feeble and if you persist, you'll be dead."

"Stop this now," Willie said in a firm voice. "Give us the frame and go your way. You've done your damage. We can't hurt you with it. But we can't let you leave with it. We won't have another Devastation."

"Is that what you think?" Callib said, and as he launched into a speech of self-aggrandizement and false assurances, Malja heard a voice call from the side.

Cole Watts waved her over from the back corner of the stable. Malja wanted to hear her fathers and see what would happen, but the urgency on Cole's face and the fact that she had climbed back down the hill could not be ignored.

"What?" Malja said when she came closer.

Cole had her saddled horse waiting. "We must go now. McKinley — he'll kill us all."

"McKinley can't even control his bladder."

"He's still capable of creating powerful magic — but he's unstable. One of my greatest fears if Willie took over was how he'd handle Old McKinley."

Malja's tone lowered. "He's handling him like a loaded gun."

"And like any gun, there's a high probability this one will blow up in Willie's hand. So get on the horse, and let's ride."

Though Malja's head still rang from being tossed, she had enough sense to listen. She climbed into the saddle, and Cole got up behind her. She heard a growing argument from the field. Callib's rage and Willie's scorn dueled like master swordsmen. But Willie broke off his words, and he and Lonnie started playing their guitars.

Over it all, a craggy voice chopped into the air. "Malja," the voice called, and it twinged something in her brain.

"Brother gods, it can't be," Cole said. "Old McKinley is speaking."

"Malja, listen to me."

She heard Callib yelling, but Old McKinley's voice echoed in the hills.

"It's the music," Cole said. "They're making him clear-headed and letting his voice become louder."

Malja said, "Is that even possible?"

Though Old McKinley looked weak and emaciated, his voice echoed with youthful vigor. "You know me, Malja. You killed my partner after I murdered your dear Uncle Gregor."

She didn't doubt his words at all. The twinge in her brain recalled the voice as its owner had held her against the wall of the shack. Her face paled.

"I told you then that Jarik and Callib ordered the death, but that wasn't quite true. Jarik never knew. Callib is the one you want. And if you can see them right now, you'll be happy at the seething anger burning between them."

"Get this horse going," Cole said.

"Enough," Callib yelled, and Old McKinley toppled to the ground. Willie and Lonnie continued to play. Someone started blowing a mouth harp and other Bluesmen plucked notes to compliment the growing sound.

Old McKinley returned to his feet. "Malja — Callib is your true enemy. Just like he's always hated you, he's always hated me. I never did what he demanded."

"You're making it easy to want to kill you," Callib said. Again Old McKinley was thrust into the dirt.

The music raised in volume as others joined in. Those without instruments sang. The sound bolstered Old McKinley back up.

"They hired me, Malja, because they were too weak to do it themselves. That's their true secret. They're weak."

A red bolt arced from Callib's hand and pulled Old McKinley into the air.

Cole leaned close to Malja's ear and said, "They're using music to build up enough power to create an explosion. They're making themselves into a bomb. They'll release it, and we'll die with them."

Malja saw it on their faces. Solemn, resigned surrender. She kicked the horse into a strong gallop.

When they reached the rocks from where Malja had spied earlier, she pulled up the horse and looked back. The music drifted up their way. She swore she could feel the magic mounting in the air.

"I've got to go back."

"You can't. Old McKinley isn't telling you this for no reason at all. He's going to—"

The music ceased, and the softest of sounds like a puff of air from a thrown pillow met with the harshest of lights like a little sun exploding from Old McKinley's heart. A wall of heat rolled up the hill and smacked into Malja and Cole, knocking them off the horse. Cole covered her head and curled into a ball. Malja, however, looked once more.

The little sun continued to burn. She smelled rotten eggs. She had to turn away — the brightness hurt her eyes.

She heard a noise building like a wild animal working itself into a rage. The full force of a new blast reached them, smashed Malja to the ground, and burned across her back. Her assault suit protected her skin from damage, but it could not protect her head from being knocked unconscious.

Malja's head throbbed. The morning sunlight penetrated her like needles poking through her eyes all the way back to her brain. Her tongue rubbed at the dry, pasty film in her mouth.

"Ah, you're up," Cole said, her voice echoing and magnified.

Malja wiped at her nose and closed her eyes. Sleep would be much easier than dealing with anything else.

"No, no," Cole said like Gregor would when she tried to shirk her daily chores. "We've lost too much time as it is. The only reason the world's still here is because McKinley's magic closed in that hole in the ground and put a sore beating on Jarik and Callib's pets. Best I can tell they're headed north."

Malja bolted up fast, fought back her spinning stomach, and said, "My fathers are still alive?"

"Dear me, McKinley isn't near strong enough to take down those two. Not even with two full bands playing behind him."

Gazing down the hill, Malja saw the flattened leftovers of a powerful blast. A clear, grassy circle marked where McKinley and Willie had stood. White blast marks streaked outward like salt strewn across the land. Bodies littered the area.

She turned back. Cole's eyes were still red and her face puffed from the exertions of mourning. "I'm sorry about all of this."

Cole carved a grin. "Not your fault, is it? Besides, there's no time for sadness. We've got to get moving."

"North?" Malja said.

"Your fathers have my frame. With their magicians hurt, they can't travel back the same way they came. The City of Ashes is west of the Yad. Closest crossing is north. If they mix their magic with my frame, well, what do you think will happen then?"

Malja gave a weary nod and groaned as she pushed up to her feet. She patted the horse's neck and breathed in its thick aroma. She mounted the horse and said, "Let's go."

Hours later, she should have stopped. The poor horse faired worse — both could barely stay awake, but the horse carried two people on its sore back. Still, Malja pushed on. She tried not to think. Too many quiet miles lay ahead. But too many had drifted by, and her mind refused to hold back.

Tommy. Always Tommy.

She wanted to wrap her arms around that boy, hug him tight, and kiss his forehead. She wanted to promise him that once Jarik and Callib were dealt with, she would build a home for them. It would be a small place in the woods, far from the chaos — a small place with a garden filled with fresh vegetables and an apple tree loaded with perfect, red apples.

Night descended as they staggered upon the way station. Malja found no sign of Tumus or Fawbry or Tommy. The fire ashes were cold. Some nuts and a bit of chewed meat littered the floor. On one wall, Malja noticed charcoal doodling — a big circle, some dots, an arrow pointing to some little circles, wavy lines. She touched the drawing and pictured Tommy standing in the same spot.

But they had gone now. They must have left before Fawbry had returned. They could have left days ago — and perhaps he followed.

Cole stretched out on the floor. "This place reeks."

"Smoke-cutter died in here."

"Good. I hate those bastards."

"Go to sleep. We'll move out soon."

Cole rose on her elbow. "You need to sleep, too."

"Don't worry about me."

"Are you guarding me? You scared I'm going to try to run away? You shouldn't be. Everything's different now. Your fathers — they're not right in the head. They're going to do far worse to this world than the Devastation. So I'm sticking with you. I think I'd like to have you there when things turn ugly. So get some sleep. I need you alert and ready."

Malja weighed the points and lay down on the counter. "If all you just said is true, then you can tell me where Jarik and Callib are going. Where in the City of Ashes? If I'm going to protect you, I need to know so I can plan the safest route."

Cole chuckled. "Rest well. I promise I'll take you there. You have my word. Tomorrow, I'll lead the way."

"Not tomorrow. We have to go find my friends first."

"We don't have time for that. We've got to stay after your fathers."

"You don't get a vote in the matter."

Cole rubbed her face, and with a frustrated exhale said, "And where are they?"

"I don't know for certain, but I have a strong suspicion. And the more I think about it, I'm as close to positive as I could ever be. It's the only place that makes sense."

"So where would that be?"

"Dead Lake."

Cole said nothing for a moment. She shook her head and turned over to sleep. "You've got strange friends."

Chapter 18

Malja awoke a few hours later, yawned, and put her head back down. Her body craved another hour or two, but her brain urged her to prep the horse. The poor beast might not survive if they maintained such a grueling pace, but Malja saw little choice. She hoped some extra care now would be enough.

Stretching her limbs, but not getting up, Malja inhaled, held her breath, and exhaled slowly. The fighter in her chastised such a lazy awakening. She should spring to alertness. But her body needed to recoup, and this was the best she could manage. Peeking at Cole to make sure she still slept, Malja scrunched her face tight, held it, and let all her muscles ease back. It was a little relaxation ritual Gregor had taught her.

I'm close, Uncle Gregor.

Knowing Old McKinley died did nothing to quiet her Beast, but it did fill a small darkness in her memories — like recalling a name after struggling for it. She hoped Gregor was pleased, but tried not to think about it. And before her mental image of Gregor could frown at her and point out how too often she tries not to think about things, she rose and headed outside to the horse.

The morning work helped busy her mind, but in case it wasn't enough, she thought about the hole into another world and the fact that she fell through it without dying. She should have been burned to dust but here she stood rubbing a horse. Perhaps Jarik and Callib had put some strange spell upon her. Perhaps Cole had done it with her machines. It was even possible that they all had conspired together when she was little.

And there was the other world itself — a world far more civilized, probably more powerful, and possibly more dangerous. Contact with this world had had enough influence to birth the Bluesmen. Malja's fist tightened at the thought of what such contact would do to her fathers.

As Malja finished with the horse, Cole awoke and readied to go. They headed out without a word.

Malja stayed alert. She listened for snapped twigs or a sudden break in the birds' melodious morning chatter. She searched the trees and rocks for a shadow or a glimmer or anything unusual. She sniffed the wind for signs of a camp or an ill-washed enemy.

"I wasn't trying to hurt you," Cole said after several hours. "I know how it looked, but you were never in danger."

"You burned off Fawbry's hand."

"That was a little personal. Besides, I had to act harsh for the Bluesmen. My place with them was tenuous. They needed to see that I had the strength and the will to follow through on my promises. Otherwise, they would never listen to me."

"I don't care about anything you want to say except for where I'll find Jarik and Callib. So let's just go to Dead Lake, make sure my friends are okay, and then head for the City of Ashes."

"You're in charge. Even if it means we'll lose your fathers. I just hope we're not going to see Barris Mont. You can't trust anything that bloated monster says."

A flock of gray and white minrits took to the sky leaving behind the skeleton of a dead birch. "What do you know about Barris Mont?"

Cole scoffed. "More than you, apparently."

Malja refused to be baited, so she let silence lap over them. That didn't stop her brain, however. Over the next hour, she reviewed her limited experience with Barris Mont, searching for any hint of his ulterior motives. Unfortunately, there were many — well, not hints, exactly, but plenty of signs to suggest he had lied or at least obscured the truth.

They camped early that night to insure the horse's survival. The following midday, they came upon the Muyaza village. Something bad had happened.

Nobody traveled across the river. No line of waiting passengers had formed. Two buildings had been squashed into rubble. Dark, soupy smoke billowed toward the clouds. Worse — a row of bodies rested at the shore and a few weeping families sat nearby. Others carried more bodies over using the river litters. Blood stained the food table.

As the two women neared the village, a Muyaza man noticed them and thrust a finger towards the hills. "Go," he said. "No cross."

"What happened here? Who did this?"

"No cross. Go."

Malja looked to Cole. "Jarik and Callib?"

Cole raised an eyebrow. "Possibly. But this world is full of violent people."

The Muyaza man continued to point, but said no more. To Malja, he looked like a sad Chi-Chun — so distraught he could raise only one arm. She surveyed the area.

"You," she said. "Magic do this?"

The man's face tightened. "You bad. Go. No come back. Ever." Wiping his hands in an exaggerated manner, the Muyaza turned his back on them and left.

Cole said, "They really love you here."

"Doesn't matter. We still have to cross the river."

"Considering what's just happened, I doubt they're doing their usual patrols against bridge-builders and such. We could easily build a boat. They won't bother us."

Malja's stomach rolled at the mere thought of water travel. "A boat will take too long."

"Nonsense. We'll go back to my cabin. I have tools and machines that can help."

"Your cabin is days away. Besides, there's nothing there anymore. Fawbry burnt it to the ground."

"He what?"

"It was an accident."

"That Kryssta-loving fool. He did it on purpose. I know he did."

"I don't care. Get that into your head. I don't care. All I want right now is to get across that river, and it won't be done on any boat."

Malja set the horse moving toward the river's edge and then headed upriver. She hoped to find a shallow or narrow area to attempt the crossing. After only a few minutes, however, she heard the clumsy steps of someone following them without knowing how to do so properly. Wrenching the horse around, she saw a Muyaza man trip in shock. Not just any Muyaza. This one bore a white scar across his chest and had almost died under Viper's sharp curves. Tommy had stopped that from happening, and now she would see how Tommy's kindness was repaid.

Malja slid off the horse and pulled out Viper. The man scrambled to his feet. "No. Please. I help."

"Help how?"

"I take cross Yad."

"You want to help us cross the river?"

With an enthusiastic nod, the man smiled. "I called Skvalan. I take cross Yad."

"Why?"

Skvalan turned cold, his brutish muscles and stern brow finally matching the bruiser she had dealt with before. He gestured back at the village. "I listen. You hate magic. I hate magic."

He choked up and Malja recalled the woman who had tried to stop him from confronting her. "Did they kill your wife?"

"Wife?"

"Your woman."

His eyes darkened as he nodded.

"How do we get across?"

Skvalan stepped close. "Wait for night. No Muyaza see. I open water."

"I thought only the old ones did that."

"I no good but I do."

Cole said, "That sounds so encouraging."

Night took its sweet time coming. As the hours passed, Cole noted several times how far they would have been in making a boat. Each mention caused Malja a second of bitter reflux in her throat. If Skvalan backed out, they would have to use a boat. The seasickness alone bothered Malja, but listening to Cole gloat would near kill her.

Skvalan arrived an hour after the moon showed its face. He wore a heavy cloak, a satchel overflowing with fruit, and he carried a litter. He looked at the two women without visible emotion. "We go," he said and dropped the litter at their feet.

Malja wanted to yell at the man, but it would do no good and she needed him. With Cole on the front and Malja in the rear, they lifted the Muyaza on the litter. Skvalan took a cleansing breath and concentrated on his leg tattoo. Five minutes passed before the protective bubble formed, and it barely covered the three of them.

"Leave the horse behind," Malja said.

As they entered the river, walls of water pressed in. Skvalan grunted as if struck by invisible foes. He strained to maintain the bubble and their safety. Malja urged Cole to walk faster, but Cole had never labored under a litter before — she grunted and strained, too. For Malja, the litter was easy. She had carried many bodies off many battlefields. The water, however, worried her. It pushed against the bubble with steady force that they had to compensate against or be swept away. Fighting the Yad, swimming to shore — it had been hard enough the first time. She had no wish to repeat the event, particularly at night.

Though the moon provided some light, the darkness beneath the water blotted out most light. The river flowed around them in muted tones. Even the river's odors seemed less pungent in the night.

Halfway across, Malja asked if anybody needed to rest. "Just keep going," Cole said and Skvalan grunted. Though Malja approved of them both for toughing it out, she suspected Cole didn't want to stop for fear of not being able to start again.

They pushed on. Slick stones and uneven surfaces threatened to topple them at every step. Malja risked a peek at Skvalan. His body shook with his effort.

As if leaving a long, dark tunnel, they emerged from the Yad and reached the shore. Skvalan and Cole dropped to the ground, sweating hard and breathing heavy. Blood dribbled from Skvalan's nose. Malja handed them fruit and treated herself to a ripe apple. She gave them a short while to recoup.

"Thank you," she told Skvalan. "I owe you for this. Cole, let's go."

As they headed out, Skvalan followed. Malja now saw the cloak and satchel for what they were — all his possessions. Skvalan must have seen her intention to turn him back for he reached into the satchel's side pocket and pulled out a long braid of dark hair. "Wife," he said. His fingers tightened around the braid as if choking the life from the bastard magicians responsible.

The Beast is in us all, she thought. She suspected he would follow them regardless of what she said. She might as well have him on her side. "Okay," she said.

Walking to Dead Lake sapped what little stamina they had left. Malja wanted to sleep. She had grown tired of being tired, but knew the luxuries of a soft, safe bed were long away. One look at Dead Lake told her that bed had moved even farther into the distance.

Trees had been toppled. Dying fires charred the ground, mixing their smoke with the growing fog coming off the lake. A Chi-Chun man hung from a tree limb, blood dripping into its own crimson puddle below. Further along the shore, they found more evidence of battle.

Skvalan tensed, and his head darted from side to side. Malja wondered if she had more of a warrior on her hands than she had given credit. Cole, on the other hand, held her nose against the harsh stink of the dead drifting like the fog.

"Stay close," Malja said. Clouds kept blocking the moon — she didn't want anybody getting lost.

She heard the mournful praying long before she saw the dark figure emerge. As they closed in, she spied a Chi-Chun woman bent over two bodies. The woman raised her arms upward and said, "Korstra, most powerful brother god, to serve you, we live and in serving, we are fulfilled. I offer you the souls of two cherished servants." She lowered her hands, touched the corpses, and began the whole thing over.

Only when they were close enough to trip over the dead did Malja recognize the woman. "Tumus?"

Tears streamed down her dark skin as she faced Malja. "There was no warning," she said. "They just came in and started killing."

"Who? Tumus, who did this?"

"They never stopped. They kept moving forward like we were in the way." Tumus got to her feet and opened a secretive smile. "Don't fear. I left Tommy with Barris. They linked so Tommy could finish his new magic easier and in good health."

Malja didn't wait for Tumus. She might have strangled the Chi-Chun if given the chance. She stormed across the stony shore, each step making her angrier. Her actions, her choices, her orders — all of it should have made her wishes clear. She did not want Barris Mont playing with Tommy's mind. Her anger at the stupidity around her only fueled her anger at her own gullibility. She should have expected this the moment she decided to leave Tumus and Tommy behind.

Of all the carnage she had witnessed in the past, nothing compared to the bizarre setting she found at the dock. Numerous Chi-Chun corpses littered the ground like smashed scarecrows. Several horses lay dead amongst them. The corpse of Barris Mont rotted in the lake. Only a small portion of his bulbous form broke the surface like an island made for vultures and minrits. One damaged tentacle stretched from the water, across the dock, to the strangest part of all — a burnt hole in the ground surrounded by fallen trees, debris, and people, and all knocked away from the hole.

Cole said, "Something exploded here."

"No," Tumus said, but she wasn't correcting Cole. She was speaking to herself, denying what her eyes told her. Throwing her body onto the hole, her words grew louder and more painful. "No, no. Please, no. I'm sorry."

Malja chilled. "Tumus? Where's Tommy?"

"I-I'm so sorry."

"Tumus," Malja said, her voice snapping the Chi-Chun name but getting little reaction. She stood tall over Tumus, as if she could will the woman to speak. "Where's Tommy?"

"He ... he ..."

"Damn Korstra, where's Tommy?"

Screaming the words out, Tumus said, "I left him here with Barris! I left him here! I-I left him."

Chapter 19

Malja couldn't feel her hands. She slumped on the dock facing the charred darkness in the ground, and her hands just went away. Her face, too. Only the icy-hot spike of loss impaling her chest convinced her that the numbing was not a return of the magic she had drunk.

She tried to cry out, scream, make some sound — but she couldn't move. Her lungs could barely pull in enough air to keep her alive. Her eyes stung from not blinking. She stared at the black dust, the blasted dirt, unwilling to look away. When she exhaled, her breathing shook from her body like a broken machine.

She had promised him. She had held that little boy's hand as Wuchev's splashes blended with his terrified tears, and she had promised him. Yet the first moment he needed someone else, she broke that promise.

She could feel the excuses mounting and shut them down. "My fault," she whispered. She had left him with Tumus. Nothing would change that. No excuse could fix that. She had failed.

Callib's right. She remained there, staring, petrified in pain as her thoughts trundled over each other, spiraling her deeper into doubt. She had slipped off that morning, so Tommy couldn't cause her discomfort about leaving him behind — and in the Freelands, no less. Perhaps Jarik and Callib had been right to try to kill her. She left Tommy unprotected. *I'm a monster.*

She had held his hand. She had made her promise. And now, she could only wet the ground with her tears.

"Who's Tommy?" Skvalan asked Cole. "Why she cry?"

Hearing Skvalan, Malja realized she was crying, and that blew her open. Every ounce of pain released like a blast of magic scorching the charred ground. She wailed and clutched at her heart. She kept waiting for everything to stop, to end, because the idea that life would continue made no sense.

But at length, her tears did stop. Her breathing eased. And a low, growling rumbled within her. Callib's not right, it told her. Jarik's not right. They're the monsters that murdered the only right one she ever knew.

Gregor.

She lifted her head and looked around. Cole and Skvalan meandered around, waiting for her to snap back, while Tumus cried on her own.

Sure. Wait for me. They're all helpless without me. The dead pain in her heart started to beat. *But if I say Left they all want Right.*

She had tried it their way. She had tried to be peaceful. She didn't slaughter the Bluesmen, she didn't kill the Muyaza, she held back all the time — especially with Tumus. The result — the Bluesmen had been decimated, the Muyaza refused to help her, and Tommy ... she had to stop thinking about that. Gregor had taught her to follow real evidence, facts not fancies. And Gregor was usually right. He believed in her. Maybe he was right about that, too.

Facts not fancies.

The only fact she had regarding Tommy — he wasn't at the dock. But her instincts told her that if he was alive, Jarik and Callib had him.

He is alive, she told herself, because the thought felt both right and necessary. Without it, no matter how angry she could be, she never would have stood again.

But she was standing. Angry, cold, even a bit dead inside, but standing nonetheless.

"We're going," Malja said, firm and strong. The others straightened and assembled. "Cole, you lead us to those bastard magicians. Mess it up in any way, I'll cut off your head. Anything gets in our way, it dies. This madness they brought upon me is going to end."

Wiping her eyes, Tumus said, "I wish to accompany you. I can help."

"No."

"Please. All I've known here is gone."

"I don't care."

"Let me help you. For Tommy. For what they did to him."

Viper flashed out and hooked Tumus in the back. Through gritted teeth, Malja said, "You did this to him. I charged you to protect that boy. You brought him here, to Barris Mont, knowing I didn't want that. The only reason I don't kill you now is because I think you'll suffer more living with your guilt."

She released Tumus. The Chi-Chun woman dropped to her knees and new tears bellowed out.

"We're leaving now," Malja said, turning away from Tumus. Cole cast a pitiful look at Tumus before heading toward the mountains and the City of Ashes. Malja felt no pity. Only one thought echoed in her head — *I've got a promise to keep.*

Malja picked up the trail with ease — a wide swath had been cut through the trees and brush. Jarik and Callib made no attempt to hide.

Cole did better than Malja had expected. Hiking long hours with little break can be hard on the most seasoned soldiers. But Cole never quit and never complained. Skvalan held his own. Malja's expectations for him were high — after all, he had spent his days crossing the Yad over and over. He should be strong.

She spoke little during the day, letting the physical exertion work away the rest of her anguish.

That night, they circled their campfire and ate the stringy but nutritious meat of a dollad. Skvalan had caught the tunneler right before it burrowed to its freedom. Whenever he met Malja's eyes he raised the leg bone in his hand. She nodded the first few times, but his pride had become annoying. She concentrated on eating to avoid his eyes.

"I didn't see any signs of Tommy," she said. She didn't mean to say it out loud, but once started, she had difficulty stopping. "If they had taken him, he would've tried something to get my attention — drop something or leave a marker of some kind."

Cole and Skvalan exchanged looks of concern. Malja opened her mouth, ready to babble more, when a thought struck hard enough to make her smile. "If he's not with them, then he's out there somewhere. He might be just fine."

Cole touched Malja's knee. "Dear, you've suffered a loss. We understand that. If you want to turn back, it's okay. We can find some other way."

Malja's eyes flared up. "We're not going back. Tommy is not dead. I know it."

"All I'm trying to say is—"

"You just want out. Guess what Miss Watts? Everybody wants out. Nobody's ever happy with the life they were given. But some of us learn to live with it, to take control of it, and make the best of it we can. Others — they just want to cry over their wounds and go back."

Cole's face hardened. "Don't you dare lecture me, little thing." She threw her bone in the fire and plopped down next to Skvalan. "I may not have the Bluesmen under my control, but don't think I'm under yours. I have knowledge to keep me alive."

"Push me far enough, and I'll kill you anyway. I can search the City of Ashes without you. May take the rest of my life, but I'd do it."

"I believe you would. But I know more than just where to find Jarik and Callib. I know all about Barris Mont and I know the core truths of the Devastation. And I know where you come from. I've even seen your mother."

Malja shot forward, kicking through the campfire and releasing Viper in swift motions. Sparks lit up the darkness and reflected off Viper's blade as bright as the blaze in her eyes. Before Cole could react, Malja had Viper pressed against her quivering neck, a slick, trickle of blood marking the skin. Skvalan watched without comment and only mild interest.

"You'd better start sharing that knowledge now," Malja said.

"If I tell you, you might kill me."

"If you don't, I'll definitely kill you."

With her hands raised in surrender, Cole pulled back from Viper and used her worn smile. "Okay. You've convinced me." Malja held still a fraction longer while Skvalan reset the campfire. With her jaw jutting in a dare, she backed off two small steps. Despite her hands shaking, Cole continued, "You're not from here. Not this place. You were born in another world."

The words froze between them. Malja's mind pulsed with memories of the other world she had seen — the green séance table, the oddities outside the window, the people staring at her. "That was home?"

"No," Cole said, lowering her voice and her hands. "The world the Bluesmen talk with is not your world."

"How do you know?"

"Because I was there when Jarik and Callib got you. I saw them create a portal — just the two of them — and I watched you fall into our world. That world you came from — it's absolutely incredible."

Malja's mouth tasted stale and her lungs constricted. Gregor had said that someday she would learn the truth — no, that she would have the *chance* to learn the truth. "The important question," he said, "is do you really want to know?" Of course she wanted to know. But he only smiled as he served up breakfast and said, "Sometimes the truth is a heavier burden than the mystery."

Although Skvalan had built a hefty blaze, Malja could not escape the cold pressing in. "Tell me everything," she said.

Cole slouched as if the weight of sadness surrounding them had been placed solely upon her. "I told you magic caused the Devastation — the magic to create a portal. There's more. See, Barris Mont was alive back then."

"I know. He showed me. He had once been human."

"Perhaps. I wasn't there. But human or not, Barris planted the seed in all those foolish magicians' heads. Made them think they were better than all the rest. He knew of the other worlds, or at least he suspected, and he persuaded these fools to play with some very hot fire."

"Barris caused the Devastation?"

"Partly, yes. And you would think that erasing three-quarters of the world would give a person pause, but not Barris. He approached it like an equation that needed to be solved. He had no luck. Until one day, he met two brothers who were also budding magicians."

"He gave Jarik and Callib their powers?"

"He *unlocked* their powers. They had them from the start. But for all his ability to look inside a person's mind, that big fool had blinded himself to what Jarik and Callib truly were. Barris wanted to be right. He needed to be; otherwise, he had nothing to show for all the death he caused."

The campfire popped and the tower of wood fell apart on one side. Malja wondered how much more she could take before she, too, crumbled apart. "So, Jarik and Callib are trying to open a portal. But you've already done that."

"Patience, now. What you saw with the Bluesmen was nothing. Your fathers had accomplished that much long ago. They've been able to open portals to hundreds of worlds. What they can't do is travel to them. We all burn up if we touch the magic. Just like Fawbry."

Malja's stomach lurched. "But I don't."

Cole tilted her head like a big sister revealing the truth about boys. "No, you don't. Oh, my dear, sweet little Malja, life can be so unfair. Your fathers opened world after world, trying to unlock their secrets. They found many worlds with no magic at all — just machines. So they came to me. They wanted me to build many things — machines to stabilize the portals, machines to boost their magic, machines to test the portals, all kinds of things."

"And you did this, of course."

"Jarik and Callib aren't the types that really offer much choice, now are they?"

"I suppose not."

"Well, there it is. I built what I could, but we still couldn't get through the portals. One morning, they opened a portal, and it must have materialized right beneath your mother because she just fell into our world."

"Fell?"

"We all stood there, just stuck in shock. We'd never had anything like that happen before. She had a baby in her arms — you. And she clutched you tightly like she knew what was about to happen. She stared at us with the widest eyes I've ever seen. Scared me into praying to the brother gods for a moment."

"What did she say? What did she look like?"

"She looked a lot like you — long, dark hair, strong face. If not for the fear in her eyes, she'd have been a striking woman. She spoke a lot, but it wasn't in any language I ever heard. Callib, though, he reacted like she had come to cause another Devastation. He saw something in that portal, and it scared him something awful. He shut down the machines and yelled out his magic. The portal sealed and sucked your mother back into it in the process. You, however, remained."

"She let me go?"

"No. The force of the portal stripped you from her arms. She screamed as it brought her back in. Most heart-wrenching thing I ever heard in my life. Callib stared at you like you were the spawn of evil. He wanted to destroy you. Dissect you, too, no doubt. But Jarik picked you up, and that was that."

"Then why did they get rid of me? If I'm the only one who can pass through the portal, if Jarik saved me, if any of what you're saying is true, then why toss me into the woods?"

Cole stifled a yawn. "Didn't know what they had, did they? I'm sure they wish they could take it all back just so they could use you. Now, I've told you enough."

"You sit there and tell me everything."

"You going to kill me? Then who'll tell you the rest? I gave you some of it, but I still have a few bits left and those'll keep me alive, thank you. So, now, I'm going to sleep. We've got a lot of hiking to do tomorrow."

Malja kicked her heel into the dirt and swore. As Cole rested her head on the ground, Malja joined Skvalan in squinting at the fire. She tried to stay angry at Cole, but the woman had given her more information than she ever had before. She saw her mother reaching for her like the campfire flames straining toward the night sky. Sleep would be a long time in coming.

The rain began before sunrise — heavy, thick drops at first followed by drizzle, then heavy again. The ground became mush in seconds. Malja, Cole, and Skvalan hiked through the damp forest and over muddy hills, keeping their heads down and saying little. Being Muyaza, Skvalan cringed under the cold droplets, but Malja refused to baby him, and she suspected he would resent such help anyway. Skvalan would push through his cultural issue, if for no other reason than to prove his toughness and his worth to the group.

Malja required no proof from either Skvalan or Cole. Hiking mile after mile in chilling rain without the aid of horses proved enough. She only wished they could move faster. Jarik and Callib had hours on them, and the bastards could float over obstacles that slowed Malja's progress. She didn't fear losing them — with Cole's help, she would find them. But with the frame in their possession, Malja feared they'd have too much time to cast their spells.

Cole stopped. Massaging her hip, she said, "My, my, my. Take a look at that."

Malja trudged back and followed Cole's gaze. In the distance, nestled discretely behind a wall of oak, stood the ruins of an old mansion. Vines had engulfed much of its front helping obscure it from notice even more.

"We should keep moving," Malja said.

"Hold on. There might be supplies in there. At the least, we could get dry, build a fire, get warm."

"We're already too far behind," she said, seeing Skvalan's longing. "Stopping here will only make it worse."

"Maybe so, maybe not. Who can know? But I know this—if I don't get a tiny bit of comfort, I won't be worth a thing in another mile."

Malja considered leaving Cole behind. She could find the City of Ashes on her own. Two powerful magicians couldn't be that difficult to locate — people talk, and Jarik and Callib were probably well-known in the city. She could do it. It would take longer, that's all. She took several steps up the path. A lot longer.

She kicked the muddy ground. "We'll rest for an hour, then it's back on the hike."

Cole had the sense to stay quiet.

Chapter 20

Skvalan broke apart another hand-crafted chair to feed the fire. They were in the foyer — a massive room of marble columns, curving stairs, and stained-glass. Two statues guarded the front door — the Prophet Galot on the left, and the magician Moonlo on the right. Moonlo looked gaunt compared to the well-fed image of Galot, but his stern expression spoke to the firm will power and unending faith that helped him write and spread the Book of Kryssta.

"Guess they couldn't make up their minds," Cole said.

"What?" Malja asked. Cole had been flitting about the mansion, commenting on its fine architecture and relatively good condition since they had arrived. Malja chose to ignore her as much as possible.

"The owners," Cole said. "Not very religious, I guess. Or maybe too religious."

"Sit down already. You're the one who said you needed rest."

"I know, but this place is amazing. People have probably walked by for a hundred years and never knew it was nestled back here like a buried treasure. You understand that? It's practically untouched."

"That's right. So we've got chairs to burn."

Skvalan tossed the last bits of wood into the fire and settled with his back against a thick column. Cole rolled her eyes. "Well," she said, drawing out the word like a disapproving parent, "the two of you may have no appreciation for the riches to be found here, but I do. Enjoy the fire. I promise to return for some rest before we go, but first I've got to see what else I can find."

"No, Cole, you stay," Malja said, but Cole continued to rummage through a pile of discarded things in one corner. "We are too close to the enemy." Cole moved on to a small wooden desk with numerous drawers. "This is not the time for scavenging."

"Praise Kryssta and Korstra and whoever else you fancy, look what I found." From the bottom drawer, she pulled out two bottles of wine. The labels were torn and faded but the distinctive pyramid-shaped bottle meant they were Luntland — among the finest wineries before the Devastation. So fine that people still knew the name. "Here's one bottle for you and one for me. Now I'm off to check the rest of the house." With a triumphant gait, Cole sped up the stairs.

Malja and Skvalan wasted no time. A clean strike from Viper cut open the bottle. Skvalan found a light, metal bowl in the trash pile. Malja raised her first toast to Cole — an undamaged bowl like this was rare. If she had a horse, Malja would have loaded it with everything she could find. Instead, she and Skvalan emptied the bottle by the bowlful.

"You don't talk much," Malja said, resting her woozy head and watching the fire's smoke weave up to the ceiling three floors above. *Didn't mean to drink so fast.*

"No speak well."

"That's okay. I'm comfortable around quiet ones."

Silence settled between them. Sounds of Cole bumping through the house mixed with the drumming rain like the beginning beat of Cole's music magic, but between Malja and Skvalan — silence. Until Skvalan sniffed loudly and said, "We go soon."

Malja opened her eyes (she hadn't realized she drifted off). "I know. I want to go, too. But I'm starting to think Cole is right. I mean, obviously, we don't have to track them. Cole knows exactly where they're going. And there's no way for us to catch them — we're too slow on foot. So, might as well rest and do the best we can tomorrow."

Skvalan placed his small pack under his head. "No good."

"I know no good. That's because I'm lying. I mean all I just said is true, but I'm not telling it all. See, I don't care if Jarik and Callib open another world. I don't even care if they destroy this one. I just want Tommy back. That's all. I should never have left him. That's why I've kept pushing us so hard. And now maybe Cole's right. She won't say it out loud, but maybe she's right. Maybe Tommy's in the middle of Dead Lake. Maybe he's dead."

Skvalan opened his bag and pulled out his wife's braided hair. "Wife dead. I see. Tommy no see. Tommy no dead."

"Don't give up, eh? Don't worry. I'm drunk and I'm babbling. Trying to convince myself. Prepare. Gregor always told me to prepare for the worst, because then you won't be disappointed. Trouble with that is you can end up lying to yourself. Jarik and Callib — I know them. I try to tell myself they were something else, but they're not. They're evil. And they raised me, influenced me for ten years. Maybe that makes me evil, too. Can a person overcome that? I know Callib wants to change everything, run the world his way. But he'll destroy everything good. Then they'll be nothing left for Tommy. So, I guess I do care if they cause another Devastation. That's something, right?" The fire crackled and Malja watched the sparks drift upward. "I do care."

Skvalan stroked the braided hair with his thumb.

"I've drunk too much. Don't listen to me. I'm just tired and angry and confused. And drunk."

Malja closed her eyes and felt her body drift with the sparks and sweet-smelling smoke. Things had been simpler long ago. She woke each morning with one easy task — hunt for food. After that, the day was hers. If she could just let go of all her rage, just forget Jarik and Callib — they never existed. Only Gregor. He was her father.

But every time she tried, reality reared in her mind. Now she saw her mother reaching out for her. Now she saw Jarik taking her away. And now that bastard had taken Tommy. He must have. Any other scenario would have left a body or blood or some evidence. To leave nothing at all but scorch marks — that's the work of magic.

Even though she heard laughter from her mouth and her body shook, Malja also felt tears trickle on her face. "It's over," she said, jerking Skvalan from his own slumber. "I can act tough forever, and it won't matter. I care. I do. But we can't stop them if we can't get to them. You want to know why I agreed to come in here, why I got drunk, why I let Cole go running around? Because it's over. We lose."

Skvalan shook his head and spit to the side. He might not have understood a lot of her words, but Malja could tell he understood her tone. Perhaps the alcohol had gotten to her or the unyielding stress — whatever the cause, she felt tears. Not crying, pitiful tears but raging, frustrated ones. She wanted to pummel something, assert her strength, remind this Muyaza why he feared her not too long ago. She watched the fire cast orange and black against the walls. She didn't move.

Cole darted into the room, her face flushed, and said, "You must come see this."

If not for Cole's urgency, Malja would have rolled over and slept. Instead, she let Skvalan help her up. They followed Cole through the elegant corridors of the mansion. These weren't the sterile white of Barris Mont's old office or the decayed grandeur of Ms. Nolan's place. These walls hinted at a youthful, new wealth with plenty of technological remnants that Malja had no knowledge of how to use. No wonder Cole wanted to snoop around here.

Cole led them into a wide open room of cool, smooth stone and sharp, musty odors. A blue, boxy contraption on four wheels filled up half the room. Cole ran her hand along the thing and slapped its metal body.

"Have you ever seen one in such good condition?"

Malja rubbed her head — she still felt a bit tipsy. "What is it?"

"Why it's a grounder, silly."

Malja inspected the grounder again, trying to imagine it as one of the rusting, hollowed out shells that dotted the world. "Didn't know they had wheels."

"They did, and a lot more. This one has been sitting here, protected from rain and wind and animals and thieves, just waiting for us. All it needs is some power and a little attention, then it'll run."

Skvalan nodded. "It is like horse?"

"Better than a horse. With this we can follow the old roads and even with stopping to clear overgrowth and as long as we don't suffer any major breakdowns, we'll reach the City of Ashes by tomorrow night. We just have to change the batteries." Cole hefted a pack of two large cylinders encircled with a coil.

"Well," Malja said, "unless one of you has suddenly become a magician and can produce electricity, this is all pretty useless to us."

"These batteries are in excellent condition. The best I've ever seen. Even if it takes us two days to find power, we'd still—" Cole stopped, her mouth agape, her eyes lost. "Willie?"

Malja turned around. Willie stood in the doorway.

But not Willie, too.

The creature had Willie's form but not entirely. One eye was clouded over like Old McKinley. And the corners of his mouth turned up like Shotgun. His stature belonged to Willie but his belly borrowed from Suzu.

With a guttural yell, Skvalan rushed forward. Thousands of insects, maybe millions, crawled out of the creature and covered him in a living armor — cockroaches, ants, tapats, silvers, and any number of bugs Malja could not identify. Skvalan punched the creature. The creature stepped back an inch — nothing more. Skvalan, however, clasped his fingers and grimaced as if he had broken his hand. A powerful back fist from Willie sent Skvalan tumbling against the grounder.

The insects skittered away. Some disappeared into his clothes. Others used his ears or nose as an exit. Some left his body for the walls and floor.

Willie lifted his arm. A jagged tattoo marked the underside.

"What is it?" Malja asked.

In a stunned voice, Cole said, "Magic I never believed in entirely — raising the dead. Jarik and Callib brought him back to get rid of us."

Willie stared at his tattoo.

"He has magic now?"

"He *is* magic. They probably didn't have time to be specific, so they just raised everything in the same ground as Willie."

"But he —"

"Dear child, are you going to stand here and let him get that spell off or are you going to kill him?"

Malja whipped out Viper and attacked. As she swung her blood-hungry blade, the insect armor reformed. Viper slashed through, splattering insects and knocking Willie back into the house, but drew no blood. Malja followed in and attacked again. Each hit knocked away insects and pushed Willie back further, but more of the bugs filled in the damage.

They entered a kitchen — sinks and counters remained as well as many metallic, boxy objects Malja had never seen before. She kept her focus on Willie. Even through her constant slashes, Willie maintained his focus on his tattoo — seeming to see through the insects.

Malja brought Viper around and attacked the tattooed arm. The insects clicked and chittered loudly. A new arm formed below the tattooed arm. This new arm also formed an insect sword. It deflected Malja's blow, spraying the walls with roaches and beetles.

The arm retaliated, and Malja went on the defensive. Blow after pounding blow pushed her abilities. Death had not lessened Willie's swordsmanship.

Malja tried to counter, but the attacks came too fast. Forced into blocking each swing, she struggled to find an opening. Her body tired, while his insects seemed stronger.

In a desperate move, she ducked under his swing and slashed at his legs. She lopped off the left at the knee. Willie broke off his assault, hopped backwards, and waited as the bugs formed a new leg.

Panting, sweating, and tired, Malja watched Willie like a wary rabbit sensing danger — still, but ready to leap.

"You can't beat me," Willie said. "I was too strong before and now, with my magic, you're hardly worth the time." The insects peeled down off his head and torso, creating an undulating mass around his legs. "But I'm a Bluesman, and we follow through when we're paid."

"You were never paid to kill me," Malja said.

"Just slow you down; hinder your progress." An electric ball burst into existence between his fingers. "Killing your friends should do that for me." He thrust his arm forward, shooting ball after ball of dazzling blue-white lightning. They sizzled and crackled toward Cole. Malja jumped in the way.

Before she could be hit, the ball broke into long, jagged strands. Each strand curved back as if a massive wind blew against it. The magic lit up the room as it passed over Willie's confused face and shot into a dark figure standing with arms outstretched.

"Tumus?"

The Chi-Chun woman continued absorbing the lightning and said, "Hurry. I can't do this for long."

Flinging forward, Malja hooked Viper into Willie's back and brought his innards toward her. He tried to summon his bugs, but Malja slashed, hooked, and tore with furious abandon — the insects could not move fast enough. Not when his focus fought in too many directions.

The lightning ended. Willie's hacked body dropped. The insects scattered.

Malja glanced at Tumus. Little sparks of lightning danced between her limbs, each time pulling a pained cry from her clenched mouth. *Good,* Malja thought. As fast as the thought arrived it brought with it the reason for her anger — Tommy.

Moving her lips the bare minimum, Tumus said, "Get away. Can't hold on to this much longer."

Malja didn't move. Cole, however, sprinted across the kitchen. "Wait," she cried, bringing the batteries to Tumus and showing her where to touch for recharging. As the magic drained from Tumus, she sighed like a child relieving a full bladder. Calmer, she recharged the second battery. When the last of the magic left her body, she dropped on the floor and wiped her drenched brow.

"You aren't welcome here," Malja said.

Tumus shrugged off Malja's words. "Korstra has different plans."

"The brother god gets no say. Tommy's gone because of you. You're not welcome."

"Do not forget that I just saved your life. And do not believe you're superior to me. I did not try to get rid of the child. You did that."

Malja's hand tightened around Viper's grip. "I was protecting him. If he had come with me, the Bluesmen might've killed him."

"What makes you think we were any safer? Stuck alone in the

Freelands? Yet we waited. For days. Barely any food. Every little sound a possible threat. Korstra looked over us, though. He was our true protector."

"Then let him protect you some more. You're not welcome, and I don't want you following us."

"I care nothing about what you want. I'm going to help save that boy."

Malja looked to Cole and Skvalan. Cole found something on the battery to draw her attention while Skvalan discovered the wonders of picking at his elbow. "They don't understand. They don't know you. You'll put Korstra ahead of all else."

"I will fulfill my duties. Korstra brought Tommy into my life, and I will get him back."

Malja turned away. As much as she wanted to lash out further, she knew Tumus was not to blame. Dangerous to a team, yes. But not to blame. "It doesn't matter," she said. "We're too far behind. Even with a grounder, we'll never get to him in time."

Tumus brightened. "So you do believe they took Tommy."

"Listen to me. We can't get to the City of Ashes in time. So go home. It's all over."

Struggling to stand like a newborn foal, Tumus let out a muted yelp. When she stood, she took a boastful breath and said, "Powerful magic takes more than tattoos and time. It takes strength and energy. Creating a creature from bits of the dead is extremely powerful magic. Imbuing such a monstrosity with lightning magic *and* the power over insects is practically unheard of. No matter how strong Jarik and Callib are, the energy they expended to stop you will have weakened them extensively. Perhaps for days."

"You're saying they've camped out?"

"Or their followers are carrying them. Either way, they will not be capable of powerful magic for a little while."

"That's good information. Thank you. Now get out of here. Go pray to Korstra or something."

"You stupid fool. I will go to the City of Ashes. I will follow you if you won't allow me to be a part of your group, but I will go."

Malja's face blazed. She wanted to cut Tumus. Shaking her head, she reined in and stomped off to the foyer campfire. She paced the wide hall and kicked any debris that dared to block her path. Though fuming, an odd grin crossed her lips — she knew anger so well it had become an old, welcome friend. Something shivered beneath her rage, however. A sense of wrong, a sense of sadness and regret — an emotion tied to the name Tommy. She mashed it well with anger. She could swallow any emotion with anger. Normally that ended it. But everything surrounding Tommy kept resurfacing.

Skvalan walked in. "Grounder run soon."

Malja nodded.

Skvalan nudged the fire with a rock until it flared up. "Tumus come, too."

Malja squatted next to him and let out a tense breath.

"I love wife. I go. She love Tommy. She go, too."

Malja closed her eyes.

Skvalan said, "She helps."

"She's a zealot. That's why Tommy's gone. She refused to follow my orders and instead follows her brother god."

"What you mean? Zealot?"

"Forget it."

Skvalan rubbed his ample belly. "We go fight magic. We need magic. She has magic."

"Look, I know you want her with us, and I know that she can help. But I don't trust her. I can't."

"Trust Cole? I think no."

With a begrudging grumble, she said, "Cole's not so bad."

"Trust me?"

"You want revenge for your wife and village. I understand that better than you'll ever know. You, I trust."

Skvalan stopped picking at the fire and faced Malja. "We need magic. Tumus come. Trust me."

Malja made a bitter face. To stand her ground against Skvalan meant at best, creating a rift between each member of the team and at worst, breaking them apart. Being alone would be nice but would not be good strategy at the moment. "Fine," Malja said, a bit more aggressively than she intended. "She can come, but she'd better be careful."

"Good." He said nothing more as they waited for the grounder to be ready. For that, Malja was grateful.

Chapter 21

Riding a horse never bothered Malja, but just a few seconds on the sea could flip her stomach. Sitting in the front passenger seat of a grounder while suffering a hangover proved an odd mix of both. She felt fine, despite the constant bumps and swerves as Cole guided the vehicle along uneven macadam, overgrown dirt paths, and rocky, dried riverbeds — as long as Malja kept her eyes forward. Whenever she chanced a peek out the side window, her stomach would lurch its bitter, acidic contents straight up her throat.

At least twice every hour they had to stop to clear out a fallen tree or dig through a wall of rocks. These hindrances provided Malja with some time to relax her stomach. Even heavy lifting or hard work chopping wood felt better to her body than the unnatural motions of a grounder. She couldn't comprehend how people once used these machines all day long.

She was a bit thankful for her hangover, because nobody bothered her. Cole drove. Skvalan and Tumus sat in back. They spoke quietly throughout the day. Apparently Tumus knew the Muyaza language — a fact she never bothered to mention before. Had Malja felt better, she would have yelled for a while about it, but being sick saved her from that foolishness as well.

And it was foolish. She had no regrets about the previous night — she truly worried about where Tumus's allegiance ultimately fell — but this day, hours later and sober, she could admit that Skvalan also spoke some truth. Tumus cared for Tommy and felt deep pain over what had happened. Yelling at the woman did nothing to help.

Cole brought the grounder to a halt and squinted off to the left. "I wonder," she muttered and got out. The others followed.

A few yards into the trees lay the wreckage of some vehicle. As Malja stepped closer, her eyes widened. It was the trader's flatbed.

Weyargo's mutilated body had been wrapped around a tree. Malja said, "I met him once. Nice man. He had a magician with him to power this thing."

Everybody glanced around. "Animals eat," Skvalan said.

"Perfect," Cole said. She had been dallying with the flatbed's batteries.

Malja perked up. "Can we use those?"

"Not directly, but we can drain some of the power to recharge ours. Shouldn't take too long."

Malja checked the sun. "Get to it. We don't want to be stuck here tonight. That dead trader'll attract plenty of attention."

Cole was true to her word. In less than an hour, she had managed to get a quarter charge added to their grounder's batteries. She complained that she had lost a lot in the transference, but Malja figured every little bit got them that much closer.

After a few hours driving, Cole pointed ahead and said, "Look at that."

They had crested a small rise and for an instant the trees parted. In the distance, they saw the City of Ashes. Endless rows of gray and black shapes sprinkled the mountains like rotting, jagged teeth.

"We probably can get another hour in before it's too dark to drive. Tomorrow, though, we'll be there."

They managed an hour and a half. Malja suspected Cole pushed the extra time not because of good light, but rather out of a desire to finish this mess she had joined. Malja didn't mind. They had made the extra time without incident and were that much closer.

Later that night while Skvalan's deep snores creaked like an ancient wooden ship, Malja watched the City of Ashes and heard violence running wild in the streets. Flashes of magic and plumes of fire rippled along the city. The sounds reached across the sky like distant thunder.

As she settled in next to Malja, Cole said, "The few clans living there go crazy over territory wars. Jarik and Callib probably keep the peace a little better, but they're absent right now."

"I thought you liked anarchy."

"In the Freelands, yes. There are miles of nothingness separating small pockets of people. One government, one set of laws to rule all would never work in a place like that. But in a city where people clash together non-stop — well, just listen to that lunacy."

As if in response, a series of green bursts popped along the streets followed by two heavy booms like massive cannons.

"Did you want something?" Malja asked. She pulled out Viper and worked the blade with a good stone she had found on the ground. She would have preferred her whetstone, but that now collected silt at the bottom of the Yad River.

Cole clasped her hands in her lap, straightened her back, and curled her legs to the side as if posing for a sculptor. After all the hiking and trudging and fighting, Malja had forgotten just how beautiful Cole could be. "When we arrive at the city," Cole said, "we'll head west for several blocks until we reach the Kryssta temple. From there we go north until we find the Skyway Bridge. There's where we'll find Jarik and Callib."

Malja continued to run Viper across the stone, creating a rhythmic scratching like a machine needing oil. "Why are you telling me this?"

"I could tell you that you need to know in case something happens to me, or I could even say that it's all about stopping Jarik and Callib. But the real reason — I don't know exactly. Aren't I just a fool? I suppose I want you to keep me in the group, even though you don't need me for information."

"Being part of a group isn't very anarchic."

"Pure anarchy cannot be maintained for long."

Malja gestured to the city. "They're doing a pretty good job at it."

"Only when their Masters are gone." Cole shifted closer, lowering her body in an apologetic fashion. "I know you've got many valid reasons not to want me along, but when I watched you and Tumus argue ... well, you both fought passionately, because you both love this boy. The only thing I've ever felt that much passion for is my work."

"And Jarik and Callib have that now."

"Yes. I suppose I want it back, but it's more than that. I want to help you and be a part of something good. I know my time with the Bluesmen became a horrible screw-up. I know that. But my heart was in the right place. I just wanted to open up the possibilities for everyone, so magicians like Jarik and Callib couldn't rule over everybody."

"You want to keep the anarchy going strong."

"Please, don't fight me like Tumus. Sweet little Malja, let me do something good."

Malja drew her head back. "I don't know why you think I could force you to go."

Cole chuckled. "Thank you."

They listened to the chirping night creatures and distant, random explosions. Malja sharpened Viper. Cole relaxed.

Many people had come in and out of Malja's life and she never minded much. Drifting through the world brought that about. As long as she thought she had a good sense of the person, she felt secure. The closer she came to Jarik and Callib, however, the more confusing the people around her had become.

Adding to her thoughts, Malja heard Tumus approach. "Can't sleep?"

Tumus huffed as she sat next to Cole. "That man's snoring is worse than listening to Barris Mont speak."

The others laughed loud enough to interrupt Skvalan's snoring, which only caused more laughter. The brief mirth didn't fool Malja, though. Tumus did not sit with them for companionship. As their laughter subsided, Malja pressed for an answer.

Tumus said, "I'm concerned about tomorrow."

"We all are," Cole said.

"I'm worried we're being led into a trap."

Cole's smile dropped. "You've the gall to accuse me —"

"Not you. Them." Tumus indicated the city. "Jarik and Callib had outrun us. They should have been to the city already and done whatever they wanted. Instead, they use exhaustive magic to send an abomination upon us. Why?"

Malja set her sharpening stone aside. "You think they wanted us to catch up?"

"It's a possibility."

"Yet you know I'm going in there anyway."

"For Tommy."

Malja inspected her blade. "Yes. For Tommy."

"Well," Tumus said as she stood, "I simply wanted to make sure we all understood. Good night."

After she left, Malja turned to Cole. "Still want to come along?"

Cole's face darkened as she peered into the distance. Malja lifted Viper and stood in a ready stance. She sniffed the air and listened for snapping twigs or crushed leaves. Cole looked at the ground like a defeated child. "The fighting stopped."

"Jarik and Callib?"

"They're in the City of Ashes now. They're home."

Chapter 22

The batteries gave out a few hours into the morning drive. Malja's anticipation fueled her legs, and she suspected the same could be said of the others. Nobody complained. They moved like ants scaling a tree to get to some leaves — steady and strong with a goal firmly in place.

When the sun reached its highest point, they took a break, each member of the team settling under a tree or an overhang for shade. All except Cole. She stood at the path's edge, gazing across the wide vista.

Malja approached and offered a swig of water from a dented canteen. Cole's cheeks were damp — more than just sweat. "You okay?"

Dabbing at her eyes, Cole said, "It's silly, but I just started thinking about Faw-Faw. I was remembering how back then the two of us lived so free of any concerns. Our days were spent following our whims and our nights were, well, passionate. Now it's all just this."

"Sounds like it was a dream, and dreams don't last forever."

"I know. See, but then I think about chubby Suzu or Rev with his big voice and charming laugh and ... I'm sorry they're all gone."

Malja threw a rock into the open air and watched it plummet. "Let's get hiking. It's going to be hard. That'll keep your mind off the dead."

As they trudged through several hours, Malja found her own dead to be kept at bay by the hike. She focused on each breath, each step, each rock. As night approached, they came upon the city streets. No gates, no arch, no bridge — nothing to signify the start of the city but a few scattered buildings.

These first structures stood tall with little apparent damage beyond broken windows and the wear of ages. Some were brick. Others smooth metal. A rare few were made of the once-white material Malja saw in Barris Mont's memory. Now, the white barely showed. A fine dust coated every surface — a mixture of dirty ash and mountain snow.

Malja saw no signs of people. Not even a furtive peek from a window corner. Nothing. She listened for a slipped foot or dropped object or a hushed voice. Nothing. The place was a cemetery.

Cole led them down one street, and Malja tried to memorize the turn. Lampposts lined this new street along with plenty of evidence attesting to the horrid nature of the city's inhabitants. From each lamppost hung a body. On each body, the skin covering the head had been removed, the head had been hollowed out, and a candle had been mounted in the skull. The dim light provided unsettling shadows across the ash-covered street. Tumus murmured a prayer.

A few blocks further in, they came upon a humble building surrounded by waist-high grass. The buildings around this one structure had been razed to the ground. An altar poked out from the grass. A statue of Moonlo lay in several pieces.

"The Kryssta Temple," Cole said. They turned north. Cole pointed into the dark and said, "Straight that way, several miles, we'll come upon the Skyway Bridge."

On the next block, Malja noticed footprints in the dust. Just a few at first. But eventually enough that the others noticed, too.

"Are we being watched?" Tumus asked.

"Probably," Malja said.

They came upon a massive, circular fountain with the far end dipping back, tilting the whole thing toward the buildings. The street bent around the structure which Malja thought looked more like a lake than a fountain. The stagnant water reeked. A statue in the middle rose several stories — or, it once did. Now it was a pair of legs surrounded by piles of rubble.

As they walked on, bullet holes marked walls and doors. Burnt-out grounders and smashed storefronts lined the streets. A flyer teetered part way in a lone wall, as if unsure whether or not to crash to the ground. Craters pocked the sidewalks. Smoldering fires scented all the evidence of the previous night's fighting.

The deeper in they traveled, the worse the city looked. Graffiti marred the cracked and ruined walls — violent and pornographic images painted in mud, charcoal, and blood. Like old advertisements, the words CALLIB IS KING and JARIK RULES weaved around the pictures. Bodies with fresh wounds decorated walkways. Worse — body parts littered the streets.

The last of dusk's sunlight disappeared. Malja ordered they set camp for the night with two of them guarding in shifts. They picked the sturdiest-looking building and settled in on the third floor. Malja denied Cole's request for a campfire. "It'll attract too much attention." So, they huddled up and attempted to sleep in the cold mountain night.

Only Skvalan could sleep. The others shivered and paced and kept watch. They listened to the skirmishes ignite and fade out, but none of the fighting reached the scale they had witnessed during their approach to the city. Apparently Cole had been right — Jarik and Callib's presence helped tame things.

During one of the lulls, Tumus came up to Malja with a stern face. "I think you truly believe Tommy is alive, and that being so, I must tell you something you don't want to hear."

The first thought to pierce Malja's mind — *Tommy's dead and Tumus has known all along.* She came close to striking Tumus. Even repositioned her feet to provide a strong leap. But she recalled that Tumus also believed Tommy was alive.

Oblivious to Malja's reaction, Tumus went on. "I know you hate me and blame me for all this, but that blame is false. I did not seek to disobey your commands. Tommy did." Tumus stepped back from the wild glower in Malja's eyes. "Tommy asked me to take him back to Dead Lake, to Barris Mont. He said if I refused, he'd do it on his own."

"It's amazing he said all that," Malja said. She leaped to her feet and gripped Tumus by the throat. "Especially considering the boy hasn't spoken a word since I've met him."

Tumus did not squirm. She spoke calmly, though straining for air, and she bore her gaze into Malja with religious conviction. "He did not speak with words. He drew pictures on the walls."

Malja thought of the huge circle, the little circles, the arrows and dots she had discovered. She let go of Tumus and turned away. "He told you he wanted to go back? Maybe you misunderstood."

"No. We spent hours going over his pictures until I knew quite clearly his desires. He can feel the changes going on inside him. He knows he has potential, and permit me to say that he has astounding potential, but he's being kept back and he wants to learn how to control his powers. Barris Mont could help him, and Tommy wanted that."

"You think you know him better than me?"

"In some ways, yes. I'm not afraid of what he is, and I don't shun him for it, either."

"I do not—"

"It doesn't matter what you say to me. I'm telling you this, because if we find him, *when* we find him, you should be prepared that he's not the boy you're trying to make him."

Before Malja could say more, Tumus left her alone. Malja leaned against a windowsill and watched the empty street below. The half-moon cast its pale light on the debris, creating grotesque shadows and illusions of depth. Good light for hiding. She poured her energy into searching those shadows for enemies — better than thinking about what Tumus had said.

An hour later, as her head lolled to the side, somebody tripped and cursed while scurrying down the street. The noise startled Malja awake. She spotted the person in seconds. Not a person, really. A griffle. And not just any griffle. This one was small — a runt — and had several white tufts on its head.

Malja checked if anyone else had awoken. Both Tumus and Cole had finally fallen asleep. Skvalan, however, stared at her with sharp eyes.

She waved him over and whispered, "Keep watch. I have to check something out."

Skvalan crossed his arms and looked around. Malja couldn't tell if he was questioning her or foggy from just waking up. Finally, he nodded and slipped in next to the window. "Don't take long time," he said.

Malja hurried outside and down the street. Following the griffle was easy. The little creature made such a racket, a blind man could catch him.

They traveled several blocks west and turned south for a few blocks more. The night air chilled Malja's nose, but her assault suit kept her body warm. She moved fast and kept her eyes searching for attacks. As much as the griffle's noise made him easy to follow, it also could attract unwanted attention.

Around a towering rubble pile, Malja saw the dancing orange light of a fire. She pulled out Viper and readied for what she might find — a horde of griffles, perhaps, or even some bizarre religious rite. She wasn't sure what she hoped to gain, but as Gregor would say, "Coincidence is just an excuse not to delve into the Why of something." That griffle could not be in this city by accident, not at the same time she sought Jarik and Callib, and she wanted to know why it was here.

As she rounded the rubble pile, she discovered her answer, and while she had no expectations, she never expected anything like this. Fawbry.

"Here, here, I've got food," the griffle said, jumping around while

Fawbry lay with his back against a lamppost. He looked tired and bruised — his left cheek puffed and dark. His lovely coat, now blotted with dirt, lacked its usual sheen. "Eat, eat. Then read, Mayor, please read."

Fawbry patted the white tufts and nibbled on something dark and round. Before he could swallow, the griffle tugged at Fawbry's coat pocket. Fawbry grinned through gritted teeth and pulled out his little Book of Kryssta.

"Okay," he said. "Calm down. I'll read one more, but then we've got to get some sleep." He thumbed the pages until he settled on one. "Listen, now.

Though Time is infinite —
Ours is a flicker of candlelight —
It is ours to burn away"

"Whee!" the griffle shouted and rolled on the ground. "That's my new favorite."

"Shhh," Fawbry said. "We have to stay quiet."

Malja surveyed the area one more time but still found no threats. She stepped into view and nodded at Fawbry. "Hi there," she said.

Fawbry and the griffle jumped to their feet. Fawbry fought against wincing, but his hand went up to his side and rubbed a sore spot. When he saw who had spoken, his posture dropped, and Malja caught a disappointed scowl flash across his face. But he broke out a smile.

"Malja. I can't believe I'm going to say this, but I'm happy to see you."

"What are you doing here?" she asked, not bothering to pretend smiling.

Fawbry glanced around. "Are you alone?"

"Are you?"

Opening his arms, he said, "It's just us two. Really."

Malja stomped toward Fawbry and raised Viper, poised to strike. "You better explain what you're doing here. How is it that you didn't know where Jarik and Callib were, yet here you are? That doesn't happen by accident."

Fawbry shrunk back. "I see nothing's changed for you. Calm down. No need for that. It's all easy to explain."

"Explain fast."

"Well, the short side of it is that after I left you, I headed west."

"Why west?"

"South is the Freelands, North is my family, and East ends at the ocean. None of those were good options. I couldn't go to Barris Mont without you. I wouldn't dare. So, I just wandered west for some time. A few days ago, I ran into two trogets. You ever seen them? Big brutes with horns running down their spines. They wanted to eat me. I tried to read them some of the Book of Kryssta because it worked with the griffles. Turns out it only kind of worked this time. They decided not to kill me, because they thought they might get a bigger reward if they brought somebody with brains to their masters."

"Let me guess — Jarik and Callib."

"They had me held near the edge of the city. Tufts and several other griffles ended up here after you broke up my little gang. He's always been loyal. So when he saw me, he helped me escape."

The griffle puffed his chest. "I did that."

"You looking for protection now?" Malja asked. "Is that why you're speaking nice to me?"

"I'm talking to you at all, because you've got that curved blade ready to eviscerate me." Fawbry put his arm around the griffle. "But we are on the run. So, we would appreciate your protection, of course, but I'm not trying to lie to you. I'm not trying to be falsely nice or anything like that." He raised his arm to reveal the stump where his hand should have been. "When I left, I was angry. I'm still angry. But I've never been outright stupid, either. I don't want to be here." He leaned close to Malja and whispered, "Frankly, I pretty much figured we were dead. I was just comforting the little guy and stalling. So if you can help me, if you're willing, then I'll gladly take your help."

Malja sheathed Viper. "You don't want to be here with me. I'll just make a bigger mess for you. Besides, I'm not leaving here. Not yet. I'm going after Jarik and Callib, and I'm going to rescue Tommy."

"Tommy? What happened to him?"

The genuine concern in Fawbry's voice, the worry bordering on fear, touched Malja. Hesitantly, she went on, "I think Jarik and Callib have him."

Fawbry exchanged looks with the griffle. "No, no, no. This can't be. We were just sitting here reading from the Book about life and why we're here at all. I was trying to tell Tufts how I appreciated the risks he took for me, and how life is about doing for others, and that if you do that, if you help others, then good things come your way."

"Kryssta says that?"

Fawbry shrugged. "Everything I've ever done was for myself. Even helping you was just a way to stay safe enough to get to Barris Mont. And in the end, all it got me was the loss of my hand and almost being eaten by a couple of trogets. But this little guy here snuck in while those beasts slept, untied me, got me out, got me food, all because he believes in the Book and in me."

"Careful, you're starting to sound like Tumus."

"Look, I don't know what I'm thinking, exactly, but something's different. You suddenly show up right when we're talking about all this. Maybe Kryssta's trying to tell me that if instead of getting you to help me, that if I help you save Tommy, maybe things'll get better for me. No, that's crazy. I've been through a lot. My brain's not working right. But still, that's how I read it."

"Me read it, too," Tufts said. "We help. We get good things. We help. We help."

Malja didn't want to take him along, but she felt wrong leaving him here. "Cole's with us," she warned.

Looking around with awe, Fawbry shrugged. "Doesn't matter. This isn't about me."

With a frown, Malja said, "Okay. Follow me. And keep that griffle quiet on our way back. I'm tired, and I don't want to fight tonight."

They returned in silence. Malja tried to equate this Fawbry with the one who had left her back in the Freelands. Something had changed, and she thought it had to be more than just coming close to dying. That could change a person, but life in this world was full of chances to die. It could be a scary, altering experience, at first, but after awhile, even danger becomes routine.

When they got back to the others, they settled in for the remaining few hours of night. Malja surprised herself — she fell asleep within minutes.

The following morning arrived to the shocked gasps of Cole and Tumus. Before they could ask a coherent question, Malja said, "I found them last night, and they're coming with us. This is about Jarik and Callib and Tommy. All your problems with each other get buried for now. Understood?"

Tumus glowered. Cole let out a sigh. But both women nodded.

"Good," Malja said. "Then let's get going."

The day passed in an arduous, silent hike. Miles of rubble piled against shells of once-towering buildings. The stench of rotting corpses flowed in and out, blending with the ever-present rich aroma of burnt wood.

Tufts had the energy of a child. At times, he would race ahead like a scout, or he'd circle members of the group — studying faces and embracing scents. Fawbry brought up the rear, keeping his distance from the others but staying close enough for protection.

By the time night approached, Malja saw something different from the monotony of destruction — an amber halo several blocks ahead. "Cole," she said, "what's that?"

Cole's features broke into an appreciative smile. "By Korstra and for Kryssta's sake, I don't believe it."

Tumus said, "Please don't blasphemy."

"That must be the factories."

"For what?" Malja asked.

"Everything. Jarik and Callib have hundreds of people and creatures living here. They need food, clothing, everything. Those factories use magic and muscle to provide."

"They run all night?"

Cole tapped her lips. "Perhaps they're making up for lost work from fighting while their masters were gone. Who knows? The factories, though, they're big. We'll have to cut west to go around them."

"How far?"

"Miles, I imagine."

"We don't have the time anymore. Jarik and Callib have had plenty of rest. Let's go ahead and scout what's up there. Then I'll decide."

Tufts hopped from foot to foot. "I scout. I scout."

"No. I need to see it myself."

Fawbry waved a finger. "No way am I staying behind. If I don't stick with you this time, bad things'll happen."

Tumus said, "What's he talking about?"

With a friendly pat, Cole said, "Don't worry. It's just some of Krysstanism coming through."

"Well, I won't stay behind if he's going. Korstra needs to be heard, too."

Malja raised her hands. "Stop it. All of you just shut up. You can all come. Just be quiet."

They proceeded along the streets, the factory lights brightening as they closed in on the location. Though they could hear the clangs and calls of people at work and see the warm lights surrounding the enormous buildings, they felt colder than any time before.

The buildings stretched off like a river and endless chimneys punched the sky. Fences made of chains, wood, and scavenged junk marked the perimeter. Thick posts dotted the ground, each with a metal arm pushed out to the side. From these hung the flag-mouths Malja knew from the Bluesmen. They sang in unison — little soft songs that appeared to lull the workers through their drudgery.

Lines of workers left the main building to either walk in the yard or deliver materials to one of the numerous, smaller buildings. Many workers had been maimed or injured. A few weren't human.

Overhead, fluttering along the fence, several crazed-looking people with dragonfly wings kept watch. Each wore a vest strapped with two powerful lamps that cut through the dark with blades of light. Malja thought of Nolan's sister, Audrex, and how the bastard magicians had caused her insanity. Clearly, Audrex was not the only one they had experimented with.

"These people are prisoners," Tumus said, and Malja shared her disgust.

"Not quite," Cole said. "They're followers — prisoners only to their belief in the magicians' powers."

Malja scoffed. "Like the Bluesmen were to you."

"Maybe. However, dear, I never would have had to treat my people like this. We worked hard in our fields, but we did it together for the common good of all of us."

"*They* worked. You sat upstairs where no one could bother you. And somehow I don't think Willie would have agreed with you. In fact, he most likely ..."

Malja stared at the factory compound, her mind weighing out an idea growing within. Fawbry opened his mouth, but Skvalan stopped him with a sharp gesture. Skvalan's intense focus on Malja told the others to stay quiet.

Finally, Malja grinned. She pointed to a long row of homes cutting through the compound. Each home stood at least three stories. From the damaged fronts, Malja could see that each home shared a wall with the next.

"There," she said. "We get inside and cross the factory compound in no time. They'll never see us because they're busy working or guarding the workers or checking the perimeter."

"And we're upstairs where no one can bother us," Cole said with a bitter undertone.

"Might as well make some good out of what you did."

"Little girl, all the problems with the Bluesmen and with you, that was the fault of Willie."

"Willie didn't order Fawbry's hand burnt off."

Skvalan snapped his fingers, quieting the two. Fawbry looked both embarrassed and defiant. But Malja detected a little pride, too, in the way he placed his stumped hand around Tuft's shoulder.

Malja flushed with annoyance at the entire group, including herself. She thought she should say some words to bring them back together, to encourage them, but she stayed silent. Too late for that. They were who they were.

With Viper in hand, she led the group across an open street. Crouching as she scurried, she brought them behind half of a car. The ragged edges looked as if some giant monster had torn the other half off with powerful jaws.

Malja pointed out a gouge in the brick wall of the second row home. The factory fence began only one house further in. Nothing between the half-car and the gouged wall — no cover of any kind. Without a word, Skvalan shot off, sprinted across the open area and slid into the house. Tufts followed as if playing a game of warrior — hunched low, moving fast, his hand carrying an imaginary weapon.

"Okay, okay," Tumus whispered to herself.

Malja heard the mounting anxiety, and when Tumus jumped to her feet, Malja yanked her back down. One of the crazed dragonflies flew overhead, his stark light creating day for a few seconds. He snorted and giggled as he passed by. Malja's skin prickled.

They waited a short while, once the dark had returned. Malja took her hand off Tumus and watched like a hovering parent as Tumus crossed to the house. Cole, Fawbry, and Malja followed up before the next dragonfly guard could fly by.

The smell hit Malja as she entered the house — something only a day dead. A rank odor that never got easier to inhale. The factory lights seeped in enough to see. The dainty songs seeped in, too. *Good,* thought Malja. *Hopefully that means it's loud enough to cover our noise.*

The room had been picked over long ago. Only a pile of bricks, glass, wood, and dirt remained as an obstacle blocking entry into the hall. Using a wide plank, Malja dug out a gap large enough to shimmy through. Dust coated the air and tasted like moldy bread. Whatever died must have been buried in the rubbish pile. Malja pushed that thought aside and tried not to taste anything she breathed.

Once all six had entered the hall, Malja picked up the pace. Though they needed to be quiet, the faster they moved, the faster they would reach the other end. Besides, with Jarik and Callib so close now, she never could have moved slower.

Down the hall, up a flight of stairs, down another hall. Malja saw a finger-sized hole in the wall at the end. She peered in — an empty room in the next house, except for a stained, beaten mattress and a pot filled with liquid.

Malja used Viper to carve a larger hole. The others paced behind her, crossing arms, tapping feet, making little utterances that did nothing more than piss Malja off. She could have torn down the wall, but feared such an action would be too noisy. But after a few minutes of hard, sweating labor, she had managed only a fist-sized opening.

"Go away," Skvalan said in a brisk whisper.

Malja looked back to see Skvalan preparing to barrel through the wall.

"No," she said. "Too loud."

"Go away." He waved her aside, but she didn't move. To Tumus, he rattled off a few words.

Tumus said, "I think he wants to use magic."

Skvalan took slow steps toward the wall. He closed his eyes and concentrated. Malja stepped away as he approached. The narrow hall forced the others to slide around him so he could pass.

Malja wondered what other magic the Muyaza knew, but when Skvalan reached the wall, she understood. He only knew the one spell. The bubble formed around him and pressed against the walls. Wood creaked like an old ship in heavy winds.

Skvalan sat cross-legged in the hall. Malja wished they had something big enough for a litter — they could have made a battering ram out of themselves and the bubble. Instead, she watched as Skvalan pushed outward with his hands, forcing the bubble forward. Dust and chalky particles trembled around the hole Malja had carved out. Skvalan groaned as he pushed again, his hands shaking. A divot formed in the wood, growing bigger as the bubble moved forward.

The idea seemed good at first, but the harder Skvalan pushed, the more Malja worried the wall might crash down, giving them away. Before she had time to complete her thoughts, the wall burst open. Wooden framing snapped like broken bones poking out of skin. Flatter wood and soft filling crumbled to the floor sending more dust into the air.

For a few seconds, nobody moved. They all looked at Malja as she listened for sounds of alarm. Workers continued to trudge. Saccharine singing continued to mellow the yard. No screams or orders or attacks came.

One look at Skvalan told Malja they would not do this again. Sweat beaded on his face, and he had trouble getting to his feet. She hauled him up by the arm and slapped a hand on his back.

"Thanks," she said before ducking through the opening.

"Yeah," Tufts said, slapping Skvalan's leg. "Thanks."

They walked into a bedroom, down a hall, and found a door where the shared wall with the next house should be. Malja placed her hand on the door — cool to the touch. She pressed her ear against it and listened — nothing. As if handling explosives, she gently lifted the latch and pulled the door open.

A dark corridor stretched off. No door or windows offering glints of light existed. Just darkness.

Malja raised a hand to halt her friends. With Viper in front, she stepped into the dark. She paid attention to all her senses to discern if anything awaited them. Nothing to see or smell or taste. But she heard it — a slight, quivering exhale. Someone trying to be quiet, but too nervous.

With a graceful shift of her feet, she lowered her body, preparing to pounce. A twist of her hand repositioned Viper for maximum damage off her initial swing. She turned her hips, winding up like a top. She held all that built-up power long enough to be sure of where to strike. And she let loose.

Three distinct strikes sliced through the dark. A surprised breath came followed by blood-filled choking. A body slumped to the floor sounding like a clumsy fellow dropping a stack of heavy books.

That's when the alarm sounded.

Chapter 23

Malja had expected the singing flags to blare out an obnoxious scream or perhaps to announce, in an irritating voice, that they had an intruder. Instead, they continued to sing and the workers continued to work. The alarm took the form of a high-pitched, rapid beeping coming from the dead man's belt — just like the frame in Cole's basement, the one that exploded.

Malja sprinted to the far wall and hacked away at it with Viper. Fawbry followed her, tossing away debris as it fell. Cole, however, did not panic. In the dark, she said, "It's an alarm, not a bomb."

A chunk of wall fell to the floor. Light streaked in revealing Cole bent over a torso while Tumus and Skvalan waited in the back. Tufts wrapped his little arms around Skvalan's knee.

"A quiet alarm is worse than a noisy one," Malja said and swung Viper into the wall again. "Means that whatever answers the call is expected to handle us without everyone knowing. It means that—"

Standing behind the group, a dragonfly-winged madman raised his arms. The lamps on his vest blasted the hall with drastic brightness. Malja shielded her eyes until they adjusted. She heard Skvalan yell, Tufts shriek, and the flat smack of Cole or Tumus hitting someone with a wooden plank. She could see the dark outlines of punches thrown and people tossed.

The Dragonfly faced Malja. He didn't kill the others. He read the team well. Malja saw it in the way he repositioned his body. He knew she posed the real threat. With his wings moving faster, creating an incessant buzz, he launched after her.

Fawbry dropped to the floor and covered his head. Malja had time for two quick thoughts. First, there was no room to evade the attack. Second, this was going to hurt.

She tried to bring Viper up to a useful striking position, but the Dragonfly slammed into her like a wild horse. Just as the impact on her front registered, the Dragonfly continued forward, using her to ram through the wall. Pain fired across her back.

They tumbled to the floor, spraying dust into the still air. They were in a wide room with a beautiful, tiled floor and tall windows lining both sides. Two huge lamps hung from the high ceiling, each decorated with glass bits now covered in cobwebs and grime.

Malja had no idea what the room had been built for, but as she shook off pieces of wall, she saw that the place was intended to impress. The Dragonfly glanced around, too, until they locked eyes. Malja raised Viper. The Dragonfly buzzed his wings.

Like before, he soared towards her with amazing speed. This time Malja didn't need to think. She had plenty of room. She sidestepped the attack and cut the creature through the waist. One swift slice. Two pieces of Dragonfly tumbled in different directions.

"Hurry," Malja called back. "More will come."

Fawbry's dust-covered face peeked through the wall. "Good to see things are as usual with you." With Tufts climbing on his back, Fawbry entered the room.

Skvalan limped in, his arm around Tumus's shoulder. Cole brought up the rear. Even in the dim light, Malja could see that Skvalan's body was not used to magic. But before Malja could speak, Tumus brushed by her and said, "He'll be fine."

Halfway across the room, the tall windows behind them shattered. Four Dragonflies — two women, two men — flew inside.

So much for the quiet way. "Run!"

Malja bolted ahead to clear the way while the others hobbled as fast as they could manage. She hoped the Dragonflies would converge on her. No such luck. But her separation from the group confused the buggers enough to gain a few seconds.

She dashed into a small room with a wide bathing tub built into the far wall and a cracked seat with a hole at the bottom like a fancy indoor outhouse. She stepped into the smooth tub and swung Viper into the wall. Tile chipped off and the wall crumbled apart as if had been made of wet, clumped sand. The damp odor of rot wafted out. Malja stood still — the walls had looked so strong.

Skvalan and Tumus stumbled in. Malja heard the rapid buzzing not far behind. They stepped through the wall and continued on. Cole charged through next.

Malja said, "Get started on the next wall. I'll be right there."

Cole nodded and dashed off. Either she was a good soldier following orders or a scared mouse too frightened to balk. Malja was happy to take either one.

The buzzing grew louder. Malja flattened against the wall next to the doorway. She raised Viper and waited.

"I'm coming," Fawbry yelled, bursting into the room and through the wall, Tufts riding his back the whole time like a panicked version of a child's game. Malja waited as the buzzing closed in. When the first Dragonfly entered, she decapitated it. The others pulled back, hissing and buzzing. She leapt over the tub, through the wall, tucked her head and rolled. Popping to her feet, she hurried on.

Before she reached the end of the hall, she saw a new problem. The entire next building lay in a collapsed pile below. Malja waved toward the stairs. "Down," she yelled and the others obeyed.

Thumping down the stairs, Malja noticed Skvalan moving with a little more certainty. At the bottom, she pulled him ahead and said, "Will you be okay?"

Skvalan shook off the arm. "I don't stop."

"We've got to run the rest of the way. Understand? No cover. You fall, that's it."

"I fine."

"Good." She heard the confused buzzing above. "Everyone follow me. No stopping until I stop. Got it?"

She made eye contact with each one. They were ready. Maybe like dollops waiting to run from their burrows, hoping nothing tried to eat them, but ready nonetheless.

Malja counted to three. She kicked open the door and sprang off. Glancing upward, she saw them — two Dragonflies leaping from the open wall three stories up. They let out a churlish cackle as they descended in a frenzy of bloodlust and sheer, adrenaline-fueled excitement. She pointed onward and let the others sprint ahead.

The singing mouths clamped shut. Several Dragonflies hovered above, casting their spotlights on Malja's team. The workers halted and watched.

"Keep running," she yelled. They had another block to go.

Malja suppressed all sounds of her feet pounding the ground and her blood pounding through her heart. She ignored the lunatic symphony surrounding her and filtered out the confused calls of the workers. She heard only the buzzing wings.

The volume and tone changed. She kept running and listening, never looking back, just listening, driving her legs and listening. She waited for the pitch to alter as the Dragonfly swooped in to attack. It came fast.

She dropped to the ground and rolled forward. The Dragonfly passed overhead — close enough to touch. As Malja returned to her feet, she followed through with Viper, digging its point into her enemy. It cried out as one wing tore off. Malja sliced down and sprinted onward. She passed the trembling Dragonfly without remorse.

Tumus and the others had stopped running. Malja cursed as she rushed to catch up. When Malja reached them, she saw what had brought them to a halt. A Dragonfly woman stood before the fence. Her greasy hair draped over her lowered head as she stared at her tattooed arm.

"I'll handle this one," Tumus said and spread her arms outward.

Malja waited. She tapped her fingers on Viper's grip. The itch to attack grew stronger, but the Dragonfly's spell might be ready. She could be waiting for Malja to launch. Better to wait on Tumus while everything remained static.

Skvalan leaned on Cole. Fawbry bent over and coughed spittle onto the ground. Tufts hid behind the legs of one, then another, in the group. His eyes big with nervousness as he rasped out harsh breaths.

They were all exhausted, but Malja's body shivered with adrenaline. Her assault suit kept her going, too.

The fourth Dragonfly landed behind them, his body taut and ready to strike. Malja attacked, her muscles thrilled to be active again. She swiped low, hoping to cut the creature near the knees. This Dragonfly, however, read her intentions and took to the sky.

"Die! Die! Die!" the woman guarding the fence bellowed as a rush of fire flowed from her hands.

The nearby workers squealed and sought cover. Tumus stood her ground, mouthing the name *Korstra* while the flames shot towards her. Though Malja had witnessed the Chi-Chun absorb magic before, she couldn't help but wonder if this time Tumus would fail.

As it neared, the fire curved toward Tumus. The Dragonfly woman raised her arms and the stream of flames reared as if it were leashed to its creator. Tumus turned her palms upward and the flames pulled down toward her. Back and forth, tugged one way then the other, the flames danced in the air like a pet caught between two masters.

Like all the others watching, Malja stood mesmerized by the display. When the Dragonfly man swooped in to hit her head, she never countered. The blow knocked her to the ground and brought sparkling lights to her vision.

She knew better than to try to shake it off. Even as she stumbled to her feet, the Dragonfly landed next to her, striking out with a fist. Though dizzy and off-balance, Malja swung Viper to block the attack. Her strike lacked power and went in a wide, wild arc, but its unpredictable wobble served her well. The Dragonfly pulled back.

In the short time he took to reconsider his next attack, Malja's head cleared. The two warriors came together in a brash display of solid weapon work meeting superior reflexes. The Dragonfly held no weapon because he had no need. Malja missed every swing. He was too fast.

But she could be fast as well. He came at her with fists and feet. She dodged most of it. Twice she willingly took a punch in the side hoping to use the closeness against him. The first time she gouged his arm. He wised to the trick the second time.

Caught between two fights, Fawbry, Tufts, Cole, and Skvalan all stood tight together, watching and waiting. Tumus continued to battle for control of the conjured flame, but Malja couldn't look long enough to tell who might win. She ducked and countered, but Viper slipped through air. She felt like a child practicing against her shadow.

The Dragonfly rose up at least twenty feet and hovered for a moment. He cocked his head to the right and opened his mouth. Rotting teeth and a sickly-gray tongue greeted her.

Thrusting his arm forward, he dived straight down. Just before hitting the ground he shot off away from Malja. She had braced for the hit, but the change in course left her confused. That is, until she understood his target had changed — Skvalan.

In a series of smooth motions, the Dragonfly threw Cole into a wall, knocked Fawbry into Tufts, and snatched Skvalan, taking him high above the ground. The weakened Muyaza tried to free himself but the Dragonfly held tight. Skvalan punched and wriggled. Nothing worked. In frustration, he let out a deep, guttural war cry.

"Let him go," Tumus yelled.

Malja watched on, stunned by the passionate power emanating from Tumus. The Chi-Chun spun her torso, her arms flowing like a seasoned dancer. The sudden shift in motion surprised the Dragonfly woman. She lost control of her fire and Tumus took over.

The flames funneled into her right hand. She raised her left and sent scorching bolts into the air. She had complete control now. The bolts circled Skvalan and the Dragonfly — only striking when they could do so without hitting Skvalan.

Malja felt Tumus's anger burn as hot as the magic above. Tumus turned back to the magic's source.

"Stand aside," she said.

The crazed Dragonfly woman giggled as if watching a silly puppet show. "Not until you're all dead."

Without further warning, Tumus released the rest of the flames. The Dragonfly woman never tried to escape. She welcomed the full blast with open arms and a sadistic smile. As it sent her crisp corpse smashing through the gate, Malja could still hear her foolish giggles.

All grew still. Only the sound of the brisk mountain winds blowing against the broken city infiltrated the area. The pungent odor of burnt air and burnt flesh drifted on this wind.

Just a few feet away, Malja saw Skvalan's body tangled in a heap with the Dragonfly man. No one moved. Tumus pushed Malja aside as she rushed to Skvalan. She dropped to her knees, crying, and carefully pulled Skvalan's body away from the Dragonfly man.

"We can't stay here long," Fawbry said as he settled up next to Malja.

"I know."

They waited. At length, Tumus composed herself, but she did not join the others. Instead, she raised her arms upward and in long, mournful tones, she said, "Korstra, most powerful brother God, to serve you, we live and in serving, we are fulfilled. I offer you the soul of a cherished friend." She lowered her hands upon the corpse, closed her eyes, and started again.

Cole looked to Malja. "She can't do this."

"She is."

"But these weren't the only guards."

"I know."

"There's bound to be more. If we stay ..." Cole's eyes and chin shivered.

Malja had seen plenty of people reach their breaking point. Cole was no warrior. She wasn't even a grunt soldier. She was a technician and a politician. That she had lasted this long impressed Malja.

"Keep yourself together," Malja said as she heard the distinct buzzing in the distance. "We don't go on without Tumus. We don't leave our teammates behind."

"But they're coming. We barely made it this far against just four of these nasty things. We've got to hide."

The buzzing had grown loud enough to pull Tumus's attention. The sound came from all directions — even above. Like a giant machine grinding its way through the city, a Dragonfly force of at least forty closed in on them.

Malja wiped Viper clean, rolled her shoulders, and settled into her battle stance. Cole's face dropped. With a worried whimper, Tufts scrambled up Fawbry's shoulder. Tumus joined them, grim understanding resting on her lips. Without a word, she handed Malja a strand of dark hair — Skvalan's wife. Cole looked at the determined faces of her allies and panic bloomed.

"Are you crazy? They'll kill us." Cole's hands shook and tears rolled along her nose. "I'll run. I can hide. I don't need you."

Tumus held Cole's shoulders. "Trust in Korstra."

Cole backed away, pointing a wavering finger. "You're both as insane as those guards. Come now, Faw-Faw, you don't want to stay here and die."

Fawbry picked up a rock as a poor weapon. "I've got to help Tommy," he said.

Tumus lifted her hands and started focusing on her magic. Cole looked at them with confusion at first, but a horrible understanding dawned on her face like a swimmer alone in the ocean seeing a massive wave towering over her. She spun to find the Dragonfly force hovering like a cicada-covered field — clear wings and incessant buzzing. She raised her hands in surrender.

One Dragonfly man landed. He wore a dirty red breastplate made from the hood of a grounder and held a machete in each hand. His cold face revealed nothing as he spoke. "I am the Factory King. You are trespassers and murderers. For you, there will be no mercy."

"I am Malja, daughter of Jarik and Callib."

A startled wave rolled through the Dragonfly force. The Factory King contorted his face and jerked to the side. He whispered to the empty space on his left. With a jerk of his head, he regained his self-control and said, "There are many of my subjects in this great world who would make such claims. But only the real Malja could defeat my entire army."

Cole dropped to her knees while keeping her hands straight in the sky. "I don't want to die," she repeated in a soft prayer-like whisper.

The Factory King laughed and pointed both machetes at Cole. The familiar burning rage Malja knew like a beloved pet snapped to life. In one rapid stroke, she cut through the King's arms. The machetes rang out as they hit the ground, but the King's screams challenged the sound. Blood gushed from his wounds leaving behind a crimson trail as he flew off.

"Put your arms down," Malja said, nudging Cole with her foot. "Grab the weapon."

Cole took a few seconds to react, but so did the infuriated army. By the time she took hold of one machete, Fawbry grabbed the other, and Malja had cut down three Dragonflies. The same panic that drove Cole to surrender now fueled her fury. She fought off her attackers with harsh strength and blind anger, but did little to reduce their numbers.

Malja moved in bursts of speed and grace. She knew her assault suit aided her; however, it could not manifest energy in her that did not already exist. Ducking one blow, striking another, feigning one attack, and following through on the next, Malja used all her skill to protect the group.

Streams of fire, bolts of lightning, and blasts of ice shot down from above. Tumus moved like a juggler, catching magic in one hand and throwing it back into the air with the other. Dancing left, reaching out right. Throwing magic without watching the result.

Fawbry did his best, but he lacked Malja's skill and Cole's rage. He parried what he could and struck a few enemies, causing an occasional cry of pain. When the opportunities arrived, Tufts leapt off Fawbry to claw at heads, eyes, arms, and wings. After a few lashes, he hurried back to Fawbry and readied for another leap.

Without warning and in unison, the Dragonfly force broke off. Malja, Tumus, Fawbry, and Cole stood back to back, weapons ready. The great cacophony of buzzing ceased as the entire army landed.

In the new silence, Malja heard her heartbeat drumming in her ears. Each deep breath she took sounded like a hurricane. She circled around her friends, waving Viper to keep the Dragonflies at a distance. Tumus pulled herself together and circled from the opposite side.

"This city is ours," a Dragonfly said.

Malja shifted her back foot, lowered her center of gravity, and cleared her mind. She turned Viper an inch more open. She searched for the one who spoke.

"Korstra will protect us," Tumus shouted.

A commotion broke out far in the back. Strange sounds like cheering and arguing filtered its way up. As it reached Malja's ears, her stomach hardened — not cheering, not arguing, but chanting. Over and over.

Zorum. Zorum.

Fawbry said, "Um ... Malja?"

"Shut up," she said. "All of you back away." She stepped forward to increase the distance between her and her friends. While she didn't know who or what exactly Zorum was, she had encountered enough battle in her life to guess. This had all the marks of their best warrior.

From the crowd of Dragonflies emerged a giant. Zorum stood nearly eleven feet tall with muscle so thick his skin tore in an effort to contain him. His wild hair shot off in all directions as if he had been struck by lighting. His Dragonfly wings lay flat and impotent against his back — a side-effect of whatever magic he had used to get this way. Blood dribbled from his oversized knuckles. Madness swam in his oversized eyes.

"I am Malja," she yelled. "This is Viper." Her voice overcame the buzzing. Her name stopped a few. Zorum's deep gasp halted the rest. She knew they sensed the tension, even those that didn't know her name.

Zorum saw the sudden pause in the group and registered his mistake. With a thunderous voice, he said, "Malja's a myth. You're just a wench."

"You're about to find out."

Without further preamble, they circled each other. The Dragonflies cleared around them and began to cheer. Roars of excitement followed each feint, thrust, and parry. They stood as one, bonded by an anticipation Malja could feel in the air. Those that knew her name, knew they witnessed the birth of legends. She thought she heard betting. It reminded her of battles long gone. Her lips cracked into a grin — just a second's break to smile, but Zorum seized the opportunity.

He charged, startling Malja into a clumsy block that left little more than a scratch on his arm. Zorum barreled forward again and grabbed Malja's free arm. He swung her around like a drunk spinning a whore, spitting laughter while his mates cheered him on. He smelled putrid, and part of Malja was grateful when he let her fly into the crowd. Several Dragonflies kicked and punched her as they tossed her back into the fight.

"I thought Malja was a great warrior," Zorum said. More laughter rippled through the Dragonflies. "Guess she's just a little girl with a big story."

Malja settled into a fighter's stance, breathing heavily but not empty of all her strength just yet. The corners of her lips raised — they always underestimated her. With a piercing scream, she launched her assault.

She swung Viper over her right shoulder, guessing Zorum would block it with his magically enhanced arm. He did. So she reversed her motion, spinning fast and slicing horizontal across his thighs. Blood seeped down his legs but he showed no signs of suffering.

"Stupid," he said. He punched downward, his fist connecting with her back. The Dragonflies roared. She hit the ground, air shoved from her lungs, her head rattling at the blow. A thick hand took hold of her braided hair and yanked her to her feet. Zorum pulled back his fist, a brutal gleam in his eye, and let out a deafening yell — his breath worse than his body. As the fist sped towards her, Malja kicked straight out for his groin. Down he went, dirt spewing into the air around him.

He rolled on his back. She leaped over him, ready to stomp on his throat and end this. Instead of grasping his privates, though, like most males, Zorum stayed present in the fight. He caught Malja's foot and twisted her to the ground, once more knocking the breath from her lungs. Gasping, she rose to all fours only to feel a crushing blow on her head, sending her face into the cracked pavement.

Her head spun. She couldn't find her balance. The ground seemed to pitch and yaw under her. She saw Dragonflies urging her to fight, others laughing at her failure. She saw twisted faces and lustful eyes. They were beyond insane.

She saw her friends. They looked at her with pity and suffering and tears. They looked at her with defeat in their eyes. She attempted to rise but rolled on her back, staring at Zorum's towering figure.

"You see," Zorum said, but the words muddled in her ears as if spoken underwater.

She saw him shake with mirth while he displayed Viper like a conqueror and then let the weapon drop as if it were a harmless toy. Her eyes closed, and for a moment, the idea of sleep sounded ideal. More harsh laughter startled her awake. Fear wrapped a chilled hand around her heart — fear for Tommy.

Fawbry babbled, pleaded, but Malja couldn't decipher the words. Zorum dropped Viper and pointed at Fawbry who raised his stump in defiance. *Good, Fawbry.*

Malja rolled to her stomach. Zorum kicked her side — just strong enough to warn her to remain still. He stepped over her, one huge leg on either side. His deep voice rumbled the ground as he yelled at her friends bow down. She didn't need to look at them now. They had to be terrified. They had to be lost.

Then I won't be. Viper lay just in front of her head. No time for hesitation.

In a series of smooth motions, she snatched the weapon, flipped it so the curved blade faced skyward, jumped to her feet, and thrust straight up, sending the blade deep between Zorum's legs. She bellowed her rage as Zorum crouched and groaned in pain. His shock afforded her a few precious seconds — enough to step on his thigh and vault herself higher, slicing up through his gut and into his chest. Arching backward, she flipped her body. She pulled Viper along, tearing it out of him in a crimson spray, and landed on her feet.

Malja's head screamed at her audacity, pounding her brain against her skull with every heartbeat, and she fought hard not to pass out. Zorum gazed down in disbelief as his innards flopped to the ground. He couldn't even muster a final word. His body dropped like a soulless bag of rotten meat.

Shocked silence hung in the air. Nobody moved.

Malja stood still. Breathing heavily. Eyeing every Dragonfly she could see — there would be no more challenges.

Before she could speak a word, the Dragonflies prostrated themselves on the ground. Malja frowned. She'd never seen this kind of reaction before. But Tumus elbowed Malja, and the answer came to her without looking. She could feel their presence like the shadow of a predator darkening over sleeping prey. She peeked over her shoulder, knowing exactly whose appearance had caused the sudden change.

Jarik and Callib.

They floated over the wreckage Malja and her friends had wrought, looking every bit as strong and virile as they had at the Bluesmen's house. Bald, shirtless, tattooed — power radiated from them like a sun. Basking below them, their entourage of magicians floated and focused.

As they neared, Jarik turned his jaded but sad eyes upon Malja. She wanted to leap in the air, berate them for all the sorrow they had caused, and slay them with merciless blows. But more than just exhaustion stopped her. A strange emotion roiled underneath her hate — a desire to curl up and go unnoticed. Not a need to hide, but rather a hope to become small.

Callib leveled a stark, penetrating glare at the Dragonfly army and said, "You have made a mess of this place. If you can't handle the simple job of being guards, what good are you?"

"W-We're sorry," one Dragonfly woman said.

"I have made you all, and I can unmake you. Don't fail me again. Where is the Factory King?"

In a sturdier voice, the Dragonfly woman pointed at Malja and said, "She cut off his arms."

Callib faced Malja, and she felt the full weight of his gaze like a boulder sitting on her chest. It sent her mind swirling backwards — seven years old, caught in one of the many off-limits rooms, a broken beaker in her hand. She never could please Callib. It proved easier to disappoint.

"All of you will follow us to our home."

"I'm not here to follow you," Malja said, her brazen words surprising her as much as them. "I came to—"

Callib's hand sliced across the air as if he held a sword. "I know exactly why you came. Jarik may not have believed you were capable of patricide, but I never doubted."

"Malja," Jarik said, his voice firm but a tinge warmer. "Come with us. You won't be harmed. You may keep your weapons. Your friends won't be harmed."

"You can't hurt us anyway," Callib said.

"You've been gone a long time," Jarik said. "Ever since you came into our lives, we've worked tirelessly to find a way to send you home. Come with us and let us show you what we can now do."

"Besides," Callib said like a konapol lowering itself to strike, "we have Tommy."

Chapter 24

They left the factory compound with Jarik and Callib leading the way while five magicians brought up the rear. They moved at a slow, somber pace as if in a funeral procession. Indeed, Tumus and Cole both cycled through fear of the magicians and grief over the loss of Skvalan.

Malja's heart hammered against her chest, but not for the same reasons — she dealt with fear through force and she knew death too well to grieve. But her fathers were a different matter. She tried to quell the emotional tornado tearing through her, but each time Jarik looked over his shoulder at her, the storm grew stronger. Callib, thankfully, never looked back.

She caught a glimpse of Fawbry and a different sensation trembled along her skin. Battle left varied scars on a person's mind. Fawbry displayed an odd serenity. She had seen that look before — a man shaken enough by his experiences that he became so determined, so confident, all logical caution was abandoned. It was the look of a warrior believing in a righteous quest. Such things could be a great advantage, but could be equally dangerous and unpredictable. And such things tended to be temporary. One other explanation existed, and Malja hoped this to be true — that Fawbry was in shock.

The block they proceeded up barely resembled a city. Only a few buildings still stood — skeletons of brick, metal, and jagged glass. The rest littered the streets in uneven piles. The blocks ahead had become a trash dump.

Callib raised his left hand, glanced at the sawtooth tattoo there, and with a casual flick of the wrist, created four balls of light. The lights each took a corner surrounding the group and followed them as they moved through the dark, empty streets. Tumus and Fawbry gasped — neither had ever seen magic executed with such ease.

Malja, however, had seen plenty of it. She would not let Callib's little display intimidate her. *They are the bastard magicians, and they deserve all my rage.*

Only thoughts of Tommy kept Malja from attacking. Callib said they had Tommy, and Malja forced herself to wait until she saw the boy. Once she knew Tommy was alive and safe, she would let this tornado within her loose.

A grave smile crossed Malja's lips. Her thoughts were bold and full of pride. She hoped she could live up to them.

Ahead, the city seemed to disappear. For just a second, Malja's step hesitated.

Cole whispered, "It's okay."

The street ended without warning — just a sheer drop as if the ground had been gouged out by an angry witch. Malja could not make out the other end. Darkness and fog filled the chasm. Out of the darkness emerged what passed for a bridge — a haphazard framework of rubble slammed together by a drunk.

Jarik and Callib led the group onto the bridge. Its rough surface creaked under their weight. Half-way across, they stopped. Jarik faced the empty darkness. He raised his right arm and cocked his head so he could focus on the tattoo wrapping around his bicep.

Callib said, "This is where everything ended and everything began. This is the true location where the Devastation erupted. Others have claimed their paltry plots of land as the true location, but even Barris Mont's Dead Lake is not big enough."

"That's blasphemy," Tumus said.

"Not at all. The Devastation reshaped our entire world. It culled the weak and created opportunities for the strong. Magic of that magnitude would leave behind a grand mark. This crater is that mark."

"The Chi-Chun do not recognize—"

"I don't care what your little cult thinks. Here is where the Devastation began. A massive explosion of magic and fire that leveled the world. It blasted in all directions, even through the ground, and no doubt burst out in many places. Even your Dead Lake."

Jarik's body grew taut as if straining under a great weight. Callib turned his attention to the side of the bridge. With a brotherly smile, he patted Jarik's shoulders.

Malja stepped closer and peered over the edge. Under Callib's artificial lights, all she saw was a milky sea of fog.

Fawbry came up to her side. "Not very impressive."

But shadows formed beneath the waves. They grew larger, darker, thicker.

First, a tower broke the surface. This connected to the blocky architecture of a building out of Barris Mont's memory. It continued to rise, growing wider and gaining several smaller buildings at its sides.

Malja remembered the smaller, earthier house they had raised her in. More than anything else, seeing barbed wire surround the roofs and iron bars block the windows convinced Malja of the threats Jarik and Callib feared. They had built a fortress to live in.

The building continued to rise causing Fawbry to audibly gasp. He leaned back, gawking at the building's height. The bottom level finally came to rest flush with the bridge. The lesser magicians wasted no time getting through the entrance's massive double doors. Several looked back at Jarik and Callib like dogs eager for permission. Others rushed ahead for sanctuary.

Jarik exhaled and let his shoulders slump. Malja expected the entire building to plummet back into the chasm with the magicians screaming all the way down, but it held steady. Apparently, moving the building required much stronger magic than parking it.

Callib kissed the top of Jarik's head. "It still amazes me when you pull off that spell."

"It's getting easier. A few more times and it won't take half what it takes out of me now."

"With Malja here now, my dear brother, we won't need this place. We'll have castles all over the world."

As they stepped inside the building, a disturbing thought flashed through Malja's head — *we might not get out again*. She clenched her fists and sneered. She should be thinking like the warrior she was — not some prissy weakling worried about breaking a bone or losing a limb.

The foyer of this floating city block could have had no other purpose than to intimidate. Huge columns rose upward to meet the ceiling seven stories away. The walls were uneven like a cavern yet they had a geometric quality as well — long, flat rectangles like crystal sticks cut at irregular heights.

Two mammoth-sized statues made up the far wall. One of Jarik, one of Callib — each sitting upright as both the guard and the ruler, each scowling as they looked upon all who entered. Between these statutes was a normal-sized door. Guarding the door stood one maxdin — eight feet tall, coarse hair, claws and teeth.

The softest sounds echoed and amplified and mutated in the open space, surrounding visitors with strange, deep tones that chilled the skin. Malja had seen many extravagant rulers build many extravagant homes, but this surpassed any of her experiences. And while this foyer succeeded in composing awe and a sense of power, Malja wondered if this boasting through architecture undercut their strength as well. The most fearsome warriors she had ever fought almost always downplayed their appearance — choosing to dress like a commoner rather than in something that showed off muscles or weapons or power.

Whatever the case, Malja had had enough. Despite the turmoil spinning her stomach and the weariness aching her bones, she found it easy to pour herself into saving Tommy. Jarik and Callib, her fathers and enemies, lost importance to her. The portal frame that could open up other worlds but Cole feared would bring about another Devastation meant nothing. Tommy was the sole thought that stood in Malja's brain unmarred by conflicting ideas.

"Where's Tommy? You said you had him, bring him to us."

Jarik said, "She is plucky."

"You should know the only reason I haven't cut you both down is because of Tommy."

Callib raised his top lip as if smelling something vile. "Be careful how you estimate yourself," he said, opening both hands towards her. "You are no more than a rat."

Malja's hand reached back for Viper even as her nerves jangled across her body. Jarik pushed between them. "Callib, control yourself," he said.

"Control myself? If you had shown more control years ago, we wouldn't have to deal with her now." Callib broke away, throwing an angry charge of electricity into the air. "*No, Callib, I promise, she's dead.* But that wasn't true, was it? Cowardice got the better of you. You took one look in those little girl eyes and just had to leave her instead of doing what you should have done. And now look at this mess."

"Just because I didn't handle it the way you wanted doesn't mean I didn't handle it."

"Leaving her for dead is very different than what I ordered you to do."

"Your mistake is thinking you can order me to do anything at all. We either work together or you can—"

Callib flapped his arms as he headed through the door by the statues. The maxdin straightened when the magician neared. "Enough already. Calm down. I'll get the boy prepared. When I come back, try to be more civil."

Jarik closed his eyes and took a cleansing breath before facing Malja. "Wait here," he said.

212 - The Malja Chronicles

As he walked out of the foyer, he gestured to the maxdin and the creature followed him, ducking low to get through the door. Cole crossed her arms and snickered. "My, my. Those two boys are gonna kill each other."

"They've been together longer than I've been alive," Malja said.

"Family can have more conflict than anybody. Let's hope we can use that to our advantage."

Malja nodded and held back the urge to cheer on Cole. The woman had found her courage once more, and Malja did not want to make her uncomfortable by pointing it out. To avoid the possibility, Malja walked back toward the entrance.

She could not see the bridge. She pressed her hands up to the glass — a strange experience, unbroken glass — and squinted. Though she never felt so much as a slim vibration, the fortress had left the bridge and now floated in the dark fog. The house had become an island.

With an echoing clang, the door between the statues opened. Nobody came out.

"Guess we're expected to go," Malja said.

"Oh, how dramatic," Cole said, melting into her superiority like an old lover. "For all their supposed greatness, these two have a lot to learn about presentation."

Despite her bravado, Malja caught Cole's eyes darting around like a bird looking for an escape. *Well,* she thought, *that's okay. A good fighter always feels nervous before a big battle.* Tumus looked worried, too. For a Chi-Chun of Korstra, however, Malja expected less fear and more of that overconfident arrogance she had come to enjoy. Fawbry merely stepped toward the door. Not a word spoken. Even Tufts noticed — the griffle chose to walk several paces behind.

They proceeded down a corridor marked with numerous closed doors on either side. The walls were stone and arched overhead. Narrow alcoves filled in the spaces between doors — focus booths, each filled with a hard-working magician.

At the far end, an open door led to one of Jarik and Callib's workrooms. Large enough to fit a mid-sized boat, the room bore the magicians' conflicting tastes quite well. The ten-foot windows along one wall belonged to Jarik. They had red drapes that touched the floor and little animal wood carvings around the frames. Callib had been in charge of the workspace. In one corner, a wide desk covered with papers and books; the rest of the space left open for experiments — practical and utilitarian.

Malja took it all in with the expectation of battle. She noted exits, defensive positions, and areas to avoid. To her left was Cole's portal frame. They had rigged it upright with large cables connected to it. The cables led to the second large object — a chamber composed of mirrored walls and hanging metal rods. More cables snaked along the floor from the chamber to the third object — a dark cylinder about six feet high and three feet across.

Both Jarik and Callib stepped forward. Their bodies glistened with sweet-smelling oil that reminded Malja of Gregor's cooking — particularly when he fried a myrit. Even their bald heads had been covered. The oil brought to life the vibrant colors of their tattoos.

Warnings spiked in Malja's head. "Where's Tommy?"

Callib turned away but not before Malja caught the sinister amusement on his face. He stepped into the mirror chamber, reflections of him on every wall, and adjusted several of its components. Jarik gestured toward the portal frame.

"Patience," he said. "We wish to show you what this is all about. We are not monsters. Sure, we've made mistakes. We are far from perfect. But, where others bemoan their failings and wallow in self-pity, we improve ourselves."

With surefire steps, Callib walked up beside Jarik. "Go get started," he said. "I'll handle this."

Jarik hesitated, the desire to explain pushing against the need to perform. With a muted nod, he acquiesced. Callib gave a little shake of the head and snickered as Jarik entered the mirror chamber.

They're like nasty children, Malja thought.

Jarik took a wide stance in the center of the chamber and focused on the mirror to his side. From here, he could see the tattoos on his back — the oil making even the smallest ones clear. As he worked on the spell emblazoned on his right shoulder blade, doubt trickled along Malja's skin. They might be nasty children, but she now saw that they were *smart,* nasty children.

Callib walked up to Cole and offered a ridiculous bow. "You have my sincerest admiration."

Cole frowned. "You have my portal frame, and I'd appreciate it kindly if you return it."

"I see the time away from us has not changed your humor. Well, I'm sorry, Ms. Watts, but we cannot return the frame. In fact, it is our deepest wish that you help us build an even better one — one that will help us connect with other worlds in more substantive ways."

"You can wish all you want but I—"

"We have glimpsed into hundreds of worlds. Hundreds. Each containing knowledge and riches that would better our world over and over forever." He raised his index finger to stop Cole from speaking again. "I understand why you're angry. But I think after you see what we can accomplish today with your frame, I truly believe you will have a new desire to help us."

With her head high, Malja said, "You get nothing from us until we see Tommy."

"You stupid brat," Callib said, spit flying from his twisted lips. "You never could wait. Never could just let us present things to you the way we had chosen. You want Tommy? You *have* to see him? Very well. But I warn you, this'll only make it harder on you."

Callib looked at a tattoo on his hand. He closed his eyes and whispered words Malja did not know. With a childish snarl, he jerked his head toward the dark cylinder that connected with the mirror chamber. When he opened his eyes, the cylinder became translucent. Inside was Tommy.

He stood in a knee-high, thick, green sludge. Green water filled the rest of the cylinder like an algae soup. Tommy's body swayed in an unseen current, his eyes closed.

"Don't worry," Callib said. "The boy is fine."

"Fine?" Fawbry said. "He can't breathe in there."

Callib pulled back, uncertainty crossing his brow. His eyes widened, and a devious grin formed at the corner of his lips. He eased back with a predatory grace. He looked at Tumus. "You didn't tell them."

Malja's eyes shot to Tumus. The Chi-Chun woman's face betrayed her. Malja said, "You have something to say?"

Tumus looked from Callib to Malja — neither appeared safe. "W-When Barris Mont connected with Tommy, he ..."

"He what?" Malja said, her skin and muscles burning with the desire to attack, to shut out whatever might come.

"He ..."

Callib cleared his throat in a loud, unnecessary manner. "Perhaps I can help. You see, when Barris realized that Jarik and I were approaching, he knew our purpose. We had come to take his power. So, he tried to trick us."

"No," Tumus said. "It wasn't like that. Barris saw a great power in Tommy, but the boy had been so abused in the past, he was too mentally damaged to unlock it safely himself. Barris simply wanted to help the boy."

An icy hand took hold of Malja's heart. "What happened? What did that bloated bastard do?"

Tumus opened her mouth but only shook her head. Callib said, "He transferred himself into the boy. That's why you're precious Tommy is still alive. Barris can breathe underwater, so now Tommy can too."

Malja pressed a hand against her chest as if her heart had been ripped out and she wanted to staunch the wound. *Stay focused,* she thought. *Mourn later.* Rubbing her eyes, she opened her mouth but no words followed.

Fawbry stepped closer to the tank harboring Tommy. "Barris took over Tommy's body?"

"No," Callib said. "They share it. And now that we have the boy connected to our chamber, we share it."

"You're using him?" Malja said, her voice cracking. "For what?"

Callib opened his arms and nodded to the portal frame. "For you." He walked into the mirror chamber and positioned himself similar to Jarik.

While Jarik appeared to be in a deep trance, Callib acted more like an impatient child. He moved about the chamber, using different mirrors for different spells. He focused on his knees, his spine, and his feet. Spell after spell blended with Jarik's singular, powerful conjuring.

The cylinder containing Tommy brightened and pulsed waves of heat. Cole pointed behind them. Malja saw more bright light as the occupied focus booths pushed their magic into the room.

"This is a lot of energy production," Cole said. "It feels like a bomb. Be careful."

"I'll do that," Malja said, her anger refocusing her even as it took on a tinge of Cole's caution.

A cracking sound like wood splintering under heavy pressure ignited the air. The cables wriggled, jolting with power. With a sizzle, an airy pop, and the smell of burnt leaves, the portal frame opened.

Jarik and Callib exited the chamber, triumphant and sweating. They both gestured for Malja to look into the frame. She stepped forward a little — enough to peer into the frame without being too close.

She saw a room made of dark woods. Shelves crammed with books covered most of the walls. A window provided Malja with a glimpse of wide, hilly grass and a vehicle passing in the sky across a huge, ringed moon. In the room, she saw the desk with blue-green lights floating above it. A woman sat behind the desk, touching the lights as if they had substance.

Jarik stepped closer to Malja. "This is your world. You came from here. You were born on those soils. And that woman is your mother."

Jarik's words slammed into Malja's head like an avalanche of stone. Everything around her — Cole, Fawbry, Tumus, Tufts, the mirror chamber, Tommy, her fathers, the fortress, the City of Ashes, the entire world — it all disappeared into darkness leaving only Malja and the portal frame. She felt as if she floated in darkness, cut off from her body's senses.

She watched the woman in the frame, searching for any resemblance, any sign to verify Jarik's claim. The woman did look like Malja — thick, dark hair and a strong body. Her face shared some of Malja's structure, and the way she concentrated on her work bore the same determined focus Malja knew well. Like Malja, the woman wore a black assault suit that fit her perfectly.

The woman looked up, her face mirroring Malja's shock. All her actions occurred in slower time. Even as she hurried around her desk and stepped closer to the portal, her motions were slowed. Her hair bouncing in the air, the chair falling backward, the papers on her desk fluttering — all moved gracefully as if underwater. She covered her mouth, but could not hide her tears.

Malja's world slammed back into focus. She looked to Jarik and said, "Can I go there?"

With a joyous laugh, Jarik said, "That's why we did this. Long ago, we wronged you. We made a mistake."

Callib leaned in. "We simply want to make things right. Go home, Malja. You've been gone far too long."

Malja glanced back at the others. Their expressions couldn't have been more different. Cole gazed upon the portal and the machinery that helped make it possible, and her hands rolled the fabric of her shirt. This small action kept her from leaping forward to examine the wondrous technology.

Tumus, however, could not take her eyes off Tommy. Her valiant chin jutted out, and her body stood firm. Malja knew exactly what she was thinking — how to save Tommy.

Fawbry lacked expression. He stood as if holding on through boredom, waiting for Malja's command to act. She knew for sure now — he was lost in his own mind for now.

I'm alone. Malja took a few steps closer to the portal frame. *I always have been.*

Except if she reached out across worlds she would find a warm hand awaiting her. One like her own. She could leave this destitute, unraveled world of misery and violence, and replace it with a cozy library, green fields, and flying machines. She could have the warm embrace of a parent who never abandoned her.

She took a few steps more.

Jarik looked on with a bittersweet expression. His mouth tightened as if to hold back from blubbering an apology. He hung his tattooed head and laced his fingers. Callib bowed as he gestured toward the frame as if to say *Accept this gift and please forgive us.*

There were no more steps to take.

She gazed into her mother's brown eyes. Tears glistened and dribbled down her mother's cheeks. The woman put out one hand, yearning to touch. Malja raised her left hand and held it just before the frame. She scrutinized her mother's features like inspecting herself after a battle. She saw the old scars and the healed bones — her reflection yet older and more worn.

It was like being inside Barris Mont's magic once more — observing herself from the outside. Except this was no memory brought to life. All she had to do was step forward.

Gregor would tell her to seize the moment. "If I could have my way," she could hear him say, "you would never fight. You would never have to. A little bit of order, and we could all just peacefully live our lives." Yes, Gregor would tell her to jump through the portal, to wrap her arms around her mother, and to never once look back at this blood-soaked world.

But she did look back — just one last time to say goodbye. She saw Cole and Tumus enveloped in their personal euphoria. She saw Fawbry grin — happy for her with unbridled affection. Tufts giggled for no clear reason. She saw Jarik and Callib smiling like the fathers they should have been all along. And she saw Tommy — his submerged body swaying and peaceful, a pleasant look on his face that promised he would be thrilled for her to go through the portal.

For a second, her shoulders slumped. She lifted her head, filled her lungs with air and strength, and said, "Goodbye."

She whirled around, unsheathed Viper, swung it over her head, and using the strength of both arms, destroyed the portal frame in one thundering blow.Sparks of electricity and magic shot up toward the ceiling. As pieces of the frame clattered on the floor, Cole and Tumus snapped out of their blissful daze. Fawbry and Tufts looked confused.

Malja turned Viper toward Jarik and Callib. Jarik had a stunned expression, but Callib seethed with rage. Cole rushed over to the portal frame, caressing it like an injured baby. Tumus watched Malja like a bodyguard unsure of what her employer required.

"You liars! I almost went," Malja said, her grip solid and unwavering. "So tell me this much — was that woman even my mother?"

Callib shrugged. "How should we know? All the women from that world look the same."

Malja sidestepped to the right. "This was your plan? Open the portal frame and cast a spell that drugged us all into bliss. Trick me into going in and then what? I'm gone and the world is yours?"

"The world has always been ours."

Jarik finally looked away from the destroyed portal frame. His expression cleared, replaced with cold stoicism. "Well, once again, you disappoint us."

Malja flinched, and the involuntary response disgusted her.

"We made it easy for you," Jarik continued. "That may not have been your mother, but it was your world. We all could have gotten what we wanted. You would have gone home and escaped from here. We would have learned how you can travel through the portal frame and saved decades more of research."

"You made it too easy," Malja said, inching toward Tommy.

Callib turned to Jarik. "You should have listened. I've always been right about her. But you promised me she would make it so we could travel to other worlds. We should have killed her from the start."

Malja said, "Now we're getting to some truth. You did want to kill me from the very first, when my mother dropped onto your floor clutching me in her arms. I've been thinking about this. Why, I've wondered, over all these years, why didn't you just blast me away with some magic?

"I guess when I was little, Jarik kept you from harming me. You need each other's tattoos, each other's magic and power, so you had to compromise. As I grew up, you saw the warrior in me, and that meant I didn't have the magic you wanted — the magic that Barris Mont had. That extra bit of power you needed to accomplish a stable portal. So you planned to kill me. Jarik promised to take care of the unpleasant details and then told you he had killed me because if you knew that he had left me in the woods and that I had survived ... well, Jarik knows your anger quite well. For some time after you didn't know I was alive.

Then one day you learned about Gregor. You couldn't kill me because of Jarik, and you couldn't kill Gregor yourself because of Jarik. So you hired Old McKinley to do the dirty work. You had Gregor slaughtered and hoped I'd fall apart without him.

"But the question remains: why am I still alive now? Surely in the last few years you heard I was looking for vengeance against you both. Jarik no longer needed prodding. He wanted me dead, too." Another few steps brought Malja into range. "The only answer I can come up with — you fear me."

"If you believe that, then you're as stupid as you are insolent. When we learned you were alive, we couldn't have cared. It was only when we learned that Cole and the Bluesmen were looking for you, that she thought you might hold the secret to traveling through the portal that we decided to use you if the opportunity arose. But we never sought you out. We didn't have to. You were searching for us. It was just a matter of time."

"No, you saw something in my mother's eyes that first day. Something that terrified you. That's why you wanted me dead. That's why you went through this nonsense about sending me home. Get rid of me without facing your fears. And you've been afraid for years of this very moment. Because whatever you saw in her, you see in me. The only thing I can think of that would scare you so greatly is power. You don't try to harm me with your magic because you know I can defeat you."

"Never!" Callib lunged toward Jarik and grabbed his hand. "You think you're so strong," he said, pulling Jarik's arm close enough to stare at the tattoos. "You think you're special. But you're not. You're nothing. And like a spoiled child, you destroy the gifts we give because they're not perfect."

"Malja," Cole said, "he's stalling for his spell."

Malja stepped forward, but Callib said, "You don't want our stable portal. Fine. Now you can feel what an unstable portal is like."

With a flick of his wrist and a deranged howl, Callib let loose a massive blast of magic. Hot, white light burned from his eyes and fingers. It shot out of him like a volcano, breaking through other parts of him until it flowed from his entire body.

Tumus raised her arms to absorb the magic. A small tendril from the blast knocked her to the floor. The magic pouring from Callib and Jarik did not seek out Malja. Instead, it struck the open air behind her.

A sound like ripping cloth magnified a thousand times cut into the air. Hurricane winds churned up from nothing, all of them blowing against Malja. But the wind wasn't really pushing her as much as pulling her. Something was yanking all the air away and trying to bring Malja with it. She planted her feet firmly, but still the forces made her step back.

Callib's harsh, satisfied look chilled her. Cole and Tumus and Fawbry had anchored themselves on parts of the portal machinery, but their wide, shocked eyes told her something ugly awaited her. With a terrified squeal, Tufts lost his grip. His body soared across the room and disintegrated upon the portal.

"No," Fawbry screamed, but the howling winds drowned him out.

Malja peered over her shoulder and discovered what an unstable portal looked like. Then Callib's storm knocked her off-balance and tossed her through the portal.

Chapter 25

Freefalling through a bitter, cold sky, Malja's stomach rose up in her chest. The wind stung her face. For the first time in her life, terror reached down her throat and ripped out a piercing scream.

She fell. Mindless to all around her. Knowing only that she screamed.

When her throat finally balked, she managed to regain some self-control. She started to think.

I'm in another world. Clouds blanketed below her obscuring the ground. Nausea swirled inside her as she dropped.

She closed her eyes, but that didn't help. She rolled onto her back feeling the cold against her like an icy chair. When she opened her eyes, she saw the jagged portal hole receding into the sky. With only the racing wind in her ears, she watched as the hole snapped shut.

Before she had time to consider the implications of that, she passed into the clouds. Moisture beaded on her assault suit and dampened her hair. Thunder rumbled close by.

She broke through the cloud cover to discover a world of raging storms. Rain and lightning thrust toward the ground, and she dropped with it like some banished god. She kept waiting to see a mountain or a forest or a city — some large object which would kill. Instead, she saw water.

In all directions spread a vast ocean. The tear that escaped her eye drowned on her rain-soaked cheek. She would die in the water, every bone shattered upon impact but still aware as she sunk beneath its murky waves. She might even feel the nibbles of fish as her chest burned for air.

She hoped some important event from her life might flash in her mind or just some pleasant memories of Gregor. She would have been happy to consider a lost opportunity or a regretful moment. But her mind blanked at the endless expanse of water below her.

She tried to makes sense of how this could be — how her life could be so abruptly ended — but it only made her feel pointless and small.

Like staring at the stars after reading her astronomy book. She became so absorbed with her lack of final moments that her mind didn't register the ripping sound overtaking the storm. She didn't notice the dark maw open below her. And as she slid through, she only thought how nice it felt to be out of that storm.

Chapter 26

The rain stopped. The wind ceased. But still Malja fell. No longer day. No longer outside. She fell from the top of a high, vaulted ceiling.

The floor zoomed up and with it came the knowledge that she had returned to Jarik and Callib's fortress. Before she could smash to her death, before she could even think about it, the air around her thickened like a stew left overnight. Her body slowed until she landed with a gentle touch, the cool floor a gift against her outstretched body.

Though her life had been saved, her stomach still rebelled. She managed to get on all fours before throwing up. When nothing else could leave her system except long strands of spittle, she gasped and coughed. Wiping her mouth, she looked upon a sight that made her question if she had indeed returned to her world.

The cylinder that had imprisoned Tommy lay in shambles, its brackish liquid drenching a portion of the floor. The mirror chamber had been shattered, littering the area with reflective shards. Tumus and Cole watched Malja with gaping mouths while Jarik nursed his bleeding jaw. Fawbry stood by the cylinder brandishing a metal pipe dripping wet. He had used the pipe to smash open the cylinder. But it was seeing Tommy that confused Malja the most.

His lanky twelve-year-old body faced Callib with a warrior's strength. With one arm raised and eyes narrowed, he pushed back against Callib's magic. Fire, electricity, black smoke, noxious gases — all balled up between the two magicians.

There. She finally had admitted it. Tommy was a magician.

Callib roared under the strain as he attempted to heap more and more magic upon the boy. Though Tommy's arm vibrated and sweat dribbled down his back, Malja saw a fighter with greater stores of power yet to be tapped. No. *Not a fighter — a magician.* He's a magician using powerful magic which will rot his mind until only insanity prevails. Perhaps he had heard her thoughts for he turned his head in her direction and raised his other hand. The door leading out burst open.

Tommy lifted the corner of his mouth and pointed to the door. Malja thought she saw a tear run down his cheek, but she couldn't be sure — trenches of sweat cut down the dirt on his determined face.

"Malja, come," Cole said from the doorway. Tumus tried to pull Malja away.

With Viper in hand, Malja said, "No. I won't let a boy sacrifice himself for me. I'm not leaving until this is over."

Drawing on all her speed, strength, and accuracy, Malja raced forward. She held Viper's grip at her stomach so the crescent-shaped blade pointed out from her side. *Run straight past him and let the blade do the work.* She came in fast and silent, hoping Callib's attention would be focused exclusively on Tommy.

But Callib saw her.

"You," he said, saturating the word with all his disappointment, fear, and hatred. Malja didn't see the motion, but she felt the pain as Callib sent a red bolt in her chest, blasting her onto her back. Tommy thrust magic from both hands, and though the ball of magic shimmered, it held.

Malja stared at the ceiling, stars dancing around her vision. *Stars.* Stars, magic, madness — it all connected for her. After a few moments to catch her breath, she rose to her feet with a satisfied smile. She had a plan.

She pointed Viper at Jarik. "I've always known you were the weaker brother. Right to the end, you make Callib do all the hard work."

"Watch your tongue," Jarik said, blood on his chin. "Standing up to my brother has kept you alive."

Malja turned to Callib. "Then you must be the weak one, hiding your shame behind all this bluster. Makes sense — you made Jarik get rid of me, hired Old McKinley to get rid of Gregor, never doing the jobs yourself."

"Be quiet," Callib said, keeping his focus on the growing mass of magic.

"You did all these things that Jarik never knew about. Haven't you ever wondered what he's done behind your back? Or do you just think he's too worthless to bother worrying about?"

Callib straightened, his eyes opening in paranoia. "What is she talking about?"

"Liar," Jarik said. "I've always been a loyal brother."

Malja looked unconvinced. "Except when you went against Callib's orders and let me live. And now look where we are? Seems to me the both of you are trying to get the better of the other."

"It's not true," Jarik said, blood sputtering from his lips. "Don't listen to her. She's just trying to turn us against each other."

"You're right, Jarik. Callib is the weaker. Wielder of powerful magic but, like you, insignificant in the end."

Callib's face twisted as he struggled against Tommy's magic. "Lies!" he said. "We are special. We are the most powerful, most unique beings in the universe. We are far more than mere magicians. Could a silly magician hold battle with another while talking with you? I think not." To prove his point, Callib sent a strong surge of energy into the ball, and Tommy slid back a few feet. "We are gods. This world belongs to us. We will dethrone Korstra and Kryssta, and all of Corlin, all of Geth, will bow down before us. We are the new brother gods."

Malja walked straight at Callib. "Brother gods? You can't even defeat a little boy."

"We are gods!"

Before Malja could change her course, before Tommy could conjure some help, Callib swept both his arms in her direction, throwing the concoction of magics at her. Though most of it dissipated from the sudden change in focus, enough made its way to hit Malja.

A stone wall of sound slammed into her — deep rumbles and high-pitched squeals. Her feet went out from under her, sending her reeling to the ground. Viper careened into the air. Her head hit the floor sparking a dazzling array of colors before her eyes.

Her disorientation lasted only a moment, but by the time she had recovered, the room had grown quiet. Callib stared off, his face frozen in disbelief. Malja's eyes darted to the left. There lay Jarik, wheezing as blood pooled beneath him, Viper lodged in his chest.

With cold, patient steps, Malja approached Jarik. They locked eyes. Jarik's paling skin flushed with life for just a few seconds. "Callib was right about you," he said. "Worthless. Disappointment."

"You can't hurt me anymore," Malja said, placing her foot on Jarik's shoulder as she gripped Viper. "But I can hurt you."

She jerked Viper free. Jarik screamed. "That was for Nolan's sister, Audrex," she said. She raised Viper over her head, but before she could strike, a blast of energy tossed her several feet away.

Callib hurried to Jarik. "It's not possible." He cradled his dying brother and made no attempt to hide his streaming tears. "We're gods."

As Malja jumped back to her feet, Callib lifted his hand and pointed a warning finger. From the corner of her eye, Malja saw Tommy preparing to defend her, and though she couldn't see Tumus, she knew the Chi-Chun woman also readied her magic. Malja held Viper at her side.

She stepped forward, and Callib thrust his arm. But nothing happened. Concentrating all his energy, Callib tried again. A few sparks fizzled from his fingers.

In a somber, respectful tone, Tumus said, "Their magic was tied together. As Jarik dies, so does their power."

"That's not possible," Callib said. "I was a magician long before Jarik."

"Once you started linking your power with Jarik's, you entwined your abilities forever."

Callib's dumbfounded eyes gazed upon Jarik's face. He stroked Jarik's cheek and nodded. "It's okay. Perhaps it's best this way." The floor lurched to the side and dropped three feet. Callib let out a short chuckle that brought a perverse gleam to his eye. He looked from Malja and Tommy to Tumus and Cole and finally, to Fawbry. He let out a barking laugh. "Jarik's dying," he yelled. "Jarik's dying, and he's the one holding our home in the air. We're all going to die together. One big, happy family."

With each successive laugh erupting from Callib's chest, his face twisted into a grotesque, maniacal mask. Like a sigh, the fight left Malja. There seemed no point now. Jarik and Callib were no longer who they had been.

"Malja," Cole said, her voice shaking more than the floor.

The left side of the building tilted for a second before leveling out. Malja sheathed Viper as she ran over to Cole. Tumus, Fawbry, and Tommy followed. Together, they rushed through the door and down the long hall lined with focus booths.

Several of the booths had been knocked open by the building's sudden drop. The magicians inside were dead. A few bore the serene expression of someone asleep or in deep meditation. But others died in horrible agony, clawing at the booth doors until their fingernails were no more.

"How could this have happened? We never heard anything," Tumus asked.

Cole said, "Sweetie, Jarik and Callib linked everyone together to create that stable portal. When the whole contraption blew, well, there are always side effects."

Malja skidded to a halt. "What? You're saying I killed them?"

"No, no, dear Malja, no, no. You were inside the portal when this happened. Callib did it, when he struck out at Tommy, when he tried to stop the boy from saving you."

Malja didn't know whether to believe Cole, but the whining sound of bending metal and a turbulent thumping in the floor reminded her feet to start moving again. They left the corridor and hustled through the enormous foyer. Bits of wall and ceiling dropped like hail crashing into the floor and spitting up debris.

Tumus reached the other side first. She pushed the large door open and stood in the doorway, blocking everybody's progress. She looked back at Malja and shook her head. "We're too late."

Malja caught up and peered out the doorway. Although the building sank slowly, the bridge was still at least twenty feet higher up.

From behind, Fawbry let out a short yelp. Everyone looked at him. He looked back, a bit dazed, a bit unsure. "What's going on?" he asked.

Cole laughed, wrapped her arms around him, and kissed his reddening cheek. "You went a little crazy, Faw-Faw. Kind of shut down for awhile. But you're back now, and you've helped save Tommy."

"I did?"

Malja said, "Yes, yes, you helped. You're a hero. But if we don't get out of here, you'll be a dead hero. So let's go. We have to climb."

Cole said, "Not at all. You don't think I spent all that time working for Jarik and Callib and I didn't learn any thing, now did you? Those boys would have a backup plan just in case something like this happened."

"You think they planned for us to come and destroy them?"

"No, but they would've planned for Jarik being incapacitated, seeing as how he's the one keeping this place in the air."

"Fine, fine," Tumus said. "So what's this backup plan?"

Cole leaned her shoulder against the wall and thought. Nobody spoke, though all of them stared at her. Fawbry shivered as he looked around. Tommy slipped his hand into Malja's. She clenched it tightly, but kept her attention on Cole. If she even glanced at Tommy, she knew she would start hugging him and possibly start crying. She wasn't sure she would be able to stop.

"A crash room," Cole blurted out. "They probably built a crash room — a reinforced section of the building that could withstand most types of impact. If they were in trouble, they could lock up inside it and just wait the whole thing out."

"Great. Where is it?" Fawbry asked, his voice climbing pitch with each word.

"If I were designing it, I'd put it at the bottom of a normal building, but this one is floating — so, I guess it would be in the middle since an impact could come from any direction. That way they'd have plenty of cushion on all sides."

The building reeled to the side, sending everyone scrambling to stay upright. Tumus braced herself in the doorway. Shattering glass and tumbling rocks echoed against the walls. Malja planted her feet in a wide stance. A moment later, the building settled.

Holding tight to the doorjamb, Tumus leaned out. "I think, maybe, we can—"

Malja grabbed the back of Tumus's clothes and tugged her back inside. "No time for debates. Cole, lead the way to the crash room. Everyone else follow."

"Look here, I don't know for sure there is one," Cole said.

"Do your best," Malja said, "because any minute now, Jarik is going to die, and this whole place comes crashing down."

"I'm just not sure—"

"Cole!"

"Okay, okay. My goodness, you don't have to be so rough."

Malja gestured to the crumbling building. Cole said nothing as she headed back through the foyer and into the focus booth corridor. She stopped without warning.

"Damn," she said, staring at the floor.

"What now?" Fawbry asked.

A wide blood trail painted a path from the far end of the corridor into one of the unused focus booths. Cole said, "Callib dragged Jarik through there. He's taking him to the crash room. We're too late."

"We can't be," Fawbry said.

Malja kicked the booth at her right three times and cursed. She took several deep breaths before speaking. "You're sure we can't find this crash room in time?"

"By the time I find it, Jarik and Callib will have it sealed up. I'm sorry."

"Then we climb. Get high enough to cross to that bridge."

"One of these doors should—"

Malja kicked down one door, then another. Fawbry had reached the third and tried the handle. The door opened to a stairwell. With a bow, he gestured toward the stairs as if inviting her to a dance. His hands shook, but Malja appreciated his attempt to not panic.

"Hurry now," Malja said, making sure everyone went ahead before going upstairs herself.

Climbing stair after stair, adrenaline pumping her legs faster than the muscles wanted to work, Malja listened to the building fall apart around her. She heard Tumus praying in short puffs. She could see the concern and bald fear on Cole's brow. And Tommy — Malja only wanted to think as far as knowing he was with them and alive.

"This door, I think," Cole said.

They entered an octagonal library. Books lined the walls and the air smelled musty. Two tables dominated the floor. Pieces of yellowing paper and moldy covers were spread across the surfaces. Some papers had been laid out like puzzle pieces that didn't quite fit. Others were stacked for later use.

"What a shame," Cole said as she led them through the room. "All this effort to rebuild lost works of knowledge, and now it's going to be lost again."

With a glimpse at the table, Malja said, "Keep moving."

Cole did as commanded, though her eye lingered on the half-completed texts. Fawbry rushed ahead, and at the far end of the library, he pushed aside two sliding doors that opened onto a narrow landing. Cole followed, leaned over the railing and by the relieved drop of her shoulders, Malja knew they were high enough.

Malja took a look for herself. She judged the distance as no more than fifteen feet and dropping. "Get ready," she said.

Cole swung her feet over the railing. Malja lifted Tommy into a similar position. She held him tight against her chest and felt his right hand pat her arm.

The building jolted and Cole lost her balance. Rather than tumble, she had the presence to push off. She hit the road and crumpled into a fetal position, clasping her ankle and crying.

Tommy wriggled in an attempt to dislodge from Malja. "No," she said. "Just a few feet closer first."

He glowered at her.

"We're sinking slowly. It'll be fine to just wait."

He shook his head and pulled up his sleeves to reveal the tattooed skin. Dark, thick-lined tattoos covered his arms like winter clothes.

Malja stepped back, unsure of what she thought of the sight. It

230 - The Malja Chronicles

revolted her, but it was also Tommy — she couldn't look upon him and feel that way. She leaned in to view the details, and he leaped off.

"Tommy!"

When he hit the surface, he tucked into a ball and rolled to a safe recovery. He glanced up at her, smiled, and went to Cole's side.

"I-I can't do this," Tumus said. Her dark skin took on a sickly hue. She shook her head over and over. "Korstra help me. I can't do this. I'll never make it."

"It's okay," Fawbry said. "I don't want to jump either, but you don't have to. When the building sinks some more, we'll be just about even with the bridge. We can just hop right off."

"No. I can't do this."

"And I thought Korstra gave you such strength. You going to let a Kryssta-loving fool like me show you up? Come on, now. We're close enough. Watch." Fawbry hopped off, hit the ground with a grunt, popped to his feet, and waved back. "Easy," he said.

Malja pressed against Tumus's back. "You can do this. It's just a little step to safety."

The building dropped fast. Malja and Tumus fell to the floor which dipped enough to slide them back into the library. Books tumbled off the shelves. Malja's cheek hit a table leg and the copper taste of blood coated her tongue.

"Tumus, we have to go now."

Tumus had wrapped her arms around a chair. "I can't. I'm sorry. I've never been in the air like this before. I can't."

"You must."

"Go without me. I'm not afraid to die. Korstra can have me."

"That's it," Malja said. She got to her feet and crossed to Tumus as the building leveled out once more. "If you aren't afraid to die, then shut up and come with me." She tore the chair away from Tumus, squatted down, and lifted Tumus over her shoulders.

The floor shivered. Malja lined up with the doorway and kicked the chair against the railing. The shivering grew to a rumble.

Letting out a primal scream, Malja sprinted forward, her tired legs straining under the added weight of Tumus. She stepped onto the chair, then the railing. The building sank rapidly. As Malja pushed off, she watched the bridge pass before her eyes. She reached out — metal and concrete scraping along her chest, Tumus screaming in her ear — and latched onto the bridge as Jarik and Callib's building tumbled into the darkness below.

Malja hung from the bridge, her fingers finding the slimmest purchase, while Tumus clung to her back like a baby cholloh. Fawbry stretched out toward them, but they were too far down. Malja let out an aggravated moan. Her fingers slipped.

That was it. She just slipped for a second, but gravity gave no quarter for such mistakes. They fell backward. Malja watched Fawbry's anguish as he reached uselessly for her. Tumus let go, weeping from the sudden darkness that enfolded them as they lost sight of the bridge.

Falling to my death twice in one day. If her body hadn't been so tired, she might have laughed.

A distant, thunderous thump reported the destruction of Jarik and Callib's fortress. A long fall. Too much time alone with her thoughts. Too much time to pay the dead their due.

Heat suddenly. First a slight warmth. Next came a full-blown hot air thrusting up from below. An explosion. The air lifted her like a doll, effortlessly throwing her into the sky. The bridge came into view and just as fast disappeared below her.

"Just kill me already," Malja yelled.

The heat beneath her dissipated, and as her body crested, she felt a familiar sensation along her arms like fingers tapping up and down her skin. Instead of falling back, her body shifted toward the bridge and descended in a peaceful, controlled manner. She looked down to see Tommy guiding her and Tumus to the ground.

When she reached the bridge, Malja and Tumus went straight for Tommy. He lowered to the ground, breathing hard like he had jogged several miles. His body shivered as the sweat covering him chilled his skin.

Malja wrapped her arms around him and kissed his forehead. She didn't wipe the tears from her face or muffle the sound of her bawling. All she wanted was for Tommy to know, to feel within his bones and heart and, if such a thing existed, his soul — that she needed him. She loved him.

"Thank you," she said. Tommy matched her grip. Feeling his small hands pulling her closer sent her into another fit of tears.

"See?" Fawbry said to Tumus. "Easy."

Tumus prostrated near Tommy's feet. Her hands shaking like a bowstring just shot. She mumbled to the ground, but Malja distinctly heard the name *Korstra.*

When she lifted her head, Tumus smiled and said, "It's over."

Malja wanted to believe that, but she heard an odd buzzing that sent uneasy pulses through her. As the sound grew louder, she let Tommy go, wiped her face, and stood. Viper itched at her back. She let the weapon free, the sight of it sobering Tumus.

"What's wrong?" Cole asked.

"Listen," Malja said. By now they could all hear the horrible buzzing of Dragonflies. "Be ready."

Fawbry lifted Cole, while Tumus carried Tommy. Despite her exhaustion, Malja led the way with Viper as a warning to any Dragonflies suddenly getting brave. She used all her energy to keep moving and not stumble. If she showed any serious weakness, she expected the Dragonflies would swarm in on them.

As they progressed across the bridge, Malja kept searching the darkness. They wound through the mounds of trash and rubble, and still Malja remained alert. Several times her head swam. She feared she might pass out, but her will refused such an easy escape.

As they neared the factory fence, she could feel the eyes watching. Dragonflies buzzed overhead but none came close enough to be seen. Zorum's split body lay in a heap not too far away. That reminder did far better in protecting them then Malja's shaking arms holding Viper.

Two workers appeared with three horses. Their terrified gazes drifted between Malja and the billowing smoke from the destroyed fortress. That thick cloud would cover the sky for days.

One worker handed his reins over and dashed back to the factory. The other swallowed hard and held his reins out. He pointed into the distance. The message was clear enough — *Take these horses and go far away as fast as you can.* Malja had set them free from the factory life and they wanted to throw her out. As she snatched the reins, she growled and the worker sprinted away.

"Easy," Tumus said. "You just killed their gods."

Malja climbed atop a brown mare and closed her eyes for just a second of relief. She didn't think she had the strength to endure another fight. She barely had the strength to open her eyes again. Fawbry mounted a horse and sat Cole across, protecting her wounded ankle with care.

Tumus tapped Malja's knee and handed Tommy to her. Malja slid the boy in front and wrapped her arms around him. His unconscious body limp and unreactive. Without a word, Tumus walked away and mounted the third horse.

Before they entered the fenced-off factory, Cole pointed them westward for several blocks. The detour would add another day's travel most likely, but Malja didn't mind. They avoided the factory workers and any other Dragonflies in that area. And they had the time. After all, there was nothing left to do.

Tommy still didn't speak, but the recent events had left their mark. Each night they made camp, he labored as hard as ever with the others, but when they finished, he curled up next to Malja, insisted she place her arm around him, and moved little until morning. Even while he ate, he did so from this position.

Malja tried to give the boy what he needed, but it did not come naturally. Besides, part of him was Barris Mont. She'd look in his eyes, searching for a flicker of that creature, and grew angry no matter what she thought she saw. After a week of travel, her conflicted feelings must have become apparent for Tumus chose to approach her one evening after everyone else had fallen asleep.

"He's all Tommy. You don't have to worry."

Malja saw no point in pretending ignorance. "Easy for you. You loved them both. This boy is double the prize for you."

"You know I don't see him as a prize. Korstra, in his infinite wisdom, found a way to save this boy's life. Barris gave himself up to Tommy, and while he lives on in the boy's body, he has no control over anything. Tommy is entirely Tommy. He merely has the essence, the power, of Barris Mont."

"This is supposed to make me feel better?"

Tumus grinned. "You need to forget about Barris. Just see Tommy. Nothing else has changed."

"I don't know. The magic he created to fight with Callib was ... if I hadn't actually seen it ... and you're saying that's all him. No Barris?"

"I'm saying that the boy is still a boy. And he still needs you."

"You wish it was you."

Tumus stroked Tommy's hair. "A little, yes. Yet I was not the one who saved him from slavery. I was not the one who protected him from the wilds."

"Some protection. He would've died, if left to me. You were the one who took him to real safety."

"Ahh, so that's it."

Malja closed her eyes and faked a yawn. "There's no it."

"You blame yourself. You think that you failed and that's why Barris is now within Tommy. You think you should have been there to stop it or perhaps never have let Tommy be in that situation in the first place."

"You couldn't be more wrong," Malja said, but she couldn't convince herself, let alone another.

Tumus clasped her hands. "I'm sorry you don't believe in Korstra for you would find great comfort and understanding if you did. You'd see that you cannot control the world, that even a brother god could not predict such things. If he could, he would have saved his beloved Elatria. I guess the best I can tell you is that this is not your fault. It is the will of the world. It is the way of life."

"Yeah? Well, life is tossing the Black Beast upon me for not being a good parent to Tommy."

A few days later they reached the well-kept mansion where they had found the grounder. Cole's foot had been wrapped and babied as much as possible — now, she could hobble along for several hours without tiring. They spent the night under the comfort of the mansion's roof, and Cole wandered its halls longer than she had spent at any stop since she broke her foot.

As Malja readied to go to sleep, she heard a strange noise. The size of the mansion caused sounds to bounce around, but she was sure she had heard a voice. She followed the echoing sounds until she reached the kitchen. There she found Fawbry and Tommy playing the Reflex Game. A wide smile covered Tommy's face as Fawbry tried to feign an attack. Backing out quietly, Malja left them to their game. She finally slept soundly.

The next morning, as they prepared the horses, Cole called the group together. "I'm not going," she said. "I want to stay here."

"What? Why?" Fawbry said.

"Bless your heart, you still just want to be with me, don't you? Sorry, Faw-Faw, but it'd never work. We were good for awhile, but I've got plans and you'd really be better off going home."

"Kryssta, you're an infuriating woman. All I asked was why. I'm not professing my undying love."

"See that? Your undying love. You've got to move on."

While Cole and Fawbry continued to verbally spar, Malja thought about the mansion. Filled with ancient technology that begged the attention of someone knowledgeable, there was a graceful logic to leaving Cole with it. One thing gnawed at Malja, though.

"What plans?" she said, interrupting Fawbry's next insult.

Cole raised an eyebrow. "Excuse me?"

"What is it you want to do with this place?"

Cole walked over to Fawbry's horse and fussed with the saddle. "Oh, nothing to worry about. It's not like I'm going to start a group of blues-playing assassins or anything."

"That's right," Malja said in cautious tones. "That would be a dangerous and foolhardy thing to do."

"Why, Ms. Malja, I think you're threatening me. Oh, don't give me any of your looks. I never was built for leading armies or anything like that. That's your area. I just want to get back to the simple things — building machines. Just because we all live by our own rules doesn't mean we have to live without comfort. It's not as if the two are mutually exclusive."

Malja stayed silent a moment, thinking it over, weighing the woman Cole had been with the woman she had become. Malja extended her hand. "Good luck. I think I'll actually miss you a bit."

"My, my," Cole said, shaking Malja's hand. "You'll have to come back and visit someday. You, too, Tumus. And Tommy. You're always welcome."

Fawbry swung up onto his horse. "Don't worry about excluding me. I wouldn't want to come back here if my life depended on it. Not unless you've got a new hand for me."

Cole raised both eyebrows, grinned, but said nothing.

Two nights later, Malja woke from a dream she could not recall. Tommy whimpered and nuzzled her side. Tumus sat by their campfire and asked, "You okay?"

Malja nodded. "What are you doing up?"

Tumus hesitated. Stretching out her legs, she said, "I'm trying to figure out what I should do next."

"Korstra's not telling you?"

A loud laugh broke from Tumus, and Tommy started, looked around and fell right back asleep. "Sorry," she said. "No, Korstra's not helping me out here. I've got to figure it out on my own."

"Any ideas?"

Licking her lips, Tumus said, "I think so. I'm going back to Dead Lake. Jarik and Callib hurt my people, killed many, and left them in disarray. Without Barris around, there's bound to be a mess, and I think I could do a good job helping clean it all up."

"You've been gone a long time."

"The Chi-Chun are not often fast movers."

Malja smirked, thinking of how most Chi-Chun could spend hours standing in one place. "We should pass the lake soon," she said.

"Then I have time to change my mind."

But Malja knew as she closed her eyes that Tumus would stay behind at Dead Lake. Malja's life did not join well with most people. If not for Tommy, Tumus would never have come along in the first place.

Sure enough, at Dead Lake, Tumus slid from her saddle and sifted her fingers through the soil. She washed her hands in the cold lake waters and breathed in the lake air as if she had entered a holy shrine.

Little had changed. Debris littered the ground and birds pecked at the few remains still scattered about the land. Barris Mont's enormous body could not be seen. Malja guessed that scavengers had consumed much of it before the rest slipped back underwater.

"Guess you're staying here," Fawbry said.

"It's best I do. Korstra wouldn't want me traveling with a Kryssta-lover like you."

Fawbry let out a shocked gasp. He jumped to the ground, stormed up to Tumus, and let his face open into a wide smile. He wrapped his arms around the woman and ignored her protests while he hugged her.

"Never thought I'd miss a Korstra fool, but I'll miss you."

When Fawbry broke away, Tumus faced Malja. "Don't pretend you'll miss me. I'm just glad we got through all this without killing each other."

"He's going to miss you," Malja said, jutting her chin in Tommy's direction. "That means I'm going to miss you. And, maybe, I just might miss you a little bit on my own."

"I couldn't ask for more," Tumus said before turning her full attention on Tommy.

Kneeling before him as if he were a king, she pressed his hand against her wet cheek. Tommy looked to Malja for guidance. She motioned with her hand — *make your own decisions.*

He tapped Tumus on the shoulder, and when she lifted her head, her broad smile set them at ease. She hugged the boy.

"You will always have a home here," Tumus said. "Promise me you'll come to visit."

Tommy covered his heart and nodded. He tapped his chest twice and brought his hand to his forehead — his military salute.

"Okay. Good." She brushed her cheeks clear and stood, but never let go of his hand. She gazed at the lake and grimaced as if the empty waters cut through her. "You could," she said, her voice quavering, "that is to say, if you wanted to, you would be welcome here ... to stay."

Malja pulled Tommy away, and to her joy, Tommy clutched her side.

Tumus held the boy's hand as long as she could, all the time speaking as fast as her mouth could move. "I'm sorry. Please, I'm sorry. It's just that part of him is Barris Mont and this is the home of Barris and I just thought part of him may want to go swim in his lake and feel his waters and know why he is the way he is now."

"Don't ruin this," Malja said.

"I know. I'm sorry. After all, I have Korstra. Who do you have besides Tommy?"

"We should go."

"Of course," Tumus said and blew a kiss to Tommy. "Please, come visit some day. I promise I'll be fine."

They rode to the Yad in silence. Tommy made a few pleasant faces for Malja — reassurances that he was fine and that he wanted to be with her. But no matter what he did, Malja still felt doubt chewing at the back of her mind.

Does this parenting thing ever get any easier? she wondered.

At the Yad, three Muyaza came out to see Malja arrive. Much of their village remained in disrepair, yet some were back helping people cross the river's rough waters. Others worked on rebuilding their homes and fixing the broken litters.

One Muyaza waited for a moment, but when no other horses followed out from the tree line, he spoke rapidly to the others. They waddled off to the main part of the village and within a few minutes, the entire community came out. They were silent and somber.

Malja dismounted and approached with her head low and her posture as non-threatening as she could muster. An elder Muyaza stepped toward her. She offered the small lock of hair Skvalan had carried. The elder snatched it from her, clutching it close to his chest, and the entire community wept.

As the Muyaza turned away, Fawbry asked Malja, "Should we stay?"

"What for?"

"The funeral — assuming they have one."

Malja mounted her horse. "You're welcome to do as you wish. I don't go to funerals."

"That's because you're usually the one who did the killing."

Malja didn't bother answering. The Muyaza were gracious enough to get them across the Yad for free and that served as their final words. Once they had gone back into the forest, Malja pulled up next to Fawbry.

"Thank you for helping us save Tommy."

"Some help. I go crazy, and you're thanking me." Fawbry's horse snorted and this appeared to be the most answer she would receive.

"Well," she said, "I assume you'll be heading back north, back home, but if you want to stay with us, we'd be happy to have you."

Fawbry snapped his head around. "Are you insane?"

"Look I know things have not been easy with us, but Tommy likes you and I think—"

Laughter burst out of Fawbry like a colorful fountain spraying cool water. "Shut up already. You're insane to think I'm going north."

"But you hate me."

"Somebody's got to protect this boy from you, and I still have one hand. Besides, after I left you I almost died out there. And I ended up back with you, anyway. This is a dangerous world. Might as well have the most dangerous person in it on my side."

Tommy snickered and that brought a smile to Malja. "That's good enough as far as we're concerned," she said.

"Great." Fawbry clapped his hands. "So where are we going?"

Chapter 27

The town of Darmen had been built on a small hill and consisted of two roads crossing. Homes lined the north-south road. Here lived the Governor, some store owners, and a few citizens. The east-west road consisted of The Maple Tree Inn, the stables, a house of prostitution, a gambling house, three bars, another house of prostitution, and three homes belonging to the true rulers of the town — the Morlina Brothers.

The Star Bar had been built around the rusting shell of a bank vault which served to keep food cold. The metallic walls provided it with a unique atmosphere and unusual acoustics. Malja, Tommy, and Fawbry sat at a round table made from an old road sign — TORSKA BRIDGE 5.

"Got any apples?" Malja asked.

The gruff owner behind the bar, heavy beard and bald head, pointed to a small basket on the far end.

"Thank you," Malja said and helped herself to a ripe, red apple. The cold Korstraprime rains had been falling for three weeks, sending rivers of grime rushing through the town streets. Finding apples in such good condition was a treat. She bit into the fruit, licking its juice before taking the next bite, savoring the experience thoroughly.

Tommy dug into a cheese sandwich, his attention fixated on Fawbry's copy of the Book of Kryssta. Learning to read had proven easy for the boy, and Malja expected him to be proficient within a few months. She would have to keep an eye out for an astronomy book or else Tommy might become a Kryssta convert.

Fawbry said, "Um, not to upset you, but what in Kryssta's name are we doing here?"

"Having lunch," Malja said.

"But this is the Morlina's town. Coming here is like begging for a fight. I thought we were done with all that."

Malja took another bite of her apple. "How long have we been wandering around Corlin?"

The question took Fawbry off-guard. "I don't know. A few months, I guess."

"That sounds right. And what have we been doing?"

"Traveling. What's this got to do with being here?"

After one final bite, Malja placed the core on the bar and returned to her table. "We've been doing nothing. Just wandering. That's because we didn't have a purpose. Before, I had a clear reason for every action, every step in my life — get Jarik and Callib. But now there's nothing."

"I see," Fawbry said, his eyes more panicked with every word. "You were feeling bored and useless, so you thought it'd be fun to provoke some nasty men and cut them down."

"No," she said, calm and patient. "We're here because I finally know how to live in this world. For me. And I hope for you and Tommy. This is the first step."

"Oh, wonderful. Just what I wanted to hear. What limb am I going to lose this time?"

The bar room door opened with a blast of cold air. Four men walked in, each wearing a dark, rain-doused coat. The first was Arkam Morlina. The second was his magician. The other two were his thugs.

Malja's nerves jangled. Arkam was a portly, unimposing fellow on the outside, but his name and the violence his brothers had attached to it kept Malja alert. The magician ate far too much and smelled of raw onion.

"Are you Malja?" Arkam asked as his thugs spread out. One edged behind her, the other slid along the wall in front. "I got a message you wanted to see me."

Fawbry nearly choked on his food. "You called this guy here?"

Malja stood in as non-threatening a manner as she could manage. "I'd like to discuss with you how you and your brothers are going to stop hurting this town."

Arkam stared in shock before breaking into laughter. "Are you threatening to take over here?" To his men, he said, "This is unbelievable."

"No threats," Malja said. "I don't want to hurt anybody. If you'd simply sit down, I'm sure we can figure out a way for you to live here peacefully, or if you don't like that, you and your brothers can leave and the town can take care of itself."

Arkam leaned against a wall and shook his head as if dealing with a naïve kid who needed to be shown who was in charge. "Do you know who I am?"

Malja raised a finger. "Do you know who I am?"

Throwing his hands in the air, he said, "Well, you've been funny, but you make no sense. I've got to go. Just be glad my brothers weren't the ones to get your message. If they had to get soaked just to listen to this nonsense, well, you'd all be dead right now." To Fawbry and Tommy, he added, "You both should run from her. She's going to get you killed."

Fawbry crossed his arms. "She's the safest bet we got."

"Come see me. I'll give you better."

Malja shifted her foot. "Don't make me hurt you. Please. Sit with me and work this out."

Arkam's face tightened. He motioned to his magician. The magician rolled up his sleeve and gazed on his tattoo — swirling smoke with bits of grit dotted throughout. Malja didn't have to look behind her to know Tommy had several spells ready to go.

Throwing his fist onto the bar, Arkam said, "Do you know what my brothers will do to you?"

Malja sighed as she saw Arkam's eyes signal his men. The one behind her died first. Malja jabbed Viper back and up, catching the thug just under the rib cage. The other one swung a short sword overhead. Malja sidestepped the attack and countered right through his mid-section.

Arkam backed up to his magician. "Y-You just killed two good men."

"These were thugs," Malja said. "They stole and raped and terrorized this town for you and your brothers. Now sit with me and talk. It can stop here."

Arkam kicked one of the bodies and slipped on some blood. He managed to keep from falling by holding onto his magician's sleeve. "You're all dead. You understand? Simple as that. All three of you are going to die."

The magician popped his head up and the ground quaked. Arkam bent over with a sadistic howl of joy. The bartender jumped from behind the bar, crying, with his arms raised in surrender.

"Fawbry," Malja yelled.

Fawbry leaped forward and tackled the bartender, bringing him to safety behind the bar. Even as the ground in front of her opened up, she listened for sounds that Fawbry had succeeded. She heard it in a giddy laugh — the sound of someone surprised to be alive. The sound that launched her into action.

She thrust forward. Viper sprayed blood off its blade as it sliced toward new victims. Before she struck Arkam, a thin stream of fire shot by her, igniting the somber magician. He screamed, but the sounds were never heard. A bubble of air had formed around him, containing the fire, the smoke, and the sound.

Malja brought Viper down and Arkam's right arm joined the bodies on the floor. With a flick of his fingers, Tommy closed the wound.

Malja placed Viper under Arkam's chin. A dark spot formed at Arkam's crotch. "P-Please. Don't kill me."

"There's only one reason you are alive right now. So listen closely. Your brothers are out of business. You go tell them that. And then, you leave this town and go to the next closest one. You tell everyone in that town that the great Malja is real, that she's sick of people like your brothers ruining life for everybody. You tell them that Malja is fair. Give up all this evil and all is forgiven. We've lived in crazy times. I understand. But fight me, and you'll die. Either way, I'm going to rid the world of all the scum like you. You tell them that, and then you go to the next town and do it again. And you keep doing it until you die of old age. Understand?"

Arkam nodded.

"And I'm going to be following just behind. If you stop, I'll catch you. So, get started."

He bolted from the bar, tripping on the fallen corpse of his magician and landing in the muddy streets.

"It's okay now," Malja said.

Fawbry and the bartender stood. "You do understand that his brothers are going to come fighting."

"Maybe not. I can hope for the best, right? If not this time, then maybe the next. Eventually these fools will get the message."

"But—"

"Tommy and I can take care of them. And I need you to keep the innocent out of harm's way."

"So this is the grand mission now? Clean up the country?"

Malja shrugged. "My fathers were Jarik and Callib. Tommy has part of Barris Mont inside him. You were a warlord."

"I wasn't any good at it."

"And I ... I was consumed by hatred. We're responsible for a lot of this mess. Fixing it seems like the right thing to do."

Fawbry looked to the bartender. "Well, can I at least get a free drink for saving your life?" The bartender passed out. Fawbry shrugged, reached for a mug, and poured himself a drink. "I suppose this'll work well. Better than your myopic revenge thing."

"Much better," Malja said as she wiped Viper's blade. "The Black Beast is dead. Now, I'm the law."

THE WAY OF THE SWORD AND GUN

BOOK 2 OF THE BEST SELLING SERIES THE MALJA CHRONICLES

STUART JAFFE

THE WAY OF THE

SWORD AND GUN

Book 2 of The Malja Chronicles

For Garrett

Malja

Malja wanted to kill the boy. Again. Not literally, of course. She loved Tommy. But over the last year, the boy she had saved from slavery, the boy she had fought for and protected, that she had sacrificed everything for, had turned into a moody, unpredictable monster.

Even as they rode through the forest toward the town of Affengar, she could feel his ever-shifting attitude in the air. He kept ahead of her and rarely looked back. Though he never spoke, hadn't from the day they met, she heard his anger clearly.

Fawbry, the third member of their trio, pulled up beside her. He held the reins in his one good hand. The other — a mere stump where his hand had been sheered off — rested in his lap. "Relax," he said. "Tommy's how old? Maybe fourteen? This is normal behavior."

Malja shuddered — maybe normal would have sufficed back when they first met, back when Tommy had only the lightning arc tattoo on his arm signifying the one spell he could cast — electrical energy. But that was a long time ago. That was before they met the behemoth, Barris Mont, before he unlocked more of Tommy's abilities. Now, a sleeve of tattoos covered Tommy's right arm and more grew each week.

Tommy snapped his fingers and pointed ahead. When Malja's roan mare crested a small rise, she saw Affengar below. The trees broke away, forming a mini-valley for the town, and as the sun leaned toward the horizon, it cast a beautiful glow on the buildings.

Compared to most towns, Affengar thrived. The two-story buildings showed little sign of the Devastation. Many towns had rebuilt amongst the ruins, creating a patchwork of scavenged metal and modern carpentry, but here the buildings smelled of sawn wood and hard work. Bits of the pre-Devastation past, the days when magic ran the world, poked their way in — ancient claw-shaped lampposts lined the street and two grounders, stripped of parts, had been parked off to the side.

Malja straightened in the saddle, letting the sunset give her a more majestic, authoritative image. Her horse reacted to the change in posture and straightened too. As with all the towns they had liberated, she would need the townspeople behind her, and they needed to see her strength in order to believe. She glanced down at the eyes watching her from the streets. Though the grit of violence clung to her long-coat and form-fitting assault suit, promising a woman of battle, she wanted to project at least a tinge of hope. It seemed that every town they had visited required her to muscle out the warlords and self-declared rulers. Perhaps this one would be different.

Tommy reined in his bay mare, pulling back just behind Malja. He should have been a masterful rider by now, but he had spent the better parts of his early years tied up in a cargo ship, forced to use his magic to power the engines. That's where his anger should go — at those who hurt him. She had done nothing but raise and protect him.

"We may have finally lucked out," Fawbry said from the rear. His black horse whinnied in agreement, and Fawbry laughed.

Sometimes, especially when she had to kill a lot, Malja loved the sound of Fawbry's laugh. "Just keep your eyes clear," she said. They had gone through so many towns that the entire experience blended into mush.

"Don't worry. I'm using my eyes well," Fawbry said, leering at two plump girls standing in a doorway. They giggled at his attention. "This town seems like a nice place."

"Tommy. Sleeves," Malja said.

She didn't have to look back to feel his anger. He thrust his sleeves down to cover his tattoos anyway. Too many people feared magicians — not only because they had caused the Devastation so long ago, but because so many lost their minds by using magic. Malja couldn't afford to have the townspeople turn against them because of Tommy.

They rode through a bustling market filled with colorful stalls and energetic haggling. Fresh breads and sizzling meats perfumed the air. But Malja noticed how the townspeople glimpsed her from the side as if they were putting on a play and wanted to see if their audience believed.

Sorry, Fawbry, she thought, *this is going to be like all the others.*

As if in response, people stopped sneaking looks. The vibrant noise died. The bustling activity ceased. Cold, staring eyes followed Malja and her companions as they pushed forward through the street.

"Tommy. There." She nodded ahead to a wide stage made of stones and concrete.

Tommy took his bay toward the left side of the stage. With a gesture of her head, Malja sent Fawbry to the right side. Once they were in position, Malja rode right up the middle, dismounted with a flourish, and planted herself center stage.

"I am Malja," she said, letting her voice boom over the heads of the gathered crowd. She paused to allow the murmur to settle. In the last year, she had been through this process so many times she could sleep through the whole thing and still know what happened. "I am here to bring you freedom. I am here to bring you law. The country of Corlin has been at war with itself since the Devastation, a playground for opportunists to bully good folk like you into submission. No more."

She paused. Usually either a joyful hope infected the crowd or an elder fired off a question designed to challenge her. This time, however, she met only silence.

"I have traveled from town to town, across Corlin, and in each town, I have defeated those that wish to control you. And when I leave, I leave behind the three laws with which you can take control of your future."

By now, the audience should have brought out their dictator or erupted into celebration. Instead, they shuffled their feet and stared at her as if she spoke some foreign tongue. She even saw one man slink away from the crowd.

Tommy and Fawbry shared an uncertain glance. She kept her face forward, cleared her throat, and spoke in strong, unwavering tones. "There's no need to fear me. Follow my laws, and we can all be free from control.

"Law one — Do nothing to another that you would not want done to you.

"Law two — When in doubt, leave the other alone.

"Law three — Before using magic, do for yourself.

"Follow these laws, and there is no need for anybody to police you. We can rule ourselves with the simple sense the brother gods, Korstra and Kryssta, gave us all."

A man's voice from the crowd called out. "Go away. We're fine here without you."

"That may be. You appear well-off and happy. I don't want to impede that. I simply want to make sure all of you are free."

She stared at the blank faces staring back. An uneasy sensation coated the space between them. This was all wrong.

A high-toned howl cut into the silence, echoing across the market, followed by a lower, nastier growl. Fear sliced through the crowd as if the earth might tremble and split open. The heinous cry came again.

A rush of activity ignited. The crowd dispersed. Sellers closed their stands. Mothers ushered their children away. Men looked into the distance, swallowing against their nervousness. In seconds, the market was deserted.

Fawbry stepped down from the stage. "Perhaps I should check on the young ladies and make sure—"

"Get back," Malja said.

Wrapping his multi-colored robe around him, Fawbry scooted back to the stage. Tommy never wavered. Malja expected no less.

At the far end of the road, two men on horseback approached.

The first wore only a satchel and a loin cloth, displaying his lanky body, sun-browned skin, and bald head with an arrogance reserved for those of the mystical arts. Malja saw at least five tattoos on his right leg. He also had a black stripe tattooed on his head — this last one, mere decoration.

The other man, dressed in a drab coat, stared at the one small tattoo on his arm. Lost in a trance, he rocked with his horse's movements but showed no other recognition of the world around him — amateur. As they came down the dim street, each lamppost ignited with a crackling lightning ball. Malja wondered if the lesser magician enjoyed being a glorified generator.

The first magician halted, rested his arm on the saddle's pommel, and from across the empty roadway, he said, "I am Eldred. Are you who I think you are? *The* Malja?"

Malja closed her eyes and tried to clear her head. "I am."

Gesturing to the town, Eldred said, "All this belongs to me. I protect this town, ensure its prosperity. And in return, they give me food, women, and once a month, they sacrifice one of their own, so that I may provide through the magic of blood."

Malja shrugged. "So you're running a protection racket."

Eldred raised an eyebrow. "These people are happy and civilized, well fed, comfortable. They have all they need. This is how it was before the Devastation. This is how it was meant to be. We magicians provide the crops, the power supply, the healing, the justice. We make civilization civilized. Why shouldn't we be paid for such services?"

"Blood sacrifices are not civilized."

Eldred chuckled. "I suspect you have an ocean of blood on your hands. Far more than I could ever match. And what have you provided in return?"

Malja pulled Viper from its special sheath. The unique weapon, curved like a giant sickle with both the inner- and outer-crescents sharpened, rested in her hand with the familiarity of her own body. Viper was part of her.

"This doesn't need to be a fight," she said. "You can walk away or even stay as one of the townspeople. All will be forgiven. In this world, people lose their way. You have. But I offer you a chance to begin again. Please, take it."

"I see," Eldred said and snapped his fingers. A burly man, struggling to control three leashed konapols, stepped out from an alleyway nearby. "This is my answer."

Half-intelligent creatures with a pack structure, konapols had thin gray fur covering powerful, toned muscles, front legs that crushed anything in their way, and old, wrinkled faces that were at odds with the vicious teeth they hid. Their hind legs, though small, could deliver a kick strong enough to knock a person unconscious. The domesticated konapols were small and used to patrol gates. These, however, were wild.

They snapped at the burly man holding their leashes. They snarled and strained against their bonds. Malja had seen the domestic versions before, but these huge creatures promised a far more difficult fight.

"Release them," Eldred said, and the burly man did as ordered.

Two of the konapols broke into a full press attack, covering great distances with each stride. Malja leaped from the stage and dashed towards the beasts. When they were in striking distance, the konapol on the left jumped into the air while the other stayed low — teeth bared, claws out, making deep guttural barks.

Malja saw her play like it had been mapped out long before. She stepped forward and swung Viper in an arc. The blade sliced through the airborne konapol's neck as if there were no bones connecting it to the body. Before the carcass could smack into the ground, Malja used the momentum of her swing to spin around and lodge Viper into the chest of the other attacker. With a surprised howl, the konapol swatted the blade out of his chest, causing more damage to the wound.

Malja kicked his front claw, breaking a bone with an audible click. He reared back, rage spitting from his mouth in a torrent of noise and saliva. Malja swished Viper across the unprotected gut, and the konapol dropped into a dead ball.

The konapol that had stayed behind paced back and forth, its eyes narrowed, its mouth dripping with saliva. Beyond the creature, Malja saw that Eldred had brought his one leg over the saddle and fixated on his tattoos.

Malja raised Viper, blood racing down its sharp edges. Her fierce eyes, her strong stance, and her unwavering focus crossed the distance to the konapol like a gunshot. The animal hesitated for a fraction of a second. Enough to let Malja know she had the advantage.

With a roar of hot, stale breath, the creature lunged forward, galloping towards her with its teeth bared. It barreled down the dirt road, spit streaming back from its wrinkled jowls. Animal rage had taken over what little thought it could muster.

Letting loose her battle cry, Malja sprinted ahead. Her legs pumped hard as she positioned Viper below her intended strike point. The world disappeared. She saw only the konapol, only the dust and dirt sputtering around it, only the muscular body she sought to cut down.

The konapol lowered its head, its powerful stride thundering against the ground. Malja pushed harder, trying to close the distance fast. And in a flash, they passed each other. Malja flicked Viper upward to the strike point, giving the blade a slight twist for maximum power, and slashed open the konapol's flank.

It slid on the dirt street, confused and trying to find its enemy again. Its momentum did not take well to the sudden turn, and the konapol's inner-gore slopped out of the opening Malja had cut. With a curious gaze at its side, the konapol halted. It seemed to consider the horror of what it saw as it fell with a wet thump.

Malja knew well the stillness that followed — a quiet comes over the battlefield for a precious moment while those left standing decide if things really are finished or if the lust for blood still boiled. From the middle of the road, she surveyed her work. Three dead konapols.

She lifted her head and shined a cocky grin at Eldred. But her grin faltered. She had made a crucial mistake.

The konapols had been more than a diversion. They provided Eldred with blood. This was all just a stalling tactic to afford Eldred enough time to cast a spell. She had to move fast.

Malja snapped her attention to the konapol corpses. The gore pooling around the dead beasts trembled. Blood pulled into a tight ball and sprouted green tendrils. A plant. It shot out runners like snakes, each one reaching out for Malja.

She slashed the first with ease. Cutting through vines would not be any trouble. But looking further back, she saw the plant's main body growing thicker, tougher. The new runners it sent out were equally thick and tough. And there were more of them.

Malja rushed toward Eldred. Kill the magician, kill the magic. She moved fast, but a quarter of the way in, one tendril wrapped around her leg and pulled her off her feet.

She slashed through it, but by the time she stood, another two had replaced it. Fury flooded her as she hacked tendril after tendril. Using Viper like a scythe, she wiped a circle around her free from the plant, but it only lasted seconds. Konapols had a lot of blood, giving Eldred a lot of material to work with.

Before she could reposition for another swipe, three thick runners spun around and took her back to the ground. She held tight to Viper but couldn't move. The plant rolled her so she faced away from Eldred. She saw Fawbry sneak off to the side. He'll pay for such cowardice. She also saw Tommy bare his tattooed arm as he walked straight towards her.

Don't do this, she thought. *I can handle this.*

But as another tendril covered her mouth, she knew she needed somebody's help. Since Fawbry ran off, that left only Tommy.

Tommy raised his arm and glanced at the tattoos for only a few seconds. The ground shook. Two holes opened and swallowed two konapols. Tommy kept walking forward.

Just like that. Malja froze. She had no idea the boy could conjure such power so quickly.

Tommy turned his attention on the third dead konapol, the one that spawned the plant. But before he could raise his arm, the plant fought back. A new set of runners sprang out and twined around Tommy's arm. With his free hand, he tried to pull them off. They were too strong and too numerous.

Eldred patted the head of his fellow magician. "You see that? That is why we magicians will always rule. We aren't feral fools who try to violently slash our way through every problem. We can use our magic and our intelligence, and we can solve problems with finesse."

The other magician beamed. Eldred then raised his voice to address the townspeople who watched from the alleyways and windows. "I will not hold Affengar responsible for this foolish assault. I know of Malja and her attempts to rule Corlin. But she is learning now that she is not your savior. She is not the law. She's just a nuisance. Your real savior, your real law, is the great Queen Salia of the North. From her palace in

Salia City, she reaches out like my plants and takes firm hold of those around her. In return for your loyalty, she provides peace and a world in which you have the chance to prosper."

Malja had wrenched her head around to catch Eldred gloating. Since the plant had not tried to smother her to death, she guessed Eldred planned something else for her — probably public humiliation designed to bolster his stance with the townspeople. Either that or a more "legal" execution.

He dismounted, and with his hands raised, Eldred spoke on, savoring his moment. Malja squinted. A shadow behind the magician moved, a shape she recognized — Fawbry.

"Never forget your loyalty to Queen Salia and she will never forget to protect you," Eldred went on.

Fawbry raised his hand high above his head. He held something — a rock. He slammed it down on Eldred's head. The magician's face locked into a sly grin as his body weaved from side to side.

Eldred's partner tackled Fawbry. The two rolled on the ground, clumsy in their inexperienced grappling. They traded punches to the ribs but appeared more winded from the efforts than the blows.

Though he wasn't knocked unconscious, Eldred lost the focus necessary to maintain his magic. The vines constraining Malja and Tommy loosened.

Tommy wrenched his arm free, glanced at his tattoos, and cast his spell. The plant lost its color in seconds. It changed from green to brown to a pale, sickly white. When he finished, the tendrils that surrounded Malja crumbled to the ground, leaving behind a chalky residue and a bitter odor.

With Viper in hand, Malja raced the final distance toward her enemy. Eldred watched her approach with a quizzical look as if he couldn't identify what she was. That look remained even as she removed his head from his body.

Fawbry pushed Eldred's partner back and when the man saw Eldred's head, he pointed at it, cried out once, and dashed for his horse. Malja, Tommy, and Fawbry stood in the street and watched this novice struggle to get his foot in the stirrup. His horse did not co-operate. After a lot of gasping, some cursing, and another weak cry, he managed to get into the saddle and gallop off.

"Admit it," Fawbry said, his unkempt hair dirtier now from rolling in the road. "You thought I had run away."

Malja slapped Fawbry on the shoulder. "Doesn't matter what I thought. You did well, and I thank you. Now, let's go before we have to deal with the town."

Too late. The townspeople hurried out of their hiding spots, all smiles and giddy laughter, and rushed over to thank Malja and her crew. With false modesty, Fawbry allowed two buxom ladies to walk him off while listening to him recount what had just occurred. Others surrounded Tommy, unbothered by his silence, and offered him drinks and hugs and even a few kisses.

Malja waved off those who approached her and scowled at any who tried to congratulate her. She knew none of it was genuine. They simply wanted to ingratiate themselves with who they thought now ruled them. Only after a few days alone might they understand they were now free to choose their own path.

Fawbry let out a high laugh and his girls tittered. Malja grinned. He would definitely get one of the girls before the night ended. She would have gladly scouted out a suitable man for her own amusement, such opportunities didn't come often to a traveling warrior, but this night, she had to deal with the boy. She brushed by a few open arms and grabbed Tommy by the elbow.

"Go celebrate," she said to those who followed her. "I've got to confer with my friend here. Then we'll join the party."

Deeper in the growing crowd, somebody opened a barrel of wine. That was enough to pull the stragglers away from Malja. No amount of celebrity could outshine free alcohol.

Once they were far enough from eavesdroppers, Malja whirled Tommy around. "Don't you ever do that again," she said.

Tommy glared at her.

Owl

The afternoon had cooled from the rains but not uncomfortably so, and Owl preferred it that way. Standing in the Great Field, an open plain that crossed the entire Penmarvian countryside, he tried hard not to bounce from foot to foot while Chief Master knelt on a mat and meditated. Soon, Queen Salia would arrive and a meeting in search of peace would begin. Owl had to make sure that meeting went smoothly.

His eyes shifted amongst the patches of overgrown grass surrounding them. While Chief Master could spend the time quieting his mind, Owl's job required vigilance. All his years of training in the Way were finally being brought to the test.

They had promoted him to Guardian that morning. They gave him a tailored tan coat that both looked sharp, with its fancy inner-lining of swirls, and allowed him the range of motion needed to fight. Their trust for Chief Master's safety had been placed upon him.

"It's perfectly fine for you to meditate now," Chief Master said, his aged voice standing out in the wide field. "We're in no danger."

"Of course, we are," Owl said, and though his voice was calm, his face betrayed his tension. For once, he felt grateful for his dark skin — Chief Master never could read Owl's face well.

When he first came to the Order as an orphan, all the Masters marveled at his dark skin. They had heard about such people living in the wild South of Corlin, but in Penmarvia, people tended to be either pale or tan. At eighty-seven, Chief Master was too set in his world view and continued to have difficulty.

He placed his bony hand on Owl's knee. "You must learn to listen to all my lessons. Not just the ones that suit you."

"Forgive me," Owl said, bowing his head.

Chief Master chuckled like a creaking door. "Being here has certainly put you on edge. A warrior is no good to anyone, least of all himself, if his mind is clouded and his body tense. Besides, this is not a day for battle. It's just politics."

"Yes, Chief Master, I understand."

"If you understand so well, then why are you still standing?"

Owl knelt next to Chief Master. The wet ground soaked through his thin pants, staining the simple gray cloth with mud. He clenched his eyes and tried to force a sense of calm. Instead, he shivered.

His hands danced over the hilt of his sword and the grip of his gun. His sword was a perfect weapon — thin, balanced, and sleek, yet sturdy and deadly. His gun had a simple design. Few remained who knew how to make guns, but simple didn't mean useless. It had a dual-chamber allowing one shot more than most, and he kept it in perfect working condition — as he had been trained.

With a huff, he got up and brushed off his pants. "I can't stop worrying about being here. When you first told me I was to be your escort, I should have been ecstatic. I know what this means. But I keep wondering — why me? Brother X is a far better fighter."

"Not as far as you think. You are probably the second best we have trained."

"But he's first. He's the best. You've trained all the Guardians in the Way of the Sword and Gun so that we could protect every magician in the Order. Why isn't he here protecting you?"

"Breathe in, Owl. Hold. Now, let it go. You worry so much. Brother X has been gone for a few weeks. So, even if I had wanted to use him, he's not around to be used. But I also know that life often presents opportunities, if we are willing to grasp them. You are more than capable of succeeding today. I have the fullest faith in you. So, why not enjoy this opportunity? All of this world has suffered in the generations since the Devastation. We must learn to find the pleasure in any moment. We've enough pain."

Owl snickered. "You never stop teaching me."

"All my pupils will always be my pupils. Since the day you came to us, I knew I wanted to teach you. That's the joy of being Chief Master. We get to focus on the most promising students."

"But the Queen—"

"The Queen is the Queen. We have no control over what she will say or do. We'll simply present our views and pray to the brother god Kryssta that she can be reasoned with. Besides, it's not like she's a follower of Korstra."

"That would be a travesty," Queen Salia said as she stepped off her transport — a huge box-shaped vehicle pulled by three magician-powered flyers tethered with long cables. The flyers, small dart-shaped crafts, made a low hum as they hovered.

She moved with grace as she approached Chief Master on his plain mat. With her shoulders held back proud like a strutting bird, she lifted a perfect eyebrow and waited to be acknowledged. Her golden hair, straight at the jawline, formed a crown that only heightened the jeweled tiara resting atop her head.

Owl snapped to attention. He should never have listened to Chief Master. How could he be excused for letting the Queen approach without noticing?

Chief Master placed his hands on the mat and brought his chin to his chest showing great respect. "May Kryssta watch over you."

Though he remained standing, Owl repeated the phrase, "May Kryssta watch over you."

"And you both," Salia said, standing a few feet before them.

With a labored groan, Chief Master rose to his feet, his knees crackling as he moved. "Oh, for a younger man's body. Enjoy your youth, both of you, for like power, it is always temporary."

Salia's eyes widened. "Are you really beginning with threats?"

"No, no, you misunderstand. I have great respect for you and for your strength. Sometimes my mind likes to make little observations, that's all. I'm sure you'll hold on to your power for a long time."

Salia seemed placated but wary. Owl felt the same. He'd been Chief Master's pupil for so long, had spent so many years seeing the man display the strongest spirit, that it seemed bizarre to watch him behave as an inferior. Chief Master had said this was politics, but just in the opening words, Owl found the whole thing confusing. Who had the real power? The old man who showed weakness or the grand Queen who showed arrogance?

"You are wasting this audience," Salia said.

Chief Master bent over unnecessarily — Owl knew the old man could stand firm and strong — which made him appear smaller. "My apologies. And thank you for meeting us without all the pageantry and soldiers."

"I have no fear of you."

"Nor should you. But it is a great sign of your trust, and we acknowledge it. Though you requested this meeting, I am most grateful for the opportunity. I come on behalf of the Order of Kryssta for I see great potential in an alliance between us."

"A bunch of magicians?"

"The best magicians. We have devoted our lives to the study of magic and a resurrection of the wonderful benefits magic once brought this world."

Salia's face darkened. "Like the Devastation. Meddling with powers you didn't understand took everything away, destroyed all the cities, killed off nearly all the life. My own scientists have calculated that the Devastation probably left our species with maybe a million people. On the entire planet."

"And we feel the full gravity of those events every day. We understand why so many fear us. But generations have passed since those days. And, if properly trained both in magic and in Kryssta, there is no reason for magicians to lose their way ever again. We once powered the world with buildings that flew and vehicles that moved on their own. We brought light into homes and created ways for people to communicate over vast distances in an instant. With your help, we can do this again. Safely. Carefully. And you, as Queen, will have the most control over this power."

"And in return?"

Chief Master stepped closer to Salia, his back straightening just a bit. "We wish to be allowed to cross the Great Field and find a safe haven in Salia City. My magicians can provide for the people, but we will not become slaves nor will we allow persecution."

"Interesting word." Salia stepped in front of Owl, moving in precise, stiff motions. She looked him over and said, "Tell me, Guard Dog, what does he teach you of persecution?"

Owl looked to Chief Master, but there was no way to receive any instructions other than a nod. "I-I know that fear can make people do many things they wouldn't do otherwise."

Raising her eyebrows, Salia said, "Let me take Chief Master's place for just a moment and educate you." She pushed close against Owl's side. She smelled of flowers — he didn't know the names — and that delicate aroma made her words more threatening. "When the Devastation came," she said, "the world fell into anarchy, chaos. Many lands, like those in the South, were sparse to begin with which made it easier for them to survive on their own terms. In Penmarvia, however, we lived in densely-packed cities. Even after the Devastation struck, even after so many millions upon millions died, there were still too many to get along easily."

Trying to sound understanding, Owl said, "I know my history."

"Do you? Did the Order teach you how they formed to protect themselves from the backlash against magic, and then, when they

264 - The Malja Chronicles

thought it safe, they descended upon the city and carved it up between them? Each Order magician claimed a section, and each magician answered to nobody. Isn't that right, Chief Master?"

"That was a different time," Chief Master said. "Long before any of us was even a glimmer of thought."

"The problem with you magicians is that you *never* bother with those glimmers, never think about tomorrow. You just satisfy your immediate desires, and you're never satisfied."

"That's enough," Chief Master said, and though his voice remained steady, Owl saw the flash of fire in his eyes.

Salia matched it with her own fury. "You and your kind's insatiable desires created war upon war within the blocks of my city. I don't care how long ago it began. It was still going on when I grew up. It was the world I lived in."

Through a forced, placating expression, Chief Master said, "You changed all that. You rallied the people, defeated those misguided magicians . . . and disposed of them. You brought Salia City into prosperity. It is the reason you are called Queen. In recognition, we retreated to the other side of the Great Field and built the Order compound. Please. I have spent my life educating my students about peace. We are ready to work for your people as equals."

Salia crossed her arms. "Strange how you've chosen now to come before me."

"How so?"

"When I first became Queen I offered to discuss terms between our kinds so that we could live peacefully. I was rejected."

"That was a different time, and I wasn't Chief Master then."

Salia raised her index finger. "I think you are here today because you know I have recruited my own magicians and use them like dogs on the outlying towns, helping me bring more people into my fold. You're here because you know that when I finish with these magicians, they'll be executed. And I think you suspect my army is closing in on the Order compound."

"Please, listen. We have much to offer."

"We have no need for sharing with magicians, and we certainly have no need for the Order. As descendants and accomplices of those who tortured us, your very existence is a constant threat to ours."

Chief Master clenched his fists and said in a voice Owl had only ever heard when he wanted to cow a student, "Listen to me now. We have a chance to create peace before there is war."

Salia patted her chest in mock surprise. "Now that sounds like a real threat."

Chief Master pulled back his sleeves and raised his arms. It was a dramatic pose, but it served a practical purpose — Chief Master could easily see the tattoos he needed in order to enact a spell. Things had turned sour so quickly that Owl's skin prickled when he saw the pose. His hands moved toward his weapons, prepared just in case.

Without losing a sliver of her amused expression, Salia said, "Just like your kind. You don't like a situation, you resort to magic. What's the matter, Chief Master? Not really good at diplomacy? Can't you handle things on your own? Perhaps dear Kryssta will help you."

"How dare you!" Chief Master's eyes blazed wide open. "You act like a Korstra-worshiper, whining that life has been hard and unfair. You're a child who has wet her pants and doesn't know what to do."

"You forget your place."

"I know our history better than you. I know what it's like to be persecuted day after day for something you had nothing to do with. And now, after generations, it seemed we had all settled into an uneasy co-existence. I came here in good faith to solidify that peace, to make it so that no man, no magician, ever needed to fear again. But if your intention is to expand your holdings while misusing and abusing my people, then you will feel the full wrath of a magician."

Salia opened her arms wide and grinned. "It's a good thing, then, that my army has not been approaching your Order. Rather my army has been decimating the Order this whole time."

"W-What?" Chief Master stumbled back as if struck in the chest.

Owl rushed to his side.

"The Order is no more," Salia said, her voice harsh now. Calculating. "The magicians are all dead. And the Library is mine."

Chief Master fell to one knee. "The Library? That's not possible. How do you even know about it?"

Salia gestured toward the darkness of the transport. "Why he told me, of course."

A man dressed in fine crimson robes stepped out. His strong frame supported an arrogant swagger that Owl had seen many times before. Even if Owl's mind refused to acknowledge the truth, seeing the fine sword and well-made gun on this figure's waist could not be denied.

"Brother X?" Chief Master said, tears filling his eyes.

Owl pulled out his sword and gun in one practiced motion. Before he had settled into his fighting stance, though, Brother X flashed out his own weapons and closed in. Owl danced backward with graceful ease, but Brother X's speed startled him.

"Now, now," Salia said and Brother X halted. "We don't want these two dead. Not yet."

Chief Master never took his eyes off his prized pupil. With his hands trembling, he managed one question. "How long?"

Brother X lifted his lip with such disdain that Chief Master's breath caught. Salia moved between the two. "Your dear Brother X has always worked for me. From the day he joined the Order, he has fed me information. All you are has always been mine. We just had to wait for the right time to strike."

Owl knew he shouldn't speak, but he could not hold back. He pointed his blade at Brother X, its tip shivering like his voice. "I-I wanted to be like you. I-I thought you were our best."

"He is your best," Salia said. "And soon he'll be even better. Now that I know of the Library and the Twelve Books; now that the Books are in my possession."

Owl opened his mouth to curse them but a grating laughter stopped him. To his side, Chief Master covered his grinning mouth like an embarrassed child. Even as his eyes continued to tear, he laughed.

"You have nothing," he said, sounding a bit drunk. Then, he stepped forward, and his stern, masterful voice returned. "You have *nothing*. The Library, the Twelve Books, the Order — you have destroyed or taken it all. Congratulations. But Brother X only knows what we tell him." Salia's gloating face faltered. Chief Master went on, "And since you've been here, you haven't had the chance to see the treasures you have won."

"What of it?" Salia snapped.

"Do you really think the learned men and women of the Order would just let our most dangerous knowledge sit around for anybody to take hold of? That was the kind of irresponsible thing magicians did in the past." Chief Master looked at his hands and shook his head. "We were bad people long ago. But no more. The Books are in code, and you'll never find the thirteenth book to decode them."

"And why is that?" Salia asked through gritted teeth.

"I suspect you've destroyed it along with everything else that was useful at the Order. Just like I'll destroy you."

With a flick of his wrist, Chief Master turned his hands outward. Too late, everyone realized that Chief Master hadn't been staring at his hands in regret but rather had been building another spell. A bolt of ice shot from his hand creating a vapor trail in the cool air.

Brother X moved so fast, so fluid, that Owl barely had time to marvel let alone react. Twirling like a Master of the Way, Brother X knocked the ice aside with his sword. As his body spun around, his other hand brandished a handgun that glinted a shred of sunlight. He fired.

Chief Master dropped to the ground, clutching his side. Brother X continued his spinning motion, whipping his sword around for a death cut to the neck. Owl finally snapped into action.

"Chief Master!" he screamed, his sword deflecting Brother X's attack.

He pointed his handgun underneath the crossed swords, but Brother X twisted in the opposite direction. As Brother X unwound, he again used the spinning motion to strike at Chief Master. Owl whirled forward, closing the distance between them, and elbowed Brother X in the stomach. With a powerful hand, Brother X shoved Owl away and both spun into a proper fighting stance.

Salia backed up to her transport. "You've been taught well."

Owl glanced toward her, and when he saw her blood-thirsty grin, he knew he had made a mistake. The glance had lasted no more than a second, but to a fighter as skilled as Brother X, it might as well have been an hour. Just as Owl comprehended his error, Brother X flashed by him. Owl could smell the sweat on his opponent and heard the blade cut into Chief Master.

"Protect the book," Chief Master said, his voice gurgling with blood, his words dying with his body.

Though not as fast as Brother X, Owl didn't just stand there like an open target. He dashed forward, lifting his gun, and leveled the weapon at Salia's head. Brother X would be attacking, but Owl couldn't look behind — Chief Master's lifeless body was there. Only one thing remained — revenge.

But before he could pull the trigger, Owl felt a blade cut his side. Brother X struck the right points to force Owl's hand open — a precision move that required great skill. If he severed a nerve or hit the wrong point, the hand might lock down instead. The gun tumbled away. Owl slipped in the mud. Brother X slashed upward, spinning Owl until he rolled against Chief Master.

"Thank you," Salia said.

Owl didn't move. There was no point. He could never move fast enough to avoid a death blow. While Brother X watched his body for signs of life, Owl kept his face buried in Chief Master's bleeding chest and remained motionless. He didn't move or breathe.

"Come now," Salia said. "I've got to see those Books. If that bastard magician told the truth, we have a serious problem."

Brother X kicked Owl in the leg and trudged off. Only when Owl heard the transport recede into the distance did he stop pretending to be dead. He checked Chief Master's body — no breath, no heartbeat, no life.

Owl cried.

Malja

With his weight on one foot and his eyes looking past her shoulder, Tommy's impertinence grated on Malja. She wanted to shake him hard, even slap him — anything to get him to listen to what she wanted to say. But just because he refused to hear it all once more didn't mean he'd get his way.

"I'm sick of dealing with your magic," she said. "I've asked you many times to hold back on it. It's dangerous and destructive to yourself. And every single time you use it, you show me such disrespect; you're saying you don't care about anything I say. You spit in my face. Do you understand that?"

Tommy rolled his eyes.

"I'm not exaggerating," she went on. "This is too important for you to pull this crap with me."

Tommy pointed to the white dust in the road — the remains of the plant that had immobilized Malja.

"Don't you try to claim that you saved me. If anything, Fawbry saved us both. You just got in the way." She knew she should stop, but her blood was hot and her mouth kept moving. "And the next time you want to cast a spell, you just remember who saves your ass over and over again. I don't ask much from you."

Tommy's eyes widened.

"I don't. But I do ask you to not use your magic. Yet you keep defying me on that one. Well, stop it or maybe I won't be there to save your foolish butt next time. What's the point if you're just going to rot your brain casting spells? Don't become something I'm going to hate."

The words hung in the air between them. Tommy tried to hold his composure, tried to look tough, but she could see the quiver in his eyes, the hurt underneath. Her shoulders dropped and she reached for him, but he brushed her aside just like she had done to the townspeople.

"Tommy, wait," she called. He ignored her, returning to the celebrating town.

She watched him go, guessing he would grab some wine and get drunk. She was wrong.

He cut through the crowd until he reached their horses. With a fierce jump, he mounted the saddle and galloped off. She rushed down the street for her own horse, but by the time she had mounted, Tommy was gone.

Let him go, she thought. *He just needs to calm down. Then he'll be back.*

But as the party raged on, Tommy did not return. Malja stuck to the less raucous parts of the street, one eye always in the direction he had left. And she waited.

Hours passed.

Though she hated to reveal any weakness, her growing unease overcame her tactical sense. She weaved through the celebrating crowd, scanning the faces for Fawbry. When she overheard a circle of girls giggling about their libidinous friend, Villy, and how she'll thank the hero seven times and then some, Malja broke in and found out where the couple had gone.

One block down. The house on the right. The red door with a half-moon carving.

Malja checked for Tommy one last time. Still nothing. She burst into the house.

Fawbry froze. He was kneeling on a thick blanket. Villy, an ample woman, had her backside pressed against him. Neither wore any clothes.

"Wait your turn, honey," Villy said in a charming shrill.

With a shake of his head, Fawbry said, "You couldn't bother to knock?"

"Get dressed," Malja said and politely turned around. As she listened to Fawbry placate Villy, promising this interruption would only take a moment, Malja felt a twinge of guilt. They had so few chances for any kind of pleasure in life. Why should she spoil Fawbry's just because she had a fight with Tommy? And Villy deserved some pleasure too, though Malja never cared for that position — too subservient. But Villy sure seemed happy.

Jerking his robe on, Fawbry stepped into the street. "What is it?" he said as Malja followed him out.

"I'm worried about Tommy."

"This is the urgent thing? Tommy? You always worry about him."

"We had a fight."

"You always have a fight."

"He took a horse and went off. That was hours ago."

Placing his hands on his hips, Fawbry said, "Oh, Kryssta. He's fourteen. Don't you understand that yet? He's moody and he's testing you. That's all. He just wants to know you'll stick by him no matter what."

"What more proof does he need? I destroyed that portal to save his life." She didn't have to explain further. Fawbry had been there when Jarik and Callib, Malja's now-dead fathers, used magic to open a portal into another world. But she did have to tell him what she saw. "A woman. There was a woman in that portal and she wore the same black assault suit that I have. I've no idea who she is, but Jarik and Callib didn't lie about this much — that was my home world. And I threw away that chance to save Tommy's life. How can he not know I'm here for him?"

"You don't stop thinking about that world, though. He sees you at night, looking off, muttering to yourself. I see it, too. You haven't given up the hope that you'll find a way back there."

Malja checked down the street to make sure nobody was listening, and maybe to see if Tommy had returned. "That part of my life is over. We've been doing well now, spreading my law around Corlin. We're making things better here." She pictured the world she had seen through that portal — civilized, structured, powerful, happy. A world that hadn't been wiped out by the Devastation, that didn't know magicians could go crazy. She could stop fighting in such a place. Even enjoy true peace.

Fawbry pointed at her. "That's the look." She glared at him with her harsh eyes and though he maintained his composure, his finger trembled. "Now, now. I'm on your side. I'm here to help."

"Then help. How do I fix this?"

"You don't. You give him time. He'll be back in the morning. And tomorrow, he'll be just as moody as he was today. You be there and you wait. And I'll even pray to Kryssta for you. Someday, he'll outgrow all this, and he'll look up to find you. So, you be there."

"What if he gets injured out in the forest? What if he needs our help now? You don't even care."

"Don't you dare," Fawbry said, jumping to a level of anger Malja had never seen in him before. "I've been by your side for over a year. I've risked my life for the two of you and watched you fawn over him and ignore any contribution I've made. I've taken your belittling jokes with a smile, and yet I stick by you. I don't run away even though you think I will, and I even saved your ass more than once. Just today, in case you forgot. And you dare question if I care?"

Malja looked away, clenching her fists. Through gritted teeth, she said, "I'm sorry."

"You should be. I want to think of us as, at least, a team. But you seem determined to make me feel worthless. Well, I care more about that boy than you'll ever understand." He stomped back to the red door. "He's growing up, and he's powerful. And he knows you don't want to be stuck here with us. So don't worry about him. He'll be fine out there. You, though, you should do some growing up yourself."

The red door slammed shut leaving Malja in the empty street. The celebration played on just a block away, and she listened to the laughter and cheering and drinking and joking as if observing a strange new species. There was a horrible, violent world surrounding them, yet these people found a way to ignore it all. They had pulled together as a true community and celebrated a simple victory.

She meandered back to the main street where a group of drunken men took the public stage and re-enacted the battle to the joy of onlookers. Many people danced to the thumping sound of a guitar and washbasin drum. Some couples walked off to darker corners, leaning on each other, holding hands, kissing.

Malja found a chair separate from the group. She positioned it to watch the direction where Tommy had galloped off. Perhaps Fawbry spoke the truth. Perhaps not. She only knew that this night would bring no answer to such a complicated question. For now, all she could do was wait. And worry.

Later, Fawbry approached with a satisfied smile plastered on his face. One stern look snapped that smile off. He followed her gaze down the street. "He's still not back?"

Malja shook her head. To her relief, Fawbry's eye twitched and he let out a shaky breath. "Okay, then," he said. "Let's go look."

The party had broken into a few straggling groups. Two stumbling individuals cleaned up some and made more mess elsewhere. Most of the town had gone to bed or had passed out in the street. Those that remained were too drunk to notice the heroes mount their horses and ride out.

Malja guided her horse at a walk. She didn't want her horse to be injured galloping in the dark. And she needed to observe her surroundings closely. But such careful scrutiny turned out to be unnecessary.

About ten minutes out, Malja's horse balked and refused to go on. A dark mound like a wide boulder blocked the road. Malja dismounted and approached the mound.

"This feels bad," Fawbry said.

Malja hated how Fawbry talked when nervous — he gave away their position and distracted her concentration. This time, however, she worried more about the mound than scolding the man.

In the dim moonlight, she could just see the scuffle marks of two men and a boy. On a nearby tree, she saw scorch marks and the air bore the sour stench of magic. A chill covered her skin.

The mound was no boulder. Tommy's horse lay on the road. Dead. Blood formed a dark pool around its body.

Malja dashed back and vaulted up on her horse. Fawbry stared at the mound, clearly afraid to ask her.

She answered the unspoken question. "Tommy's in trouble."

Owl

Owl stumbled out of the little town's tavern and weaved around two men coming in. The night air braced his skin while his stomach argued against the alcoholic abuse he had self-inflicted. As his body convulsed, he caught the porch railing in time to avoid falling face first into the mud and retched.

Wiping his mouth with his sleeve, Owl patted the railing. Even drunk, his reflexes still worked.

If only they had worked as well against Brother X.

From a few windows, Owl saw people spying on him. Late-night gossips. Easy to dismiss under normal circumstances, but gossip about him would alert Brother X. He would know Owl was alive. Owl had no doubt that Brother X would search for him — might be searching right now. Not only was Owl the last living warrior trained and true to the Way of the Sword and Gun, but he was probably the only real threat to Brother X. And Brother X heard Chief Master tell Owl to protect the book.

"Except," Owl slurred to the night, "I don't know where it is. I don't even know what it looks like. If I saw it, I wouldn't know."

Wobbling toward the stables, he laughed. "Oh, Chief Master, you sure bungled this one. You picked the wrong man to protect the Order's secrets." Stopping in the middle of the road, he raised his hands to the sky and shouted, "Look at me! I failed you. I had a job to do — and now look."

He heard the familiar pattern of thumping hooves. Brushing aside the tears on his cheeks, Owl teetered toward the nearest alley. To his drunken eye, the ground kept rolling, and anyone observing would have seen a man taking wide, unsteady steps, but he managed to get into the shadows before the riders arrived.

From his vantage, he watched them tramp by. They never even stopped to look around. Either they weren't after him, or they thought he had gone farther away than this town.

I should've gone farther. I should've run all the way to the other side of the world.

Except he knew he never would. Despite all the thoughts and feelings that led him to get drunk, he knew when he sobered up, he would start looking for that book. Chief Master deserved that much and countless more.

A strained, muffled cry came from deeper in the alley. Owl peered into the dark as he walked toward the cries. Most people would have run off, but an entire life of training — training that Brother X had betrayed — pushed him further down the alley.

On the back end of the alley, Owl found a woman held down by a man and a diseased creature — boils and puss covered its leathery, green skin. The man held her legs; the creature choked her from behind and held her mouth shut. With her clothes torn and her face bruised, she reached toward Owl. Her eyes implored his aid.

"Turn around," the man said to Owl. "You don't want to mess with us."

"Yeah," the creature said, sniffling every few seconds. "Go get your own woman. We ain't sharing."

Though Owl's head lolled as he stared at them, his body reacted with little thought. He pulled out his blade. The metal rang in the alley, and he pointed it at the man — the greater of the two threats. Twice, he tried to speak but his muddled brain couldn't remember the right words.

At length, he said, "Get out or I'll kill you."

The man pulled a hand-ax from his belt as he stood. "I ain't afraid of swordsman. I killed plenty of you with this ax."

"He has," his partner said. "I seen him."

The woman tried to get up but the man backhanded her to the ground. "I'll deal with you in a minute."

Owl sheathed his sword. "I can see you're tough. You don't even blink at the sight of a sword."

"That's right. I ain't scared of blades."

With a swift motion, Owl pulled out his gun. "How about bullets? You scared of them?" The two thugs stepped away from the woman. Owl went on, "Run away now, little boys, or I'll shoot you both."

They were gone before the woman had a chance to move. As Owl holstered his weapon, she hurried up to him. "Thank you," she said. "Thank you so much. They would've . . ."

"No problem," Owl said and headed back up the alley.

"Wait," the woman said. When Owl turned, she paused, her face a mixture of confusion and relief. Finally, she put out her hand. "I'm Galba."

Owl frowned as he stared at her hand. He tried to focus, but the image kept blurring, then doubling. He wanted to introduce himself, but his mouth felt like it was filled with feathers.

"Are you okay?" Galba asked.

He saw her concerned expression for a moment, but then the edges of his sight clouded over. The clouding closed in, crowding out her face. And bright — the clouding was a bright mash of white and purple and blue and green.

"I'm drunk," he managed to say.

Then he passed out.

From the depths of his sleep, Owl dreamed of his youth. The Korstraprime season had been upon him — cold winds, dry air, and nothing growing in the ground. Owl had been sitting with his back against a building in the town of Retic's Grove. He was just a kid. His parents had abandoned him to an orphanage — or what passed for an orphanage — when he was born. The place forever smelled of rotting fish. And as he grew, as soon as he thought he could survive on his own, he left that awful place.

Except there were plenty of things they did for him that he never thought about. Even with the big things, like food, he had assumed he could fend for himself. But the world slapped down those who thought they could do better than everyone else, and Owl soon found himself crying in an alleyway, desperate with hunger. That's when Brother X walked by, picked him up, and brought him to the Order. If Brother X had not stopped, had not acted, Owl would have starved. Yet as his brain recalled what a wonderful man Brother X had been, it also recalled the horror the man had created.

With a startled snort, Owl awoke.

He sat up in a hardwood bed, and his head spun with his stomach. He had never been much of a drinker. The previous night returned to him in bits — a lot of alcohol, an alley, and sadness. Great, overwhelming sadness. That part hadn't left him.

Before he could dwell on the loss of Chief Master, Owl rubbed his eyes and tried to figure out where he was. A patched, stained blanket that smelled of old cedar covered him. He was in a small room — he could almost touch the opposite wall — that held the bed and a three-drawer dresser. A closed, green-chipped door and a filthy, curtained window blocked out the rest of the world.

Though clothed, his coat, shoes, sword, and gun had been removed and laid on the top of the dresser. He heard muffled voices coming up through the floorboards. Wherever he was, he was on the second floor.

With shaky legs, he rose from the bed and put on his shoes. His mouth tasted of stale vomit, but he couldn't produce enough spit to change that. His body wavered, and he grabbed the dresser to steady himself.

Pathetic. He had been too slow, too weak, to protect Chief Master. He had been worthless fighting against Brother X. He had to play dead like a coward. Walking miles alone until he reached a town only pounded in how worthless he was — the horses didn't even wait for him. And he got pissed-drunk.

Owl put on his weapon belt, sheathed his sword, and picked up his gun. He stared at it a moment. From his pocket, he pulled out a red-painted bullet — the Honor Bullet.

Everyone trained in the Way of the Sword and Gun carried an Honor Bullet. It was a totem, a reminder, and a threat. It was a symbol of one's accomplishments in training and of one's honor. And should one shame the name of the Way, it was to be used on oneself.

Owl loaded the gun with the Honor Bullet. He inhaled sharply and placed the gun at his temple. He closed his eyes.

"Chief Master," he whispered, "forgive me for failing you."

Owl's finger put pressure on the trigger, but before he could set the gun off, someone knocked on the door.

"You awake in there?" a soft voice asked. "Breakfast'll be ready in just a few minutes. Why don't you clean up and join us?"

The savory aroma of cooking meat hit his senses — churning his stomach and sparking a memory from the night before. Somebody had helped him while he had wandered the streets. He was in somebody's home. He would only further his shame by committing an honor suicide here. And though his stomach rebelled, it was enough to lower Owl's hand.

Besides, if he had learned anything growing up, it was never to walk away from a good meal. He wanted to find out who had done this cooking and what she wanted.

He could kill himself later.

Holstering his weapon, Owl opened the door, and headed downstairs. His balance had not fully returned, and he found negotiating the narrow stairs to be a challenge. But when he entered the kitchen, he knew he had done the right thing — this was no place for suicide.

Watching the kitchen activity was like watching a song performed by expert musicians. A young lady moved from a wood stove to a chopping board and back, dashing ingredients and stirring a pot, cutting a vegetable and tasting a sauce — all with a dancer's grace. A wooden table took up the center of the room, and seated there, Owl saw an old couple. They also watched the young lady with expressions of admiration.

When the old lady looked back and saw Owl, her face brightened. She brushed her forefinger across her forehead — a quick prayer — and said, "Praise Kryssta, you're okay."

All eyes turned to Owl. The faces smiled. The old man, far more wrinkled than his wife, took her by the hand. With his free hand, he pushed back a chair. "Please, join us."

Owl gratefully sat. His legs had already grown wobbly. The young lady plated breakfast and served the food — a mound of seasoned blue-roller eggs with a light vegetable sauce on top.

"For my hero," she said. "Don't worry if you can't eat. You were quite unwell last night."

"Your hero?" Owl asked. His stomach surprised him by suddenly craving the food. He dug in, the flavors delightful on his tongue — even if he needed a bit of water to get it down.

"You don't remember? You saved me from those disgusting scum. Scared them off with your gun? I'm Galba. Remember?"

Owl rubbed his head, his finger lingering on the small indent left from his gun. "Thank you for the food."

"It's the least I can do."

To the older couple, Owl said, "You've raised a fine daughter."

They laughed. The old man said, "Galba's not ours. We rent a room upstairs."

"We do have a child, though," the woman said with eagerness in her eyes. And sadness. Both glistened there in a way the worried Owl. "He's a man now, but he's always a child to me."

The old man patted her hand. "Forgive us for imposing, but we couldn't help noticing your weapons. You are one of the Guardians of the Order of Kryssta, yes? The sword and gun?"

Keeping his eyes on his food, Owl forced down a bite of egg and nodded. The old couple both let out a relieved sigh.

"You see," Galba said to them. "I told you he's for real. He'll help. He's a true hero."

Owl cringed inside.

"I've always heard about you men," the old man said. "Lots of stories, but I figured there had to be some truth. I just never had the chance to travel the distance to find you."

"Don't fawn, dear," his wife said.

"Oh, sorry. She's right. I get carried away. But you're really here. Kryssta has helped us greatly today. So, let me get it out then. This is all about our son. He ran off to the Southern countries about a year ago," the man said. "I suppose he was looking for an adventure or was acting like a wild youth. I'm guessing a woman was involved."

The man's wife hit his bicep, glanced at Galba, and dabbed at the tears on her cheeks. "We hear such terrible things about Corlin. That country is crazy. No police, no law, total anarchy. He could be killed and nobody would care."

"Please, help us."

Owl frowned. "What can I do?"

"Only a strong man, a man trained in the Way, could survive down there. Please, go find our boy. Bring him back."

Owl placed the forkful of eggs back on his plate and pushed away from the table. "I'm sorry," he said. "There's a lot that's happened and I don't think I'm the man you want."

Panic filled the old woman's face. "You must. Please. I beg you. Our dear son. Our Fawbry. He's not a warrior. He's not brave like you. Those animals down there will destroy him. We heard that he might've even gone into the Freelands."

"If he can go there, then he's stronger than you think."

"It's that wretched whore he's with," the old woman said.

The old man glanced at Galba, then spoke in a lower tone to Owl as if Galba couldn't hear in such a small room. "A merchant came up from Corlin a few months back and described this group of vigilantes led by some woman called Malja. A man in that group sounded a lot like our Fawbry."

Owl's attention snapped into focus. "Did you say Malja?"

"Supposedly she and Fawbry and some kid have been causing a lot of trouble down there."

The old woman rubbed her red eyes but couldn't stop the tears from falling. "He's a good boy. He wouldn't be doing any of that on his own. She's manipulated him."

"You're sure the name was Malja?"

The couple nodded. They wanted to say more but Owl's sudden intensity stopped them. He could see it on their faces — hope.

Owl had heard about Malja, the great warrior woman of the South. The Order always figured that any serious threat to Penmarvia would come from the South, and she was the name that continually found its way up to them. Part of his training had been in dealing with attacks from primitive warriors like her. The Masters always said that was the real threat. They never had expected to be hurt by their own Queen.

Now they were all gone. All the Masters, all the Guardians, the entire Order. Only he and Brother X remained.

And yet, like a sign from the brother god Kryssta, the name of Malja returns. If he could get her to help him, he could bring to Queen Salia the very attack the Northern countries feared. He could clean off his shame and put away his Honor Bullet. And if he died in this attempt, it would be with honor of its own.

"Yes," he said to the stunned couple. "I'll find your boy."

Malja

Whoever had attacked Tommy made no effort to hide their tracks. Throughout the night Malja and Fawbry followed the hoof prints in the dirt road, and the trail never once left. When dawn arrived, they were able to ride faster.

"What kind of idiots take a boy and just follow the road?" Fawbry asked.

"They want to be found or they don't fear being found. Either way is not good."

Throughout the night, Malja's focus had been on following the trail. She blotted all else out for fear of losing Tommy in the dark. With the sun up, seeing the trail with ease, her brain had the chance to wander, and though she wished otherwise, she kept seeing that portal, that woman, that world.

Her Uncle Gregor — the man who found her in the wild and raised her as his own — taught her that she had to pay the dead their honor. He said that whenever she killed a man or a beast, she had to spend a little time thinking on this life she took. If not, the dead would haunt her. But the portal haunted her more.

This wasn't a life she took, and no matter how much she thought on it, it wouldn't leave her. It only got worse. This was another world she had denied herself — sacrificed. That she had done so to save Tommy and to hurt the evil magicians Jarik and Callib, only heightened her sense of loss. After all, what choice did she really have?

Except she had been truly tempted.

If she had just stepped through, she would have been free from all this. She would be in a civilized world instead of traipsing through the morning, hoping not to see any more blood. She might even be happy. And, without a doubt, she wouldn't have to kill people or worry about paying them their honor.

"Over here," Fawbry said, pointing to an opening in the trees.

Malja had been so wrapped in her thoughts, she missed when the trail broke off. Fawbry didn't comment but she could tell he knew what she had been thinking about — when she was supposed to be looking for Tommy no less. Scowling, she turned her horse around and followed Fawbry into the forest. Within minutes, they heard voices.

"Dismount," she whispered.

They tied the horses to a tree and headed toward the sounds. Malja pulled Viper from its custom sheath. Fawbry crouched as they moved in, pulling out a skinning knife. When they heard an angry shout, they ducked behind some pines and spied on a small campfire surrounded by two horses, two men, and Tommy.

"You ain't listening," the one man said. He had a thick beard that obscured his mouth and huge feet that stomped with each word. His unwashed odor permeated the camp and its surroundings. "This kid's no farmer."

The other man, bony and unkempt, said, "Then why was he partying with a bunch of farmers? That make any sense? Of course not. Now calm down, have a drink, and let's stay with what we said."

The bearded man squatted and passed gas loudly. "He's gonna be worth a lot, right?"

"Those people love their kids. You'll see. They'll pay to get him back."

"What if they don't? What if they don't like him and that's the reason he was out all alone last night? What if—"

"Then we'll sell him. Always somebody looking for slaves. Relax. It'll be fine."

The bearded man rubbed his backside and glanced at Tommy behind them. "I hope we can sell him. That bastard hurt me."

Malja could see they had tied Tommy's hands behind his back and blindfolded him. Being shot by a bolt of conjured electricity does tend to make one cautious.

Fawbry pursed his lips as he thought. "The way I see things, we've got two good options," he whispered. Malja kept a serious face. Fawbry was smart and worth listening to, even if he tended toward the less confrontational methods. "First, you can stay here, keep watch, while I hurry back to the town and get some people to come pay a ransom. Or we could wait until their asleep and—"

"I've got a better idea," she said and stepped away from the tree. Sometimes confrontational was the most efficient choice.

As she walked by Fawbry, he brushed his forefinger across his brow, glanced up to the brother god Kryssta, and said, "Please don't let her get me killed." He followed her, keeping several steps behind. That was another thing she liked about him — even though he whined about it and wanted his share of recognition, he stayed with her.

Since Malja made no attempt to be quiet, the two kidnappers jumped to their feet at her approach.

The bony man held a long piece of metal with the business end cut into jagged teeth. The bearded one picked up a large wooden club. They took a few steps toward her, leering as if they had not seen a woman in years.

"Well, well," the bony man said. "What a fine present to send us. I think I'll enjoy—"

"You have stolen that boy and that is against the law," Malja said.

The bearded man scratched his belly. "What law?"

"Law one — Do nothing to another that you would not want done to you. I think you boys wouldn't want people stealing you, tying you up, and threatening to sell you."

Raising the metal weapon above his head, the bony one said, "I don't know no laws, but I know a sweet ass when I see one. You got a name? I like to call out a woman's name when I take her."

Malja raised an eyebrow. "My name's Malja. I am the law."

Both men froze. The bony one looked from Malja to Fawbry to Tommy, matching up the members of the crew and their descriptions with the stories he no doubt had heard. Then he took a hard appraisal of Viper. His head tilted back in recognition and he dropped his weapon.

"What you doin'?" the bearded man said.

"Shut up. This is her. The real Malja."

The bearded man leaned forward and squinted. As his brain finally caught up with the situation, his mean countenance melted away. "Oh, lady, we're sorry. This your boy? We thought he was a dumb farmer. You can have him back. We didn't mean nothing."

Malja kept watch on the man with the club. "Fawbry," she said, and Fawbry scurried by everyone to attend to Tommy. Malja side-stepped a few times to reposition the men away from Tommy. Just in case. "You two don't need to live like this anymore. I'm bringing laws to Corlin so that we can all be free to live like we want to without troubling each other."

The bony one shrugged. "What if I want to rape women and steal kids? Am I free to do that?"

Malja opened her mouth, ready to deliver all three laws, when a man with a sword and a gun dropped from the trees. He shouted loud as he sliced straight through the bony one. The bearded man stared dumbfounded at the bloody mess that had been his friend.

Startled, Malja snapped Viper out in front. The man moved with grace and purpose like a well-trained dancer. In a swift, spinning motion, he cut open the bearded man's belly.

And it was over.

He sheathed his sword, holstered his gun, turned to Malja and bowed. "My name is Owl," he said. "I've traveled very far just to meet you."

Owl

Malja swung Viper overhead and came down in a clean ax cut. Owl dodged to the side, his face a soup of confusion.

"No, no, I'm on your side," he said.

Again, Malja attacked, but Owl had grown up evading great swordsmen — Brother X, for one. A grin rolled across his lips. He was being attacked by the great Malja and her famous weapon, Viper. But the fun of it passed just as quickly as the thought. She had massive power — he could feel Viper slice the air as it passed him by — and he wouldn't last too long just dodging.

"You don't understand," he said.

"Those men were no threat," Malja said, her body bristling with rage. Owl stepped back, amazed at the sheer power behind her eyes. She went on, "You murdered them, and I don't need a murderer on my side. Get out of here before I get really angry."

"I'm from Penmarvia. Queen Salia is after you. You're in danger."

"I fear no queen. I'll send her your head as a warning."

Malja launched at Owl with a ferocious yell. In a blur, Viper streamed out from her side, heading right for Owl's neck. He stood his ground, watching every movement, keeping his breathing calm, letting his years of training gauge the timing.

At the final moment, he snapped his sword out and up, clanging with the inner-crescent of Viper and stopping Malja from cutting off his head. She pressed hard and he pushed back. He had to use both hands on the sword — one at the hilt, one pressing against the back of the blade — to keep Viper from completing the cut. Metal against metal screeched. He locked eyes with her.

Grunting out the words, he said, "I came here for your help."

"I don't care." She barely had trouble speaking, and Owl wondered just how much strength she hadn't used yet.

He saw her shoulder move just an inch, but it was enough to signal her release. A second later she broke off, attempting to knock him off balance by using his own force against him. But he had been ready —

instead of stumbling forward, Owl broke off as well, moving in time with Malja as if dancing.

"I thought you were a great warrior," he said, keeping his eyes on his opponent. "Aren't you trying to take over Corlin?"

Malja scoffed. "I'm letting people be free enough to make their own choices. Nobody gets to rule over anybody."

She lunged forward, but Owl anticipated the attack. He moved to the side and slapped Malja's shoulder with the flat of his blade. Since he couldn't match her strength, he'd have to settle for grace. He prayed Kryssta would let him outlast her and not slip up.

"Queen Salia has taken over most of Penmarvia," he said. "She wants Corlin, too."

"Tell her she can't have it."

Twisting her body, Malja used Viper's outer-crescent as she pivoted around, sweeping low for the knees. Owl jumped over the attack, and tapped Malja's head with the flat of his blade. He said, "I don't work for her. And she tried to kill me." He could see the fury lighting her eyes. "I want you to help me free Penmarvia just as you are doing here."

"Not interested," she said, stepping off and slicing at the waist. Owl moved aside, but Malja changed motions in the middle of her swing. She jabbed Viper forward, an astonishing shift in momentum, and cut through Owl's shirt, taking off a small bit of his skin.

Owl had hoped to show her he was no threat, but Malja's face displayed such animalistic fervor, he had to admit he was wrong. This had been a bad idea. Too late now, though.

Without hesitation, Owl launched into a flurry of attacks. Left side, right side, straight ahead — stepping forward with each strike. Malja parried the attacks with ease, but he was not interested in making contact. The sword was being used to open a path for him to get close.

And there it was. He twirled away from Viper, curving in fast, forcing her to swing Viper in an awkward manner in order to deflect the attack. The moment the weapons clashed, he spun around the other direction. Before Malja could adjust for the expected strike, Owl ripped his handgun from the holster and pointed it at Malja's head.

"I'm sorry about those two men," Owl said, breathing hard. "I thought you were fighting them, and I only wanted to help."

Like a Kryssta statue, Malja maintained her pose of action but didn't move further. He saw her eyes checking out the weapon, trying to determine if the gun would actually fire.

"I clean it every day," he said. "Make sure every part works. I assure you, it's quite deadly."

From behind, a wild-haired man with one hand and wearing a colorful robe let out a gasp. Owl had spied the man from the beginning. He had to be Fawbry. No other would fit the description so well.

"Oh my Kryssta," Fawbry said, rushing up next to them. "Y-You're from the Order of Kryssta. You really are from Penmarvia. You know the Way of the Sword and Gun."

"Yes," Owl said. "And you all will listen to me or I'll have to shoot Malja in the head."

"You might want to reconsider that plan," Malja said.

Owl felt a sharp pressure on his inner-thigh. He didn't need to look to know — Malja had Viper set between his legs, pointed upward. If he shot her, she would most likely castrate him as her body flew backward. A sly grin rose on her lips.

Fawbry waved his hands between them. "Will you two stop with this nonsense? Malja, he's not a thug. He's one of the great legends I heard about growing up. Well, not him specifically but the Order and the Guardians and the Way of the Sword and Gun and I just can't believe it."

Looking into Malja's eyes, Owl knew she would never break the standoff first. So, he holstered his gun and waited for Viper to be removed. She waited a moment, and Owl's heart quickened.

"Malja," Fawbry said both pleading and accusing.

"Fine," she said, removing Viper in a smooth motion as she backed up. Her wary gaze never left Owl though, even as she attended to the boy.

Fawbry shook Owl's hand. "It's a great honor to meet you."

Owl had heard about this type of reaction but he had never experienced it before. He'd never been far enough away from the Order before for such an encounter to occur. He tried not to smile, but his mouth refused to listen.

"Don't worry about Queen Salia," Fawbry went on. "We can handle a dozen Queens. Right, Malja? She's incredibly tough. And Tommy, too. He's more than you think. Not that you can't handle the Queen yourself. I'm sure the order has lots of men like you."

The joy swept away from Owl and he lowered his head. If the Order had been filled with men like him — cowards who played dead upon the body of their Masters — Salia would have taken over long ago. He glanced at Malja and Tommy. They fussed with each other like a mother and child. He thought of all the parents and children in Penmarvia.

"Listen to me," he said, and the force of his voice sparked the others' attentions. He intended to tell them of Fawbry's parents, to use that connection as motivation for their help, but watching them together, he paused. Instead, he told them of the Queen's trickery, the betrayal of Brother X, the death of Chief Master. The rest he left unsaid. "She has destroyed the Order, killed off the magicians, and is coming here. But it won't be a simple fight against an army. She's got control of the Library."

Fawbry gasped.

"What library?" Malja asked.

Fawbry rushed toward Malja, tripping in his excitement. "The Library. It's a legend even greater than the Order. After the Devastation, some members of the Order of Kryssta discovered a powerful location in Penmarvia, far to the North. It pulsed with magical energy. They built a temple around it and studied it. Over the years, they wrote the Twelve Books about what they learned; forming a Library that holds secrets to great power."

"And Salia has these books?" Malja asked, rising with a stern look on her face.

"She does," Owl said. "But the books are useless to her now — they are in code. Chief Master told me of a thirteenth book that should offer the key. I've got to find it before Salia. If she gets the key, she'll use the Library."

"And?"

Owl shrugged. "Nobody's ever used it before."

Fawbry paced from Owl to Malja and back. "You don't get it. This Library is massive magic. It can be used for just about anything. It's like a direct conduit to the brother gods."

"You're talking legends," Malja said.

"Your man might be right," Owl said.

Malja, Tommy, and Fawbry broke into laughter. "My man?" she said. "Fawbry is not and never will be my man."

Trying not blush, Owl said, "The reality is that the Library is barely contained power. If Queen Salia gets control of it, she'll have an incredible weapon to use against Corlin. She could cause a miniature Devastation throughout your lands. She might even open holes into other worlds and drop all of your people in."

A strange look crossed Malja's face, and Owl feared he had, once more, said something wrong. Fawbry's smile faltered and Tommy crossed his arms. This was a complex trio. Owl had to navigate them cautiously.

He decided to bring Fawbry's parents into the conversation as a way of regaining some control, but Malja narrowed her eyes and said, "Are you talking about portals to other worlds?"

"I-It's only what I've been taught. That the Library could possibly do that. But there's plenty of myth mixed in with the facts of the Library. Portals may just be some Master's imagination. I've never seen such a thing."

With a dark expression, Malja said, "We have."

Owl's chest knotted tight as Malja's expression and words crashed into him. If Queen Salia could open a portal, then his failure on the Great Field was more than a personal failing against Brother X. It was more than a failing against this world which would end up under Salia's control. His failure may destroy world upon world. He wanted to throw up.

"Please help me," he said so quiet he wondered if he had spoken at all.

"Think about it," Fawbry said to Malja, whining just a bit. "Help defeat Salia and I'm sure they'll help you use the Library. Maybe they can find your home world."

Owl caught the slight waver in her attitude. That Malja was from another world was something he'd have to think on later. For now, the idea that he might succeed in recruiting her, pushed him onward. "The boy could benefit, too," he said, hoping to entice her. "He's a magician, right?"

"Why?" she asked.

"I thought so. Growing up around the Order, all I ever saw were magicians. I feel like I have a sense for spotting them." Fawbry waved cautioning hands from behind Malja but Owl didn't understand what part to avoid. "The Library might be able to help him grow stronger. Maybe even unlock a new spell or two."

Though Tommy brightened at these words, Fawbry deflated. Malja looked angry enough to spring Viper at him again. Owl sighed. He knew too little of their dynamics, but he saw clearly that Fawbry was the only one among them who could talk to her even a bit. He needed Fawbry — even if he had to forget his promise to Fawbry's parents. Someday, he promised himself, he would tell Fawbry, but for now, he couldn't let this key man go running off to Mommy and Daddy. Lying to Fawbry, even a simple lie of omission, didn't sit well with Owl, but he saw no other option. Without Fawbry, Owl felt sure that Malja would take Tommy and he would have to return to Penmarvia alone.

Malja

Malja turned away from the group with her fists clenched. She heard Fawbry tell Tommy and Owl to stay back. When he approached her, she could hear the shake in his voice as well as his body.

"Y-You should consider this," he said.

"No."

"This might be the answer you're looking for."

She looked over her shoulder at Tommy. "There are more important things than just finding my home." Then she faced Fawbry. "Why should we even believe this man? He jumps into a fight he has no purpose in, messes that all up, and then while we're still trying to catch up with it all, he plays out this little scenario that just happens to feed in with some childhood fantasy of yours. You don't find that suspicious?"

Fawbry walked a few steps further away. Malja suspected he wanted to be just far enough out of Owl's hearing range. "Of course I'm suspicious," he whispered. "That doesn't change much. The fact is that if he's telling the truth, we'd be fools to go away. Especially if this Queen has any real intention of taking over Corlin."

"That's only if he's telling the truth."

"If he's a liar or maybe walking us into an ambush, then we'll deal with that. I've noticed you're quite good at handling that kind of thing."

Malja snickered. "So I'm just the muscle?"

Fawbry shook his head — not in denial but frustration. "You've been asking me all about Tommy lately, so listen to me now. Tommy wants this. Take a close look into his eyes. He believes Owl, and he wants to see the Order. We've spent the last year traveling all over this horrible country, and I don't think we've done much good. It seems there's a never-ending supply of bastards trying to rule over everybody, and no matter how many we take out, another comes along. Tommy and I know you don't want us around."

"That's not true," she said, Fawbry's words stabbing through her chest.

"You don't need us, that's for sure. Look, the important thing is that if this Queen is for real, then we can do something big again. Not just against petty little crap like Eldred, but something as big as we did before when we took down Jarik and Callib. And if you can admit it, that's what you're looking for every time you fight in these little towns. That's what you're after with your laws. We all want that greater sense of purpose we had before. Well, Owl's giving us that chance."

Malja raised a hand before Fawbry launched into a longer, more enthusiastic speech. "Let me be alone."

With a quick nod, Fawbry eased back to Tommy and Owl. Malja walked to her horse, grabbed her whetstone from the saddlebag, and sharpened Viper. Each stroke let her mind release from the tensions of this decision. She knew that she would have to decide soon, always it was up to her to make the big decisions, but for the moment, she could let all thoughts congeal into one simple idea — sharpen Viper.

What confounded her wasn't the responsibility of a decision, but rather her reaction when her decisions included Tommy. In battle, she had faced hard choices numerous times. Lives were gained or lost based on the paths she chose for her armies to follow. In direct combat, her mind had to evaluate an enemy, find an opening, and exploit it to the fullest — all while defending every incoming attack. She had faced these challenges more times than she'd care to recount, and she had done so with great success. But when it came to choices concerning Tommy, she felt stymied. Except it was more than that. It wasn't just Tommy — it was anything involving Tommy and magic.

She kept seeing him from that first day — dirty and chained to the fuel cells of a thief's ship; the dark, churning sea; ready to jump into an unknown future with her simply because he knew a good chance when he saw it; the pounding rain; the way he curled around her leg as she rowed a lifeboat to safety. He was small and innocent but, even then, had the fierce bravery she loved.

That was it, really. She wanted to keep him like he was back then. Malja silently laughed at herself. She suppressed her emotions and personal thoughts so often that it took a long time for her to see what others picked up on right away.

Fawbry had it figured out already, she guessed. At least, he thought he did. Except another thought gnawed just underneath. Magic. It corrupted souls and twisted minds and destroyed people. And it was powerful.

"Tommy, come here," she called over her shoulder.

The boy paused long enough to send her the message that he chose to come. When he sat, she observed him for a moment. He had shown her too many times now just how powerful he had become. And yet ...

"Why did you let those fools capture you?" she asked. "You could've stopped them easily."

Tommy firmed up his chest, pointed at her, and then raised three fingers. Her third law — Before using magic, do for yourself.

"You got caught because you tried to not use magic?"

He motioned with his head in an unclear way. He didn't want to admit anything to her.

Malja's heart split. Happy that he had even attempted to follow her ways. Sad that he had so clearly needed his magic. And what would have happened had she not arrived in time? Would Tommy have used his magic then, more than just a jolt of electricity, or would he have let them sell him into slavery once more? She knew the answer even if she didn't want to know. If any serious danger had threatened the boy, he wouldn't have blinked at annihilating those fools.

"Okay," she said, and the other men walked over to her. She put away the whetstone and grabbed some gear lying on the ground. "I don't think this Library is going to be an issue. Nobody has the key book, so nobody gets to use the Library."

Fawbry looked as shocked as Malja felt. "We're actually going to help him?"

She glanced back at Tommy. "It doesn't seem to be working well the way we're going now." She wheeled around to Owl and pointed her finger at him, the threat of her words equally matched in that simple gesture. "I don't trust you, but I will make you a promise. If you're lying to us, if you try anything, I won't just kill you. I'll make you suffer something awful first."

Owl had the brains to stay quiet.

The next day passed by in the monotony of travel. Because Tommy's horse had been killed, he rode on one inherited from the dead kidnappers. It fought his inexperienced technique, causing him to utter numerous grunts and groans as he used the reins and braced against the horse's movements. Malja had offered to share her horse, but Tommy refused. She tried to hide the hurt she felt — she had carried him on her horse for almost a year — but seeing the sympathy in Fawbry's eyes made her press in her heels to speed up. For much of the day, she rode ahead of the group.

Fawbry had said that Tommy behaved typically for his age, but that had to be wrong. She didn't recall ever being like that. When she lived all those years with Uncle Gregor, did he have to suffer through constant defiance? And when he died, her loss was so great it clouded the rest of her life. Tommy wouldn't even care if she died.

Twice during the day, Owl rode up by her side and attempted to drag her into a conversation. She rebuffed him both times. He was a handsome man — his dark skin and strong features fit in well with Corlin — but she had no interest in him beyond getting rid of Queen Salia. And the Library. If even that.

The following night, they set camp under the ruins of an old factory — two moss-covered walls forming a corner and rows of dilapidated focus-booths were all that remained. Tommy found a dented sign that read: DUNSON METAL & MAGIC. While Malja took her turn keeping watch over the camp, Fawbry read to Tommy from the Book of Kryssta:

> *To understand all there is,*
> *One must strive to know nothing.*
> *Clear all from one's soul,*
> *Become an empty vessel.*

She liked the sound of his voice when he read to the boy. He sounded protective and loving, like a big brother. Perhaps he would take care of Tommy if anything should happen to her.

Malja shook off those thoughts before they managed to latch on. Bad luck to think about dying. Not that she believed in such superstitions. For her, the only truth was the reality around her. She certainly never believed in the whole "brother gods" idea, though she enjoyed the stories for what they were — good stories.

Fawbry closed the book. "Let me tell you a story," Fawbry said in a low tone as the campfire colored his face with its orange glow. Tommy snuggled against his chest and listened. "There are several versions of this story," Fawbry went on, "but this is the one I grew up hearing over and over. So, there were the two brother gods, Korstra and Kryssta, and they ruled over all of existence together. But one day there came along this woman, Elatria, that both gods fell in love with. Their jealousy of each other tore apart the world. Earthquakes, hurricanes, all kinds of destruction. Made the Devastation look like a mild afternoon.

When they finally settled down, they saw that they had accidentally killed Elatria in all the violence. Overwhelmed by grief, they poured their pain into hatred of each other. They split up the world, each taking a season — Korstraprime and Krysstaprime — to rule alone. The short time between — the pre- and post- prime seasons — well, that's when they hand over power to the other. And you'll notice that those times are when we have the worst storms because the brother gods are fighting. Of course, the brother gods do more than control the weather, but if you ever wonder if they are watching us, taking care of the world, you simply have to look around."

A few minutes passed without a word. Malja glanced over to find Fawbry and Tommy both asleep. Watching them, a fraction of the tension she always carried lifted away. But that moment of semi-peace was short-lived — Owl approached her. He had managed to get quite close before she heard him, but when she did, she bolted to her feet and brandished Viper.

"It's just me," he whispered.

Malja eased down on a rock, letting the dim campfire warm her back. "You're very quiet," she said. With a begrudging huff, she added, "And you're very good with a sword."

"Gun, too," Owl said, sitting beside her. "The style is called the Way of the Sword and Gun."

"I haven't seen you shoot yet."

"I suppose not," he chuckled. The deep sound warmed Malja more than the campfire.

"You should go back to sleep. Your shift starts soon enough."

Owl didn't leave. He stretched his legs out. "I've always wanted to meet you. Stories about you travel far, and I've held this strong belief that you and I could be good friends. We have a lot in common."

"Stories are just stories."

He stayed quiet for a while but he wouldn't leave. She held back from scolding him. It would do no good. And, in truth, she didn't mind his presence — as long as he kept silent.

It was Malja, though, that broke the quiet. "Besides being good fighters, what could we possibly have in common?"

"We're both orphans, for one. Like you, I never knew my parents. They abandoned me. I lived on the streets of Salia City for a while — scrounging food and joining up with other kids stuck in the same situation. Until Brother X found me. The Order took me in, and I never regretted it. As I got older, it became clear that I didn't have any magical ability, so they taught me to be a Guardian of the Order. I learned the Way, trained hard, and here I am. Our lives, while different in the details, are very similar."

Malja's skin prickled as her heart chilled. "We aren't the same at all," she said. "I wasn't abandoned. I was stolen. I wasn't brought up in some lovely temple. I was raised by two ruthless magicians who wanted to use me for their schemes. And when they thought I couldn't help them, they threw me away. I was ten and left in the woods to die. It was only the kindness of one man that saved me. And those bastard magicians killed him, too. There's nothing similar about us."

Owl stood, readjusting his coat. "At least you know where you came from. Right? Isn't that what Fawbry was saying? You want to use the Library to get back to your home. Me — I walk down a street and wonder if the people I pass are related to me. Maybe an uncle, an aunt, a grandmother. Could that couple be my parents?"

"You want pity? Is that it?" Malja stood chest to chest, though she had to look up to meet his eyes. "You won't get it. Everybody in this world has had a hard, crappy life. Tommy's had enough pain for two lives."

"I just wanted—"

"You wanted to buddy up to me, to be part of our team. But you're not. If you're telling the truth, you're a messenger. Got it. If you were more than that, you'd be back there fighting against this queen, instead of running for my help."

She could see Owl's shock — not at her venom but at her final words. He stared at her a moment, his eyes glistening, before storming off. He returned to his spot by the campfire and pounded the ground with his fist.

Damn. Why should she feel bad that she upset him? She didn't trust him — although no ambush had materialized, lending his story some credence. Which meant she lashed at him not because she didn't want to hear, but because she wanted to shut down the conversation.

She sat. Though she had held them back, the words had almost burst out of her — words she barely wanted to think about — that she truly wanted to leave this world.

Of course, Tommy and Fawbry knew, or at least suspected — but they didn't understand how often she thought of that woman reaching out for her. Not a day passed without Malja wondering what would have happened had she just stepped through the portal. Because one truth she told Owl never changed here — the world was crap. Nobody lived well. Everyone suffered. With magic, without magic — it didn't change anything. And all her efforts to make a better place, for Tommy, for herself, were soaked in blood.

"Did you hear that?" Owl said.

Malja jumped at the sound of his voice, hating that he had sneaked up on her again. She opened her mouth to berate him when she noticed the look in his eye and processed what he had said.

She listened to the night air.

Rustling leaves but no wind. A crackling of wood but just hot coals on the fire. A sharp breath. Something was out there. More than one thing.

Malja leaned toward Owl. "Wake up the boys and get your weapons."

As Owl dashed off, Malja released Viper. She looked out into the darkness trying to locate her enemy. She listened. She looked. She sniffed the air.

She heard a rock tumble to the right. She spun, caught sight of a fast-moving shape, but then it was gone. Fawbry and Tommy were awake and alert now, and she saw them also looking in the same direction.

"What is it?" Fawbry asked.

Malja didn't answer. She didn't know. Owl pulled out his handgun and held it steady with both hands. For the first time in her life, she was happy to see a gun.

Usually, a gun meant a false sense of security, a misfire or a wild shot that often did more harm than good. Owl's was different. She had seen it too well when he held it against her head. This gun would fire true. Anything leaping out of the woods at them wouldn't get much of chance.

Another noise behind them. As they whirled around, hissing emerged from the left. To the right, she caught the sound of a stick being stepped on. They were surrounded.

Yet, still, Malja had not seen a single foe.

"Over there," Fawbry shouted, but when Malja stepped toward the spot, she found nothing.

"Here," Owl said. Again, nothing. Owl looked at Tommy. "This is an illusion. Magic."

"You think Tommy's playing with us?" Malja asked, turning her frustration on Owl. "How dare you."

"Tommy's isn't doing this. But he can flush out the culprit."

Malja shook her head. "We don't need magic to solve this."

"I recognize some of his tattoos — at least, the general idea of them — and the one on his wrist should do well for us."

"I said No."

Tommy looked at his tattooed arm for a few seconds, and just as Malja reached for him, sunlight poured out of him in all directions. The woods lit up with shadows and light, and standing just to the side of Owl, they all saw a young magician. Malja didn't stop, though. She grabbed Tommy and shook him until the light faded.

"Get him," Malja commanded Owl. As he ran after the fleeing magician, Malja held Tommy's shoulders tight enough to leave bruises. "Stop it. Please. You don't have to use magic. You can be more than that."

Tommy raised his chin, and Malja saw a fire in his eyes she had hoped never to witness.

Owl

Owl tore into the wood. Sprinting through the dark, he ignored the limbs whipping against his body. Twice he stumbled but his training provided him the excellent balance needed to keep from slamming into the ground.

At first, he only saw the moving branches that said something had just run through. His heart pulsing hard, his breathing strong and steady, he raced after the magician. As he shifted to the right to avoid a row of thorny saplings, he caught a glimpse of his enemy.

With the moonlight restricted by the trees, Owl prayed he hadn't picked up the trail of some scared animal. He pushed on. Sweat stung his eyes and his stomach tightened.

"C'mon," he said. "Faster." He tried to coax more strength from his legs. He had to catch this man. The pain of his heart beating into his chest was nothing compared to the pain he knew he would feel if he failed again.

He jumped over a fallen tree and skidded to a halt. The magician stood there like a shadow fully formed. A stream glistening with moonlight trickled behind him.

Owl raised his gun. Though breathing heavily, he said, "Don't make me shoot you. I'm a Guardian of the Order. I will not miss."

The magician spun and tried to escape. Owl fired. As the echoes of his gunshot receded, the only shadows that remained came from the trees.

Owl didn't move for three minutes. He stared at the empty spot that should have contained a dead body. He used all his remaining energy to keep back the shameful tears that welled from deep within.

When he returned to the campsite, Owl found Malja, Tommy, and Fawbry locked in a heated argument.

"You don't know," Malja said to Tommy while Fawbry hovered around them. "I've lived longer than you. I've seen what magic does to people."

Tommy raised his shirt, displaying the jagged scars he suffered while a slave. Owl had never seen such an abused child before. He sickened at the sight.

Malja shook her head. "I'm not saying you don't know anything. I'm saying . . . do you remember Audrex? The sister of that Nolan woman? She was deranged. Magic had done that to her. And she only had one spell she could do. How many do you have? Do you even know? I don't even want to think about what having that bit of Barris Mont inside you can do. I'm not telling you never to do magic again. All I'm asking of you is to take it slower." Malja pointed at Owl. "He said the Order and the Library and all that might help you with your magic. Wait until then. Okay?"

Tommy stood there and listened, but Owl could tell the boy wanted to be anywhere else. Owl was pretty sure Malja could tell, too. It only served to anger her more.

Fawbry jumped in with a muttered joke that Owl missed but it was enough to crack the tension for a second. They all stepped apart, the joke already fading into their confrontation, but it was enough to diffuse the moment. What could Fawbry have said? The fact that Owl would never know further proved to him just how removed he was from this group. Malja finally faced him. Her expectant look weighed heavy.

"He got away," he said. She grimaced and Owl tried not to lower his head. "I had him. I did. I even shot at him. But he just vanished."

"A scout?" Fawbry asked.

Malja nodded. "Fast moving, shadowy, and can dodge a bullet? That's a good spy and a good scout."

Fawbry moved to his pack. "We've got to get moving. The Queen'll know now that we're here."

Malja shot a nasty look at Owl. "You should've had him."

Though he was the tallest in the group, Owl felt smaller with every word. "Whatever spell he was using, he knew it well. He cast it very quickly," he said. Even his own words felt weak.

Malja squinted into the darkness. Owl watched her calculating, and though he wanted to speak, he feared interrupting her. At length, she faced him. "How much longer until we reach what's left of the Order?"

"A day or two."

"Which is it? One or two?"

"One, if we go fast. Otherwise, you'll have to camp another night and you'll arrive before midday. There won't be anything there, though."

"It's a place to start. Load up," Malja said. Tommy went to Fawbry to help with the work. "We'll go slow through the night so the horses last. The moment we hit dawn, we'll push hard the rest of the way."

Owl lugged his saddle over to his horse. "I'm sorry," he said to Malja. "I tried."

Hewing her saddle onto her horse, she said, "I don't understand how somebody so skilled with a sword and a gun could fail to get one scout." She pulled the girth hard and her horse complained.

Later, they rode through the forest in silence. Malja led the way. Owl and Fawbry clumped together a few feet behind. Further back, Tommy rode in a constant state of annoyance.

The long, isolated ride left Owl with too much time to think. Just picturing Brother X and Queen Salia irritated his stomach. Trying to equate that vile monster slaying Chief Master with the idolized student who had saved him from the streets spun Owl's brain in ways that he could not fathom. He tried to focus on his meditation training, but the calming emptiness would not come. He had never been good at it to begin with, and the stone of tension in his chest did not help. The constant inner-turmoil left him wanting to go off alone and never come back. Forget the world. Forget the other worlds. Just drift away.

Fawbry pulled alongside and said, "Don't let Malja get to you."

Owl took a moment to excise from his thoughts. When Fawbry's words sunk in, however, it served to remind him of his most recent failing. "She's right," he said. "I should've had that scout. I've endangered all of us."

Fawbry lifted his stump so Owl could get a long look. "She's endangered all of us many times." Fawbry stared at the empty space where his hand had once been, and his eyes glazed over in thought. A moment passed before he shook off his own troubles and said, "The thing to understand is that I've endangered us, too. Tommy's managed it recently. It's the way of things. We live in dangerous times."

"Not me, though. That is, not since I was a kid. Once I joined with the Order, they took care of me. I didn't have to fight for food or shelter. The only dangers I faced came from annoying the Masters and training. Life behind their walls was safe."

"When I was a kid," Fawbry said, gesturing with his good hand as his excitement grew, "I remember hearing stories about the Order and its Guardians. I always wanted to join you guys. Learn the Way."

"You should have. I think we would've gotten along well," Owl said with honest regret. He never had made too many friends, but Fawbry seemed so accepting that he could picture the fun they would have had together. And Fawbry wouldn't have betrayed him.

"I'm not Order material," Fawbry said. "I never would have made it through the first week."

"Nonsense. You've lived out here on your own and this is a truly dangerous world. I don't see how you manage to handle it."

Fawbry nodded forward. "I have her."

When the dawn arrived, Malja kicked her horse into a gallop and the others followed. The exhilaration of speeding across the Penmarvian landscape blotted out all of Owl's concerns. He concentrated on keeping control of the horse and enjoying the rush of air against his face. It was something the Masters had taught him — savor the immediate moments of one's life. Times to worry always come eventually.

Not only did such wisdom prove to be freeing to Owl's tensions, but focusing on the immediate moment made the morning soar by as fast as the horses galloped. When Malja raised a hand to slow the group, Owl eased back in his saddle. His thighs ached and his body had become slick with sweat.

A small stream curved nearby, and they let the horses drink up and rest. As Owl filled his canteen with water upstream from the horses, he heard a rider approach. Before he managed to stand, Malja had Viper out and readied herself for a battle. A boy no older than Tommy rode in on a small but fast horse.

"It is you," he said, smiling at Owl.

Without taking her eyes from the boy, Malja said over her shoulder, "You know him?"

Owl waved Malja down from her fighting stance and rushed to the boy's side. "Sprint! You're alive!"

"I was about to say the same of you," Sprint said with a hearty laugh. His dark hair had been cut short and spiky so that it looked like a dangerous helmet at first. Owl remembered the day the boy had shorn his waist-length hair. He said it made him faster, and it earned him the name Sprint.

"I thought Queen Salia killed you all," Owl said.

"She tried, but we're the Order, by Kryssta. You think some half-wit Queen and a two-faced betrayer are going to get the best of us?"

"They killed Chief Master. And they said—"

"The Order is still here. We're in bad shape, I won't lie to you. All the Masters are gone except Master Kee. Only a handful of magicians and Guards survived. But we're still here. And by the looks of your friends, you've brought us some reinforcements."

Owl looked back at Malja, Tommy, and Fawbry. They made for a shabby bunch, but it would have to do. And despite a boy who refused to speak, or a man without a hand, or a woman ready to kill at the slightest provocation, for the first time, Owl felt a spark of hope in his heart.

Malja

The boy, Sprint, led them out of the forest and along the tree line. A vast open plain spread out before them. Owl called it the Great Field, and the name served it well. Nothing but wide swaths of grass as far as she could see.

The Order compound, what remained of it, stood like a blemish on this ocean of grass. Black smoke rose from various points along its gated walls. From the outside, the compound reminded Malja of the more fearful places she had come across in Corlin — the ones that built walls around the entire town, kept guard at all hours, and deeply mistrusted any strangers that came their way.

Fires smoldered, filling the air with a rich aroma. The main gate had been blasted open, the stench of magic surrounded it, and the ground had been churned up by a hundred horses. Bodies of man and beast were strewn about the rubble. Malja wondered if the first days after the Devastation had looked like this.

Among the few people still alive, two worked together to clear the dead away. They wore long, tan robes that hid their features, but Malja caught a glimpse of tattooed arms. They stopped long enough to watch Malja and her team pass by. Owl waved but the disheartened expressions the two wore stopped him from speaking. They ran a finger across the forehead and nodded when Owl and Fawbry returned the gesture.

"Up ahead," Sprint said, pointing to a crumbling structure built against the compound walls.

They pulled up to a hitching post and dismounted. Owl fussed with his clothing and combed his hair with his fingers. To Malja, he said, "Wait here. I'll be right back."

Malja watched him approach a heavy door with Sprint at his side. He hesitated, let out a shudder, and entered the building. She looked to Fawbry. "You know anything about what goes on in there?"

Fawbry raised an eyebrow. Malja knew this look too well now — an attempt to appear knowledgeable whenever Fawbry had no clue what he was talking about. "I think—"

"Forget it," she said. "Go help Tommy rub down the horses."

Fawbry stepped toward Malja to protest, or at least complain, when Tommy slapped a brush in his hand. The two had a good rapport and worked well together. She wondered if she should be concerned that Tommy showed no interest in Sprint — a boy close to his own age.

She walked away without looking back. There were more pressing problems, and she didn't want them to see the concern on her face.

First, she had to get her mind straight that Owl had been telling the truth all along — he was not a potential enemy. That also meant this queen was a real threat and that the Library — she didn't want to think further about that. Better to focus on more immediate concerns.

After letting that scout escape, Malja had kept an ear open for any indication of an attack. Soon Queen Salia would learn that not only was Malja nearby, but that the Order had not been entirely razed. Her army most likely marched toward them.

She looked around the shambles of the compound. The only thing not damaged was a statue of Moonlo, his gaunt face and stern eyes watching over his followers. In Moonlo's hand, the sculptor had carved the Book of Kryssta which Moonlo wrote, supposedly, after being visited by the brother god Kryssta. The statue stood in the center of a cracked fountain.

Everywhere else, debris and blood littered the ground. Five Guardians stood atop a ledge on the wall keeping watch. A robed woman stood amongst them — a magician, no doubt.

At the far end of the main courtyard, a young woman passed by carrying bandages and water. The moans of suffering rose in volume when she opened a door to a small building. It was a sorry mess.

At least Malja understood how to deal with all of this. Far better than having to deal with Tommy. No. Easier not better.

As she made her plans, her eyes grabbing every detail, Fawbry and Tommy finished with the horses. At length, Owl re-emerged from the building. He took a few steps and simply waved for the others to join him.

Malja's men waited for her to lead the way. Good. No matter what else, Tommy and Fawbry knew who to get behind in an unfamiliar situation.

Little light found its way inside the building. The damp, cool air carried that sour odor of magic that permeated everything. Even the walls stank of it.

Owl must have seen her wrinkle her nose. He said, "Please forgive the air if it's bad. The Order is first one of magicians, and they practice their abilities a lot. Or they did before all this."

"How do you stand it?" Malja asked.

"I don't even notice it," Owl said. He gestured toward a hall and led them up a staircase.

Malja had been inside many temples before — particularly those that followed Korstra. But she had never stepped foot inside a Kryssta temple before — didn't even know they had temples. In fact, she didn't realize that was the building's main purpose until she noticed the numerous small rooms on either side of the hall.

Each room was big enough to fit a single person in a seated position. Kryssta followers rarely congregated for a religious service. Prayer was always considered a private matter — sacred in its solitude. Though Malja never felt the need for religion, she thought she would prefer this type of prayer instead of the mass gatherings of the Korstra.

They climbed the stairs, and Owl pointed to an arched doorway. "Master Kee is in here. Thank Kryssta. It's a miracle he's still alive. Now, I've told him all that has happened to me and he has been very understanding. Please, give him your fullest respect."

Master Kee's room looked gigantic compared to the tiny prayer rooms. He had a small bed in one corner, a desk and chair next to it, and a wooden stool by an unadorned window. The green paint on the walls peeled away like flakes of skin.

The Master displayed surprising vitality when he sprang to his feet to welcome his guests. His arms, though wrinkled with age, still showed firm muscle. Malja suspected he could still break a few bones with a punch. Even his long, white hair appeared full of life — thick and flowing — despite the color.

"Welcome," he said, gesturing to the chair and bed. "Sit, please."

Malja took the chair, leaving the bed for the other three to squeeze in. She said, "We've come to—"

"No." Master Kee waved his index finger, his eyes as stern as the statue of Moonlo. "We won't begin this with posturing. We don't have that kind of time, and I hate those kinds of games."

Malja already liked the man. "Fine. Clearly, some of you survived Queen Salia's attack. Is the Library really in her possession?"

"Yes," Master Kee said and lowered to the stool. "She has the Twelve Books and she knows the Library building is just north of here."

"But she needs the thirteenth book, right? And then the building will give her great power."

"The building is just a structure. It's what's inside that gives the power."

"And what's inside?" Fawbry asked like a child caught up in a bedtime story.

"A rock — a boulder, really. The Stone of Antow. When the Devastation struck, it infused this massive rock with great magical energy. At first, the magic would shoot out in dangerous flares and pulses. Chief Master Antow took it upon the Order to serve mankind by watching the rock, making sure nobody got hurt, and to study it. It wasn't much, but he had hoped the people of the world would see this as a small apology for the failures of magicians."

"Hard to see how that's much of an apology. If the Order studied the Stone of Antow, and we know they did, then he was just pushing on in the way earlier magicians had done."

"Except these studies, decades later, led to the Twelve Books which detail how to control the rock's properties."

Owl added, "It was Chief Master Ginto who had the Library built around the rock."

"That's correct," Master Kee said, and Malja saw the pride slip across Owl's face. "And it was also Chief Master Ginto who had the Twelve Books written in code. He foresaw the days that would come when others would try to use the power of the Library for their own gains."

"And the thirteenth book," Owl said. "That has the answer to the code."

"I expect so."

Trying to sound casual, Malja asked, "What exactly can this rock do? I mean is it just magical power to enhance a magician's spells or does it do something on its own?"

Master Kee folded his arms and gazed out the window. "It can enhance a magician's power, certainly, but it has a far greater purpose. You may find this difficult to believe, but it can actually create a hole in our existence and through that hole, it can connect us with other worlds."

"I don't find that difficult to believe at all," Malja said. Fawbry and Tommy looked away, both snickering.

"Good," Master Kee went on, "because it's true. The same energies that caused the Devastation were thrown into this rock and are just waiting to be released. Magicians have tried over the years to get hold of its power, but we've always fought them off. Even the mad brothers Jarik and Callib attempted it once. I suspect seeing the rock is what spurned those two to hunt down every promise of portal magic they could find. But opening portals, though it takes an enormous amount of magical power, isn't the worst thing this rock can do."

Malja's gut hardened. "What else can it do?"

Master Kee didn't speak at first. His mouth moved as he continued to stare out the window. When he finally spoke, his voice sounded far away. "Losing control of a portal can cause a massive blast of power — the kind that caused the Devastation. But that blast left much of the world intact. More people died from falling buildings and being trampled in panics than from the magic. The blast itself was like a giant wave of air. A storm of epic proportions but still just a storm.

"This, however . . . if Queen Salia deciphers the Twelve Books, if she tries to use the power of the Library, and if she fails to control it, the result would make the Devastation look like an afternoon shower. There will be nothing left. No buildings, no forests, no animals, no people. We'll be as dead as the moon above."

Owl stood, his chest heaving with tension. "Then we've got to find that thirteenth book."

A knock at the door drew Master Kee from the window. With short, calm steps, he crossed the room, opened the door, and lowered his head to a young man. When the man left, Master Kee faced Malja and her team.

"Brother X and his army are approaching."

Owl

Through all his years of training — listening to Master Kee lecture, listening to Master Kee count reps, listening to Master Kee demand more effort — never had Owl heard such defeat in that old man's voice. The strong-bodied man aged before Owl's eyes. He even bent forward a little as if the weight of his words pressed against his back.

"How far out are they?" Malja asked.

Master Kee looked lost for a moment, then embarrassed. "I forgot to ask," he said.

Owl wanted to step in front of the Master, to somehow protect his image, but he could see Malja and Fawbry and Tommy. Their faces spoke enough — they had seen the change in Master Kee as well. A thought sprang into Owl's mind, a memory of this wonderful Master teaching a class on tactics. Owl smiled. Only one thing to do when all sides are blocked and the retreat is cut off —

"Go forward," he said, pulling all eyes onto him. With a stronger tone, he continued, "The thirteenth book. We've got to find it. It's all we have left."

Malja gave a single nod. "It's got to be somewhere you're capable of finding; otherwise, your Chief Master wouldn't have left it to you. Wouldn't ever have told you about it."

"Which means it has to be close. He knows I rarely ever left the compound, so if he wanted me to find it, he would put it somewhere here in the Order."

"Good," Malja said. "Tommy, Fawbry — you two help him figure this out. I'm going to secure the defenses of this place as best as can be done. You all go find that book."

As she left the room, Owl felt a surge of energy fill his chest. This was something he could do. Chief Master had entrusted him with this book — he had to find it.

Master Kee appeared rejuvenated by the assignment as well. Sometimes just having a task could fill one with hope. "Let's start in the kitchen," he said, setting a brisk pace out of the room. "That's the closest of Owl's three most frequented places."

Fawbry grinned. "Likes food a bit much?"

"Training uses a lot of energy," Master Kee said before Owl could rise to the bait. "All of our people are healthy eaters."

Over the next half hour, the group tore apart the enormous kitchen. Designed to feed the entire Order three-times daily, plus all the large groups walking in for food, the kitchen was actually four fully-equipped kitchens united by a central island made of marble. Knives and bowls, metal pots and metal trays, mixers and choppers — all lined up, ready for use. Half the room, however, had been wrecked during the previous attack. Rock, wood, glass, and rubble covered the floor. Though they exhausted every possible nook, they found nothing resembling a book beyond a handful of cookbooks.

A thought gnawed at the back of Owl's mind — they'd never find the book in time. Too much has happened. When the first attack had come, the Order was unprepared. There most likely had been a panic. Anything could have happened to a book during the mayhem that followed.

Owl shook off the thoughts. Those that persisted in plaguing his mind, he shoved down where he could ignore them. He had to hold out a bit of hope. Otherwise — he didn't want to consider that.

"I don't think it's here," Fawbry said.

Master Kee tapped his chin. "Let's try the dormitory."

Each step closer to the dormitory encouraged Owl. It made more sense than the kitchen, and he knew just where amongst his possessions to look. He had blundered a lot since being promoted to a Guardian, but now he could make up for that. Redemption took the simple form of a book.

The dormitory room consisted of a long, open area filled with beds. A waist-high bookshelf stood to the right of each bed. Small trunks were at the foot of each bed. All very precise and controlled. This had been Owl's home for most of his life.

"I'll check my own things," Owl said.

He walked to his bed, a quarter of the way in, and opened his trunk. While Master Kee, Fawbry, and Tommy rifled through the rest of the dormitory, Owl carefully checked his folded clothes. No book hid between them. He reviewed every title on his bookshelf, looked under his bed, and ran his hands over the sheets. He neither saw nor felt any sign of a hidden book.

Finally, he reached under the bed and pulled loose one of the floorboards. He hid personal items here, things that he didn't want others knowing about. Most of the items had to do with girls. A stolen garment. A braid of hair or a napkin with a distinct lip imprint. Though Owl had been careful to never get caught, it wouldn't surprise him to discover that Chief Master had known all along. And it would be a perfect place to hide the book.

He reached in, his blood tingling as his fingers danced over the dusty items. But there was no book.

Owl slammed the floorboard in place and slapped his bed. "Nothing," he said. The others kept working through the dormitory, turning over beds, opening trunks. An urge to stop them hit Owl — they shouldn't be going through all this personal property without permission. Except the people who had slept in these beds were all dead.

"Lots of books," Fawbry said, "but nothing that's about a code or anything."

Master Kee frowned. "You and Tommy go to the sparring room. It's a place Owl has spent a lot of time. Just across the compound — you won't mistake it."

"If we find something, where will you be?" Fawbry asked.

"Right here. We'll keep searching."

Owl caught a look between the two men before Fawbry ushered Tommy out of the dormitory. Master Kee waited a few moments in silence. When he walked closer, Owl didn't bother hiding his frustrations. Master Kee knew him too well for that.

"We're not going to find the book here," Owl said.

"No," Master Kee said as he sat on the edge of Owl's bed. "Chief Master would never leave something as important as this book just lying around for anybody to pick up."

"It's not in the sparring room, is it?"

"I doubt it."

Owl's face reddened and he let at a garbled growl. He kicked his bookshelf hard, knocking it onto the neighboring bed. "Then why are we wasting our time?"

In a voice so calm and quiet, it forced Owl's attention, Master Kee said, "Because you are showing so much uncontrolled emotion that I fear for you."

Owl looked at the toppled bookshelf. "Of course I'm emotional. Everyone we cared about is dead, and we can't find the only thing that'll help us."

"I think it's more than that. You've been trained, and trained well, to handle stressful, combative situations. The loss of our friends is horrid, and we will mourn them when the time is right. But Kryssta and the Way show us that we must control ourselves, even at the worst of times, or else we are controlled by irrationality."

"You don't understand."

"I'm a Master. I understand a lot more than you realize."

"Then tell me — why was I made a Guardian? I've done nothing but mess up."

"You earned your position just like all Guardians."

"You lie," Owl said, surprised at his own vehemence. "Other Guardians had to formally test for the promotion. They appeared before all the Masters in closed ceremony. Or they were challenged in a tournament. When did a student ever get the rank of Guardian just like that?"

"I admit your case was a bit unusual, but—"

"Tell me the truth. Was I promoted just because Brother X had left and Chief Master needed an official Guardian?"

Despite Owl's abrasiveness, Master Kee remained calm. "It was Chief Master's decision. We discussed who would make a good candidate, but he made the final decision — you. Not a different student. You were the one he chose."

"And he's dead because of it."

"He's dead because he was betrayed by Brother X. We all were." Master Kee peered deeply at Owl. "Something has happened to you, something more than Chief Master's death, more than the loss of the Order, more than Brother X's betrayal or his march upon us. Whatever it is, it's clearly hurting you. And if you don't let me help you with it, if you let it overcome your ability to think clearly, then I think we'll lose any chance of surviving."

Trust and warmth poured out of Master Kee, yet it made Owl cringe. He wanted to believe Master Kee, on some level he knew the Master was right, but he couldn't reveal the full extent of what happened on the Great Field, how he feigned death, cowering against the lifeless body of Chief Master. Master Kee would despise him for such acts. No amount of explanation would bring forgiveness. If anything, Master Kee would demand Owl use his Honor Bullet.

Owl bowed his head, and when he straightened, he made sure to be as stoic as possible. "I am a Guardian of the Order of Kryssta, trained in the Way of the Sword and Gun. I have full control of my body and my mind. You have nothing to fear."

Master Kee stood with a sad gaze. He looked as if he might say more on the subject but instead just shook his head. He stepped away from the bed. "Come. We have to get to safety."

"But the book."

"It's not in here. We must collect Fawbry and Tommy, and I will show you a safe place where we can use our brains for a while. See if we can figure out where Chief Master would have hidden such an important book."

Owl didn't move at first. He ached inside. He almost blurted out the truth of his cowardice, almost crashed to the floor crying and begging for mercy. But his training kept him still. Though he tried to think through the problem more, his emotions made it difficult. He kept seeing Master Kee's sad eyes.

But nobody had given up yet. Owl held on to that. He had managed to get Malja on his side. Surely, that had to be worth something. Malja had to be able to help.

Malja

Malja walked along the wood planks that formed the narrow ledge against the compound wall. Though barely adequate room to mount a defense, it would suffice. The wood showed signs of decay — running or fighting on this would be dangerous, at best, but it would be more so for the invaders who would be unfamiliar with where to step.

The few magicians still alive took to her orders well. Perhaps it was the glare in her eyes betraying her disdain. Perhaps they just understood that their lives depended on doing as she commanded. Either way, they worked surprisingly hard at blocking the gaps in the wall and gathering anything useful for weapons.

She had the Guards collect guns from their fallen friends. Those were loaded and set at intervals along the ledge. With only two shots per weapon, they wouldn't last long. But they would do some damage.

As she watched from above, the magicians stopped mid-stride. Malja could feel the reverberations straight up through the wall. The magicians looked at each other as if one of them might be able to dismiss what they felt. But Malja knew those vibrations too well. They came from hundreds of feet tramping the earth. Brother X and his army had arrived.

She hurried along the ledge until she reached the east wall. Even without her dented spyglass, she could see the dust on the horizon. With it, she saw the crimson clad betrayer astride a black horse and hundreds of soldiers behind him.

Malja looked at her meager force. Not even twenty Guards and a half-dozen magicians. When the vibrations took on the enormous sound of a hundred armored bodies, she expected them to fall apart. Especially if they continued to stand still and wait for the army to arrive.

"Get back to work. We can still have things ready before they get here," she said, snapping them into action.

Though they moved with purpose, the magicians became clumsy

from nerves. Had they been new recruits to a fledgling army, Malja would have berated them, using sheer force to make them fear her more than any threat outside the walls. But these magicians were not soldiers. They were barely useful magicians. One of them was so raw, he could only produce electrical magic.

The Guards worked steady and strong, but Malja was not fooled. She could tell they were green when it came to real battle. Queen Salia's earlier attack probably summed up their first full experience in raw combat. No sparring gear. No Master to intervene. No rules. Some of them looked eager to fight again. She noted those faces. Others had a sickened expression. She noted them as well.

Beyond the few extra handguns, the pile of weapons amassed consisted of rocks, rusty nails in moldy wood, a few arrows, a pipe, and little else. Two magicians sat on the ledge, focused on their tattoos, prepping their spells. Malja didn't have time to inventory all the spells at her disposal, and even if she had, she would have balked at the idea.

"Doesn't matter, anyway," she muttered to herself. If she had more time, she could have set up barriers and obstacles to funnel her enemy's progress through a narrow point. From there, a handful of magicians with rocks and spells might stand a chance. But the pounding of Brother X's army grew louder, underscoring the lack of any sufficient defensive measures.

By the time Brother X's army arrived and broke off into three groups, Malja thought her force had enough power to feign a good defense. They could put on a show, but she had no illusion that they would be able to fight. Looking over all they had, she thought they could put up enough of a defense to stall. Sometimes that's all it took. Stall defeat long enough, opportunities opened up.

Trotting back and forth in front of his soldiers, Brother X thrust his sword skyward and his army cheered. Malja knew this kind of display well. Her own force paled at the sight. The army stretched far back, so numerous they had replaced the grass of the Great Field with their unending bodies.

Malja waited until the noise died down. Then she said, "You've marched a long, tiresome way for nothing. There is no victory for you here."

"You must be the greatly pathetic Malja," he said, and his army laughed. "You'll find Penmarvian soldiers far tougher than the scraps that call themselves civilized down in Corlin." Brother X pointed to a soldier who rushed back into the crowd. Seconds later, three cloaked figures were carried in, each one concentrating on a tattooed leg or arm. They were set down far apart, and the soldiers gave these magicians a wide berth.

Malja looked to her own magicians. "What are they doing?"

The oldest magician, a portly woman, said, "There's no way to tell from here. Whatever it is, it's taking a long time to conjure and that can't be good."

Brother X pointed his sword at Malja. "Surrender now and we can avoid bloodshed."

"You first have to give us something to be afraid of," Malja said. She didn't feel so brash, but she knew better than to let a superior force get away with any kind of belittling or weakening comment.

Flashes like lightning on a pitch black night snapped from the magicians' hands. The ground before each one rippled and reformed as if invisible hands sculpted the earth. The soldiers stepped further back.

Malja's magician watched with wide eyes. "Lava-spitters," she said.

The sculpted ground finished changing. They looked like a giant blisters cut open. Steam trailed out of them and the thin membranes that made their skin expanded and contracted at odd intervals.

At Brother X's command, soldiers tossed anything they found on the ground into the creatures: rocks and sticks and dirt, as well as broken weapons and severed limbs left from the previous battle. These items melted down inside the lava-spitters, and even from the wall, Malja could see the molten balls forming in the creatures' mouths.

"Fire!" Brother X called out.

All three creatures threw up the molten balls. Three fiery spheres sailed through the sky. Molten goo dripped from them as they passed over the wall. Though high in the air, Malja felt the burning heat pass across her.

They hit the bell tower first, splattering like an egg thrown against a tree — but this yolk ignited the walls, spewing hot gray-black smoke toward the sky. The second ball set the stables aflame. The last struck the statue of Moonlo, melting it into a formless blob.

This defense would fail if Brother X could manage a few more volleys. "Guards," Malja said. "Shoot those things dead."

Five Guards pulled out their handguns and aimed at the lava-spitters. Nobody shot off at random. Instead, they each steadied an arm and waited, patiently seeking out a perfect shot. Malja was impressed.

"Defend the spitters," Brother X said. Twenty men lowered to one knee and aimed guns as well as crossbows at the wall. They were either less experienced or more nervous — they shot right away.

Bullets spat into the wall and arrows whizzed overhead. Malja and her men crouched until the last bullet fired. Now, while Brother X's soldiers reloaded, they had plenty of time to aim.

Malja paced behind them, waiting to hear at least one gun fire. They were amazing — stoic and still like a statue of Moonlo. Malja peered through her spyglass. More and more debris found its way into the lava spitters. The next set of molten balls formed with steady growth.

She wanted to yell at her men, force them to fire, but she held back. If these Guards had even half the skill she had seen in Owl, then they didn't need her to guide them. They had training in the Way, and she would have to put her trust in that.

Brother X swung his sword down and yelled, "Fire!"

The lava-spitters convulsed to throw up another volley.

Malja only heard the rapid report of gunfire seconds after. Smoke from the fired weapons wafted by, obscuring her view. But she could hear the screams.

A moment later, she saw the aftermath. The Guards had shot the lava-spitters just as the molten balls were about to leave their bodies. The result — the lava-spitters never got the chance to put any force behind their weapon. The balls fell back and splashed their burning liquid across Brother X's army, forming a long line of orange fire sizzling in the ground.

The Guards and magicians cheered from the wall. Malja quieted them down and made sure they were prepared for an attack. They waited and watched. To her relief, Brother X called back his soldiers. He brought the magicians out front again and had them start the arduous task of creating new lava-spitters.

"We've got a little time," Malja said to her men. "Ready your weapons for another strike. When the time comes, they won't do the same attack. They'll storm the walls, give us much more to deal with, so we can't shoot out their spitters. Get ready. The real battle is coming."

Owl

Owl, Tommy, and Fawbry trailed the old man through the winding halls and down several flights of stairs until they entered an underground bunker. Two rooms and a bathroom. A large table and four chairs. Nothing else.

Master Kee pressed a button next to the door and a tube mounted in the ceiling lit up. It cast a pale light upon the room. "We still have a few storage cells left and a handful of magicians to recharge them, if needed."

Fawbry said, "This is how you survived the Queen's first attack?"

Master Kee raised an eyebrow. "Many of us. Yes."

"It's hot," Owl said as he removed his coat and tossed it on the table. "You fit everyone in here?"

"No," Master Kee said. "If we had, more people would have survived. Some refused to come down, insisting on fighting. Some found other safe places to be. Most died."

"It'll be perfect," Fawbry said, taking a chair and leaning back enough to put his feet on the table. "So, let's figure this out. What exactly did the Chief Master tell you?"

The others each took a chair and settled in — Owl and Master Kee on opposite sides and Tommy on the end. Owl's voice caught as he recalled those final moments. Though it hurt to discuss, he detailed Chief Master's death.

When he finished, Master Kee stretched across the table, placed a hand on his shoulder, and closed his eyes in prayer. It was unorthodox to share a prayer, and awkward in this position, but Owl didn't mind. Part of him actually found comfort in it.

Fawbry scratched his head. "You said this was the first time Chief Master took you out as his escort?"

"That's right," Owl said.

"Did you ever spend much time with him before that?"

"No. That's part of what made it so odd. Usually he assigned Brother X to be his guard. But, of course, Brother X was busy betraying us this time."

"Do you think Chief Master knew that?"

"Knew Brother X had betrayed us? I can't see how he'd know," Owl said. He remembered the horrified look that twisted Chief Master's peaceful face into one of sheer disbelief. "No. He couldn't have known."

Master Kee said, "But he did. I remember just a few days before the meeting when a messenger from Queen Salia's court came to the Order — a young girl with striking gray eyes."

Sweat beaded on Owl's forehead. "I remember her, too."

With a chuckle, Master Kee said, "I suspect all of the Order noticed her. We have females in our ranks, but not many."

"I'm glad I never joined then," Fawbry said.

"She arrived to request the parlay in the Great Field that we know now was a delaying tactic and a trap," Master Kee continued. "I rushed to Chief Master with the news. Tensions between the government and the Order had been so high that I honestly thought this was a crack we could exploit to bring peace about Penmarvia. But when I opened the door to Chief Master's study, he merely nodded and waved me off."

"He knew?" Owl said.

"I think he suspected. And he looked sad, I think. He looked like he had been expecting the news all along but had also been hopeful that it would not come. Sort of resigned."

Owl's hands covered his stomach as if he had been punched. "When he saw Brother X at the Great Field, the betrayal became undeniable. He knew the whole time but only then was it real."

Fawbry said, "That's when he knew you were being set up."

"I just don't understand why," Master Kee said. "If he knew Brother X had betrayed us, if he knew this meeting was most likely a trap of sorts, then why did he go? Why not warn us?"

Fawbry's face brightened. He stood and paced the cramped room. "First, he only suspected. But even if he knew, he had to go. If he had ignored the message, Queen Salia would have guessed that he had figured out the betrayal. Without this Brother X fellow in place, there'd be no reason to hold back. She would have brought on a full-scale assault."

"You think he went along with the meeting in hopes of delaying this situation?" Owl asked.

"He may simply have figured out this way cost less lives."

Master Kee nodded. "That sounds like something he would do."

Fawbry leaned on the table, his face filled with excitement. Owl didn't see exactly where this odd man was headed, but he could feel Fawbry's attitude catching within. "But it only made sense if Chief Master could ensure that the Queen wouldn't get hold of the full power of the Library." He pointed to Owl. "You said you hadn't had much contact with him before. So that would suggest that he gave the book to you recently, maybe even on that day."

"But he didn't. I never got a book from him," Owl said.

"You did. You just didn't know it."

Planting his hands on the table, Owl stood and glowered. "I would know if I received a book from the Chief Master. One doesn't forget such a thing. Especially on the day that he died."

Fawbry pulled back, his lips quivering. "Calm down. I'm not accusing you of anything bad here. All I'm saying is that perhaps Chief Master got this book into your possession without you knowing about it." To Master Kee, he asked, "Could Chief Master have had somebody put the book in Owl's belongings?"

"I checked my things already," Owl said. "You were there."

Master Kee shook his head. "The books are sacred. We don't just leave them on somebody's bed."

Three loud slams on the desk brought all attention onto Tommy. At first, Owl thought the boy's fierce expression was one of frustration at the bickering going on. But then Tommy thrust a finger toward Owl's coat.

"The coat?" Fawbry asked.

Even as Tommy flipped it inside-out, Owl knew. "Of course," Owl said. "My Guardianship."

Master Kee popped to his feet. "Your Guardianship. That clever little man."

"By Kryssta, what're you talking about?" Fawbry said.

While he spoke, Owl leaned closer to the coat and Tommy. "When you begin learning the Way, you are called Novice. That's your name. Only after passing the first level of tests do you acquire an actual name. Second levels allow you to call others by name. The highest level you can achieve is Chief Master. Below that is Master. Below that is Guardian. Most of us only ever make it to Guardian."

Brimming with excitement, Master Kee said, "The night before the meeting with Queen Salia, Chief Master came to me and asked what I thought of Guard Owl. That's what we call the level before Guardian — just Guard."

"See," Owl said, unable to wait for Master Kee's patient cadences. "Only a Guardian or higher could leave the Order compound and be tasked with protecting the Chief Master. So that morning, he made me a Guardian."

"And," Master Kee continued, "the tradition is that the Chief Master presents the new Guardian with a gift. Often a new sword."

Fawbry said, "He didn't give you a sword, though?"

"Nor a book," Master Kee said.

Owl pointed to Tommy and the coat. "He gave me that coat."

Tommy raised his hand and glanced at his tattooed arm. A ball of electrical energy formed. It cast a pale light directly on the coat. All four hunched over. There, sewn into the lining, they saw words.

"This is it," Owl said. "This is the thirteenth book."

Malja

Malja stared out at the ever-growing numbers of Brother X's army, her mind blanking at the sight. Tens of thousands of soldiers and magicians marched in on the fields. She had never seen so many people in one place.

"Why don't they just attack us and get it over with?" a woman asked. Her name was Bell, or maybe, Beel. Malja couldn't recall.

"They don't know how many of us there are. They certainly don't know how few. Look at the size of that army. They got word that I had come and assumed I brought some kind of army with me. So, they're being sensibly cautious."

"But with that many, it doesn't matter how large our force is."

"Don't forget, they still plan to conquer Corlin. They can't afford to lose too many lives messing around here."

Mocking her words, a loud, raspy barking noise rolled in from the distance. Malja pulled out her spyglass. "Crap," she said under her breath.

Three muscular men led in a green sodik. The army parted for the massive beast with its rock hard skull and wooly hair. It had six thick legs like ancient tree trunks and a hide that took no notice of gunshots. Twelve feet high, the beast had only one clear purpose — a giant battering ram.

"Don't look scared," Malja said, though she knew it was a futile command.

In unison, the three muscular men dropped the chains. From behind the sodik, soldiers fired their guns into the air. The noise scared the creature into a blind run straight for the wall. Its legs thundered into the ground as it lowered its head, putting its hard-boned skull into a battering position.

"Clear out!" Malja called.

Three Guards and two magicians hurried out of the way. The sodik galloped ahead, crushing anyone stupid enough to get in its path. It let out another raspy cry.

And it hit the wall. The far left corner. Shattered concrete and glass sprayed into the air. Stone and wood and every little bit of scavenged metal crumbled to the ground in an avalanche of debris. Because Malja's forces were so small, nobody was hurt, but had her army been properly sized, the creature would have taken many lives.

The wall breach was damage enough.

The sodik pulled free from the rubble and snorted. The jolt appeared to have calmed the creature for it settled down against the wall and groomed itself.

Master Kee stepped into the courtyard, scanned the area until he found Malja, and rushed toward her. His fast, agile motions continued to impress Malja, and she let her lips curl up briefly. He wasn't even breathing hard when he reached her.

Before he spoke, Master Kee peered over the wall. With a grim face, he placed his hands on his knees. Malja thought he might vomit, but then, with a sharp inhale, he straightened.

"It still hurts to see my former pupil on that side of the wall," he said.

"The giant sodik and the hole in the wall don't bother you?" Malja asked.

Master Kee ran his forefinger across his brow. "He was family." Then, with a triumphant glow covering him, he said, "We found the book."

"Finally some good news."

"Your boy found it, actually."

Malja couldn't have stopped the warmth of pride filling her chest. "Good for him," she said. "I should go down and see what we can do with this."

Master Kee must have caught the way she looked at the magicians and then Brother X's army. "Don't worry," he said. "I'll take care of things up here."

"Make sure that gate is reinforced with whatever you can find."

"I'll make sure."

"And have those three men over there build two more barriers so we can retreat into the buildings when it becomes necessary. Once that sodik clears out, they'll attack."

"I've fought in armies before. I know what to do. You go see the book."

"I only meant—"

"I appreciate what you've done. Now let me show you something."

Master Kee stepped around Malja and whispered to the portly magician. She turned to him, her brow drawn deep, but he urged her toward the edge of the wall. Licking her lips, the magician stepped closer and lifted her robe to reveal her tattooed belly. She concentrated on the tattoo for just a moment.

"Cover your ears," Master Kee said loud enough that all on the wall could hear.

Malja did as told. The magician inhaled for a long moment. Like a blowing the seeds of a twirl-flower into the wind, the magician puffed out her breath.

Though Malja did not hear a thing, she felt it. A strong vibration as if a deep-voiced singer sang a note right on her chest. All of Brother X's army fell to the ground. They shook as if jolted with electricity. Brother X managed to get off his horse before succumbing to the magic. Then they stopped altogether.

Master Kee uncovered his ears. To Malja, he said, "I told you I could handle things." He laughed.

Malja pushed him with one hand. "Why didn't you tell me about her? Why have I worked up this defense when you could simply—"

"We need your defense. We're still in trouble. The effects of that blast are not long and she won't be able to do it again for half a day. When Brother X gets up, he's going to want our blood. Their full assault will be next. So get downstairs and go see about that book."

Malja gripped Master Kee's hand. "Good luck," she said. The look in his eyes told her he understood — this was it. They were going to die. After one long gaze at Brother X unconscious on the ground, Malja climbed off the ledge and headed toward the bunker. When she entered, she found Owl, Tommy, and Fawbry clunking heads as they huddled over Owl's coat. They pointed at it and spoke in rapid utterances.

"There," Owl said.

"Yup, yup," Fawbry said.

Tommy grunted and slapped the coat.

Malja broke their concentration with a snap of her fingers and said, "Master Kee said you found the book."

Fawbry stepped back and gestured to the coat. "It's all here in the lining."

When she saw the markings on the coat, she shook her head. "Clever."

"The text is in an old dialect," Owl said, "but I think I'm getting it."

Malja shrugged. "What's to get. It looks like a map."

"But of what?" Fawbry said. "These circles and connecting lines don't following any roads or lands that I know."

"Me neither, but it certainly is a map," Malja said.

Owl nodded toward the stairs. "How are things up there?"

Malja's face darkened. "Not good. So, if you can use this book to run the Library, now would be a good time."

"It's not like that," Owl said, a fearful look in his eyes.

Fawbry and Tommy shared the look. Part of Malja didn't want to know why, and for a moment, that part won out. "I don't care what the problem is," she said. "Without that on our side, Brother X's army is going to slaughter us."

"Unless . . ." Fawbry said, his voice shrinking as he spoke. "Well, there are old traditions in the Order. Right? I mean, the stories I grew up listening to often talked of entire wars being settled by two warriors. Their fight would be agreed to represent the entire armies."

"Single combat?" Malja asked.

"Exactly. Single combat."

Owl lowered his head. "I can't go out there and challenge Brother X to single combat."

"He'll accept," Malja said. "He's a warrior, after all."

"He nearly killed me the last time we fought."

Malja stepped in front of Owl, grabbed his shoulders, and looked right up into his eyes. "We don't have a choice. Master Kee has made a bold strike, but it won't be enough. We don't have the forces to fight back. And since you're all just guessing about that book, we can't even use that. You need to challenge Brother X."

Fawbry said to Malja, "You should do this. You'll beat that bastard easily." He sped through his words in a way that bothered Malja — as if he wanted her to leave.

"No," Owl said with such force that Fawbry shied back. "Brother X would never accept her as our representative. It would have to be a Master or a Guardian."

"Master Kee's strong," Malja said, "but not enough to fight Brother X. Not from what I see. Single combat is our only real chance of surviving this."

Owl looked at Tommy in a strange way. "Not our only chance," he said.

Fawbry's cheeks flushed under Malja's scrutiny. Tommy wouldn't meet her eyes. "What's going on?" she asked.

"Tommy has an idea about this map," Fawbry said. "It's a good idea, but you won't like it. But please listen. He thinks the map shows specific focal points for magic. Sort of like his tattoos."

Owl said, "I'll go outside. I'll face Brother X, and I'll probably die. But I'm willing to risk that, if doing so gives you and Tommy enough time to find out how to decipher the code."

Malja scrunched her brow. "What are you talking about?"

"The map," Fawbry said, swallowing hard. "Tommy thinks it gives focal points for creating portals. This map is the thirteenth book and it's leading us to open a portal to another world."

Owl cut in, "That world must be where the code is."

Fawbry looked at Malja with a mixture of guilt and grief. He raised his stump. "And since you're the only one who can travel through a portal—"

Owl

Malja paced the bunker like a trapped animal. "You've all gone crazy. Absolutely insane. I will not have Tommy opening portals. That level of magic will destroy his brain faster than anything. I won't have him do it."

"Just listen," Owl said.

Malja thrust her forearm across his chest and pressed him against the wall. "You are not part of this."

Owl reached up and grabbed her wrist. With a simple turn, her arm had no choice but to bend forward and down. Stepping to the side, he had the arm behind her, pushing painfully against her back. "Since you need me to stall Brother X with my life, I suggest you treat me a little kinder."

When he let go of her, he stepped back, ready for her to attack. She whirled around, seething, her fist jabbing towards his gut. He blocked it. Rather than attack from another angle, however, she jabbed again, catching him with a hard hit.

Fawbry made a show of clearing his throat. "If the two of you are done, I'd like to point out that we only have a little bit of time left until that army is upon us."

"I won't have Tommy—"

Tommy grunted and gestured toward Malja. He scowled and pointed at the map.

Fawbry said, "I know you hate being reminded of this, but part of Barris Mont is inside the boy. With that extra power, Tommy can easily control a portal. He did it once before to save your life."

"Be quiet."

"I'm just pointing out that when he did that, he had no focal point to draw on and the world wasn't destroyed. But with this map, he won't have any problem. It's like a specially made tattoo."

"Fawbry, I swear I'm going to kill you," Malja said, but Owl thought it more an expression than a real threat. Maybe he was starting to understand this group after all.

Dust drifted off the ceiling as Brother X's army pounded the ground above. Tommy and Malja watched the ceiling and listened for a moment. Tommy then snatched a piece of paper and a pencil from inside the desk. He started copying the map. But Owl took greater interest in Malja. If he couldn't get her on his side, they had no chance.

In as firm a voice as he could muster, Owl said, "I'd like to speak with you in private. Now."

Malja's head shot back, her eyes wide with what Owl assumed to be surprise and anger. Through tight lips, she said, "Wonderful."

He led her into the stairwell, ignoring the stunned expressions of the others. Once alone, he said, "I know you don't like me, but we don't have time for me to charm you. And I suspect you prefer a more direct approach anyway."

"So stop blabbering and get to your point."

"Right," he said, avoiding her cold eyes. "It's clear to me that you hate all things having to do with magic. At least, when it comes to Tommy."

"Don't tell me how to raise the boy."

"Magic is merely a tool. It's like a big rock. It can be used to build incredible structures and make our lives better. It can also be a weapon. Neither good nor evil — it just is. And before you go on about Tommy going mad, I've seen the madness that can happen when an untrained magician delves into the stronger powers. But it doesn't have to be that way. That's what I learned growing up here. That's why I wanted Tommy to come here. The magicians here spent their lives learning to control magic, to make it do what they wanted without harming themselves."

"Didn't do them much good, did it?"

Owl leaned against the wall as if he had been pushed. "You can attack all you want, it won't change the fact that Tommy is growing up, discovering more power within himself every day. And he is determined to help you, help all of us. He won't let you keep him away from danger. Especially when he sees you take risks all the time."

"Don't you dare—"

"There's an army up there and it wants to raze us to the ground. Queen Salia wants to rule everything, even if that risks destroying it. Why do you insist on thinking this is about you or Tommy? Are you that selfish?"

Malja clamped her mouth and stared through him. The quiver in her eyes told him that his words had struck. She wasn't going to say anything more, that much was certain, but he prayed that she wouldn't dismiss him too quickly.

He watched her eyes as she considered the situation. Though she had a wicked temper, he was impressed by the way she recomposed herself and thought like a leader. She reminded him of several Masters — Masters now dead.

"Come on," she said and returned to the room.

Leaning over the table, she looked at the map Tommy had drawn. "One of these circles is the world that holds the code we need to read the books, right?"

"Yes," Owl said, coming to her side. "And if Queen Salia attempts to use the Library without the books, the magic won't work properly. She'll go mad, and if she loses control, we could have another Devastation."

"I know, I know," Malja said. "But we can't even know which world has the—"

"Barris Mont knows," Fawbry said. Tommy nodded, never taking his eyes off the map. "I'm sure of it. He's always been smarter than everyone. And now that he's part of Tommy, he can guide Tommy to get you to the right place."

Malja said nothing for a moment. Her hands gripped the table's edge, her knuckles turning white as she stared at the map with Tommy. Her lips drew in tight, until she finally shoved back, kicked a chair into the wall, and said, "Damn Kryssta! Damn Korstra! Damn it all!"

Owl started at the outburst, but he noticed that Fawbry appeared to relax. Then the strange fellow said, "Okay, then. You and Tommy should get ready. And Owl, you should go outside to meet Brother X."

"What about you?" Malja said with a touch of venom still in her voice. "You planning on finding a little nook to hide in?"

Fawbry squirmed a little. "I can do whatever you need of me. You know that."

"Then go with Owl."

"Now wait a minute. I'm just going to be a target out there."

"Your presence, having anyone by his side, will give Owl's offer of single combat an appearance of authority. Grab at least two others to go with you — one magician, one Guard. If this is going to have any chance of working, we have to make sure Brother X believes Owl speaks for the Order."

Fawbry let out a nervous chuckle. "Of course. That makes perfect sense. I knew you didn't want me fighting. I can put on a show,

330 - The Malja Chronicles

though. That I can do."

"Go," she snapped.

Fawbry turned to Owl. "Don't dawdle," he said, giving Owl a light push on the shoulder.

"I need my coat," Owl said.

Tommy raised his index finger. When he finished copying the map, he lifted the paper and inspected his work. Satisfied, he tossed the coat across the table.

As Owl and Fawbry climbed the stairs toward the surface, he slipped on the coat. It draped onto his body like a second skin. He thought of Chief Master and the book in the lining. And as he saw daylight ahead, he thought of Brother X and the coming battle. Maybe this would make a difference. Maybe he could earn a little forgiveness.

"Do you find it hard," Owl said, unsure of why he suddenly felt the need to speak, "to follow Malja?"

"Not anymore," Fawbry said.

"She confuses me. She is a warrior, strong and tough-minded, yet she can't accept the boy doing his part in all this. She attacks me for speaking the truth and then acts like it never happened. Is she always so difficult to understand?"

"You have no idea," Fawbry said.

When they entered the courtyard, Owl looked up at the wall. Small rock piles lined the wooden ledge running the parameter. Near the South wall, he saw a group of Guards praying. He took three steps towards them, intending to admonish them for group-prayer when everyone should know that prayer to Kryssta was meant to be done alone. Except he stopped.

He recalled the comfort he had felt when Master Kee prayed with him. Perhaps he shouldn't cause these brave men any grief right before they risk their lives for us all. It seemed that there were times for single prayer and times for a group.

"You ready?" Fawbry asked.

Nighthowl and the magician Bennet volunteered to escort them out. They were good people, though inexperienced, and Owl was pleased to see them. The anticipation on their faces, the fear, was not well hidden.

Owl tried to think of encouraging words to say, but in the end, he adjusted his coat, checked that his sword and gun were in place, and took three cleansing breaths. "Let's go," he said.

Two men, one with a blood-stained bandage wrapped around his ribs, opened the main gate just enough to let them through. Owl moved with a confident stride, but his stomach twisted inside. He could feel his chest constrict as they turned the corner to face the army.

All Owl could see was an ocean of armor and weapons. The voices melded together into a steady roar. Thousands.

His heart sank.

Thousands.

Malja

Tommy leaned against the bunker wall. Malja sat on the table, her arms propping up her head. The incessant thundering of Brother X's army was the only sound.

Malja struggled to think of another way out of this. They lacked a force large enough to fight through the sieging army, and they were using up the little defensive resources they had. Eventually, they would be overrun. At length, she simply lifted her head, and in a soft voice, she said, "I don't like this."

Tommy moved close to her and smiled as if to say, "Trust me." He took her hand and placed it on his head. She stroked his hair and fought the mounting emotions. He had grown so much in just the last year. He was almost taller than her, and though she didn't like to admit it, he had taken on that same cold expression she knew so well — the one she always wore.

"Listen to me," she said, and thank the brother gods, Tommy didn't glaze over. "When I go through that portal, I don't want you trying to be a hero. If you start to feel pain or weakness or maybe even some kind of damage to your brain — if you feel any bad effects from this magic, I want you to stop. I don't care if you strand me in that world. I've been stranded before. I'll survive."

Tommy's face contorted with horror and he shook his head.

"I'll be fine wherever I go," she said. "But if I come back here to find that doing this turned you into something other than the great young man I know you to be, I just couldn't live with that. You understand? I won't do this if it'll hurt you."

Tommy gestured upward and shrugged.

"I know there's an army up there. That's not more important." To the surprise of them both, she lifted Tommy's hand and kissed it. "Not to me. I don't know what other options we have, but if you can't make me this promise, I won't go. We'll have to think of something else."

For a moment like a brisk wind, Malja thought he would give up on this portal idea. But the same wind blew it away. Tommy ran his hand over the paper copy of the map, and Malja gulped down the last of her tears.

"Okay," she said and got to her feet. "You sit here. You shouldn't have to worry about standing when trying to deal with something this big."

Tommy agreed. He sat cross-legged on the table, laid the map over his lap, and concentrated on the circles and lines.

At first, nothing happened. Malja knew this would be the case. To conjure a portal took skill but not a lot of time. To conjure a portal to a specific location and to do it with enough care that there would be no danger of destroying the surroundings — that was a different matter.

Yet long before Malja thought it possible, Tommy's arms glowed a rusty brown. The air filled with a horrible, acrid odor. Crackling, like dry wood on a fire, erupted a few feet behind the boy.

Tommy swung his tattooed arm toward the back wall, never taking his eyes from the map. Malja planted her feet, unsure of what might happen when the portal formed. She forced her eyes forward. *Don't look at Tommy.* She didn't want to know what this was doing to him.

And the portal opened.

Malja took a quick survey of what she saw — night, a field, a withered tree off to the side, no creatures, no immediate danger. The warrior in her wanted to study this a little longer — get a feel for what she was about to do. But the more time that passed, the longer Tommy had to keep the portal open using magic.

"Check back every half-hour," she said. "I'll be there eventually."

Letting loose her war cry, Malja leaped through.

The air was cold. Malja's breath puffed out in moist, white clouds. A sharp crackling announced the closing of the portal.

She remained still for some time. Her heart hammered in her chest. Her skin tingled as if she had been soaked in cold water and thrust into warm air. Like a snuffed candle, tendrils of smoke lifted from her body. She tried to let her well-honed senses observe the area, but her mind had difficulty grasping that she actually lived.

The only other time in her life she had experienced something like this, the Bluesmen had forced her head through a portal. That had felt weird and confusing. This was far stranger.

She lifted her feet and set them back down. Left then right. Again and again as if to make sure the ground wouldn't disappear. She inhaled — sweet, clean air with a touch of burnt wood from a fire in the distance somewhere. That meant something intelligent enough to create a fire. *Could this be my home world?*

"Don't be stupid," she whispered. There were hundreds of circles on that map. The odds that this one belonged to her people was remote. Besides, she couldn't stay here long. She had to find that code before Tommy started up the portal again.

The longer she took, the more times he would have to use his magic to open the portal. She couldn't keep putting him at risk. Time to get moving.

She turned around. As expected, the portal was gone, but a large, wooden house on a wide hill had taken its place. It had three sections — the middle rose four stories high while the sections on either side only rose two. Lights inside flickered — candlelight. Silhouettes passed by the windows.

Malja crouched low in the field and slipped Viper free. She watched the house, her tensions growing. Though there appeared to be a lot of activity inside, nobody exited.

From beyond the house, she heard sporadic drumming — muted, yet fast and harsh. Keeping low, she scurried up the hill and around the house, keeping a healthy distance from the windows. Hiding behind a tree with long strips of furry bark, she saw that the hill dropped off sharply into a valley. And in the valley, there was war.

Every time she heard that distinct, rapid drumming, she saw flashes of orange light down below. Whatever kind of weapon produced that sound and that light was something Malja hoped never to be on the wrong side of. She heard terse commands demanding attention and injured bodies scream for help. A fiery plume exploded amongst the trees, briefly illuminating the dark valley. Hundreds of bodies scurried through the forest. It looked more like chaos down there than any attempt at strategy.

When Malja turned back toward the house, a little girl stood in the shadows. Neither moved. Malja didn't want to scare the girl, but before she could do anything more than lift her hand to wave, the girl dashed off — all four arms, gray skin, and backwards-bending legs of her.

With control, Malja hurried around the house. The girl-thing yelled, and the front door banged opened. More of these creatures poured out of the house.

They scanned the area, their heads bobbing in balance with their movements, and their clothing — strips of fabric that hung like vines

— flowed too. They spoke in an effortless language punctuated with trilled sounds, and they moved in a coordinated fashion. Groups of five spread out, each peering into the distance.

Malja looked behind. The field was too open and empty to make a run. They'd see her with ease. She wanted to observe them, evaluate their aggressiveness and their fighting ability, but there was no time. Tommy would be opening a portal eventually. Besides, she had to trust him — trust that he had put her in the right spot.

Sheathing Viper, Malja stepped into the open. "I don't want to hurt anybody," she said with arms out, her palms up.

The creatures moved back, their surprised trills and calls sending the younger ones scrambling into the house. One creature, sporting strands of skin off its chin like a seaweed beard, squinted and leaned closer. With two hands clasped behind its back and two hands in front, it bobbed a few steps toward Malja.

Without thinking, Malja slid her right foot back into a fighting stance and lowered her center of gravity. Her right hand reached behind and rested on Viper. Her left stretched toward the creature as a warning. The motion caused her long coat to open, and her black assault suit reflected the low light from the house.

The creature's eyes widened as it stared at her clothing. It jumped into the air, spun around, and raised all four arms. "*Ahna lo larro*," it said.

A murmur of shock rippled through the crowd. The creature said its words again and pointed at Malja. The crowd repeated the words as if by saying them out loud, the words held new meaning. And then they dropped to the ground, prostrating before her with their heads lowered in the dirt.

Malja stood straighter and let go of Viper. None of the creatures spoke. She watched their behavior and wondered what was so special about her to cause this.

The front door opened, and a tall version of these creatures stepped out. This one wore similar strips of clothing to the others, but these strips were patterned with gold, green, and black. It observed Malja as if unsure she was real. It waited — tense and worried. At least, Malja thought it was tense and worried. For all she knew, the expressions she tried to read meant the exact opposite on these creatures. Finally, it trilled and walked toward her with controlled grace that limited the bobbing motions.

When it reached her, it bowed its head but not its body. "Follow," it said, over-enunciating, clearly trying to make sure it got the word right. Then it headed back toward the house.

Malja walked behind the creature, careful to step around the prostrated ones. Inside, the house was a massive temple to the art of woodwork. Everything had been carved from wood — beautifully so. Ornate moldings, candle sconces, tables, chairs, every aspect of the house had been carved into striking images of animals Malja did not recognize and of the creatures themselves.

More of these creatures lined the halls. When they saw Malja, they all dropped to the floor, heads pressed down. The specially dressed creature waved her onward, leading her up a wide staircase that curved around an abstract sculpture — at least, it looked abstract to Malja.

On the fourth floor, Malja's escort stopped before a simple, wooden door and lowered to the floor. One arm gestured toward the door. "Enter, please," it struggled to say.

Malja reached for the handle, but the door opened by itself. As she entered the large room, her boots clumping dull tones on the floorboards, she noticed the numerous books lining the walls and the rich wooden furniture taking up half the room. Another of these creatures, this one wrinkled and pale, sat behind a wide desk.

"It is an honor to meet you," it said, straining to articulate a few words but far better at speaking than the escort.

"Thank you," Malja said, knowing it would be better to play along than prove from the start that she wasn't whoever they thought she was.

"I know you have little time," the old one said as it stood. "I have practiced this speech for many years, so I would be ready. Please don't ask questions because I do not understand what I am saying. I've learned these words that were prepared for me, but I do not speak your language. Please clap your hands once if you understand what I have said."

Malja clapped her hands.

The old one visibly shivered. Malja suspected it never thought this would happen. The old one's expression sobered and it said, "Welcome to our world, traveler. Your arrival signals the beginning of peace. When your kind first came here and asked us to protect the code, we were a young race. For generations we have passed down this speech, the code, and all of us have believed in the promise — that one day, another of the black suit would visit us and ask for the code. That day is now."

Malja's lungs forgot to take in air.

"The war that hurts us," the old one went on, "will now end. Those who believed will be rewarded. Those who denied will know they were wrong. Your time is short. I will give you the code and light the beacon."

"Wait," Malja finally said. "You people got this code from someone dressed like me?"

The old one listened closely but clearly had no idea what she had said. Malja pointed to her assault suit. "Like this?" she asked.

The old one clapped his hands once, and the sound chilled Malja's skin. Reaching under the desk, the old one produced a piece of paper and motioned Malja closer. "This is the code. Learn it well."

Malja looked at the paper. It consisted of three concentric circles, quartered by intersecting lines, and in each quarter was a symbol. A fifth symbol — composed from the other four — marked the center. She closed her eyes, redrew the code in her mind, then looked at the paper again. Close, but not quite right. She tried three more times before the image in her mind matched the one on the paper without fail.

When she walked away from the desk, the old one's shoulders drooped. "We hope we have helped save your world as you have helped to save ours. Now we can light the beacon so all in the world, those that believe and those that doubt, will all know that the world-hoppers returned. There is no need for dispute. Peace can return to us once more. Knowing this, our sacrifice will be rewarded."

The old one shuffled its odd-shaped legs toward a tall candlestick. It took the flaming candle, raised it above its head, and in a loud voice, it said, "*Salloo mala reesi!*" The others in the house echoed these words, followed by those outside. There was relief in their voices — exultation, even. The old one repeated the phrase in a reverent manner and let the candle fall to the paper-littered floor.

"Go," it said. "Leave the beacon now."

Malja had met zealots before, but never for her. The old one stood motionless as flames spread out across the floor, up the book-laden walls, and onto the ceiling. It opened its four arms and wriggled its mouth into an attempt at a human smile. The dry wooden house crackled as the air choked with smoke.

"Go," it said again and the flames licked the edges of his strips of cloth that served for clothing.

Malja stepped out of the office and closed the door. Despite all the horrors she had witnessed in her life, she couldn't watch this being burn up because of its belief in her. She rested her hand on the warming wood and closed her eyes. She had seen sacrifice before but not like this. How could she ever be worthy of such a thing?

In the hallway, she found the escort still prostrated by the doorway. Fires had ignited further down the hall. Black smoke poured out of one room at the far end.

"You've got to get out of here," Malja said.

The escort raised its head. "Thank you," it said and lowered its head once more.

Malja attempted to help the creature up, to take it to safety, but it yanked its hands away. She moved in again, but the creature jumped to its feet and dashed down the hall. When it reached the room belching smoke, it dove in without hesitation.

Though Malja understood what she had been told — that this entire house was the beacon, that these creatures had developed a religion based on a visit from one of her people, that these creatures planned to die in flames to signal this world of her arrival, of her true existence — she could not process the ideas with any sense of depth or reality. The whole thing seemed foolish to her. It was distant, like a myth told around a campfire. But the flames were real and the noxious smoke was real. The heat rose with every second she waited.

"Damn," she said, going down the stairs two at a time.

On every floor she saw the followers of this insanity sitting, waiting for the fire to consume them. They were placid, accepting, even happy — if their proud postures meant the same as a human's. The ceiling had become a mass of fire. Burning bits of wood dropped down, spreading the flames faster to the other floors. Yet not one creature even flinched.

The strong smell of burning wood overpowered all other odors, and for that mercy, Malja felt thankful. She didn't want to know how these creatures smelled when cooked.

It wasn't difficult to get out. The creatures left a clear path for her to follow. When she stepped into the clean air and felt the heat pressing at her back, she let out an anguished cry.

It lasted just a few seconds, and though it wasn't enough to relieve the hardness in her chest, it would have to suffice. She could only think that they had died because of her, for her, and that meant she had to honor all those souls. Until she did, Malja worried she might never sleep again.

Though she heard the crumbling of the house and the raging fire bellowing into the night, she never turned to look. She kept her eyes focused on the field. Tommy would open a portal soon. She wanted out of this world.

That's when two vehicles on wheels raced up towards her, screeched to a halt, and four burly beasts jumped out. Each one was loaded with straps of bullets, belts with knives, and objects that could only be guns.

Owl

Walking through the throngs of Brother X's army, Owl tried to keep his eyes forward. They parted for him but sneered as he passed. They shouted insults and feigned attacks. Nighthowl and Bennet each walked at his shoulders while Fawbry kept close behind. Owl could hear his whimpering as they went. It didn't bother Owl. His mind had shifted into a fighting mode. All his troubles, his guilt, his fears — all had to be suspended. As Master Kee had pointed out, emotions can make clear thinking difficult, and in a fight like the coming one, he had to be clearest of all.

He planned to walk until either he found Brother X or they attacked him for real. The longer it took, the more time he gave Malja. Unfortunately, the army had a different idea. They stopped parting for him and instead encircled his group. Still, they gave a wide berth.

"What are they doing?" Fawbry asked.

"They're making a ring for the fight," Nighthowl said.

Fawbry inched away from Owl, but he had nowhere to go. The hooting and jeering from the soldiers rose in volume. Owl pulled out his sword and eased into a fighting stance. Brother X had to be around here somewhere. Looking back, Owl saw the Order wall and the sodik that had smashed the end into a heap. If he lost this fight, that wall would be leveled.

"We can't fight yet," Fawbry said. "We need more time."

Owl snapped his attention onto Fawbry just long enough for the man to cower. "We don't get a choice."

"Malja needs more time," Fawbry said, and he screwed his face into a stern look. To Owl's surprise, Fawbry marched into the center of the cleared circle and raised his hands. "Listen here," he shouted. "I want to tell you something."

The soldiers lowered their voices, curious about this unexpected event. Fawbry looked around and threw open his colorful robe. He pulled out a small book and raised it overhead.

"This is the Book of Kryssta," he said. A flurry of fingers swiped the brows of the soldiers. A sly grin crossed Fawbry's face, and Owl nodded his encouragement.

"This warrior," Fawbry said, waving a hand toward Owl, "is one of the greatest to have ever mastered the Way of the Sword and Gun. And like all great warriors, like hard-working soldiers such as yourselves, it is vital that we praise the brother god Kryssta before entering any combat. To do otherwise is to invite evil into our hearts. Like Kryssta tells us—" Fawbry made a show of fumbling for the right page. He read:

Each day is a day for life
Each day is a new birth
When a stranger claims to know all
Tell him you live only for each day

He closed the book. "Let us take a moment to pray alone so as not to let the stranger claim our hearts."

Fawbry lowered to one knee. The soldiers around all dropped to the ground and prayed silently. It was the closest thing to a service the followers of Kryssta would allow, and it devoured plenty of precious time.

At length, the soldiers stood, as did Fawbry. He walked back to Owl and said, "That's the best I can do."

Owl rested a hand on Fawbry's shoulder. "That was incredible. You're smarter and braver than I ever realized."

Fawbry let out a short laugh. "Just don't tell anyone." He looked at the fighting circle as his laughter died. "It's up to you now. Good luck."

Owl nodded and returned to his fighting stance. "Brother X," he called in a strong voice. "I challenge you."

Owl's eyes darted from soldier to soldier. He wondered where Brother X would come from — on horse, most likely — powerful and commanding. He was wrong.

Just before Brother X's blade would have cleaved through Owl's head, Owl saw a shadow moving on the ground. He looked up to see Brother X's crimson cloak fluttering like a crazed bird. Owl got his sword up in time to deflect the attack but the sheer force of Brother X's attack sent Owl to the ground.

He rolled backwards and onto his feet, releasing his gun at the same time. Brother X also had his gun out, and the two warriors settled into their fighting stances. The soldiers roared with excitement.

"You fooled me. I was sure you were dead."

"Almost," Owl said, shoving thoughts of cowardice deep within.

"You know, we don't have to do this," Brother X said. "If you surrender, I'll spare the life of Nighthowl, Bennet, and your fancy friend here."

"You betrayed us," Owl said, his teeth locked tight together.

Brother X shrugged. "You can't betray something you never belonged to in the first place. I never was a real part of the Order. I had been a spy for Salia from the beginning."

Owl lunged, but Brother X parried away his attack with a nonchalant flick of his sword. Flowing with the deflection, Owl stepped closer and spun through his attack as he had been trained. He barely had to think about it. His body just knew to come round for another strike. Brother X met this one, too, but was forced into a serious response. They locked swords.

"You didn't have to kill him," Owl said, his taut muscles pushing his blade forward. "Chief Master wanted to create a peace."

"When the marauding beasts and petty warlords raped and killed my parents, where was his peace?" Brother X said, breaking loose and leaping into another attack. "When I lost my brother and two of four sisters, where was Chief Master and his magicians?" He faked right, spun left, and struck hard. "Never was he there to help us."

"Chief Master helped hundreds, thousands. If he had known, he would've been there for you, too."

Brother X launched a flurry of attacks, spinning off every parry and returning with more crushing strikes. Owl had sparred with Brother X many times and had fought him outright once before, but the speed and ferocity of his opponent astonished him. Only the rush of adrenaline kept him from freezing up. Owl dropped low for a leg sweep, but Brother X jumped over the attack and brought the butt of his gun down onto Owl's head.

Training saved Owl's life. Though disoriented, his body shoulder-rolled out of the way of Brother X's follow up sword strike. He stumbled to his feet and regained his focus.

"You won't win," Brother X said.

Blood dribbled down Owl's forehead. He let it run. With a slight hop forward, Owl raised his blade for an ax-strike. He watched Brother X's eyes follow the blade, and he brought up his gun with his other hand and fired.

Brother X's speed continued to impress. Though his eyes gazed upward, his own blade swung out, catching Owl's wrist and knocking the gun off target. Brother X then kicked straight into Owl's gut. He aimed his own gun right between Owl's eyes.

Owl could hear the Masters in his mind teaching that when faced with a gun, one that there was no doubt would be fired, any action, no matter how desperate, was worth taking. Even only a one-percent chance of living was better than a one-hundred percent chance of death.

Owl thrust his head toward Brother X's chest, rolling the gun's muzzle upward along his scalp. Brother X involuntarily shot. The blast rang Owl's ears and he felt the singe on his skull, but the bullet went off into the distance.

Brother X shoved him backward and attempted to aim again. This time Owl swung his gun-wielding hand to knock Brother X's weapon away. Both guns discharged into the ground. Neither of them had another shot.

Huffing, Brother X stepped back to regroup. "You say you want peace but you fight me. Queen Salia will bring peace to this world through force. Give her the power of the Library and there will be an end to the suffering of the innocent."

Though exhausted and sweating, Owl didn't want to let Brother X rest. He attacked again. Both warriors moved fast, but Owl could tell that Brother X had slowed considerably.

They struck with vicious abandon and used the thicker parts of their guns to deflect the incoming blades. Sparks shot out at every clash. The soldiers cheered and hollered at the awesome sight. Such a thought distracted him, and he failed to see the butt of Brother X's gun until it hit him in the cheek.

All went dark.

His ears continued to ring but the sound died out. He floated in darkness. A breath later, it all came back. Copper taste of blood. Rumbles of a large crowd. Rough stone under his hand. Sharp odor of sweat. His vision returned last. He sat in the dirt, blood filling his mouth, Brother X standing over him.

"When my sister was only sixteen years old, she saw how horribly the people were treated," Brother X said. He sounded muted but Owl heard enough to understand. "She saw the abuse every day. And she had had enough. She began taking control of our town. And when she brought peace to our people, then Chief Master showed up to take over. That was when I was forced to join the Order. That was when my sister and I planned for this day."

Owl stared at his opponent with his jaw slack open. "Y-You're Salia's brother?"

"I've been her spy since the beginning," Brother X said and thrust his sword through Owl.

The blade came out Owl's back and blood spit from his mouth. Fawbry cried out. The soldiers cheered. Owl looked into the amused face of Brother X and wanted to scream at the depth of the betrayal.

Brother X cocked his head to the side. "Look at that," he said with an impressed nod. "You've trained well."

Owl looked down at the sword piercing his body. The butt of his gun pressed against the blade. He didn't recall doing so, but it appeared that he had pushed the blade to the side so, though it sliced through him, it failed to damage any organs.

Brother X pulled his sword free, wiped it off, and returned it to its sheath. He singled out two men. "Wrap his wound and take these enemies to the prison grounder." To Owl, he said, "After we take your book and destroy what's left of the Order, my sister will want to meet with you."

Malja

The four creatures bearing guns stared in awe at the burning house. The gold light flickering on their faces did little to improve their gruff features. Flat, wet snouts and bristle-haired bodies. Thick muscles and gray skin. A row of spikes along the spine. They looked at Malja, and she could practically see their thoughts — wondering, since the house now burned as a beacon, if she could really be some magical prophet returned.

Malja decided to take a chance and hope they answered yes. She put her hands on her hips, parting her coat enough to show her assault suit that had made such an impression on the other creatures. These brutes, however, showed no reaction.

She then slipped out Viper but instead of holding the dear weapon as a threat, she placed it vertically before her like some holy symbol. "Put down your weapons and pray before me," she said, mimicking the cadences she had heard from the Korstra leaders in the South.

The creatures look to each other in confusion. The biggest of these brutes thrust a meaty finger at her and garbled out a few short sounds. The others aimed their guns in her direction.

Malja sighed. "Wonderful," she said, and in one graceful motion, brought Viper back to a fighting position.

The leader let out a noise that had to be mockery, and when it spoke, the others joined in. Malja couldn't blame them. If this had been Corlin, she would be the one laughing — low-quality guns and limited shots meant she would have a good chance of taking down four bandits. But here — she didn't know.

The guns looked to be in excellent condition. They also looked far more dangerous than any weapon she had ever seen. Two were handguns that made even Owl's well-maintained weapon look like a paltry imitation. One reminded Malja of a shotgun, only bulkier and more compact. The last weapon required two hands to carry and had so many parts that Malja couldn't begin to guess what it was capable of.

No way was she going to get a step closer to them like this. She

346 - The Malja Chronicles

needed something to disrupt the flow of the moment. So, she laughed. She let Viper hang at her side and she laughed. The creatures let out hesitant sounds and watched each other for leadership.

"Guess you're not in charge," she said to the one she thought had been the leader. She stepped forward, smiling and forcing out as much laughter as she could. "Since you can't understand me, I thought you should know that I'm not really this friendly."

She moved to the side, essentially placing the one on the end in front of her, and the others lined up behind. The advantage wouldn't last long, but it would give her a little extra time. She turned Viper so that its point faced her first target.

The one creature she had mistaken as the leader stopped laughing. His tone dropped and his guttural words erupted in rapid succession. He knew something was wrong.

Malja gave them no time. She swung Viper upward into the first creature's chin. Yanking downward, she removed her blade. Viper's force thrust the shocked creature to the ground while its lower-jaw rolled several feet away.

The next in line raised its gun, hands fumbling with some control on the weapon. Malja sliced diagonally upward. The creature tumbled back which saved its life — though Viper did cut a line across its chest.

The other two had enough time to fan out, flanking both sides of her. One held a handgun, the other the two-handed gun. Had they simply shot her, Malja thought they might have killed her. But they were scared and unsure. And, she suspected, they thought merely holding their guns on her was enough of a threat to stop her.

They were wrong.

Malja leaped toward the one with a handgun. She saw its face scrunch up just before she hooked Viper on its hand and pulled through. The hand and the handgun flopped to the ground. Malja kept moving until she was behind the creature.

She heard a high-pitched sound followed by a whomp, and the creature fell over, a hole the size of her head burning in its chest. The one on the other side held its smoking weapon. Whether it had killed its fellow soldier on purpose, she couldn't tell. By the way it trained its weapon on her and showed no sign of panic, however, she thought the thing could fire again without reloading.

Sweat fell down her side. Her assault suit lowered its temperature to cool her but the heat of the burning house continued to intensify. The roof fell in with a crash, sending sparks hurling into the air. With firelight dancing on its face, the creature used its weapon to gesture to one of the vehicles.

Malja calculated the distances between her and the creature — too far to take a gamble. If she could maneuver closer as she walked toward the vehicle, she might be able to use the extra reach with Viper to hit the creature. But she saw no other choice at the moment. Getting in the vehicle was not an acceptable alternative. Once inside, she was dead.

The creature barked out a few words. Malja stepped around the body at her feet, using it to position closer. She casually let Viper swing in her hand. Just a few more steps closer.

The air sizzled but not from the fire. *Tommy!* The creature's awed eyes confirmed what Malja already knew — a portal had opened behind her. The creature threw its weapon aside and dropped to the ground, burying its head under its hands. She thought she heard it whimper.

After putting Viper away, she backed toward the portal. But before she entered, an idea struck her — Viper had come through the portal with her unharmed. So had her clothes, for that matter. Whatever made it possible for her to travel through the portal without burning up like Fawbry's hand, also appeared to protect things on her body. And that meant she could bring a few items back.

Crouching down, she swiped the handgun and the one that looked like a shotgun. "Thank you," she said quickly before the creature changed its mind, and she entered the portal.

When she stepped into the bunker, Malja's skin froze and her heart nearly stopped. Tommy stood at the bunker entrance with one hand stretched out toward her and the other stretched toward the stairs. His face had drained of blood. Sweat soaked his hair. A third eye blinked from his cheek and a fourth from his neck. Eyes like those that had once covered Barris Mont.

Tommy looked at her a long time — those eyes empty of recognition. Her heart skipped but then he shivered, raised his lips into a relieved smile, and collapsed. A dim field of magic in the stairs dissipated. The extra eyes closed and faded back into his skin as if they had never existed.

She rushed to his side while the portal shut behind her. "I knew this was going to be too much. Damn Kryssta, I knew it." She cradled the boy and brushed his hair aside.

He was breathing, thank the brother gods, but his skin burned with fever. She rocked him gently for a few minutes. When his eyes fluttered to consciousness, Malja let out a long held breath. Tommy patted her arm.

Struggling to stand, he pushed Malja away.

"You need to rest," she said but he struggled anyway. She wanted to hold him down, yet his eyes blazed with a determination she knew well. Better to let him have his way a little longer. He looked up the stairs and then motioned for her to follow.

Malja checked that both guns she had brought with her had survived the trip. They appeared to be good — she wouldn't be sure until she fired them, and since she had no extra ammunition, she didn't want to waste bullets. She strapped the guns over her shoulders and followed Tommy.

Blood stained the stairs. On the first landing, she found Tommy on his knees, wrapping Master Kee's bleeding arm with strips of the man's robe. Master Kee's bruised face trembled.

Malja sniffed the air — burning, blood, and bowels. She knew that combination. The army had ransacked the Order. But she didn't hear any sounds of occupation.

She closed her eyes. "Thank you, Owl, for you sacrifice," she whispered.

"No," Master Kee said. "Owl lives. And your Fawbry, too. But Nighthowl and Bennet were not so fortunate."

"I will pay them their honor," Malja said.

"Thank you."

"Where are Fawbry and Owl?"

"Brother X took them prisoner. He has the book now, though I don't know if he's aware of it. I hope not. For as long as he and Queen Salia think those boys have answers, they'll be kept alive."

"So he defeated Owl, took him and Fawbry prisoner, and attacked here? It seems your bunker is well hidden."

Master Kee shook his head. "It was your boy who saved us."

"Tommy did?"

"Brother X's army tried to finish us for good. But when I came down to the bunker, Tommy didn't hesitate. I simply wanted to know if you had returned, if there was any hope, but this boy of yours — he created an illusion around this building. Made us look dead. Fooled me until I reached the stairs and saw him at work. Those of us who managed to get in were safe."

"Illusions? I didn't know you could do that."

Tommy shrugged. Apparently, he hadn't known either.

"I'm impressed," Malja said, and she could see Tommy's chest swell. He kept his eyes on Master Kee, but she didn't want to draw attention to the boy's pride. That much she had learned — leave the boy alone in situations like this. Besides, she didn't fully understand what an illusion spell meant nor what damage it could cause the caster. Best to keep quiet and observe.

Master Kee raised his head to get a better look at Malja. "Did you find the code?"

"I did."

He fell back. "Thank Kryssta. We're all safe now."

"Don't get too happy," she said. "There's still an army to deal with."

"They left."

"Left?"

"They saw we were all dead. Though they didn't know they had the book, they left because they had a means to get the book — their prisoners. Beyond that, the Order compound has no strategic value — we're far from anything other than the Library. Despite the numbers they brought, Queen Salia can't afford to leave anyone here — not when she plans to take Corlin."

Malja looked at Tommy. "If he can create illusions, maybe they can, too. Maybe their army isn't as big as I saw."

Master Kee closed his eyes. "That would be a gift from Kryssta. Just like you."

Malja tried not to laugh, and Tommy smiled. "No sleeping, Master Kee. We've gained some time, but they took Owl and Fawbry prisoner. They'll be tortured until eventually they'll tell what they know, which is more than just the book. Our enemy will find out what we've attempted to do. This isn't over yet."

Owl

Consciousness came and went like a tide within Owl's mind. All sense of time and direction floated on clouds just out of reach. He felt movement. He heard horses and shouting. He smelled manure.

When he woke and stayed awake, he was resting on a pile of hay in a cramped cell. Fawbry sat by a metal door, his arms wrapped around his knees. Slivers of light poked through slits in a boarded window high above.

"Where are we?" Owl said, his throat parched and sore. When he spoke, his side ached and he remembered being skewered by Brother X.

"What's it look like?" Fawbry said.

"I know we're in a prison, but where exactly?"

"Salia City, I think. We definitely traveled east, so if this isn't the city, it's somewhere close by."

"Malja?"

Fawbry shrugged and let his head fall back against the wall.

Owl put a hand on his wounded side and sat up. It stung like an animal bite but the damage was minimal. Far worse than the wound — he didn't have his coat anymore. "So, not only did I fail to defeat Brother X again, now he has my coat, and I probably didn't even give Malja enough time to succeed. This just says everything, doesn't it? Stupid ol' Owl can't do anything right." With a groan, Owl clambered to his feet. "I'm sorry. I really am. I thought I had been trained to be a great warrior, but I'm just a failure. And now, I've let Queen Salia have the power to destroy the whole country."

"You sure have an ego," Fawbry said.

Owl snarled. "I failed. I'm telling you I'm a sorry excuse for a warrior. How's that having an ego?"

"You really think the future of Penmarvia is all up to you? That losing a fight or two is the destruction of all the Masters' hard work training you? I know you're part of a great legend and all, but nobody's that important." Before Owl could protest further, Fawbry got up close and said, "If you had succeeded things might've been easier, but that doesn't mean all hope is lost. And besides, failure is good for us. It teaches us how to be better. Sometimes it opens us to opportunities we'd never have come across otherwise. By Kryssta, if I hadn't failed as a griffle warlord, I'd never have met Malja." Fawbry frowned. "Of course, that might have been better for me considering I lost my hand because of her."

"I appreciate what you're saying, but I have been raised for this one purpose — to protect the Order. Twice, now, I've been tested by the real world, and twice I have failed. There is no excuse."

"Stop worrying," Fawbry said, but Owl detected the nervousness in his voice. "So what if Salia has the thirteenth book now? She probably doesn't even know that's what your coat is."

"She's got plenty of brilliant minds on her side. They'll figure it out. And why even take the coat unless they already know?"

"Doesn't matter. She's not going to understand it. And if she does, so what? It's all useless without the code. She'll never get to use the other books."

Salia spoke as the metal door clanged open. "Not so," she said. Two guards watched Owl and Fawbry as Salia entered the cell. Fawbry cursed under his breath.

She looked harsher than when Owl had met her before. Not just because her blonde hair had been pulled back tight enough to stretch her scalp. No, she looked stressed. Tired. He wondered if that was just because he saw her as an enemy now or if the rigors of leadership had taken their toll.

"My magician-slaves," Salia continued, "are very bright indeed. They've already figured out that your coat is a map. There are a few symbols on the edges of the coat. Did you know that?" She walked closer to Owl, gloating as she spoke. "With that little bit, my magicians have deciphered the Order's pathetic code. A shame, really. I'd been looking forward to torturing the two of you for information."

Owl spat at her feet. "You're a liar."

Salia's face darkened and the entire cell seemed to grow colder. "Tomorrow, the two of you will join me and a few of my best soldiers. We will cross the Great Field and go to the Library. And I will use its power to save this world from itself."

"It's not possible," Owl said. "You're no magician and you don't trust their kind."

"I'm more than you know. And there's more than one way to cast a spell. There are all different kinds of magic power. Incantations that prime the air with magical energy. Musicians that can create spells by plucking their strings. And even powerful spells derived from the essence of life — blood."

Fawbry snapped his fingers as if he had caught her in a lie. "Ah, there's your mistake. Blood magic requires fresh blood. And for something like the Library, an animal would never do. You'd need the most intelligent, most dominant type of life. You'd need—"

"Two full grown men?" Salia said.

Fawbry's face dropped. "W-Well, no, not really. I misspoke. I meant you need a corpse. Blood magic is based on death not life. What you need is—"

"Stop babbling."

"B-But blood magic is more a fantasy than reality. Nobody can really do it. Not with any accuracy."

"I believe you and your slut warrior dispatched one of my best blood magicians in some little crap town in Corlin. How was his accuracy?" She turned away from them. "Regardless, we'll find out tomorrow when I cut your throats on the Library steps." She left the cell.

Brother X walked in next. His towering body had to bend over in order to fit. Owl glared at him but knew Brother X didn't care. He never really did. It all had been an act.

"First," Brother X said, holding his fist out towards Owl, "even though I never once cared about the Order, I did train in the Way, and I do believe in its tenants." He opened his fist. In his palm lay a single, red bullet. "If my sister did not require your blood for the Library, I'd gladly give this to you, so you could die properly."

"Aw," Fawbry said. "You're just a tender guy, huh?"

"You, I'd torture mercilessly."

Fawbry held back any further sarcasm. Owl, however, said, "Go away. We have nothing to say."

"Don't hate yourself for losing to me. While you and your brethren trained in your forms and your techniques, each one of you hoping to get a little better so you could win in controlled sparring competitions, I excelled in the Way. I studied you all, too. I observed everyone closely."

"You had to report to your Queen," Owl said, letting each word overflow with his hatred.

"Yes," Brother X said. "I also watched because I knew that someday, I would have to face the strongest of you all. It was no mistake that Chief Master chose you to guard him. After me, you are the best the Order has to offer."

Owl turned away. "I don't need your pity nor your gloating."

"I offer neither. As a matter for my own honor and peace, I wanted you to know that you never had a chance to defeat me. I know your moves. I know your strengths and weaknesses. I've defeated you twice because I've studied you. Our battles were never on even ground."

"Come, Brother," Salia called from the hall.

As he exited, Owl whirled around. Ignoring the pain in his side, he stepped forward, his muscles straining. He pictured leaping into the air, wrapping his arm around Brother X's neck, and slowly choking away the man's life. Instead, he watched the metal door clank closed and heard Fawbry let out a sigh.

Owl bowed his head. His entire body shuddered. "It's all over," he said. "We failed."

Malja

The sun fell, casting brilliant colors across the remnants of battle. Malja and Tommy stood on the wall and viewed the pitted earth. Swords and spears littered the ground alongside bodies and streams of blood.

All was quiet outside. Inside Malja, however, a storm raged.

She kept thinking over what Tommy had done — opened a portal while simultaneously shielding an entire building with a massive illusion. She kept picturing him with those extra eyes. The damage such magic would cause the caster nauseated her. But the fact that Tommy showed few aftereffects other than exhaustion terrified her.

At his young age, he should be a quivering mass of brainlessness. Magic that powerful should have robbed him of any hope of sanity. And yet, he seemed fine.

Perhaps that beast, Barris Mont, somehow had protected him from the inside. Back when they first met Barris Mont, he had told her that Tommy held the potential for great magic. And Tommy had shown that promise several times before. So why did she feel so filthy, so guilty?

Uncle Gregor often told her that guilt was the mind's way of policing itself. "We don't always listen to ourselves," he would say while slicing fresh-picked apples for lunch. "Often our bodies ignore our brains. Guilt helps us know when we've done something that, deep down, we consider wrong."

If Gregor was correct, she had wronged Tommy from the start. That couldn't be right though. She only wanted a good life for Tommy.

Together, they walked along the blood-stained ledge until they reached a small platform with a pile of unused rocks. Malja settled on the pile while Tommy sat lower down so he could wrap his arms around her leg and rest his head on her knee. She fought against the twisting in her chest and the welling in her eyes.

"I'm sorry," she said, and he tightened his grip on her leg. "Fawbry once told me that I endangered all my friends. I think he's right. I can't say you'd have been better off as a slave on that ship where I found you, but it might've been better if, after I had saved you, I left you with some nice family. All the magic you've been doing, all the spells that must be hurting you in some way, you only do them to help me."

Tommy wouldn't look at her, but she knew he listened.

"I should go after Fawbry and Owl," she said, her hand shaking as she stroked Tommy's head. "We've got the code now. Queen Salia is still out there. I know I should go. But — I don't know what I know anymore. I've always been so sure of myself. Even when I didn't have the answer, I could make a decision. After seeing what you had to do, though — keeping both powerful spells going — after knowing how that must have hurt you, I just don't know anymore. It's not fair to you."

Tommy got up and walked to the wall. He stared at the last gasps of daylight. When had he grown so tall?

Malja continued, "You can't go with me this time. You're still pale from those last spells. You're not ready to fight again. And you shouldn't have to. You're a kid."

Tommy snapped his head around, shooting a stern look at her.

"I know, but you really are young," she said. "I hate the idea of leaving you — here of all places. But if you come with me, if you continue to do magic . . . well, I hate that idea more. You're too important to me."

Tommy appeared to get an idea. He urged Malja to wait as he limped away. Malja watched, trying to recall when he started limping. *Just how strong was that magic?* she wondered.

Alone on the wall, she breathed in the evening. Though she wouldn't admit it, she enjoyed the mixture of clean, forest air with the ruins of battle. It smelled familiar and comforting. She understood battle far better than anything else.

Battle was like mathematics. In math, the answer either was right or wrong. Add two and two and there was only one answer. In battle, one either lived or died, triumphed or surrendered, dominated or was dominated.

If only relationships could be as simple. She might even figure out why she refused to tell the whole truth to Tommy. Because the full truth was that she couldn't stop thinking about that other world she had been in. She couldn't get it out of her head that they had mentioned another like her. She had seen such a person before — the woman who had reached out to her, dressed in an assault suit, from a portal Malja closed to save Tommy and defy Jarik and Callib. And remembering all of that saturated her with a desire to go home — to her real home.

The real truth, the ugliness inside that she hated to look upon, was that part of her had no qualms about ditching Tommy, Fawbry, Owl, and the rest of the world. Let the putrid mess die. If she could be free from here, if she could hold her mother, if she could return to where she truly belonged, then why suffer in this forsaken land? Before going through the portal, that nasty idea had been no more than a notion, a fleeting thought that nagged her like a fly, but she could easily shove it away. Now that she had been to another world — it all seemed possible.

As Tommy returned, the exertion tolling on his face, Malja buried her thoughts. To do any of those things required using Tommy's magic. No matter what, she wouldn't do that to him.

The boy stopped in front of her and motioned for her to close her eyes. Malja did so. She felt him pull her hand out. He placed something cool in her hand and tapped her shoulder so she'd open her eyes.

In her hand, he had left an apple.

Malja's eyes welled. "Thank you," she said, her voice cracking at the end.

He hugged her, and she let him. She stared at the apple as if it were a golden chalice or a fragile relic from before the Devastation. She brought the apple to her mouth, but Tommy pulled her hand back. He pointed toward the east.

Malja understood. "Not until I get Fawbry and Owl back, right?"

Tommy smiled.

Putting the apple into her coat pocket, Malja gazed eastward. "I'll get my things ready, catch a little sleep, and then I'll head out. Don't worry. I'll get to them before the morning sun finishes rising."

Owl

With his forehead against the metal cell door, Owl knelt on the hard floor. He closed his eyes. Nothing made sense anymore.

All his life, he had believed in the brother god Kryssta. As a child, suffering on the streets, bullied and beaten, he told himself that if he prayed hard enough every night, someday Kryssta would answer. When Brother X found him and took him into the Order, when they offered him a safe place to stay and belong, Owl thought Kryssta had listened to his pleas. Even when things were difficult at the Order, Owl believed not only that Kryssta had saved him, but he embraced the idea that he served some greater purpose. It blossomed within and covered him like a shield. By the time he had reached the height of his training, he had no doubt that he followed a true calling.

But it was all a lie.

Kryssta had not given him the strength or skill to defeat Brother X. Kryssta had not intervened to save Chief Master. Queen Salia would destroy the lives of so many, maybe of everyone, and where were the brother gods? Silent.

Owl couldn't hold back the tears. Everything inside him broke. He lifted his head and wailed. He guessed somewhere nearby Salia and Brother X laughed at his anguish.

Fawbry came to Owl's shoulder. "Please," he said, "you mustn't give up."

"It's over," Owl said. He wiped his cheeks, but they were wet again soon enough. Everything had become a mess and the urge to set something, anything, right filled his heart. The timing was wrong, but it would be worse to let Fawbry die without knowing his parents love him, that they searched for him.

He inhaled, ready to speak, when Fawbry said, "I've lived through some tight times. I know what I'm talking about. I've seen Malja do incredible things just by not giving up."

Owl held back. Fawbry was wrong, of course, but why should Owl burden the man further by summoning images of his parents? Especially when Fawbry never mentioned them. For all Owl knew, Fawbry hated his parents and mentioning them would only hurt him. Watching Fawbry interact with Malja had taught Owl that it was all too easy to say the wrong thing. Better to hold back until he felt sure.

With a disgusted huff, Fawbry said, "You're a trained warrior in one of the greatest fighting styles there is. Stop this self-pity and do something. You can overpower the next guard that comes in here and—"

Owl turned his soaked face toward Fawbry. "You know nothing. You think I'm some children's bedtime story. Oh, the mystical Way. But like everything else, that's a lie. There's no mysticism, no magic to it. Learning the Way of the Sword and Gun is a simple matter of practice. Years of practice. Any idiot can do it."

Fawbry let out a frustrated groan. "You're the idiot, if you believe that."

"If I'm such a great warrior, then why have I failed?"

To Owl's surprise, Fawbry smacked the back of his head. "So what if you lost a fight? I wouldn't have lasted two seconds against him. You made that bastard sweat."

"But—"

"You're upset because you failed at this or that? Look at my life. I've practically turned failure into an art form. It doesn't matter. We all fail, all the time. Life stacks the odds against us, so to succeed is always amazing, and even then, another failure is coming up fast. What matters is how we deal with it."

Owl sniffled and laughed. "You must think I'm not doing so well then, huh?"

"You'd do well to stop worrying about what others think. That's your only true failing — looking for validation from without. Stop comparing yourself to Brother X or Malja or Chief Master or whoever you think is so great. Just do the best you can with what Kryssta gave you."

Wiping his face, Owl felt his chest loosen and his nerves relax. "I'm sorry," he said. "You're right, of course. The Book of Kryssta teaches us as much. But somehow I just thought Kryssta wanted more from me."

"Ah," Fawbry said, wagging his finger. "Now I see what's going on. You think you have a special purpose."

"I did. No more."

"Didn't you ever go to school?"

"Of course. The Order raised me with a full education."

Fawbry shook his head. "The Order educated you, but you never went to school. You lived behind the walls of a compound, and everyone there was a devoted student of magic or a disciplined trainee of the Way. You weren't surrounded by a diverse group of kids, some who had no interest in what was being offered."

"You were?"

"There were twenty-three of us. And one thing I learned was that we all thought Kryssta looked over us in particular, that Kryssta had some special purpose for each of us. I outgrew that belief, though. I mean, how could Kryssta be bothered with the tiny details of every single life? Surely, the brother god has more important things to accomplish."

Owl rubbed his temples. "Now my education is lacking. Please, stop. I can't take any more of this."

"Relax. Stop worrying about all of it. Life is fairly simple. Do your best and know that things have a way of working out. It may not be the way you want it, but it'll work out."

"I don't want to be killed and have my blood used for magic. What's your great philosophy say to that?"

Fawbry brought his face close to Owl and said, "That you should stop crying and help me get us out of here."

Perhaps it was Fawbry's words. Perhaps it had been the look on his face. Owl couldn't be sure, but it all combined together and clicked in his mind.

The Masters often spoke of how the world never stopped, and so no horror, no failure, no event would end things. Life always continued. Or as Fawbry had said, things had a way of working out — one way or another.

"Guard," Owl called and scrambled to his feet. "Guard!"

The metal door opened and the guard walked in. Before he could speak, Owl jabbed his throat. He swept the guard's legs and punched him in the groin while he fell to the floor. The guard never uttered a sound.

Owl took the single-shot handgun from the guard's belt and nodded to Fawbry. "Let's get out of here."

As he left the cell, he could hear Fawbry's stunned utterances. "W-Wait. How did you — I mean, that was incredi — You mean you could have done that this whole time?"

Malja

Riding through the night to Salia City reinvigorated Malja. She finally had a bulk of time alone with only the rumbles of her horse to bother her. The hours provided her more than enough quiet to do as Gregor always asked of her — to honor those she had slain. Usually, she detested thinking on all the violence that comprised her life. This time, however, the alternative was to think of Tommy and the eyes of Barris Mont. She had enough difficulty dealing with the boy using such heavy magic, this new development made her want to yank Barris Mont out of Tommy and slaughter the bastard. But even if she knew how to do that, she suspected the separation would harm Tommy as well.

She rubbed her head. Better to pay honor to the dead. She did her best to recall the faces of those strange creatures in another world. A warmth of peace overcame her for just a flash. She had not sought to kill them. They were not attempting to harm her. Though their deaths resulted from her arrival, she had actually brought them joy. She had validated their faith. To think on them now, truly paid them their honor.

Except to recognize these creatures also meant recognizing that she had encountered them in another world, one she could never have reached without Tommy's magic. She could hear Owl and Fawbry simultaneously offering her their advice in a cacophony within her head — the boy can handle it, let him try, let him grow into the magician he is. But they didn't know what they were talking about. They hadn't been raised by truly powerful magicians. She knew firsthand what magic did to a mind.

Tommy did appear to be stronger than any magician she had ever faced, though. She could admit that. Maybe that's why she let him get away with the bits of magic he did. No. That was a lie. She allowed far more than just bits. The honest answer, the thing she didn't want to hear even from her own heart, was that as much as she hated what magic could do to a mind, sometimes they needed it.

Her chest filled with a pressure bordering on pain and her throat closed up as if she had become sick in just seconds. The ugliness had to be faced, and perhaps that ugliness was her. Because she could stop Tommy from using magic, couldn't she? Was she really trying hard enough? Perhaps she held back because of that day when Barris Mont transported her into his memories — when she saw the world as it had been before the Devastation. The things magic could do were, well, magical.

All her fighting, her laws, every aspect of the last year had been for what? Just some pathetic attempt to remake the world into a sliver of what it once was? But she had left the world no better as far as she could see. Magic had once provided a clean, safe world. All she had ever done was spill blood. The truth — she used Tommy, and then thrust her hatred for having done so right onto him.

Malja clutched her chest and fought back against the tears welling in her eyes. It was no use, though. She couldn't suppress anymore. She turned her head toward the sky and let out a howling scream.

All her frustration, anger, and hatred burst forth. Tears streamed down her face as her horse trudged on, and still she screamed. She gasped and coughed, but even that did not stop her cry. Only when her throat ached and her voice cracked into silence, refusing to produce more sound, did she lower her head.

She thought little more during the rest of her ride. Her mind was exhausted from the most self-confrontation she had ever let happen. And she feared that if she started to think on it all again, she wouldn't be able to stop another outburst. There was no more time for that this day. She had to be Malja, the great warrior, once again.

When she reached the outskirts of Salia City, she dismounted and walked the horse in. The city was an odd mixture of old and new, ruined and rebuilt. Even from the far edges, Malja could see the Queen's palace high in the air, its towers and walls reflecting the morning sun. Whether it floated like the buildings of long ago or merely had been constructed large enough to tower over everything, she couldn't tell — too many burned out shells of buildings blocked the way. That was the city.

The urban epicenter was the palace. Radiating outward were blocks upon blocks of buildings that had been rebuilt, refurbished, or simply torn down for something new to take its place. The further one went out, the more the buildings remained ruins.

"Hey," a little voice called from an alley. "Lady."

Malja watched a young girl, probably no older than Tommy, scurry toward her. The girl appraised Malja's horse and said, "There's a stables over a few blocks. I'll take your horse for you. Won't even have to pay me now. The charge'll go on the stable bill."

Malja was about to tell the girl to go away, but she thought about how Fawbry would handle this. He understood cities better than her. And, much to her chagrin, he understood people better, too. He would use this little thief to his advantage.

"Come on now, lady. I won't hurt your horse."

"Take it," Malja said.

"Really?" the girl said. "Okay. You won't regret it. I promise I'll take extra special care. You have my word. What's her name?"

"Don't know. You name her."

The girl smiled so genuinely, Malja thought the girl hadn't smiled in years. "I will," the girl said. "I'll have to think about it. She'll be great for me. Er, that is, until you pick her up."

"Fine, fine. Just go."

The girl took the reins and led the horse further down the street. Once she was out of view, Malja trailed her, always keeping just out of sight. They headed deeper toward the center of the city. She watched as the buildings became nicer and the population more numerous.

People walked about, some working on rebuilding, some hurrying to another location, some laughing or singing. Malja had never seen such a busy place. So many people and all of them paying little attention to her presence. Oddest of all — nobody fought.

There were no threats or shouting or drawn swords. No screams of abuse. No smells of death.

Four women and their children walked by. They never acknowledged her. Malja tried to smile at the children, but they kept their eyes looking ahead.

Maybe Uncle Gregor had it right living alone in the woods. He hated it when people got industrious. Even when she had tried to widen their shack so he might have a private room (also, amazingly enough, giving her a private room in the process), he fought the idea. Gregor wanted to live free and simple. Yet he took Malja in when he could have easily let her fend for herself.

At length, the girl led the way toward an open square which was fenced off and filled with several horses. On the far end, a large stable crowded against a bar and a shabby residence. As the girl neared the stables, an ugly man stepped out to meet her.

He had greasy hair that seemed to be cleaner than his body. His ample paunch strained the buttons of his stained shirt, and every few moments, he coughed up phlegm to be spit on the ground. Most importantly, he had a dented dagger in his belt.

With a pat on the girl's head, the man pulled out several coins from his pocket and handed them over. The girl gave him the horse, making the trade with a cautious eye. She tried to say something about the horse and the man raised a hand to smack her. She jumped back out of reach, and feeling safer with her coins, she skipped off down the street as if stealing horses to survive made for a happy existence.

Malja could imagine all kinds of suggestions from Fawbry now, but this was something she knew how to handle best. Without any effort at hiding, she marched straight toward the man.

"Interested in a horse?" he asked, opening into a welcoming grin. From several feet away, Malja could smell the alcohol on him.

She stiff-armed him in the chest, grabbed his grime-ridden shirt before he could fall, and tossed him into the stables. She didn't need anybody outside to see what happened. At least she didn't have to worry about the man doing anything stupid — not yet. He was a seasoned criminal, apparently, and knew better than to attract unwanted attention. It would only make things worse.

"Look, if I accidentally picked up one of your horses, I apologize," he said while turning his back toward her. "I deal with a lot of them and sometimes they start to look alike."

Malja knew what was coming. Before the man had a chance to whip around with his dagger, she reached over, grabbed his wrist, yanked his arm back, and slammed her palm into his elbow — not enough to break the delicate joint, but enough to stop the man from doing anything more.

"Just take a horse, okay? No need to hurt me."

"What's your name?" Malja asked.

"Skeen."

"Well, Skeen, you've just volunteered to be my guide."

"W-What?"

"Two very important prisoners have been brought into the city," she said, pushing him away — his rank odor lingered behind. "You're going to take me to them."

Skeen's jaw jutted to the side as he thought. "I don't know about any special prisoners. Honest."

"But you know where such prisoners would go. The palace, perhaps?"

"No, no," Skeen said, puffing up with a little importance now that she had made it clear she wasn't going to kill him. "Queen Salia doesn't bring filth like that into her palace. Wouldn't want to dirty the floors. No, she has a guard station nearby though. It has a few holding cells that can be used for interrogations. Mostly so that she doesn't have to lessen herself by going into the main prison."

"Sounds like where I want to go. Take me there."

"Lady, I can't do that. If I leave, my horses'll be stolen."

"Not my problem. Let's go." Malja pushed Skeen toward the door.

"Please. I'll give you information but I won't leave these horses unguarded. I'll lose everything, and I won't lose everything for some no-name thug of a woman."

Malja raised her chin. "My apologies. I didn't introduce myself. I'm Malja of Corlin."

Skeen paused and then burst into a spit-filled laugh. "Oh, well then, Malja of Corlin, allow me to introduce myself. I'm King Skeen, the Queen's secret lover." He clutched his belly as he bent over laughing.

In a calm, smooth motion, Malja placed Viper right under Skeen's chin. The cool touch of metal cut away all his humor. She pressed Viper a bit harder. "I don't care if you believe me. I'll still kill you if you don't start helping me."

Skeen didn't move as the situation sunk into his alcohol-soaked brain. Then his entire being deflated — body and soul — right before her eyes. Never before had she seen such a complete loss of confidence occur so fast. Fear, worry — yes. But the way Skeen transformed from a blustering thief to a whimpering drunk amazed her.

"May I please send for my partner? He can watch the horses while we go."

"You've wasted a lot of my time."

"Aren't you going to need a horse or two when you want to leave? If my partner is here, he can have a few ready and waiting . . . in case you need to leave faster than you planned." His lack of subtlety did nothing to undermine his point.

"Hurry on it," Malja said.

"Yes. Yes. I will." Skeen ran out of the stable, crossed the street, and grabbed one of three boys leaning against a wall. He berated the boy, poked him in the chest several times, and slapped him across the head. The boy sprinted off. With a placating grin and enough hand gestures to start his own fighting style, Skeen returned to Malja. "It'll just be a moment."

Malja looked up and down the street, searching for trouble. The place actually looked rather peaceful. From one window, a woman leaned out and called a friend in another window. They two rattled off some words, both laughed, and they returned into the building.

As Malja walked over to her horse and pulled out the two guns she had pilfered from the other world, she said, "What's it like here? Living under Salia."

Skeen fished out a bag of seeds from his pocket and tossed a handful into his mouth. "We got food," he said and offered the bag to Malja. She shook her head. "And the city itself ain't a mess of crime. I suppose that's something."

"You're a thief. She hasn't stopped everything."

"Yeah, but I'm harmless. It's the killers and the rapists and that kind that you got to worry about. Salia's stopped a lot of that. Oh crap, are those guns?"

Malja winked as she strapped the weapons over her shoulders. "You like living under this crazy woman?"

"People here, they live decent."

"Not free, though. They have to follow whatever insane rules the Queen comes up with, right? I mean, isn't she just a glorified dictator?"

Skeen licked his filthy fingers. "Doesn't really matter. She's in charge. And since most of her rules are basic and obvious — things like, don't kill each other — well, we're okay with that. The kind of thing you're talking about, she reserves those laws for the magicians. I wouldn't want to be a magician around here, that's for sure."

The boy returned followed by a man that had to be Skeen's brother. He shared the same thick waist and the same greasy hair. Both men had bloodshot eyes and smelled like feces laced with alcohol.

"Allow me to introduce my brother, Allart," Skeen said with a silly bow.

Malja shoved Skeen. "Let's go." To Allart, she said, "Have three horses saddled and ready when I return."

As they walked off, Skeen pointed out the three horses he wanted prepared. His finger shook enough that Malja figured the brother would do as told.

"It shouldn't take us too long," Skeen said, leading her down an alley and toward the city. "If you don't mind, once we get there, I'll be leaving."

"This whole thing with the Order of Kryssta — is it because she hates magicians so much?"

Skeen picked his nose and flicked off his find. "Don't know anything about the Order. But when it comes to magicians, everybody knows Queen Salia hates them. I'd sooner be a murdering child rapist than a magician around here. Course, the real crap of it all is that she's a magician."

Malja stopped. "What?"

"Oh, yeah. Everybody knows that one. I mean, ain't that always the way of things? The person who hates something the most usually is that something."

Skeen headed down a street, the palace filling most of the sky as they moved closer in, and Malja trailed along, her mind trying to catch up with this new view of her enemy. "What spells can she do?"

"Who knows? She probably doesn't even know herself. By Kryssta, after magicians kill off all you care about and destroyed any family you loved, you may not be wanting to be one yourself. The way I see it, she's got a right to hate that side of her."

A rough voice, a military voice, barked out commands loud enough to be heard at least one street over. Skeen stepped against the wall and pointed toward the corner.

"Is that it? Around the corner?" Malja asked.

Skeen looked nauseous. "This is as far as I'll go. The army's been getting ready since the morning. I don't know what it's all about, but from everything you've been asking, I'm guessing I don't want to know. So, good luck, whoever you are. I promise the horses will be waiting for you."

Malja inched along the wall, trying to hear more. With her focus on the voice, she forgot about Skeen. Not surprisingly, when she turned back, he was gone.

The rough military voice came again. Malja shoved away all thoughts not directly connected with the voice. She backtracked and cut down another alleyway, then moved in closer, now at a better vantage. She pressed against a smooth wall.

"Load up those two grounders," the voice commanded. Malja peeked around the corner but nobody noticed her.

Several soldiers loaded horses and grounders and even a few flyers. Most of the grounders were open bed, dented, and rusting. A few had a closed cab.

Magicians sat on the vehicles, priming the engines with their spells. Other soldiers sharpened weapons, loaded quivers, and attached sheets of wood or metal to the vehicles. A thick-armed man, bald and sweaty, shouted the orders — he owned the voice Malja had followed.

"Hurry up with that armor," Baldy yelled. "We'll be taking the Queen to the Library soon. I want that flyer cleared off. We need to fit our prisoners and three guards on it."

Malja perked up and a tinge of joy rushed through her. She hadn't realized it until that moment, but somewhere in her mind, she had decided Owl and Fawbry were dead. Of course, the man only said the prisoners, but Malja couldn't imagine what other prisoners would be important enough to bring to the Library.

A loud bell clanged urgently. All the soldiers stopped and looked toward Baldy. Malja didn't have to look. That bell rang of trouble. A young soldier rushed up to Baldy, and the worry on his face as he broke the news confirmed Malja's thoughts — her boys had escaped.

Baldy pointed at two men. "Krig, Banrog — go help find those prisoners. The rest of you get back to work. We've got to be ready to go anytime now."

Krig and Banrog, both the kind of men most people feared, jumped off a grounder and jogged passed Malja's alleyway, heading further down the street. Malja let them go for a few feet before following as fast as she dared. The palace loomed in the sky.

Owl

Two bodies dropped to the floor. Owl stepped over them and peered down a hall lined with sculptures of Salia. He motioned for Fawbry to follow.

"Wow," Fawbry said, looking at the unconscious guards as he maneuvered around them. "I should give up all this and just travel around motivating people."

Keeping focused ahead, Owl said, "You certainly helped me." Somebody rang a bell rapidly.

"That would be for us," Fawbry said.

"Come on." Owl led them to a T-junction, his eyes roving the walls, looking for a specific door.

"Owl," Fawbry whispered behind him. "Over here."

Looking back, Owl saw that he had mistaken a life-sized carving for another piece of art. It was actually a door, and Fawbry's grin told Owl they had found his weapons. Quite a few weapons, it turned out. The room was loaded with confiscated swords and guns.

While Fawbry picked out a sword he liked, Owl saw his familiar blade just behind an official's desk. His skin tingled — though the Masters never allowed the trainees to name their swords, he still felt a kinship toward the object. He picked it up, felt the perfectly balanced weight, and a small bit of the tension he held fluttered away. Next to where the blade had lain, Owl saw his gun and holster. He examined it carefully — no damage — and he thought they might get out of this after all. That's when the official who sat at this desk returned.

"Hey," he said. "Stop right there."

Owl moved fast. He didn't want to kill, but he had to make sure the guard couldn't cause them trouble. He kicked a roundhouse to the guard's knee, stepped in as the man crumpled, and popped him in the temple with the hilt of his sword.

"Kryssta," Fawbry said. "You really are like the legends."

Owl's keen ears heard light footstep approaching. He pointed at the doorway with his sword and brought a finger to his lips. Fawbry's eyes widened. He crouched behind the desk and waved Owl onward. Owl stepped closer to the doorway, raised his sword, and waited.

The footsteps halted a few feet before the door. Owl flexed his fingers and readjusted his grip. He cleared his mind, ignoring Fawbry, ignoring the pressure of trying to escape, ignoring the worries of what they had to accomplish. His mind thought of nothing but listening for any cue that the time to attack had arrived.

He heard breathing. Lowered his body. Readied to pounce.

The attack came so fast, Owl should have died. Only the fact that he had his sword positioned up saved him. It blocked the curved blade from severing his head. Curved blade?

"Malja?"

Malja slipped through the doorway, pulling Viper away. Her eyes took in the room and her shoulders let loose a little tension. "Good to see you alive. You, too, Fawbry."

The colorful robe waved from beneath the table. His head poked up just to the nose, just enough to look around. Then he stood with a huge grin. "Malja! Thank the brother gods."

"The code?" Owl asked.

"Of course she got the code," Fawbry said. "You really think she'd fail?" To Malja, he added, "You did get it, right?"

Flyer and grounder engines rumbled through the air. Horses whinnied. A deep voice yelled out commands.

"Damn," Malja said and peered out of the room.

"What's happening?" Fawbry said.

"Salia's leaving for the Library."

"But she needs us."

As Owl opened a drawer, removed two bullets, and loaded his gun, he shook his head. "She only needs blood. With us having escaped, she must have decided to use two other poor souls."

"Let's go," Malja said. "If we let her get to the Library, rescuing you two will have been pointless."

Following Malja into the hall, Fawbry said, "We're pointlessly fine, thanks."

Malja led them through several corridors, ducking them into an office while soldiers tramped by in the opposite direction. She led them with such brazen confidence that Owl understood how she had earned her reputation. It was more than just killing. She could be inspiring.

They entered a stairwell drenched in blood, and Owl had to rethink his image of Malja. Two gutted bodies had been draped over the railing, their gore dripped down several floors.

"Krig and Banrog," Malja said.

"Kryssta," Owl said, trying to picture the sheer animal nature in Malja.

As she led them down another hall, she said, "I warn you. It wasn't easy getting in here. The entrance has a lot more blood."

Owl took a few steps down the hall but stopped. His skin prickled. He knew without turning around that Brother X stood in the hall not too far behind.

"Fawbry, Malja," he said, his voice a steady rock. As they turned to face him, as he saw their reaction, he knew his senses had told him the truth. This time, however, he would not be afraid. He looked straight into Malja and said, "You and Fawbry must stop Salia. I will stay here and stop this man."

Malja walked up to him, and to his relief, she did not protest. Instead, she gave him an unusual looking handgun. "I brought you a little present from my trip."

Owl inspected the gun. He didn't understand a lot of what he saw, but he understood enough. "Thank you."

"Just be careful. It's a lot stronger than you think."

"So am I."

Fawbry closed in, keeping his eyes on Brother X. His lips quivered. "You don't have to do this."

"Salia has to be stopped, and you two can't do that with him in the way."

"But after all you've said—"

Owl tapped the side of Fawbry's head. "You were the one convincing me to not let failure destroy me."

"I didn't tell you to go crazy, though."

"You're wasting time. Go after Salia." Owl looked over his shoulder at Brother X who stood with his arms folded and his legs unwavering. "Live or die, I have to do this."

"Listen to me, please."

Malja took Fawbry's arm and spoke fast and quiet in his ear. Owl, though, still heard her. "If you want him to have a chance at living, stop weighing him down with your doubts." In a louder voice, she said, "We have to go."

As Malja and Fawbry rushed down the hall, Owl turned to face Brother X.

"You won't make it through alive this time," Brother X said with a smirk.

Owl bent his knees for balance. He raised his sword in his right hand and aimed his new gun with his left. He stared at Brother X with stoic eyes. He said nothing as he watched Brother X's cocky smirk falter.

Malja

The mass of grounders, flyers, and horses had gone. Not too far though — Malja still heard the rumbling convoy in the distance. The churned up ground made a distinct path that could be followed as did the sharp odor of the magic used to fuel the vehicles.

Two horses, saddled and ready to go, stood by a long hitching post. *Probably belonged to Krig and Banrog,* Malja thought. They wouldn't be returning.

"Looks like we're riding," Malja said as she picked the dappled gray. She unwound the reins and mounted up. Fawbry, however, hadn't moved. "What's wrong?"

Fawbry looked up at her, his face drained. "What am I going to do? I'm no fighter."

"You've been with me for over a year. After all we've done, you think you can't fight?"

"You fight. Tommy fights. I usher people out of the way. I sneak around back and get our enemies when they aren't looking. If I get on that horse and ride out with you, there's no place for what I do. All that'll happen is I'll get killed."

"We don't have time for this. Get on the horse."

"Go without me. I'm a liability."

"Get on the horse."

"Why do you care? You don't need me. Just go."

Malja dodged the idea of telling Fawbry about the things she had discussed with Tommy. Instead, she said, "At the least, you'll be my decoy. Especially in that robe."

"Very funny."

"Maybe this'll help," she said, offering the other gun she had brought back through the portal.

When he took the weapon, its weight surprised him, lurching forward. But when he regained his footing, he looked like a child getting a special reward. His eyes roamed the weapon.

"How does it work?" he asked.

"Don't know for sure. But like all guns, you pull the trigger and something goes boom. Just make sure the end with the hole is facing your enemy."

Ducking his head under the strap, Fawbry said, "Thanks."

Malja didn't respond. That she might have done this as some gesture more than needing another fighting body disturbed her. Besides, there were more important things to deal with at the moment. "Get on a horse and let's go."

"Right behind you," Fawbry said, and to her surprise, Malja found his words energizing.

Together, they galloped off toward the convoy.

Owl

Owl and Brother X stood still, their weapons poised and ready, their eyes locked on each other. Facing off in a corridor had its problems. The narrowness of the space meant Owl and Brother X couldn't circle each other. Nor could they come in straight and significantly alter direction at the last instant for a surprise flanking attack. Broad sweeping strikes were useless, too.

Owl had his feet set in a classic 'L' stance taught to him by Master Kee long ago — his feet balanced so that he could launch into an attack as easily as leap out of the way. He saw that Brother X chose a more aggressive posture — one that afforded him greater power when attacking but lacked the ability for a fast defense.

He pictured the fight. Brother X would leap forward, but Owl would jump to the side — and hit the wall and have a blade slice through his back. Owl shifted his feet and lowered his body. This position slowed his offense (he'd have to raise his body a bit before he could move forward effectively) but it meant he could withstand Brother X's frontal assault without evasion or falling to the ground.

In reaction, Brother X changed his stance. He took on a straighter pose, almost standing, designed for a fast overhead strike. Owl altered slightly to accommodate.

In this way, the two battled without striking. Each shifted to a new stance only to be countered by the other. As they stared at each other, as they planned out the battle before it occurred, any one mistake would leave a deadly opening.

Owl controlled his breathing. He had to stay calm. Once, he had the privilege of watching two Masters spar like this. It lasted two hours — only one strike. The losing Master fell to the ground and was rushed to the infirmary.

As Owl mentally prepared for a long fight, both he and Brother X stepped into the same beginner's stance. They both recognized it at the same time. Both dashed ahead.

The clash of blades rang throughout the corridor as they passed each other. Two distinct hits — one high, one low — both blocked. They whirled around. Owl set in a defensive posture in case Brother X hurried into another attack. Brother X, however, would not be so foolish. He took on a simple fighting stance, and their face off began again.

This time was different. Owl's arms shook from the jolt of Brother X's attack. Twice before Owl had faced this man, but this time, the strikes came in faster and harder. Brother X had been toying with him earlier.

As they shifted into new positions, Owl watched his enemy's gun hand. In the Way, a fighter fired his weapon only either when facing multiple enemies or when the sword failed. With only two shots, each bullet had to be considered precious. Owl glanced at the gun Malja had provided. How many bullets did it hold?

His eyes had only checked his gun for less than a second, but that was too long. When he looked up, Brother X was upon him. Owl raised his sword, deflecting the incoming blade but not with any control. Brother X's blade slid across Owl's, jumped the hilt, and took off Owl's index finger. Brother X leaped by and rolled forward. As Owl turned around, Brother X finished his roll, spun back, and aimed with his gun.

Owl's finger screamed, but he made no sound. He regained his focus. He saw Brother X's trigger finger move. As the bullet ripped into the air, Owl let his body drop backward, and he watched the bullet sail above him — where his head had just been.

Popping back to his feet, Owl whipped his new handgun forward and shot. The enormous bang deafened him. The sheer force of the weapon shoved Owl's arm to the side, destroying any aiming he had attempted.

On the wall, a hole the size of a fist opened next to Brother X's shoulder. Brother X looked at the smoking hole and then at the weapon. For the first time, Owl thought he saw a flash of uncertainty. He shot again.

This time, Owl was prepared for the powerful recoil. His aim, for Brother X's chest, did not waver. Brother X raised his sword to take the bullet — something a common swordsman could never accomplish — but a true Master of the Way was no common swordsman. The bullet struck the sword, sending sparks off to the sides, and pushing Brother X back.

"That's two," Brother X said.

Owl pulled the trigger again. A third bullet shot out and Brother X's shocked eyes gave Owl great satisfaction. Brother X deflected this bullet too, but he fell to one knee in order to absorb the powerful shock.

A fourth bullet blasted out. Owl's arm shook to the bone and his wounded side burned, but he held firm despite the pain. Brother X blocked again, the shower of sparks flickering against the sweat damping his face.

Owl shot a fifth bullet. Brother X missed a clean block. He changed the bullet's trajectory away from his heart, but it still cut through his gun arm, spraying the corridor with blood.

Owl raised the gun to aim at Brother X's forehead. He focused all his energy on holding that gun still. "This is for Chief Master," he said and pulled the trigger.

Beeeeeeeeeep

The long tone coming from the gun was matched with a red light. Both Owl and Brother X stared at the gun, unsure of what the sound meant. Before Owl could realize that it didn't matter, what mattered was that the gun no longer fired, Brother X lunged from his crouched position, his sword leading the way.

Owl batted the blade away. Brother X's face was as red as his clothes. Sweat and spit flew off him as he barraged Owl with one sword strike after another. He grunted and shouted. Owl stepped back with each attack, doing his best to defend, never getting a chance to counter the attacks.

"You're pathetic," Brother X said and sent his blade after Owl's neck. Even as Owl blocked it, Brother X tried to redirect his attack lower to the shoulder. "You can't even kill me with five bullets."

Their swords clashed and the sheer force behind Brother X's blows pressed Owl against the wall. Brother X spun his gun sideways and held it by the back end. He thrust the weapon at Owl's neck, the move intended to damage Owl's throat while pinning him against the wall.

Owl knew the move well. He lowered his head, taking the painful strike on his chin. Brother X pulled the gun back and flipped it around, using it like a metal glove over his fist. He punched Owl in the chest. Then again, lower to the wounded side.

Owl cried out, his voice blending with the incessant beep of his weapon. His torso convulsed and his legs buckled. The sudden loss of control saved his life. Brother X instinctively jumped back, assuming Owl's movements had been planned. That mistake gave Owl the time to re-grip his sword and strike at Brother X.

The swords clashed, the guns blocked. Controlled rage fueled the men. But Brother X always managed the better strike, the better defense. No matter what Owl tried to do, Brother X countered.

Owl parried the next attack and spun around, but Brother X knew these moves too well. He caught Owl's sword on the barrel of his gun and kicked Owl in the thigh, knocking him back several feet. Owl tumbled to the floor.

"You'll never beat me," Brother X said, not even bothering to settle in a stance. "You're too slow, too weak, too predictable."

The throbbing pain in Owl's thigh deadened the leg. He tried to stand but couldn't get his leg to co-operate. He rifled through his mind trying to remember how the Masters had taught him to handle this kind of situation.

"It's over," Brother X said. "Now you die."

As Brother X launched into his attack, time slowed for Owl. He watched his enemy leave the ground, his red cloak fluttering like a flag behind him. The bloody sword turned downward for a skewering thrust. Brother X's face turned into a twisted mix of lust and hate.

The sword moved just a hair to the side. Brother X's eyes looked off that way, too. And in the sliver of a second, so much that Owl had been trained to do collided with what the Masters taught that he had not understood.

Owl's body had leaned to the side. It was doing as he had been trained — a simple roll to evade the attack. But Brother X was already looking at the spot Owl would roll to. He knew. Because he had been trained the same.

The Masters taught that the greatest fighters never had to fight. It made sense now. Owl decided that he would not do as he had been trained. Instead, he would sit still with his sword pointing upward in a traditionally meditative state — just as Chief Master always asked of him.

The last thing Owl saw before time returned to normal for him was something he knew he would never forget — Brother X's eyes as he realized his mistake. Stuck in the air, he couldn't change direction. Brother X came down, impaled on Owl's sword. Blood streamed along the blade and over Owl's hand.

The long beep of the gun ceased and the light changed from red to blue. Owl pressed the muzzle against Brother X's temple.

"P-Please," Brother X said, his voice weak and wet. "Please, let me die honorably."

"No," Owl said and pulled the trigger.

The blast shot Brother X down the corridor with Owl's sword still stuck through him. Brother X's head, however, went straight against the wall, leaving a smear of blood and a pile of shattered bone fragments.

A few minutes passed before Owl dared to move. He didn't think, either. He just sat there, letting the immediacy of the moment wash over him. When he finally attempted to stand, he found that the pain in his thigh had left. His finger and his side would take time to heal, but he could still move.

As he retrieved his sword from Brother X's corpse, he noticed a paper sticking from a pocket in the cloak. Owl snatched it out. As he read it, he knew he wasn't done yet.

Malja was in serious trouble.

Malja

For Malja, galloping on a horse was both exhilarating and terrifying. She had great respect for the animal and loved the feeling of all that power thundering her across the land. She thrilled at the wind whipping her braided hair like the horse's tail. But knowing that the only control she truly had over the animal was the control it allowed to be given made her tense.

They were closing in on the convoy when her horse veered to the right. Malja used her heels to guide the horse back, but it was frightened by something. A glance over her shoulder showed that Fawbry's horse had a similar reaction.

Pressing harder and tugging on the reins, she forced the horse toward the left, but when it reached the target direction, it continued on to the left. Fawbry pulled up next to her, pointing out the three magicians on the back of an open bed grounder. Damn magicians. She didn't know what magic they were using, but clearly the horses had a distaste for the spell.

The grounders rolled on wide, patched wheels, and the body's edges were covered in broken glass and sharp metal bits. Whether that was meant to protect the magicians or to keep them under control, Malja couldn't say.

"Split and flank," Malja said. If it took three magicians to cast this spell, then they probably didn't have enough power to follow two targets.

"See you there," Fawbry said and took his horse off to the right. Malja kicked her horse on, speeding along the left.

As they closed in, she heard panicked shouting and the harsh whine of a flyer making a tight turn. Malja pulled Viper loose and kept her eyes straight ahead. The closer they came, the more noise she heard. Between the pounding of the horse she rode and the non-stop rumble of the convoy, Malja found it difficult to hear much else.

The flyer, a snub-nosed craft with two wings out like a bird of prey and two wings perpendicular to the ground, sputtered off to Malja's left. A sole magician powered and operated the craft. It came in low and fast, stirring up dust in spiraling plumes.

Malja ducked, pressing her body flat against the horse. The flyer soared right overhead. The heat it generated pressed down, causing the horse to stumble. It took two halting steps before it regained its rhythm.

Malja made it a point never to learn a horse's name — they never lasted long enough around her. But after that feat, one that would have lamed most horses and sent her rolling in the dirt, she thought she might learn this one's name. As the flyer curved around for another pass, she reminded herself that she had to live through this first.

The craft came in low again. This time, however, Malja was ready. She flicked Viper's sharp tip skyward. As the flyer passed over, Viper squealed as it cut through the metal underbelly. Malja felt several tugs as Viper sliced wiring and cables.

Black smoke belched out of the back end of the flyer. The magician strained to get control of the ship, but it was too late. It arced off to the side and smashed into the ground.

Malja would have loved to inspect the wreckage but that would have to wait for another day. She set her horse racing onward. In short time, she saw the back of the convoy with the flatbed carrying the three magicians that were causing her horse a lot of trouble.

She rushed ahead, unsure of how to stop them, when she saw Fawbry approaching from the right-hand side. His multi-colored robe whipped behind him. He let out a meager war cry as he raised his arm toward the magicians. Malja's eyes widened — the gun.

Malja had heard many different handguns and rifles before. Never had she heard anything like this. The weapon let loose a rage of bullets, spraying them like a fountain. She heard the steady *tat-tat-tat-tat*, delivering death at speeds she never imagined, and watched the three magicians arch backward. Blood spurted into the air and they slumped over each other. Fawbry's war cry morphed into a scream as the gun's recoil knocked him from his horse.

Without anyone to control it, the flatbed wobbled and then curved off toward a large rock. When it hit, the bodies soared several feet beyond.

Malja's smart horse knew that the disturbing spell had vanished. The horse cut right into the path Malja had been wanting to go this whole time. As she neared Fawbry, he got to his feet and shook his body.

"Get ready," she called out.

Fawbry saw her, shouldered his weapon, and put out his arms. She leaned over and as the horse passed by, she swooped Fawbry up and onto the back of her horse. He was lighter than she had expected and ended up hanging off the opposite side. With her leg, she shoved him back up, keeping her hands on the reins and pushing her horse after the convoy.

When he settled behind her, Fawbry wrapped his arms around her waist. "Thanks for getting me," he said.

"I still need you. And that gun," she said.

"It's amazing, isn't it?"

As they neared the convoy, Malja got a clearer look of the set up. Lots of horses and several grounders spread out over a wide area. A handful of flyers led the group further up. In the middle of it all rode an enclosed transport with rope ladders swinging from either side. Sunlight glittered off its metal body. A flatbed of soldiers trailed behind. Tethered to the transport, three flyers pulled it like horses towing a cart. Atop the transport stood Baldy.

"There," Malja said. "That's where Salia is."

"Makes sense," Fawbry said. "There's faster ways to get to the Library but they're through the forests. Very narrow. If she wants all this protection, she has to cross the Great Field."

They were close enough now that Malja could see Baldy pointing to several of his men and shouting orders. Three horsemen broke off and headed back.

"They don't have many magicians," Fawbry said.

"Hard to use them around here when you say you hate them so much."

Fawbry tapped the gun. "I got a little magic right here."

"Then use it," Malja said. "And don't fall off this time."

Fawbry lifted the weapon as Malja loosened the reins and squeezed her heels to spur the horse on. The three horsemen closed the distance — two pulled out clean, shiny swords, and one pointed a gun.

"Look at this," Fawbry said as a red light emitted from the gun. "It's like a pointer to wherever I aim."

"Then aim at the enemy!"

Malja watched the red light dance on one of the horsemen. When Fawbry pulled the trigger, the noise shattered around her. Her assault suit stretched itself from the neck up over her ears. She knew it could alter its shape — it had grown with her since she was little — but never had it reacted so fast. Flashes of gunfire continued at her side. Her horse kept steady, but she could feel its body shudder under her.

Fawbry fired more, and one horseman fell back, blood popping out wherever the bullets struck. With the gun still spitting out, Fawbry took down the other two horsemen. In just seconds, he had cleared them out.

Malja could see the faces of many of the soldiers in the convoy. They stared back in shock. She sympathized. Whatever this weapon was, Fawbry had shown that with it, even a weak clown could become deadly.

"Get to Salia," Fawbry said. "I'll take care of anything that comes our way."

Baldy sent several more waves of horsemen. Each time, Fawbry unleashed a barrage of bullets that leveled the enemy before it came close enough to engage. But Malja saw that Baldy wasn't a fool. He stopped sending men to their deaths and instead commanded most of the soldiers to break off back toward the city. They were useless now.

The way Baldy stared at Malja as she approached told her enough. He knew she was coming for Salia. And since he couldn't stop her from reaching the transport, he might as well wait and prepare.

Malja's horse tried to slow its gait, but Malja pressed it onward. "Almost done," she said, stroking its neck.

Baldy climbed down the back of the wagon, reached below for a moment, and then saluted his men standing on the flatbed. At first, Malja saw nothing change, and her confusion was matched by the soldiers questioning their captain. Then the wagon continued ahead but the flatbed fell behind. Baldy had uncoupled the flatbed.

Most of the soldiers dropped to the flooring. Any magicians onboard wouldn't have had enough time to cast a significant spell. Seven, however, lifted long-range rifles and took aim.

"Keep going," Fawbry said. As they passed the stalled flatbed, Fawbry pulled his trigger. Once more, the weapon belched bullets with deafening bursts. Five of the seven soldiers fell. The last two fired back. Malja couldn't tell where the bullets struck, but she knew they had missed her, Fawbry, and her horse. Beyond that, she didn't care. All that remained was the transport.

Fawbry tapped Malja on the shoulder. She turned her ear toward him. "I think I'm out of bullets," he said.

It was a shame to lose such a great weapon, but Malja hadn't expected it to last so long. She'd never known any gun that held so much ammunition.

"I'm going on that transport. You steer the horse," she said.

Before Fawbry could object, Malja swung her left leg over the horse's head and stood in the right stirrup. She motioned for Fawbry to scoot onto the saddle. Though his eyes looked at her like she had lost her mind, his body did as she commanded. He inched forward until he could hold the reins and had his left foot in position. Malja then put her hands on his shoulders, shoved down hard and popped herself onto the horse's back just behind Fawbry.

Sitting fully in the saddle now, Fawbry looked over his shoulder and said, "Don't ever do that again."

Malja readied Viper and nodded toward the transport. "Get in as close as you can."

Fawbry did as instructed, his hands shaking from both the galloping horse and his own nerves. Malja brought her left foot up, getting ready to jump onto the transport. Just a little closer.

She never heard the loud twang of the crossbow. Baldy had plenty of time to set up his shot, and he hit her in the right bicep. She yelled out both her pain and aggravation. She dipped forward but Fawbry pulled her back from falling off.

"You okay?" he called back.

"Keep going." She glared at Baldy. He laughed and blew a kiss. As she wrapped a fist around the bolt and yanked it from her arm, she kept her eyes on him.

Her assault suit tightened around the wound like a bandage. In seconds, the pain numbed enough to be ignored.

Fawbry brought the horse right next to the transport, and Malja jumped onto the rope ladder hanging over the side. She looked up to see Baldy patiently waiting for her. Smart. No point in struggling to load another bolt on a bouncing transport. If he dared try to harm her on her climb, she would be on him fast and Viper's reach would cut him down. Better to take the best possible location on the roof, get balanced, and ready a sword.

When Malja swung onto the transport's roof, Baldy made another excellent move. He attacked before she had time to gain her footing. Viper clanged with Baldy's sword, and Malja's back foot slipped. She fell back, tucking her leg underneath, saving it from twisting and herself from falling off the side.

Baldy growled as he jumped toward her. Malja swung out with Viper, catching Baldy's sword and tearing it out of his hand. It spun off into the distance.

And then she saw his eyes. Tight, slitted, reptilian eyes. Whatever Baldy was, he wasn't human.

Malja rolled over and kicked out as she rose to her feet. Baldy didn't take the bait. He stood back and settled in for another bout.

The transport jolted but Malja now had her balance. She held Viper low with both hands and measured her opponent. To go with his eyes, he had a thick hide. No tail she could see — good. Tailed creatures often had better balance. What concerned her most, though, was the fact that he hadn't produced another weapon since losing his sword. He eyed her, muscles pumped and ready, and snarled. The only possible dangers he posed besides pure strength were the metal bracers he wore on either forearm.

She stared him down, watching his shoulders and his waist, waiting for the signs of attack. Baldy lowered slightly as if to pounce. Malja stepped in, bringing Viper forward and upward.

Though Baldy's eyes betrayed his surprise, he reacted well. He swung his arm into Viper, letting the bracer take the blow. Viper rang out in a sound both strange and uneasy — not the usual sword against sword sound, but a duller noise like hitting a grounder.

Baldy followed the blow up with a backhand. Malja ducked to the left and jabbed with Viper. Again, Baldy blocked. Back and forth they attacked and dodged and blocked. Neither seemed able to hit the other with any significant force. Twice Malja thought she had him, but the transport would sway or bump and destroy her opportunities.

Stepping wide to the edge of the transport, Baldy came in for another punch. Right before striking, he changed course and pounded her foot into the roof. As she staggered under the pain, Baldy cranked back and smashed his fist into her wounded bicep.

Malja screamed out. The transport bumped into the air and slammed down on the ground. Malja lost her balance. She dragged her feet for friction but Baldy could not be stopped. With his foot, he kicked her over the edge.

She rolled, trying to grab hold of the rope ladder as she dropped. She missed as the coarse rope scratched her face. Tucking her head, she prepared for a hard hit on the ground. It didn't come. She wasn't falling anymore. She looked up to find her right foot caught on one of the rope ladder rungs.

Her body banged into the transport's side. She flipped Viper into its sheath and grabbed the ladder with both hands. Her wounded arm throbbed, but her assault suit had dulled some of the ache already.

Below her head, the ground raced by.

"Malja," Fawbry called. Despite the pain, she lifted her body enough to see Fawbry's horse keeping pace with the transport. Fawbry held his gun at his shoulder and aimed in her direction. "I think this'll be big."

Malja put out one hand and felt the word No rising in her throat, but she didn't have time to speak. A cylinder of smoke poured out of the gun. She never saw what it shot, but she felt it.

The transport lifted into the air, taking Malja with it. An eruption of fire and noise plumed out of the side. As it descended, it toppled over, turning the side Malja was trapped on into the roof.

She held tight to the rope ladder while the transport dragged along the ground. The tethered flyers twisted with the turning transport. Two crashed into each other with explosive force. The third strained in a foolish attempt to keep moving until flames flared out of its engines. It plummeted to the ground, its magician pilot screaming the short way down.

Black and gray smoke streamed out of a huge hole in the transport's side as Malja untangled from the rope ladder. She crawled toward what had been the roof only moments ago and peeked over the edge. Baldy's head rested on a few churned up stones. The rest of him had been pinned under the wagon.

"Did you see that?" Fawbry yelled, looking around him as if searching for an audience. "Did you see what I just did?"

Malja stood. Her legs wobbled worse than when the transport was in motion. "Korstra and Kryssta, split me in two."

Fawbry laughed. "Never heard that one."

"What did you do?"

"There was a little switch on the side that seemed to suggest this gun had another shot or two in it. Didn't know it was going to launch a bomb. But by Kryssta, that sure was something." Fawbry froze as his thoughts caught up with him. "Hey, there's no way Salia survived that. I just saved us all. I'm the hero." He twirled with his gun raised in the air. "I'm the hero," he sang.

Malja stepped to the edge of the burning hole and squinted. She fanned away the smoke. That's when she knew things had gotten far worse than she expected. "Wonderful," she said, peering into the empty transport.

Owl

Faster. Faster. Owl urged his horse onward, his mind calculating and re-calculating how much time they had wasted chasing the convoy. Salia could have left during the night, taken a small contingent through the forest — paralleling the Great Field but avoiding being seen — and arrived at the Library before dawn.

No. If she had done so, and assuming she had used her contingent for the blood magic, the world would have known by now. At best, she would have risen as a goddess to rule over them. At worst, another Devastation would have swept through the lands.

That neither of those horrible situations occurred suggested that she left at a later time. She had to be at the Library, but she hadn't completed her magic yet. There was still a chance.

Smatterings of debris dotted the plains as he galloped through. Between the smashed grounder, the loose horses grazing in the distance, and the numerous bodies littered around, Malja had left Owl a clear path to follow. Up ahead, smoke dirtied the sky.

When he reached the source, an upended transport with a gaping hole in the side, Owl dismounted to check it out. If Fawbry or Malja lay injured nearby, he had to help. Being quick was key. Check the transport, scan the area, and if he didn't find them, assume they had moved on to the Library.

With his sword out, he walked the perimeter of the transport. Other than lots of ground metal, three crumpled flyers with three dead magicians, and the head of some bald creature, Owl found nothing. No evidence of Malja or Fawbry being injured or in trouble.

"Watch over them, dear Kryssta," he said, passing his finger over his forehead, and headed to his horse.

That's when the dead rose from the ground.

It began with moans of pain. Whatever brought them back, and only Salia's magic made any sense at this point, the reincarnation was not easy on the body. All the dead — the magicians, the swordsmen, even the animals — stood and shuffled their way toward the Library.

They limped and dragged and pulled their limbs along, wincing with each step.

Two thoughts struck Owl: First — Salia had reached the Library and raised the dead, but she still hadn't used its full power yet. Second — if allowed to continue, these dead creatures would come upon Malja and Fawbry from behind.

"Unless I stop them," he whispered.

Owl sprinted ahead until he was in front of the line of the dead. He raised his sword, inhaled sharply, and settled into a fierce offensive stance. "Time to die again," he said.

Malja and Owl

When Malja and Fawbry reached the Library, Malja slipped off the dappled gray before it had a chance to slow down. She brought out Viper, whirling it above, and sprinted ahead. Several feet away from the wide, stone stairs of the Library, Malja skidded to a halt.

At the top of the stairs, Salia raised her arms out to either side. The Library overshadowed her like a twisted thorn that touched the clouds. It had been constructed from scavenged ruins — concrete, wood, glass, pipes — to form a cylindrical tower with barbed spikes surrounding the top like a crown.

Not a Library at all. More like a bizarre military post or a prison.

Fawbry dismounted and walked up beside Malja. He inspected his weapon. "I think this thing's got one more bomb in it — maybe two."

Malja didn't respond. Her attention was on Salia and the warped expression the Queen wore — a crazed look Malja had seen before on many magicians. "We're too late," she said.

Salia never blinked though her eyes teared. On the left side of her face, her jaw drooped as if the skin were melted wax. Purplish bruises dotted her cheeks. She turned her head to one side, revealing the hair had been burned away. Blood stained the bottom of her gown, and she stood barefoot in the entrails of two soldiers. Their gutted bodies had been tossed behind her.

Four more soldiers stood with her, two on each side. They didn't show any signs of life. Malja's gut told her these soldiers were controlled by Salia's magic.

"I am the Queen of all," Salia said, her voice shivering like the tips of her fingers. "I've been given the power of the brother gods. Worship me." The four soldiers bent to their knees in praise.

"I'm just guessing," Fawbry said, "but something tells me her magicians didn't quite decipher the code correctly. She's a mess." Aiming his gun, he added, "Stand back. I'll take care of this."

Fawbry shot a bomb into the air. With a loud whoosh of suction, it left a smoking trail. Malja watched the bomb climb and curve back down toward Salia. About ten feet away from the target, while still mid-air, the bomb bounced off to the side, hit the ground like a ball, and rolled away.

Malja broke into a sprint. She wielded Viper with such deadly intention that the weapon jittered in her strong grip. Salia looked down at her, but the Queen's eyes seemed to look through her, as if she saw not with her eyes at all.

The ground jumped. Just once, as if one of the brother gods had bumped into the countryside by accident. The full on trembling came next.

Malja pushed forward, but every step increased the intensity of the violent shaking. About halfway up, she had to stop moving just to keep from falling. But stopping wasn't a choice. She lifted her leg, nearly fell over, but managed another step closer.

"Worship me," Salia said and pointed a clawed hand at Malja. The stench of magic swirled around the stench of the dead. Salia motioned and Malja felt a full blast of pressure in the chest. She reeled back, fighting to keep upright.

She spun back and pushed off the stairs. When she hit the bottom, she tucked her head and rolled. A few stairs dug into her back, but she didn't crack her neck, so Malja figured she should be thankful. She returned to Fawbry. The look on his face and the fact that the ground continued to shake told her things were about to get worse.

Turning back toward the Library, Malja heard a sharp bang. The ground between her and the Library steps cracked open. Dirt and rock slid in like water through a hole.

"That gun have any more to it?" Malja asked, focusing Viper on the widening hole.

"Don't know. But I'll keep trying with it."

Salia let out an agony-filled scream and a crimson light pulsed around her. Two of the soldiers sprinted down the stairs, and without consideration, they leaped into the widening chasm. As they dropped, Malja caught a glimpse of them changing. Limbs burst from their sides and their skin rippled and altered.

Seconds later, two fitulags hurdled out of the hole and skidded on the ground. They had six legs, large fangs, horrible smells, and an attitude to match. They hooted at each other before facing Malja.

"Are those the soldiers?" Fawbry asked.

"Now would be a good time to try," Malja said.

Revolted by the creatures, Fawbry aimed the weapon and pulled the trigger. Nothing happened. He looked over the metal casing, the barrel, every aspect of the gun. Something had to work on it.

A loud huffing erupted from the hole, shaking the ground and even causing the aggressive fitulags a moment of confusion. The eel-shaped beast that emerged, however, made the enormous sound seem too small. It snapped up one fitulag in its over-sized jaws before gazing down at Malja and Fawbry.

"Any time, Fawbry," she said. But waiting for Fawbry to be lucky was never going to work. Instead, she charged the giant beast.

No matter how many maneuvers Owl performed, no matter how many grabs he evaded nor how many slashes and gouges and lunges he unleashed, the undead soldiers continued to walk. If he cut down their legs, they crawled. If he hacked off their arms, they wriggled. If he mutilated them to the point of immobilization, the others stepped over the corpses and moved forward. They were of one mind, one purpose, and Owl had exhausted himself trying to stop them.

He struggled for breath, each inhale igniting the pain in his side. His hand numbed where his finger had been severed, but his chin and chest throbbed from the abuse of fighting. There were so many to slay, Owl prayed his body would last long enough to see the job through.

From several feet behind, he heard a horrible sound like tiny bits of metal clattering down a pipe. The headless leader's body stood atop the overturned transport. It was covered in sticky blood, ribs poked out of one side, and one of its legs bent at an odd angle. Yet it stood. And from its throat came that awful, grating sound. It was a horror only the insane mind of a magician abusing magic could bring forth.

Though Owl couldn't understand its words, the undead around him responded. They stopped their steady gait toward the Library. They looked around for a moment as if trying to identify a strange song that only they could hear. In unison, they caught sight of Owl. Then they started walking toward him.

Viper cut through the eel-beast without resistance, and the thing let out its loudest roar. Malja had to cover her ears for protection. Apparently her assault suit only reacted to certain sounds. The beast slid off, gaining some distance while it prepared for another strike.

"I hear the voices of Kryssta and Korstra within my skin," Salia said, practically singing the words. "I hear the brother gods and I see the universe as they do. I call upon the powers of magic, the powers that once hurt my people, I call upon these powers to aid my people now. Cut through this universe and free the worlds beyond."

Like a bolt of lightning tearing into the night sky, the space behind Salia cracked open. A wind struck up as if the air leaked out of their world and into this opening. Malja stepped toward the hole in the ground, her focus locked on Salia.

"It's a portal," Malja said to Fawbry, yelling over the roar of the wind.

When she faced him, however, she saw the eel-beast darting right for her head. Malja dropped to her knees. Crashing into the hard ground sent needles of pain through her legs, but the eel-beast shot overhead. Before it could alter its direction, Malja used Viper to remove another chunk from its hide.

It cried out, but the force behind its voice had weakened. Malja's ears could handle it now. She brought Viper back, slicing through the eel-beast again before it whipped off into the distance once more.

To the side, Fawbry had one foot pressing the fitulag close to the ground. He bashed the creature's head with the butt-end of his gun until it didn't move. By the time Malja had joined him, Fawbry had finished the job.

"We're too late," he said.

Malja glanced back at Salia. The crack had widened. "No," she said. "I won't let this happen." She sprinted toward the Library.

He couldn't hack at them fast enough. Owl's muscles burned and sweat covered him in a wet film. He had lost count of the number of undead that he felled. Not just the soldiers. Even the horses. Anything in the area that had been dead came at him.

Even after he disposed of a soldier, he found himself facing the same one again. With so many coming in, he didn't have time to cut them up into small enough pieces to stop them all. And all the time, the headless leader stood on the transport and sang its horrid, grating metal tune.

This was no fight of grace and skill. The undead did not pose a threat of speed or talent. They just fought through attrition. They fought by wearing him down.

As Owl decapitated another soldier, he glimpsed the leader swaying to its tune. Before that thing had begun its noise, the undead had ignored Owl and moved toward the Library. Simple enough.

Summoning the little strength he had left, Owl twisted his hips, winding his body tight, and let go. As he spun around, he pushed off with his legs like a dancer, keeping the momentum going, spinning and spinning. With no need to block a sword attack, no need to change direction, Owl spun with his sword out, slicing every object that crossed his path.

The only way not to succumb to dizziness was to find a steady point to focus on and whip the head around when necessary to return to that point as fast as possible. For Owl, the focal point was clear — the headless leader. As he spun, he could see bits of undead fly off in chunks of blood and bone. They pressed in, killing themselves again and again.

Owl spun. When he finally stopped, he felt as if he had been spinning for hours though less than a minute had passed. Gore piled around him, but no more of the creatures pursued him.

The headless leader never stopped swaying and singing. Perhaps it didn't know, couldn't tell that its army had been demolished. No matter.

Owl strode right up to it and cut it to pieces. He screamed out with every slash, tears rushing from his face. He thought of Brother X and Salia and Chief Master, and he cut down this abomination. Even after the leader had become little more than a motionless pile of flesh, Owl struck. He chopped and hacked, each blow letting a little more rage go.

He only stopped when his body lacked the strength to continue. He collapsed. His sword dropped from his cramped hand and rolled in the dirt. He fell back against the transport. His wounded side, his battered body, his bruised and tired muscles all cried out at once.

"I did it," he said, his voice as quiet as the gentle breeze. "I did it."

As he exhaled slow and deep, he dared to let a satisfied warmth fill him. But a chilling sound banished the sensation. A few legless corpses kicking against the ground. A few armless torsos bumping amongst the gore. Some just hands or pulsating organs. Whatever could find a way to move began to tremble its way towards Owl.

He stared at the body parts with his jaw slack. He reached for his sword, but it had rolled two feet beyond his fingers. Owl stared at the weapon as the undead closed in. He couldn't find the energy to get his sword. He had no more in him.

* * * *

The chasm in the ground looked too long to jump across and too wide to waste time going around. Malja dashed ahead anyway. She had her assault suit to help.

The suit did a lot for her — kept her dry in the rain, cool in the heat, warm in the cold; it grew with her; it kept her toned and strong — but she had never called upon it to act for her. When she was younger, she refused out of defiance toward Jarik and Callib because she thought they had used magic to create the suit. But now she knew that wasn't true. The suit came from wherever she was born. It was all she had to prove who she really was. And if it was magic, she'd have to deal with those consequences later. She had to stop Salia or they'd all be dead and there would be no later.

Pumping her legs and arms, she neared the edge of the gap. Her heart hammered as she tried to connect with her assault suit. She had no idea how. All she could think to do was close her eyes and say the words like a prayer.

Grant me the strength to cross the distance ahead.

She opened her eyes, saw the edge just steps away, held her breath, and jumped.

Her legs felt strong as she launched into the air.

Emptiness passed beneath her.

She saw motion — more creatures from below.

The wind fluttered in her ears.

The opposite side of the crevasse approached.

Her body descended.

She wasn't going to make it.

Although her mind looked on, stunned by her failure, her body reacted. She windmilled Viper up and around, stretching out as far as her arms would allow. The weapon's tip hit the gap's edge, knocked loose rocks and dirt, and scraped down the side as she dropped.

The harsh sound of blade against stone grated in her ears, but Malja held on. She used her legs against the rock wall to help stop her descent. Dirt fell beneath her.

She glanced up. Through the dust, she could see the top of the gap. She hadn't fallen far. Just a few feet. The wall had plenty of jagged bits and jutting rocks.

She climbed.

"Malja?" Fawbry's voice echoed as he called out from the opposite side. "That portal's about to open. Hurry."

Malja kept silent — kept her mind on securing the next foothold. And the next. And the next. When this was over, she'd have a word or twenty with that clown about annoying her when she was working. For now, she only had to find a place for her hand to latch on and pull up.

When she reached the top and dragged her legs over the edge, she rolled onto her back and allowed herself a few seconds to catch her breath. No more though. If nothing else, she wanted to shut up Fawbry's encouragement. A little slower but still with enough energy to fight, Malja got to her feet.

The two remaining soldiers scooted close to the blood at Salia's feet. They each pulled out their swords, and showing no sense of emotion, they slit open their own throats. Salia laughed. She rocked her head from side to side. Blood from her victims drenched the stairs like a red pathway leading straight to her. Her mouth twitched.

"I am the goddess of all worlds," Salia said, but her voice no longer sounded human. It echoed and modulated as she spoke. "I have risen from the scraps of the streets to bring peace through my rule. Follow me and this and all worlds will live in peaceful obedience. Deny me and pain will be your only pleasure until death."

Behind her the portal opened further. A storm raged in the world glimpsed through the portal. Lightning flashed, but the rumbles of thunder could not be heard on this side.

"Brother gods, I hate magic," Malja said, trudging up the stairs. From behind, Fawbry screamed her name — with panic not cheering. She glanced back. Another eel-beast slithered from the gap in the ground.

Malja broke into a full sprint. She lifted Viper towards her side, ready to cut through Salia. Even as the eel-beast followed her up the stairs, its mucous-filled mouth breathing hot stink at her back, Malja's battle sense assured her she would reach Salia before the beast could strike.

Two steps at a time. Heart pumping. She groaned and swore and spit and did anything to keep her body climbing. The eel-beast hissed from behind — closer than she expected.

She adjusted Viper one last time. Salia was in range. Malja pushed off into the air and bellowed, "Die!"

Salia raised her hands upward as if tossing flower petals into the sky. From the bloody mess beneath her rose hundreds of tiny vines. They shot up and twined around Malja, spinning around her torso, immobilizing her arms, locking her in the air.

Unable to move, Malja could only stare into Salia's mad eyes. She had conjured the vines, the hole in the ground, the beasts, the expanding portal, all without a single tattoo or even a moment's hesitation. She just drew on the unlocked power of the Library and did whatever she wanted. Like a true goddess.

Malja had seen magic warp magicians. She had even seen it destroy the mind of a young non-magical woman. But never had she witnessed the insanity she saw in Salia. The Queen's eyes — never blinking, never seeing — burned a thought into Malja's heart she never imagined capable of existing.

We're going to fail.

For Owl, life had broken down into breaths. Inhale — the undead inched closer. Exhale — the undead moaned. Inhale — he watched their approach. Exhale — he tasted blood in his mouth.

A slight smile crossed his lips. Even after they killed him, he knew they would never reach Malja and Fawbry in time to do any harm. If only Chief Master could see him now.

There was only one thing left to do.

Owl shifted to the side, his bones popping as if he were an old man, and he pulled out his gun — the one he had trained on, the only real gun he ever cared about. He looked it over. Only two-shots, not as sleek as the handgun Malja had given him, but it was his. The only gun worthy of taking his life.

Settling back, he pulled out the red Honor Bullet. As he placed the bullet into the chamber, all his tensions lifted from his body. No regrets. He had lived a full, meaningful life. It had its share of pain and disappointment, and he never reached the level of greatness he thought he should, but he had tried.

The Masters had once said that success or failure was never important. All that mattered in life was that one try. Funny that he should only recall that now. "It would've been helpful a little while back," he whispered.

He brought the muzzle to his temple. In a traditional honor death, a Master would be present to record his final words. Though Owl knew nobody would hear him, nobody would write down his thoughts, he still spoke. "The length of one's life is without purpose. What we do in our time defines the value of that time. Dear Kryssta, I pray I have used the life you gave me well. I pray you will take me into peace. I tried."

Inhale — the fingers of one undead soldier touched Owl's foot. Exhale — Owl's finger settled on the trigger. Inhale — the undead with mouths slobbered as they readied to feed. Exhale —

The vines squeezed the air from Malja's lungs. Spots formed wherever she looked. Still, she strained to move her arm, to cut through with Viper, to do anything that might stop Salia.

Fawbry's incessant babbling changed. It sounded excited, hopeful. Malja craned her neck around, and from the corner of her eye, she saw something both wonderful and disturbing.

Ten feet above the ground, Tommy floated in — cross-legged, eyes locked in deep meditation upon his tattoos, his face serene yet purposeful. Below and to the side floated Master Kee in a similar position. Energy shimmered between the two magicians like a desert mirage.

Salia noticed the boy, too. She flicked her right hand, sending both eel-beasts at him. With another motion, she sent the body parts of her sacrificed soldiers into the chasm. Seven fitulags popped out and zipped by Fawbry on their direct course for Tommy, their numerous legs clicking against the debris-filled ground.

Like a great singer belting out the final note of an epic song, Master Kee opened his mouth and released a long tone. The creatures rushing towards them smashed against an invisible barrier. Wherever these beasts made contact with the barrier, fire burst out. The poor things wanted to run away — they whimpered as they attempted to do so — but Salia's magic kept them attacking and burning.

Tommy reached out with both arms and made a motion as if he were pressing down upon the portal. Salia scowled, bringing both her hands around to keep the portal open. But every time Master Kee repelled her creatures, Salia had to snap her magic after the fitulags or else they would run off. Tommy pressed harder, forcing her to move between spells faster.

Malja noticed the vines loosening around her. Not enough to free her, but clear evidence that Salia had difficulty juggling all she had to deal with. Malja struggled more against her bonds, hoping to either free herself or add to Salia's troubles.

"You cannot do this," Salia screeched. "I am the goddess of all the worlds." She thrust her arms forward, and Malja caught a glimpse of Tommy tumbling away. "None can—"

The edges of the portal trembled and contracted, and Salia had to focus her energy on keeping it open. Though Tommy and Master Kee had been hit, Malja could hear Fawbry cheering them on. They must have regrouped quickly.

Malja leaned forward, her eyes ignoring Salia. Her mouth dropped open as she tried to accept what she saw. Deep in the portal, amidst the lightning and rain, a man stood — a man wearing a black assault suit just like her own. He seemed to see her, too. He stared right through the portal at her. He took three steps and stopped at the portal's edge.

And he put his hand through the portal.

Tears welled in Malja's eyes. She pulled hard against the vines, trying to free just one arm. Her muscles strained and if not for her assault suit, she would have pulled or maybe even torn them.

She opened her mouth but couldn't come up with words to say. As the portal edges closed more, Salia fell, her right hand dropping to the blood-soaked floor to keep her steady.

Malja looked to the man in the portal. Whether or not he understood what he saw, she could tell one thing — he knew she could not take his hand. He pulled back and walked away.

Tommy hovered above. His eyes remained closed. With a forceful motion, he brought his arms down and the portal slammed closed.

The scream that ripped out of Salia matched the thunderous crash of the portal. She wailed like a mother losing a newborn. Her cries cracked as she shattered her vocal chords, yet she did not stop.

The vines holding Malja fell apart, dropping her to the stairs. She landed hard and her limbs tingled as blood recirculated. Despite her pains, Malja knew not to waste any time.

With just a few steps, she stood over Salia. The mad queen raised an arm. Before she could cast any spell, Malja hooked Viper underneath the woman's rib cage and lifted her overhead. The screams no longer were those of failed magic or anger at her enemy. They were screams of pain and terror.

Mixed with laughter.

No trace of sanity remained.

With both hands gripping Viper, Malja held Salia hooked overhead. The queen gibbered and laughed and spit and screamed. Malja rushed down the stairs, not wanting to lose her momentum. At the chasm's edge, she hurled Salia into the deep darkness. The eel-beasts, the fitulags, and the unseen creatures below cackled and crowed and hooted their joy at finally receiving a meal. Even as they feasted, Malja heard the Queen's cackles of madness.

From across the open ground, Fawbry shouted, "Is it over?" When she nodded, Fawbry collapsed with an exhausted sigh.

Malja eased to the ground and joined her companion in a few moments of quiet.

Owl

As Owl rode up to the Library, he wasn't sure which looked worse — Malja or himself. Fawbry and Master Kee were clearing the stairs of blood and rubble while Malja stood before a wide gouge in the ground. She held an apple and took a big bite. Tommy sat near her, dangling his feet over the edge, with a dazed expression and his arms wrapped around her leg.

"You're alive!" Fawbry said, running all the way around the gouge to reach Owl. It took a while, but no other greeting could have pleased him more. "Thank Kryssta. When you didn't show up here, I was sure you had died."

"I think it was close. But I'm here."

"You are here. Which means you did it — you defeated Brother X. And you said you weren't a mythical warrior."

Owl dismounted and patted his horse. On his way to the Library, he had decided not to share all that had happened with the undead. In any normal circumstances, the use of an Honor Bullet held a supreme sense of privacy. More so than prayer. He saw no reason to break that tradition. Besides, how could he explain it to those not trained in the Way?

He had been sitting against that transport with the gun pressed against his head. The undead wriggled toward him. And he pulled the trigger. Only a click and nothing happened.

The undead crept closer. He could smell them surrounding him — a foul odor of bile and blood. Those that still had a voice moaned.

Fumbling with the gun, he checked it over, but he saw nothing wrong. A Guardian always kept his weapon in excellent condition. It should have fired. He reset the gun and put it to his head.

Then the undead stopped. They just fell. Once more dead.

Owl remained with the gun at his head, ready to fire. He waited for several minutes, unsure what to think of this change. At length, when the dead did not rise again, he entertained the possibility that Malja might have succeeded. If Salia's power had been cut, nobody was keeping the dead animated. Still, he did not move.

Only when his horse meandered by did Owl enter a clearer sense of consciousness. He lowered his weapon and gazed up at the beautiful animal. Sometimes, Kryssta didn't bother with subtlety. He holstered his weapon and climbed the horse.

Without command, the horse headed for the Library. Good thing too, because Owl required most of the ride to return to full awareness. Seeing Malja and Fawbry somehow made the whole experience a bit surreal, though. Better to leave it buried within for now. Maybe, someday later, he might ask Master Kee about it, but for now, he merely let it lay beneath the surface.

Malja and Tommy walked over. She shook his hand. "Y'know, with Salia and Brother X gone now, there's nobody in place to take charge. Penmarvia is going to end up a lot like Corlin, and I can tell you firsthand anarchy only works in small groups. Salia City's going to be a bad place for a while."

"I'm still here," Owl said. "Master Kee is still here. We'll just have to rebuild."

Master Kee heard this and scurried over. "That's wonderful. I didn't want to impose my hopes upon you but I'm thrilled you'll stay with me."

"Where else would I go?"

Kicking at the ground, Fawbry said, "We were thinking of asking you to join us."

Owl clasped Fawbry around the shoulder. "You're very kind to offer, but I belong with the Order. Please, always consider me your friend, and know you'll forever find a safe haven at the Order."

"There is one problem," Master Kee said, his face turned down.

"Problem?" Owl said.

"The Order is going to have to recruit new students — both magicians and trainees in the Way. That's a lot of work for me. Not to mention all the regular duties of a Chief Master."

"That's right. You've inherited the role."

"And its duties."

"You'll be fine. Besides, you know I can teach the Way."

"No," Master Kee said, and Owl's hurt was palpable. "Only a Master can teach a student." Malja crossed her arms but Master Kee held up his hand to stop any protests. "Therefore, when taking into account your defeat of our most skilled practitioner, Brother X, as well as all your contributions to helping stop Queen Salia, I see no reason not to award you the title of Master. Master Owl, do you accept?"

A smile broke across Owl's face so wide, he thought his skin might split. "Yes, Chief Master. I accept with humbleness and honor."

"Marvelous." Chief Master clapped his hands, and Owl thought the man would have loved to open a bottle of wine if they had one. "Then there is one more matter we need to put in place before we can truly rebuild our Order. Malja, you have the code to decipher the Library texts. Please share it with us, so that we may prevent this from ever happening again."

Malja's face took on a strange twist. She stepped back as if ready for another fight. "No," she said.

"Don't do this," Chief Master said, his old face aging more. "You can't possibly be thinking of using it for yourself. I know you want to find your home world, but it's too dangerous. You've just seen that yourself."

"I'm not going to use it. Magic like this is too powerful for any one person. Or any group." She looked directly at Owl. "You want to rebuild? You do so without the Library."

"It's not right to lock away knowledge."

"I won't share the codes. If I could forget them, I would."

Chief Master's face scrunched up. "This is wrong. How are we supposed to become responsible magicians, how are we to learn the proper methods of control, if we can't have access to a true source of magic?"

"Both of you," Owl said, "stop it. Chief Master, she is right that we must tread carefully. If anything, Salia has proven that the power of the Library is vastly dangerous. And Malja, Chief Master is right that we shouldn't lock away knowledge just because it's dangerous in the wrong hands." Owl took Malja's hand and bowed, hoping that a little subservient behavior might quell the rage he feared his next words would incite. "Look into your own past. Did you fare better having Jarik and Callib withhold knowledge from you? Was it right for them not to tell you of your mother or the world you come from? Should you have—"

"Enough," Malja said, pulling her hand free in one rapid motion.

Owl lowered his body even more and prayed to Kryssta that when she hit him, he would survive. But no stunning blow came. Instead, he felt her soft lips against his ear. She described an image to him, a group of symbols that she had memorized.

"A fifth symbol," Owl blurted out. "That's why Salia got it wrong.

The markings on the map only showed four symbols."

"What symbols?" Chief Master asked.

Malja gently lifted Owl's chin. "I put my trust in you," she said. "Don't ever make me have to come back here and regret that decision."

"Well, then," Fawbry said, stretching his arms, "I suppose we should get going. There's plenty of ladies, er, towns in Corlin that require our help."

Malja whistled and the dappled gray cantered over to her. Tommy made a face that caused Malja to grin. "Yeah," she said. "I like this one."

Fawbry said, "Then give her a name."

Malja looked at the horse a long time. Owl could tell that this meant something to her and that the others knew about it too. It reminded him how little he ever understood of these three.

"I've got it," she said. "I'll name her Horse."

"Horse?" Fawbry laughed and Tommy joined in. "That's the best you could do?"

"Well, she is a horse."

"You named your weapon Viper and for this wonderful creature — Horse?"

"Stop laughing," Malja said, but she was laughing too.

Owl couldn't imagine a better time to ask about Tommy.

"I, um," he said, putting out his hand. "I have an offer for the boy."

Malja's pleasant attitude shifted fast like lightning across the sky. "What offer?"

Owl crouched in front of Tommy. Though the boy had performed incredible feats of magic, he looked much the same as before. No sense of madness lay behind his eyes. Not yet.

"Tommy, you heard us, yes? Chief Master and I are going to rebuild the Order. It will be a place that's safe for magicians. Safe for them to learn how to control their skills. A place where they can be amongst those like them and where they can help others like them. Most of all, the Order has always been a place where magicians could further their collective knowledge, so that perhaps someday, they can stop the harm magic does to the body and mind. This is the perfect place for you to live. You wouldn't have to worry about food or shelter. You could spend your days learning with friends. Would you like that? Would you like to stay with us?"

Tommy brushed his fingers along Owl's cheek, and for a fleeting second, Owl thought the boy meant to stay. But Tommy turned to Malja and took her hand. He clung tight as if he feared somebody might force them apart.

Owl bowed to Malja once more, this time as a sign of respect. "As it should be," he said.

"I know you meant well," Malja said, "with the best intentions. But Tommy and I won't be split up. We're family."

Owl jolted straight in shock. "Oh, no. I can't believe I forgot," he said. "Fawbry, please forgive me. With all that's been happening I never explained how I found you in the first place."

"It doesn't really matter," Fawbry said.

"But I found all of you in Corlin because I ran into Fawbry's family."

"M-My family?"

"Your parents. They've been worried about you. Hoping to find you. You must go see them. Please. I promised I'd get you to them."

Malja must have noticed the same apprehension Owl had detected for she laughed. "Don't worry. I'll see that he meets them."

Malja

From the moment they entered the low-ceilinged house, Fawbry's parents never stopped nagging. They were upset that Fawbry had taken so long to come home. They thought his colorful robe looked weird — not like that of a respectable young man. They worried about his safety, especially considering the stories they had heard about *that woman* and the deplorable condition of the sweetest, darling little boy the mother had ever laid eyes on since her own Fawbry had grown up.

Malja ignored as much as she could. She chuckled at the thought of *sweetest, darling* Tommy — these folks would petrify in fright if they ever glimpsed that little boy's power.

The rest she swallowed down without comment. Because as annoying as this old couple was, Malja couldn't help but warm at the way they fawned over Fawbry. Even as they picked on his every step (or misstep as they would see it), they saturated him in kind attention. The old woman baked his favorite sweet rolls and hummed a tune she said was his favorite as a little boy. The old man listened to tales of the little towns Fawbry had helped out and with a lascivious wink, asked about the women.

The big surprise was Galba. Fawbry's parents had arranged for him to marry this lovely but awkward girl. Apparently, as far as they were concerned, Galba was his girlfriend.

"Mother, I don't even know the girl." Fawbry paled and looked to Malja as if begging her to take out Viper and slash through his family so they could make an escape. Malja just shook her head and enjoyed the couple's banter as they talked up the girl — about the only time they weren't nagging their son.

"Don't look so," his mother said. "Trust us. We picked good for you."

"That's right," his father said. "Galba's a good cook. She works hard. And she's got a healthy bosom on her too."

"And excellent birthing hips. I want some little ones from you two.

That's the right of a mother."

"You'll be a grandmother, dear."

"Not if my boy keeps gallivanting in the company of *that woman*."

That night, Malja tucked a blanket around Tommy and watched him sleep in an actual bed. She wasn't sure she could sleep on such a soft mattress, but Tommy's slumber came swift. He had slept heavy every night since defeating Salia, and Malja worried this might be a side-effect of all that magic. Not that sleep itself was so bad. But if this was a permanent side-effect, then what other damage might have been done?

Except he really hadn't displayed any significant sign of damage. He never did. That bothered her even more.

The bedroom door opened a crack, and Fawbry poked in his head. "Can we talk?"

Malja followed him downstairs to the kitchen. Sitting at the wooden table, Fawbry looked terrified.

"Take me with you," he said. "I can't stay here. They'll drive me insane. And while I'm sure this girl they want me to marry is wonderful, I don't want to be married."

Malja frowned. "I've been upstairs looking at Tommy and thinking about family. It's strange what that word means. He and I, well, we've just got each other. We need to stick together; otherwise, we're just empty."

"That doesn't mean this part of my family is the important part. They raised me, but Jarik and Callib raised you."

"They kept me alive, but they weren't family. They used me like an experiment. And, don't forget, they threw me away, left me in the forest to die. Did your folks try to kill you when you were ten?"

"No," he said, picking at a splinter in the table.

"I look at you here with your folks, and I see a loving mother and father. I know they annoy you, but trust me, you wouldn't want them gone. If I truly believed in the brother gods, I would beg them to bring back my Uncle Gregor."

Fawbry shook his head slowly. "I know all that. I suppose you're right. I just . . ."

"What?"

"I just thought you and Tommy were my family, too."

Moonlight peeked around some clouds, casting its pale light into the kitchen and across Fawbry's face. Malja thought he might cry. And she felt a tug inside her chest unlike anything she had ever experienced in life.

"I didn't realize," she said. "I mean, we are your family."

"You are? You feel that way too?"

She didn't know. But she considered how Tommy would answer, and that much was easier. "Yes," she said. "You're part of our family."

Fawbry rubbed his eyes. "Thank you."

"But you've got family here, too."

"No," Fawbry said, hitting the table harder than he intended. "I mean, yes, I do have my family here, but I can't stay here. Not after all I've been through with you and Tommy. How could I live a life of being a husband and working a farm or whatever job my parents set up for me? I can't do that. How do I do that after Queen Salia, after Jarik and Callib? I've seen too much to just go back."

Malja got up and paced the kitchen. She understood exactly how Fawbry felt. But she had worked out the next several steps for her and Tommy, and it seemed wrong to take Fawbry where she planned to go. But it also seemed wrong to sentence him to a life of boredom with a nice girl he didn't really care for. Didn't seem fair to the girl, either.

She placed her hands on the table and leaned in with an intimidating glare. "Listen to me," she said and proceeded to tell him of what she saw in the portal — the man in an identical black assault suit, the way he reached through the portal for her, the final look on his face. She then gestured to the kitchen and said, "You have more than a family. You have a home here. The people here are like you. They understand you. I don't have any of that. I want to find my home."

"Then go back to the Order. Use the Library and—"

"I won't risk destroying this world — that's something I could never live long enough to pay honor for. I have a plan though, and if it works, I'll use the maps Tommy copied and I'll find my world. And I'm taking Tommy with me."

Fawbry looked at his stump. "Through a portal? How?"

"I'll find a way. I'm not losing another family."

Then Malja saw something that astonished her. Fawbry swallowed hard, stood, and put out his good hand. "Me neither. I don't care what you say. I'm coming. We're family. And, besides, you always need me."

Malja chuckled as she wrapped her arms around Fawbry. She let the hug hold long enough for him to know she cared but no more. That kind of affection still always felt awkward.

Sighing with relief, Fawbry said, "So, now what? You want to have

Tommy open a portal?"

"Never. That's the kind of magic that's hurting him now. Maybe you and Owl are right that magic isn't all bad, but portal magic isn't any good that I can see. No, I think we've got a lot of traveling to do."

"Good. The further from here the better. I've had it with girlfriends."

Malja wrinkled her brow. "That might be a problem."

"Wait, now," Fawbry said, suspicion leaking into his voice. "If we're not going to use magic to open a portal, then—"

"I only know one person who's smart enough and crazy enough to try to build us a portal without using magic."

Fawbry's face dropped. "Don't say it."

"I'm sorry, but if you're going to come with us, we've got to go see your old girlfriend — Cole Watts."

Fawbry let out a short laugh. Then he flopped into his chair and howled laughter until tears rolled down his cheeks. "It's never dull with you," he said. "But that's how I like it."

"Let's get some sleep. Tomorrow, we set out."

"As a family," Fawbry said.

Malja placed her hand on Fawbry's shoulder and thought of Tommy. "As a family."

THE WAY OF THE

BROTHER GODS

BOOK 3 OF THE
BEST SELLING SERIES
THE MALJA CHRONICLES

STUART JAFFE

THE WAY OF THE

BROTHER GODS

Book 3 of The Malja Chronicles

For Zackary

A great nephew and Marine.
We're all proud of you.

Chapter 1

When Malja returned to consciousness, she was upside-down, tied up, and hanging from the rafters of a study. Her blood raged. Her head throbbed in the back, and though she couldn't move her arms to feel it, she knew a large bump had formed where she had been struck.

The study was immaculate in design, with ornate shelves and a high ceiling. Open beams cut across, and the coarse rope that bound her had been tied off on the center beam. Books filled the room. A dark-wood desk covered with papers, bits of metal, and colored wire, had been pushed against the wall to make an empty space below her.

To her right, she saw Tommy — blindfolded and bound to a chair. Though only fifteen, he was the most powerful magician Malja had ever known. Even Jarik and Callib, once extremely powerful magicians, had to rely on each other to produce their best magic. Tommy needed only himself. That was the reason for the blindfold. It kept him from seeing the tattoos that grew on his body. They were used to focus and create magic. When she had first met Tommy and saved him from slavery, he had only one tattoo on his forearm. Now, both arms and his entire torso were covered in intricate designs.

To Malja's left sat the dark-skinned man who had ambushed them when they had entered the mansion. He wore a tailored black suit and matching hat. Sitting on a wooden stool, he rocked back and forth as he played his guitar — a Bluesman. The thumping rhythm pulsed with Malja's blood and the moaning sound the man made reminded her of a wounded soldier. He never sang any words, just moaned a melody and played his steady rhythm.

She scanned the rest of the study. No sign of Fawbry. Good. That clownish fool could be a lot of trouble at times, but she had learned that he was loyal. If he wasn't tied up here, then hopefully, he had managed to avoid getting caught. And that meant she had someone out there trying to help her.

Breaking off from the song, the Bluesman eyed Malja and his mouth opened into a sadistic grin. "Well, you sure took your time waking up. I didn't think I hit you that hard."

"You didn't," she said. "Just catching up on my rest."

Honest amusement crossed his face. "Name's McGhee. I'm guessing you know I'm with the Bluesmen."

"There are no Bluesmen anymore. I was at their farm. I watched them all die at the hands of the magicians, Jarik and Callib."

"We weren't all there. Some of us, many of us, were scattered throughout Corlin and Penmarvia, doing our jobs."

"Murdering people."

McGhee flashed his smile again. He picked up a small device and pointed it at the fireplace. "Watch this," he said and pressed a button. A fire appeared and warmed the room. "Isn't that something? Cole Watts is the smartest lady I ever met. Makes me think that life before the Devastation must have been incredible. I mean she can't do magic, but the machines she can build — well, they're magical in their own way. That's probably why you came here looking for her. Not me, though. No, ma'am. I came here for the same reason I snuck up on you and cracked your head."

The heat from the fire wrapped around Malja, agitating the ache in her skull. Tommy stirred his thin body but not enough for Malja to know if he was awake. Then she spied movement from under the desk. Watching from the corner of her eye, she tried to make out if it had been nothing more than a shifting shadow or if ...

McGhee set his guitar aside. "I'm here to make things right. You and Cole Watts are responsible for the deaths of a lot of my brothers."

"We didn't kill them."

"Sure you did. If the two of you had never come into our lives, we'd all still be living. But Cole Watts had to have you for her experiment. We searched all over, and when some of my brothers found you, you killed them. But we caught you eventually."

"I was looking for her at the time."

With a chuckle, McGhee poked Malja causing her to swing a little. "You don't seem to fair well when you go looking for her. And it don't matter how you came there. We had you. I know she thought you were special, said you're the only one who can go through a portal without being burnt to ash, but the fact is, you only brought us trouble." Malja recalled when they had forced Fawbry's hand into an open portal and the hand seared off. Was he really under that desk right now? McGhee grabbed her chin and turned her so she faced him straight on albeit upside-down. "Jarik and Callib came because of you and that portal. They may have done the killing, but you and Cole Watts created the problem. And Wolf's right — how is it that the two of you survived? Nobody else did. Just you two. That's what bothers the rest of us Bluesmen."

"Wolf?"

"Sorry, but you won't live long enough to meet him. Shame, too, because he's a great man. He should've been leading us all along. He's smart, tough, and braver than any of the fools we've had in the past. Wolf's got the plan to get us Bluesmen back to where we want. It's going to be glorious. But before we can do anything, things got to be set right. You should've died back there on the farm. So, it's time to fix that situation."

Malja knew better than to argue the details with McGhee. Instead, she nodded towards Tommy. "Let the boy go. He wasn't there. He had nothing to do with any of it."

"I'm not going to kill a boy. But I'm not above using him either. He's going to make great bait to bring out Cole Watts." McGhee reached over to the desk and picked up a small book. As he did so, Malja snatched a sharp look into the shadows under the desk — Fawbry was there, for sure. McGhee went on, "Turns out this boy might be quite powerful. See this book here? Cole Watts kept a journal since she's been at this mansion. I think you'll find some of it to be quite interesting."

He tilted his head back and flipped through the pages. Malja struggled against her bindings but McGhee had done a professional job tying her up.

"Here," he said, pointing to a place in the book, "listen to this. 'The boy displayed such easy command of his power as if it required almost no effort at all to cast. He opened a portal to save Malja and did so without hesitation. If ever I can find Tommy again, perhaps he'll show me how he does it so that I can learn how to replicate the event mechanically.' You hear that, boy?" McGhee kicked Tommy's shin, and Tommy startled awake. "Good ol' Cole had something in store for you. I know her too well. When she talks about you showing her so she can learn, that means she's wanting to experiment on you, maybe even cut you open and have a little look at your innards."

"It's okay, Tommy," Malja said, keeping her voice firm and clear. From behind the blindfold, Tommy cocked his head, listening for clues to the situation.

McGhee turned through many more pages and then said, "I got here another little passage I think you'll enjoy. 'Today I met a very special man. A man named Harskill. He wore the same odd clothing that Malja wears.'

Malja's attention snapped to McGhee hard enough to send her body spinning on the rope. All thoughts of Fawbry and escape vanished. McGhee steadied her with one hand. "That's right," he said. "Wasn't expecting that one when I walked in here. I was just looking for her or you. We're looking all over for you two. Now I find out you ain't the only one like you in this world no more. In fact, I think Wolf will find this very interesting, if he don't already know. Seems he knows lots of things I never expected. But having another like you — well, that's a serious threat to the Bluesmen, as far as I can tell. Wolf might just be a little happy with me when I show him that. Well, that and your head." He snapped the book shut and tossed it on the desk. Rubbing his belly, he stood. "Another little thing Cole Watts put in this house — a room for pissing and crapping. Can you imagine? Don't have to go out and dig a hole in the ground. Not an outhouse or anything. I swear, since I got here, I find every excuse to go." He walked to the door. "I'd let you give it a try, but the whole point of keeping you alive right now is so I can make you suffer for every one of my brothers you killed. And when I punch your gut and you're all full of pee, well, that's going to hurt real bad. In fact, when I get back from my luxurious piss, we're going to start your suffering in earnest."

As a last thought, McGhee picked up the journal again. "Might be fun to read while I go," he said and flashed his awful smile one more time before leaving the room.

A second later, McGhee returned wearing a ridiculous grin. "Fooled you. You really think I'm gonna just leave you here while I piss?"

"It wouldn've been nice."

"I'm sure." Before he could say another word, a loud crash came from below. Shattered glass and banging pots. McGhee's face dropped as he looked out the door. He glanced back at Malja, clearly stuck. Pinching his lips, his eyes darted between the direction of the noise and Malja.

Malja wiggled her tied body and yelled, "Fawbry, we're upstairs!"

McGhee stomped right up and backhanded her mouth. "Why'd you do that? You know better. Now, I've got to go kill your friend."

Fawbry waited until he heard McGhee's footsteps echo down the hall. With a slight groan, Fawbry rolled out from under the desk, his unkempt hair looking particularly wild. "If he played one more song, I was going to scream."

"Hurry up," Malja said. "Get my hands free first."

Fawbry slipped a knife from his belt and went to work on the ropes around Malja's hands. He wore a stained tan shirt — his usual multi-colored robe would have stood out even in the shadows — and the odor of stress wafted around him.

"We're going to be fine," Malja said, keeping her eyes on the door. When her hands were free, she let her arms hang. Blood rushed straight through to her fingers, pinpricking her skin and relieving the pain in her shoulders.

Fawbry pulled a chair over and stood on it to reach the rope holding her overhead. As he cut, Malja readied to fall to the floor — no way could Fawbry catch her, though he might be able to slow her down. Either way, there would be noise enough to get the Bluesman's attention.

"Almost through," Fawbry said.

"When you finish, get Tommy free. I'll take care of McGhee."

"Already planning on it."

The half-cut rope snapped and Malja crashed to the floor. Only a deaf man would miss that amount of clatter. Fawbry froze, staring wide-eyed at the door. Malja pulled up to her feet, but the numbness in her legs made walking awkward. "Get Tommy," she said, and her voice brought Fawbry back. As he attended the boy, Malja looked around the study for Viper — her large sickle-shaped weapon with both inner- and outer-crescents capable of deadly strikes.

"Well, well," McGhee said from the doorway. He held his guitar in one hand, and with his free hand, he pulled a short sword from the instrument's neck. "There was a rat downstairs. Seems there's one up here, too."

No time for Viper. Malja launched toward the doorway, but her wakening legs moved too slow. She stumbled against the desk, knocking papers and books to the floor. McGhee backed into the hall, chuckling at her clumsy attack but keeping a careful distance between them. He could have cut her down with ease, but his knowledge of how dangerous she could be caused his caution. Sometimes, Malja was grateful for her reputation.

He stepped with grace as he backed toward the wide staircase that wound down to the huge foyer. Over a balcony railing, Malja saw two statues at the bottom. She remembered them from her last visit — one was of Moonlo, author of *The Book of Kryssta*; the other was the Korstra prophet, Galot. Korstra or Kryssta — she could have used the help of either brother god, except she guessed they wouldn't help a non-believer like her. Instead, she'd have to fight a weaponed opponent the way she always had in the past — by herself.

McGhee eased down the stairs, keeping his eyes on Malja as he inched backward. He never stopped smiling, but Malja thought she saw a twinge of concern in his eyes. Not fear. She knew that look too well to be mistaken. No, this was *concern*.

"Worried you won't get away?" Malja said.

"I'm the one with the sword. I don't care how fast you are — you ain't strong enough to knock me out with one hit. Even if you land a punch, I'll still cut you open."

"Then why do you keep backing up?"

They were halfway down the stairs. Malja's leg strength returned and her fingers curled into fists. She could feel the moment of attack upon her.

McGhee sensed it, too, for he feigned another step back and shot forward instead. Slicing down with his sword, he displayed agile footwork and good control. Malja dodged to the side and smacked into the wall. She tried to kick McGhee in the ribs, but her legs were still too slow.

McGhee swung around, the blade whipping towards Malja's neck. She ducked and lunged, barreling her head into his gut. She heard a satisfying *Oaf* as they hit the railing. Though the old wood held, she knew she couldn't pull off that trick again without sending them both crashing into the statues below.

After two fast jabs to the gut, Malja jumped back and readied for the next attack. McGhee took a moment to shake off his surprise and then settled into a solid fighting stance — legs well-separated, sword in front, free arm back for further balance. Though his body calmed for the fight, McGhee's face twisted with rage.

"You're a murderer," he said. "You killed all my brothers, good men, for nothing."

Malja glared at him, saying nothing, letting silence eat away at any confidence he dared to hold.

McGhee cried out and swung his sword overhead. Malja side-stepped, punched hard at the kidneys, and pulled back only to realize that McGhee had set her up. He had planned for her to dodge and strike. As she moved backward, he winced at the pain in his side but still managed to jab hard with his blade.

The short metal cut straight into her left side. He stepped close up against her, pressing the blade through to the hilt. Placing his mouth against her ear, he whispered, "Wolf wants you to know that the Bluesmen never forget."

He yanked the blade out and let her fall to the stairs. Though she could feel her black assault suit close around the holes, enough blood had gushed out to glisten on the stairs. McGhee stood over her, held his sword with both hands, and lifted it over her head.

Lightning cracked through the air, arcing from the second floor, and reached into the blade McGhee held. His eyes popped wide as his body jolted back. Another bolt smacked into him, and the smoke of burnt skin rose around him. A third bolt shot him into the railing, splintering the wood, and sent him flailing to his death below.

Malja looked back but she already knew what she would see. Tommy stood at the top of the stairs, ready to create more lightning if necessary. She wanted to say something but her blood continued to run down her leg and onto the stairs.

Her head lightened. She wondered if she might fall to the ground when she remembered that she already sat on the stairs. Fawbry and Tommy were next to her now. They looked worried. Malja closed her eyes. They were talking but she couldn't make out the words.

Chapter 2

Malja's eyes fluttered open to find Fawbry looking over her. His mouth curled up offering comfort, but his chin trembled and his brow knit tight. The mural on the ceiling told her they were still in the mansion and the sunlight streaming in suggested mid-morning. She lay on a bed — too soft for her comfort — and she noticed some furniture covered with sheets and blankets.

Fawbry helped her sit up. She winced in expectation of pain, but nothing happened. Examining her side, she found the wound not only healed but non-existent. As if she had never been struck at all.

With her stomach twisting, she glanced at Fawbry. He had the sense to look guilty. "I tried to stop him. I told him you would want to heal naturally," he said, "but I can't order Tommy around any more than I can order you."

"Where is he?"

"Across the hall."

Malja swung her feet off the bed and stood. Her head swam a little but overall she felt fine. She brushed by Fawbry and crossed to the other bedroom.

Tommy lay on a bed big enough for three people. Fawbry had swaddled him in blankets yet still the boy shivered. The air around him had a bitter, stale odor. His skin had paled and sweat beaded on his forehead.

"How long's he been like this?" she asked.

Fawbry patted down Tommy's head. "Since he healed you. He's getting worse, too."

Malja approached Tommy and touched his arm with two fingers. He deserved more than her. She pressed her whole hand down and rubbed his arm. He deserved better.

She held her face still as she digested Fawbry's words. *Since he healed you.* The idea that Tommy's repeated use of magic might someday cause something like this had never ceased roiling inside, but seeing it in reality cut into her heart like a cold blade. She stared at the two of them in silence before muttering, "I hate magic."

She walked out of the room, down the hall, to the stairs. McGhee's body had not been moved. She checked and found Cole's journal in the coat pocket, then returned to Tommy and Fawbry without a further glance at the dead man.

Malja sat beneath a window, keeping one eye on Tommy, and skimmed through the tightly written pages. Lots of details about experiments and machinery. A few comments about missing Fawbry — even some regret over having destroyed the man's hand.

"What are you looking for?" Fawbry asked.

Malja glanced up. She saw the tremor in his eyes. Different than before. No longer just about Tommy. After these last few years, she knew Fawbry's looks — he was mustering the courage to challenge her verbally.

Confirming her suspicions, Fawbry said, "You still want to find her, don't you? Even after you nearly died and Tommy's suffering because of it. Even though you know there are more Bluesmen out there just waiting to kill you. And they're organized again, right? This Wolf fellow?"

"Would you rather settle down here? Make a lovely home? I'm sure we could find your parents and the arranged bride you ran from. You could have a calm little life here. Make a few little Fawbrys even. Until the Bluesmen find you anyway."

"All I meant was —"

"Cole Watts kept detailed notes in this journal. What she thought, what she was doing, and where she was doing it. We're going to follow it like a map until we find her."

"She's not a healer."

"She'll be able to help," Malja said with too much force. "Besides, she can work with us to open a portal. That's the important thing. You can make a home here because this is your home. But I'm not from this world."

"I know, I know," Fawbry said, scowling as he turned to Tommy. "No need to tell me all of it again."

Malja didn't respond. She wanted to, though. She wanted to assure Fawbry that her strong desire to find her home would not turn into anything like the obsession that had driven her years before. At that time, she had wanted revenge on the bastard magicians, Jarik and Callib, for stealing her from her world, for raising her knowing only violence, and for abandoning her in the woods at age ten.

But she had her vengeance. This was different. She would not sacrifice Tommy or even Fawbry for a chance to get home. They had become a family and that was just as precious.

She couldn't tell him any of that, however, because he would ask more questions. And the fact remained that the deeper one looked within her, the more damages one would find. All the people she had killed. All the anger. If Fawbry knew just how dark she was inside, this fragile family would crash to the ground and shatter. She wanted to reach out to them, to comfort Tommy, protect them, but the thought of destroying what they had built was too great. She refused to take this bit of family away from Tommy. It wasn't much, it was far from perfect, but it belonged to them.

"Here," she said, pointing to the last written page in the journal. "Cole traveled South to a town she hoped would 'meet my unique requirements.' What does that mean?"

"Knowing Cole, we don't want to find out."

"If there's a town just south of here, we might find help for Tommy."

Fawbry scrunched his face but nodded. With a resigned slouch, he walked over to a closet door. "I found something for you that you'll need," he said.

From the closet, Fawbry pulled out Viper. Malja brightened as if seeing a lover return from years away. She took the weapon in hand, felt its well-balanced weight, and inspected it for any damage. Viper looked good.

"Thank you," she said.

"Guess we should head south then."

"Relax," Malja said, giving Viper a few practice swings. "We'll be fine, now."

They rode out. Despite his size, at fifteen years he reached Malja's chin, she cradled Tommy as she guided Horse through the woods. Until Horse, she had never connected with an animal before, but this particular mare had proven itself in battle and responded to Malja's needs often before Malja could express them. Even now, Horse appeared to move with a gentler gait and to pick out a smoother path as if the creature sensed Malja's worry over Tommy. She hoped Tommy could sense it, too.

The land flattened as they traveled further South. They passed several burned out buildings — mere skeletons to remind passersby that once, long ago, the world had been a civilized place filled with technology powered by magic. Back then, a group of magicians attempted to open a portal to another world, but they couldn't control what they had created. The Devastation resulted. The generations that followed had only these remains to remind them that there was time when they didn't live as scavengers amid the scarred ruins, the mutated creatures, and the fouled lands.

Malja pulled out Cole's journal and while holding Tommy tight with one hand, she held the book with her other. The Bluesman McGhee had read to her about a man dressed like her, a man named Harskill. Fawbry had been wrong to worry about her obsessing over finding Cole Watts. If there was anything Malja couldn't stop thinking about, it was Harskill. Another person wearing an assault suit like hers? She had thought it impossible.

The suit, until now, had been unique in this world. She had worn it since she was a baby. It grew with her. It reacted to her needs and adjusted for her — kept her warm in the cold nights, cooled her under a blazing sun, and dried her during a heavy rain.

The only times she had ever seen another person with such a suit was when looking through a portal to another world. Never had she heard of somebody here having such a thing.

Malja glanced over her shoulder at Fawbry. He watched the trees and a few white-spotters flying overhead, their wide wing span lending them uncommon grace. He had no idea that she was thinking about Harskill over and over.

Scanning through the journal's pages, she found the name she sought and read:

> *Today has been the most unusual day of my life, which is saying quite a lot. While working on the details for the Dish, a man was brought before me. He wore an odd black suit, the kind I have only seen once before in all my life and never thought I'd see again. But there he was. Another from Malja's world. His name is Harskill. He said he sought me out because he had learned of my attempts (and somewhat success) at creating portals. He wants to help me and he's the perfect person to do so. Until Harskill, Malja was the only person I knew who could enter a portal without dying. But Harskill is one of her kind and seems to believe that he can do what she can do. If so, my research will progress faster than ever before.*

Malja had to close the journal. There was more about Harskill and she planned to read it all later, but just seeing the reality on paper — another like her in this world — filled her with such a hurricane of emotions, she had to digest it all before reading on.

Two days later, they came across the scattered remains of a paved road. Black chunks marked the path where nature had yet to take over. They followed the road, noting the lack of ruined grounders or rusted road signs — even before the Devastation, this was apparently a remote area — until they saw a figure standing ahead. Clad in the scraps of a moldy tarp, the figure waved at them and shuffled closer.

"Go back," the figure called out — the voice of an old man.

Malja pulled up Horse and Fawbry halted just behind. Malja eased Tommy into Fawbry's arms. She made sure Fawbry held the boy tight and secure. Then she turned toward the man and watched as he continued his approach. No need for Viper. Yet.

Thin, filthy, and bruised, the old man pointed northward when he reached them. "Go back. The evil brother god, Kryssta, has forsaken this land. Go back, and Korstra will protect you." The old man's gaze fell onto Fawbry and took in his reaction. "You curl your lip. You don't believe me?"

"Kryssta doesn't forsake lands."

"Oh, I see. You're a fool. Well, then, go forth and see what your beloved Kryssta has wrought upon a town of good people just because they follow Korstra."

"Kryssta doesn't —"

"Of course, He does. He brought on the Devastation when he couldn't steal the love of the Goddess from Korstra, and then He has you all believing that the only way to praise him is in solitude. Right? You aren't allowed to pray together? It's all about the self."

"It's about improving the self."

"Selfish is what I call it. Korstra teaches us to ban together, to work as a family, so that we are stronger together. That the tribe is more important than the individual. And down here, in this little town, the tribe worked wonderfully together. So, Kryssta destroyed it. You go there. You see for yourself what that evil brother god has done. And I praise Korstra for I know it will be the last thing you'll ever see. Kryssta has no love for anyone. He'll kill you the moment you understand His true nature."

Fawbry shook his head. "I'm sorry you are filled with such hatred, but you are wrong. Kryssta doesn't kill, doesn't destroy, doesn't do anything like you suggest."

The old man laughed. To Malja, he said, "You watch out for that one. He'll kill you in your sleep if Kryssta commands it." He laughed again and walked up the road.

Malja checked on Fawbry. He looked more angry than shaken. "You okay?"

"Let's go," he said, setting his eyes on the road.

Malja took Tommy back into her arms. Burning with fever and flush in the face, he didn't seem to be aware of his surroundings. But he did snuggle closer against her chest, and despite her tendency to stiffen at such contact, she didn't pull back.

As they moved on, Malja heard Fawbry pull out a book and leaf through it. Fawbry owned only one book — *The Book of Kryssta*. She was happy for him that he found comfort in its words, but for her neither brother god meant much. She had seen too many evil people on both sides to become a believer.

By the end of the day, they reached the town. It sat in the open which suggested either a brazen attitude or a lack of enemies. Malja guessed the latter since she had not seen or heard anything to suggest other towns nearby.

The town had a grid pattern of streets forming orderly blocks of two-story buildings. As the road they followed merged into one of the town's streets, Malja noticed the construction was not the usual mashing of scavenged materials. These buildings had been built from the ground up — not found and re-purposed. Clearly the design of this town had been planned from the start.

Fawbry nodded toward an open door. Peering in as they passed by, Malja caught that the room inside was empty. The whole town appeared empty.

"I think something bad happened here," Fawbry said.

When they turned the corner, Malja brought Horse to a halt. "I think you're right," she said.

Before them, a dozen burned bodies had been strewn across the street. Shattered windows and splintered doorways marred the orderliness of the town. Bricks had been yanked out of the walls. Paint had been peeled back.

"Look," Fawbry said. "It all goes in the same direction."

He was right. All the destruction reached out toward them as if something closer to the town center had exploded, blasting everything and everyone down the street.

"It's getting dark," Malja said. "We'll pick a building for the night."

"That one still has a window."

Malja led the way with Viper held in front. The building turned out to be a home with little furnishing and plenty of dust. An empty picture frame was the only decoration. A foul odor permeated the air.

"Upstairs," she said.

They climbed the creaking wood and settled in the bedroom with the intact window. Layers of dust and grime coated the walls, and she couldn't see much through the filthy windows, but Malja felt more secure for Tommy than out on the street. Tommy fell asleep right away. Fawbry watched over him like a mother while Malja checked out the house.

"I'm going to find us some food," Malja said when she returned to the room. "There's another stairwell in the back. Anything happens — grab Tommy and use those stairs to get out. And scream. This town isn't that big and everything's quiet. You scream, I'll hear it."

"Don't worry. I can scream loud," Fawbry said but neither of them laughed. Then, with a shiver, he added, "This place. What was Cole doing here?"

Chapter 3

Fawbry's question stayed with Malja as she slid through the empty streets. But where Fawbry asked in fear, Malja felt hope. The only thing she could think that would cause this kind of destruction was an explosion of magic. On its own, that could mean a lot of things, but this was all about Cole Watts. Couple this town with the journal and it seemed obvious that Cole was experimenting with something powerful and dangerous. With Harskill in the picture, Malja knew for sure that Cole Watts had started messing with portals once again.

The town proved her right when she reached its large town square. In the center, she found a circle of odd, charred machinery with thick cables linking it all together. One wide cable ran straight into the center where Malja saw the scorched remnants of what looked like a large picture frame. She knew it well. A portal frame — Cole Watts had developed the technology to control a portal with the aid of magic created by the Bluesmen's music. This one clearly hadn't worked.

A strange sound caught her attention — a low moaning sprinkled with high-pitched whines like a wounded animal. Malja followed the sound down an eastern road. One side of the road had a long gray-brick wall. About two-thirds of the way down, Malja spied a huge hole in the wall dripping with blood. A konapol corpse draped the entrance.

Konapol were strong creatures. Whatever killed this one would be stronger.

Malja peered into the hole. With the sun down, she didn't have enough light to see much. A little movement, perhaps. The hole didn't seem that deep — more like a tiny cave.

A whispering voice traveled from the darkness. "Come in," it said.

Malja raised Viper so whatever had called her would know she had a weapon.

"I won't hurt you. Come in," the voice said.

Looking up and down the street, Malja searched for signs of other life. Tommy needed a good meal to regain his health — something more hearty than found berries and tree leaves. If she had to, she could take back a bit of the konapol, but its meat was tough and tasteless, and she had no idea how long ago the beast had been killed. Tommy hated the stuff, too. It seemed that this creature calling her was the only meat around. But it had some intelligence, enough to speak and not just attack her out of instinct.

She knew going in would be risky and dangerous, but if she walked away, she doubted whatever was in there would leave her alone. She could hear the desperation in its voice. This thing had to be dealt with, and if the result was food for Tommy, then all the better.

"I'm coming in," Malja said. "Don't make any quick motions or I'll kill you."

"I won't hurt you," the voice whispered with such desire that Malja could practically hear the creature salivating with hunger.

As Malja crouched and walked in, she felt the ground crunching under her feet. The snaps of small bones accompanied every step. A dim light flickered ahead — a fire. Thankfully, the deep aroma of burning wood masked the nauseating odor of rotting corpses.

The hole went further in than Malja had expected, a tunnel really, but she reached a point where the space opened into a wide room — one of the other buildings. A small fire surrounded by rocks and skulls crackled in the center of the room. Just beyond sat a gnarled figure, human in basic form but far from human. Close enough, though, that Malja dropped all thoughts of eating the thing.

It was tall and gangly with mottled skin stretched tight against the bone. No fat. No meat. A line of sharp bone ran along its spine, and its hands and feet looked more like sharp talons. It had a freakish face — childlike eyes but with the deadly teeth of a predator.

It sat on a wooden stool. Nothing else in the room. Malja entered.

"Who are you?" it asked, though it appeared to suffer pain in the attempt to speak.

"Malja."

"Really, now. I've heard that claim before. Even ate a few who said as much."

"Make your move and you won't have a mouth to eat with ever again."

It coughed for a moment. "I can see the revulsion in your face. You look at me like I'm some ugly beast. A monster to be destroyed."

"What are you then?"

"I ... I don't know anymore. I *was* a worker. I was human like you.

We all were. We worked here every day until this happened. Another Devastation came and like before, we were changed, mutated. Maybe we are beasts and monsters. But we're not the real monsters. No, no. We worked for Cole Watts. She is the true monster. You watch out for her. She'll sacrifice you without a care. Turn you into something evil and disgusting. She caused another Devastation."

Malja shook her head. "There wasn't another Devastation. The world is as it was. Except here."

"Cole Watts did this," it said. A fit of coughing followed. It hacked up and spit out a glob of blood. "She plays with powers she doesn't understand. She thinks she's a god, but she's a fool. She's no Kryssta, and she's certainly not the great Korstra. She's just a mad woman, and we all suffer for it."

"There are more like you?"

It nodded. "Over half her workforce was in town when she let her experiment loose." It turned its big eyes on Malja and lost all sense of threat. "P-Please," it said. "If you are Malja, then you understand the horror I'm feeling. I've been made into something less than I was. Malja, the real Malja, is a great warrior. She would have mercy on me. Kill me even. She could end my pain in one swift stroke. Is that really you? Are you really Malja?"

In the flickering firelight, the creature's face shifted between weak pleading and hideous aggression. The conflict within this former-man played out not just on its face but in the room as well. Malja noticed now that all the bones were covered in uneaten flesh. The corners of the room had been fouled with vomit. This creature's hunger drove it to attack and eat these animals raw, but the vestiges of humanity left within it caused it to rebel against its body's desires.

"Please," it said, exposing its neck for a killing blow. "Have mercy on me."

Mercy. Malja had killed for many reasons: survival, defense, and revenge. She had led armies and toppled rulers. But to take a life for mercy? On the surface, it seemed fine, perhaps even moral, and could be done with ease. Except that Malja knew no killing was free of complications. At the least, she would have to pay the dead their honor as Uncle Gregor, her guardian growing-up, had taught her. How could she pay honor to a half-human/half-mutated beast? Especially when such a creature existed because it was helping Cole Watts do things she had been warned never to do again — opening portals. Then again, Malja sought Cole Watts to open a portal for her, so perhaps she was no better than the creature before her.

"Okay," she said, and the tension holding the creature firm eased away. It sighed, and Malja swore she could see a smile on its jagged mouth. She raised Viper, watched the creature close its eyes, and she struck true.

A pained cry erupted in the distance. Another joined it. Soon a chorus of howling screams echoed from outside, and Malja knew the other workers that had been mutated were still around. Somehow they had sensed this one's death.

The screams turned into angry growls. And they were coming closer.

Chapter 4

Malja peered down the tunnel she had arrived by. Something was in there. Approaching fast. A quick scan of the room offered no other exits.

With a resigned huff, she said, "Wonderful." She held Viper in front of her, the blade turned horizontally, and crouched into the hole. Cackling echoed around her.

Moving as fast as she could manage in the awkward position, she pressed forward. The bright moonlight that should have marked the end of the hole had been blocked out by whatever creature came her way. The double-strike odor of sweat and feces rode in on the constant noise of the creature.

Though her thighs, knees, and ankles cramped from trying to hurry in a crouch, she pushed her legs harder, faster. The only light came from the dying fire behind her. It was enough, though.

She saw a hairy mound of muscle and teeth ahead. Letting out a guttural war cry, Malja charged forward as fast as her legs would allow. Viper jabbed into the creature's gut. With more momentum, she would have cut straight through, but the confined space and awkward crouching lessened her impact. Instead, Viper lodged into the creature's spine.

She shoved forward, pushing the creature backward as it howled in pain. It slashed at her with sharp claws, but it couldn't reach. It tried to dig into the wall, but that only let Viper cut deeper. Hollering in agony, the creature started stepping backward, helping Malja reach the exit.

They burst onto the street, the night air cool and bright. The creature tripped on the curb and fell. Malja followed through, pushing Viper straight into the street and separating the creature in two. As she yanked Viper from the gore, she heard more creatures behind her.

Looking over her shoulder, Malja saw a vast array of deformed and mutated people. Some stumbled toward her on stumped legs. Some crawled out of the windows, adhering to the walls with ease. Others sped toward her on a belly of fingers. Their skin reflected in the moonlight — silvers, greens, blacks, and browns. They were a mass of burn victims, leather-skinned lizards, oddities and peculiarities, and even one woman who appeared to be made of glass. They shared only one common trait — they all were coming for Malja with teeth bared and hunger in their eyes.

The first to attack had four arms, several rows of teeth, and ghostly white hair. It leaped into the air, spreading its claws and opening its mouth. Malja jumped back. When the beast hit the ground, she kicked forward, knocking it into the crowd.

Another creature, this one with a head of bumps and bruises and no neck, threw a wide punch. Malja dodged it with ease and swiped Viper, cutting off the creature's forearm. The first attacker returned, and this time, it spurred the others on.

Malja's focus intensified as she fell into a rhythm of evading blow after blow, her body twisting and ducking, and then when the openings could be found, she struck out with Viper, causing damage and pushing back her enemy. There were too many. And they all had the one target — her.

Taking a chance, she whirled around, letting Viper slice at anything in its way. Two heads rolled and the rest of her attackers stepped back for a second. It was all the time she needed.

Malja dashed away from the group, sprinting until she reached the crossroads. "Fawbry!" she bellowed as she turned down the street.

Many of the creatures were too deformed to chase after her, but enough of them had speed to be dangerous. Their sharpened claws clicked against the cracked pavement as they closed in on Malja. Slobbering and snarling, they would catch her before she could reach Horse and the boys.

"Fawbry! Get —"

Something wet and strong wrapped around her throat, yanked her off her feet, and smacked her into the ground. She looked back. The same four-armed, white-haired bastard stood with its mouth wide open. Its huge, muscular tongue stretched out from its mouth to Malja's neck. With her free hand, she tried to pull it off, but the tongue tightened its grip. She struggled for air.

More creatures arrived, circling Malja, waiting for White Hair to kill her so they could feast. Malja rose to her knees, ignoring the jeering of the crowd, and tried once more to pull the tongue off her neck. No good. White Hair laughed — a disgusting sound with its tongue out.

Lack of air slowed Malja's thoughts, but one idea stood out — she had only used her left hand to pull at the tongue. Why? *Because I'm still holding Viper in the other hand!* Not wasting time to chastise herself, she flicked Viper over and slashed upward. White Hair laughed no more.

She pulled the severed tongue from her neck and watched White Hair run off, its clawed hands covering its mouth as it blubbered in pain. It left behind a trail of blood that a few creatures decided to lap up. The others had grown cautious, but hunger still ruled them. They inched forward, closing any gaps around her.

Bright flashes erupted from one building. The building Tommy and Fawbry were in. Sizzling sounds and anguished screams followed more flashes. All the creatures and Malja looked up.

The windows on the second floor exploded outward. Flames shot in the air. A fiery ball soared out of each window and struck the ground. Just before they hit, Malja realized they were not balls of fire but bodies of fire. The odor of cooked flesh pulled many of the creatures away from her.

From the hole where the window had been, Tommy floated out. Malja had seen him do this before — sitting cross-legged in the air with his hands resting on his knees — but she had never seen the way his eyes blazed in concentration. Fawbry peeked out from the second floor as Tommy hovered just above the street. All the creatures were mesmerized by him. They even stopped eating their charred friends to watch.

Nothing more happened for a moment. The still night air lacked any noise — all the surrounding animals waited to see the outcome. When the creatures attacking Malja seemed to think nothing more would happen, they attacked again. Two grabbed for Malja while four others charged Tommy.

Malja dropped to the ground, sweeping Viper through the legs of her opponents. Tommy raised a hand, his eyes fixated on his tattoos. Flames shot from his hand, lighting up the street. All four fell — one of them burned to ash.

This proved to be enough of a threat to outweigh their hunger. The creatures rushed away, whimpering like wounded pets. A few bold ones dragged the cooked corpses with them, but none dared to look at Tommy. In seconds, the street emptied except for Malja and Tommy.

Pulling debris from his hair, Fawbry stepped from the building and said to Tommy, "They're all gone. You can stop now."

But Tommy continued to float. Though the look in his eyes no longer blazed, it had not returned to normal either. His eyes had turned pinkish, and he looked ahead as if focused on nothing. And his sickness was gone. All the fever, all the weakness, had mutated into a floating magician.

"Tommy?" Malja said, her voice shaking a little.

Reaching out a hand, Fawbry said, "Come on, now. The threat's all over."

Tommy turned toward the south and glided down the street, his feet never touching the ground.

"Wait," Malja said but Tommy continued his steady pace. Malja kicked at the rubble on the ground. To Fawbry, she said, "Get the horses."

"Where's he going?"

"We'll find out if you get the damn horses."

From the Journal of Malja:

I don't know why I'm starting to write in this. I'm not the type and it's not even my journal. But I'm stuck on Horse with too much time, and if I read through this thing one more time, I'll go crazy. Though to be honest, and I suppose that's part of what writing in this thing is about, I've avoided reading a few sections. But there are lot of empty pages and there was a pencil in the book so here I am.

And if I don't do this, I've got to deal with the dead and I'm tired of that. I've tried to always listen to Uncle Gregor's advice and pay the dead their honor, but more and more I find myself killing things like those mutated creatures. How do I pay them their honor? They weren't warriors met on the battlefield. They weren't human. Not anymore. I don't know what they were. And that one that asked for mercy. Maybe writing in this will help. Maybe this is another way to pay them honor.

We've been traveling for a few days now. Tommy's been leading the way while Fawbry and I dutifully follow. I hate watching him float. He never touches the ground. I suppose burying myself in this journal keeps me from seeing what he's become. He only stops when we refuse to go on and that only happens in the evening when the horses need a break and we need food and sleep. I have to force Tommy to eat. I'm not even sure how much of Tommy is still in there. He's used so much magic in the last few years. Powerful magic. Opening portals and fighting superior forces. If he's lost his mind to magic because of me ... I can't think like that. We'll get him help. He has to be okay. Cole Watts understands magic and machinery and can get the two to work together. She'll be able to help us.

The other thing is Harskill. I've always been good at keeping these kinds of thoughts shoved far down and only dealing with them as needed. The sections of this journal about him, I avoid. Mostly. But as I write this, it all is pouring out. Harskill is a big part of what I think about. How can I not? Not that I think he's a sibling or a real family member. That would be crazy. But it's become clear to me in the last few years that my people, whoever my people are, have the ability to travel through portals. So why couldn't one of them come here? And if one can come here, then it must be possible to find my home. So why do I keep hesitating to read too much about him?

Chapter 5

Malja had seen most of Corlin and even some of the northern country, Penmarvia, but as far as she knew, nothing was further south than the Freelands — the land most ruined by the Devastation. Yet not only had Tommy taken them further south, but he had led them around the Freelands altogether. Malja had assumed the Freelands encompassed everything that was south for that had been her experience. Tommy, however, had avoided that desolate land and brought them into the most bizarre place Malja had ever seen — a waterless swamp.

The land consisted of deep runs where swamp might have once been. When she pictured all these natural chutes and paths filled with water, it made sense. What were now miniature buttes had once been the little islands of trees, dirt, and rocks that dotted the swamp. Lacking enough water to support the area, most of the land had become desert-like in vegetation. Some of the trees still stood, though, with thick roots that stretched far down into the pathways like aged fingers, digging deeper, searching for whatever bits of water flowed beneath.

"It's like walking through the skeleton of a giant monster," Fawbry said.

That would have been a comfort. It would have been evidence of something once alive around here. Fawbry held on to Tommy's horse, and whether from being riderless or being tugged along, that animal did not seem comfortable with their surroundings. Even Horse acted uneasy, and twice Malja had to redirect the mare back to following Tommy. She couldn't blame Horse, though. Not only was this land eerie on its own, but Tommy's floating form surrounded them with a tension like being prey.

She pulled out the journal. She knew what parts she hadn't read, and she needed every bit of information that might be relevant. With a hesitant hand, she opened the journal.

Harskill continues to be of immense help. He's understood the project from the start and has, once or twice, nudged me away from making crucial calculation errors. Clearly, his people understand mathematics and portal physics quite well. He's also a darling young man, and I'd be lying if I said he hadn't piqued my interest. It's been a long while since I've enjoyed a man. I'm not sure if his interest in me goes beyond the scientific, but I think I'll find out tonight.

Malja closed the book, unsure if she should read on. It bothered her that Cole Watts might sleep with Harskill. It bothered her more that she was bothered at all. What did it matter? Yet, however rare, Malja had felt jealousy before, and she recognized the sensation again. She wanted Harskill for herself. Not sexually. Probably not. But she wanted him untainted by this world. And of all people, the idea that Cole Watts would be his lover bothered her more. Refusing to give in, she snapped open the book and read on:

This afternoon we finished all the preparations for our first full test of the new portal frame. If all goes well, we will form a controlled portal within the frame near the center of town. Everyone on my team has worked hard this last year and I can see the excitement among them all. And since we won't run the test until morning, I decided to seduce Harskill. Well, I tried, at least. It appears he is not persuaded by my charms. I've gotten old, I suppose, and for many men, age is not as attractive on a woman. It's a shame because my years of experience could have given us both a passionate night that would not be forgotten. Not ever. I must admit, though, he was most gracious in declining me. Makes my desire even stronger.

Malja put the book away and tried not to smile. Fawbry trotted up next to her. "Something amusing?" he asked.

Shaking her head, Malja said, "Just a bit in the journal about Harskill."

Fawbry shifted in his saddle. "I don't mean to upset you, but perhaps you shouldn't read the rest of that journal. You might be building up an image of Harskill that he can't fill."

"I'm not a child."

"But you are alone, and he's one of your kind — supposedly."

"Supposedly?"

Fawbry tapped the pommel of his saddle, his face scrunched as he made a decision. "Don't misinterpret this, but you may not like what you find in Harskill. Before you say anything, please listen. See, when I was little, there was a boy at my school, Teeco, and we weren't great friends but we got along at school just fine. He was an orphan. One day he told me that he found some paper in his adoptive father's desk. This paper was about his real mother, the one that gave birth to him.

"It wasn't much. Just a tag that had been attached to his coat when he was left at his father's door. He spent weeks going over every little detail he could remember from that slip of paper. Each day, he told me more and more. His mother had been born in a fishing village, so he built up an image of her based on that fact — she must be hard-working, she must be strong, she probably needs a good night's sleep but is beautiful nonetheless. He talked on for days.

"I guess his father discovered that he was sneaking peeks at the paper and confronted him. Teeco told me that after their long talk, his father agreed to let Teeco meet his mother. That boy was so excited, he practically danced in the classroom. Well, I'll never forget the day he got back from this wonderful visit. He didn't want to talk, he didn't want to play, he didn't want to do anything but sit on a rock. And, of course, he didn't smile.

"I never found out what went wrong exactly, but my own folks told me enough about the fishing villages that I could guess."

Malja said, "She was a whore?"

"I think so."

"Those fishing villages are an ugly life. With so few people left since the Devastation, the waters are filled with food, and the women come thinking they'll get security. But fishing is hard work and you have to love the water, too. Not as many men are interested. Most of these villages I've seen had three, maybe four, women for every man. No man needs to settle down to one woman. Lots of whores there, and most do it for food."

"The point is," Fawbry said, ducking beneath a low hanging vine, "that you shouldn't guess at what Harskill is like from the little you find in that journal."

Waving off his words, Malja said, "Don't compare me to some pampered kid you once knew."

"My Kryssta, you're an idiot," Fawbry said, not making an attempt to hide his frustration. "Or maybe I'm the idiot for thinking you might have grown a bit, changed at all since I first met you. You are so selfish that you actually convince yourself that you do these things for others. You don't really care about me or Tommy."

"Don't you dare say —"

"Look at that boy!" Fawbry's face turned red as he jabbed a finger in Tommy's direction. "Something terribly wrong has happened to him and you just want to contentedly follow him? I understand fully that you hope to find Cole and Harskill and a portal to your home. And that's what I'm saying. That is all you hope for. If Tommy or I get killed in the process, so be it."

Malja backhanded Fawbry, knocking him to the ground. Her skin boiled with rage, and she had to stop her hands from grabbing Viper. "I have changed. I'm not that single-minded thing you met years ago. But even back then, I always loved Tommy and I've always worried about what might happen from his use of magic. You are the idiot, if you can't tell that much about me."

Brushing off his multi-colored robe, Fawbry said, "It's just that Tommy's in trouble. You can see that. And yet here you are reading that journal and dreaming about Harskill. I know those things are important, but we shouldn't be doing this. We should turn around, take Tommy back north for help. Maybe find Tumus. She helped him once before and she knows all about Barris Mont, and since Barris Mont is inside Tommy, she could tell us what to expect, what to do. That plan at least has some logic behind it. You're just leading us toward a wish."

Malja reined in her anger and in a tight but quiet voice, she said, "My guess is that we've gone more than half the way to wherever it is we're going. There can't be that much further south before we hit ocean. So, if we turn back for help, it'll probably take longer to go that way than to just push on. I don't know what's happening to Tommy, but don't think that I don't care just because you can't see it. I think the faster we get to Cole, the faster we get to helping Tommy. Besides, if we chose to go back, who's going to turn him around?"

Fawbry looked ahead at Tommy hovering patiently for them. The boy didn't turn around while he waited, but his shoulders were high with tension. It physically hurt him to wait.

"Come on," Malja said. "Get on your horse and let's go."

With his only hand, Fawbry patted his horse and whispered a calming word. Malja moved in to hold the horse steady so Fawbry could remount. "You'd think this would get easier," he said, "but I swear, every time I mount up, it gets worse."

* * * *

That night they camped under a low overhang — roots and rocks formed their ceiling. Malja spent her time attending Viper — cleaning, sharpening, oiling. She had neglected the blade for too long.

Fawbry stood in front of Tommy and tried to reach the boy. He told jokes and stories and even danced a little. Nothing evoked a response. At one point, Malja glanced over to see Fawbry's arms tangled up.

"You okay?" she asked, worried that Tommy had conjured Fawbry into a knot out of annoyance.

Fawbry untangled his arms and walked over. "I'm fine. Just playing a simple game to show him that our minds are strange and sometimes unreliable. I'm hoping he might be able to come back to us if he realizes he has more control than he's using."

"How's a game going to show that?"

Cracking his knuckles, Fawbry said, "Give it a try. See what happens."

Malja set Viper down and stretched her arms. "What do I do?"

"Put your arms straight out in front of you and place the backs of your hands together. Now, cross your arms so that you can clasp your hands together. Good. Now, bring your clasped hands to your chest and roll them towards you so that you are staring at the tops of your fingers."

Following the instructions, Malja ended up with her own arms tangled together. "I still don't see how this is going to show me —"

"Shh. Pay attention." Careful not to touch her, Fawbry pointed to one of Malja's fingers. "That finger there. Move it."

Malja shrugged and tried to move her finger. It didn't move. She stared at it a moment, but her brain couldn't quite figure out how to reach it. When she finally managed to get some motion, she not only moved the wrong finger but the wrong hand as well.

"You see," Fawbry said. "It's not so hard to confuse a brain. Maybe that's all that's going on with Tommy. Maybe his brain's gotten all confused from the magic, and he just needs to untangle. That's what I'm hoping, anyway."

Malja played this finger game a bit longer. "If it works, great. You've got until we find Cole Watts. Then she better be able to help him."

"Thanks," Fawbry said and went back to Tommy, tangling up his arms once again.

* * * *

The next day, as they traveled through the swamp, Fawbry rode next to Tommy, continuing to play mental games in his effort to bring the boy's mind back. Malja said little while she led Tommy's mare along.

She tried to keep track of their route despite the numerous twists the dead swamp took. When her stomach grumbled, she checked her saddlebag and counted another two days of food — mostly hard rolls and a few potatoes.

"Let's take a rest," she said. "Have something to eat."

Fawbry hopped off his horse and walked toward her, reaching out for the reins to Tommy's horse. A long-wailing siren pierced the air. Fawbry's horse spooked and galloped off. Fawbry still held the rein and was snagged along with it. Reaching down fast and gracefully, Malja grabbed Fawbry's robe and yanked him free. He stood on the ground, pale and breathing heavy.

"Thanks," he said. "That could've been bad."

"What is that noise?"

Fawbry's horse galloped back their way — whinnying its confusion and fear. With its head low, the horse barreled right by. As the siren continued its long tones, the ground swelled, causing the panicked horse to rear on its hind legs.

"M-Malja," Fawbry said, staring at the horse as the ground opened up. The horse fell in, cried out in agony, and the sound of crushed bones and chewing followed. "Get me out of here."

Malja released Viper from its special sheath. The swollen earth settled back, but Malja remained vigilant, her eyes searching for any sign of another attack. In mid-wail, the siren cut out, its final call echoing into the distance.

Shaking, Fawbry said, "What happened? What was that?"

Just behind them, dirt spewed into the air along with half-digested horse bones. They came up with forceful puffs of air, spraying grit in all directions. Malja bent down to pick up Fawbry, but the smell of horse flesh terrified Horse. She bolted forward, her mind completely taken over by instinct, and ignored Malja's attempts to control her.

They dashed by the hovering Tommy and slammed hard into a barrier neither could see. Horse took it the worst, crumpling to the ground, dazed. The abrupt hit sent Malja over Horse's head and into the invisible wall, knocking the air from her lungs. She rolled to the ground, popped back to her feet, and held Viper in a sturdy fighting stance.

Two long tentacles broke through the dirt, each one like a dead root flailing around for nourishment. Malja wasted no time in cutting them. When she struck, a deep moan vibrated through the ground.

Fawbry rushed over to Tommy's unused horse, trying to calm it enough to mount. Malja glanced at her own mare. Horse had stood up but still looked wild-eyed. And just beyond Horse, Malja saw the long roots of a tree hanging over a mini-butte.

"Fawbry," she said. "Climb!"

As Malja made for the root system and Fawbry hurried to follow, the ground underneath Tommy's horse swelled. Malja hated to see it happen, but in seconds the earth opened up and pulled down the horse. Climbing up the roots, Malja peeked over her shoulder and saw row upon row of teeth, rolling up to the surface like waves.

"Help me," Fawbry said from below. With only one hand, he couldn't climb the roots well.

Malja jumped down and placed her shoulder underneath Fawbry. As she reclimbed the roots, Fawbry reached up to anything he could hold on to, helping lighten her load a little. She groaned under the weight but managed to get off the ground and into the roots.

Horse blew air through her nostrils and paced beneath them. Malja strained her muscles to hold position even as her heart beat against her ribs. She didn't want to see it happen, but the ground beneath Horse rose.

"I'm sorry," she whispered to Horse.

Whether or not Tommy reacted because he heard Malja, she never knew, but Tommy did react. He spun around, checked the tattoo on his left pectoral, and waved his right hand at the swelling ground. Four tentacles shot out, but they lacked purpose and strength. They shot out more like a gasp for air.

And they were stone.

In fact, Malja now saw that the ground beneath her, beneath Horse, also looked like stone. A light-gray mass of rock. Tommy had petrified the creature.

As simply as he had acted, he returned to his hovering position and waited. Malja and Fawbry eased to the ground, avoiding the hard surface of petrified creature as they attempted to regroup. Fawbry's face reddened as he stomped over to Tommy.

"Korstra's bed-mate! You couldn't have done that sooner? We were almost killed."

Malja hiccuped a laugh. "I've never heard 'Korstra's bed-mate' before."

"I just made it up and don't try to change my thinking. Tommy can be awfully selective about when he decides to use his magic to save me. For you, he does it without a thought. But me? I don't appreciate him holding back like that."

"He holds back because I've asked him to do so," Malja said, all trace of amusement leaving her. "Look what's happened to him because of magic."

"I know, I know. I just —"

"You were almost eaten by a ... whatever that thing was. It's okay. Just don't take it out on Tommy. He's a good boy."

Fawbry's face pinched in but before he could speak, a familiar rumbling came in. It was a sound they all knew well — an engine.

A grounder with a hardtop drove in and skidded to halt, its engine idling loud as dark smoke poured out its back. The door opened, and a tough-looking, helmeted figure emerged. The figure pressed a button on its belt and the invisible barrier flashed blue. The figure stepped through where the barrier had been, observed them for a moment, and pulled off the helmet.

The lovely, dark-skinned face of Cole Watts peered out. "Faw-Faw? Dear, is that you?"

Chapter 6

Cole Watts drove through the twisting passages of dried-out swamp with familiarity while Malja leaned back and watched the landscape soar by. Tommy floated above the seat behind Cole, and Fawbry kept him in place with a safety restraint.

"Don't worry about your horse," Cole said, her voice as smooth as her beautiful, dark skin. "I'll have my people bring her in. I'd have my assistant Garros do it but he's been avoiding me lately." She snatched a quick look in the back. "My, my, Faw-Faw, you sure do look handsome. I know we had a rough patch but I must tell you, you've been on my mind lately."

"Rough patch?" Fawbry said. "You burned off my hand."

"Bless your heart, you don't forget anything, do you? Now I know I was wrong, and I think I've shown y'all that I've changed when I helped you get rid of those nasty magicians, Jarik and Callib. What you don't know, though, is that part of that change was realizing all the good things I gave up along the way. And, Faw-Faw, my dear sweet man, you are one of those things."

Fawbry blushed. Malja knew Cole Watts had charm to spare, but she was amazed at the brazenness the woman displayed.

"We need help for Tommy," Malja said with a firm voice.

"I certainly think so. One look at him and it's terribly clear he's in trouble."

"Do you know what's wrong with him?"

Cole chuckled. "Sweetie, I've only just seen him. He's grown quite a bit in the last few years, that's all I know. When we get to my place, we'll have him checked out. Don't worry about it." She patted Malja's knee. "Now, tell me all about what you've been up to. I do miss your darling way of handling things with such brute force."

Malja swiped away Cole's hand. "We know about your town up north. Is that an example of you changing your ways?"

Though she still wore a pleasant mask, all the warmth left Cole's face. "See, dear, right there. Brute force. Guess you haven't changed much either. Well, truth is, I've tried. When you all left me at the mansion, I spent months just playing with all the old technology there. The kitchen had ways to keep food fresh and cold as well as a machine that cooked food without a fire. Quite impressive what life had been like before the Devastation."

Fawbry said, "We heard all about your special room for peeing."

"There was one of those, yes," Cole said, glancing back with an amused wink. "Problem was I figured out how it all worked, what parts needed a magician's touch and what parts needed a mechanic's. It was fun and interesting but it didn't take long, and then I was bored. And my mind just kept turning back to the idea of a portal. All those worlds. I had come so close to doing it myself — I had done it really, just not in a way that could easily be repeated. Not without a roomful of musicians.

"I tried to forget about it, do other things. I want you to know that. I really tried everything I could to leave it alone. I even prayed, which is not something I've ever done seriously — once to Korstra and once to Kryssta. Still, my mind toyed with me. Worked on the math in my head without creating the physical portal. That kind of game where you see how close you can get to what you shouldn't, and see at what point you feel guilty. It's a terrible thing to play, because eventually, you get comfortable with that sharp edge you walk, and so you step farther and farther out.

"That's what happened to me. And one day, I walked too far. I just started up again. I knew you would be mad if you ever found out, but I also think you knew I'd do it. Maybe you even wanted me to do it. After all, you can't find your way home without a portal."

Fawbry closed his eyes and shook his head. "Did you even see what happened to the people in that town? What you did to them?"

Cole's mouth set into a thin line. "It was a horrible accident. It shouldn't have even come close to happening. We didn't realize that the power required to open a portal without magic was too great for the frame to hold. All my math suggested it would hold. It exploded so unexpectedly, and fire swept through the streets."

"Why weren't you injured?" Malja asked.

Cole lifted her chin as she drove on. "I ... I regret what I did. I admit that. Even though I underestimated how much power we would need, I still knew the power involved was immense, so I purposely set up our control station just outside the town. I should have warned people. I intended to do so when we tried a full run. That time, though, we were just checking some basic functions and running about half the power into the frame. I had no idea there was any danger that day."

"You did more than burn people. They mutated. As if it had been another Devastation," Fawbry said, but his voice held more compassion than anger.

A tear wet Cole's cheek and Fawbry placed a hand on her shoulder. "When the portal frame exploded," she said, "We searched for survivors. That's when I learned of the mutations. I'm sure you don't need to be told that the townspeople had not taken kindly with me. I was lucky to have this grounder or else they would have torn me to pieces. As it was, I drove off South and barely got away. I drove and, I admit it, I cried. Bawled like a little farm girl having to kill her favorite chicken because it got ill. I drove for hours. And I thought to myself that this had to be it. I had to stop messing with such powerful things. The Bluesmen were destroyed because my experiments attracted Jarik and Callib. An entire town was burned and deformed because of my experiments. And," she said, resting her hand atop Fawbry's, "I lost a man I loved because I wouldn't stop my experiments."

Malja expected Fawbry to pull away, maybe even protest. Instead, he let out a short, bashful giggle.

Cole went on, "That was it, right then. I was going to stop the whole project. Even thought about finding you all and offering my help in whatever you were doing. But then the brother gods blessed me with a sign. I knew they wanted me to continue because I had never driven this way before and yet, somehow, I ended up facing this —"

Cole stopped the grounder. Malja looked off to the left where Cole pointed. An enormous building could be seen in the distance — long and wide, it looked like a giant bowl sitting in a metallic grid-like structure.

"What is that?" Fawbry asked.

"We call it the Dish," Cole said, staring at the building with a seductive eye. "And it's going to make my portal frame work." She turned the grounder to the left and headed straight for the Dish.

Malja could not believe the size of it. "You could fit a whole town in there."

"We have. It takes a lot of people to operate the Dish, and the only town nearby is the one you came through to get here. So, anybody working on this project has to live here. We have all the facilities needed for such a large group of people."

"How did you find enough people?" Malja asked, her eyes never wavering from sight of the building.

"We put the word out and they found us. Lots of people out there are tired of fighting just to live. Here, they have safety and purpose. Most of them don't understand or even care what the overall project is. They've just been told that if we succeed, we can end the horror that is daily life in Corlin. That's all they need to hear. So, we have people who specialize in various things that need to be done in order to let the more scientifically gifted people do their work. We have cooks and farmers, of course. There's also many who are willing to do anything we ask. The Dish itself was not in good repair when I found it, and it's taken us many months just to clean it up so it's functional."

"What does it do?"

"Later. There's something far more important to you, Malja my dear." Cole stopped the grounder and turned it off.

They stepped onto a smoothly paved road. Malja and Fawbry gazed skyward at the enormous building towering over them. A few birds nested in the crooks of huge metal beams. Fawbry pointed to a piece of cloth tied to another beam — fluttering in the wind though the air on the ground was calm around them. Tommy slipped out of the car and hovered next to them. Cole, however, scurried to the main gate, said something to a guard, and then came back.

"Everything I've done here, back at the old town, and even much of what I did at the mansion, could not have been accomplished alone. I had help from a man I happened upon. I think he might seem a bit familiar, Malja, for he is from your world. I'd like you to meet Harskill."

From the main gate stepped a tall man with a slight frame. He wore an impossibly clean white shirt, tan pants without a single rip or stain, and peeking out from underneath, the same black assault suit as Malja wore. When he reached out his hand, she felt her pulse quicken. In a voice rich with experience, he said, "Hello, Malja."

Chapter 7

Malja couldn't move, could barely find the strength to breathe. She heard Cole Watts as if from far away. The woman mentioned something about Harskill and Malja spending a little time together, Fawbry mumbled some comment, and before Malja realized it, the two had taken Tommy into the building, leaving her alone with Harskill.

He was older than she had imagined, gray hair adding a note of wisdom to his short sideburns, and his mouth showed the hard cracks of age chasing down a man. "I'm sorry," he said, lowering his hand. "I thought it was customary here to shake hands when meeting."

Malja snapped out of her daze. "It is. Most places. I just was taken aback."

"I imagine so. Ms. Watts explained to me a little of your situation."

She looked toward the door they had taken Tommy through. "I have to make sure my boy is okay."

"Don't worry. They'll take excellent care of him. You have my word. Now, as I understand it, I'm the first Gate you've ever met."

"Gate?"

"Our people are called the Gate," he said, opening his arms in a warm welcome.

Part of Malja wanted to rush into his arms like a child taking in a parent's embrace. Another part of her, however, the part of her that had helped keep her alive this long, sparked up a note of caution. As well as Harskill presented himself, something itched at Malja.

She put out her hand. "I'm happy to meet you."

Harskill lowered his arms with a knowing grin. He shook her hand, firm but not attempting to crush her bones. And there was a tenderness, too — an intimacy in the way he gazed at her as their hands touched. "Let me show you the Dish," he said and headed into the building.

They climbed a series of metallic stairs before entering a huge, vaulted walkway that appeared to run the entire perimeter of the Dish.

Like spokes on a wheel, corridors periodically shot inward, and Malja caught sight of focus booths lining the way. Long ago, those booths would have housed magicians paid to spend hours sitting in darkness, creating energy for this building. Everything around her was metal. Though there was some rust, a few twisted supports, and even a section blocked off with a mountain of debris, the majority of the building showed little damage from the Devastation.

"Is it true?" Harskill asked as he led her up another stairwell, "You were raised by magicians who accidentally pulled you through a portal?"

"It wasn't much of an accident. They didn't return me, after all. Stole me right from my mother's arms. I don't even know her name. Do you? Do you know about a woman whose child was stolen through a portal?"

"I'm sorry, but we are not like that. We don't know each other that way."

"What do you mean? Please, I don't know anything about the Gates."

"Just Gate. And it's a bit complicated. For one thing, you haven't been raised in the same way as the rest of us. You've never learned of our responsibilities. I'm not sure how much I should tell you. I could end up ruining your life here."

Malja let out a short chuckle. "My life was ruined the day Jarik and Callib stole me."

"But you have friends and a son."

"He's not my son. And when is friendship anything more than a matter of using each other to survive?"

"It's just that —"

Malja grabbed Harskill's arm and spun him around. She climbed two steps so her eyes were level with his. Just above a whisper, she said, "You need to understand a few important things, and if you repeat any of this, I'll kill you. I've traveled a long way to find Cole Watts because I knew she'd be the one who could open a portal. I've risked the lives of my friends to do so. I did this because I'm going through the portal, and I'm going to find my way home. Now I didn't learn about you until just a few days ago, but it seems to me that you can answer a lot of my questions, save me a lot of time and trouble, and maybe even help me avoid hurting my friends. So, you better start telling me about the Gate and who I am or you'll find out just how many of the rumors about me are true."

Harskill didn't move, didn't flinch, didn't show the slightest sign of fear. With a stoic face, he returned every ounce of the cold strength pouring out of Malja. A strong wind rattled metal on metal. But when Malja frowned and backed up a sliver of an inch, Harskill winked and said, "It seems Ms. Watts was accurate when she told me how tough you are and how you prefer to solve your problems by force."

"Tell me —"

Raising a hand that, to Malja's surprise, stopped her, Harskill said, "Give me a little of your trust and I promise that all your questions will be answered. Even though when I'm finished, you'll probably wish you hadn't asked."

Before Malja could say another word, Harskill continued up the stairs. At the top was another wide hall. Harskill led the way through a heavy door to the outside. The floor sloped upward, ending on the edge of the Dish.

Malja gasped. This high up, the air was cold and strong. It whipped around causing Malja's assault suit to heat up in an effort to maintain her body temperature.

"Look behind you," Harskill said.

When Malja turned around, she gasped again. From this vantage, the Dish laid out before her like an enormous, smooth crater. The light gray surface had been made out of endless tiles, each one the size of a large bed. Three crews of workers walked to various spots — patching or replacing damaged tiles. A platform had been erected at the bottom of the Dish in the center, and on that platform, a large portal frame sat.

"When this is complete," Harskill said, placing his hands wide apart on a chipped, metal railing, "the Dish will focus all the energy Ms. Watts can produce onto that single point in the center. From there she hopes to be able to crack open a portal inside the frame that will be controlled and sustainable. Unfortunately for her, she wishes to achieve this without the aid of magic. I've never seen such a thing successfully done. And I've seen many attempts."

Malja took a deep breath, trying to control her impatience. The best she could manage was to sound calm when she asked, "Who am I?"

"You are one of the Gate," he said, never taking his eyes from the Dish. "And if your goal is to find a way home, well, then you share the same goal as most of the Gate. I regret having to tell you this, but we have no home anymore. Ours has been gone for generations."

A sharp pain burned in the center of Malja's chest. "W-What?"

"Surely, you understand by now that, for most people on most worlds, playing with portals is more than just dangerous. It can be catastrophic. To the best of my knowledge, our people are the only ones to ever successfully reach a level of control over portals that we can travel through them without the physical consequences others have experienced. Like the Devastation that Ms. Watts told me about. But all things still have a price."

"Are you saying the Gate destroyed their world?"

Harskill patted the metal railing as if assuring himself of its sturdiness. "I never thought Ms. Watts would get this far, but then again, I've never quite seen a world like this one. Despite the horrible repercussions you've suffered from attempting to control portals, you all still keep trying. And, if what I understand is correct, you've had some limited success as well. But that won't last. If this Dish gets close to working, it'll make your Devastation look like a little bruise. Nothing will remain." He straightened and faced Malja. "We were lucky. We already knew how to operate a portal safely. But every time our people take a step forward, they want to take another step. We couldn't be satisfied with simply having the portals. And it was when we tried to take things even further that our world vanished. You won't be so lucky here. Everything on this world will be gone."

Malja looked at the crews working on the Dish and tried to absorb all that Harskill had said. He waited without a word. At length, she said, "If this is all true, then why have you been helping Cole build this thing."

That odd grin returned to Harskill's lips. "I haven't. That is, she doesn't know it, but I've done all I could to impede her progress. I had hoped when I sabotaged her last experiment at that little town, she would have given up. I almost succeeded. But then she found this place."

Malja grimaced as if she had bit into a rotten apple. "Why would you tell me these things? You've just met me."

"Because you are Gate. You weren't raised as such, but deep within you, you are Gate. I know that soon enough you will understand who we are and thus, who you are. I have no fear to reveal these things to one of my own. That's why I left Cole's journal at the mansion for you to find. You were bound to come looking for her, and I thought the journal might ease you into all of this better. Besides, we Gate are powerful. If you want to run off and warn Ms. Watts, go right ahead. It won't matter."

"I won't say anything. Not when you caused an entire town to be destroyed to protect your secret."

"An unfortunate but necessary outcome."

"How was that necessary?"

"Because those of the Gate have a strict purpose. Understand this now before you cast judgment. We have been scattered across the infinite worlds, traveling from one to another, making sure no other world suffers our fate."

"You insure that you're the only ones who can use portals."

"It's not selfish, I assure you. Not only do we protect worlds from destroying themselves, but we protect worlds from worlds. There are numerous places out there that are filled with horrible, evil creatures. Should they get control over a portal, they would embark on a mad attempt to take over everyone. World upon world would be lost to war and all the horrors that go with it. We stop that from happening."

Malja crossed her arms. "You didn't stop it here."

A flash of hurt crossed Harskill's face, and for that, Malja was thankful. "There are not a lot of us left," he said. "We can't be everywhere. And we make mistakes. After we missed the first portal here, we saw the destruction that happened and figured you wouldn't be able to do it again for centuries. We moved on. I only noticed this world again because of the short proximity of time between attempts to open a portal."

"And you came to stop us?"

"Exactly. If I do this right, Ms. Watts will determine that safely opening a portal is not possible and she will abandon future efforts. The problem I've encountered, however, is that Ms. Watts is tenacious to a degree I had not anticipated."

"And if you can't convince her?"

Harskill shrugged. "Then I'll have to kill her and destroy any record she made of her work." Without realizing it, Malja must have made a face because Harskill said, "You need to understand that it is not our desire to thoughtlessly kill people. We try to solve these problems as non-violently as possible."

"Then just bring her up here and tell her everything you've told me. Cole's a very smart woman."

"She'll never give up. Not that way. Knowing that we exist and the extent to which we've advanced would only make her more determined. Think about yourself. If someone told you not to do something for your own good—"

Malja laughed.

"Exactly," Harskill said. "Besides, we've tried to be open in the past. The results are rarely positive. That is, if you follow the strict rules of the Gate."

That tension returned to Malja, that sense of something unsettling underneath. "You don't follow the rules?"

"Not anymore. The goal of the Gate is to be the caretaker of all worlds. We are the protectors and the controllers. The Gate believe that we should stop there, but after traveling these worlds and seeing how few contain anyone with even reasonable intelligence, I know we can be so much more than caretakers. We far surpass all others in knowledge, in technology, in magic. We have gifts that can bring peace and prosperity to all. And we can crush with ease those who stand in our way or threaten the worlds with blood conflicts and unbridled atrocities. We can be the true gods of the universes." Harskill's face brightened with his words. He started to speak again but faltered. He closed back up, glancing around as if afraid someone might have heard him. With an embarrassed chuckle, he put out his hand. "You have been lost to us for so long and we never even knew. Now that you have been discovered, I can show you the wonders of the worlds. But before I can do that, I need your help in stopping Ms. Watts from using the Dish. Please, will you help me?"

A high-pitched noise squawked from a mesh circle on the post by the stairwell. "Malja?" Cole's voice — fuzzy and distorted — called out. Harskill brushed past Malja, clearly annoyed at the disruption, and pushed the single red button next to the mesh.

"This is Harskill. Malja's here with me."

He gestured for Malja to come over. She put her mouth close to the mesh and said, "Cole?"

Harskill let go of the button, and Malja heard Cole's voice. "Have Harskill bring you down to the Infirmary. Fawbry and I have Tommy here and ... just come down here. You've got see what's happening to him."

Chapter 8

Malja left Harksill, hurrying down the stairs, skipping as many as she could without falling, and worked her way through the long series of halls until she reached the main entrance. From there she followed instructions Harskill had given her before she left the lip of the Dish. A few people walked the halls doing whatever business they had. They got out of Malja's way, looking at her with concern or confusion.

When she burst into the Infirmary, Cole and Fawbry stood against the back wall, watching Tommy as if he were a dangerous creature. The room had two rows of cots and several devices that Cole, no doubt, had made. One of them glowed orange and gave off heat. Another beeped every few seconds and had numbers on its screen. Above Fawbry's head was a monitor displaying the main gate and several hallways. On the other side of the room, Tommy floated. Catching her breath, Malja walked toward the boy, and she saw what had caused Cole's urgent call.

Dozens of snake-like appendages had grown out of Tommy's arms. They started around the elbow, and a few reached to his wrist. They wriggled back and forth as if attempting to escape his body, but they never appeared able to detach from his arm. Worse — Tommy's head had angled back with his mouth open, and a line of drool streamed down his cheek.

"I-I think," Fawbry said, his voice shaking as much as Malja's heart, "this has something to do with Barris Mont being inside him."

"Don't get too close," Cole said. "If Fawbry's right, those tentacles could link you with Barris Mont's mind just like they would've when he had his own body."

"Except it's Tommy's mind, isn't it?"

"It is. But all that Tommy's been through recently, and what I saw when I was with you in the mountains, suggests that Barris Mont is more than just a presence inside Tommy. He truly shares that boy's body and mind."

As Cole and Fawbry talked, Malja watched Tommy closely — searching for any sign, any flicker of the boy she had spent so much time protecting. The things on his arms made the sickening sound of wet innards sloshing from an open wound, and the smell reminded her of an enemy's bowels let loose in battle. This all started after Tommy had healed her. Had she caused this? She turned away, hoping her face didn't look as tortured as she felt inside.

"It's been a few years since Barris Mont entered him," she said. "We've seen bits of Barris surface before, but nothing like this. If Tommy's been able to keep control of himself for all that time, why would it change now?"

"Dear me, if I knew that, I'd be able to do something to help, now wouldn't I?" Cole said. "Perhaps there's something Barris Mont wants or needs. Perhaps he's always been fighting for control all these years and Tommy is finally weakening. Perhaps Tommy is the one doing this, somehow permitting Barris Mont access to his body. At this point, we can't really know."

"Then what do we do?"

Cole walked up to Malja and offered a patronizing pout. "Oh sweetie, it's possible that there's nothing we can do. The only persons I ever knew who could handle this sort of thing were Jarik and Callib, and well, they're no more."

A deep clunk echoed and the lights went out. Several of the devices continued to operate but most of them also died. The heating device dimmed but managed to keep going, providing an orange hue to the otherwise dark room.

Cole raised her head toward the ceiling. "The brother gods must hate me. That's the fifth power disruption in the last three days." She let out a resigned sigh. "Y'all just sit tight here. I've got to go fix this."

Fawbry said, "I'll go with you. I'm sure you can use some help."

Cole smiled. "That's kind, but you may not want to. This project requires a lot of power, and the only source I've found is an old magic depository. There are so many wires and junctions and places for problems to occur."

"Why wouldn't I want to see a relic like that? I've only ever heard about those things. They were used before the Devastation to store up magic-produced power, right? Kind of like a safeguard in case the magicians all went on strike."

"It is fascinating. But it's also underneath the ground through several long sewer tunnels. I'm sure you wouldn't want to walk through all that."

"Sewer tunnels?"

"Long tunnels that were built to dispose of all the human waste created in a city."

Fawbry turned green. "Oh." Then he shrugged. "If that's what I've got to do, then that's what I've got to do. It'll be wonderful, er, that is, interesting having you show me this old technology."

The genuine joy that flashed across Cole's face surprised Malja. It showed her that all the grins and smiles she had seen before were empty. They weren't lies so much as a brave face. Something was wrong with Cole, something she hid from everyone — Malja felt certain of that.

"You'll know when we've fixed it. The lights'll come back on," Cole said with her fake smile back in place. "Come on, now, Faw-Faw. Let's go." She took him by the hand and led him out into the dark hall.

Malja was alone. Not literally, though, since Tommy — and to some extent, Barris Mont — hovered nearby. She watched him in silence for awhile. The snaking tendrils coming from his arms never stopped moving, and his head never changed its uncomfortable position.

"It's not fair," she growled between clenched teeth. "Not fair at all. Kryssta? Korstra? Any of you brother gods actually out there? Because if you are, you best change the way you've been doing things. Look at this boy. You allowed him to be a slave, be abused, be exploited by a bunch of soulless fools. And when I saved him, you left him so damaged that when given the chance, he chose to stay with me. That's how screwed up this world is. A sweet boy wants to stay with a killer like me. What good are gods if this is the kind of thing you allow? You should have to answer for that."

She sat on the edge of one cot and rested her chin on her fists. She looked at the boy and fought against the tears that wanted to gush from her. "Tommy? You in there at all? I wish you were able to talk with me. You've always been a smart boy and I've been very confused lately. Harskill just makes it worse. If even a little of what he said is true, then what am I? Some protector of worlds? That doesn't seem right. How could I protect an entire world when I can't even protect you? Seems like the only thing I've ever been able to do right is kill. And now Cole is in trouble with Harskill and she doesn't even know it. I don't know what's going on in Fawbry's mind. He should be hating Cole for the loss of his hand, but he acts all smitten with her."

Stretching her arms, she stood and pulled out Viper. She looked at the well-maintained blade and thought of some the battles she lived through. *It was much easier when it was just us two, just trying to kill my fathers. I understood things back then. Now, I don't even understand people.*

That thought resonated in her, dancing across her skin with a chill — she really didn't understand the world around her. It seemed the more people she had let into her life, the more complex and painful life had become.

But she could hear Uncle Gregor as he stood over a bowl peeling potatoes and carrots. His deep voice rambling on from thought to thought in a never-ending stream of education. "Too many people," he would say, "they all look for the easy way. It's always been like that. That's why we had the Devastation in the first place. If the magicians who caused all this had slowed down, taken the time to really work at what they were trying to do, the Devastation might not have happened. But they thought that they knew better, and they wanted to get to their results as fast and as easy as possible. They wanted recognition and fame. And they wanted it now. But you remember this well, nothing worth anything in this world comes fast or easy."

Malja tried to smile for Tommy but she only made her lips tremble. "I won't give up on you," she said, her voice cracking. "I know you can hear me. If you're fighting Barris Mont in there, just hold on. Keep fighting. I'm not giving up."

A loud buzz came from down the hall, and the lights popped back on. Squinting at the sudden brightness, Malja sheathed Viper and inhaled sharply. Cole and Fawbry would return soon. She only had a few moments to clear her mind and pull herself together.

That's when she saw the man on the monitor. He stood at the main gate. Though the image wasn't clear, it was enough for Malja to make out dark skin, dark suit, and a guitar strapped to the back. The Bluesmen were here.

Chapter 9

Malja sprinted through the halls, pulling Viper out as she moved. Workers jumped to the side to avoid being trampled. When she reached the main doorway, she kicked it open and saw three Bluesmen up ahead stringing up a hooded body.

One Bluesman sat on the shoulders of another, trying to secure the thin rope to hang the body. The third Bluesman stood underneath and held the body still and slack. They all froze at the sound of Malja's approach.

She didn't give them time to do anything more. She leaped through the air, swinging Viper across. Though Malja never felt the blade make contact, she heard a yelp cut short and the sharp twang of a taut line being severed. She hit the ground, rolled, and popped to her feet.

The Bluesman holding his friend looked up to see his friend's head missing. His eyes widened as the full weight of the body dropped back. He let the headless corpse fall, blood staining his fine suit. The third Bluesman dropped the hung body and pulled out a sword.

"Look at this, Bronzy," the man said. Bronzy still watched his dead friend. "Hey, snap to."

Bronzy looked up at Malja like a rabid animal. She stood in a low fighting stance with Viper cocked to the side and angled up, ready to hook one of them by the jaw and rip off his head. Malja studied her enemy. She knew the face on Bronzy — a man enraged to the point of making senseless, dangerous choices.

"You didn't even give him a chance," Bronzy said.

Bronzy's partner noticed the state of his friend, too, and used it against Malja. "That's right. She just cut him down. Just like she did all our brothers. This here is Malja."

"Really?" Bronzy said, leaning in. "This really her?"

"Tell him. You really are her, aren't you?"

Malja turned her back foot an inch to give more power when pushing off. "Come and find out."

The partner lunged forward with his sword, but Malja held still. He pulled back at the last moment and repositioned. He feigned another attack. Still, Malja remained motionless. She tracked him with her eyes. When he lunged again, she saw the shift in his shoulders — he meant it this time.

She pushed off with her foot and swung Viper upwards. The extra power clashed their blades sooner than he had expected, jolting straight into the arm, and causing him to lose his grip. The sword clattered to the ground. As Malja came down, she swung Viper back, its outer-crescent sharp enough to hack the Bluesman's arm clean off.

Screaming in pain, the Bluesman fell to his knees, blood spurting out of the hole in his shoulder. Malja turned her focus on Bronzy but not before seeing the Bluesmen pick up his arm and scurry into the night. Bronzy lifted his right hand. It shook as if he were a drunk, one week dry and desperate for the simplest drop of fermented anything. In that unsteady hand, Bronzy held a gun.

Malja set Viper in front and readied to strike. The Bluesmen had lots of guns, but from all that Malja had seen in the past, their guns were no better than any other scavenged from ruins. It might fire. It might fail. But even if Bronzy managed to get off a shot, even if his wavering hand managed to point in the right direction, the chances of a gun shooting straight were small.

"How many more of you are out there? Tell me that and I'll let you run off."

Bronzy shook his head fast enough to pull a muscle and his eyes darted around searching for an escape. "I-I'm the one with the gun. I-I'm telling you nothing."

Blood dripped from Viper, and Malja let Bronzy see it before she spoke. "Last chance. How many of you are left?"

Bronzy straightened his elbow, a novice's motion before firing. He never got to pull the trigger. Malja shot forward, cutting twice as she sped by him. The familiar sound of a body falling to the ground in several pieces followed.

Malja stood still for a moment, letting the adrenaline seep out of her with every breath. When she felt calm, she used Bronzy's shirt to wipe Viper clean. Then she approached the body they had been trying to hang. The hood slipped off. It was a young man with wiry brown hair and gentle lips. The face of a sweet disposition. His neck was cut from the hanging — not by the rope but by a guitar string tied to the thin rope like a garrote. They had intended to hang him at the door and run off without being seen. But the guitar string was the message.

No need now. Malja had already sent them a reply.

"Oh my Kryssta," Cole Watts cried out, bursting through the door and falling beside the dead man. "No, no, no."

Fawbry followed close behind but froze at the sight of carnage. When his eyes landed on Malja, he nodded as if her presence explained everything. He pointed to the young man. "I think he's the missing assistant."

Cole lifted her head, her mouth open in a cry so strong she could make no sound. Tears drenched her face. Back and forth her body bobbed until she inhaled a deep breath and let out a wretched scream.

"You!" Cole said, rising to her feet and pointing at Malja. "You're a poison to me. You're the one who led Jarik and Callib to the Bluesmen. If not for you, they'd still be on my side instead of trying to kill us. And now you've led them here. And I see it on your face. You don't care. You don't care about anybody but yourself. You force Fawbry and Tommy to go wherever you want. Who cares if it might kill them? If Malja wants to find a way off this world, then by Kryssta and Korstra, she's going to do it. Even if it kills everyone else along the way."

Fawbry placed a hand on Cole's shoulder but she stepped away from him. "Look at him," she said, pointing to the dead man. "He had nothing to do with you. All he wanted was to work for me, learn from me. He was smart, too. He would've been able to pick up wherever I left off when I grew too old to continue. The Bluesmen would never have touched him, would never have even known about him if you hadn't brought them here. You killed him."

As Malja listened to Cole, she never looked up from the dead man. There was no point in arguing or even fighting back. She had seen such outbursts of emotion before. Nothing would change her mind. And maybe nothing should. Maybe Malja *had* brought this onto them all.

Cole bent over, sobbing and taking in raspy breaths. Malja raised her head enough to see Fawbry approach Cole again. "Come," he said. "We'll get somebody to take proper care of him." This time, she let him put his arm around her. He murmured to her and she nodded. Taking short, stumbling steps, they walked back into the Dish building.

Malja's mouth tightened in anger even as her chest shuddered to hold back any sadness. She stood in the silence, surrounded by the dead, blood and gore pooling around her feet. Maybe they were all right about her — straight on back to Jarik and Callib. After all, death seemed the only consistent result around her.

Even Tommy.

He was alive for now, but being with her had not saved him. She rescued him from one hellish life and brought him into her own. What good did that do? As a slave, all he had to do was make magical power for a thief's ship. He got fed, somewhat, and if he behaved, no harm came to him. With her, he had been forced to share his body and mind with Barris Mont, had been mentally and physically strained, his magic usage had wasted away his sanity, and he'd been at risk of death on numerous occasions. How could she ever have thought that it was a good idea for him to stay with her?

An earthy aroma came from behind. She turned to find Harskill leaning against the doorway. His clean clothes, weathered face, and sophisticated aura stood at odds with the carnage painting the ground.

"They don't understand our kind," he said. "It's not their fault. It's not prejudice or even willful hate. It's that we seem just like them on the surface, so they assume we are the same. But that's not true. The power we hold comes from far more than technological or magical advancement. Our power is borne deep within. That's why you don't fit in here even though you've been raised in this world."

With more of a plea in her voice than she ever wanted to hear, Malja said, "I don't know who I am. I don't understand anything anymore."

Harskill reached out toward her. "Come here. Let me show you something that will tell you exactly who you are."

Chapter 10

Harskill walked a few steps ahead of Malja, his body upright with a confident gait. He turned down one corridor then another without pause. He knew this building well.

Malja followed, her heart beating hard and her mind jumbling too many thoughts. She could hear Cole's brutal accusations echoing in her ears. She also replayed her battle with the Bluesmen, trying to pick out her mistakes that she could improve upon. It was a reflex, her brain's way of calming herself after battle. But then she thought of Harskill, the Gate, Tommy, and Barris Mont. It was too much. A gray numbness settled in.

"In here," Harskill said, opening a door to a simple office — plain desk, two chairs, and a cabinet. Nothing on the walls; dust covered the desk. "Several floors above us is the Dish — this massive piece of technology that Ms. Watts hopes to fill with magic and create a stable portal. The amount of raw power she requires is staggering." Malja opened her mouth but Harskill raised a hand to quiet her. "To create a portal is easy. The people of this world have done it several times already. But none of those portals were stable. And with one exception, that being the portal Tommy created to send you through and then recreated to bring you back, none of them could be repeated, not exactly as before. But a stable portal, one that can be opened and closed at will, one that can be controlled and relocated, one that won't rip apart a world and mutate its creatures — that's far more difficult."

He rolled up the sleeves of his shirt, closed his eyes for a moment, and when he opened them, he placed his hands in the air as if on a glass window. Then he spread them apart and the emptiness between opened up into another world. Malja's astonishment could not be hidden. Harskill held a portal between his hands right before her eyes.

"This world is called Sheng-Lo," he said.

The portal opened onto a sunny day by the ledge of a valley. Lush, green hills rolled into the distance, a few dappled with hefty, grazing animals. Below, in the cool shadows of the valley, soft plumes of smoke rose from a bustling town. Birds rode on the heat. The air was quiet and peaceful.

"This world was learning portals when I arrived. I offered my 'assistance' and in doing so, I was able to lessen the damage of their experiments. They learned from their mistake, they understood the danger of what they had embarked upon, and they wisely gave it up. As a result, instead of a world destroyed, they live in a world of gentleness and sufficiency for all."

"It's beautiful," Malja said.

"I've often thought that if I ever live long enough to become too old for my work, this would be a wonderful world to end my days upon."

Harskill brought his hands together, closing the portal. He concentrated again, spread out his hands, and opened another portal. The world Malja saw consisted of endless towers reaching into the clouds above. People were everywhere. Noise was everywhere. But it wasn't ugly or undesirable. Like the town on Sheng-Lo, this city bustled with vibrant energy, a lifeforce all its own. It smelled fresh as if a warm rain had washed through, leaving the world cleaner than before.

"This is Wodros," Harskill said. "There's a lot of fun to be had here. All kinds of exciting, strange, and unique people. You can see just from this little bit that they have a lot of technology. Where Sheng-Lo focused almost exclusively on magic, the people of Wodros relegated magic to the realm of religion and healing. Everything else they do for themselves without magic. They chose to make this distinction because they had begun to play with the idea of portals. I arrived and since they fully accepted me as I am, I was able to show them directly what horrors they would unleash. They turned away from portal research and have prospered for a long time since."

He closed the portal. "One more," he said, and after a moment, opened another. This time, Malja saw a land as wild and free as Corlin. Except there were no cities, no towns, no villages. No ruins of anything either. Just a lush forest filled with the sounds of animals unseen.

"This," he said, his body dazzling with the light from the portal, "this is Ti. And as I'm sure you've noticed, there are no people here. I did that. I came to this world to find it like this. Virgin from humankind. I spent a few years here, basking in the freedom of its wilds. Its unadulterated world. No governments, no economies, no religions. Just the simpleness of the wild. And then I found a few isolated tribes of people, too primitive to be considered human by our standards. Every time I discover they have made an advancement, I retard it. I stop them from ever becoming more than animals. They are being given the greatest gift — the purity of the wild — and they will never know how lucky they are to have encountered me."

Malja must have grimaced because Harskill brought his hands together with a sharp clap, closing the portal, bringing them back to the dull office. He looked disappointed in her, at first, but then shook it off. "You have a lot to learn," he said. "The Gate are a special people. We have special skills, special knowledge, and special responsibilities. But the first thing you must grasp is that the rules don't apply to us. We're smarter. We're better. We can rule and create peace everywhere."

That strange sensation returned to Malja — a feeling that there was more underneath Harskill than she could discern. Yet his words held some truth. It wasn't something she thought of often, and when she did, she shoved the thought away, but the thought never left her — I'm better. Just as she knew she was a better fighter than most any opponent she ever faced, she knew she was smarter than the countless self-titled Mayors, Governors, Chiefs, and Kings. They all fought and bullied to maintain power over one little town or one large city. They terrorized and cajoled, threatened and bribed, and did whatever low thing needed doing in order to keep control. She was better than that and Harskill confirmed it. The Gate ruled not over towns and cities but entire worlds — and they did it by helping the people save themselves from events like the Devastation. To Malja, that made sense. It felt right.

Harskill moved closer to Malja. He smelled as clean as he dressed. "Don't let Ms. Watts upset you. It's been my experience that people often lash out at the one who saved them. Mostly it's fear striking at whomever is closest."

She had intended to stay silent, but her mouth opened anyway. "I know. I've gone through it before. But living the life I have, I don't have many close friends. And while I don't think I can consider Cole Watts a friend, she wasn't an enemy."

"It feels a bit like betrayal, doesn't it?"

"Maybe. Mostly, it makes me feel alone."

Harskill put out his hand as if she had said something profound. "Then all doubt is gone. You are of the Gate. We're lonely. We live apart from each other, never permitting more than one of us in a world at any time. We leave messages for each other in religious texts or monuments or even deep in a cavern somewhere. It's like a game and it's the main contact we have with each other except for mating. Every other year we meet on Mullgolus for several months — it's the closest world to the one we lost, and we mark our time by its revolutions. There we court and pair off and mate."

"I thought there were no rules. Why can't more than one of us be on a world? Why —"

"It's a self-imposed punishment for the crimes of the Gate that existed long before I was born. And as far as I'm concerned, that rule doesn't apply either. I want to change things from this lonely existence. Why should we suffer for the sins of generations ago? We don't have to continue to do things their way. You're evidence of that. You are of the Gate yet you don't act like us, you don't think like us. Yet you'll always be one of us." Harskill opened his hand. "Join me. Forget all these petty rulers fighting and dying over little chunks of land. Let me show you world upon world."

"Will you show me how to create a portal?"

Harskill's lips curled into that odd grin. "I'll show you how to be a god. Take my hand. Be my Goddess Queen. Help me rule the worlds and bring peace to all."

From the Journal of Malja:

Loneliness is only part of what I keep buried within. Harskill understands that. He does it, too. But he also understands me in ways that I don't even understand. He knows who we are. He can teach me so much. He's smart, handsome, and seems to desire me. So why do I hesitate? Why did I leave him standing there with his hand reaching out for me? He asked me to be his bride and I stared at him for a long time until the pressure of my silence became too much to hold. I didn't run away like a little girl, thank Kryssta and Korstra and any other god that's out there. But I did turn away. I did walk off without a word. Why do I like the idea of Harskill but not Harskill himself?

Maybe I'm just scared. Well, no maybes, I am scared. How could I not be? I've spent my life learning how to survive in a world bent on destroying me. The things Harskill talks of are so different. I don't know if anything I've learned in my life would be useful. I'm not sure I'm ready to be a naïve pup again.

If I could write laughing at myself, I would. Here I've spent so much time seeking out a way to find my home, and now that I have it right before me, I'm afraid to do it. I'm a bigger fool than Fawbry.
Maybe I shouldn't write in this thing. Maybe Uncle Gregor had the better idea. Pay my honor and be done with it. Writing my thoughts just gets my head spinning one thought, one emotion, after another and once it gets started, it seems so hard to stop. Even after my hand cramps and I don't want to write anymore, my head spends the rest of the night going over all these thoughts.

Me, a Goddess Queen? It sounds ridiculous when I hear it. Even worse when I see it written on these pages. But the Gate are my people, and if this is who we are, then perhaps I should embrace this. Travel worlds, bring peace, and be treated like Kryssta and Korstra. Maybe the brother gods aren't gods at all. Maybe they were two of the Gate who came to Corlin and fought over this world. The people here were just digging out of the rubble of the Devastation, so perhaps that's where the brother god religions began.

I'm stopping for tonight. My head hurts.

Chapter 11

Malja sat in the infirmary watching over Tommy. Several hours had passed since Harskill's offer — no, really a proposal. The idea that anybody would propose to Malja, no matter the circumstances or intentions, filled her with both confusion and dread.

Even if the idea of romance could somehow be part of Malja's existence, one look at Tommy reminded her that she could never be a successful wife or (and this part still sounded weird to her ear) a Queen. Her stomach rolled. Here Tommy floated, suffering, fighting for his life, and Malja's having little girl fantasies of being royalty.

Except she knew herself better now than ever in her life. She didn't care about a title like Queen any more than she cared about ruling over people. She liked the anarchy of Corlin where she could find it. Wild freedom. But these thoughts were all just a mask, a way to hide from the boy. That's the real pain, the real confusion, the real dread.

She had saved Tommy only to fail him. She had tried to protect him from magic only to watch him use it again and again to save her. And now, he suffered for it.

Rubbing her face, she discovered her eyes were damp. She got to her feet, swiped a bowl of soup that had been left for Tommy, and approached him. She spooned out a mouthful and raised it to his lips. "Okay. Time to eat. Please. You haven't had anything since we got here. You need to eat." She wasn't sure how long it had been. There were no windows in the Dish, but she had the sense that they had stayed at least a full day, maybe two. "Come on, Tommy. Wake up and eat." Tommy did not respond. Malja dropped the spoon in the soup making a small splash. She grabbed the bowl and raised it, ready to hurl it across the room. But she held back. A moment passed while she stood frozen, ready to throw the bowl but still holding back. At length, she placed the bowl on a table. When she looked back at Tommy, he opened his eyes.

"Tommy?" Malja moved in slowly.

He did not seem aware. His eyes locked forward without searching his surroundings. As Malja stepped closer, another eye opened at Tommy's neck. A fourth opened on his forehead. She even saw one on his tattooed bicep open up.

"Barris Mont," she said, her teeth clenched, her throat growling out the words. "You leave that boy alone."

The infirmary door opened and Fawbry entered. He glanced at Tommy and Malja before he said, "It keeps happening. Barris Mont is getting stronger inside Tommy."

"You should know," Malja said. "You're the one who brought us to Barris Mont in the first place. None of this would be happening if you hadn't —"

"Don't you dare blame me. I've proven myself to our little family more times than should ever be necessary. You're just angry and scared."

"I don't —"

"Of course, I forgot. The great Malja doesn't get scared. Then you're angry. Don't take it out on me. I'm the only one ever on your side."

Malja scowled. "Then why does it feel like you're against me?"

Fawbry sat in a chair and let the fight dissipate into the air. When things seemed calmer, he said, "We're a family, and families work in odd ways. Some are full of affection and pride. Others are all anger and bluster. We fall into patterns that allow us to work together no matter how different we all are. That's what makes us a family. That we're willing to find those patterns."

"What's our pattern? You annoy me and I get angry?"

Fawbry chuckled. "A little, maybe. I think we work best when we ignore each other, build up until we're ready to let it loose, we argue, but eventually we realize the other is right."

"How can we both end up being right?"

"Because whenever one of us is right, the other figures it out quick and we don't argue."

Malja thought on this for a moment. "So in this fight, you're saying that soon you'll realize I'm right — that you are responsible for bringing Tommy to Barris Mont and causing all this?"

"I can't deny that, though it hurts me to think it's true. But you'll also soon realize that I love Tommy. By Kryssta, I even love you. You'll remember all the times I've risked my life for you two, and you'll understand that when I say you're my family, I mean it. If I could take back all that happened when we first met, not just Barris Mont but all of my stupidity, I would. Seeing those eyes all over Tommy, those tendrils out of his arms, all those tattoos — I pray to Kryssta all the time to save him and hope that it's not all my fault."

Malja ruffled Fawbry's shaggy hair as if he were a child. "If that old man on the road is right, Kryssta is to blame for all this." Before Fawbry could respond, she raised her hands in mock defense. "I'm kidding."

"That man was the fool. *The Book of Kryssta* tells us to improve ourselves so that we can bring a better world around us. It teaches us not to follow leaders blindly, but to follow our own leadership within. Isn't that what you believe? We've gone all over Corlin and Penmarvia trying to get people to lead themselves."

"Doesn't seem like we've had a lot of success."

"*The Book of Kryssta* never suggests that self-improvement is easy."

"You really believe it all? I don't just mean the ideals, but do you really believe Korstra and Kryssta exist? That there are two brother gods fighting each other over the scraps of us left on this world?"

"I have to."

"But what of the portals and the other worlds and all of that?"

"I don't know. But just because I can't comprehend it, doesn't mean it isn't that way."

Malja's brow pinched. "I'm sorry I said those things. This isn't your fault. And back at the beginning, I would've ended up seeking Barris Mont even without you. He was the one who got us on the right track when I was hunting Jarik and Callib, and nothing was going to stop me from that. You have nothing to feel guilty about." Fawbry nodded, and Malja put on a false tone of levity. "So tell me what's going on with you and Cole? Are you two falling in love again?"

"No," Fawbry said with a surprising amount of shock. "Not at all. Not like that. I mean, after all, she did this to me." He held up his stump.

"Then why are you acting so affectionate to her?"

"You don't see what's going on at all?" Fawbry checked the door to make sure nobody approached the infirmary. When he returned to Malja, he said, "This entire building and the Dish require a lot of power. When she first mentioned a magical depository in the sewers, I had hoped it was simply a large collection of battery storage units. But it's not. It's a *schuco*."

"Which is what?"

"You've never heard of one?"

"I've been busy killing off every threat Corlin has to offer."

"The schuco are boxes made by magicians for the purpose of storing and enhancing magical power. Before the Devastation, they were used to help power cities and such. Cole's been tapping into that schuco in the sewers because it's the only way she can get that kind of power nearby, and those things poison the air around them. Every time she goes near it, her skin, her lungs, her entire body is exposed to whatever magical residue surrounds that thing."

"Magical residue?"

"I don't know what to call it. I just know what it's doing. It's killing her. Cole is dying."

"And you're being by her side?"

"She's a person who I once cared for a lot. I know she's done some terrible things, but she did them with the hope of helping people. She just got lost along the way. And she's tried to make up for it."

Malja gestured to the building around them. "This is making up?"

"She deserves a little compassion. When Korstra broke the great chalice and brought upon the world a year of unending rain, did Kryssta forsake him? No. He offered open arms to his brother and forgiveness. *The Book of Kryssta* is filled with examples where Kryssta shows compassion to Korstra, and there are even times when Korstra does the same for Kryssta. If the brother gods can do so toward each other, then surely we can, too."

Malja sighed. "You just don't give up on any of us. I suppose we don't deserve you."

"I'm sure of that," Fawbry said.

Cole Watts entered the room, and Malja thought she saw a slight limp. Maybe she had imagined it, though. Knowing that Cole was dying, Malja wondered if she might be seeing things in Cole's health that weren't there.

Cole looked over Tommy and read the data her machines provided. Then with a huff, she turned around and said, "I apologize for the things I said outside. I was upset at the loss of a good person, and I admit it, I was also a little frightened by the appearance of the Bluesmen. Though nothing can permit me to behave so rudely. So, I'm sorry."

Malja hated hearing an apology. She never knew what to say or how to react. It was easy to give an apology when she was wrong, but hearing one — especially one which she thought might not be required — left her feeling uncomfortable. She did nod, so Cole would know the apology had been heard and accepted, but beyond that, Malja said nothing.

After a lingering moment, Cole finally said, "I noticed you've spent a little extra time with Harskill. It makes sense, of course, that you would seek him for answers. I just want to warn you to be careful around him. I wouldn't trust him too much. He thinks he's subtle and powerful, but I see through him. He's been against me from the day I met him. I suspect that if he had never come along, I may have already succeeded in opening a portal."

Fawbry put out his arm for Cole to balance on. "Why keep him around then?" he asked.

"Once he arrived, I couldn't get rid of him safely."

"Just tell him you don't want him here. You have a whole bunch of people here. He's just one."

Cole raised an eyebrow toward Malja. "She's just one."

"Besides," Malja said, "if Cole openly got rid of Harskill, he'd come back in force. She hoped to keep him close by in an effort to control and minimize his obstruction."

"Exactly," Cole said. "And with the Bluesmen around, I only want to have to manage one enemy at a time. So, be careful around Harskill. Don't believe everything his says. But also, please, don't anger him. Keep him coddled as long as we can manage."

Malja pictured his reddening face as she turned away from his proposal. "We might be a little late on that one," she said. Before Cole could inquire further, alarms broke out.

With his finger shaking, Fawbry pointed at the approaching figures on the monitors. "Looks like the Bluesmen are back."

Chapter 12

Malja watched the monitors closely, counting each Bluesman she saw. Twenty. Twenty-five. Thirty-two. They covered each exit, armed with guns, swords, and even an ax.

"I thought they were all dead," Cole said. "A few stragglers but there weren't that many off the compound when Jarik and Callib destroyed them all."

"That was almost two years ago. More than long enough to do some recruiting," Fawbry said.

The screeching alarms cut out, leaving them surrounded by the sounds of the Bluesmen preparing to strike. Malja continued to observe them on the monitors. It appeared that they had organized into four man units with two units at each exit. Those with guns trained their weapons on the doors while the others crouched in the back, waiting for either an order or a set time to attack.

But they didn't attack. Every flick of the monitor to a different camera view showed Malja the same thing — Bluesmen ready to move but waiting.

"Why aren't they attacking?" she said.

Fawbry tapped the monitor, pointing out a Bluesman missing his arm. "I think they're worried about the great Malja."

"Maybe. But I don't see a lot of fear. I see patience."

In answer, the monitor switched to a view of the main gate where she had fought the Bluesmen earlier. There she saw them escort an elderly man forward. A magician.

"There," Malja said.

"I see him," Fawbry said. To Cole, he asked, "You know that one?"

She nodded. "Walker. Don't be fooled by his age. He's one of the Bluesmen I had purposely sent off on assignment as much as possible. I never wanted him around. Never struck me as a stable sort of mind. He's got power and he's always wanted to rule over us all."

Walker pointed to the ground and two Bluesmen squatted to pick at something there. They looked to be collecting something small — dirt or pebbles maybe. Then the monitor moved on to show an empty corridor.

"Get it back," Malja said. "We've got to see that."

Cole repeatedly pressed a button on the side of the monitor, cycling through all the cameras. She moved slow and deliberate like an old woman.

Fawbry crossed his arms and shivered. "I know this isn't the usual way for us, but considering that we're out-numbered and that they're bringing out a magician, maybe we should think about escaping before it's too late."

"It's already too late," Malja said.

"Are you sure? I can move really fast when you're trying to save my life."

"Here it is," Cole said and pressed another button locking the image.

Malja tried not to show any reaction. Fawbry, on the other hand, cursed and turned away to hide his fear. The Bluesmen had been collecting insects. Walker had already turned two of them into beasts the size of large dogs — six-legged, hard-shelled creatures with sharp pincers and constant clicking noises.

Concentrating on his tattooed forearm, Walker worked at another insect. As it grew, its thin legs buckled under the new weight of its carapace. Walker raised his other arm and conjured another bit of magic. New muscles bulged around the legs, and in seconds, the giant insect lifted its body off the ground.

"We can't just stand here and watch," Fawbry said, his voice raising in pitch. "Come on. Go fight them or let us run away or something."

Malja's steady gaze did little to calm Fawbry. "You're right," she said.

"I-I am?"

"I just don't see a good way to fight them until they attack. And unless you know of another way out, they've got us surrounded."

Cole smiled. "Why dear, you just have to ask. I can get us out, if you can give me a little time."

"Um, Malja," Fawbry said, his attention glued to the monitors. "I think they're attacking."

Malja checked the monitor for a second — Fawbry was right. "Fawbry, help me block this door. Cole, I'm asking — do whatever you're going to do."

Pursing her lips, Cole said, "Sounds more like ordering, but I'll take

476 - The Malja Chronicles

care of it."

Malja ignored the taunt as she tipped over a nearby bed and slid the furniture in front of the door. Fawbry grabbed anything he could manage — chairs, equipment, even a blanket — and tossed it in front of the door. He snatched glances at the monitor. With his hand shaking and his movements hurried, Malja worried he might start screaming in fear, alerting the enemy to their exact location.

"T-Those bugs are coming," he said.

On the monitor, Malja saw Walker had grown at least eight insects and his fellow Bluesmen were turning the things loose in the Dish building. "Anytime now, Cole," she said.

Cole ran her hands along the far wall, mumbling to herself the whole time.

A heavy thud hit the door. Malja rushed over and pressed her shoulder into the pile of furniture. Another thud. Strong enough to push Malja back an inch.

"Fawbry!"

Letting out a whimper, Fawbry joined Malja. Together, they shoved the door back. The awful sound of insect legs tapping and scratching and trying to break in filled their ears.

"How'd they find us so fast?" Fawbry asked.

Malja's stomach chilled. "They knew where we'd be. One of Cole's people must have told them." To Cole, she added, "You've been betrayed."

Fawbry grunted as he pushed harder against the door. "We'll be dead, if she doesn't hurry up."

Malja looked at Cole — no closer to getting them free. She checked out Tommy — still floating, still catatonic. When her eyes turned to Fawbry, the insects pounded the door hard enough to knock him over.

Two spiny legs poked in around the open edges. They were sharp and fast-moving. Malja pushed back, but she kept slipping on the smooth floor.

To his credit, Fawbry jumped to his feet, and with a high-pitched cry, rammed the door. The insect shrieked like rusted metal torn in a storm. It snatched back one of its magic-enhanced legs, but the shutting door pinned down the other.

"Cole?" Malja said.

"Just be patient," Cole said as if calming a pestering child.

The insect leg flailed about, smacking into the wall and the loose chairs near the top of the furniture pile. Fawbry laughed, wide-eyed and shaking, and straightened in his triumph. Before Malja could say a word, the leg whipped downward and smacked into Fawbry's shoulder. He shouted, surprise and pain blending, and he fell to the ground clutching his bleeding shoulder. Without Fawbry's help, the door opened a crack more and the insect pulled its leg free.

Slapping her hand against the wall, Cole said, "Here we are." She pushed against the wall, and a large square panel slid open. "Access to the air ducts that'll then lead us into the sewers." Cole took Tommy's hand, careful to avoid the tentacles, and pulled his floating body into the duct.

Malja looked down at Fawbry. "Go, already," she said.

Though tears covered his face, he looked more confident and determined than at any point since the Bluesmen had arrived. Even as the insect continued to slam into the door, widening the opening with each strike, Fawbry took the time to look back at Malja. "Don't be a hero," he said. "You follow me in there, okay? We're going to need you."

Malja jutted her chin toward the open wall panel and watched Fawbry scurry in. Just as she could no longer see Fawbry, the insect smashed the door even wider, sending Malja to the floor. She rolled back up to her feet and whipped out Viper.

The insect barreled into the room. Around its mouth were numerous little appendages like fingers that never stopped tapping out rhythms. In an awkward motion, it turned its two-part torso in Malja's direction, placing it between her and the air duct. Without hesitation, the insect shot forward.

Malja leaped to the side as she swung Viper. The outer-crescent smacked the top of the carapace and slid off. No damage. But the insect now faced the wrong direction. It tried to turn around but its new, bigger body was too cumbersome for its old, smaller brain. Malja swiped underneath the torso, slicing through two of the creature's legs. Though strong, they lacked the same hardness of the carapace.

The insect scrabbled forward to the nearest wall as if it could slip into a crack at the bottom. Walker may have made the thing a giant, but it still operated on little bug instincts. While it attempted to escape, Malja crouched into the air duct, closed the panel behind her, and hurried off to join her companions.

Chapter 13

Malja followed the group, all the time listening for the tell-tale clicking sounds of the giant insects. Cole led them through a maze of ducts, turning at one interchange, going straight at another. There seemed no discernable pattern to their path, yet Malja saw little choice but to push on.

"Here," Cole said, stopping in the middle of a long passage. She pointed down. "Cut through here and we'll enter the waterways."

Malja scrunched her forehead. "Waterways?"

"Sewers. But don't worry. There's little water running through them anymore."

With a roll of her eyes, Malja wriggled by Fawbry and placed the tip of Viper at the spot Cole indicated. The sharp blade cut in without trouble. Malja made a long incision and then another one crossing the first. After putting Viper away, she put her arms around Fawbry's shoulder and said, "Help me balance." Then she kicked the duct flooring hard. It bent outward, wafting a horrible odor their way.

Cole leaned her head in. "I never promised it would smell good. Drop in here and this will take us where we're going."

"Where's that?" Malja asked, but Cole had already slipped through the hole.

Working together, Fawbry and Malja slid Tommy down the hole. He never showed any sign of understanding what was going on around him. He just continued staring off with empty eyes. Cole took hold and pulled him the rest of the way. Once everybody made it through, they set off.

The sewer was a long brick tunnel thick with noxious odors. Though no water washed through anymore, the ground was still a muddy sludge. Malja tried not to think about the reasons for that.

As they rounded a curve, Cole moved toward the tunnel wall where a tiny alcove formed shadows. Malja jogged to Cole's side. A metal door with rivets running along a seam in the middle blocked their way. Cole lifted her head and smiled. "I found this place when I first explored the sewers. Never thought I'd really need it, but after all we went through with Jarik and Callib, I figured I should be better prepared in the future." She pulled out a key, unlocked and opened the door.

Inside, Malja saw a small room with a single cot and boxes of provisions piled high on one wall. Containers of water lined the opposite wall. Under the cot, Malja spied some types of machines and several books. Above the cot, mounted on the wall, was a monitor similar to the one in the infirmary with two smaller monitors above.

"You've got a little hideaway," Fawbry said, flopping onto the cot. "This is wonderful."

From the doorway, Cole watched the others settle in. She wore an odd expression as if she were reliving a sad memory. She saw Malja observing and said, "I'm fine. I just expected that this might be where I went to die."

"That might still happen," Malja said, turning her focus to the main monitor. Though it didn't cycle through as many cameras as the previous one, it did provide her with the ability to see more of what was going on above them. In a battle, every bit of information helped.

Over Malja's shoulder, Cole watched the monitors. A few cameras relayed stark images of workers dead on the ground. The picture flicked to an empty hall, and then to a young woman being devoured by a giant insect. Cole sniffled and rubbed away the tears dribbling down her cheek.

"They deserved better," she said before turning away.

Fawbry surveyed the room and patted the brick wall. "This should be safe for awhile. And now that we're not in immediate danger, what're we supposed to do?"

"I've got to carve a way through them," Malja said, her eyes turning icy as she watched the monitor. "Kill enough of them, and they'll either give up and leave or they'll want to negotiate some kind of truce. Either way, we'll get out of here alive."

"Sounds good to me," Fawbry said with extra-enthusiasm. "I'll watch over Tommy and Cole while you're gone." He raised his hand to fend of Malja's concern. "I'll watch them carefully. I won't let anything happen to Tommy. You've got my word."

Malja looked over Tommy. He had a small cut on his forehead from banging around the air duct but appeared fine, otherwise — for a boy sharing his body with a powerful creature, sporting multiple eyes and undulating tentacles, and being locked in some kind of catatonia. *I can't fail him,* she thought. Then she closed her eyes and cleared her mind. She was about to go into battle. Worrying about things beyond her immediate control only served her enemies.

"With so many Bluesmen spread throughout this entire building, I'll have to take them out one or two at a time. And it'll have to be done quietly so I don't alert the others until I've reduced them by at least half. The rest will get nervous or even panic. That'll make them hesitate when they face me, and that will give me the extra seconds to kill each one with ease."

Fawbry paled. "Isn't there a more direct approach?"

"You don't like my plan?"

"It's just that it relies on stealth. And you've never been one for quiet, sneaking around. Every time I've ever tried to do that kind of thing with you, you just walk right up and start slashing."

Malja tucked her long braided hair under her collar and opened the door. "I'll be fine."

Fawbry nodded and pulled out his copy of *The Book of Kryssta.* He flipped through the pages, urgently searching.

"You're going to pray before I go? You've never done that before."

Looking up from the book with a chilled expression, Fawbry said, "You've never done something like this before."

Chapter 14

Malja skirted down the edge of the sewer tunnel until she reached the opening in the ceiling that led to the air ducts. A few turns in the ducts and she had passed beyond the reach of the sewer's stench. Crawling in the tight space, she moved with careful precision to avoid making too much noise.

Whenever she found a vent, she held still and peered through. Twice she came upon Bluesmen, but they walked in a full four-man unit. Though she didn't want to do so, if she had to, she could take on four enemies at once. But the attack would be very risky.

Awkwardly slipping out of the duct without losing the element of surprise would be hard enough. But against four, it would be near impossible to engage them all at once. Somebody would be free from her attacks, free to run off and warn others. That was unacceptable.

She would have to be patient.

Further on, she saw another unit followed by two of the giant insects. Two more Bluesmen followed, each holding leashes tied around the insects. They didn't look any happier than the bugs.

At length, she came upon a curved hall that was empty. She waited. She listened. Nobody came by and she never heard the echo of a voice or a footfall.

Her instinct was to kick open the vent and drop to the floor, but as Fawbry had pointed out, this mission required stealth. Moving slowly, trying to be quiet, Malja eased the vent loose and pulled it inside the duct. She paused long enough to listen once more before slipping through the opening and onto the floor.

The ceiling sloped sharply. Just above must be the Dish. A thick tube large enough to crawl through ran parallel to the floor along the inside of the curved hall. Every few seconds the tube pulsed.

Malja placed her hand on the tube's surface. Warmth shot up her arm like putting on a shirt that had been in the sun all day. When she took her hand off, the comforting feeling left just as fast.

"It shouldn't feel good, should it?" a male voice said from behind.

Malja turned slowly but kept her hands at her side. The Bluesman held a gun on her — single shot handgun with a dented barrel and chipped wood on the grip. His dark skin hid his features in the shadows, but she could still make out his fine suit and a glint of the guitar on his back.

"It's just a big mass of wires," he went on. "So why does it feel good to touch? Personally, I think it's because your friend, Cole Watts, keeps on messing with things she don't understand, and this is just one of the side effects. Course, not everyone agrees with that. Some think there's no harm in using magic like this. But you and I know better, don't we?"

"We do?"

"Magic is the power of the brother gods. Did Kryssta come down here and say that we should meddle in the ways of gods? Did Korstra tap babies on their heads to grant them such power? No. We've stolen the power and misused it. It was never meant for people. That's why we go insane when we use magic too often."

"What about your music? I've seen it cast spells before."

"The old Bluesmen did that. The ones that followed Cole Watts to their grave. Ones like my brother," he said and stepped closer.

Malja recognized him right away — practically a twin. "You're Willie's brother."

"That's right. My name's Wolf."

A chill rushed through Malja, but she did her best to hide any outward reaction.

Wolf went on, "You ought to understand right now that the only one reason I haven't shot you dead is that I want you to take me to Cole Watts. Some of the Bluesmen want to tear you apart, too, but I don't care about you. It's Watts I want. You're nothing. You just got in the way. But that old betrayer — she promised us many things, great power, the chance to leave this ruined world, and we gave her everything — most of us even gave our lives. My brother gave his."

"Your brother didn't die for her. He followed Old McKinley. They tried to take power from Cole, not give it to her."

"Because she was failing us. She has to pay. And once she's dead, we'll tear this place down. No one should have power like this. We are not gods."

"Sorry," Malja said, taking two specific steps into the center of the hall — one foot forward, one slightly back. Not quite a basic fighting stance, but enough that she could maneuver into a better position with ease. "I won't take you to her. If it helps any, she's probably going to die on her own fairly soon."

Wolf raised the gun. "You will take me to her, or I'll shoot you."

"You've got a serious problem, now. I've been shot at before by guns that were in far better condition than that thing, and you only get one shot. Chances are that gun won't do much. Even if one of the brother gods smiles on you and the bullet hits me, you'd have to be really lucky to kill me. And that's when your problem gets worse. Because if I'm still alive after you shoot, I'll have Viper cutting open your throat before you have time to get your sword out."

Though Wolf did not move, his eyes scanned over his gun. Malja watched closely, but Wolf gave away nothing in his face, and his body language was equally silent. She couldn't tell what he planned to do.

Raising the corner of his lips, Wolf lowered the gun to his side and let it clunk on the floor. "I was hoping the threat would be enough. Too bad, really. Now, I've got to actually kill you."

Malja felt a twinge of pity. These Bluesmen loved their sword-hidden-in-the-guitar-neck trick. But she would cut him down long before he could get his hand up to the guitar neck. He didn't know it, yet, but he was dead.

As if reading her thoughts, Wolf shook his head and with the flick of his wrist, a long blade slid from his right sleeve, it's narrow grip stopping perfectly in Wolf's hand.

As she spun Viper free, Malja's battle grin rose. "Cute," she said.

"You liked it? Then you can see it again." Wolf flicked his other wrist, and a second blade slid from his left sleeve. He bent his knees and lifted both blades into a ready position.

Malja lowered into her full fighting stance and let out a calming breath. More than anything in life, she understood this. All her troubles, concerns, and fears vanished as her focus limited the world to the man holding two swords.

Wolf raised one sword overhead and charged, betraying a lack of experience. If not for the second sword, Malja would easily block the attack and cut down her enemy. But fighting two swords means two different attacks at the same time. If she blocked the overhead blade, the lower blade would cut upward and gut her.

When Wolf reached the strike zone, she lowered Viper and spun it so the inside-crescent faced upward. Then she blocked straight up, using Viper like a giant hook to catch both blades. Wolf tried to swing his blades free, but Malja followed the motion. They looked like dancers making large circles with their weapons.

After three revolutions, Wolf wised. He stepped backward, freeing his swords by pulling them straight towards him. Malja reset, preparing for the next attack.

She caught a quiver in Wolf's cheek — perhaps doubting his ability, wondering if he could survive this confrontation. But his eyes never looked away from her. She understood that look of determination. He had a brother to avenge. Nothing but death would stop him.

"I've been down your path," she said. "Vengeance will not bring you peace."

Showing no interest in words, Wolf thrust towards her neck and waist at the same time. Viper's curved blade covered a wide enough distance to deflect the attack, but Malja knew her opponent would adjust on the next strike. She couldn't give him that time.

Stepping out to the right, Malja swung for Wolf's head — a smaller target than the body but also awkward to defend with both blades. Wolf ducked. Before he could pop back up, Malja kicked with her left leg. She connected with his chest, sending him flailing against the thick tube running along the wall.

He pushed off, unable to hide a shiver from the odd sensations of the tube, and quickly returned to his senses. Lunging forward, he thrust his right blade for her face and left blade at her knee. Too far apart for Viper to catch both.

Malja raised one leg high and stomped down on the knee-striking blade. At the same time, she shoved Viper upward for the block. When she heard the metal clang, she turned Viper in a practiced motion that slipped her enemies blade down enough for Viper to rotate back and lock the sword. She put all her weight forward, pressing the other blade into the floor.

Wolf's shocked eyes met her calm gaze. He was bent over but still gripping the two swords that he no longer had control over. Malja looked over his face for a second, seeing Willie and remembering all that had happened years ago. That second was a mistake.

Wolf let go of both weapons and shot forward, tackling Malja to the floor. When she hit the hard surface, the air in her lungs coughed out. She kept hold of Viper, but with Wolf straddling her, she didn't have enough leverage to swing the blade. Nor enough air. Wolf punched her chest, her jaw, her shoulder. He didn't aim at all. Just pummeling his fists over and over. And tears fell.

Malja tried to bridge, arching her back to upset Wolf's balance, but he was heavy and she needed a full breath. She tried again anyway. To her surprise, Wolf flung back as if she had punched him hard in the chin.

When she jumped to her feet, an unseen hand pressed against her, keeping her from attacking. Two Bluesmen entered, each holding a gun that looked more capable than Wolf's ever did. Behind them, the Bluesmen's magician stood. Staring at his tattoo, he raised one hand and Viper yanked free from Malja. It drifted across the hall and settled into the magician's hand. Bowing slightly, the magician stepped aside.

Harskill walked in.

Wolf dropped to the floor and pressed his head down. "I was trying to force her to get me to Cole Watts. I'm sorry I failed you, O Lord."

"You may rise," Harskill said.

Wolf gratefully stood. "Please forgive me."

"No need. You never had a chance at success against her. She is almost a god like me. When she accepts that, nothing you have will stop her."

Wolf eyed Malja with a strange mixture of awe, hatred, and fear.

"Go join the others," Harskill said. "Lead the search."

Wolf bowed and hurried out. Harskill smiled and opened his hands to Malja. "You still haven't answered my question. Will you be my goddess Queen?"

Chapter 15

C ome with me," Harskill said. "I've set up a room for us to work in."

"Us?" Malja said, the venom in her voice unmistakable.

Harskill raised his hand and moved close to the long tube near the wall. He stepped with the enthusiasm of a teacher about to make a key breakthrough with a student. "Look at this," he said, hovering his hand above the tube. "This is not natural. It's not right. Cole Watts needs these half-living conduits in order to amplify the limited magical energy she has access to."

Malja recalled when Cole had teamed with the Bluesmen. Back then, she had used things that looked like flags with mouths, half-living conduits that amplified the Bluesmen's music magic.

Harskill went on, "As a practical point, these things are unstable and will collapse under the pressure of opening a portal. As a moral point, do you understand what she did here? She grew these things — mixing magic, machinery, and dead tissue. If ever there was a meaning to the word abomination, you look upon it here."

"I don't defend Cole's actions."

"But you want her results. You want all the benefits of having access to the portal she'll create, and you'll just ignore the consequences. Ignoring something, pretending it doesn't exist, only makes you naive. You can pretend gravity doesn't exist, but you'll still fall."

Malja crossed her arms. "I don't pretend and I don't ignore."

"Then join me. I can show you how to make your own portals — safe ones that don't harm the world around you."

"Safe from destruction, but not safe. Not when you use the power to control others. We have no right to do such a thing, to take away people's freedom, to make them slaves. Why would I want to be a god like that?"

Harskill opened his hand toward her. "I'll show you," he said, and led her down the hall.

They turned a few corridors and entered a wide office. At one end, an empty metal desk. At the other, a table covered with papers and books. Harskill escorted Malja toward the table while the magician escorted Viper to the desk. He laid Viper down, pulled back a sleeve to reveal an intricate, serpent-like tattoo, and he began a spell.

"Don't worry about him," Harskill said. "That one will take him quite awhile to perform."

"What's it going to do?"

"Just giving the Bluesmen a little boost. Nothing that matters."

"He better not do anything to my weapon."

Harskill pulled back his sleeve to show his skintight, black assault suit underneath. "This is our greatest achievement. It aids us, heals us, makes us stronger, better. It allows us to become the gods we are. It's called a *do-kha*."

Malja inspected her own assault suit — no, her *do-kha*. She should learn to call it by its proper name. The suit did protect her from cold and heat. It kept her dry and clean. But that it could make her stronger? Better? Godlike?

"You've never learned to use it, have you?" Harskill asked.

Malja frowned. "I knew it was different — special. But it's always done what it wants. I've never really had any control over it."

He looked at her with an odd warmth. Malja detected lust — everybody had a touch of that — but there was something more behind his eyes. It reminded her of the way Uncle Gregor had looked upon her sometimes, but it wasn't so paternalistic. Love? Malja choked back a laugh. He hardly knew her. How could he be in love with her?

"There's so much I can teach you," Harskill said. "How to use your do-kha is just the beginning. I can show you how to open portals, how your do-kha will protect you when crossing through, how to help world after world."

"Enslaving people is not helping them."

"What if I changed my ways for you? What if I said I would stop being a god to these people? If you come with me, be by my side, I will do that. I will show you worlds I have helped and those I have not yet visited. You can see for yourself whether my actions are good or not. After you see, after you understand, if you still want me to step back from being what the Gate were meant to be, I could honor your choice. I suspect you'll understand things differently."

Malja looked at her do-kha starting with her wrists, her arms, her chest. She stared at it as if it were a tattoo and she a magician. She didn't understand the first thing about being of the Gate. Could she really judge Harskill for suggesting they were gods when she knew so little? Maybe they were gods. Maybe that was all a god amounted to — a person of extraordinary power.

"I know you're not ready for all this," Harskill said. "I wish we had more time. But Cole Watts has accelerated matters. I have an idea, though, one that might help you comprehend who you are and what we are capable of."

A familiar sense of danger reached into Malja, but she remained quiet.

Harskill walked toward the door, gesturing at the magician as he spoke. "Your weapon — Viper — is protected by my magician. I lied. He did perform a boosting spell, but that only took a moment. The rest of this time, he's been setting up guardian spells around Viper. Any mortal of this world will fail at retrieving that gorgeous blade. Not you, though. I have the fullest confidence that you will succeed because we are the Gate. We are gods."

Harskill exited, but as he walked out, Malja spied two Bluesmen standing guard. They closed the door, a click of the lock, and Malja was stuck with a magician.

Crossing her arms, she sat on the floor and glowered. This was the same kind of crap Jarik and Callib would force her through. They called them 'little tests,' and she hated every one. Not because they were too challenging or painful or even threatening. But because it was evident from the start that the tests were less about her learning how strong she was and more about them proving themselves right. Nothing different here. Harskill set this up to prove she was a god like him. He could look at her with boyish love in his eyes for the rest of his life, and she wouldn't believe the test to be anything else.

"Fine," she said, getting back to her feet. She had no desire to play this game, but she wanted Viper back. No Bluesmen magician was going to stop her.

She marched right up to the desk and reached for the weapon. Electricity arced out of the air and into her hand. Her muscles seized and her skin quaked. With a crack, the magic broke off and Malja was flung backwards across the room.

Shaking off the vibrations coursing through her, she snarled. "You'll regret that," she said. The magician winked and continued his spells.

Malja inspected her arm. No damage to her or her do-kha. *And that's Harskill's point.* He wanted her to learn to use it. Pacing across the room, locking eyes with the magician every time she came forward, Malja racked her brain for an alternative. There had to be some other way to get Viper without using the do-kha. Anything to avoid giving Harskill that satisfaction.

She glanced up at the ceiling. She could go into the vent and drop down on the magician — but any competent magician would protect all sides including above. This man struck her as more than competent.

She could barrel forward and let momentum carry her through the electrical field. It might work, but the jolts going through her would most likely leave her unable to fight at best and incapacitated at worst. Plus, that assumed there wasn't another layer of magic underneath. The longer she took deciding what to do, the more time the magician had to create such a layer.

She looked at her do-kha. A few times in the past, she had tried to make it do her bidding. Nothing ever came of it. At least, nothing she was aware of.

But it had protected her before. Not just keeping her comfortable but real protection. When she chased after Queen Salia up in Penmarvia, Fawbry had fired a gun right next to her. The do-kha had extended over her ears to protect her. It reacted quickly — how could it? It didn't know what was coming. Did it?

Unless it was somehow linked with her. A chill crossed over Malja. Had this do-kha been more than just a piece of her lost life? All along, had it actually been a true part of her, connected to her, within her, perhaps?

If that could be, then why hadn't she been able to use it? Malja thought of Fawbry's finger-twist game. Just because she could see her fingers didn't mean she could make them work right. In fact, it was the act of seeing that confused the brain. Perhaps she had always been "seeing" the wrong part of the do-kha, trying the wrong way.

Then what's the right way?

In Fawbry's game, trying to move a specific finger failed when she concentrated on doing so. She could succeed by ignoring the specifics and focusing on the overall goal.

Malja closed her eyes. As a test, she tried to warm the suit. In the past, she would have stared at it and attempted to command it to warm her. This time, she simply thought about the end result — the comfort of warmth.

The do-kha warmed.

The warrior in Malja understood tactical advantage very well. She lowered her head and looked up at the magician — a dangerous, blood-thirsty look. The magician blanched but quickly returned to his spell-casting.

Malja walked forward, her eyes shifting to Viper. She forced her mind to ignore the do-kha but rather envision herself walking through that magical wall. She pictured the arcs of electricity going into her without harm. She saw herself taking Viper.

Only when she lifted the weapon did she realize that none of what transpired had been in her head. As she had imagined it, so it had happened. Viper sat within her grip. She felt whole again.

The magician — his eyes wide, his chin shaking — pressed against the back wall. "Guards! Help!"

Malja heard the door open behind her. She couldn't give them time to settle into the room. Before they had both entered, she squatted to the floor. If they had guns and shot reflexively, the bullets would sail overhead. She pivoted on her left foot, slicing upward as she shoved off.

She caught one guard in his armpit, the momentum of her strike cutting straight through. His arm thumped on the floor, and the man screamed. His partner froze — astonished. Twisting Viper sideways with the outer-crescent facing her enemy for a fast cut, Malja sliced across the air, taking the top off of the second guard's head.

As she turned toward the magician, a familiar smile crept onto her lips. Though the act of killing never appealed to her, she enjoyed her strength, her ability, and the speed and flow of battle. All the conundrums and confusions life brought her way left as if she were meditating, lost in the immediate moment — nothing else existed.

The magician threw up. Tears dribbled from his eyes, and when he could breathe, he gasped out his plea. "P-Please don't kill me."

Malja was about to answer when she saw that the magician looked passed her. She spun around. Harskill stood in the doorway holding a rifle. The long barrel would insure an accurate shot in such close proximity.

The magician dropped to the floor, pressing his head down, mumbling prayers as fast as he could.

"You've disappointed your god," Harskill said as he pulled the trigger. Flames flashed out of the barrel along with a loud report. The magician went limp — a wide red hole opened in the back of his head. Harskill lowered the spent gun. "He promised that he could challenge you, but I should've known better. How could a puny mortal challenge a god?"

Malja repositioned her feet and held Viper between them. Harskill leaned against the door jam, calm and casual.

"Now this," Harskill said, "is truly a disappointment. Unless threatening me with your weapon is some form of courtship I don't know." His lips rose, and any doubt Malja had concerning Harskill vanished. She saw evil in that face.

"You're a sad, lonely man," she said. "I won't be your plaything."

"I get what I desire. That's one of the joys of being a god."

"You forget," Malja said, lowering her body just enough to pounce. "You've said I'm also a god."

Malja burst forward, swirling Viper in huge half-circle, over the shoulder, and down at Harskill's head. Without moving from the door jam, he raised his left arm to block. Viper landed right in the middle of his forearm. It should have cut through and embedded in his head. Instead, sparks flew out at the point of contact, and Harskill continued his nasty grin.

As Malja pressed down, trying to force Viper through Harskill's arm, she saw the black do-kha peeking out from beneath his shirt. The do-kha had protected him, hardening into a steel bracer according to his need. Malja whipped Viper away and back in at Harskill's ribs. Again, sparks flew from the clash with the do-kha. Whirling around, she went for his head on the other side, but he brought his arm up and used the do-kha once more to block the attack.

Harskill said, "Just because you broke a spell and got your weapon back, doesn't mean you know how to use the power you have. You are no god."

Bringing up his other arm, Harskill slapped away Viper. The force knocked Malja off-balance and she stumbled to the side. As she righted herself, Harskill slammed his palm upward into her sternum. She had never felt such a hard blow. It sent her back several feet. She rubbed the bone, pressing in to make sure it had not cracked.

"It's not too late," he said, putting out his hand. "This has been an upsetting experience. I understand. But now you see what you've done, and in me, you see what you are capable of. And you are right. I am lonely. So join me. Be my Queen. Be a goddess. Together we can reshape all the worlds we lay eyes on."

Malja swung at his hand, but the pain in her chest retarded her motions. He dodged with ease. His do-kha grew over his hand and he slapped the blade aside, the reverberations shaking up her arm. He backhanded her across the face, dropping her to the floor.

The world spun around her. She tried to stand, but her ears rang and a fuzziness surrounded her head making simple thoughts difficult. She knew she was in trouble, but she couldn't get her body to respond properly.

A hand reached down, grabbed her under the arm, and lifted her up. "You've squandered my greatest gift. I could've made you something incredible," Harskill said. The sound of his voice snapped Malja's brain back. She raised her head, but before she could think enough to block, he punched her in the chest.

She flew back through the air, hit a wall, and kept going. She slammed into the hallway and crumpled into a heap. Bits of wall covered her. The pain in her chest flared with every struggling breath as if she were drowning.

He's going to kill me.

The thought hit her harder than Harskill's fists. If she stayed, she would lose. She had been in tough fights before, but never once had she fully accepted such a possibility. There was no doubt, though, and her heart ached more than her body.

Despite her pains, she forced herself to her feet. She picked Viper off the floor, stunned by the idea that she had let the blade go, and staggered down the hall. Using the wall to keep her balance, she moved as fast as possible, taking any turn that presented itself, putting as much distance as she could between her and Harskill.

The lights flickered as Malja stumbled onward. She weaved like a drunkard and fought back the nausea churning her stomach. Footsteps approached.

Malja ducked into a shadowed recess and waited. Two Bluesmen stormed by. This wouldn't do. By now, she figured the entire group had been summoned to find her. She didn't know her way around the Dish, and she had been hurt. She needed a place to rest.

Slipping out of the recess, she took the first left she came upon and started trying doors. Three of them were locked, but the fourth one she tried opened. Inside, she found a cot and a set of drawers. In the corner, rubble piled under a hole in the wall. Malja peered into the hole — empty. She closed the door, locked it, and collapsed on the cot.

She tried to picture herself healed, but the do-kha did not respond. Apparently, some uses of the do-kha were not as simple as just imagining the outcome.

Three minutes passed, and during that brief moment, Malja thought she might actually have a chance. Then she heard the Bluesmen in the hall. They were trying the doors, yelling out the word Locked, and kicking them open.

Dragging herself off the cot, every muscle weary and aching, Malja pulled out Viper and positioned in front of the door. No room to hide or attempt an ambush. She would have to face them head on.

The door rattled. Malja flexed her fingers and settled her hands into the proper grip. A voice called out, "Locked." She took shallow breaths so as not to aggravate her wounded chest. The door banged as somebody kicked it. Malja raised Viper and prepared to strike. Two more kicks, and the door ripped open.

As Malja growled, surging forward with her blade, the Bluesman only had time to open his mouth in surprise. She sliced from shoulder to hip. One cut. One kill.

A gun shot out, its bullet striking the doorway just above Malja's head. She ducked back into the room, and the other Bluesman followed. He had a long-barreled, one-shot handgun which, upon seeing Malja's sizable weapon, he tossed to the floor. From a hip scabbard, he pulled out a sword.

Malja should have attacked as he entered, but she had used up too much energy taking out the first Bluesman with one strike. She couldn't let any more time slip by. She stepped forward and cut upward. The Bluesman jumped back and deflected Viper with his sword.

With a facile step, he stabbed straight at her. Malja managed to side-step and raise Viper for an overhead strike. Everything moved slowly for her as if magic had thickened the air. Viper felt heavier than ever before. The Bluesman stepped into the attack, blocking it with a clang of metal, and then jutted out his elbow, catching Malja in her wounded chest.

She gasped and doubled over. The Bluesman slammed his knee upward, connecting with her cheek, and rocking her backward onto the cot. The room spun out of control.

The Bluesman said something but the words did not make sense. Malja only heard an echoing muddle of sound. Her mouth felt loose like her jaw was stuck open, the effort to clamp it shut too strenuous. She tasted blood and spit. The Bluesman stood over her. He spoke again and the word *Die* made it through into her head.

But before he could strike, she saw the strangest thing. A rainbow of color opened up behind him. It burst out of the vent, spread across like colorful wings on a bird, and jumped upon the Bluesman's back.

She heard a voice — Fawbry. In his multi-colored robe, he rode the Bluesman's back and locked his arm around the man's neck. The Bluesman stumbled backward into the wall. Then purposely stepped forward and slammed back into the wall. Fawbry held tight, yelling his war cry even as tears streamed down his face.

The Bluesman reached up and grabbed a handful of Fawbry's wiry hair. Fawbry held tight — wincing, yelling, crying, pulling back on his arm. The Bluesman's eyes rolled upward and he fell backward onto the floor and Fawbry.

Wiping his wet face, Fawbry extricated himself from under the Bluesman. "You okay?" he asked Malja. She could focus enough to nod. Putting her arm around his shoulder, she stood.

Fawbry said, "I don't think you can climb up into that vent. We'll have to find a floor level access." From his pocket, he brought out a folded paper. "Cole gave me a little map. Can you stand on your own?"

"I think so," she managed.

Fawbry peeked into the hall. He looked at that map, the hall, then the map again. "I think I got it. Can you walk?"

Malja took a few steps and didn't fall over. "Yes."

"Follow me," he said and ducked out of the room.

Chapter 16

Fawbry led the way — scurrying down half-lit halls, holding up at corners, peeking around doors, sticking to shadows. If he heard voices or footsteps, he turned around and went a different way. Malja followed without question. Her throbbing head allowed for little else. Even if she wanted to fight, she was in no condition to do so. Drying blood stuck to her cheek. Her nose felt swollen. Her sides were dull with aches.

"In here," Fawbry whispered, his voice booming in her ears. He pulled her into a storage closet filled with boxes, a few tools, and bits of unused metal and wood. In the back, low to the floor, he pointed to a wide intake vent. "Help me with this."

Malja took one step and everything went dark.

She couldn't open her eyes. She didn't think so, at least. If they were open, everything around her was dark. She heard the echoes of heavy breathing and something dragging in short motions. She felt tugging at her shoulders.

Somebody (*Fawbry?*) cursed.

Dull light.

People staring at her from above — Fawbry and Cole Watts.

Malja tried to sit up but she was tied down to a cot. Cole Watts moved closer. Her arms shook as she approached, and she paused long enough to turn away before coughing.

Fawbry's concern shifted to Cole for a moment. When he looked down at Malja again, he managed a friendly sigh. "Sorry we tied you. You kept trying to punch us."

"Where?" Malja said, her mouth dry and sticky.

"One of Cole's little hideouts. This one's actually in the vents. I couldn't get us to the one in the sewer. Too many Bluesmen blocked access that way."

"And," Cole said, wiping at the corner of her mouth, "he had to pull you along."

"Thank you. That was brave," Malja said, and though Fawbry waved off the praise, she could see it fill his heart. "Now let me up or I'll rip you to pieces," she growled.

Flustered, Fawbry undid the ropes. "Don't get up too quickly or —"

Once free, Malja shoved up, glimpsed Tommy floating in the corner, and the world spun around her head. She fell back onto the cot.

"Bless her heart," Cole said. "She's always been a determined gal."

Rubbing her temples, Malja said, "We don't have time for this. Harskill has control of the Bluesmen and he's using them to get to you."

"I told you. I couldn't trust him from the start. He's been trying to sabotage my efforts all along."

"I know," Malja said, but something gnawed at her. She sat up again, much slower this time, and took a few breaths. "Why are we still here? Why are we still alive?"

Fawbry smacked his hand on the top of his head. "I know we've had our share of religious talk but now's not the time for debating Kryssta and Korstra."

"I'm talking about Harskill. He claims to be godlike and that he wanted to stop this portal project from happening. Except now he's got control of the Dish and he hasn't done much to stop you. I mean he could've killed us all and just been done with it. He had plenty of chances."

"Oh dearie," Cole said, "you're not that naive. The man's lost his mind for you. He wants you. Probably dreams of you popping out a few little Harskills, too. It's the only reason the rest of us are alive. If he killed us, he'd lose even a sliver of a chance with you."

Malja shook her head, sending a new wave of pain across her brow. "I think there's more to it than just that. Maybe that was true at the start but he's got something bigger in mind than me."

"All the more reason to do my plan."

Malja gripped the edge of the cot. "What plan?"

"Hear her out," Fawbry said.

After a few short coughs, Cole sat next to Malja and placed a hand on her knee. Malja smelled Cole's perfume — honey and a strong flower she couldn't place. Even in this dank, depressing hideout, Cole had to have her feminine side. Maybe that's what had been at work on Fawbry — moreso than sympathy for Cole's illness.

"Well now," Cole said, her drawl thickening in her attempt to charm. "I think you may be right about Harskill, and I say this because, as you say, we're all still here. So, if his motive is no longer love and it is no longer destroying this place, then there is only one viable choice. He wants to use the Dish for himself. Why else would he have an occupying army of Bluesmen in here?"

Malja held still. "He likens himself to a god. Perhaps he wants to use the Dish's power to enhance his own. Make himself more like a god. Is that possible?"

Cole lifted her drab clothes and looked at the hideout's stained walls. "In my life I've learned that just about anything is possible. Even situations you never thought you'd step into. And when it comes to power, everybody wants more."

A grin passed Malja's lips, but she corrected that fast. She knew Cole well enough — this was all just the lead up to her plan.

"Okay," Cole said, patting Malja's knee as she stood. "I can see that you know it's coming, so here it is: You want to fight someone with god-like powers, then you need someone with god-like powers." Lifting a hand with melodramatic flare, Cole gestured to Tommy.

Malja knew they expected her to protest. She could see it in Fawbry's frightened gaze and in Cole's patronizing smile. But what was the point of that argument anymore? All her efforts to protect Tommy from the ills of magic only led him here, and here was an awful place to be. If Cole had a plan to reawaken Tommy, to give him a chance to be saved from whatever had happened to him, Malja gladly agreed. Anything would be better than the state he was in.

"What do we do?" she asked.

Stunned, Cole said, "W-Well, I seem to recall Fawbry telling me about how you once linked with Barris Mont. His tentacles are, to a degree, right there growing out of Tommy's arm. If you could establish a connection through them, you might be able to help Tommy come back. With him at your side, you should be able to bring a true challenge to Harskill."

"That seems like a lot of conjecture."

Cole crossed the room and stroked Tommy's head. His skin had turned a mottled gray and more eyes appeared all over. "He's a lovely young man. And so powerful. Barris Mont is powerful, too. Both of them share their power within this one body. And it's magic." She paced the room, speaking more like a priest trying to sway the congregation and less like a scientist bent on having her way. "You know, when I first decided to do this project, I didn't want to use any magic at all. Look where it got me when I used the Bluesmen. No magic, this time. That was to be my rule. But then I kept running into power supply problems, and I found the underground shuco. So, I convinced myself to use that little bit of magic. I'd just bend the rules a little — after all, I made the rules." Cole chuckled and coughed. "But that never really works. We lie to ourselves, but those are the worst kinds of lies since nobody can refute them. They are within us and that's it."

"What are you saying? That I should follow your plan because you've convinced yourself it'll work?"

"I'm suggesting that this Dish will never work right for me because I built it with one power source in mind, but I lied to myself and used another. Someone else, however — someone who has the knowledge of portals because he was there during the Devastation, someone who understands magic because he spent decades helping magicians unlock their powers, someone like that could take my work and see it to completion. Only Barris Mont fits that description."

"And that can only happen if I get him and Tommy free of whatever is going on inside them, so they can help me defeat Harskill."

Cole brought a hand to her mouth. "Oh my. I must be feeling worse than I realized. Forgive me for being so bluntly honest."

"It's refreshing," Malja said, but a part of her worried that Cole's frank admissions were just a step in a more elaborate plan. That would be more typical of Cole. Though she did look unwell.

"Aren't you cute," Cole said, playfully wagging a finger at Malja.

Her eyes widened for an instant, and she collapsed to the floor. "Cole!" Fawbry said, rushing to her side. By the time he had reached her, Cole's body shivered in a seizure. Malja tried to help, but her movements were slow and pained. Fawbry cradled his old love, holding her tight against his chest. With each violent shake, Cole let out a groan. The sound echoed around them. As fast as it began, it tapered off until she looked like a child sleeping in her father's arms.

Fawbry gazed up at Malja, his face screwed up with too many simultaneous emotions. "She's going to die. Soon. Please, try with Tommy and Barris Mont. Get them back, so Tommy can fix this."

"Isn't healing me what caused him to lose it in the first place?"

"Please," Fawbry said, unable to produce any more sound than a whisper.

Though her entire body protested, Malja nodded. Fawbry was family, and sometimes that was all that mattered. Besides, if she was going to lose Tommy forever, she wouldn't let him go quietly. She'd fight it every step.

She stood straight, sheer willpower keeping her from falling back. Without looking down, she said to Fawbry, "I know Cole's dying, and I'll do what I can. You've got to watch me closely if I manage this link. Tommy's very powerful but clearly he's not the only one in charge of that body. And I don't trust Barris Mont ever. If it looks like I'm in trouble, you take your knife and cut me free. If Barris Mont fights you off, then take Viper and cut off my arm. You understand?"

"Y-Yes," Fawbry said.

She stroked Fawbry's head once. "We've come a long way. There was a time you would've been screaming at me for even suggesting any of that."

Fawbry pulled her hand down, almost taking her to the ground, and he kissed her palm. "I trust you now more than I ever have. I'll do exactly as you say."

"Good," Malja said and unsheathed Viper. She placed her wonderful blade on the cot, ran a loving hand across its grip, and closed her eyes. As if Viper could hear or think, she mouthed the words, "Watch over me."

When she approached Tommy, a shiver of doubt chilled her gut. This close, she now saw how lost in his mind he had become. Covered in sweat, stinking and shaking, with his eyes locked forward, he not only looked insane, he looked terrified.

"Tommy. Barris Mont," she said, and all the eyes on his body focused in her direction. She pulled back her do-kha sleeve and placed her arm next to the undulating tendrils of Tommy's arm. "I want to speak with you. If this is like the time at Dead Lake, then I will not resist."

The tendrils continued to move like weeds underwater, but now they stretched and squirmed and reached for Malja's arm. They sounded like a thousand maggots crawling over a corpse. She refused to react. She braced herself as the first tendrils made contact and the world around her disappeared.

Chapter 17

Before she saw anything, Malja smelled the ocean. Next, her legs wobbled as the waves rose and fell. She tasted salt and felt the spray of a water against her cheek. Finally, the world appeared around her — a world from years ago.

She stood on the deck of Captain Wuchev's ship. The same Captain Wuchev who had tried to kill her for a few precious trinkets hidden in the hold. The same Captain Wuchev who had enslaved Tommy, chaining him in the front battery room and using him as a power source.

The ship was a large hunk of salvaged scrap with a half-shell rounded back, a wide main deck, and three makeshift masts cut into the rusting deck. The smell of rotting fish stuck to every surface. Nobody, not even Wuchev, could be seen.

The choppy water spoke of a storm brewing somewhere in the distance. Another storm brewed within Malja — part anger, part nausea. She hated the water.

"I can't say I ever thought we'd meet like this again," a smooth voice called from behind.

Malja didn't need to turn around to know Barris Mont stood there. He came up beside her, leaned on the railing, and looked out at the ocean. He was the same as when they had first shared mental space — gray suit with a brilliant green tie, clean beyond anything capable in the real world, handsome and smelling as if he had emerged from a spice-scented bath. It was a mental image — a memory of what he had looked like before the Devastation mutated him into a multi-eyed glob of a monster and before he abandoned that enormous body for Tommy.

Tapping a steady rhythm on the rail, he said, "I don't wish to sound pushy, but if you recall, being in another person's mind can have rather intoxicating effects, and you in particular, reacted quite strongly. I suspect you don't have much time until you're rolling on the deck, drunk senseless."

"You're right," Malja said as she stepped behind Barris Mont and locked her arm around his throat. She yanked back, lifting him off the ground, and held him as he struggled for air. "How dare you take advantage of this sweet boy. Jarik and Callib attacked you at your lake and instead of protecting Tommy, you used him as a surrogate body. And now you've been slowly turning him into you. Seems to me, if I kill you, all we be fine."

The ship lurched atop a large wave, but Malja held tight. Barris Mont pulled down on her arm, straining to speak. "Look ... around. This is ... Tommy's mind. You're ... hurting him."

Malja released her stranglehold and the waves settled. Barris Mont fell forward, catching himself on the railing, and gasped for air. Malja grabbed him by the coat and hauled him back against a pile of crates. "You better start talking because time is going fast. If you don't help, you aren't worth much, and that means —"

Barris Mont raised his hands. "No need to threaten. We both want the same thing here. For Tommy and I to be free. But understand that the boy and I are, for the moment, a shared entity. Hurting me while in his mind hurts him as well."

"Fine. But don't plan to wait me out until I start acting drunk because I'm angry right now. The last thing you want to see is me angry and drunk."

"Of course," he said with an oddly proper bow. "The first thing you need to understand is that I did not use your boy as a way of escaping Jarik and Callib. I entered him because he was going to try to fight those two powerful magicians himself. They would've killed him with barely a thought. By entering Tommy, I was able to control some of his power for a short time, enough time to make his usefulness evident to the magicians, so that they would take him along — as they did. I saved his life."

"You used him."

Barris Mont's eyes flared. "I've protected him all along. He has tremendous magical gifts and wants to use them. He holds back sometimes because he cares for you and knows you disapprove. But there is part of him, a strong part, that dabbles with his powers anyway. From here, inside the boy, I've been able to lock away many of these talents, to protect him from himself. Yet my power is limited in this form, and as you've seen, the boy has grown strong. But to say that I've used him when all you've ever done was use him, when it was his magic saving your life time and again that pushed him toward insanity. I've kept him sane at least a year longer than he should've managed, and I put him in his current state not to turn him into me, but to keep him alive. You should be ashamed at how you've treated Tommy. So, forgive me for ignoring you, but I give little credence to your view."

Malja's anger rose up her throat but she kept it in check. Through gritted teeth, she said, "At least we both agree we don't care about each other. But we both want to help Tommy. Right? We both want to stop Harskill. Right?" The boat rocked to the side, and Malja stumbled a bit before regaining her balance. "I think I'm already starting to get drunk. So stop posturing and tell me what I have to do."

Barris Mont made a show of mulling over the idea before finally nodding. He clapped his hands twice, and a young man dressed in a formal black suit with a white bow tie came around the central mast. He carried a covered silver tray. He bowed before Malja and removed the covering.

In the center of the tray, Malja saw an empty glass bottle. She had never seen one so clean and clear. For that matter, she had never seen one completely intact before. Even the best bottles had cracks along the sides or chips around the mouth.

Barris Mont lifted the bottle and dismissed the servant. He inspected it with care before setting it at Malja's feet. "Tommy is suffering from an imbalance," he said. "The magic side of him is overpowering the non-magic side. It's what happens to all magicians when they aren't properly trained. And ever since the Devastation, few people really train magicians anymore, so we have many more cases of this kind of insanity."

"Get to the point."

"Stop acting like a brat," Barris Mont said. "This isn't a case of you getting to kill something or bash someone. This is a delicate matter. If you don't fully comprehend the situation, we are certain to fail and the damage to Tommy could be permanent."

Malja swiped the bottle from the deck. "Fine. What do I do with this delicate object?"

"Not you. Us. We have to do this together. If done right, we can stabilize him which will allow me to let go of the limited control I've exerted to keep him going this long. Then he should be okay for the short term. He'll need more help later, but this will suffice. Now understand that this imbalance is represented all around us. That bottle is nothing more than just such a representation. Our task is to awaken Tommy's sense of self to the point that he recognizes the difference between this representational existence and the real world."

"I don't know what that means."

"It means you have to take this bottle to Tommy's representational soul. The heart of his magical being. When you arrive, I'll be there doing my part. Place the bottle correctly and the rest should handle itself." To stave off Malja's protest, Barris Mont walked to a hole in the deck that had not been there before. "Down here, okay? Go down there and keep going down until you find Tommy and myself. That's when you know you'll be at the right place."

"And I put the bottle where?"

"You'll know when you see."

Malja rolled her eyes. "Why didn't you just say so?" As she passed him by, she bumped her shoulder into his chest.

"Be careful in there," Barris said. "It's made up of Tommy's mind, and he's not all that stable at the moment."

Malja peered into the hole. It stretched down quite far. Orange firelight flickered at the bottom. Shadows and silhouettes filled the hole with legs and wings. Whatever creatures occupied that drop, there were a lot of them.

Malja looked up to Barris Mont — but he was gone.

The wind picked up and the ship churned from side to side. The ocean waves grew choppy. The clouds darkened. Little dark marks dappled the deck — raindrops.

Malja checked down the hole again. If anything, she swore the number of creatures had increased. This better work. As she put the bottle in the pocket of her coat, lightning cracked across the sky.

And she jumped in.

Gravity, if such a thing existed in this place, pulled her down fast while the arms, legs, wings, and tentacles crowding the hall slowed her down. Too fast for them to get a hold on her but slow enough to avoid breaking a leg when she hit bottom. Whatever these creatures were, they cried and screamed as she dropped out of reach.

The bottom of the hole came up fast. Malja readied herself for a hard jolt to her legs. Instead, she passed right through the dirt floor like passing through a cloud. The sensation of falling lifted, and she felt a firm, metal floor beneath her feet. It came about so gently, so suddenly, that for a moment she had no idea that she had stopped falling, just that the internal sensations had changed.

"You little weasel," a voice called from behind.

Malja turned around. She was in the cargo hold. A few feet away, Captain Wuchev shouted at a young version of Tommy. Wuchev stood in his threadbare clothes, sweat flying from his dirt-caked cheeks, as he held a frayed leather strap in his hand and slapped it across Tommy's bleeding back.

"When I give you an order, you'll obey me and you'll obey quick," Wuchev said, punctuating his words with repeated blows.

Tommy cowered beneath the abuse, curled in a ball. Though he covered his shaggy head, the matted blood showed dark through his fingers.

"Leave him alone," Malja said.

Wuchev looked up, his face soaked, and spit at her. "This is my ship, and the boy is my property. And, by Korstra, nobody is going to order me around on my own ship."

In one swift motion, Malja slid Viper free. As Wuchev raised the leather strap for another strike, Malja cut his forearm clean off. Wuchev screamed as blood geysered from his open wound.

Malja swung Viper for the kill, but when she should have felt her blade hit bone, she sliced through air. Captain Wuchev was gone. The ship was gone. The ocean was gone. Malja stood in an empty field of waist-high grass.

A cool breeze crossed her skin. Meat roasted on a fire nearby, its savory scent wetting her mouth. She took three steps toward the aroma when she heard a young boy scream from the opposite direction.

Darting across the field, she scanned for any sign of the boy. He continued to cry out but she couldn't pinpoint where the sound came from. Every time she turned one way, the voice shifted to come from another direction. The field seemed to flow forever, and it all looked the same. The more she changed direction, the more confusingly similar it all appeared.

Breathing hard and getting nowhere, Malja stopped. Though she had never heard his voice before, her instincts told her it had to be him. "Tommy!" she called out, but now there was only silence. "Tommy!" The empty bottle in her pocket grew heavier with every passing second as if it could drag her under the ground, drown her in the grass, make her know that no matter what she ever did, she never would save the boy.

She gazed up at the passing sun. Three enormous winged-beasts circled the air in the distance. She had never seen such things before —

wide, leathery wings attached to a furry torso; white spots dappled the fur while a long, feathered tail whipped in the air like a war standard; a blunted beak did little to mar an already hideous head.

One broke its circling pattern, folded in its wings, and dived. It disappeared from view for a few seconds, re-emerging several feet away. From its mouth, a tan cloth dangled — Tommy's shirt.

Malja tore off for the boy. Keeping her eyes on the sky so as not to lose sight of the winged-beasts or of her direction, she pushed her legs harder. Cawing, another dived toward the ground. She heard a painful yelp.

Breaking through the grass, she entered a cleared area. Tommy lay face down. The winged-beast perched on a fallen log a few feet away. It watched Tommy, waiting for him to die.

Malja raised Viper and let out her war cry. She shot forward, leaping over Tommy, and swiped at the beast. It shot into the air, but Viper caught its tail.

Except the blade found only emptiness. The beast had vanished. The field was gone. All had disappeared again. All was dark.

She heard the steady rumble of a ship's engines, the vibrations coming through the metal floor. Rain and thunder raged outside. Stale urine and rotting food assaulted her nostrils. As her eyes adjusted, she knew exactly where she had been taken. The battery room on Wuchev's ship — the place she had first met Tommy.

It was a small room with two large storage batteries composing one wall. Rusting pipes and thick wires decorated the rest. Chained to one pipe, huddled in the darkest back corner, Tommy whimpered and watched.

Malja took a step toward him, remembering how she freed him from this horrible situation. And she stopped. This was the point, the moment in time when she changed his life forever — sent him on a path to Barris Mont. Sure, she freed him, but was it worth it? His life had been in constant danger with her. He rarely slept with a roof over his head. Sometimes food was scarce. Worse, since being with her, he had been using all kinds of magic — not just producing electricity — and that magic had led him to the edge of insanity.

She didn't fool herself into thinking that staying on the ship would have been anything wonderful, but at least the only threat Tommy faced would have been Wuchev. Not the host of lunatics that confronted them all the time. Not the regular attempts to use, abuse, and kill them. She made the choice to take the boy — her decision. She could have left him. She changed the course of an entire life merely by acting on the thought that she could set him up for a better life. But why should she be the one to decide which life was worse for the boy? That's something a god would do.

Tommy leaned out as far as his chains would allow. He seemed to recognize her. He smiled, but the darkness crept in around them, and all disappeared.

Bright daylight blinded her at first. At length, she found herself standing in the middle of city ruins. Once-tall buildings had collapsed to the ground. A few that managed to stay intact leaned into others like dead trees. Debris coated every inch of the city, piled high enough to block easy passage in most areas. In fact, Malja saw that only one path had been cleared away.

She wound her way along until the path opened into a strange scene. Frozen in time, Tommy and Barris Mont stood on opposite sides of an ornate pedestal. On the pedestal, Malja saw a pillow — clean and shiny, smooth like nothing that ever existed since the Devastation. And the pillow bore an indent just the right shape to match the bottle in her pocket.

This was it. Barris had said she would know when she got there, and she knew.

She walked straight to the pedestal, her chest lifting at the idea that she had reached the end of this experience, and pulled the bottle out. Though nobody else could move, she swore she heard Tommy's soft tones. She looked over and saw how he struggled so hard to stay sane. The toll was evident in the stressed lines of his face.

She looked at Barris Mont. He stared right at her as if urging her to finish her task and save the boy. But he also seemed hungry for her to act.

She let out a pitiful laugh. Here she was again, holding lives in her hand, deciding the fate of so many. Maybe Harskill was right. Maybe they were gods — just not in the mystical sense of Kryssta and Korstra. Maybe being a god meant having the power to make these choices and acting upon that power.

Lifting the bottle, Malja peered through the glass. She frowned. Of all things, why should a bottle represent Tommy? The places she had been — the ship's hold, the field, the battery room — were all from Tommy's head. Why would he choose a perfect bottle, something he had probably never seen in his life, to represent him?

She glanced at Barris. He also possessed some of Tommy's body and mind, and he had lived before the Devastation. He had seen bottles like this one before. Couldn't this bottle really be Barris looking to free himself?

She looked upon Tommy again. Fighting insanity? Possibly. But concern, worry, maybe even fear seemed to paint his face.

Malja let out a barrage of curses and kicked at the rubble on the ground. Why make her figure this out? This wasn't where she excelled. She knew Viper. She knew fighting. She knew how to read an enemy's intentions and counter the attack. She knew how to rate a weapon. She understood blades. That had always been the way for her. The blade.

"The blade," she whispered. "Is that what I am? *The Blade?*"

Uncle Gregor had taught her to seek out her true purpose in life. He often said that such things were never easy to find, that many never discovered what they really were, but that if she found it, she would know because it would make sense when all else was confusion. That's exactly how she felt and thought.

The Blade. She was a force of strength, of a warrior, of power. Of course, she always knew that fighting was her best asset, but now she saw it as more. It wasn't just fighting but the entire art of it all. It wasn't simply slashing at an enemy. Viper was an extension of her. And there was a purity in the fight, a clearing of all confusions. In those moments, the movement of the body, the strategy of the opponent, the precision of the strike were all unified into action without debate. No worries over the future, no regrets over the past, just that moment in time. That purity. That's what she thought of when she repeated *The Blade* in her head.

Fawbry read books and prayed to Kryssta, all in some effort to understand how he fit in the world around him. Despite her protests, Tommy explored magic for the same purpose. But she rejected those methods because they didn't make sense to her — they didn't feel right. She had hers all along. She just didn't know it. The Blade was her way. That was her power. And perhaps, like Harskill said, that made her a god.

She looked at Barris Mont. Her fighting instincts screamed that he was a liar. He had used Tommy to survive and now he wanted to take the boy over. She needed no other thought. All her life with Tommy, all her instincts, all her training, every aspect of her unified into knowing exactly what to do.

She threw the bottle to ground, happy to watch it shatter into countless shards.

Chapter 18

Malja slammed backward, her arm ripping from the tendrils that connected her to Tommy, and slumped to the floor. Every inch of her singed with pains both new and old. Her chest still ached where Harskill had struck, and her mouth tasted bitter with blood.

Fawbry rushed to her side. "This was stupid. I'm sorry. Please tell me you're okay."

Unable to open one eye, Malja lifted her head. "Better than ever," she said, and part of her believed it. Something wriggled along her arm. When she looked down, she saw the tail-end of a tendril slip under her skin.

She pinched her skin around the tendril, trying to squeeze it back out. It slipped in further. She dug her finger in, leaving a gash as she tried to get at the thing. But her do-kha moved in fast, sliding down her arm and under her digging finger, so that in seconds she could no longer touch her skin. The do-kha would heal her wound, maybe it would get rid of the tendril, too.

She snapped her focus up, ignoring the pain the sudden motion brought with it, and asked, "Is Tommy okay?"

Fawbry slid to the side, and they both looked across the room. Though his head hung low, Tommy opened his eyes — his real eyes. They glowed and shifted colors. His tattoos glowed as well. And there were more. Tattoos covered every visible part of him as if shattering the bottle had not only shattered Barris Mont's bindings, but released every spell within him.

Tommy opened his hands and swirls of magic pooled in his palms as if he carried puddles of steaming power. It dribbled between his fingers and wherever the substance hit the floor, small flames shot upward before disappearing. The bitter odor of magic engulfed the room.

"W-What happened?" Fawbry asked.

Malja looked to Fawbry but suddenly saw herself and Fawbry from across the room. *She was floating with her arms out, palms open, and magic seething through her body. She was seeing through Tommy's eyes.* Shaking her head, she returned to her own sight.

"Oh no," she said, looking at the tendril wriggling under the skin of her arm.

"Don't say *Oh no* and then nothing." Fawbry's voice raised pitch to near panic. "My Kryssta, what's going on?"

Malja looked upon her bruised body and saw all her injuries. Everything below the skin. She could see Fawbry's heart beating rapidly and hear her own rasping breaths. She strained to hear Tommy but heard the entire world instead and had no way of knowing what sounds belonged to the boy. She raised her hand filled with magic and pointed at her body.

"What's he doing?" Fawbry asked, his arms spreading out to protect her while his legs scooted him away.

"It's okay," Malja said. "I think he's going to help me."

A green-tinged light spiraled from Tommy's hand, stretched across the room, and layered over Malja. When it touched her, every nerve in her skin fired off. She screamed, her voice rattling the thin walls. She desperately wanted to switch back into Tommy's head but didn't know how it had happened before. Tears flowed from her and her body arched toward the ceiling. From the corner of her eye, she saw Fawbry curled in the far corner, crying out, reaching out but unable to get any closer.

And then it was over.

The green-tinged light fell apart like a breaking fog, and with it, so went the pain. She felt refreshed like she had enjoyed an uninterrupted night's sleep. Malja jumped to her feet, her body restored — maybe better than it had been in years. She looked up at Tommy. Had he destroyed the tendril, too? No. She could still feel it in her arm. She could still feel the connection to Tommy.

In his head, floating on the opposite side, she saw her own astonished face looking back.

"I'm not a god," she said. "He is."

Fawbry crawled over to Cole, asleep near the air duct entrance, and said, "Heal her, too. If you can do that for Malja, heal Cole, too."

A hard scrabbling sound came up the air duct. Fawbry peeked around the edge and jumped back. He didn't have to explain. One of the giant insects crawled in, its legs clicking as it reared back and hissed at them.

Casually turning, Tommy flicked his fingers in the insect's direction.

It paused long enough for Malja to see a change overcome its body. If it were human, she would've thought it was confused and worried. Then it bent backwards with a loud snap. Its body lifted into the air and its sides folded in. What now comprised its torso, which included some legs and a bit of its head, crushed inward and it folded yet again. With every successive fold, it snapped and crunched. Blood and goo splashed out only to be caught mid-air and thrown back in. The same amount of matter continued to be shoved into a smaller and smaller space until the giant insect had been crushed into the size of a stone good for skipping along a quiet stream.

The stone dropped to the floor with a thud. Fawbry bent over it, sniffed, and then tried to pick it up. He couldn't budge it anymore than he could have lifted the creature at its original size.

Tommy raised his head with an approving expression and his body lifted upward, slipping through the ceiling as if nothing blocked his path.

"Where's he going?" Fawbry asked.

Malja looked to the monitors but heard the painful screams first. Bluesmen patrolling the halls found themselves being compacted into ever smaller bits until they became dense stones. Every image the monitor brought up displayed a similar scene.

"I wonder," Malja said and closed her eyes.

When she opened her eyes, she saw through Tommy again. She watched as he drifted through walls and floors and ceilings. Every Bluesmen, every insect, every threat that came after him met the same fate. He passed above the building into the main Dish itself. He floated along its smooth, open surface until he reached the center. Stretching out both hands, he looked to the night sky. Streams of power surged through the air, from every edge, every panel, every part of the Dish. They pooled in a central point hundreds of feet above him and poured down into his hands.

The entire building shook as if the ground quaked. Fawbry grabbed Malja's shoulder and shook her extra. "This building isn't safe. We've got to do something." He turned to Cole. "Get him back in here to heal her so we can get out." The walls rumbled.

"It's him," Malja said. "Tommy is drawing in all the power Cole's Dish can produce."

The shock on Fawbry's face matched the shiver in his hands. "We've got to stop him."

"Why? He's a god. Let him have the power. He's destroying our enemies with little effort and besides, he's Tommy. He loves us." Metal whined in the distance echoing up the vents like a lonely cat. "This is who he is. This is purity to him. With this kind of power, he can bring peace and security to this world. He can end the brutal lives and all we've endured since the Devastation. And, he can open the exact portal to my home."

"Kryssta and Korstra are our gods. He's just a boy. And this much power might destroy him."

Malja shook her head. "I've seen inside him. He is more than you know."

Fawbry dabbed at his eyes and turned away with a huff. He knelt beside Cole and stroked her hair. "I can't believe this is how it all ends. Not only Tommy, but Malja goes insane. Even Cole is mentally gone. How did I end up the only one left with a brain?"

"I'm not insane," Malja said. "Tommy won't let anything—"

"How do you know it's even Tommy? Barris Mont is still in there. Did you even consider that unleashing Tommy like this, giving him all this power, more power than a young boy knows how to handle, it all might be the very thing Barris Mont wants most?"

"But Tommy's still in there. Barris can't —"

"If the bit of Tommy that's in that body gets burnt to pieces by all this magic, then Barris is in there to take over."

Cole awoke. She touched Fawbry's cheek and mumbled. Fawbry looked down, offered a loving smile, and stroked her hair. "Please," he said to Malja while never looking away from Cole. "Do something to stop this."

The Dish building jolted to one side. The monitor fell from the wall and smashed into the floor. Sparks and electricity crackled off the open wires dangling from where the monitor had been mounted.

Malja had one hand on the wall to steady herself. "It's Tommy in there," she said. "Trust me. I was given the bottle. I freed him and all his power. It's Tommy. He's going to make all this right. He's going to get me home."

"You selfish fool," Fawbry said. "I thought you really cared about us. I thought we had become a family. But even now, you're willing to risk this entire world just so you can see your home."

"You don't understand."

Fawbry opened his mouth, and Malja fully expected him to yell at her. He had done so before and often gave her the perspective she needed. But he didn't say anything. He closed his mouth with a sad expression, disappointed, and returned his attentions to Cole.

Magic energized his skin, coursing through his blood, pumping in his heart and brain. Tommy felt stronger, loving, powerful. He wanted to suck in all the Dish could provide. He wanted to draw in all the magic of every magician. The world could be his to mold. A figure stepped out on the Dish's edge. A Bluesman. Tommy couldn't dispose of him during this moment. Too dangerous while all this power streamed into him. Another Bluesman stepped out. And another. More and more until they had spread around the entire edge of the Dish, surrounding him from a wide distance. Each one had a little metal box and a flat guitar. Harskill stood with them, too. He raised and lowered his hand in one strong motion — a signal. All the Bluesmen strummed their guitars. From the metal boxes, a huge sound erupted. The electrified guitar sounds continued as the Bluesmen played. The air around the edges shimmered. One more Bluesman stepped forward — Wolf. He played atop the complex rhythms and rhythmic lines of the others. As he did so, as the pace increased, the shimmering air became a magic force like a wall that blocked the energy Tommy tried to absorb.

"What's that noise?" Fawbry asked as the muffled music reached into the air ducts.

Malja rubbed her eyes. "The Bluesmen are using their magic to try to stop Tommy. Harskill's with them."

Though weak and sounding more like an elderly woman, Cole Watts commanded attention just by speaking. She pointed at Malja and said, "The schuco system. If you shut it off ..." She dropped back against Fawbry and closed her eyes.

"She's right," Fawbry said. "If you go down into the sewers, follow the conduit line back to the schuco junction box, you could shut down all the power to the Dish. Cut off the power and all of this threat goes away."

Malja didn't move.

"You've got to do this," Fawbry said. "We'll find some other way to get you home, but I know you too well. You won't sacrifice Tommy for this. You never have before."

"He was never a god before."

"He isn't now. He's just a magician — a terrifyingly powerful magician, but still a magician."

She leaned forward, letting her forehead press against the wall. "I don't want to hurt him. We have no idea what cutting his power off might do."

Fawbry's tone softened. "But we do know he can't keep taking on more power. Eventually, something bad will happen to us, to the world, to him. And you know very well that the real worry isn't

Tommy. It's Barris. That's who you should stop."

Malja closed her eyes. She had hoped to be transported back to Tommy, but it didn't happen. She stayed in that air duct, listening to the muted tones of Blues music and the growing wheeze of Cole's struggled breaths. And she felt something in the back of her eyes. A strange sensation as if someone were back there, touching her eyeballs, tickling or stroking, them. Irritating them, too.

Barris? She didn't know why she thought his name but the odd feeling left right away. He had been spying on her through her own eyes just as she could see through Tommy. But why would he care at all what she was doing? Unless Fawbry was right.

"Okay," Malja said, turning to Fawbry and Cole, the familiar determination back on her face. "How do I get to the schuco?"

Chapter 19

Many years back, when Malja lived with Uncle Gregor and dreamed of vengeance, she came across a vacant vemmer hole. Vemmers were long, wide-bodied serpents that burrowed into the ground and waited to ambush prey. Feeling a sense of adventure, Malja poked her head down the hole. Numerous skeletons of numerous creatures littered the bottom — some half-eaten, some still with flesh rotting away. The atrocious smell caused her to vomit and nearly pass out.

Standing over a rough-cut hole in the Dish air ducts that led to the defunct sewer system, Malja wished for that odor. The sewer she had walked through before had smelled bad, of course, but it was a field of flowers compared to this one. She held back from vomiting but didn't know if that success would last. No matter. She had an important task ahead of her — she couldn't care about personal comfort.

The climb into the sewers was easy. Cole had installed footholds some time ago and a knotted rope hung down as well. When Malja set foot on the muddy floor, the sound of slushing and oozing destroyed any chance of holding back. She threw up. To her surprise, she discovered that purging her stomach made the sewer easier to take.

Wiping her mouth, she scanned the area. No more than ten feet across, the arched tunnel had two metal walkways lining either side. Most of the walkways were covered in slime but a rusty railing would help to keep from slipping. What would have been the waterway long ago, now was a mix of dry beds and foul slurry. A long line of lights strung on the side marked the way to the schuco.

Malja followed the trail, one hand hovering just above the railing should she need it. Normally, she would trust her balance and not care if she fell, but the thought of being covered in aged feces and rotted corpses made her want to throw up once again. She moved fast but not as fast as she was capable. Too much mold and slime everywhere. She felt like she walked on ice.

Her eye twitched, *and she was inside Tommy. The Bluesmen continued to cast their music spell, pushing back against Tommy's attempt to gain more and more energy. But some energy slipped through. She could feel him growing stronger. With one finger, he pointed toward an older Bluesman. The guitar strings snapped, and as the Bluesman looked at his instrument, his body liquefied — the watery remains flowed into the Dish.*

One down.

Back in the sewers, Malja's skin prickled. That last thought wasn't hers and wasn't Tommy's. Barris Mont. Of course the connection would reach to him, too — it was his tendril, after all.

You're a gullible fool, Barris said in her head.

Malja quickened her pace, lowering her hand to the rail just in case. "Fawbry was right. You want to take over Tommy for yourself."

I just needed to break the hold he had on me. Had you put that bottle on the pedestal, I'd have taken over safely and with ease. But you messed it up. You do that quite often.

"This whole time he wasn't crazy. He was fighting to keep you locked away."

And now that you've opened up all his potential spells, my freedom is certain. He can't control that kind of power. He's just a boy.

"He's a lot more than just that." The sewer tunnel seemed to have no end. She sped up to a light jog, her heart pounding. Thinking of the moment she shattered that bottle, Tommy and Barris frozen and full of odd expressions. She thought she had been doing the right thing. Always she had tried to help Tommy, but it seemed she always failed. "Not this time," she whispered to herself.

You won't make it, Barris said. *I've killed two more Bluesmen. When I finish them all, the power flooding into Tommy will overload his mind. Burn out his internal circuitry. And I will finally have a body that I can make use of. Trying to cut off the schuco won't matter. It's too far away. That and the fact that I have enough power now to send you a little present.*

A thick growl and a strong snort echoed from further down the tunnel. Malja vaulted over the railing and landed on a dry section of the waterway. She slipped Viper free and listened. Heavy footfalls followed by another snort. Whatever creature Barris had conjured, it sounded big.

An orange light grew in the distance, bouncing as the sounds of galloping neared. Malja shifted her feet back and forth, digging them into the soft ground, as she readied for a rough impact. The creature arrived with a thunderous cry. Shaped like a massive horse, it bore a brown exoskeleton that clattered as it moved. The gaps between its tough exterior plates burned bright orange.

It was nothing but fire inside.

It lowered its head and headed straight for Malja. She tried to hold her ground, but the beast whipped its head and flung her aside. It smelled of burned wood and flesh. She hit the railing, her lungs expelling every bit of air she had, and she dropped into the muck below.

The beast turned around and pawed the ground. Malja popped back to her feet and spit her mouth clean. With a fierce bellow, the beast leaned forward. Fire glowed inside its mouth and a molten liquid sprayed out, sizzling wherever it fell.

The beast tore down the waterway, snorting as it lowered its head once more. Malja held still, letting it think she would take another hit. At the last second, she jumped high and to the side, kicked off the railing, and landed on the creature's back. Though it let out a grunt of surprise, it reacted just as fast as Malja. It bucked hard. With nothing but smooth bone plates to hold onto, Malja was thrown upward into the ceiling and back down into the muck.

She refused to let the creature have another run at her. As it turned around, she launched forward. With an upward swing, she dug Viper into the creature's belly and ripped the weapon back. Gobs of molten liquid dropped to the ground, burning a hole beneath the beast. It screamed at Malja but even as it completed its turn, the battle had ended.

Its back legs became unsteady like a newborn. More fiery liquid burned through the ground. It tried to push off, to attack Malja one desperate time, but the pressure broke through the weakened ground. The hole opened up like an uncovered well and the beast fell to its demise.

Malja took one quick look down the hole — she couldn't see the bottom. She jumped over this new grave and hurried on her way. She had a boy to save.

Another Bluesman melted, his fine clothing sliding down the Dish's side along with what little remained of his body. Though Malja couldn't command Tommy's eyes to look in any particular direction, she still seemed to be able to watch Tommy's vision with her own eyes — picking out details that she wanted to see. And she saw no sign of Harskill. Either he was outside of Tommy's focus, or he had run off as the Bluesmen perished.

The string of lights guiding her way in the sewer flickered. She pushed on, but she could feel Barris behind her eyes, watching her progress. Waiting to harness enough energy for another attack.

It came sooner than she expected. The railings on both sides of the tunnel pulled off the ground with a rusted whine. They stretched across the waterway like metal ribbons and twisted so their jagged, torn ends pointed in all directions.

A rumbling began — quiet at first but building in intensity. Malja dug in her feet again, wondering what type of creature Barris would throw at her this time. Except for getting louder, though, the sounds didn't change. In fact, no animal sounds came. Just the growing rumble.

Malja looked over her shoulder. From ground to ceiling, all she saw was a massive wall of water rushing toward her.

She sprinted ahead, but her foot slipped in the mud. Though she kept upright, precious seconds whisked by. The rumble grew into a roar. When she reached the twisted railing, she climbed up. It took too long, though. There was no point in looking back one more time. The raging waters fell upon her.

She expected the water to be cold and hit into her back like a solid wall. To her disgust, the water was warm, foul smelling, and oily — but it did smash her hard. It slammed her into the railing, her cheek cut open by the rough cut metal, and pressed her in as if trying to pass her through the object.

She reached up until she found a grip and pulled herself toward the top. Three strained reaches. Three strained pulls. And the waters took over. Thrust over the railing, shot forward and deeper, tumbled and tossed, she fought to find the way to air.

As she paddled her arms about, she struck unknown objects washing by in the dark waters. She hoped never to know what they were. Her lungs burned. She kicked and stroked, working against the rough current. Her fingers touched something solid. The floor. She had been going the wrong direction.

Ignoring the increasing pain in her lungs, she shoved off, now heading in the right direction. In seconds, her head burst above the polluted waters. She gulped in air as the current whisked her along, the tunnel's ceiling inches from her head.

Below she saw the string of lights that had been her guide. Barris thought to drown her, but he had actually helped speed her along — unless she had passed by the schuco.

Bringing Viper up, she slammed it into the ceiling. Sparks flew out and a horrible shriek came from metal grinding into brick. The strong waters pulled Malja along, dragging Viper across the ceiling, but slower than before. As Viper dug deeper in, the waters could not fight. Soon, Malja stopped moving and held tight to Viper.

As she waited out the waters, she saw bits of wood and trash drift by. And corpses. Rats and small animals and even a human hand.

Only half the Bluesmen remained but they still managed to hold back Tommy from draining all the power. He could kill the rest with a strong blast, end this right now — except to do so meant dropping all other spells, including his control on the power source. It might dissipate or even go off wildly and destroy something or someone innocent. And something else pulled on his resources. Another part of him cast spells far below.

Malja concentrated on Tommy, tried hard to not only see through him but let him know what Barris was doing. He had to know, though. With the kind of immense magic he had displayed, he had to be fighting Barris, holding that monster at bay. If not, Barris already would have folded her into oblivion and taken over all of Corlin.

Wolf played faster and harder now, trying to compensate for the lost Bluesmen. He was good, too. Not as talented as his brother had been, but strong enough — his bloodthirst driving him harder. Malja saw it clearly. The Bluesmen's magic was gaining power. Barris saw it, too.

The water surrounding Malja slowed and began to die out. Not wanting to get stuck hanging from the ceiling, Malja dislodged Viper and swam toward the side. Once the waters lowered enough, she latched on to the railing and waited out until the water was no more.

When her feet finally touched the ground, she took a few deep breaths, ignoring the reek, and went on her way. The lights she followed ducked into an alcove that ended in a metal door with large rivets around its edge. It creaked opened.

Inside, she found the thick conduit wire poking through the ceiling and running down a corridor. This was her guide now. Even without it, though, she knew where to go. She could feel the energy pulsing in the corridor.

At the far end, she opened another door and found the schuco. It was a large white box, at least eight feet tall, with conduit wires entering it from the top. Off to the left, Malja saw a desk with another box on it and a flat object covered with letters and numbers. Strange technical instruments surrounded the schuco, and Malja imagined that Cole Watts was in heaven whenever she stepped foot in here.

A small staircase had been set up next to the schuco to offer access to the top. Malja climbed these stairs and inspected the conduit connections. The base where the connections occurred would be the most effective location to strike. Cutting through once would sever all the conduits, and since she couldn't be sure which ones supplied the Dish, that seemed the best solution.

As she raised Viper, however, she saw movement from the corner of her eye. She looked back at the entrance. Harskill watched her with an arrogant shake of his head.

"That may not be such a good idea," he said.

Chapter 20

Try to stop me," Malja said, heaving all her power behind Viper.
Harskill moved faster than any creature Malja had ever
known. Viper cut through the air with an audible swish, but the
blade never landed on its target. Harskill had crossed the room and
climbed the stairs in time to block with his do-kha.

Fire raged within Malja. She lifted Viper and whirled back, striking
as she completed her turn. The move was flashy and usually surprised
an enemy. Harskill looked amused while he leaned away from the
attack. As Viper passed by him, his face turned grim. He shot forward
again and jammed his knee into Malja's gut. She doubled-over.
Grabbing her shoulders, Harskill tossed her over the stairwell and
watched as she crashed to the floor.

"It's sweet that you want to save this world," he said, descending
the stairs like a king. "But this isn't the way to do it. You can't save a
people from themselves. Certainly you've figured that much out by
now. Look at Cole Watts. This Dish marks how many times she has
attempted to control a portal? Three? Four? Despite her failures that
have taken so many lives, despite the obvious risk of causing another
Devastation, she still pursues this foolishness."

Malja wanted to get to her feet, to fight back, but her muscles
resisted. Her mouth dried as she struggled for air. *The do-kha.* She tried
to picture herself standing firm and strong, tried to will her do-kha into
helping her. Though she sensed warmth soak through the suit, nothing
else happened. Someday, if she survived this, she would practice and
learn how to use this thing she wore, but it was no help now.

Harskill went on, "You want to save this world, you have to take
control of it. And it's not just this puny world, or even the multitude
like it. We can do so much more."

Leaning her back against the schuco, Malja got her feet underneath
her and scooted up until she could stand. She picked up Viper and
waited. Like her breathing, her other pains slowly eased.

"I know," Harskill said, "you don't want me. And though I think you'll change your mind some day, for now, I accept the situation. What I cannot allow, though, is for you to stand in the way of the Gate. We were once the greatest beings in all the worlds. I refuse to continue being punished for the failures of our ancestors. I refuse. It's time for the Gate to reunite — not just for a mating ritual, but to rebuild our lives as a single civilized society that rules over all."

When Harskill reached the floor, he placed his hand on the schuco. "When you are ready, when you understand the true nature of the worlds, you'll help me unite the Gate. I have no doubt. Until then, I'll have to go alone. I'll have to prove myself to you. So, when I take the power from this world, banish the ideas of Kryssta and Korstra, and have all creatures bow before me, perhaps then you'll begin to believe me."

"Doesn't look like you'll get that chance," Malja said, though the effort hurt. "Or didn't you notice that my boy is up there destroying your Bluesmen?"

The area where Harskill's hand contacted the schuco glowed as if heating up. Smirking, he said, "Really? I think you might want to look again through your boy."

Ignoring the fact that Harskill knew she was now connected to Tommy, Malja reached out with her mind to see through Tommy's eyes.

The fury of music had gained in power. It appeared to be layering upon the magic created before. But Tommy did not show any signs of weakness or stress as he pushed back against the Bluesmen. In fact, he had the strength to fight hard against the Bluesmen and fight still harder against Barris. Except — Wolf had stopped playing. He actually removed his guitar from his shoulder and held it like a club. He stepped from the edge onto the actual Dish, walked about twenty feet in, and battered the tiling with his guitar. Two powerful strikes and the tile broke away. Wolf paused to lock eyes with Tommy. Malja willed her warrior's gaze into Tommy's eyes, hoping she could use it to intimidate Wolf, but Wolf licked his lips instead. He thrust his hand into the hole he had opened, felt around, grabbed something, and yanked back. The conduit wire. Not the whole thing, it was far too big, but he had managed to rip free some of the cables.

"Did you tell him to do this?" Malja asked.

Harskill focused on the schuco and said, "I may have explained to him what great power was being held within these wires, tubes, and dead tissue."

Wolf raised the cable in the air like a tribal priest offering an enormous snake to the gods. While the Bluesmen continued to play, they bowed to Wolf one at a time.

Music and magic swirled around him, and Wolf pointed at Tommy. With wild passion, he shouted something, but Malja couldn't hear it. He smiled — a crazed, bright smile — and he plunged the wire into his side.

"You told him to kill himself?" Malja said.

"That wouldn't help me very much, would it?" The glowing area on the schuco expanded, radiating heat in pulsing waves.

Wolf let out a triumphant cheer even as his body shook from the magic pouring into him. He grew. Muscles thickened and limbs elongated. Bones became stronger.

Malja had seen magic do this before, knew the kind of enhanced strength it could produce. "Stop this," she said. "If that bastard hurts Tommy."

"He can't. Not yet. He's just keeping Tommy busy, so I can finish this."

"What are you doing?"

Harskill held up one finger, concentrated on the schuco, and then stepped away. He sighed and touched the wrist of his do-kha. A portal opened behind him. Malja glimpsed a sandy beach with a purple and orange sunset.

"You have choices to make," Harskill said. "You can join me now. Chase me and try your best to stop me — though, you will fail. Or you can attempt to save your friends from the explosion that's coming. I've overloaded the schuco. It'll send a massive jolt of power through the conduit that will be the end of the Dish. You may fail at that as well, but your chances are far better." Moving like light, he snatched Malja's hand and kissed it. "Goodbye, Malja." With an earnest bow, he stepped backward through the portal, leaving it open for her to follow. "For now."

Though she would loathe admitting it, Malja hesitated. Just a fraction of a second — a tiny thought of how she longed to step through to that beach, to be rid of Corlin and magicians and the constant threats to her life, to begin a search for her home. But the schuco emitted a low, unhealthy hum, and Malja's thoughts shifted to Tommy.

She darted up the corridor into the tunnel, slipping Viper back into its sheath as she moved. Though tired and sore, her legs found the energy to run. The do-kha must have finally responded. Maybe she could make use of it after all. She filled her mind with images of greater strength in her legs and arms — not outright healing but readiness.

Barris Mont's flood had churned up the ground, releasing long forgotten odors of decay and rot far worse than any she had encountered yet. The sickening smell made breathing difficult as her lungs revolted against the poisoned air, but still she pressed on — slower, slogging through the muck, but making progress.

From behind, she could hear the schuco. Its hum raised in pitched like a singer building to an impressive final note. She heard the snap and static of electrical discharge, too.

As she rushed through the tunnel, she tried to will a message to Tommy warning him of the overload. Each time she started to make the connection, however, her ability to keep balanced while running left her. She tumbled into the sludge twice before abandoning the idea. Instead, she just ran.

Up ahead, she saw the twisted railing Barris Mont had attempted to impale her on. It took a few extra seconds to climb over, but every one of those seconds bore in on Malja with the entire weight of the Dish. Running again, heart pounding, she pushed out all thoughts. Just run. Even the do-kha would have to wait. Any other thought would slow her down, make her doubt, cause her fear.

The schuco continued to raise its pitch, sounding less like a singer and more like a whining brat.

Malja's leg muscles complained but her do-kha sent massaging warmth to keep them strong. She tried to stay focused, but her heart leaped at the idea that her suit was responding to her — delayed from her immediate needs but responding nonetheless. She fell on the slick ground, rolled through a putrid puddle, and popped back to her feet. Cursing, she hurried on. A part of her mind, however, lingered over the idea that some day, she would master her do-kha. Covered in filth, she bolted through the tunnel until she saw the opening in the ceiling and the knotted rope dangling from it.

As she climbed, the schuco screamed. Her hands slipped and the schuco wailed. When she pulled into the air duct, the schuco let loose.

A wave of magic broke out of the schuco and soared along the conduit like a galloping horse. It passed several feet under Malja, but the power of it knocked her to her stomach. Her head hit the soft metal of the air duct.

And she saw through Tommy. The Dish vibrated hard enough to catch the attention of the Bluesmen. They didn't stop playing their music. They couldn't. But they exchanged looks of concern and confusion. Tommy's focus, however, shifted to his feet. He watched the tiles on the Dish intensely, and though Malja could feel him struggling against Barris Mont, Tommy managed to stop pulling magic from the Dish. The Bluesmen stumbled as their magic no longer fought against anything.

Without hesitation, Tommy raised an emerald bubble around himself. And he watched as the Dish exploded.

Malja kicked out a vent cover and shimmied from the air duct. She flopped to the floor of a room lined with benches and metal storage containers. The building shook so hard, she couldn't stand.

First, the edge of the Dish erupted. Metal, concrete, stone, and Bluesmen geysered into the sky. In the next second, another ring closer in erupted. Moving in concentric circles, the Dish shattered into the air, nearing to Tommy with each explosion. Thick smoke billowed and fire plumed as the deafening storm of destruction surrounded him. Tommy took one last glance at his feet. Just in time to see the tiles beneath him explode.

Malja screamed.

Chapter 21

Sunlight. It warmed her like a memory of Uncle Gregor filling their little shack with the aroma of sizzling eggs. Her eyes fluttered open, and for a fleeting second, she wondered if she had been dreaming this whole time. Then reality slammed into her.

Chunks of stone and metal covered her, and chalky dust filled the air. Half the ceiling had disappeared letting the morning sun break through. How long had she been unconscious? A huge metal beam had fallen and now ran from floor to ceiling like a narrow ramp. And that wonderful aroma turned out to be the cooking skin of someone down the corridor.

Malja extricated herself from the debris and checked over her body. She seemed okay, though she still had the constant throb of aches and several cuts on her hands and head. Looking at the damaged room, she thought how every time she had a chance to heal, something else tore her apart.

Closing her eyes, she concentrated on Tommy. She had to make sure he was okay.

But nothing happened.

She tried again.

Still nothing.

"Tommy?" she called out, her voice dying in the debris-cluttered room.

Nothing.

As she stepped toward the fallen beam, her eye noticed something pale and thin on the ground. She knew it at once — the bit of Barris Mont that had wriggled its way beneath her skin. It had been the way she connected with Tommy, and now that it was gone, so was her connection.

She kicked at the beam, testing its sturdiness, and then climbed. At the top, she stepped out on the surface of the destroyed Dish. What once had been a giant bowl of smooth, organized tiles now looked like the ruins of any city found anywhere in Corlin. Rubble and smoke, blood and bodies, metal and tile — all strewn about the Dish with no sense of order.

Malja clambered over and around the mounds and worked toward the center. "Tommy, are you okay? Tommy?"

When she saw the boy, tears welled in her eyes. He lay still and unconscious but breathing. The ground around him was untouched as if the explosions she had witnessed through his eyes had chosen to stop in a neat circle around him.

And the madness was gone. He wasn't floating. He wasn't catatonic. He wasn't glowing with magic. He simply slept on the ground like any boy might.

She crouched next to him and stroked his arm. With a grunt, he rolled to the side, and Malja pulled back at what she saw. A gray tube as thick as her arm snaked out of Tommy's right side. No blood, no gaping wound, but one end of this thing burrowed deep beneath Tommy's skin. The thing was covered in veins and eyes, and at the end not connected to Tommy, Malja saw a mop of tentacles. She knew exactly what it was — Barris Mont.

"Malja?" a voice called out. "Malja?"

"Fawbry! Over here!"

Fawbry staggered in, his unruly hair covered in dust, his face stunned. "What is it with you? Everywhere we go, things like this happen." Circling, he gestured toward the destruction all around. He glanced down at Tommy and nodded. "Thank Kryssta."

"Cole?" Malja asked.

Shaking his head, he said, "She heard the schuco screaming, building up its energy, and knew what would happen. We were laying on the floor — she asked me to hold her. I thought that was it. We were going to die like that. I was certain of it. But just before the explosion, she rolled to the side and shoved me under the table. Then she rolled on top of me and took the brunt of the damage. I don't know where she found the strength to do any of that, she acted possessed, but she saved me. She kissed me. Actually said she was sorry." He rubbed his stump.

"I'm thankful you're okay," Malja said. The words sounded awkward but Fawbry smiled anyway.

"Let's get something to carry Tommy out," Fawbry said. "I'm sick of this place."

After a few minutes searching, they found a wooden tabletop missing a long plank down the middle. Otherwise, it seemed fairly sturdy. Working together, they eased Tommy onto the table, positioning the still-connected Barris Mont at his side, and lifted. Fawbry groaned but managed his end well enough. As they maneuvered around the numerous obstructions, Fawbry took the backwards walking end so Malja could concentrate more on Tommy.

"He'll be okay," Fawbry said.

"I know. He's the strongest boy I've ever met. How about you, though? Are you okay?"

He raised an eyebrow. "Considering all that you've put me through, this isn't so bad. Though I must admit, you've got me thinking I should've taken my parents up on that arranged marriage. I could be home right now in a warm bed with a warm wife."

Malja chuckled. "We can head back up there, if you want."

"Don't you dare," Fawbry said, and Malja laughed outright.

It felt good to let her stresses go that way — rare and good. If nothing else, Fawbry brought that side of her to the surface. She looked up to tell him as much when she saw his face drop. Paling as his eyes drifted beyond her — and raised high above. She heard the sound of falling stone and metal. Rubble cascading to the ground like hale as something large emerged from the piles.

Gentle and slow, she lowered the tabletop and pulled out Viper. Fawbry did not move. Malja whirled around thinking she was ready for anything.

Then she saw what had become of Wolf.

The magic infused into his body, the magic that had smashed into him with the schuco's overloaded pulse, had altered him into a gigantic beast. He rose from the rubble until he stood nearly twenty feet high. His pigment had changed to crimson. His hair fell out, replaced by numerous horns — sharp and pointing in all directions. His fingers had reformed into three vicious claws. Even his eyes had lost all human quality becoming yellow, vertical slits. Covered in skin-bursting muscle, he bared sharp, animal teeth, and roared loud enough to shake the ground.

"M-Malja," Fawbry said.

"Take Tommy to safety," she said, striding toward Wolf. "I'll handle this."

Chapter 22

While Malja circled Wolf, she listened to Fawbry's moans as he dragged Tommy away. Though Wolf had become a monstrous beast, he still showed enough intelligence to keep his focus on her — the real threat. That would make the battle more difficult but not impossible.

Malja whisked Viper back and forth, loosening up her arm and wrist, getting herself ready to defeat yet another monster of Corlin. Why was she lying to herself? Fighting a twenty foot, magically enhanced killer and surviving felt fairly impossible. She had been through enough battles in her life to judge the odds.

"No," she said in a short bark. "That's not the way." She forgave herself the small lapse of doubt. This was her first creature of this size, but she knew that being a warrior depending on never considering death as a possible outcome. Only one result could be plausible in her mind — success.

Wolf lifted his two meaty fists and smashed them on the ground. The jolt knocked debris off its piles. He bellowed hot breath, mindless rage in his eyes, and charged at her.

Malja stood her ground, feeling the pounding of his tree trunk legs reverberate up her bones. Her breathing shook and sweat coated her hands. A hurricane raced toward her, yet she held firm.

Though he was now a giant, Wolf's brain had not fully adjusted. He threw a right cross as if he were a normal-sized man in a normal-sized fight. The motion was extremely powerful but slow.

As his fist tore up the ground like a runaway boulder, Malja danced to the side and sprang onto Wolf's arm. She ran along the muscle toward his shoulder, his enormous eye following her even as his body struggled to change its momentum. At his shoulder, Malja plunged Viper deep into his skin.

Wolf straightened, pressing Malja with a rush of cold air, and moved to brush her off like a bug. Malja gripped Viper as tight as she ever had before and dropped down Wolf's back. He roared as Viper sliced down his back, slowing Malja's descent, tearing open skin and muscle. She turned toward his side, continuing to gouge out pieces of his thigh until Viper slipped out.

Malja fell the last six feet and smacked into the ground. Chunks of the Dish dug into her side and she bit her tongue. Spitting blood from her mouth, she got to her feet — slower than she wanted — and reset her body position for the next attack.

Wolf flexed his muscular arms toward the sky. The skin on his back, slick with blood from the jagged crevice Malja had cut, began to pull back together. "Korstra!" he shouted. "Korstra!" Malja didn't believe in the brother gods, but she understood that uncontrolled magic could do unpredictable things. No god healed Wolf. The magic that changed him also healed him. In seconds, the wound was no more than a scar. Wolf faced Malja with a pitying shake of his head.

He jumped into the air — all twenty-feet and thousands of pounds — leaping to crush her with his body. Malja sprinted to the side, trying to get out from under the shadow of the giant's body blocking out the sun. Like an aged tree falling to the ground, he crashed just behind her, sending a shockwave through the air powerful enough to throw her across the Dish. She tumbled into the rubble, feeling every jagged rock, every metal bar, every bit of tile as it all slowed her down and cut into her.

All of her aches ignited, but she forced her body to move. She grabbed what once might have been a chair and used it to get back on her feet. Wolf also struggled to stand. Unfamiliar with being so huge, he had failed to judge the damage such an impact would have on his new body.

But he would heal.

Her do-kha rippled around her body, and she felt a burst of strength fill her like an adrenaline rush. Her aches dulled and her balance returned. Not perfect, but she could fight on.

Wolf coughed in the cloud of dust around his head — a deep, rumbling sound. When he stood, he had grown taller. At least another foot. Stranger still, two arms had formed out of his stomach, each ending with a five-fingered hand. The new arms reached down and picked up a large chunk of rock. They tossed the rock to his upper arms, and he held it over his head. He turned in a slow motion, scanning through the destruction, until he saw her. Then he hurtled the rock towards her.

Malja dodged it with ease, but as she moved, she saw his new arms grab another rock. Wolf threw this one right away, and the new arms grabbed another. Again and again, he tossed these slabs of stone, bits of stairway, broken chairs, and metal chunks at her.

Malja dashed through the maze of debris as fast as she could manage without spilling over or twisting an ankle. The projectiles smashed into the ground behind her, breaking into bits that flew off in all directions. Little stones and chips of wood pelted her back as she ran.

A large desk rested on its side a few feet ahead. Malja sprinted for it, diving behind and tucking in as a wide door crashed nearby. She couldn't keep this up — not when Wolf had an enormous supply of weapons all around.

And he had grown arms and gotten taller. How, by Kryssta and Korstra and all the gods of all the worlds, how had that happened?

The answer lit in her brain right away — magic. When Wolf plugged in to the schuco, he took on a massive amount of magical energy. Especially when Harskill overloaded the whole thing.

An idea formed, risky and dangerous, but the only other option was dodging until she made a mistake. She peeked over the table's edge. Wolf was scanning again. His rapid assault had covered the Dish in a fog of dirt. It would clear fast enough. No more time to debate.

Leaping over the table, Malja charged the giant Wolf. Her plan required two things she had no control over. As she ran, she did her best to look around for the first. She passed right under Wolf's legs and headed up the other side. Wolf growled while heaving a bit of ceiling at her. She pushed on, her entire focus now on the second key to her plan — Tommy.

"No, Malja!" Fawbry yelled. "You're leading him to us. Turn! Turn!"

Malja pumped her legs harder, feeling the shaking ground behind as another bit of the Dish smashed down. "Tommy!" she screamed. "Wake up and help me!"

As the blood drained from Fawbry's face, he waved her away as if shooing a scavenging animal. But then Malja's words seeped in, and Fawbry lit up with understanding. He turned to Tommy and slapped the boy's face. He shook Tommy's shoulders and yelled his name.

Panting, sweating, aching, Malja pushed on. So close now. If Tommy didn't wake, Wolf would kill them all.

"Come on," Fawbry said, pouring his panic into this one task. "Wake up."

Malja took the final steps and collapsed at Tommy's feet. Fawbry cried over the boy. She looked back and saw Wolf pick up an entire wall. He spun, building momentum, and let loose. The wall pinwheeled through the air, perfectly thrown. It was over.

As it closed in on them, Malja stretched her hand out and rested it on Tommy's leg. They were about to die. The spinning wall covered them in shadow as it descended. She felt Fawbry's hand cover her own. Though she smiled, a sadness flowed through her — regret that Tommy had not enjoyed a better life. But part of her hoped he felt the love of family surrounding him. She certainly felt it. It was unlike anything in her entire life's experience. Fawbry and Tommy were with her. They would die together. Had she believed in the brother gods, she would have thanked them for this moment.

A thick blast of energy shot out from behind and the wall exploded into tiny pieces. Tommy. Malja faced the boy. He strained to keep his right arm raised while he focused on the tattoos marking his left knee. Malja caught a glimpse of Barris Mont's slug-like body, his eyes fully open and staring at the tattoo as well. Another blast emitted from Tommy's hand. As it soared by Malja, she felt the air chill around her.

The blast smacked into Wolf and his body stopped moving. His skin turned bluish as if frozen. He was still alive, and Malja knew he would heal from the attack soon enough. But for the moment, Wolf had been stopped.

Tommy let out a long breath and fell back. Before Fawbry could open his mouth to admonish her, Malja took off. Tommy had come through for her; she wasn't going to let his actions go to waste.

The first part of her plan, the most important thing she needed, still hadn't surfaced. As she looked for it, she brought Viper out and prepared to do the last part she had full control over. She raced down to Wolf, got behind his legs, and hacked into the tendons at his ankles.

Three strong hits — and nothing. She flipped Viper over, and instead of hacking, she swung the hooked blade's point into the soft skin behind the tendon. Viper sunk in with ease. She dug in deeper before summoning all her strength to yank the blade out, severing the tendon from behind. The task required four hard pulls, but when she broke free and blood spurted out, Wolf let out a horrible shriek — satisfaction to Malja's ears.

She hobbled the other leg in the same method. It wouldn't last. Wolf would heal and be ready to attack, but she had bought time on top of that given by Tommy's magic. Hopefully enough.

"Fawbry," she called out, "help me find the schuco's conduit."

To his credit, Fawbry jumped to his feet and started looking. Malja climbed over rubble, searching for the key piece to her plan. Every other second, she peeked at Wolf's tendons. They had begun to reform — sooner than she had expected. She searched on, staying close to Wolf. If they ran out of time, she would attempt to hobble him again.

Fawbry muttered as he scrambled around the Dish. "I don't see it," he said, wringing his robe as he hurried along.

"Don't give up," Malja said, though she didn't see how they were going to have enough time to find the conduit and drag it over.

When she heard the sound of shifting rock, she knew Wolf was starting to move again. She glanced back to see him lift his left leg but his right had not healed enough yet, and he stumbled forward. Malja dashed towards him, raising Viper to cut the right tendon again, when she saw it. The conduit. Wolf had been standing on it.

Without missing a step, Malja slipped Viper back into its sheath, bent down, and wrapped her arms around the conduit. Her entire body tingled from the strange sensation. Her skin prickled. She heaved the large bundle of wires out of the ground and dragged it toward Wolf's open tendon.

Her teeth ground together, but she refused to let go. There was no time to readjust. No time to let her body free from the magic surging through it. Another heave. Another few inches. Almost there.

"You," Wolf said, his ability to talk rough and ugly but developing as the rest of him continued to grow. "You ... are ... dead."

Malja sneered and let out her own roar. She pulled on the conduit one last time and plunged its head into the open wound at Wolf's ankle. Wolf's body stiffened as if struck hard on the back of the head.

"Take cover," Malja yelled to Fawbry as she sprinted away from the giant.

She found the sideways desk ahead and jumped behind it. From there she watched as the ankle covered over the conduit with new skin. Wolf popped up, triumph on his face, and raised all four arms in a show of strength. He had grown to thirty feet and his muscles stretched against his skin. His fingers burst into flames and he laughed.

"I'll burn you all down," he said, pointing toward Malja. A stream of fire shot out. She tucked behind the table, saw the flames leap over her, felt the scorching heat surround her, and waited it out. "You've made me stronger," he said. "You're a fool."

When the fire stopped, Malja peeked out again. Wolf's face had lost its sense of superiority. Instead, he looked worried and ill. His lower arms clutched his stomach. His upper arms thickened, puffing up at the fingers and spreading upward towards the shoulder. His head snapped to the left, snapped right, back and forth.

"What?" he said like a small boy.

And he exploded.

From the Journal of Malja:

I've been afraid in my life before. Everyone is afraid at some point. But most of my life, most of the challenges I've faced, have thrilled me or given me the feeling of anticipation. Even the times I worried for my friends or thought I might not live to see another rising sun, most of those times were not faced with fear but something else. I don't have a word for it. My dear Uncle Gregor never told me that one. Yet today I am truly afraid about what we're going to attempt.

In this journal, the parts that Cole Watts wrote, I've discovered a lot of entries about me. Ever since I fell into this world, clutched in my mother's arms, Cole was fascinated by me. And when I became an adult and our lives intersected again, she thought I was the key to her success. So, she researched and pondered and did all she could to learn about me — all because I could go through a portal without burning up. I wonder what she would think now, if she knew the truth — it's not me, it's my do-kha. It protects me in many ways, including travel through a portal. Cole even suggested that possibility in one entry, but for some reason she discounted it. Well, Cole, if it helps you to know this, you were not only right, but you've provided us with an idea to help save Tommy from Barris Mont forever.

Cole considered that if the suit protects me in the harsh portal environment, it must do so by creating a field of energy around me. That's why my clothing and my hair and anything on my body also survives the experience. If I hold Tommy close to me, he should be within that field. He should be fine. The key question, the part that makes me afraid, is that Cole also thinks there exists an in-between area from one portal to the next. Though stepping through seems instant, Cole wrote that mathematically, there had to be something in-between — and I think that's where we can get rid of Barris Mont.

It scares me that if I'm wrong, Tommy could be maimed like Fawbry. Or worse. I don't know what I'd do if I was the cause of that boy's death. When do I stop feeling responsible for him? Maybe never. Maybe that's what it's like to be a parent.

I have a greater responsibility, too. It's why I must attempt this, fear or not. Harskill is out there, traveling between worlds, trying to dominate all of them, and somehow bring back the Gate. Who else is there to stop him? Who else even knows this is happening? If I found it within myself to fight for the wasted lands of Corlin, then surely I will fight for all the worlds that exist.

I will.

And I can't do it without Tommy.

Chapter 23

Malja placed the last stones on the burial mound of Cole Watts. She was just outside the Dish building in a clearing with plenty of sun. She hoped Cole would approve.

In silent respect, Malja paid her honor. She recalled the little she knew of Cole's life and, more importantly, Cole's final, brave actions that saved Fawbry. At length, she fished the journal from her coat and set it atop the stones. "This belongs to you," she said.

Fawbry stepped out of the Dish building — the main entrance had survived the explosion somewhat intact — and combed his hair back with his fingers. He lowered his head when he arrived and said, "Tommy's resting inside. Other than that disgusting thing that's Barris Mont, I think he's okay."

"Good. You look like you could use a little more rest, too."

Fawbry cocked his head, silently pointing out that they all needed rest. After pieces of Wolf had descended from the sky, after Malja knew for sure the threats had ended, all three of them fell asleep on the Dish. They had no way to tell for sure, but Malja thought an entire day had passed before they awoke.

Breaking the silence with a sniffle, Fawbry said, "Thank you for taking care of Cole. I don't think I could have done it without falling apart a dozen times."

Malja nodded.

Pressing his palm against his eyes, Fawbry coughed. After a sharp breath, he pulled out his copy of *The Book of Kryssta*, and though awkward to do one-handed, he found a specific passage to read.

> *Watch the body in death.*
> *Watch death join the earth.*
> *Watch the earth in life.*
> *Watch life rise above.*
> *All in all is all.*

He closed his eyes and prayed. Malja stood by his side in silence. That was what family did sometimes — be there and stand together.

Later, Fawbry composed himself and turned away from the grave. "I'm worried about Tommy. He's okay for now, but he's very weak. I think Barris Mont is draining him, trying to get back inside his body. I'd say you should just slice Barris off, kill him, but I think that would do serious damage to Tommy. After all, they've been linked a long time."

"That's why I went to Cole's journal for an answer. It's pretty simple, really. My do-kha, my assault suit, will protect us in the portal. That's why I can travel and you couldn't."

Fawbry rubbed his stump. "You want Tommy to open a portal?"

"More than that, he'll have to slow down time."

"Are you crazy?"

"Cole wrote that there's a moment in between when you are neither in one world or the next. You're just floating between worlds. It happens so fast, you don't even know it. But if Tommy can slow us down in that moment between, he could give us enough time to set Barris just outside the field of protection."

Fawbry shook his head. "Why not just open a portal and stick Barris in from here?"

"Same reason I don't cut Barris apart with Viper. But in the portal, my do-kha will be doing all it can to protect me. And since Tommy will be in my arms, the do-kha will protect him, too. If I concentrate hard enough, it will even heal him from any damage that Barris attempts to inflict. I hope."

With nothing more than sheer exhaustion, Fawbry said, "Haven't you done enough to that boy? I know you love him, but why risk his life this way? There are so many ifs that this plan has no more chance for success than chopping Barris into bits and a lot more risk. And let's say you do succeed — what then? You'll be off on some other world. How are you going to get back without knowing how to control these portals?"

"We still have Tommy's copy of the map from Penmarvia. That should help us at first."

"At first?" Fawbry pointed at her as he started to understand. "You don't plan on coming back. You're going out there — for what? Harskill? And don't think I didn't notice that I'm not being included in this plan. You just want to take Tommy and go away from me?"

Malja set her jaw. "I didn't think you'd approve of any of this."

"Of course, I don't approve. When has that ever mattered before?"

"It's not some wild dream. This comes from Cole's journal. It's right over there. You can read it for yourself. This will work. It'll save Tommy." She sounded so confident, she almost believed it.

Crossing his arms, then unfolding them, Fawbry paced in front of Malja. "How can you be so stupid?" He sputtered as he tried to get out his thoughts. Malja braced herself for an onslaught of arguments against her plan and Cole's ideas. To her surprise, Fawbry said, "How can you not understand what I've been trying to teach you all along? We are a family. After all these years, you still pretend you're alone in all this, that you have to carry the burden of us by yourself. It's not like that. Listen to me because I'm sick of you acting this way — I am not leaving you and Tommy. Got it?"

"But family doesn't harm each other just to —"

"You don't get to decide what I do. If Cole said this'll work, if you can't be deterred, then I'm going with you. Will your fancy suit protect me, too?"

"I think so."

Fawbry paused but shook off his fear. "Good enough. Either we save Tommy, or he and I die trying." He winked and added, "You get to live on with the guilt." As she reached toward him, Fawbry flapped his arms to ward her off. "I hate when you do this to me. I've got to be alone. Go convince Tommy. None of this happens without him."

Muttering to himself, Fawbry trudged off. Malja watched him leave, feeling smaller with each step further he went. By the time she turned toward the Dish building door, she imagined herself being crushed by an ant. Convincing Fawbry had been easy compared to what she expected from Tommy. After all, how could she tell him to use his powerful magic after all her years standing in his way?

"Look at me. Fierce warrior once again fearful of a boy."

The Dish building foyer smelled of smoldering destruction. Black smoke had stained the walls, marking where it had traveled up and pooled in the ceiling corners. Further in, the ceiling had collapsed, blocking the corridor leading to the rest of the building.

Tommy rested atop a cleared-off reception desk. From the doorway, Malja watched him sleep — one of her favorite things to do. She coveted these moments of untarnished peace. But like all peace, sleep never lasted long enough. Wincing, Tommy's eyes jolted open.

He saw Malja right away and reached for her.

An emotion unlike anything she had ever felt surged up her body and launched her to Tommy. She wrapped her arms around him, hugging him tighter than ever, and showered the top of his head with kiss after kiss. "I'm so sorry," she said, unable to stop tears from drenching her face. "I'm so sorry. I fought you and fought you and never let you use the gifts you've always had. I doubted you so much but it wasn't you at all. It was all me." Her heart raced, and she couldn't stop the words from spilling out. "Ever since I met you, I doubted I could survive if I let anything happen to you. I just couldn't live with you going mad because of magic. I didn't know it was Barris Mont. I didn't understand. I'm sorry. I just wanted to protect you." She tried to say more but the words balled in her chest.

Tommy pulled back and smiled. He pointed to the Barris Mont appendage and then mimed reading a book. He tapped his head and smiled again.

"You read Cole's journal?"

He nodded.

"Then do you know what I plan to do?"

With two fingers, Tommy tapped his chest twice and raised his hand to his forehead in salute.

Malja caressed his cheek and nodded. "You really are a god."

He shook his head no and looked like her boy once again.

They waited two days. Malja insisted that Tommy regain some strength before attempting her plan to remove Barris Mont, and nobody argued. She could see the reason in their eyes — they were all scared. Any viable excuse to hold off sounded like a good idea. And they all made use of the time to rest.

Horse showed up after the first day. Cole's people had taken good care of her, but when the Dish exploded, several of the stable walls were breached. Horse managed to escape. When she arrived, Malja and Fawbry acted like children, fawning over the mare, feeding it grass, and enjoying the good fortune of this animal. All the excitement, however, died down, and they were left with the hard choices they could not escape.

After two days, there was no way out. They had to either open a portal and take the risks, or they would have to start the long trek north back to the world they knew.

They gathered in an open field. Malja walked Horse in and leaned her head against the animal's neck. She stroked Horse for a little, and without ceremony let the creature go. A firm swat on the backside sent Horse running toward its freedom.

"I guess we're ready, then," she said.

Tommy stood with Barris Mont in a sling fashioned from a torn shirt. Other than that gray, sickly appendage, Tommy looked quite well. He watched Fawbry fumbling to get his robe just right. Fawbry reached for the robe's belt and made a circle like a dog chasing its tail. Tommy giggled.

"I might throw up," Fawbry said, "but otherwise, I'm ready to go."

Malja waved them closer. "Tommy, stand in front, and Fawbry, get behind me. Now you both press in close to me. I'm going to do my best, but this is all new to me."

"M-Maybe we should test this somehow."

"It'll be fine. The suit knows what to do."

Fawbry rolled his eyes. "Oh, well, if the suit knows what to do, then why are we waiting? Let's go jump into a portal and burn off my other hand."

Pulling Tommy closer to her, Malja said, "Just hold tight. Tommy, once we get in between worlds, I'll put all my thoughts and energy into having the suit get rid of Barris, but you have to help, too. You need to shove him out of you, not just what's left of his body, but his mind, too. I don't want any trace of him returning. Can you do that?"

With a teenager's scowl, Tommy raised his hand and checked his tattoos. He started a countdown on his hand — 5 ... 4 ...

Fawbry's hands wrapped around Malja. He dug his head into her shoulder.

3 ...

He said, "Whatever happens, I don't regret a single moment. You're the best thing that's ever happened to a fool like me."

2 ...

Malja reached back and patted Fawbry's head. "I love you, too," she said.

1 ...

Tommy opened a portal.

Chapter 24

Birds chirped. A simple high-low-high pattern floating on the air. And the fresh aroma of plants in bloom sweetened the music-filled breeze.

Malja opened her eyes to find herself on a bed of green grass. She was alive. White, puffy clouds drifted by a green-blue sky. She sat up, though her body wanted to remain on the comfortable ground, and took in her surroundings.

Orderly rows of trees stretched into the distance separated by wide swaths of dirt and grass. Hills to the north (if the sun could be counted on for direction) and a barn to the west. Some kind of farm.

"Tommy? Fawbry?" she said, not too loud though — no telling what kind of world they had entered. She heard rustling from two tree rows over.

As she approached the noise, images flashed in her head — twisted faces like animals that never existed, clawing, slobbering, growling. No up or down, a void of gray. And a screaming like metal forced to bend in ways it shouldn't. The in-between had been a horror to see even for a moment, and the little she recalled convinced her that she never wanted to see it again.

"Fawbry? Tommy?" She knew she would survive. The do-kha made sure of that. But the longer she waited to get a response from her men, the more she recognized that her entire plan had rested on the imagination of Cole.

Staying low as she scuttled from row to row, she searched for her family. Hopefully the farmers were far away or done with this section for the day. She didn't want to deal with those issues until she found Tommy or —

"Malja? Over here," Fawbry said.

She crossed another row of trees and found them both sitting calm and quiet. Fawbry looked much like she felt — reinvigorated but a bit shaken by the in-between. Tommy looked wonderful.

Though he rubbed his side, most signs of Barris Mont were gone.

Only a reddish patch remained, and Malja guessed that would heal soon enough. But the fact that she could see the red skin amazed her — with the exception of the sleeve on his left arm, all the tattoos had vanished.

"I think," Fawbry said, "Barris Mont had forced Tommy's body to create more magic than it could do on its own."

Tommy checked over his sleeve of tattoos that were left. He pointed to a few and sighed relief. Malja couldn't be sure which spells remained, but from his reaction, she suspected he could still form a portal. She didn't really care, though. If having her Tommy back, sane and healthy, meant being stuck wherever they were, that was okay. After all, she had spent her entire life on a world that wasn't her own. What did it matter if she spent the rest on another world not her own?

Fawbry put his arm around Tommy. "You really had us scared for awhile. Seeing you with all that power pouring out of you was probably the closest I'll ever come to seeing a god. Must be weird to lose that."

Tommy shrugged and nestled his head against Fawbry.

"He hasn't lost a thing," Malja said. "He knows who he is now. That's a tremendous gain. I didn't understand who any of us were before, even myself. Because of that, I pushed back every time you wanted to be what you were meant to be. What any of us were meant to be."

"What are you talking about?"

"Tommy is the Power. You, Fawbry, are the Soul. And I am the Blade. We each have our part to perform, and if there's ever been a godly power among us, it is only when we work together that it takes a true form."

Fawbry smiled. "I like the sound of that."

Tommy clapped his hands in approval.

"Me, too," Malja said.

"We're like Kryssta and Korstra," Fawbry said. "In all the stories, they were always greater when working together than against each other or even as individuals. We're the brother gods, now."

"I'm a sister god."

Laughing, Fawbry and Tommy rolled on the ground. They giggled and coughed and laughed some more. Malja's chest swelled as she watched them in complete surrender to joy. At length, though, Fawbry stood and brushed leaves off his robe. "So," he said, "what do we do now?"

Malja reached up to a tree and shook a branch. Large, red apples rained down. They each picked one up and bit in. Sweet and juicy and crisp. Perfect.

"Well," Malja said after swallowing a delicious bite, "we've done our best to help Corlin — no more Jarik and Callib, no Queen Salia, no Barris Mont, no Dish, no portals. We've saved a entire world. But Harskill got away. He's out there and he's causing trouble. I want to find him."

"Harskill. Of course," Fawbry said, his shoulders dropping.

Malja took another bite of her apple and headed down the lane. Tommy and Fawbry followed on either side of her. She looked at them and felt a confidence rise different from anything she had ever experienced. The Blade, the Power, the Soul — a true team. A true family.

"This won't be easy," Fawbry said.

Malja kept her eyes forward. "Nope. Saving one world was hard enough. Now, we've got to save them all."

About the Author

Stuart Jaffe is the award-winning author of *The Malja Chronicles*, the *Max Porter Paranormal-Mysteries*, the *Bluesman* serial, the *Gillian Boone* novels, *Real Magic, After The Crash*, and *10 Bits of My Brain*, as well as numerous short stories appearing in magazines and anthologies. He was the co-host of *The Eclectic Review* — one of the longest running genre podcasts about science, art, and well, everything. For those who keep count, the latest animal listing is as follows: four cats, one albino corn snake, one Brazilian black tarantula, three aquatic turtles, seven chickens, and a horse. Thankfully, the chickens and the horse do not live inside the house.

Made in the USA
Middletown, DE
06 January 2022

57979303R00324